The Other Side of Fear

A NOVEL

MARY HITCHCOCK GEORGE

authorHOUSE®

AuthorHouse™
1663 Liberty Drive
Bloomington, IN 47403
www.authorhouse.com
Phone: 833-262-8899

Published by AuthorHouse 09/22/2020

ISBN: 978-1-6655-0013-5 (sc)
ISBN: 978-1-6655-0012-8 (hc)
ISBN: 978-1-6655-0014-2 (e)

Library of Congress Control Number: 2020917718

Print information available on the last page.

This book is dedicated to the men and women in the military and law enforcement who live lives of valor every day. My thoughts and prayers, as well as my heartfelt gratitude and appreciation, go with you and your families.

In memory of
Thomas Kinkade
"Painter of Light"
1958 - 2012

After finding "the other side of fear,"
Thomas Kinkade
used his artistic talent to bravely put
God's Glory to canvas,
even in the face of an unbelieving world.
Thank you for your gift, Thomas!

Self-trust
is the essence of heroism.
It is the state of the soul at war,
and its ultimate objects
are the last defiance of falsehood
and wrong,
and the power to bear
all that can be inflicted
by evil agents.
It speaks the truth,
and it is just,
generous,
hospitable,
temperate,
scornful of petty calculations,
and
scornful of being scorned.

- Ralph Waldo Emerson
Essay VIII
Heroism

PROLOGUE

1

On a rugged mountain crest in Afghanistan, near the Pakistan border, two lone survivors of a heat-seeking, missile attack stood awaiting the Chinook helicopter to lift warriors out of the danger zone as prearranged. One, a young Special Forces Ground Commander; the other, standing loyal and at attention by his side, his Siberian husky, militarily trained and ready to rip apart any threat that might come upon his master.

Hours earlier, the remote camp, clandestine and temporary in nature, had been set up deep inside enemy territory, its six-member team tasked with a do-or-die, one-way mission to take place at 0-dark thirty that evening. Two hours before sunrise, the team's on-duty sentry returned to the slumbering camp ahead of schedule. He tapped his sleeping commanding officer on the shoulder, stealing away the man's last precious moments of shuteye. In cold, rasped exhaustion, the sentry grunted through chattering teeth, "You're up, Hero ... I'm frozen to the bone." With that said he quickly collapsed to a bare spot on the cold floor and wrapped himself in a Mylar blanket a mite too small for his ample body size.

The officer had felt the tap, and woken to the murkiness of night; but he was alert enough to hear the snarky taint of jealousy in the man's voice, one that followed him wherever he went due to his large collection of awards and Medals of Honor. He could smell the cold and snow on the man's clothing, as clearly as the strong whiff of Jack Daniels on his breath. Already dressed in camouflage, and battle-ready for his lion's share of responsibility, the officer rose to his feet and checked his watch. The hour was late, too late to deal with this latest rules infraction; each and every man was essential to this mission.

The officer rolled his blanket, then turned and took aim at the shivering sentry. "Better layer up, Tex," he advised as he delivered a long pass to the man. "I'm not stripping down to my 'seriously soft' Mack Weldon's to thaw out your frozen carcass," he groused in razzing, military banter. He gave his head a wry shake, knowing full well that he would put his life on the line for any of these five courageous men. Now his eyes settled on the man's upper body, at his non-regulation, gray T-shirt. "I'll take that…." he said simply, gesturing towards the man's chest, his fingers waggling the universal 'give-me' message.

The surprised marine hesitated, glanced down at his shirt, thumped his chest and spat out, contemptuously, "My mama gave me this shirt!"

Now, the tenor of authority and conviction rose in the officer's voice. "And Mama can get you another one once we're all home, tucked in our beds," he offered.

The slumberous warrior lying beside the contemptuous man groaned in aggravation. "Just give the man the damned shirt, asshole … and shut the ef up." He rolled away from the annoying chatter, making a big show of his annoyance by pulling his blanket over his ears.

Begrudgingly, the pouting marine pulled the shirt over his head, wadded it into a tight ball, and threw it at his commanding officer.

"Thanks," the officer grunted in return, "and a very Merry Christmas to you." He walked away, stuffing the shirt into his inside jacket pocket with plans to burn it, later. Should the marine be killed or captured by the enemy, the shirt's messaged lettering could easily lead the enemy straight back to their own backdoor.

Before stepping out into the blustery wind, the ground commander whistled softly for his highly-trained combat dog, and turned an envious eye on the slumbering men in all stages of loud, symphonic snoring, air-gulping snorts, and gaseous explosions. He suppressed a good-natured chuckle. Little did he know that the scene he was leaving behind would haunt him for the rest of his life.

Once outside, he held in his breath as he scanned the terrain in steely-eyed surveillance, listening. He heard nothing unusual or threatening beyond the melodic wind swishing through the trees. With gratitude, he exhaled slowly.

He preferred this darkest-before-dawn hour in the rotation. It gave him time to reflect and steel his soul towards any unexpected dangers that might complicate his day. It also gave him opportunity to watch one more glorious sunrise, and to acknowledge his maker with a prayer and a time-honored salute—should his life end on this day.

As he waited out the dog's tree-watering ceremony, his eyes embraced the heavens. He studied the handful of twinkling stars, yet to be gobbled up by fast-moving clouds, a strong indication that there would be no sun-gilded dawn to start his day; instead, his mind flashed back to the exhilarating experience of free-falling through the night sky with the 65-pound sled-dog tethered to his back in a tandem skydive, both dropping silently onto the boulder-riddled ground in silence, darkness and complete euphoria.

He screwed the cap off a water bottle and chugged most of its contents, remembering the satirical Navy Seal mantra, "Get up ... drink water ... and go save the world." He chuckled softly at the pure audaciousness of the message.

His sharp eyes roamed the sands in the far distance. He had studied this historical part of the world in depth, a world most Americans knew very little about; but over the last couple of decades, the U.S. military had analyzed it, as though it were a world-wide, pandemic virus as seen through a high-powered microscope. Down through the centuries, a never-ending civil war had been fought on this land. Eons of scorching heat, hate and extreme poverty had left the land lying in utter waste.

In exasperation, he lamentably acknowledged that, over the last half-century, tons of American blood had also drained into this soil, breaking the hearts of his countrymen half-a-world away.

As he took steps around the camp, his gaze dropped to the ground, to a fissure in the rock. Closer inspection proved it to be an underground grotto, one large enough for an enemy combatant to climb into. The thought was a bit unsettling.

Suddenly from afar, and through the opaqueness of the early morning, came the faint crow of a rooster; hauntingly so, as though issuing a warning on this dreary Christmas morning. The warrior's eyes followed the sound to a peaceful little villa. To the naked eye, it appeared to be a prime example of the country's middle-eastern culture; but the warrior knew from his own prior experience that this was not a fair representation of hearth and home. He knew the villa consisted of make-shift, mud housing, quickly hobbled together to give the appearance of benign family domesticity; but in reality, it was the entrance to Hell—the enemy's headquarters, and one extremely large terrorists' hidey-hole. He focused his high-powered binoculars on the valley floor, bringing the villa in for closer scrutiny—a villa that served as camouflage for what lay buried in labyrinthine tunnels throughout the mountains and beneath the surface of the sand.

He also knew from previous tours that the air at ground level stank—not just from animal shit, but of human waste, and the putrid stench of unclean bodies, commixed with foul-smelling spices, drugs and disease. In essence, the village was a walking, breathing launch pad for abominable, blood-curdling evil—an evil turned against western civilization—his sole reason for being here.

He drained the last gulp from his bottle, and stuffed it down a leg-pocket. Suddenly, the faint wail of a distressed, hungering infant echoed off the mountainside in the same way as the rooster's crow—hauntingly so. "Aw … hell!" the warrior whispered, his jaw dropping at this new complication. In disgust, he spat out his last sip of water onto the ground—his enemy was hiding behind children.

With vacant eyes, he raised his head. He quoted Clement C. Moore's famous line, under his breath, "The children were nestled all snug in their beds." Through gritted teeth, he added a line of his own, "while visions of opiates and heavy ordnance danced in their heads."

He looked again at the huts, at the high mud walls built around each lodgment, and left to dry in the sun, forming a rock-hard security barrier around each abode. He grunted, incredulously, at the number of such walls he had personally vaulted over during the course of his military career. He noted that each one looked to be a little higher than from his last stint here. Or maybe they just looked higher because he had just turned a year older.

As he awaited the return of his tail-wagging buddy, he lowered the glasses and, once again, lifted his eyes towards the brooding sky, now starless and foreboding. When, at last, the canine returned to his side, the warrior slung his rifle and backpack; and with the dog leading the way, the two tromped off in tense, but quiet comradery towards a tall rock formation on the far side of a deep ravine—a nature-made watch tower.

Together, they descended into the ravine, waded across a shallow trickle of water, then climbed back up the other side. On the trail ahead, a tail flickered. In a rare display of disobedience, the dog instantly took chase, leaving the chagrined officer with a churned-up sense of uneasiness as he followed the ancient, goat-trodden trail—a simple path, narrow but fraught with the possibility of IED's planted along its rocky, needle-strewn surface. When the "something" emerged as a scraggly squirrel, the experienced operator scolded the dog severely for chasing tail, and then turned to retrace his steps towards the tower.

Suddenly, the frigid air began to vibrate, and the, all too familiar, sounds of an incoming missile shrilly thrummed its way across the roguish sky. Literally caught between a rock and a hard place, the officer could only watch as, in a matter of seconds, the missile shredded the treetops overhead, crossed the ravine, and burrowed deep into the sleeping, unsuspecting camp. Instantly, the ground beneath the tent swelled, and the entire camp erupted into hellish flames.

The bottom dropped out of the seasoned commando's stomach, and his ears filled with the sounds of the explosion—as well as the deep, guttural screams of his brothers as the last breaths of life left their ravaged bodies. Benumbed, he battled to stay afoot amid the force of the shockwave that slammed his body backwards, and into a boulder, cracking the back of his head against the hard rock. The loud, shrill whine of the, once-fearless, canine rivaled that of the missile as he shot between his master's legs with insufferable trembling. Totally traumatized, the dog fell to the ground, unable to stand of his own accord.

At last, the warrior planted his feet and righted himself, shaking off the wooziness. Pain shot to his head as he bent down, and in the way of a gentle shepherd, scooped the shuddering animal off the ground, draping its trembling form across his strong shoulders. Without missing a beat, he charged back up the side of the ravine, and followed his tracks back to the very spot where he had stood, sky-gazing, just moments before.

Clutching his quivering, canine collar, he entered what remained of the tent, heedlessly stepping through flames; but then, he came to a complete and sudden halt. Time stood still as he realized, in those first seconds, what littered his way— the blood and guts of his fellow warriors. He poked through the flaming debris with woeful diligence, hoping to find survivors. When he shined a light, its beam fell on the remains of severed appendages. Sickened by the reality, he turned and vomited; then, dutifully and literally, took a head count—all were dead.

There was nothing, absolutely nothing the warrior could do to help them— not even collect the IDs of these honorable men, these sons, husbands and fathers, for they wore nothing in the way of identification.

In stunned mindlessness, Lieutenant Colonel Matthew J. McCormick stumbled away from the carnage, to a boulder half his height. There, he dropped to his knees in brokenness. "My God!" he bellowed as his face fell like lead into his hands.

How long he'd sat in unconsciousness, he didn't know; but when he finally came around, it was to the sound of the canine's frenzied whining and incessant licking of his face, trying to coax a response from his master. The bereaved warrior lifted his head, now thrumming like the missile that had completely obliterated his world. He cocked a ringing ear. Between temporary deafness and the swishing of trees in the wind, the voices of the approaching enemy went unheard; but the same wind carried, to the canine's nose, the strong scent of the enemy, slowly moving up the side of the mountain. With urgency, he began to paw and pace around his master.

Recognizing this trained behavior, the warrior ordered the dog into silence. He reached for his weapon, but ruefully remembered that he'd dropped it when all hell had broken loose. Standing to fight would be pointless, he quickly realized, not to mention a waste of two valuable military assets. With undue haste, he shoved and slithered both he and the dog into the small underground grotto. Through a fissure in the rock, and the murky, grey-green darkness of a concussion, the soldier sat for hours in raw fear, listening and watching the abominable warmongers trample the ground overhead.

After a very long while, the enemy began to shout and shoot their weapons into the air in celebration. Amid medieval chants, and cacophonous laughter, they finally left the site—the tips of their weapons brazenly adorned, as in ancient times, with the charred heads of his brothers.

When all had gone quiet, the officer gathered the dog to himself, and vigorously rubbed his ears and throat. With heavy-hearted gratitude, he whispered, "Good work, soldier!"

Black on food, shelter and communications, they waited for two, long days to be lifted off the frigid mountaintop by the designated chopper, a chopper with the capacity to carry over five squads; but it never showed—and the squad no longer existed. Meanwhile, the bloody slaughter of his men replayed behind dark, hollow eyes, and the septic stench of burnt flesh still cleaved to his nostrils.

His mind seethed. The military had spent millions of dollars on equipment and new technology, scrambling their signals, and hiding their covert location; still the enemy had known they were here—known they were coming—and fired upon them. There was no mistaking the evidence—either their plans had been intercepted, or someone had sold them out! He had a suspicion as to who might have sold them out.

Not yet counting himself among the dead, the warrior stood with purpose and determination. Certain that the details of this mission would never make headlines back home, he gave a sharp whistle for his dog, and set out on foot to avenge the deaths of this elite, military team. Each valorous man had been exceptionally educated, expertly trained, and highly decorated. They were the best the world had to offer. Each one was a hero in his own right. In their honor, he would complete their mission—alone.

In the months that followed, the young officer returned to service for missions too numerous to count; but as he fought, he realized that the war zone was moving—not to another hellish, dried up country, but to the lush, tropical forest of the Western Hemisphere. Spreading their ideology along the way, foreign terrorists, drug runners, and cold-blooded, mercenary killers had united, and were now working in concert with the illegal drug trade, using the American drug sales as funding as they plotted and carried out their atrocities all over the world. Over time, the brave warrior had watched his country grow weaker, while the enemy grew in strength and numbers. One thing became unmistakably clear—saving modern civilization depended, not only on stopping and destroying the enemy in this foreign land, but on stopping the funding of the illegal drug trade in his own beloved country, as well.

When an American name popped up near the top of the enemy list, taking credit for the missile attack, as well as other terrorists' atrocities, the young warrior realized that he, and he alone, possessed not only a particular set of skills and qualifications, but also knowledge that could infiltrate this particular international group of terrorists, both on U.S. and foreign soil. He knew this turncoat, this Benedict Arnold, mind and body. He'd worked with him, and fought beside him. The man was treasonous, a traitor by nature.

In addition, the warrior had learned through back channels that the DEA suspected a high-level mole within their ranks, someone leaking secrets, and crippling their efforts to fight the enemy. He took his findings to his superior military officers, asking permission to go after the terrorist. Suspecting that in finding one, he'd find the other, he agreed to go undercover. With their blessings, he quietly left the military, and hired on as a battle-tested, sheep-dipped, government agent.

PART I

CHAPTER 1

F orest Hills Daily News Assistant Editor, Andrea Daye stood, hands on hips, in the large, dank basement, gaping at the stacks upon stacks of unsold newspapers. Bundled and tied with hemp, the fusty-smelling heaps all but filled the sizable space. Wandering deeper into the mounds of ink and wood pulp product, she breathed out a heavy sigh, sickened by the sight of failure. Suddenly, the light flickered as though compassionately sharing her pain. She looked around with concernment. Seeing nothing to alarm her, she leaned over a bundle to better read a headline, in bold, large font, above the fold—the most impactful spot in a newspaper's layout. Suddenly, the entire underground cellarage went black.

Anxieties surfaced as she stood in total darkness. Willing herself to stay calm, she gripped the thin strap to her small shoulder bag. *Too late in the year for a power surge,* she thought. Intuitively, she sensed someone watching her—a gift she'd had since early childhood. She listened for distinctive sounds—sounds that could be perceived as threatening. Only the familiar whomp of the persistent, overhead presses invaded the early-morning stillness. Still, a shudder crept up her spine, and remained until long after the lights had flickered back on.

It wasn't only imagined dangers, lurking in the shadows, that fed her angst or the fire hazard created by the stacks of unsold newspapers; nor was it the single, bare-burning light bulb swaying from the ceiling on a single cord, casting sinister shadows like something out of a best-selling, international thriller. No, it was the dread that, one day, she just might find her troubled boss hanging by the neck at the end of that very power cord, as was his inclination, and constant threat; but having inherited her father's predilection towards positivity, she turned her back to the cord and grunted, gratefully, "But not today."

Unfortunately, the haunt of emotional anguish clung to her. With haste, she grabbed the nearest stack of papers, hoping to brain-storm story ideas for the Sunday edition. Balancing the weight between her arms, she quickly retraced her steps. Throwing a backwards glance over her shoulder, she skittishly hot-footed it up the rickety, old staircase as it creaked and groaned, complainingly, threatening to fall away beneath her feet—to collapse, just as her entire freakin' life had collapsed.

With a shiver running up her spine and arms heavy-laden with newspapers, she stood outside her office door. "Sheesh," she muttered, impatiently jiggling the stubborn key in the lock, "why do I always have such trouble with locks?" Finally, she pushed against the door. It yielded, giving her access to her small, unlit office. She plunked the papers down on the corner of her desk, fully intending to peruse them immediately. That thought, however, was quickly pushed aside as her boxy, antiquated phone clamored, annoyingly. Reaching across the desk, she picked up the receiver, and gave a short answer to a lengthy question, all-the-while penning a reminder to call the electrician. She walked around the desk and hit the startup key on her computer, waiting for the monitor to come alive. In the dim light, her gaze fell on her *To Do* list from the previous day, a list the length of a $200 grocery receipt. Still feeling raddled, she plunked down in her roll-away chair, its well-worn leather, faded and tattered.

In silence and pre-dawn darkness, she sat, allowing her mind to travel back to her cellar experience. She leaned back in frustration, blowing out an exasperated breath. "Since when have I become such a freaking, fraidy-cat?" she chided, aloud.

In time, the smell of printer's ink snaked its way through the building, reaching the nostrils of the young journalist, bringing an end to her lassitude. She snatched the list, fully aware that yesterday's news already had been forgotten in the minds of most of her readers.

She clicked on the TV, raised her eyes towards the screen's glow, watched it flicker to life and quickly tuned in to the day's weather forecast. Dark hued radar images showed an active hurricane in the Caribbean Sea, along with accompanying film footage of a previous event. Now, as she sat before the screen, watching vehicles and houses being demolished and washed away in real time, she said a silent prayer for those who might be caught in the path of this latest weather assault.

She watched, mesmerized by the devastation, taking it to heart, her own feelings of insecurity cleaving to her like mud. She sucked in a deep breath, comparing the visual, on-screen destruction to the havoc in her own life. She too, had been slammed by ill winds, flushed downstream, and left to flounder alone in a swirling pool of ugly debris, and irreplaceable loss.

On to the national news: the report on the number of Covid-19 deaths led the procession of stories, as usual. Another officer was reportedly gunned down in cold blood. Andrea wondered why any sane person would want to be in law enforcement in this current culture. The armed and dangerous shooter was believed to be wounded, heavily armed, heavily tattooed, and headed north—north being Andrea's direction. Trying to stay calm, and within herself, she spewed her thoughts aloud to the screen. "Thanks a bunch guys, but you can just keep your big city despots in the Big Rotten Apple." For some reason, the sound of her own voice kept her grounded in reality.

Next up, but getting scant attention, came a warning from DEA Headquarters in Virginia: persons impersonating Special Agents were using blackmail and extortion to cover up illegal drug purchases. Andrea bristled and fell back against her chair. "Well, who in the hell can you trust," she whispered in all seriousness, "if not a federal agent?"

Soon, the screen was haunted by a story on a horrendous middle school shooting, following long months of pandemic shutdown and street rioting. The story tugged on her heartstrings, causing her to pause.

When the commentator switched to the political scene, Andrea's emotions sank to gut level. She hated politics, but raised astute, world-savvy eyes to the screen. "So what deceptive fallacy are you trying to seed into my little brain today?" she inveighed to the TV anchor.

Andrea was aware that her window-on-the-world, so to speak, was far different from that of most women—women her age who got their news explicitly from social media, which focused on opinion, gossip and innuendo. She, on the other hand, was constantly fed breaking news from around the world by legitimate news services, reporting only cold, hard facts.

No. She was convinced her mind wasn't being brainwashed by propagandists.

She listened, half-heartedly, to the never ending drum beat—to a world turned upside down by elections, pandemics, race relations, riotous protests; and finally, the drum beat of those hell-bent on destroying the fabric of the nation in order to establish a society ruled, not of the people, by the people, or for the people, but a country ruled by socialist, Marxists and illegal drugs dealers. But the thing that brought it all home, making it personal, was the fact that her young, lawyer husband had, to Andrea's chagrin, gleefully jumped, head-first, into the fray by declaring his run for office.

She closed her eyes, momentarily, in dismay. "My God," she sighed, worrisomely, "what a world for a young kid to grow up in."

When her eyes finally popped opened, her gaze fell on her cheerful, little desk calendar, still displaying yesterday's date. As she ripped away the dated page, she found a small pink envelope tucked under it. Lit only by the glow of the computer, it had gone completely unnoticed until this very moment.

"How'd this get here?" She bounced a dubitable glance off the door, the one she'd just unlocked; but her spirits rose as she read her name in bright, cheerful letters. Supposing it to be a party invitation, she smiled. It had been months since she'd been to any kind of celebration, or gathering, for that matter. She lifted the flap and tugged the card out of its envelope.

Suddenly, she blanched. Large, bold letters jumped off the card: ***Die Bitch!***

"W-u-t?" she chuntered. "Didn't I spell your name right in the police reports?"

She replaced the card, dated the envelope and dropped it into the catch-all box under her desk—preserving the evidence.

Threats had become, almost, a daily occurrence in the newspaper industry. Today, however, her mind filled with thoughts as to how all this insanity was actually affecting her—her mental state. Since no one wanted to read about good people, doing good things while living wholesome, productive lives, the very nature of reporting the daily news almost always went to the dark side; depraved and perverted people, knowingly, got involved in surreptitious circumstances, but balked, and cried foul when proof of their corruption turned up in black and white—and read all over.

She clicked on an icon, and while waiting for her beleaguered, slow-running computer to respond, her mind flashed to the damsels-in-distress in the romantic movies she occasionally watched on weekends, snuggled under the red logo of her plush, gray blanket. Those particular women had problems, for sure; but the consistent theme seemed to suggest that any problem could be resolved with a kiss from just the right guy—a presupposition totally out of touch with todays be the man culture.

Her own problems were far more—far more what? "Complicated," she decided, "and of the sort," she added wistfully, "that no mere mortal can kiss away."

Like the unnerving basement experience, her world had descended into utter darkness following her marriage. Normally one to set things straight, or move on, she'd accepted her role in this troubling relationship, fully aware that there was simply no way she could ever dig out of the suffocating avalanche of misery threatening to bury her every last shred of happiness— at least not in the foreseeable future. She was willing to make the sacrifice; but what troubled her the most, as she mulled over the sordid details of a life totally gone sideways, was that none of it made sense. The question foremost in her mind was not, how to get out of a dreadful marriage and move on to a better life, but rather, would she even have a life?

She swung her chair around, gazing numbly through the tall, antiquated window. Her fingers raked, stressfully, through her hair as her sleep-deprived eyes took in the massive chain of mountains, veiled in early morning mist, and haloed by the first autumnal glow of pre-dawn light. She feasted on the rugged peaks formed eons ago, Monte Verde—the Green Mountains of Vermont. Her heart swelled and a sense of awe stole her breath away. A verse she'd learned as a child came to mind, "Be still … and know that I am God."

A melancholic smile crossed her lips as an over-whelming avalanche of memories wiped out all other thoughts. She'd never lived in the mountains, but her family had visited them often, camping each summer in the primitive campgrounds, hiking the rugged trails all the way to the Canadian border; then taking the *Vermonter* train back home.

Suddenly, she shifted her weight forward, and straightened her back. "But that was then, and this is now," she spouted, in an effort to regain her focus. Still her mind wondered. In those earlier days, during the long winter months, her family could be found on the slopes, schussing down ski runs—shreddin' fresh powder—their joyful taunts and peals of laughter clinging to the cold, frosty air. They'd even snow camped, adventuresomely, in the pristine Northeast Kingdom over one entire Christmas break, hiking trails, pitching tents, digging pits and cooking over an open fire. When it came time to go, no one wanted to leave. Andrea smiled remembering the acrid smell of smoke, as it spiraled, upwards, towards the early morning sky, the aroma of bacon sizzling in a pan, and the sound and smell of freshly ground coffee percolating over an open flame in an old, blackened pot. She remembered how she and her much younger sister would gleefully mug for each other, giggling breathlessly as they broke through the ice of a frozen stream to wash their hands and rosy cheeks before breakfast. Now her head dropped back, and her lids closed, solemnly. Her throat constricted, as a tight ball of sorrow gnarled the pit of her stomach. *Those were happy days,* she thought.

Her misty gaze returned to the streaks of pink and gray clouds stretched across the horizon, gilded by the kiss of the early morning sun, giving it the splendiferousness of enchantment. A wistful sigh escaped her lips, felt a tug on her heartstrings as though being summoned to the mountains. She wished, no she yearned to escape this world, to wander along the trails and gurgling streams, to sit beneath the trees, and scramble over boulders, to restart her life in the same gentle way the mountains began each day—fresh and awesome. In an epiphanic moment, she realized that the mountains were the only place she called home.

Hysterical laughter, much too loud for the early morning hour, came from the TV screen, interrupting Andrea's ruminations; but it wasn't just the uncontrolled chortling through tears of the female anchors, or the deep guffaws of manly laughter coming from somewhere off camera that captured the journalist's attention. Turning her eyes back to the screen, she witnessed the new male, anatomically correct, robotic sex doll, sitting nude in a chair with his back turned to the audience as the camera traveled in and around for a close-up shot of the doll's sexy, steely jawline. Entertainment news, she thought, shaking her head in pure peevishness. In a fit of incredulity, she flipped her tiny remote into the air. "Wut?" she said, scrunching up her face at the irony. "God makes man ... then man makes *sexbots? What a rip-off!*"

Feeling naïve and completely deficient in the ways of the world, she shot to her feet. With an eye to the time, and in serious need of her wayward remote, she shuffled through a stack of press releases. In the meantime, the TV discussion went from the titillating subject of sex dolls, to the rising threat of terrorism around the world, with an emphasis on the US homegrown variety. The anchor was asking in a tone of befuddled cluelessness, "What constitutes a homegrown terrorist?" as though it was the first time she'd ever heard the term.

Spewing out words in a mechanical tone, as though learned by rote and rehearsal, a panel member gave an explanation straight from the dictionary. "It's usually a feeling of alienation, and almost always, ties to a radical group in one way or another."

Grown weary of intentional time delays, and do-overs of some news outlets, trying to grab headlines and slant the news towards their own political view, Andrea popped off with sarcasm, "Where have you guys been for the last twenty years, messing with a Rip Van Winkle sex doll ... or in bed with politicians?"

The screen filled with violent, reprehensible scenes from the Middle East. War porn, the millennials liked to call it. A retired Army General, long on knowledge and experience, was discussing the rapid growth of terrorism across the globe. Lamentingly, he offered, "Our enemy has openly declared war on us ... and frankly, we can't seem to stop them."

Continuing her search for the illusive remote, Andrea tapped her fingers, exhaustively, around the tall stack of archival newspapers she'd brought up from the basement. Her search came to a halt as her eyes rested on a headline. She lifted the top issue from the stack, studying the front page image of a soldier dressed in full, desert camouflage, along with his war dog—both heroes, the headline said. The caption under the picture read: *Camping out in Hell.* Sophisticated tactical gear covered the man's head and chin, giving Andrea only a small glimpse of the warrior's face, but she took special notice of his bodacious smile. *He looks a little gaunt,* she thought, *and a bit ... haunted, perhaps.* A glimmer of possibility for a story idea raised her brow; but when she checked the date of the issue, she found the photo had actually been taken three years earlier—before she'd come to work for the *News.*

In disappointment, her gaze dropped, and she caught a glimpse of the small remote lying beside her sandaled foot, and brightly painted toes. Bending down to rescue it from the floor, she heard the TV anchor ask the General if it was true that our elite, specially trained military, our special forces, the core of the military, were still camping out in Hell, as some were reporting.

Suddenly feeling overly-marinated in news, and recognizing it as a replay of a much older interview, Andrea closed one eye, and knavishly raised the clicker, aiming at the TV screen. The last thing she heard before hitting the *Off* button was the dispirited General, answering in disquietude. "Our military men and women are always in grave danger … they have been for years … and will continue to be."

Letting the paper drop to her lap, she sat back, clutching her coffee mug between both hands. Silence filled her ears. She took a slow, thoughtful sip, allowing the idea of writing an updated piece on the impressive war hero to battle around inside her head—a *what is he doing now* kind of story. She liked the idea, but would her readers; many were anti-war activists.

She took a long sip. *Finding the guy might be a problem,* she thought. She wondered what he might have been doing for the last three years. Was he still in the military … or was he, perhaps, somewhere distilling whiskey, raising goats and legalized marijuana with his bivouac full of kids? According to the main-stream news media, he would, most likely, be found on the dark side of the mountain in a drug-induced stupor, holding his gun to his head in unguarded disillusionment. She grimaced at the image, feeling heartbreaking compassion for all the young veterans. She knew from her reading that the truly brave ones came home and continued in some kind of service to their country, be it military, law enforcement or in some kind of trade, like gunsmithing; but, unfortunately, the pandemic and bad politics had swiftly and cruelly stolen away their jobs.

She glanced at his photo with concernment. Thinking pragmatically, she said, "Of course, there's the very real possibility he might be dead."

At last, she made the decision—she would track this guy down, dead or alive, and write, either a prize-winning story, or a glowing tribute to his memory.

When her cellphone rattled atop her metal desk, and ominously lit up with the name of the new copy editor, all thoughts of the story were wiped away. *God … I don't even have time to read what's already in print,* she lamented. She clicked the Accept button, and spoke in a professional, but friendly, tone. "This is Andi."

Andrea listened. "What do you mean, you quit? This is your first day." Andrea shot a glance at the clock, "You just got here.… What can I do to help you?" She listened, taking the woman's complaints to heart. "I'm sorry you're unhappy … yes, the column is about dead people … I agree, writing obituaries does get depressing; but we hired you, and you agreed to write the obits.…" Andrea listened a while longer. "No, the word sepulcher is not a new term ... it's been a part of the English language for centuries ... read your classic literature. I understand ... yes, I'll be sure to go to hell ... but if you want to tender your resignation, you'll need to talk to Editor Rudd."

After listening to further abusive rants made quite personal, Andrea spoke with finality in simple, no nonsense terms, "Tender your resignation ... or be fired ... the choice is yours ... I'll give Marty your message." With that she clicked off and scribbled a note to her editor on her message pad:

To: Editor Martin Rudd
From: Andrea Daye
Message: Copy editor quit/fired
Reason: She refuses to work with dead people.

Andrea shoved her pad aside in disgust, and let her gaze fall to her lap, where a swatch of golden sunshine streamed through the transom window, and fell across the newspaper as though highlighting—*or glorifying,* the photo, she thought. Lifting the paper, she squinted for a closer look at the soldier's handsome image. *Really nice smile,* she thought, but what was that shadow lurking behind his dark eyes? Was it solemnity ... obstinacy ... maybe even grief? Her brows knitted, and her chin ticked up. *Nah ... he's just a smartass,* she surmised, tossing the yellowing paper back on the funky-smelling heap. A slow, wry grin crossed her lips as a second thought quickly followed: *Smartass might make for a very impressive interview.*

Finally feeling a caffeine lift, she set her mug aside and turned her focus to her computer screen where she got to work editing a piece on the upcoming election for the opinion page. No time to analyze it, but judging by the number of crackpot letters populating her email box, the craziness promised to continue unto perpetuity.

She finally clicked on the Obituary icon, trying to come up with a more favorable way to view the undesirable job at hand. Mocking the tourism industry's rhetorical tautology, she hoped to read about *"the death of a wizened, old centurion, who had lived a long, fruitful life; and while still wearing his muddy, Gortex boots, died blissfully of natural causes while staring into a glorious, gilded sunset."*

Instead, she found herself reading about a drug overdose.

A sense of apprehensiveness permeated her thoughts as she leaned into the monitor. Her eyes narrowed in on the small font. Her mind bogged down with the realization that she was staring at the obit of a mere child. A fretful gasp escaped her lips as she read about a twelve-year-old boy who had died, overnight, of a drug overdose. With professional haste, she corrected the many errors on the extremely short accounting of a young life ended by tragedy.

She slumped against the back of her chair, inwardly groaning with compassion for urban kid who had recently moved into the neighborhood. Just yesterday, she had waved at him as he had struggled to ride his skateboard to the end of his unpaved driveway. Now, she couldn't stop the images of the fresh-faced kid—his bed not slept in, his chair at the breakfast table, unoccupied, his desk at school, abandoned; nor could she stop her feelings of compassion for a mother's grieving heart at the loss of her son.

She swiped at the gathering moisture in her eyes; then pushed out of the chair, chiding herself. *Why hadn't she offered the kid her hilly, paved driveway as a place to skateboard?"*

She walked to the window and gazed out at the long shafts of magnificent sunlight filtering through the trees, and glistening like diamonds across the lightly frosted blades of grass; but she saw none of this. She imagined the world beyond the gently rolling foothills surrounding the mountain, wondering if anyone was out there, trying to put an end to all this insanity. Was anyone really trying to stop drugs from reaching the hands of innocent kids—kids too young, or too dead, to make wise decisions?

Was anyone out there? Her question, on its face, seemed naïve, stupid even; but as an erudite journalist with street smarts honed sharply by her education and profession, she was more than aware of the hordes of policemen, law enforcement officers, federal agents and even the President, trying to push back against the drug culture. She was also aware of the billions of dollars allocated to get the job done. It was a huge sum of money, but it still wasn't solving the problem.

She pushed her grief aside long enough to allow an idea for a second article to quicken in her mind, something of benefit to her readers. *Wouldn't she dearly love to meet, to interview someone who honestly put his life on the line between the dangerous, corrupt culture and America's cherished youth, to get to know the home life and motivations of one of the truly good guys? She could watch him in action … maybe even do a ride-along?* "That would be the story of all stories," she said breathlessly, "especially in this anti-cop culture." She considered the details, and gasped at the audacity of the idea, wondering, *where she might find such a guy.*

Finally, she exhaled with unmitigated determination—she would do it.

Editor Martin Rudd slammed the phone down on his desk and bellowed for his right-arm man. "Andi!"

His harsh tone shook Andrea from her ruminations and clever stratagem. She turned to glare, begrudgingly, through the glass wall separating the two offices.

"Good g-a-w-d...." he whined, egregiously, "I'm going to h-a-n-g myself!" He yelled a second time, his voice sounding irrational. "Andi ... get in here!"

Andrea shook her head and chortled, aloud, "That man has a knack for sucking the life right out of you." With synchronic timing, her desk phone clamored noisily, just as the head of the graphics department suddenly appeared in her doorway, his jaw set, scowling angrily. Without pausing, he spoke, determinedly, ignoring the jangling phone. "I need to have a serious talk with someone around here about Jolene Jorgenson."

Andrea shot him an understanding nod, crossed the room, putting her hand to the phone, "We'll deal with it ... postdeadline," she assured him, bringing home the realization that her story idea would have to be put on hold until things in the newsroom slowed down a bit.

Harrumphing at the probability of that actually happening, she spoke into the phone. "This is Andrea Daye ... how may I help you?" she said, while laying the photo of her smartass soldier, back on the stack of smelly papers. Jolene, the state and city editor—another recent hire— was calling from outside the building. Andrea sat mute listening to the long, abusive diatribe of childish, whiny complaints assaulting her sensibilities like the sound of explosive flatulence across an open mic. When she demanded the day off, and an extra-day's pay, Andrea advised, "Talk to Rudd."

"Good g-a-w-d," Andrea grumped, in Rudd fashion, realizing that this meant another long day for her.

The weary journalist had barely cradled the phone when Laila, the newspaper's photographer rushed into her office, panic stricken. "Andi ... Jolene borrowed my digital camera last night and never returned it. It's got shots of the protest march on it ... I need to file them for today's edition. She's not here, and she doesn't answer her phone ... I don't know where she is. On top of that … Sally's gone into labor … I don't know what to do," she said, frantically.

Andrea immediately hit Jolene's call-back number on her phone. No one answered. "Why'd Jolene take your camera?"

The chagrined photographer spat, "Absolutely no sense of propriety!"

Andrea nodded her understandingly. "Don't you have a backup camera?"

She grimaced. "Yeah, but it's in the shop getting cleaned."

"Okay," she answered with rapidity, "this is an on-going protest. I'll keep trying to reach Jolene … in the meantime … take my smartphone … get several action shots that tell the story … then go support your daughter and welcome your granddaughter into this crazy, upside-down world. I'll crop the photos tonight … and we'll run a full page tomorrow … will that work?"

She laid her phone out in front of the fretting woman. "Be safe."

"Andi, you're the best," she said, smiling.

"File the photos … and don't forget to return my phone," she teased.

Realizing that she would, most likely, be here all night, Andrea grasped the arms of her chair as though lifelines, her head thumping against the headrest. What was she going to do with Jolene? The woman had an immense talent … for sucking the marrow right out of your dead, dry bones!

Andrea's crestfallen gaze slowly brushed across the unlit room, following the wisp of travelling sunlight, now settled between her desk and doorframe. In her disheartened state, she imagined there a figure, a phantom figure—an elusive warrior dressed in sand-colored camouflage, and all but coming alive for the world-weary journalist. In a soft, wistful tone, she spewed her thoughts aloud to the image garnered from the dated, front page headlines.

"Hey … soldier," she whispered, commiseratively, "you're not the only one still camping out in Hell!"

Once the deadline had come and gone, and the presses were running, full-speed-ahead, a set of questioning eyes, blue with pluckily knit brows peeked over a mask and around the door frame. A voice rippling with devilment asked, "Who's still camping out in Hell?"

Andrea lifted her lackluster gaze to take in the newspaper's Lifestyle and Social Media editor, Zoe Coleman. "Andi are you talking to yourself again?"

"Always and forever," she said with embarrassment, deliberately lifting the phone off the hook, and laying it aside, silencing it, temporarily. She tossed her friend a frazzled, questioning glance, and scratched at the nervous rash on her neck. "You heard that in the newsroom?"

Zoe lowered her mask, and shot her a lopsided grin, "No, of course not ... I was lip-reading."

In her own defense, Andrea offered, "You know ... Ernest Hemingway wrote, in *The Old Man and the Sea*, that if a person talks to himself, and actually knows that he's talking to himself, it proves he's not insane."

Zoe chortled, and raised doubting brows. "You had no idea you were talking to yourself ... did you?"

Andrea batted her eyes shut, and shook her head. "Nope ... and what's worse ... good ole' Ernest ended up killing himself, possibly disproving his own theory."

Zoe laughed, "Haven't you finished that book, yet?"

"Rereading...." She answered, "Once for content, once for style and pleasure."

Zoe shook her head in astonishment, "You know, Andi ... you're the only person I've ever met who does that."

"What's next on your reading list?"

Andrea's mouth shot up at the corner, "The Complete Works of Ralph Waldo Emerson."

Zoe shot her a vacuous stare, then glanced up just in time to catch the eye of a young man in a cardinal red-gridded, button-down shirt leaving the editor's office, taking quick steps past Andrea's door. Zoe tossed her head in the guy's direction, and whispered, "Andi, watch out for the new sports editor ... he's buff, he's brash, and he's extremely bright...." she leaned in and lowered her voice, "but, ooh ... is he ever full of himself!"

"Really? David Jennings?" Andrea had already suspected as much. "So you're saying the only available guy around here is a Tool?"

"Well ... I wouldn't go that far, but he's already planning to ask for a raise."

Andrea laughed, sardonically, as she walked to the file cabinet and began rummaging for background information for tomorrow's issue. "O-kay," she offered. "So he's brash and bright, and it sounds like he's already picked up on the official reporter's chant. So, that makes him either a quick study, a hopeless optimist, or...." she snarked, "or he's hungry."

Zoe stepped around the corner of the desk to pluck a long, white cat hair off Andrea's black sweater. "People around here think he looks like a young Chris Pratt." She sucked in a deep breath and her eyes began to shine. "Confidentially ... I wouldn't mind ... if he wanted to guard *my* galaxy," she offered, provocatively.

Andrea slammed the drawer shut. "So you're saying you like your money-grubbing Tools brash and bright?"

"Yeah ... and don't forget buff ... I especially like them buff," Zoe laughed, feigning rakishness.

"I'm confused." Andrea teased, deliberately. "Are we talking about Pratt or Jennings?" She turned around in time to see the sudden deer-in-the-headlights look on Zoe's face.

Again, Andrea turned to the files, grinning and hiking a brow in concealed amusement. She'd never heard Zoe go on about a guy like this. She finally faced her friend, assuming a more professional tone. "So what's up?"

Zoe lowered her voice to a level of confidentially. "Andi ... tomorrow is Mom's night to host her euchre club. They go till midnight, and everybody brings in gobs of food. Mom can't get around, ya know, so I'll help her set up, but after that I'm free to do something else for a few hours. Want to meet for dinner at the Writer's Block Lounge ... say about 6:30? We haven't had a chance to talk much since you've been married ... and I sure can't afford to pay a reputable shrink. Maybe we could even catch the latest superhero flick afterwards?"

Andrea shot her young friend a challenging look. Zoe was the most sane, mature, young woman she knew, but she did have serious financial problems stemming from the care of her aging mother, widowed and physically disabled. She considered her friend's request. Finally, "Yeah, sure ... that would be great, Zoe ... tomorrow ... 6:30." She entered the date in her phone calendar.

Zoe smiled her gratitude, and then peevishly nodded towards Rudd's office. "He's really in a snit today...." She mocked his words and tone, "I'm gonna ... *h-a-n-g* myself!"

Andrea shot her friend a suspicious frown. "You got these offices bugged, or something?"

"Not that interested," Zoe offered, flippantly.

"Yeah ... you'd think he'd been asked to do something ... *journalistically*."

A glance askance showed Rudd about to hyperventilate. "Andrea grabbed her notebook, and the one thing she absolutely could not work without— her coffee mug, which, she figured, also kept her grounded in reality. "Okay Zoe ... I'm locked, I'm loaded, and I'm going in," she said with dramatic flair.

Honing in on her friend's post-deadline whimsicality, Zoe stood erect, and clacked her heels together. "For God and Country!" she said, in feigned solemnity.

Andrea shot her a puzzled, squinty-eyed look.

"It's on the calendar you gave me for my birthday ... the one just like yours," she gestured towards Andrea's desk calendar.

Cradling the phone, Andrea glanced at her beloved, little calendar. "Well it's good to know ... we're on the same page." She smiled, impishly, as she marched out, savoring the moment of levity in her day's routine, but as she exited her office amid the jangling of an incoming call, her heart still grieved for the young kid lying in the stone cold morgue; and her mind clung, commiseratively, to the image of the distressed warrior on the battlefield.

CHAPTER 2

"Raid!" A grizzled, disembodied voice yelled out in warning, followed by gunshots ringing out in the hot, midday sun, echoing off cliffs, and across the white, glittery sands of a forgotten resort on a long-forgotten island. A raid was in progress against a well-orchestrated organization, delivering illegal drugs to the rest of the world. Interrupted by the call-to-arms, the resort's open-aired concert, unplugged and informal, featuring the deep, rich baritone voice of their very own talented, quick-witted manager, slowly ground to a musically, dysfunctional halt.

Disregarding the gunshots, the singer stood down from his tall wicker stool, and in an act of pure showmanship, humorously jacked his knee and guitar to his shoulder, grand finale style. With rare talent and unusual expertise, fingers slid rapidly up and down the strings. Strumming out an exaggerated last chord, he belted out the final note, holding it for an indefinite length of time. At last, he turned laughing eyes to his house musicians, shooting them all a wry, closed-mouth grin, and jocosely offered words in the way of a final farewell, "Sorry mates … but I've gotta run."

He slipped the strap from his shoulder, and handed off the guitar to the youngest band member. "Consider it a gift," he said simply, starting to step away, but not before catching the look of awe and wide-eyed appreciation shooting from the kid's eyes.

"What about my request?" The whine of dismay came from a swooning fan, sitting in a round, wicker chair; both overly large and heavily cushioned. Of obvious wealth, and old enough, and wrinkled enough, to be his grandmother's mother, the woman slurped the end of her third rum *Painkiller,* and fussed, "You promised to sing, *I Can't Forget Her.*"

One to keep a promise, the handsome crooner stopped mid-step, and shot the woman an apologetic, if not patient, grin. "Ma-am … Dierks Bentley did a smashup video of that song a few years back; but if you really like my sound, there's a stack of my latest CDs on the registration desk." Preparing to quickly exit stage left, the crooner chuckled, duplicitously, "I suppose we could say they're on the house."

"I like the sound, alright," she answered, her speech slurred by drunkenness, "but I like your hot, sexy body even better," she offered shamelessly, giggling and poking her female companion with puffy, multi-ringed fingers.

The singer groaned, inwardly, dropping his head to knuckle-swipe sweat from his brow—he hated this kind of attention; nevertheless, he shot her, what amounted to, a hot, sexy wink.

With pressed lips, purplish but puckish, the woman scolded, "Why haven't *you* made a video?"

Moments later, at the rear of the multi-building complex, the same young man squared his body, grabbed hold of the sharp, cutting rock of a steep cliff and hoisted himself off the ground. Using moves he'd first learned as a pre-teen, he climbed above the roof lines, towards the top of the steep, rugged cliff. With hands stretching out, one after the other, he searched for his next finger hold; and by the pure force and strength of his muscled biceps, pulled his weight straight up, one tormenting inch at a time. His grip strength had been developed at a very early age, as well, but he had to admit, it had been a long while since he'd been rock climbing.

Now his dark brows furrowed in concert with each flex of his sinewy leg muscles. Sweat, profuse and salty, rolled off his forehead, and into his eyes, burning and stinging, before dampening his smartly-groomed beard.

When, at last, he found himself perched upon a high ledge, he let his hot breath escape, and allowed his taut muscles to relax. For the first time since leaving the military, he was more than grateful he'd continued the chin lifts and the thousands of pushups. With hands too bloody to swipe away the annoying sweat, he breathed out a grateful sigh of relief at the sudden gust of tropical wind hitting his face.

Panting heavily, he lay back against the cool rock, laughing at his predicament. For two long years, he'd been floating around in this cesspool, this sewer below the level of ordinary life, working in this particular job for only three months. In reality, he'd been preparing for this escape his entire life. Unfortunately, as fate would have it, his gloves had suddenly disappeared, and his last pair of thick, "Made in Vermont" socks had gone missing from the resort's clothes dryer that very morning, as had all his socks. They were favorites among the pilots flying in from the south, and heading north to colder temperatures.

Upon discovery of the missing socks, he'd let out a troubled breath, but quickly reflected on earlier training: *a good soldier always takes care of his feet.* Figuring himself to be a damned good soldier, he understood from experience why taking care of your feet held such high priority.

Training from another source kicked in, as well—*use whatever resource you have available.* He'd searched the Lost and Found, and pulled out the only thing that might be of possible use: knee socks left behind by an octogenarian, gay couple on their honeymoon—bird scientists. The aging couple had celebrated their marriage; and he, as resort manager, had toasted them with champagne and showered them with best wishes.

He'd held the socks up for closer inspection, one in each hand, wondering if the colorful hosiery could actually work for him, knowing, full well, that their owner would prefer they not be worn by a straight dude—LGBTQ stripes, the symbol for all gender differences other than straight. He frowned. He'd always accepted others as they were, but his facial expression bespoke his attitude towards those who wanted to make his penchant towards masculinity a mental health issue. He gave his head a half shake and snarked aloud, "It's not a choice."

He considered his image, his *manly man* image as those in the military preferred to call it, and he'd snickered at the thought. Gay, straight—or any otherkin—what difference could a pair of socks make? In straight, blunt mansplaining terms—his libido was all but dead, anyway.

He'd strapped a sheath and ankle blade to each leg, and then sat staring, at the socks especially marketed to gay men. Finally, he'd reasoned, "It is what it is … camouflage." He slipped the socks over his straight, narrow toes and long, tanned feet, finally tugging them up over his multiple weapons, up to his knees. Imperative that he look authentic, he had grabbed his field glasses from his office.

While trying to make his quick get-away, he had, grievously, run into the same little, old lady by the outdoor sauna. Her hand had shot high above her head in aggrievement, brandishing his CD between her stubby, little fingers. "Your picture, bud…." she squawked in loud, unforgiving terms, "isn't …

anywhere ... on ... here!" She'd given the CD a shake to accentuate each and every taunting word.

"Sorry, ma'am," he offered, shooting her an unpretentious grin, "I guess I'm just a little camera shy." Her head twisted and her mouth opened for another sour diatribe, but by then, the crooner had vanished. Backtracking to the Lost and Found, he grabbed a camera left behind in the breakfast nook. Then he latched on to one more item belonging to the adorable couple—a tan, crushable, safari hat. Amusement settled on his face. Had the happy, absentminded ornithologists left with any of their possessions? He shook his head and chortled at his good fortune.

Now, with no time to waste, the climber continued to move upward. When sporadic gunfire rang out from a closer range, he grabbed a handful of vines to take pressure off his fingers. He froze in place, leaning against the sweltering rock. Careful to keep his feet tucked, he wondered if the butt-ugly, fern-print shirt he'd picked up at a Good Will dump was blending in with the thick, verdant foliage. The shirt, a size too small, hugged his biceps and gapped open at the chest. He gave his head a half-shake, recognizing the irony: he looked like something on the gawd-awful cover of one of his sister's hot romance novels—one that, as a tween, had given him great pleasure in the merciless teasing.

He got a tighter hold on the vine and looked across the water. Every time he'd gazed upon the shimmering, blue water and its translucence, a fleeting image of a young girl's laughing eyes had fluttered across his mind, along with some old emotions. He'd met her by chance, and by chance he'd saved her from drowning.

"Why can't I forget her?"

Eyeing the ever-darkening sky, he studied the direction of the storm gathering to the south. It looked threatening. He hoped to be gone from the islands, and out of its path, before it hit. Tamping down his concern on that count, he switched his focus to a large, V-shaped squadron of brown pelicans. His eyes followed one particular female as she soared high into the air, then plunged, head first, into the water, finally surfacing with a beak load of small fish. Apparently happy with her catch, she now flew in his direction.

Suddenly, both man and bird, simultaneously, heard the crack of a rifle and the loud burst of rapid gunfire. With wings flapping and webbed feet dangling lackadaisically behind, the pelican flew a short distance across the shimmering water to a tiny, uninhabited isle off the coast, taking shelter in a mangrove tree as gunshots pinged sharply both inside and outside of the building. The climber hunkered down, wishing that getting off the island could be as easy for him. He was, unfortunately, not a pelican; nor was he a drug dealer.

In just a matter of minutes, Matthew J. McCormick, an honorably decorated Special Forces war hero, had become the proverbial man without a country, with the very real possibility that this whole thing could still go sideways. Not only was he fleeing the island, but the US agents involved in the raid, who knew nothing about his undercover work.

His mission had been to track the origin of the drugs, identify the brains and muscle, and locate the point-of-entry into the US—which he had done successfully. Following two long years of fact gathering, and the lost lives of several agents, the US had, finally, triggered an all-out raid on this sparsely populated island. Unfortunately, their massive laboratories—their feeder system, hidden deep in the South American jungle—still remained intact, and a continued search for numeral Uno's whereabouts would take more investigative effort, more agents, and certainly, more money; but for all practical purposes, his job here on the island had come to an end. Protecting his identity, however, was vital, for stored in his head was a wealth of information that had yet to be passed on to headquarters. His actual contribution to the over-all crime world was infinitesimal; still, should he be arrested along with the drug runners, he would be tried and sentenced to life imprisonment for trafficking in drugs. The US would not own up to their ties to him; nor could the agency or the military come forward to claim him without blowing his cover. Now he was left with only one option: don't get caught!

From his heightened view, the astute climber watched as brother agents combed the white-sand beaches with precision, skill and dedication, gathering up the drug-running pilots lodging at the resort—the very same rascals who had absconded with his socks. When they seized McCormick's bungalow, perched high on a cliff, over-looking the shimmering, paradisial water, he breathed out a heavy sigh of mixed emotions; but only one thing mattered: all the dangerous undercover work and the lost lives of the agents who had gone before him, were finally coming to fruition. Thus far, no one had spotted the man dangling, daringly, from the ledge by one hand. He could've easily been spotted—had they only looked up. And so he continued to climb to the only place he deemed safe—the lush tropical forest at the top of the lofty precipice.

Soon, a renewed crack of gunfire brought his mind back to the present danger.

He hung for a beat by his bloody fingertips, breathing air deep into his lungs. When pain shot through each finger, becoming almost unbearable, he groaned, and began to mimic the old lady, "Why haven't you made a video?" he quipped, using his ire, and her voice, to fuel the necessary fire within. Like a well-oiled machine, he again pulled his weight straight upwards. Panting heavily, he fell to the floor of a small, hollowed out cave gasping for breath. He lay prostrate with exhaustion.

In time, he rolled over, his glassy eyes staring at the hard rock ceiling, dripping with moisture. His eyes dropped to his fingers, dripping with blood. He choked out a ragged whisper, "This ... is ... why ... I haven't made ... a fuckin' video."

After a short rest, McCormick continued to climb. Upon smelling freedom, he reached for his next finger hold on a jagged out-cropping. As he prepared to fling his body over the top, gunfire chattered out from below, stirring the air and sending bullets whizzing past his ear. He sniggered at the humor in the situation as bullets glanced and binged sharply off the ledge all around him. *Damned if someone hadn't finally looked up!*

Suddenly, the slimy rock exploded, sending a barrage of debris in all directions. Rain pelted his back as the ledge fell away beneath his feet, leaving him grappling for the only thing left to grab hold of—a single twining vine. Aware that the weight of his body could pull the vine's roots right out of the rocks in a matter of seconds, he scrambled to the top of the plateau, and quickly dropped to his belly, hugging the ground amidst a reign of ricocheting bullets. Who in the hell was trying to kill him, and why? It was imperative that he stay out of this fight. In sheer dauntlessness, McCormick inched closer to the edge, his piercing glare cutting through the heavy rain. Raising field glasses, he made instant recognition.

Brantley Stone!

CHAPTER 3

Editor Rudd waggled his arthritic finger towards the chair, "Sit," he bellowed, but Andrea remained standing at the front of his desk. "Marty, don't forget … you're addressing the state-wide, high school Honor Society after school … in the gym … six-thirty … you might want to freshen up and put on a clean shirt and tie for that one."

Rudd nodded his head, indicating that he'd heard her, but he kept her waiting, as though time had no value. Having tons of work to do, she sat, impatiently sipping coffee, intermittently checking her phone messages, and then finally the news. As the minutes wasted away, and after she'd checked the temperature, weather radar, and the long-range forecast for the next two weeks, she found herself picking white cat hairs, long and disgusting, off her short, gray skirt. The impish idea to kill the cat crossed her mind. *Scratch that,* she thought, revising her thinking. *I love cats—just not this particular cat.*

Just as she was about to choose a new farcical emoji to accompany an email to Zoe, her editor spoke again without raising his head, "It seems Miss D-a-y-e," he stretched out her name and held on to it, "that your story on yesterday's front page has stirred up quite a controversy."

"My story?" A look of feigned disappointment crossed her face. "Marty, I'm crushed … I thought we were a team," she teased, lightly.

Her editor bristled. "Some of our more sensitive readers have been offended."

She let out her breath. "Let me guess … soccer moms … right?" She offered, "Isn't there anyone left in the world not offended by the truth?"

Rudd continued in a blustery tone as though Andrea had not spoken. "And there have been complaints about your drug series in the Sunday edition."

Complaints? Andrea braced for the coming admonishment. She leaned in towards her boss, giving him a gentle reminder. "Marty ... you do remember giving me the assignment ... and signing off on the finished product, right?"

He shot her a dismissive glance.

She leaned back in her chair, impatience clouding her face. When her own state had been catapulted into the country's number one position for overdose deaths awhile back, her editor had tossed the story in her lap. She had—in no way—wanted the assignment, and had tried, desperately, to escape it by hiring a new reporter; but that move had exploded into a long, drawn out saga of bad news. The minute the reporter had been threatened, he'd quit, and filed a lawsuit against the *News* for putting him in harm's way; and the story had been tossed back to her like a hot potato, and a fine mashed mess that turned out to be.

Now, her voice waxed serious, and she leaned in towards her editor. "Why are you ... all of a sudden ... so concerned about John Q. Public? I thought newspapers aspired to tell the ugly truth, and let the chips fall where they may ... at least, that's what I was taught."

Rudd's face reddened, as he felt the sting of her insult. He swiveled his chair away from her. His voice loudened. "Andrea ... we're not in Kansas anymore ... we're living in a new era."

"Are you saying I don't understand the world I'm living in?" she challenged.

"People's opinions about drugs have changed a lot over the last few years. Many don't see them as the evil they once did. Others think we've lost the war on drugs ... they think we should stop wasting our money on the fight and simply legalize them."

With the young boy's obit still fresh in her mind, Andrea slid to the edge of her chair and countered, indignantly, "Oh, p-u-l-e-a-s-e! What we're living in is the Era of Misinformation ... drug use has skyrocketed by a whopping one hundred-percent, plus; and now heroin, crack cocaine, and new synthetic, killer drugs in powder and pill form, are flooding across the border; and not just into the cities, but into the rural areas as well. They don't see them as an evil, Marty, because they're getting filthy rich from the sales. Trust me ... they're still a negative among people who expect to live a quality life without being sucked down a giant, hell hole. Marty, our very own state has led the country in heroin over-dose deaths ... how can that be accepted by any sane person?"

Andrea, working alone, had devoted the last three months to her investigative series, doing extensive research on other cities, and reporting their methods for dealing with the problem. She had even gone so far as to interview governors and mayors all across the country, proving that her own town was looking pretty bad by comparison; yet now her state was bragging that drug use was down. Was that actually the case, or were an inordinate amount of drugs finding their way into their communities, and being covered up by politicians, as she suspected. She did agree, however, that drug use was no longer a problem; *it had become, instead, a full-blown, killer epidemic!*

Rudd considered her words, refusing to meet her hot gaze. "Alright, I'm going to level with you." He tipped his head back and looked at the ceiling in deep thought. "I've started getting calls from the feds, and they're breathing fire down my neck. They want to send some hot-shot agent all the way from D.C. to talk to you. The guy is highly educated—supposedly a real dynamo. He's had some kind of special training and experience in these matters."

Andrea quickly dismissed Rudd's concern. "The feds send agents all over the country, and they're all specially trained dynamos."

Rudd's eyes hardened. "They want to know where *you've* been getting your information, and I want to know what you're going to tell them?"

What was Andrea going to tell the feds? She stiffened with anger. "I'm not telling them a damned thing!" She set her mug down with a thud and jumped to her feet. She leaned against Rudd's desk. "Marty, my sources are ... as always ... confidential under the law. I will not divulge who they are—that would put *them* in danger—but I'll tell you what they're saying."

She stood to pace the floor. "I've already mentioned our state's high standing in the nation; well, now I'm being told that this thing exceeds our wildest nightmares. Marty, we're talking about cartels and international terrorists groups—working together! Marijuana sales are peanuts compared to this thing ... they're dragging in an excess of $15 million-plus a year—and that's just for one group alone ... there are *thousands* of groups."

Andrea turned to face Rudd. She planted her feet and reiterated, "There are *thousands* of groups ... and there are whispers that this thing goes all the way up the food chain, and has for several years." She paused and turned away, deliberately giving Rudd time to digest the implication of her words.

"All the way up the chain, meaning what?" Rudd asked, a little too contemptuously.

She slid into her chair, "Meaning … all the way to the top."

Rudd rolled his eyes, and sighed, deeply.

"Marty, I know that some of these locals are deliberately trying to mislead me, just to get me off their own sordid trail."

In the back of her mind, Andrea had begun to wonder what an interview with a federal agent might entail. Being deliberately obstinate wasn't normally her way of doing business, but as far as the agent was concerned, her stance on not sharing the names of her contacts would stand. She fully intended to hand over every bit of information she'd gathered to the proper authorities; but, not right now. Trust was a big issue here—too many things were askew. She and she alone, had to determine who would be the recipient of that wealth of information.

She knew it was useless to try to reason with Rudd; but he was right about one thing—they sure as hell weren't in Kansas anymore. There were rumors that some of the government's very own agents had sunk to drug-running, as verified by the morning news; even her husband had alluded to that fact on several occasions. She believed the claim that 99.9 percent of agents were honorable and true blue, but with the report of imposters in the morning news, it wasn't without reason to believe that perhaps one or more had gone rogue. Even the agent Rudd had talked to on the phone could not be above suspicion; it was certainly a possibility. Drug money, she knew, didn't just speak; it sang a loud, Siren's song especially during this time of pandemics. She took a deep breath, realizing for the first time that she was afraid to trust anyone with what she knew, and that included her boss.

"Marty, if I leak this information too soon, before the feds are prepared to act on it, *my* life could be in danger!" She looked long and hard at her editor. "See the problem?"

Rudd's face remained stoic. He didn't doubt her story for a second. If Andrea Daye made an accusation, he knew she had the proof to back it up. It was just that simple.

At last Andrea saw understanding flicker across her boss's face and she let her breath escape slowly, not realizing until that moment that she had stopped breathing. She shot out of the chair. "Before I talk to the feds, I've got to know, beyond a shadow of a doubt, that we can trust them … that they've done their homework … and that they're ready to move in and make arrests; otherwise, it's simply too dangerous—for all of us, Marty."

Rudd shifted his considerable bulk in his large, over-stuffed, leather chair, and stared back at Andrea with dark eyes, hollow and baggy. "Well, Ms. Daye … it looks like you've written yourself into a hell of a mess."

CHAPTER 4

After a short rest, McCormick continued to climb. Upon smelling freedom, he reached for his next finger hold on a jagged out-cropping. As he prepared to fling his body over the top, gunfire chattered out from below, stirring the air and sending bullets whizzing past his ear. He sniggered at the humor in the situation as bullets glanced and binged sharply off the ledge all around him. *Damned if someone hadn't finally looked up!*

Suddenly, the slimy rock exploded, sending a barrage of debris in all directions. Rain pelted his back as the ledge fell away beneath his feet, leaving him grappling for the only thing left to grab hold of—a single twining vine. Aware that the weight of his body could pull the vine's roots right out of the rocks in a matter of seconds, he scrambled to the top of the plateau, and quickly dropped to his belly, hugging the ground amidst a reign of ricocheting bullets. Who in the hell was trying to kill him, and why? It was imperative that he stay out of this fight. In sheer dauntlessness, McCormick inched closer to the edge, his piercing glare cutting through the heavy rain. Raising field glasses, he made instant recognition.

Brantley Stone!

McCormick watched the man in familiar dress pull an AK-47 semi-automatic assault rifle over his shoulder, and aim in his direction. An amused chuckle rattled McCormick's chest at his good fortune. He had found his man—so to speak.

His mind began to whirr at this sudden turn of events. This was the man who had sold out his team in Afghanistan, a mission that had gone gruesomely sideways; but that was only where the irony began. McCormick was convinced that he and he alone, had been the sole intended target—when, in truth, he had been the only survivor.

Two years ago, the warrior-turned-agent had found this man surprisingly working as a member of the agency's very own legal counsel, and passing classified, top-secret information on to one of the country's most ruthless enemies. McCormick, with the help of his brother, also a federal agent, had followed the greedy, dark-eyed lawyer into Mexico and then into Central America. Unfortunately, as the feds had ranks on the man, he had mysteriously disappeared, as though vaporized.

Not one to accept failure, the warrior's next move was to take on multiple false identities. His incessant island hopping had put him on the enemy's trail, starting from South America, and leading, surprise-surprise, back to the beautiful equatorial waters of the warm tropical islands.

Abandoning his own unsullied persona as an officer and a gentleman, and then later forfeiting his good reputation as a U.S. Federal Agent, he went deeper undercover. Passing himself off as a brooding, washed-out veteran, disgruntled with his country and unable to provide for his wife and very large extended family—a loser with a capital L—the young War Horse grew his hair and beard long, tatted his body, pierced an ear, and hired on with one of the West's newest and largest criminal elements.

Now, Stone, his long-time nemesis, stood before him in living color, wearing the Agency's blue windbreaker as camouflage, and blending into the sea of agents in an effort to avoid capture.

Clever, McCormick thought—*diabolically clever.*

A disturbing thought hit the agent. Had Stone just happened upon him, today, or had he deliberately turned the tables, making McCormick the hunted one. The answer to that question could present major problems for him later, should they both be lucky enough to make it off this island alive. Stone, once a fellow warrior and colleague, could identify him; but McCormick's own welfare today was inconsequential. It was imperative that he make it back to the states alive to file his report.

A second, more troubling thought followed. Had Stone gotten inside information about the timing of *this* raid? *It certainly looked that way.*

Meanwhile, another blue-jacketed agent heard gunshots coming from the rear of the Inn, and cornered the building. Startled to come face to face with Stone, the agent froze.

Even from this highest point, McCormick immediately recognized the second man as the dedicated, hardworking father of four young kids. His memory flashed back: the Washington, D.C. skyline had turned to dusk, and this man had spread a soft, blue blanket under the trees lining the scenic walkway along the Potomac, anticipating an awesome display of fireworks. McCormick and his older brother, Clint, had stood under the low-hanging branches, dripping sweat, and guzzling down bottles of cold water after spending the afternoon jogging trails along the historic river, just for the novelty of doing it as patriots—and as brothers.

Their colleague had sipped his way through a six-pack, burping right along with the newborn son he bounced, belly down, across his knee. Papa had talked to them about the joys of family after returning from a wild goose chase across the country for the last two weeks. Eventually, his brother had wandered off and the colleague had to pee. He, unceremoniously, handed off the sweet-smelling, fuzzy-headed infant to McCormick, not returning for a full thirty minutes—just long enough for the kid to spring a leak, and the sweet baby smell to turn to stink. At first, McCormick had bristled under the responsibility, frantically searching the crowd for the kid's mother; but by then the fireworks display had begun. McCormick had stood with the squalling kid shoved up tight against his chest, his man-sized hand cupped over the infant's tiny ear as the babe was first exposed to the noisy, patriotic explosions of fun and frolic, all-the-while wishing he could cover his own ears. After a time, the two had bonded. McCormick figured the little urine dispenser would be about three years old, by now.

With crimson-stained fingers, he drew his gun from his shoulder holster. "Bring it on," he sniggered, blinking away a drop of burning, salty sweat, and taking aim.

Suddenly, his stomach lurched, and his throat gurgled, "Aw … hell!" In the two short seconds it had taken to blink for a clearer shot, Stone had raised his 9 mm Glock to arm's length, and at close range, shot the unsuspecting ground agent in the face. McCormick scrambled to his feet, watching the body fall away. His heart hammered against his chest wall, already grieving the loss.

Once again, Stone took shots in McCormick's direction, now laying low, playing possum, but watching the man's every move, memorizing every detail about his enemy. After a while, he watched Stone shoulder his rifle. With his ego obviously slaked, mistakenly thinking he'd killed his long-time nemesis, Stone picked up a backpack and walked out of gun range.

Now, McCormick became inflamed in self-directed anger. *Damn ... he knew Stone ... he should have seen this coming.* He ran a hand down his hairy chin, and swallowed hard at the rancid taste in his mouth, realizing that he would've willingly traded his own life for that of the agent. He would have made the sacrifice—for in his heart he held great respect for a father's place in a young kid's life.

McCormick holstered his gun, all the while making a mental note to visit the now-fatherless child.

-◄O►-

An over-whelming feeling of abandonment washed over Andrea, as she sat staring perceptively at her editor. Very early in her career at the newspaper, she had learned not to expect support from Marty Rudd. He was totally dysfunctional in his role as editor. In order to maintain a low budget, he hired only young inexperienced reporters; but he had neither the patience, nor the perseverance necessary to create the nurturing atmosphere the young reporters needed to develop their skills

At one time, Rudd had been the best newspaper columnist in the state, cultivating an obsession for getting awards. He had certainly gotten his lion's share, as verified by the many plaques upon his wall. Unfortunately, after years of heavy drinking, he was tired and irritable—burned out. Lately, he had become withdrawn and aloof, abdicating most of his editorial responsibilities to his young staff; and because of his lack of dedication to his profession, the newsroom had quickly gone to shambles.

Every newspaper needed a strong city editor, someone capable and willing to do the hard, arduous task; the *News* didn't have one. Instead, Rudd had hired Jolene Jorgenson, a woman dressed from head to toe in haughtiness, and over-dosed on her own self-worth—and maleficence. This woman was not only uneducated in language arts and journalism; Jolene was simply uneducated.

As a result of that hiring, each day brought a long series of crisis, which proved to be a source of contention and constant frustration for Andrea, who had left that position months earlier to become the Assistant Editor. Now, because of the shortage in personnel, she had been forced to take back many of the responsibilities of writing front page material. Out of necessity, she did much of the editing of the inside pages and special sections—not to mention the column she wrote, and the editing for the Sunday edition. She feared that if this down-hill spiral continued, she would end up a one-man newsroom.

The young journalist often wondered why the owners tolerated Rudd's running such a shabby paper; she thought it looked as though they didn't want nor care if the news got out to the public; and the truth was, at this point, Andrea had started to feel embarrassed at bearing the title of Assistant Editor for this newspaper.

But in spite of all her problems, one loomed larger than the rest: someone—she figured it was Jolene—had started hacking on her stories, deleting key sentences or paragraphs, changing the tone and overall focus of every story. She couldn't figure out how she was getting her hands on the articles, since she was rarely in the building; not to mention the fact that she lacked the education, talent and ability to do the job. It was all very troubling.

Now, she pressed Rudd, repeating her argument, making sure her editor understood her precarious position. "Sir ... I suggest we keep our sources confidential until I feel comfortable sharing them."

Rudd pondered her position for a moment, and then finally answered, "Alright ... we'll go ahead and run the articles, but I'm warning you Andrea ... I'm not getting *my* ass caught in the middle of this thing."

Andrea had always wondered if Rudd would be there for the really big one; now she knew—he wouldn't. She took a sip of coffee gone cold, regretted it, and set the mug back down on the table with a thud. "Trust me...." she replied, as hopelessness settled into her being, "I never assumed otherwise."

She stood up, and headed for the door. Suddenly she stopped, and spun back around. "While I'm here, Marty," she said, determination creeping into her voice. "Jolene has been chopping on my stories ... I don't like it. She butchered the hell out of yesterday's copy, and completely changed the focus of the whole article. Frankly, I didn't even know she was in the building." She paused, and crossed her arms, defensively. "I don't normally care where we run my stories ... yesterday they ran between breast implants and penile augmentation ads .... but I don't care about that ... just don't let her mess with the *content* of my stories!"

"Well, she's the city editor; it's her decision to make...."

Angrily, she cut off his words. "And *I'm* the Assistant Editor of this newspaper, and I'm saying she doesn't know a lead paragraph from the inside label of a man's pair of jockey shorts. If we don't start running things with some kind of professionalism, we're going to get our asses sued … again!"

"We can always print a retraction." Rudd offered, dismissively.

Andrea had heard enough. "Yeah … right. A few more mistakes and our entire front page will be an effin retraction!"

She hissed, "How many awards will that getcha, Marty?"

Andrea's eyes combed over the packed gymnasium full of young, energized, students—her audience. "My name is Andrea Daye … I'm the Assistant Editor of the Forest Hills Daily News … and I have never, deliberately, taken anything stronger than an aspirin."

Stepping away from the microphone, she paused for the polite round of applause.

At the back of the room, stood the principal and assistant principal, as well as the dignified, silver-headed teacher who had drafted Andrea, at the very last minute, to step in and speak to the already assembled crowd of high school students. Marty Rudd had originally been scheduled to speak; but when he had failed to show up, the overwrought educator had called the Daily News assistant editor. Meeting her in the school's front office, the spry, older woman dressed in khaki-colored leggings, a long, peachy top and orange kicks, had hustled Andrea down the hallway at a breakneck speed, delivering her to the gym just in the nick of time to shake hands with the principal and a visiting politician, before stepping onto the stage.

The woman had been a riot, cracking jokes, and feeding encouragement to her fainthearted, substitute speaker. Andrea tried to recall her name, but with all the uproar and rushing excitement, it had completely slipped her mind. She'd look it up later, give her a call, and make her a friend; but as for Rudd—he had just better be dead!

CHAPTER 5

McCormick cocked an ear. He heard no crackle of gunfire, no yelp of menacing dogs coming after him—nothing but silence. Had he escaped?

The rain stopped, temporarily, and for a long moment he stood breathing the pungent, humid air deep into his lungs. At long last, exhilaration gurgled up in his heart and soul, and a wry grin settled across his lips. *No drug— heroin or anything manufactured—could ever imitate this God-given feeling of freedom.*

In heartened mindlessness, he walked until he came upon a giant spider web blocking his path. He stopped to admire the creation, studying the angle of sunlight filtering through the clouds and trees, and observing the shimmering raindrops, still clinging to the dewy, gossamer webbing.

His thoughts returned to the girl who had stolen his heart the moment he'd first laid eyes on her … the girl he'd carried with him to West Point, to Afghanistan, and onto this island. *I don't even know where she lives … by now she'd either be married and knee-deep in kids, or as his salty military buddies liked to joke, deep in lesbian knees.* He chuckled at the military's way of clearly getting to the bottom of things.

Suddenly, a blizzard of frolicking, white-winged butterflies swooped in around him, fluttering as though in a world of fantasy. They completely surrounded him; and then, as one, quickly swished away like a whimsical breeze, and were gone, leaving him staring at a struggling Great Southern White caught in intricate, but lethal webbing. "Aw hell," he groused, knocking away the silky entrapment, setting the resplendent butterfly free.

"I didn't even get her name," he said, his mind still consumed with the girl.

McCormick sought out his route to the airport, tromping through dense undergrowth, not particularly liking the fetid smell of the fading blossoms. The euphoria that had, so profusely, accompanied his freedom was gone. As pain shot through his fingers, it brought him to the realization that it would be a long while before he could ever make another run up and down guitar strings—if ever; then came the hard-hitting realization that he wasn't the indestructible, young man he had once been. This thought weighed heavy on his heart, for he had almost always been the tallest, the strongest, and the best at whatever he did.

He had volunteered for this mission. Neither his skill-set, nor his moral code had required him to be a cold-blooded killer—he wasn't, and never would be; but he was constantly reminded of the hardening of his emotions as he'd been forced to forsake almost every honor code oath he had ever taken in his youth, just to stay alive. For the last two years, he had been shrink-wrapped in camouflage, skulking around, hugging the shadows, seeking truth. Unfortunately, in so doing, his entire life had become a lie. Before this mission, he had always liked himself—today, he didn't.

Another memory came to mind: as a young boy growing up in the church he had sat, squirming, through sermon after sermon hearing about the Light: a loving, caring savior with the ability to keep his soul from Hell. His grizzled grandfather often sat in the pew beside him in full military dress, his chest loaded with medals—chest candy, he called it. He would tap his grandson's jiggling knee impatiently, and whisper in a breath smelling of coffee, cigarettes and bold authority, "If you don't sit still, kid, I'm going to dunk you in the creek."

One Sunday morning the kid bristled and sassed back, "Bring it on Old Man."

Two things had happened as a result of that one audacious remark. Following the service he'd gotten, unceremoniously, dumped in the swollen, rapidly churning creek, as promised. But as he'd sunk deep into the fast moving water, shocked by the cold temperature, and holding his breath, he'd begun to flail, stubbornly, beneath the surface. At that moment, something both strange and wonderful had happened to him. He'd discovered that he loved rising to the challenge, finding a new strength and confidence in his ability to stay alive; not just in the swollen waters, but in the world, in general. He'd also found a new respect for his grandfather's way of delivering a message, and thereafter, happily answered to the nickname, McCreek. He chuckled at the memory, at his grandfather's living example of tough love.

As young McCormick came to a better understanding of the Light, the summer following his high school graduation, he'd gone into his dad's pastoral study and talked at length about something worming its way through his heart; then he'd asked forgiveness for his sins, and dedicated his life to Jesus Christ.

The following day he left for West Point, and was soon trained to suppress his tender thoughts and to tamp down his emotions. His life had become rough and real, but his military training and his diverse physical skills helped him escape uncommon dangers. He possessed all the skills sorely sought by the military: tenacity, and the ability to assess situations and make decisions, quickly and soundly. Those non-emotional, split-second decisions and the ability to keep calm under battlefield situations had kept him alive time and again. It also helped him rise rapidly in rank; but it had been his undying, never give up attitude that had earned him his *Badass* title in a very honorable way.

On the down side, his life had become lonelier than he could have ever imagined. In Afghanistan, he had enjoyed the comradery of his brothers-in-arms, but as they'd loaded body bag after body bag onto transport planes headed back to the States, the soldiers had dubbed it, "Camping out in Hell" which had been widely covered by the news media and written about extensively at the time. Most recently, he had used the catchphrase to describe his life of the last two years. He had worked completely alone, living amongst the enemy as one of their own. To his way of thinking, you couldn't get any lonelier, or closer to Hell's door than that. He'd clung to his sense of humor and his easy-going manner; but for all practical purposes, McCormick felt like a walking dead man.

On dark days, his faith had been his polestar. While he'd never seen visions, or burning bushes; nor heard the voice of God, he'd escaped dangers, miraculously and inexplicitly, while others had not. He never talked about it, but his close-call experiences kept him clinging to a belief in a higher power.

And now, he still believed enough to gratefully gaze up at the awe-inspiring, star-studded sky, expecting to be heard—heard by someone other than roving, rogue satellites, governmental listening devices, and high-tech cameras with the ability to make eye and facial recognition in order to instantaneously determine his exact position.

He spoke quietly, sincerely, "Father, forgive me my sins."

Moisture lurked at the base of his thick, dark lashes, but finding that particular emotion unsettling, he quickly shook off the tender feelings, replacing them with ones of deep satisfaction towards the completion of a difficult mission. He took in a breath of fresh air, and let it out slowly. Even if he never made it off this island, alive, his mission, with the help of God, was one hell of a success.

Reaching a pre-tagged clump of trees, McCormick listened for a moment then dropped to his knees. *Just maybe,* he thought, as he pulled a trash bag full of clothing from the lush, pungent undergrowth. He backed away from the shrub, and straightened, brushing away a cluster of red bugs. *Just maybe I've gotten lucky enough that only my socks will go to prison.* Somewhere in the stillness behind him, a twig snapped. Hearing the fall of light footsteps, he cautiously turned around. Dark eyes, bulging with anger, glowered back at him.

A dark-skinned kid, somewhere within the age and range of a boy scout, began to dance around on bare feet, wielding a very large machete around his head and across his denuded chest, as if in warning. Coming to a sudden halt, and with wide-spread legs and bent knees, he thrust the machete high into the air as though preparing to strike down on something hard. "You are the Stone?" he asked in broken English.

Surprised to hear the name, but maintaining a stoic countenance, McCormick spoke as though hearing it for the first time, "Stone? Hell no, man … who's Stone? I'm Robin Goldfinch … er. I'm an ornithologist." He lifted his field glasses and shoved them forward, towards the kid. "You know … bird watcher … on vacation … staying at the inn. I'm checking out all the local tourist traps around here." When the boy looked puzzled, he added, "You know … the ruins, the artifacts, the ancient buildings. I was hoping to photograph an exotic bird or two, but hell…." He grimaced and looked around at the tops of the trees in feigned disgruntlement, "The only ones I've seen, so far, are those … damned, ugly, brown pelicans."

As McCormick's voice dropped with disappointment, his hands dropped to the straps on his field glasses, fingering them, testing for strength and durability should they need to be put to use later.

He dropped to one knee, and made a big show of latching his sandal and pulling up his colorful knee socks in a veiled action, all-the-while loosening the ankle blade hidden beneath.

At last, he stood, smiling, hopefully projecting innocence. He continued his line of spoofery as he reached for his camera. "Do you … do you mind if I take a selfie … a photo of the two of us," he asked. "I love the simple authenticity of your costume, but I don't understand how you can stand to go barefoot," he rambled. "Are your parents throwing a house party or something?" He grinned from ear-to-ear, mocking a tourist awash in ignorance. McCormick was well-practiced in role playing; he'd been doing it for years.

"No!" the boy answered, emphatically. "No photo … no party!"

Having earlier witnessed the kid's display of fancy footwork, McCormick decided to save his own dance fight for another day. Instead, he brought his hands forward, preparing for hand to hand combat—should it come to that.

The boy asked, "Are you the Stone?"

"No-o-o!" McCormick shook his head, his tone and denial intensifying.

"You are … you climb cliff." He stared at McCormick's fingers, dripping blood. "Man shoot at you. My father … waits … on you order. We watch … up there." He pointed to the sky.

Figuring the kid to be of Middle Eastern descent, McCormick glanced up. *Yeah … on an effing flying carpet, no doubt,* he thought. He began to enunciate slowly, repeating himself, his voice coarsening with each word spoken. "Kid … I'm … *not* … Stone! I'm a bird watcher … on vacation … I've lost my t-r-a-i-l … and my m-a-p," he offered, slowly, emphatically.

The boy looked at him, skeptically, and began to speak in perfect English. "The only trails around here are donkey trails, and wild goat trails. If you're not Stone, you'll just have to turn around and go back the way you came."

McCormick's flinty eyes shot an amused glance over his shoulder at the edge of the steep precipice he'd just scaled, leaving a long, bloody trail behind. He gave the kid a satirical smile. "Yeah, right … I'll just do that."

Seeing his uninvited visitor unfazed, the kid ordered, "Go now." "Strangers are not welcome here … if my father sees you…." He dragged a grubby finger across his throat in a lethal manner, and went back to swinging his weapon as an obviously trained, militant. Preparing to vanish into the dense foliage in the same stealthy manner he'd first appeared, he turned just long enough to shout over his shoulder, "Fuck off!"

McCormick blew out his hot breath. This island boy—if, indeed, he really was an island boy—was extremely well-trained in the use of the machete, and he knew no fear. He counted himself lucky that the confrontation had gone no further. The thought of having to take a kid's life to get home was a down-and-out bummer.

McCormick considered the situation, his curiosity piqued. What possible connection could this child have to Stone? Suddenly, the loud, oscillating rotation of a high-tech helicopter pricked the air. McCormick took a quick step back into the dense foliage. Through crabapple sized fruit, oval shaped leaves and the limbs of a highly poisonous Manchineel tree, he watched the chopper pass overhead—going the same direction as the boy.

Stone!

Since rappelling down the cliff was not an option, he decided to follow the kid.

Thirty minutes later, McCormick emerged from a seldom used goat path, gasping for breath, sweat pouring from every pore. Evidence of a bone-chilling experience rode high on his flushed cheeks and knotted brow. A new worry clouded his steely eyes as he clutched the kid's machete between fingers dripping blood.

He'd followed the kid to a camp, an enemy camp on US soil, where bold, black flags billowed, over huge tents in the warm, tropical breeze—a camp where Brantley Stone met, once again, with the enemy, except for one major difference. This time, he wasn't merely consorting with the enemy. Today, he was the enemy. Some way, somehow Stone had managed to blossom into a full-fledged narco-terrorist—homegrown and dangerous as hell!

McCormick quickly skinned out of his tropical shirt, trading it for a dark, gray tee-shirt with silk-screened letters on the front. He traded his khaki cargo shorts for faded jeans. Pulling his running shoes from the bag, he knotted the strings together, and slung them around his neck. He had planned long and hard for this day, needing to be ready to literally hit the ground running once he reached the tarmac at Reagan International.

He shook out an ankle boot, checked the insides for spiders, and pulled the boot over one colorful foot, replacing the damned, slippery sandal that had turned climbing into such an exercise in determination.

Distracted by a rustling noise, but in a hurry to move on, McCormick reached back into the foliage. Surprisingly, a pair of yellow-breasted banaquits fluttered out of the bushes, and flitted straight for his face. He batted them away, before reaching, again, into the bushes. Suddenly, he jerked his hand away as a long, copper-colored, ground snake slithered towards his unshod, varicolored, striped foot. Swifter than the snake, McCormick grabbed it by its head, and nonchalantly tossed it back into the bushes, aware that there was likely a whole nest of them just a stone's throw away.

Undeterred, he pulled out a large, bulky package, checked it for free riders, treating it in the same careful way a seriously licensed archaeologist would treat a treasured artifact. This package was his most prized possession, and the only thing of value worth carrying off this sweltering, god-forsaken island, stinking and slithering, as it was—this place some people called paradise. He checked the water-proof, shrink-wrapped package for damage, then batted away swarms of annoying mosquitoes before shoving his other foot into the second boot.

He identified an old abandoned passage, once used by donkey-drawn carts, now overgrown with scrub vegetation, and began hacking through the thick undergrowth using the boy's machete to clear his way to the airport. Suddenly, he stopped thrashing, and listened. Behind him came the loud, harsh braying of wild donkeys, and a loud cacophony of disturbed macaws. He slowly straightened his back, and chuckled softly at the commotion, knowing exactly what had them all a frenzy. Soon a wide grin shot across his mouth. Hoping the worst was behind him, he continued thwacking. Light was waning.

McCormick walked gingerly, sidestepping skittering geckos and the occasional shy, mongoose that crossed his path. The need to duck his head arose in order to avoid colliding with late-arriving, low-flying birds, swiftly swooping down to roost in trees for the night. He grunted—every last one was exotic.

Ruefully, he thought of Lauren. She had been exotic; but their marriage had been a mistake from the get-go. She had insisted they make their home in Miami, but that had only added to his travel time, and time away from her. Apparently, she had never been happy with him, or anyone, for that matter. She'd grievously deceived him, breaking their bond of trust, and he had been hell-bent on getting out of the marriage. Still, her accidental drowning had nearly destroyed him.

She had taken his small sailboat out while he was on a mission in the mountains of Afghanistan; a storm had come up suddenly, and capsized the boat just off the Florida coast. Not one, but two nude bodies had been pulled from the water: Lauren's, and that of a male companion, later to be identified as her long-time lover. Mac had not been especially shocked by this revelation. Lauren had always been a flirt, and he had suspected others; but having opiates found in both their bloodstreams shocked him beyond grief. His bleeding heart would not allow him to think about the other facts revealed by the autopsy.

CHAPTER **6**

McCormick hated the feeling, the taste of failure. His footsteps slowed, reflecting his mood. As memories of his year of marriage surfaced, he tried to pinpoint a time when everything had gone sideways, feeling certain that things had never been right. Still, he searched his soul. His failure was universal, but just the same, the job had come first, and he'd been away from home one night too many; but none of that mattered. When a man signs on with Uncle Sam, he goes wherever and whenever Sam tells him to go. Families are expected to ruck up, and to have a life strategy and a contingency plan for dealing with their soldier's absence, and possible demise. Lauren had never rucked up, even though she had been well aware of the demands of his job when they married, as well as his 289 days away from home.

He walked a little farther, before his head drooped and he stopped short. Maybe she had sensed that part of himself he kept camouflaged. Maybe she'd found that hollow spot left empty by someone else—an emptiness she could never fill. Guilt tried to possess him, but deep, down inside, where it counted the most, McCormick knew the fault was not his alone. *Lauren had married the hero, but not the man.*

Yes, there had been plenty of opportunity for other women since Lauren, women like Lauren: island women, women of style, of paint and polish, of little or no substance—like his sister's empty-headed dolls, all dressed up to be undressed, women whose souls were so shallow they left him empty and yearning for the real thing. He had literally run from them all. He needed someone who could share his life's passion for his work, while understanding the longings of his soul.

His soul. The driving force of his life had been to protect his country from its enemies, and the destructive, killer drugs draining the nation of its strength, its vitality, and its natural resource of young minds. His only

41

mistresses had been his agency, his educational studies, his hobbies—not to mention, his loneliness. McCormick shook his head and groused, "God ... when did I become such a nerd?

Now, as he walked, he wondered if he would ever, again, love life as he once had? Was there any kind of normal life left for him to live? In his many hours alone, he had often wondered if it were possible to meet a woman who could make sense of his complicated life, duplicitous and dangerous, as it was. Was it even possible to meet someone who could understand his dedication to his job with a degree of intelligence and autonomy that could afford them a stable life together—someone who could respect him, and the job he did? Could anyone love him? Or for that matter, could he even be there for someone else?

Andrea's voice carried across the long expanse of hardwood flooring, into the ears of some of education's finest students. "I've heard politicians say that people like me are as extinct as the dinosaur, but then, in the same breath, claim that drug use is down." She smiled mischievously at her audience. "Hey, Mac ... back that rusty, old, truck up. Truth is ... drug use is up by over one hundred percent." She longed to give a name to this misdirection of information—propaganda; but this crowd was too young for the brutal truth. The statistical proof was at her fingertips, but she knew the kids would be bored by numbers. She'd stick with humor; it had gotten her through a lot of difficult times in the past.

Her eyes followed an attractive man in his early thirties as he entered the gym, walked the length of the flooring, and mounted the stage, taking a seat in the metal chair behind her. She gave no acknowledgment of his presence. "Actually, we know most of these drugs are coming from countries to the south; but seriously, don't you wonder how it's possible for so many to get into our country? I know I should leave speculation up to the professionals, but if you're still thinking this stuff is crawling across the border in the diapers of babies, as it's been suggested, you're crawling in the wrong direction."

A twitter of laughter rippled through the audience. The older man sitting behind her, to her left, laughed heartily.

"There are reports that drugs are being carried across the border on little drones ... or stuffed inside the tiny bellies of caterpillars or canaries." She raised her hands, palms up. A comedic, sardonic look flashed across her face. Chortles, twitters, and chirps gushed from the audience. Stepping back from the podium, she allowed the kids their moment of fun, while noticing that the two politicians were wearing out the seats of their pants in squirming discomfort. The man to her right noted the pause. Recognizing his moment of opportunity, he stood up and approached the speaker. He grabbed her elbow and squeezed hard. "Introduce me," he demanded in a low tone.

She ignored him, and he returned to his chair, his face flushing crimson.

Andrea paused just long enough to allow the cacophony of chattering voices to wane—and to recover her equilibrium. At last she blew out a hot breath. "Maybe you've heard this one … in the recent past, crystalized meth has come into the country packed inside knock-off versions of cartoon characters, but today … they're more likely to be found on human behinds?" The look of puzzlement manifested itself across the floor. She nodded, and offered, "You heard me right … bags of illegal drugs are being packed into fake Fannies and worn, fraudulently, into this country." She turned to look at the older politician. "Now that's what I call dragging your ass across the border!" The teenaged crowd went wild, jumping up, and wiggling their slender, little butts at each other, in pure, youthful rowdyism.

"I'm wondering … if anybody here has heard of attack squirrels." A couple of hands shot up. "Well gosh-darn, wouldn't you know it … users have started feeding drugs … meth and cocaine, to be exact, to their pet squirrels, turning them into dangerous attack animals." She chuckled, sardonically. "By comparison, they make that squirrely little character in theaters look like the Statue of Liberty."

The audience laughed, and began to imitate the frenetic movements of the hilarious rodent they all grew up loving. Now, she leaned into the microphone, her voice serious, but dripping with chumminess. "Guys … all jokes aside … with the amount of drugs being sold on our streets today … you better believe they're roaring in on jumbo jets!" Her voice dropped an octave. "Miracle drugs have healed, and lengthened the lives of millions of people all over the world. But to purchase illegal drugs, in this day … and in this culture, is to purchase death … your death; and it doesn't matter if the problem chirped, buzzed, waddled, roared or kick-boxed its way into our backyards—the problem is here."

Fueling her next comment was the realization that this age group lived in an increasingly unstable world. They needed encouragement and inspiration. "Guys, I am a young...." her hands rose and wavered in mid-air, lending an air of scrutiny to her claim, "college-educated journalist ... and I still have never taken anything stronger than an aspirin. I say, we do exist ... hear *us* roar!" She left her comment to hang in the air. Soon a wave of decisive, hearty, applause swept through the audience.

As she waited for the din to subside, Andrea's eyes brushed over her audience, at their high-spirited faces. She wondered if were possible to ever feel that light-hearted, again.

Turning a shoulder to the crowd, she surprisingly extended her outstretched hand towards the man sulking in the folding chair. "Allow me to introduce you to my *late* husband...." she paused, jokingly, and the kids laughed, "that is, my late *arriving* husband," she corrected, "Shaun Fitzgerald ... a contender for a seat in the US House of Representatives." Polite, moderate applause followed her introduction. Andrea blushed with embarrassment as the spurious Fitzgerald stood, and arrogantly struck a stately pose. Forcing his mouth into the semblance of a congenial smile, he threw her an air-kiss, and gave the crowd a flamboyant, campaign wave before strutting across the stage to shake hands with the older politician.

Once he'd returned to his chair, Andrea smiled into the faces of the crowd, making it personal. "I have to tell you guys ... you've been an awesome audience ... thank you so-o-o much for allowing me to be a part of your lives today." She stepped in front of the podium and put her hands together, applauding them. A fresh-faced girl with a most winsome smile stood up first, leading the crowd in a standing ovation. Andrea's eyes locked onto her, sensing something vaguely familiar.

When Andrea turned to exit the stage, Shaun was, once again, obtrusively at her side. He shoved his mouth, annoyingly, against her ear. "What-in-the-hell do you think you're doing here?" he hissed.

She turned his harsh glare back on him. "Living everyone's dream but my own!" she hissed. "What are you doing here, Shaun ... and where-in-the-hell have you been for the past ten days?"

He evaded her question, but caught her off-guard with his next comment. "You're a good speaker ... I'm going to add you to my campaign circuit."

She stepped back, totally aghast, "Like hell, you will!"

At last, McCormick's foot landed on a muddy, dirt road, lit by the huge, silver moon. His countenance lightened, and he grinned. The mud reminded him of home. *Another good omen,* he thought. He walked through puddles, and crossed to the other side, entering a small clearing. To his surprise, he found that he had wandered into the middle of a herd of wild goats bedded down for the night in the tall, lush grass. Silently, he started to work his way through the herd, but soon they were all standing on cloven hooves, and bleating in chorus. He slowed his steps, eyeing the head ram, not wanting to draw his ire, and possibly get head-butted by his hollow, but powerful, horns.

The term for goat came to mind from his high school Latin class: haedus kid. He took a look around, and chuckled, wryly, at his situation. The internet was loaded with off-colored sheep and goat jokes, and he was certain that should his old, high school buddies get wind of this, they would turn it into a raunchy joke that would follow him for the rest of his life—like the time he had taken a job modeling suits for the sole purpose of building a resume in the fashion industry. It had been his first undercover job. On his last trip home, one of his old teammates had ribbed him, mercilessly, pointing out his paper doll image still being used as a newspaper advertisement. He shook his head in bewilderment. There was no denying reality, he thought, as he walked through the herd—his looks did get him a lot of attention.

McCormick's image got him a lot of attention, alright; but it was in extreme conflict with the man he really was. In his line of work, being ruggedly handsome could be dangerous—it could even get you killed. Therefore, he bristled every time someone reacted to him on a purely physical level, forcing him to keep to himself more than he really should.

A whiff of putrid stench suddenly wafted up from the ground, reaching his nostrils. He lifted his foot and held it mid-air. "Aw shit!" he said, studying his boot and the dung-strewn pathway in front and behind him with disdain. A quick second look told him that more than dung littered the trail. Haedus kid was at his back.

Using caution with each new step, he continued his reminiscence, letting his mind wander to his other commercial ventures. At least with the car commercial, his grizzly, bearded image had flashed across the screen for only a few seconds— night after night. He had completely bulked at the acting job offer—there was no way he would let his life go in that direction. His thirst, his quest, was for real life.

McCormick remembered, and halfway regretted, the book he'd written in honor of his brothers from Special Ops. Written to shore-up surviving family members with good, wholesome memories of their brave, fallen heroes, the book told the story of their war experiences in Afghanistan, their comradery, and the dog that had stepped up to save, not only his life, but the many lives of his military brothers. Several photos were included within its pages, and at this point he realized that someone, along the way, was sure to see them and recognize him. He let out a slow breath. *Too late to worry about that now,* he thought, ruefully.

He stopped to adjust the jungle hat, having decided months ago, to keep the ponytail and stubble until he was off the island, but he'd have to keep the mass of hair hidden under his hat to avoid being recognized. At least now, he could acknowledge just how much he hated that damned ponytail, and the decadent lifestyle it represented. Drugs and corruption reigned supreme on this island, and from his experience, it was only one step away from total anarchy.

He watched dark, ominous clouds roll in, hiding the moon and stars. If Stone's goons weren't waiting for him at the airport up ahead, he would call Chief Straker as soon as he landed in D.C. He fully understood why the agency could not, would not, come after him.

Would he call his family? No—he would surprise them.

Home. His mind filled with precious memories and feelings that had been tamped down for two long years, his way of preventing loneliness from becoming unbearable. Suddenly, his heart beat with anticipation as he remembered *them.*

He switched his bulky package from one arm to the other, wondering if they would even recognize him? He knew he would have to get rid of his tattoos, and seriously clean up his foul mouth. His parents would never tolerate the strong, crude language he had become accustomed to using in the military and around Hell's own soldiers, here on the island.

The profanity, the tattoos, the ponytail and the guns had all helped him fit into the world's underbelly; but to McCormick, they were simply tools of the trade.

Suddenly, he stopped abruptly. "Aarrgh," he groused, as though waking from a nightmare. He leaned the bulky package against a tree. With emotion, his hands shot up to his pierced earlobe, removing the hated, expensive jewel he'd worn in his earlobe for the past two years. He hurled it deep into the thickest undergrowth. His days of looking like a pirate were over.

Responding to his sudden movements, the ram stopped in his tracks, and lowered his head in serious contemplation, giving his intruder the evil eye. McCormick turned. The ram moved forward, preparing to attack. Suddenly, McCormick's arms flailed to the side, and he began tromping towards the animal, flapping and clopping his feet. When the growl of a bear roared from his throat, the ram quickly slid to a halt in the muddy, manure-strewn trail, turned, and high-tailed it, in the opposite direction.

Laughing, McCormick decided to never speak of the goats—he wouldn't set himself up to be the butt of tawdry jokes. Feeling punch-drunk, he laughed at his own joke.

He wiped his boots, diligently, in the grass, and picked up his package, as well as his pace, as worry and more serious thoughts of his family flooded his mind. *Would they, did they blame him for what had happened a year ago?*

Frost, the quintessential work of autumn, had settled over the trees and lawn, completely covering the windshield on Andrea's car. As she scraped away at the frozen mist in early morning darkness, she breathed deeply, finding, in her heart, a rich appreciation for Mother Nature, as well as forgiveness towards herself for neglecting to pull the car into the four-car garage the previous night.

Maneuvering the many curves on her drive into work, she took special notice of the magical transformation of lush, green foliage into a profusion of vivid, autumnal colors. Knowing that its handiwork would soon be evident to late-rising Vermonters, as well as to a very large stampede of Leaf-Peepers, Andrea felt pleased. She liked seeing people happy.

Andrea left her car and walked to the *News* building through the unlit parking lot, and warily through a large gathering of loud, aggressive protesters. "Shame … shame," they chanted, mindlessly, pushing into her personal space, and screaming into her face. She tried to read their indecipherable, misspelled signs, and listen to their infantile shouts, using their 1st Amendment rights to silence her 1st Amendment rights.

What was her crime?

Andrea had written an opinion piece championing a man's God-given right to be masculine, not brutish nor boorish, but masculine; especially those defending the country, and this was the result. Now the protestors shoved past her, blocking her entrance into the building, cursing her and calling her ridiculous names. She clutched her purse and spun around to face them. "Okay ... I get it ... you can get up early and make a lot of noise. Now ... go take a shower, move out of Granny's basement, and go get a job that shows some self-respect. If you have a legitimate complaint against this newspaper, take it up with the editor or the publisher like a responsible adult... otherwise get the hell out of my face." She raised her phone, hitting law enforcement's number on speed-dial. The crowd backed away, and quickly dispersed.

Once safely inside her office, she settled into her chair and clicked on the TV. The Category 4 hurricane had hit the Caribbean Islands overnight, and after taking several lives, was headed for Florida.

Sensing movement, she raised her heavy lids, and glared into her boss's office, likening his lethargic form to that of a lumbering bear.

So he's finally surfaced, has he, she thought. Where had Rudd been, the previous night, that he hadn't honored a commitment that large and that long on the calendar? She had even reminded her aging boss of his scheduled commitment as keynote speaker.

She studied him through the glass; the sight was not a pretty one. Still dressed in the yesterday's attire, he sat hunched over his desk—his tongue hanging as loose as his stained tie. His thinning white head was cradled, woefully, between his large, swollen hands; his headache, no doubt the result of an alcohol-induced hangover—his broken body, the unspoken testament to a hard life lived.

She recalled her speech. When Rudd had failed to show up, and she had been recruited in his stead, she'd had no time for preparation. Her speech had been entirely impromptu; but her statements had been factual—based on the proven data she lived with daily.

She remembered the senior girls on the front row. They had been her sister's friends, and would have been in her sister's graduating class. She didn't know the girl in the front row, center seat, the one with the million-dollar smile. Wearing a cheerleader's jacket in a rival school's colors, she had clung to Andrea's every word throughout the entire speech. Upon seeing her smile, Andrea's mind had come to a sudden halt, sensing a familiarity about her. For the remainder of the speech, she'd wondered where she'd seen that smile before.

"This just in from the southern border," a news anchor chimed with urgency, using serious, anxious under-tones, "ICE officials are reporting that they have confiscated a very large cache of fentanyl. The overnight confiscation of the drug, which kills on contact, is said to be enough to kill every American in the U.S.!"

Andrea froze. The horrifying report was simply too grave, too frightening to comprehend this early in morning.

A short time later, the phone on Andrea's desk rang. It rang a second time and a third. "Whose damned phone is that?" Jolene whined from the back of the newsroom. "Andrea, answer your phone!"

Andrea threw the tall redhead a heated glance. Her concentration had been broken, and her ire had been raised by the newsroom's antiquated telephone system that dated back to the early 1980's, allowing phones to ring, incessantly, all day long. She had asked the new receptionist to take all her calls while she worked on the finer points of her column, but now the young girl was nowhere in sight. Andrea smirked. "She's probably quit because she doesn't want to work with phones."

As she pushed the door shut, she watched Jolene walk towards the library in the back of the room. From the woman's insolent demeanor and her bazaar attire, Andrea surmised that Rudd had repeated, word for word, their private conversation. This morning the woman was dressed entirely in witchy black with sequined netting running partway down the length of her black skirt, in the style of a very young girl. Her shoes, however, were four-inch, stiletto heels, flaming red and all cute and sparkly.

Andrea recalled Rudd's statement about not being in Kansas anymore. *If I were the editor*, Andrea mused, *I would show that one where the bricks begin.* She picked up the phone on the fourth ring. "Andrea Daye," she answered into the receiver, turning her attention to the caller.

"Ms. Daye?" questioned a male, smoker's voice, harsh and raspy.

"Yes, how may I help you?" Andrea asked impatiently, stretching across the desk for a notepad.

"Ms. Daye, I'm calling to give you some health advice." The caller paused.

"That sounds more like lifestyle material." Andrea offered as she checked to see if Zoe was at her desk. "I can transfer...."

"No ... no ... no, Ms. Daye," the voice interrupted. "You don't understand ... this advice is for you personally. His voice dropped to his chest, "Listen up."

"What now, she thought, plopping into her chair, knees spread, exhaling fiercely through her nose, and fighting off feelings of annoyance, preparing to hear a long, threatening diatribe. Andrea sucked in her breath, and held it as she picked up on the lethal sound in the onerous voice as it dropped its bomb shell, "If you don't stop writing your series on drug crime in this area, you are going to be a very sick woman ... are you still there, Ms. Daye?" he asked. "Stop writing—or you will *die!*"

Andrea sat, for a moment, in silence; then, instead of ending the call as most people would have done, she corralled her emotions, and laid the receiver on her desk, locking in the connection. Without a word to her fellow staffers, she walked into Rudd's office and shoved the door shut with her hip.

"Marty ... I just got a death threat ... I think this one's for real."

CHAPTER 7

It wasn't the threat or the protesters that had the journalist so unsettled; nor was it the news of the huge fentanyl confiscation. It was instead, Rudd's AWOL performance the night before that left Andrea too upset to even speak of it. In no mood to listen to any more news, or deal with his dribble, she spent the afternoon working on her laptop in the conference room.

Deciding to do some research gathering, she first pulled up a State of Vermont website. A lot had changed, as of late; but so far, the old, quaint Vermont was still alive and kicking, and still an active part of the state's culture, or so read the tourism ads.

She typed *Leaf-Peepers* into the search bar. A chuckle tickled her throat. This time of year always brought a herd of rubbernecks chasing leaves. They were friendly, but sometimes naïve city dwellers, road trippin' along country back roads for entertainment, searching for, and scratching off their list, the names and locations of the hundred, or so, covered bridges hidden amongst the state's rustic quaintness, and good, ole' country charm. For the most part, they were humorous, good-hearted people, if not newsworthy subjects; but Andrea highly suspected that the thing they were most in search of was, not leaves or bridges, but rather a culture that gave purpose and meaning to their lives.

Another stampede would thunder through the state in search of its number one product—maple syrup; but no report would come on that front until the sap started to run in late February or March. Everyone, of course, knew Vermont had its share of cows, goats, milk ... and mud.

Mud. Evidence of Andrea's high-spirited nature flared her nostrils, and flitted across her lips. The one thing Vermont really had more than its fair-share of was mud. Playfully, yet sometimes ruefully declared the 5th season, this time of the year always provided an abundance of laughs, hilarious photos, and sentimental writing fodder for a journalist—as long as you weren't the one stuck on a lonely, dark road, buried axle-deep in mud. The kids, on the other hand, flocked to the mud pits in their old, rusty, beat-up trucks for the simple pleasure of music-lovin', beer guzzlin', mud splattin' fun.

Now Andrea stopped to listen to the latest financial report blaring from the TV someone had left on: Aside from the pandemic, Vermont's economy was improving, somewhat; but considering the high cost of food and rent, diminished jobs, and stagnant salaries, the report still remained bleak. She blew out a dismal breath, critiquing the report from a journalistic point of view. Missing from the report was the real reason for the uptick in prices: outrageous, exorbitant taxes put in place by socialist-leaning politicians, dying towns and escalated drug use—things no one wanted to read about. Those three subjects certainly wouldn't sell newspapers to the upper income city dwellers known as Soccer Moms; and if you couldn't sell newspapers— well, you might as well turn out the lights and go muddin'.

Andrea worked, uninterrupted until the mail clerk stuck his head into the room, giving her a big smile. He spoke pleasantly. "Do you want your mail in here, Ms. Daye?"

"No thanks, Deegan … just put it on my desk … I'll be there, shortly. Thanks."

Once he had gone, Zoe suddenly hurled herself through the door, her fingers grabbing the framework as though she were a jet landing on an air force carrier going full-speed-ahead. Anyone watching would see that she had the physical productivity thing going, but her lackluster eyes showed somberness. "Andi!" she gasped.

Andrea looked up, noticing her friend's ruddy cheeks. "Protestors?" she asked.

"Oh yeah," Zoe answered, breathlessly, "Girl … you're goin' to have to put a cork in your penchant for free speech."

"I will…." Andrea offered, matter-of-factly, without lifting her eyes from her laptop, "when Hell freezes over." She thought about her editorial concerning men's God-given right to be masculine. At least the article was being read.

"Why are you working in here," Zoe asked, curiously, glancing around at the smelly room.

"Burnout."

Zoe turned caring eyes on her friend, but spoke with hesitation, "Andi ... you are meeting me for pizza tonight ... right? I've got a b-i-g scoop for you."

Andrea hopelessly shook her head at the girl's outdated newspaper lingo.

Finally mollified by her work, and with an eye to the clock, Andrea scooped up her notes, preparing to return to her office. On second thought, she sat back down and spoke in friendliness, "You've been watching *Superman: Grown Man in Tights* again, haven't you?" referring to the old black and white '50's TV version, now running in reruns, of the reruns, of the reruns on Cable TV.

Zoe plopped down at the table, "Yeah ... I'm guilty; but I can't help it, Andi. I just love that show ... it's a classic."

Andrea studied her friend, finding her amazing. At the age of 21, Zoe seemed to be stuck almost seventy or eighty years in the past. Her impish nature confirmed that fact, with bright-eyed innocence, and exuberance oozing from every pore. But that's where the description ended. The girl was extremely savvy, and wore her beautiful strands of blonde hair in a severe, tight bun. Her clothes with the padded shoulders were reminiscent of a much earlier time. It had taken Andrea a while, but she'd finally figured out that she was actually wearing her mother's clothing. She was quite bright, and quite normal—and one of the few people who could make Andrea laugh.

Just at that moment, Jolene walked past the door. *Who's to say what's normal, these days,* Andrea thought.

"Tell me the truth, Zoe. I'll bet you spend your evenings watching *I Love Lucy* and *Happy Days*. Am I right?"

Zoe tossed back her head, and cried, "Yes, Yes!" She hid her eyes behind her hands, totally embarrassed at being found out. "I'm just like the Fonz ... I need my friends," she crowed.

"Both of our lives should be flushed down the syndication toilet," Andrea groused. "I wish they would run the old Christopher Reeves movies, though. He had a sharp sense of humor, intelligent eyes and a wonderful, winsome smile." *My* mother really liked *him*," she replied, suddenly feeling melancholic.

Zoe sighed, and reached across the table for the half a chocolate bar being offered by Andrea. "Those shows help me unwind. I don't have to worry about what's going to happen next, like I do in real life ... or at the theater. Nothing is going to jump out and grab me in 3D ... and Mother's been watching them since she was a kid. All the movies today are so dark and intense, or pure evil." She took a bite of chocolate. "Everything is just too ugly … and too damned frightening," she said, shoving chocolate past her lips. "I sit in the theatre with my eyes closed, and my heart racing, mad at myself for wasting my hard-earned money on tickets."

Now, a blush came to her cheeks for having revealed her fears. Andrea watched her use her palms to smooth her hair back in place, trying to control, at least, some part of her life.

"Zoe, why don't you find yourself a big, strong, macho guy … a military guy … to take you to the movies?" she suggested, shooting her friend a cleaver grin. "You could share your popcorn—he could share his polished boots and shining armor."

Zoe raised her eyebrows, in jest. "Oh sure … and the next thing you know, he'd be telling me who to vote for." They both laughed. "So where exactly do I find someone like that? The only guys around here are mud-slinging, pot-smoking, beer guzzling rednecks, protesting socialists … or flaming gays."

Andrea frowned. "Oh Zoe … you're a beautiful, intelligent, young woman … why don't you go spend a weekend with your friends at Boston University?"

"Nah … I would just feel … left behind. Besides, what would I do with Mother?" she added dejectedly, a tinge of hopelessness sounding in her voice.

Andrea hadn't intended to sound insensitive, but it seemed to her that constantly watching old reruns *every* night might be just a little unhealthy. She tried to imagine what it must be like for a young woman to sit at home, night after night, with her invalid mother, feeling insecure and afraid of what tragedy might befall them next.

Well, duh Andi, she thought, quickly realizing the scenario was a perfect depiction of her own lackluster life—minus the invalid mother.

At this point, Andrea felt concern for Zoe. Her father, an acclaimed county sheriff, had been shot and killed by drug dealers while his daughter was still in high school. The young girl had been forced to forgo college in order to help support her mother. Now Andrea wondered if there was a way she could help her find some kind of peace and contentment in her life. At last she said, "Zoe, tell your mother I'm coming for a visit … soon; and I'm bringing Henry Cavill, Hugh Jackman, Chris Pratt and a very large pizza with me!"

"Mother wouldn't know who they were if they bit her on the neck," she lamented, her voice laden with pathos.

"Maybe not," Andrea exclaimed, her eyes twinkling, "but you would!" She winked, understandably, and pulled out a copy of Thursday's theatre section from beneath her laptop. In a teasing tone, she continued to read the names, "Jensen Ackles, Chris Pratt, Jake Gyllenhaal, Gerard Butler ... Chris Pratt."

Zoe smiled inwardly, knowing that one evening soon Andrea would, indeed, show up at her shabby, low-rent apartment complex, carrying a bag full of just-released DVD's. Secretly, she welcomed it. Andrea was good company, as well as a good therapist.

She looked up, surprised. "I thought you didn't go to the movies."

"I don't ... anymore." Andrea's head dropped. "I just sit around here until midnight, editing the Theatre Review page because Jolene can't remember that it has to be done." She tossed the paper onto the table with growing indignation.

A bell went off in Andrea's head just as a curious Jolene walked past the door a second time. She rose to her feet and pushed the door shut. With pen in hand, she made scratches across a sticky-note; then ripped the page off the pad, handing it to Zoe who, in her confusion, read it aloud, "Beer Geeks' Paradise?"

"Yeah, it's a micro-brewery the readers have been asking about ... I'm giving you the story." She pulled out a brochure from her stack of work-related items and handed it to Zoe. "Research their history, get some people photos and interview the owners ... see if you can come up with some kind of awesome reader connection; you better take Pratt along ... to guard your...."

Zoe came out with a negating chortle, "To guard my gal...." Her disbelieving eyes settled on Andrea. She stopped laughing; she could tell the boss wasn't joking. "Are you saying ... you'll pay David to go with me?"

"Well ... yeah ... he's not Pratt, but I'll bet he could guard anything that needed guarding. It'll be overtime, of course ... you'll want to go on a weekend, right?"

Zoe's eyes dropped to the sticky note. At last she smiled wide, and gracious.

"Thanks ... but what about Mom?"

"I've got your back on that one. Mom and I will spend the evening watching a flowing red cape and blue tights zoom through star-studded sky."

Zoe gave Andrea a hug. "Andi, you're wonderful."

As she left the room, Zoe remembered her first day at the *Forest Hills Daily News*. She'd been fresh-faced and green as grass, straight out of high school. Rudd had scared the bejeezus out of her; but when she aced the grammar test, and got hired as the newsroom receptionist, it was Andrea who had taken her under her wing; and it was Andrea who had, voluntarily, become her mentor, showing her how the newsroom operated—and it was Andrea who had sat up with her all night at the hospital when her mother was in danger of not surviving her second stroke. When the Lifestyle editor position opened up, it was Andrea who had recommended her for the position. And since both had lost loved ones, they had often gotten together after work to share their heavy load of grief. Because of that commiseration, and in spite of their huge economic differences, they'd become solid, supportive friends.

But Andrea had changed in the few months since her marriage. She had become withdrawn and tight-lipped, throwing herself into her work with such fervency and dedication that even Zoe couldn't pry her away from her desk.

Now, she looked up and yelled at her friend as she entered the newsroom, "Andi, you *are* going to meet me for dinner tonight, right?" She watched her assistant-editor glance at the clock, her mouth forming a moue of doubt.

Zoe's heart filled with sadness, and a sense of urgency. "Andi, p-l-e-a-s-e!"

Hating to see her friend beg, Andrea agreed by flipping her a quick thumbs up. Zoe breathed out a sigh of relief. "Great … meet me at the Writer's Block Lounge at 6:30 … on the dot … don't be late," she added with insistency."

"If I can get past the protestors, I'll be there…" She grinned with devilment, "I'm really curious about your big *S-C-O-O-P!*"

When Rudd, mindlessly, shuffled out of the building for an early lunch, totally dissing the staff, Andrea stepped up to do his job.

At one o'clock that afternoon, the phone rang on Rudd's desk. Having just returned to the building, he answered, gruffly, "Rudd."

"Mr. Rudd, my name is Matthew McCormick … I'm a special agent with the Federal Drug Enforcement Agency."

He wouldn't tell Rudd that he was in a hotel room just up the street, only a few blocks from the newspaper building; nor would he tell him that he'd spent the entire night out-pacing a Cat 4 hurricane, and dodging body-piercing bullets. "I understand you spoke with my supervisor a few days ago and agreed to work with me."

A shiver went up the editor's spine at the agent's stern, no-nonsense voice. "Hold on?" Rudd said, impatiently.

The agent said he would, and Rudd hobbled to the door and closed it—an act of privacy he seldom used.

Feeling claustrophobic inside the small, stuffy hotel room, the agent carried the phone to the window. When he looked out, past the profusion of autumn leaves, he could actually see the gunmetal gray roof of the newspaper building.

At last, "What can I do for you, Agent McCormick?"

"Before we begin, sir, do I have your permission to record our conversation? That would be entirely for your benefit, not mine."

There was a long pause, and then finally, "Yeah, sure … why not … what do you want to know?"

"I'd like to get a little background information on one of your employees."

"And who might that be?" Rudd asked, speaking through an after-dinner mint and a belch.

"Andrea Daye," the agent offered with indifference.

Rudd sighed. "What kind of information," he asked, suddenly begrudging the inquiry. "Andrea does her job—what more is there to know?"

"Just tell me who she is."

Rudd thought the agent sounded winded, as though he'd been running sprints.

McCormick thought the editor sounded drunk.

"Well, all I know is that Andrea is the daughter of the late Andrew Daye, the founder of Daye Pharmaceuticals, the largest company of its kind in this part of the country … pharmaceuticals got their start right here in Vermont, you know. She moved here about four or five years ago. I think I remember hearing that her paternal grandfather was somehow related to the man who invented the original printing press, or something, back in the 1600's. I've been told that Andrea is pretty proud of that fact. I guess that's the reason she still uses Daye on her bylines; she figures she's paying it forward … or backwards."

Or sideways, the agent thought, problematically. Rudd's grating voice set McCormick's already frayed nerves on edge, and the oaf was giving him second hand information—information unusable in a court of law. He hadn't risked life and limb, losing a whole night's sleep just to sit, unproductively, in a stinking hotel room to get this stuff. He walked over to one of the few amenities offered by the low-budget hotel: a two-cup coffee maker. "Keep going," he encouraged as he poured his second cup, knowing he'd need a lot more before the day was over.

Following his escape from the Islands, McCormick had called his boss in Virginia from Reagan International, only to be redirected and temporarily reassigned to this case, until another agent could be freed up, they had promised. Agents had died in the raid; and, their memorials would take men away from their posts. So, after being away for two long years, McCormick had agreed to delay his much needed trip home in order to make some basic inquiries.

He'd been met on a remote corner of the wet tarmac by a couple of goons, and unceremoniously handed a small laptop in a black leather case, complete with a slender, urban-style shoulder strap. Checking out the technology, McCormick had asked, bluntly, distrust sounding in his voice, "Where's my gun, my satphone … my cred pack?"

When handed a 9 mm Glock, McCormick had eagerly wrapped his raw fingers around the holster-wrapped gun, having discarded his while on the island-hopper. All else came in the form of a promise. "We'll have to forward the rest to you," offered a squat man with a fresh slash across his cheek, his voice totally lacking conviction as he shifted his eyes away from the menacing McCormick.

They had given him no additional information about the case, and this in itself left McCormick wondering what was really at play. All he knew was that some featherbrained reporter was writing newspaper articles about the distribution of illegal drugs in the area, and the articles were kicking up a lot of dust; and now Rudd was giving him history book material. A secretary, a newbie, or any amateur dick could have gotten this stuff, McCormick thought, as seeds of doubt began to take root.

"She's an Indiana University grad with an English degree, with a Journalism Minor; but she had never worked in newspaper. She applied for a general assignment reporter position, but she was overqualified, by a mile. I remember the interview. We talked mostly about Bobby Knight. He's long retired now, but you're probably old enough to remember Indiana's infamous coach?"

"I was just a kid...." McCormick offered, "but yeah, I've heard of him ... he was the basketball coach at Army, then for IU ... great coach, but he had a nasty temper ... liked to throw things. He moved to Texas, coached awhile, wrote books, and endorsed presidential candidates." He offered, "I understand he's moved back to Bloomington now ... showing signs of age."

McCormick took a long, doubtful sip from his Styrofoam cup. A little quick math told him that there was no way Ms. Daye would have been on the IU campus at the same time as Knight. The coach would've been leaving IU, while Andrea was just a young girl—and yet, she'd been able to carry a conversation on the subject during a job interview. Impressive, but as far as this editor was concerned, he was just an unverifiable, name-dropping blowhard, confused about which decade he was living in. Impatience sounded in his voice when he asked, "Can we get back to Ms. Daye?"

"Sure ... sure. You know, Andrea is a beautiful, young woman, and frankly, I had my doubts that she was tough enough to cut it in this business. The world's gotten to be such a brutal place with all the crime and corruption, racial tension, terrorism ... and all this drug crap."

Tell me about it, the weary agent thought with exasperation, his heavy lids drooping shut, then instantly shooting wide open. To McCormick's chagrin, the man's whiny voice droned on.

"Journalism is a complicated business, these days, and the average person just doesn't understand all this shit."

McCormick willed himself awake, but his wry sense of humor instantly rose to the surface. "Yeah, you pretty well have to have a doctorate just to figure it all out ... I'm guessing you don't have one?"

Taken aback by the taunting question, the editor's voice hesitated a moment, "I have my BS."

BS—education's acronym for bachelor's degree—and the world's youthful acronym for Bull Shit! The exhausted agent stifled his snort, suddenly aware that he had never actually mastered that last tenet of the Boy Scout Creed—reverence. Oh sure, he gave reverence to God, deeming him sacrosanct; but as a trained thinker, finding it increasingly difficult to find people to hold in high regard, McCormick's thoughts were not always respectful, reverent, nor sacrosanct. However, in this line of work, his irreverent attitude served him very well as a tool. Playing the smart-assed, devil's advocate often paid off in spades.

"It's all hard news, 24-7," Rudd was saying. "Even the weather is working against us these days, but Andrea convinced me of her ability to handle the job when I sent her to D.C. to do a follow-up story on the 2016 election ... you remember all the hell-raisin' that broke loose on that day?"

"Who could ever forget?" McCormick said, drily.

"Cable news stations have been courting Andi ever since ... she's turns them all down." Rudd took another puff from his pipe. "She worked her way up to Senior Reporter and City Editor, and now she's the most valuable member of my staff as Assistant Editor. If you're up against a deadline, Andi is the one you want handling the pressure. She could work for the Boston Globe, New York Times or the Washington Post anytime she wanted—they would hire her in a New York minute." Rudd chuckled to himself, "Hell, she must've been influenced by Knight though."

"A bit of a bitch, is she?"

"Well...." Hesitation preceded his answer. "Yes and no ... yes, she can be a bitch when she wants to be. She uses it as a ... uh...."

"Tool of the trade?" the restless agent offered.

"Yeah, that's it ... a tool of the trade; but otherwise, she's a first class lady. Hey, she's not in any serious trouble is she?" suddenly the clucking mother hen.

"None that I know about," the agent assured him, in all honesty.

Rudd continued, "Now that you mention it, I suppose her temperamental disposition could stem from the work she's doing on illegal drugs. Did I tell you her articles have won a lot of awards for the paper?"

"No, you didn't."

"Yeah, that girl can really write. She's got style ... a voice ... and she's selling a lot of newspapers for me. Funny thing though," Rudd continued, "Andrea doesn't give one hoot about awards. She even sent me to the State Press Association banquet to accept her last one. She's got a whole desk drawer full of the things ... refuses to hang'em."

"So ... she really is a talent?" the agent asked, a shade more attentive.

Suddenly, Rudd's voice took on a stronger, more professional tone. "Her work is excellent. She's painstakingly accurate and she writes rings around anyone in the business around here."

As Rudd elaborated, it became obvious to McCormick that the editor both admired and envied Andrea's talent, but something began to nag at him as the man began to describe the tragic deaths of Ms. Daye's family members. Andrea's younger sister had died mysteriously over two years earlier, and then, just a couple of months after that, her parents had died in a freak bus accident.

Rudd blew out a woeful breath, "Sad thing ... but Andrea inherited a fortune, and lived alone on the family estate until just a few months ago when she up and married the family lawyer." He paused, "What else do you want to know?"

McCormick rubbed his hand back and forth across his mouth and bristled face—a habit that accompanied his deepest thoughts and revelations. He detected something nefarious in the details—three dead family members, two different accidents, family estate, family lawyer, pharmaceuticals—drugs.

Now, something else was puzzling the agent. McCormick knew that newspapers were notorious for paying low wages, so obviously, Ms. Daye wasn't working for awards or money; and if she was an over-qualified, moneyed heiress married to a lawyer, and CEO of a giant company, why was she working at this killer of a job, for a rag of a newspaper—for that matter, why was she working at all? What was driving the young journalist—and if not awards, what drove her to such a standard of excellence?

The editor continued before giving McCormick a chance to speak. "You know, this whole drug thing has been a major pain in the ass for me ... no one wants to read about this crap; and now I hear the government's taking millions more of our federal tax dollars to start up some senseless new taskforce."

Senseless. McCormick took note; and if no one wanted to read about this stuff, why was Andrea selling a lot of papers for him? He noted the inconsistency, and began to pace around the room.

"Hell, I'm getting calls from people all over the place, people you would never suspect of having an interest. I have one community pillar who swears that Andrea is using the paper to help her husband's position in the upcoming election."

A ping went off in McCormick's head. "Election?" the agent asked. "She's married to a politician?"

Rudd removed his glasses. "Hell yes! She's married to Shaun Fitzgerald!"

The steely-eyed agent stopped his pacing and planted his feet. His jaw muscles flexed, and his breath pushed out his words. "Tell me about Fitzgerald."

"Fitzgerald's a lawyer," Rudd droned. "He worked for Andrea's father, helped him move his company down here from the northern part of the state, but that association didn't last long. I understand the old man just didn't like the way he did business." Rudd breathed out a heavy sigh. "Fitzgerald's an extremely aggressive, controversial fellow, running for a seat in the U.S. House of Representatives."

McCormick winced.

"Some folks are saying that Andrea is using the newspaper to turn votes in his favor, but I think he's using *her*. Personally, I don't believe Andrea would even vote for the man, let alone use the newspaper to help him get elected."

As Rudd spoke, the agent's interest in Andrea quadrupled. "Not exactly sharing the same bed of roses?" he asked, thoughtfully, adding pressure to the hand he rubbed across his beard.

The editor heard the tension building in the agent's voice, "Frankly, I don't understand why she even puts up with the guy," he offered, his tone indicating that he was ready to dish some dirt. He sighed, and reached into his top drawer for his pipe. "Hang on while I light my pipe ... I'm having tobacco withdrawal."

McCormick gave an impatient, half-shake of his head; but he had no choice but to wait while Rudd took time to fill his pipe. Again Rudd asked, "This is all confidential, right?"

The agent's fingers ran through his hair in restlessness, but he reassured the editor, "We'll keep what you tell us in the strictest confidence ... unless we need your testimony in court." McCormick looked at his recorder, hoping his tape wouldn't run out before this gasbag got finished.

Grown weary of the chair, too small for his ample size, the agent moved to the foot of the bed. He encouraged, "Please ... continue."

"Well, something's just not right." Rudd gossiped.

"How so?"

Smoke gathered and swirled above the editor's head as he peered through the glass wall, and straight into Andrea's office, where she sat toiling away on the news for the following day. "For one thing, Shaun's got this voracious appetite for power; Andrea doesn't. I just seriously doubt that the two of them even keep each other's company—if you know what I mean. Andi is a gorgeous woman, a true jewel, but her husband is always hanging out with all kinds of low-life. He shows up in public with other women, bar tenders, lounge singers and the like … and hell, she knows it."

"So what, exactly, are you saying, Mr. Rudd?" the agent asked. "Are you suggesting that he might be unfaithful to his wife?"

It wasn't the sweet, fruity scent of cherry tobacco that caused Andrea to look up from her computer screen, nor was it her gnawing hunger; it was, instead, a sense of being watched. She glanced around, spying Rudd sitting with his feet propped up on his desk, sucking on his pipe stem, and blowing smoke rings in her direction out the corner of his mouth. Momentarily mesmerized by the plume of gray-white haze spiraling over his head and upwards toward the faulty ceiling vent that allowed the smoke to filter straight into her office, she noted his unusual chattiness today, and wondered who might have the power to hold his attention for so long. Rudd's eyes shifted, and rested on her. Why did she feel like a fish in a bowl; why did she feel she was the topic of conversation?

Rudd hacked out a deep, throaty laugh, along with his smoker's cough. "I'd bet my best Captain Black Cherry pipe tobacco on it."

Sensing a possible crack in the Fitzgerald façade, McCormick crushed his empty cup into a tight ball and hurled it into the small trash can. This was a good place to start his investigation.

The agent prompted, "And?"

"And … I don't like this man, Fitzgerald—not many people do," Rudd continued. "One day, a few weeks ago, he invited me into his office on the pretense of discussing campaign issues; but during the course of conversation he suddenly switched the subject to Andrea's job here at the newspaper. At first, I thought he was wrangling for more money for her; but the son-of-a-bitch tried to talk me into *firing* her. He offered me a very handsome amount of money, too, explaining that Andrea would never quit of her own accord, and that her position with the paper wasn't in *his* best interest."

Complex thoughts filled the agent's mind.

"I'll be very candid with you, Mr. McCormick … if it had been any other member of my staff, I would've taken him up on the offer, dismissed Andrea, and whistled all the way to the bank."

Two immediate questions came into McCormick's mind: *Why would Andrea's job not be in her husband's best interest, and why would Fitzgerald think Rudd could be bribed?*

Rudd blew another smoke ring, and again looked through the glass at his Assistant Editor. "Unfortunately, Andrea has become my right arm man. She's a very talented journalist … dynamic and bold … a real risk-taker. I don't think she's ever faced a story she was afraid to tackle. She's well-travelled, got base knowledge on many different levels, with a real sense of the world around her—she's far too valuable for me to let her go."

Dynamic, bold, and a risk-taker—McCormick made a mental note. "So how did you explain that to Fitzgerald?"

"Oh, I simply begged off," he said. "I spouted something about wanting to stay out of family matters." Rudd took another long drag on his pipe and blew a large ring into the air, to the consternation of the impatient agent, and to Andrea, watching from the other side of the glass. "I don't trust the man … Andrea, on the other hand, is different. Her feelings sometimes run a little too close to the surface, but she's forthright and honest." Rudd thought for a moment. "Oh sure, I get angry with her at times—mostly because she's always right—but I trust her completely."

There it was—everything the agent wanted to know. He thanked Rudd for his time and cooperation, telling him he would soon be back in touch.

CHAPTER 8

McCormick cradled the phone, his nerves raw from being on a plane for more than twelve hours, and talking so long to this dunderhead. Nevertheless, he sat down at the desk, and filed two reports to his boss on the laptop the agency had provided—one in regards to his conversation with Rudd. He had actually amassed a large amount of information—information that needed to be followed up on, and of course, verified, immediately. The second report took considerably longer. It concerned his two years of undercover work.

When he had finished the reports, the weary agent sat on the side on the bed, and tugged off a boot. Oh, gawd, it still smelled of goat—and he'd used his sneakers, as he recalled, to bat a gun out of the hands of a psychologically, disagreeable goon back on the island. He threw down the smelly boot, fighting against his military training to polish and shine—he was still in camouflage mode. He glimpsed his colorful sock against the cheap, gaudy carpet, and grimaced ruefully, remembering he had no change of clothes. Using a gentler touch, he pulled off the second boot.

Shivers ran through him as he stripped down in the bathroom. It would take him awhile to adjust to the colder temperatures and a life other than the paradisial one he had been living; but today he was grateful for a hot shower, eager to scrub off the whole undercover experience. He flipped on the nozzle, and waited—no water.

Too late, he found the notice concerning a water-main flush. This, too, he wadded into a tight ball and threw into the trash can; then he threw off the disappointment. Having, long ago, adopted the attitude of gratitude, he dressed in the same clothes, and adopted a more positive attitude towards his situation. At least he had a door that locked, and the chance to catch a few winks back here in the good ole USA.

His eyes grew heavy as the weight of the last couple of days fully hit him. In his mind's eye he replayed his narrow escape, being shot at by Stone, watching his fellow agent's head explode into pink mist, and his run-in with machete boy. He hadn't made it as far as the Island's airport, before he'd been spotted and fired upon by Stone's minions, making it necessary to shoot his way across the tarmac and onto a small island hopper, still in the process of lifting off. Otherwise, he would be spending this moment dead.

He reviewed his phone call to his boss at Headquarters, and then finally, his reroute straight to Forest Hills, Vermont, before given the chance to leave Reagan International Airport.

This day was stacking up to be the same kind of day. He'd have to catch a few winks, and a quick meal, and then fly straight back to Washington for a very long, detailed debriefing. He'd grab a sampling of Ms. Daye's columns to read in-flight.

He set his watch alarm to sound in three hours; then laid his body down on a hard, squeaky mattress in complete exhaustion. He tried to empty his mind, but the adrenaline was still pumping. He rolled over on his back, and stretched his sun-bronzed arms behind his head, and crossed his long legs at the ankles. He thought, *Andrea Daye Fitzgerald—who is she, really?*

He closed his eyes and tried to visualize her face and figure. Rudd had called her beautiful—gorgeous even, a jewel and a lady, although a bitchy lady, he thought, correcting himself. He was quick to realize that there were many different kinds of bitchy and just as many different causes. He'd learned each and every one from the women in his life. She was talented—but working for a rag of a newspaper at a level she should have transcended by now, if one could believe Rudd. *Bitchy reason number one,* he thought. She was married—but probably not sleeping with her adulterous husband; that was bitchy *reason number two.* Reason number *three?* She'd lost her entire family.

The agent gave out a low whistle. "Andrea Daye Fitzgerald … you must be one lonely lady," he whispered, suddenly aware of the emptiness of his own bed.

At 6:15, Andrea glanced around the newsroom. Everyone else had met their deadlines and left the building, but she was stuck editing front page copy. She couldn't understand why Rudd didn't just fire the incompetent for—incompetency.

◄◦►

At 6:20, he watched the TV news coverage of the hurricane's destruction of Haiti, and the severe damage to the Islands; then flipped off the TV, not caring to hear the banter between commentators. He'd brushed his teeth with the complimentary toothbrush, and scrubbed up using bottled water, and the tiny, floral-scented bar of soap. Now, out of habit, he checked the hallway for goons with guns, locked his door, and walked to the corner drugstore to purchase the latest issue of the *News*. As he removed a copy from the wire stand, he read the large headline: *Candidates Battle for Congressional Seat*. He tri-folded the paper and stuck it into his back pocket. He'd read it over dinner.

At 6:30, his world exploded like an IED.

Andrea stood outside the door of the Writer's Block Lounge, pacing back and forth, hesitating to enter. It wasn't the socialization that had her so indecisive, for she loved being with people; nor was it a lack of hunger, for she was way beyond famished. No, it was simply the fact that, at this very moment, she felt fragile. She had these strong nagging feelings that something was wrong; that somehow, the ground was about to open up and swallow her alive. A forewarning, she wondered, or was she just picking up on Zoe's insecurity?

Suddenly, she was totally surrounded by screaming protesters, and then just as suddenly, she was not. The sound of booted, authoritative footsteps pounded the pavement behind her. Without looking around, she shoved both her feelings and the door aside—a promise to her friend took precedence over her own ill-fated feelings. As she entered the Lounge, she was only vaguely aware that someone had caught the door and was following her into the building.

The aroma of hot, cheesy, Italian tomato sauce immediately tickled her nose as she quickly stepped inside, and the smell of warm, yeast, pizza dough, all but pulled her through the entryway.

CHAPTER 9

Inside the Writer's Block Lounge, loud, rock and roll music from decades past, blared from the jukebox. Andrea's computer-weary eyes strained through the dimly lit room, searching for Zoe. Immediately over-come with claustrophobia, she spun around to leave, bumping into someone who felt like the Rock of Gibraltar; but before she could look up, a clamor of voices rose from the darkness, "Surprise, Happy Birthday!"

She glanced over her shoulder at the jubilant, yet barely visible faces of the entire newsroom staff. She gasped with astonishment. "This isn't my birthday," she said with incredulity."

"Oh yes it is," argued Zoe, appearing from out of nowhere. She grabbed Andrea's elbow, handing her a card and a small, wrapped gift, complete with a teal-colored bow, all sparkly and cutely tied. Zoe argued, "According to personnel records … today is your birthday. When you didn't celebrate last year, I got curious."

"You got nosey," Andrea corrected.

"Curious," Zoe repeated, unrelentingly, looking extremely smug. She had done her due diligence.

Andrea shot her a snarky grin. "Well, you nosey little bitc…." At that moment a tall stranger, deeply tanned and most attractive, walked up behind her, and cleared his throat. Having listened from a couple of feet away, he'd been thoroughly entertained by the push-and-shove of their conversation. They argued like siblings.

"Pardon me," he said in a deep, baritone voice, every bit as rich as his golden tan. Slowly, but observantly, he stepped around Andrea.

Unable to pull her eyes away, Andrea watched the rakishly handsome man take long, confident strides across the floor towards a table in the back of the room. Distressed jeans, old but snug, covered his slender hips, and a dark gray, tee-shirt, faded but form-fitting, revealed broad shoulders and muscular, tatted up arms. Her breathing went shallow. Not normally a fan of tattoos, she had to admit—on this guy's biceps, tats ruled.

Zoe folded her arms across her chest, and leaned on one leg in awed appreciation. "Now there's a guy with real armor," she said, laughingly.

Andrea's eyes followed the man, "Serious armor," she whispered, too low for even Zoe to hear.

Seeing Andrea's reaction, their eyes locked in mirth, and they exclaimed in unison, "Superhero?" Andrea laughed, but suddenly felt embarrassed by their schoolgirl banter. Zoe, having already judged him to be too old for her, teasingly gave Andrea a playful little shove in feigned competition. "Move aside girlfriend, you're an *o-l-d* married woman," she said, deliberately baiting her friend. "Just go celebrate your special day ... I had to do some really heavy lifting to get everyone here tonight ... so go ... schmooze."

Throwing her friend an insipid look, Andrea responded, "Yeah, I'm an old married woman, alright." Her heart weighed heavy, but for the sake of her guest, she put on a happy face. The party mood picked up quickly as she began to make the rounds between tables, greeting her friends from the newspaper, exchanging brief hugs and air kisses.

As she approached Jolene's table, the woman chose that precise moment to stand, abruptly, and leave the table in a total rebuff of Andrea's friendly gesture. Surprised that the woman was even here, Andrea moved on, undeterred, continuing to bounce glances off the preoccupied stranger with the rugged demeanor—glances off his firm, manly lips as he patiently sipped water, holding his glass between bandaged fingers. Becoming aware of appreciative whispers around the room, she realized that she was not the only woman aware of this man's presence, his unusual masculinity, his deep, tropical tan, his short-clipped full beard, or his sun-bleached hair combed back from the forehead and fastened at the nape of the neck in a very masculine man-tail.

When the music ended, he stood up, put his hands to his lower back, and slowly stretched out his muscles. Then he walked to the jukebox, and surprisingly selected the Home Free version of *How Great Thou Art*, showing no concern for the disgruntlement expressed by the crowd at his music selection. He sat down, deeply concentrating on the lyrics.

Andrea's lovefest with the last table of co-workers brought her within inches of the stranger, and her soulful gaze brushed over his downcast eyes. Sensing eyes fixed upon him, he warily lifted his. Through the dim, smoky haze, their eyes met and locked—as though for all eternity.

He shoved his chair back and stood to his full height, facing the suddenly flustered young woman. He stepped away from the table and shot her a roguish grin. "I could use a hug about now," he said, his voice low and unabashed, his dark eyes dancing with mischievous incandescence. With a playful roughness, he drew her into his arms, claiming a teasing rollicking hug for himself. Andrea's blushing cheek brushed against his gray, faded t-shirt that read: *Pain is just weakness leaving the body.* She breathed in the man's masculine scent, along with the fresh scent of soap, and a faint scent of something that brought with it, the image of goats.

As his arms tightened around her waist, she could feel the extraordinary strength of his body. Under normal circumstances, warning bells would be clamoring, sounding an alarm; but for reasons without explanations, here in this dimly lit room, this man's arms felt like the safest place in the world.

Andrea returned his infectious smile and started to pull away. "Nah … nah, nah," he said in a teasing air of possessiveness and good humor. He pulled her closer, and in a totally unexpected gesture, lowered his head and, ever so gently, dropped a light, but lingering kiss on her lips. Andrea's knees weakened, as his warm lips claimed her own laughing, trembling ones. Suddenly, tightening his hold, he pulled her closer, smothering her mouth in a long, hot, passionate kiss. The crowd hooted, hollered, and crudely banged on the tables.

Reluctantly, he released her.

Always one to own up to his bold actions, the stranger wrapped a protective arm around her shoulder, and slowly spun her around, away from the loud, boorish crowd. Ignoring the din, he lowered his head and spoke softly into her ear. "Please don't be offended. I thought you needed a kiss like that … I know I sure as hell did." He paused, his eyes of molten gold drinking in her beauty. "Happy Birthday," he offered, shooting her only a slightly abashed roguish grin.

"Thanks," she whispered, demurely, suddenly speechless and starry-eyed.

His eyes began to travel downward; but instead stopped to rest on the beautiful chain necklace she wore around her neck, with its twinkling pendant perfectly displayed below her collarbone.

The grin returned to his lips, and Andrea thought it most charming—but where had she seen that mischievous, wry grin before? Did she know this man? She wondered what he looked like without the beard.

Now Marty, already heavy into his liquor, clanged his spoon against the side of his glass, and began to mumble out a toast, never mentioning Andrea by name. His voice was pitched so low that even Andrea struggled to hear. She found herself much too distracted by the man standing behind her, his bandaged fingers still resting lightly on the small of her back. What she did hear in snatches, was Rudd's crude reference to PDA, public display of affection, and a motel room. Annoyance flamed her cheeks. Again the crowd hooted. Rudd looked at Zoe, and roared with laughter at some private, inside joke.

So this had all been Zoe's doing, Andrea surmised, disgruntledly.

She turned to question the stranger about his bandages. To her dismay he had slipped away and returned to his table; but, once again, he lifted his gaze, and their eyes locked in the midst of blaring music and the cacophonous chattering of loud voices. With his dark eyes dancing with risibility, he gave her a showman's, polite, abbreviated nod of appreciation.

With cheeks burning, and feeling as though she had been kissed by a god, she sat down next to her friend and fussed with her napkin. "Okay Zoe, fess up. How much of your hard-earned money did you pay *that* guy? Don't I get a little song and dance routine, as well?" Suddenly, she went pale, and horror traveled the entire length of her face. "Oh my gawd! Zoe, if that man takes off his clothes, I swear, I'm out of here forever … you know how I hate showy exhibitionists."

Zoe gasped in shock and grabbed Andrea's arm, "Andi, I swear … I had nothing to do with that man being here."

Seeing the distress on her friend's face, Andrea breathed a sigh of relief and backed off her words. She took a quick sip of wine. Her cheeks felt incredibly hot. She blamed it on the drink.

Willing herself to not look again at the man in the back of the room—the one with the uncanny ability to draw her attention—she tried to focus on something else. Finally, she admitted, if only to herself, that she had totally spaced her own birthday. Had she, actually been so wrapped up in her work that she had forgotten—or was it her heart's defense mechanism protecting her, knowing her day of celebration was simply too painful to bare alone?

Zoe interrupted her thoughts. In a reluctant tone, she began, "Andi, you'll never guess who I saw last night…." Her eyes quickly skittered away, and she paused before whispering the last taunting word, "together."

Andrea shook her head in cluelessness.

"Shaun…." She answered, her cagey eyes coming back to settle on Andrea, "and Jolene." Andrea's eyes widened, as her friend explained further, "I went out to the Lodge for an after-dinner interview with a couple celebrating their 60th wedding anniversary, and Shaun and company were leaving through the side door. They must have had a dinner meeting…."

Andrea shook her head. "Those two would have no reason to meet for dinner," Andrea reasoned.

"They left in her car." Zoe's words dropped like a lead balloon.

Andrea sat studying her friend's face, long and hard. Shaun hadn't come home the previous night, but she said nothing as she digested the information.

After a long while, Andrea asked, "Why aren't you eating?"

Zoe blushed. "Financially embarrassed."

Without further comment, Andrea shoved her personal, Hawaiian pan pizza to a spot between the two of them. Their eyes met with understanding on all levels as they both reached for a slice of pizza, and ate in shared silence; she'd deal with this latest revelation, later.

Andrea's mind wandered. She couldn't help but notice that almost everyone was having financial difficulties, these days. The cost of living had skyrocketed. Because of the pandemic, families were still struggling and losing their homes. Kids were going hungry. How could people survive and live successful lives if they didn't have money to buy the bare necessities? Lack of money only shoved people into lives of crime, she reasoned. Her mind began to seriously spin with ways to help Zoe out of her financial trouble.

From his table in the back corner, the stranger caught an occasional glimpse of the stunning woman with the long, shimmering, dark hair, and the gorgeous eyes, deep and intelligent, sitting with her cute friend, and now engrossed in seemingly serious conversation. To his surprise the kiss had left him light-headed and a mite uncomfortable. Now he wondered who she was, wishing the music would stop long enough for him to catch her name. He wanted to approach her … ask her to share a drink, a dance—to share his life; but she was with friends. When they, as a party, presented her with a cake, he knew his moment of opportunity had slipped away—he had some last minute investigating to do, and a commercial plane to catch.

It's really warm in here, Andrea thought as her knife creased the thick layer of icing and cut deep into the cake. She felt eyes upon her, and looked up. The perfect man was looking straight at her. Feeling flustered, she carved ample slices for her party guest. Once the task was finished, she looked up again, stealing a quick glance at the dark, handsome stranger. This time there was no doubt as to what had set her afire.

He doesn't look like an exhibitionist, she thought. In fact, he appeared serious, and quite intelligent, she noted with a degree of satisfaction. Then she noticed that he was reading a copy of today's *News,* and from where she sat, it looked like her front page article. A bolt of satisfaction shot through her at the thought of this guy reading something she'd written, and gazing upon her picture; but her smile quickly faded as she remembered that today's front page article hadn't included her headshot—just her byline.

The man casually perused the front page headlines, skimming the photos. Suddenly his eyes froze on one photo in particular. His jaw clenched, and he snapped to attention.

Second shot from the left was the likeness of a man he readily recognized. The malevolent image was all too fresh in his mind: *Brantley Stone.* Strangely, the caption listed him as Shaun Fitzgerald, but this monstrous killer sure as hell wasn't of Catholic Irish descent, as his new name might suggest.

A deep, sober frown parked on his face as he gulped down the last of his coffee and chased it with water. Stone had been running from the law for more than two years, and now, here he was—plastered, front and center on the front page of the local newspaper. According to the article, he was living in Forest Hills, running for public office—and married to *Andrea Daye Fitzgerald*—the woman he'd been sent to investigate!

The agent ran a hard hand across his mouth and beard—thinking. *Stone, a known narco terrorist, a murderer ... Stone the man responsible for the deaths of his brothers in Afghanistan, and in Mexico—and the monster was hiding out in the open—right here in Forest Hills, Vermont. Incredible!*

It took him no time to realize this investigation had already gone sideways, and he found it impossible to believe the agency didn't know about this turn of events. Either he was deliberately, and blindly, being catapulted into the Stone/Fitzgerald case, or he was being set up—maybe even both!

From the corner of her eye, Andrea watched the serious, highly evolved man push his chair away from the table, tug at the knees of his slim-legged jeans, then settle into a true macho position with one foot resting across the opposite knee. He opened the paper to the middle over-flow section, held it high between his hands, and leaned into the pages, devouring the long columns of print. The guy exuded a ton of manliness, eliciting an appreciative response from the young journalist.

Andrea's gaze settled on his boots and legs, and then on the tops of his socks. *Wait a minute....*

She stopped and did a double-take.

Wait just a damned minute!

Her mind came to a screeching halt, as she forced her eyes into a squint for a better look. *Is he wearing ... rainbow striped socks?*

She looked again and confirmed—*he is*! Her perfect man was wearing socks expressly designed for actively gay men. She had ordered a pair just like them, per request, for the mail clerk's birthday last week.

Now Andrea's blood ran hot, but for a totally different reason. Without hesitation, she shoveled ample servings of cake onto paper plates, as though at a kid's party, and quickly spread them out in the center of the table. In her haste, she all but threw forks onto the plates. Slinging her purse over her shoulder, she rose and slipped into the powder room to wash the chocolate, buttercream frosting from her fingers—and to hide her total disillusionment.

Zoe followed. "Andi, I have one more thing to tell about," she said enthusiastically.

Andrea groaned and squirted foamy soap into her hands. "Don't go breaking my heart," she said, with extreme sarcasm, having a sum of zero tolerance to waste on the Shaun/Jolene caucus. Leaning against the wall, she pulled a paper towel down from the dispenser.

For the first time, Zoe noticed Andrea's small, tangerine purse hanging from her shoulder. "Hmm, nice purse ... is it new?"

"Nah, I haven't shopped in ages ... it's from last year's fall collection," Andrea answered with little interest as Zoe fingered the long, thin straps, appreciatively.

"I just might have to borrow that sometime," she taunted, shooting her friend a hopeful grin.

"What's mine is yours," Andrea droned, listlessly, disengaging from the conversation. She'd had no interest in *things* for quite some time.

"Andi, you are teaching your adult dance class at the Y again this year, aren't you? I can't wait to learn that…." her body gyrated, "*Anaconda* thing."

Andrea glanced at her self-image in the mirror, wondering what the stranger might have seen. "Yeah, sure," she said, pulling a dark tendril down to chin level. "I'm ready to go with that and some newer dances … but I need to get some things settled, first."

Zoe picked a hair off Andrea's shoulder. "Girl, you better get rid of that cat," she teased, holding up the long, white hair between her fingers for Andrea's inspection.

Andrea snatched the hair. "Can't," she answered, sullenly. "It's Shaun's."

Zoe watched her toss the hair and her wet towel into the trash can, catching the momentary flicker of unhappiness seething just below the surface. She grabbed her friend's arm, and looked at her, full-faced and full-savvy. "Then get rid of Shaun," she said, brazenly, without humor.

Shocked by the rawness of Zoe's words, Andrea stood mute.

Her friend continued in a care-laden voice, "Andi, it's more than obvious that you're not happy with Shaun … just get rid of the jerk … and go find *your* Superhero." She nodded towards the dining room. "You could start with that one out there." With a teasing lilt, she added, "The net claims that men with long hair and beards make the most romantic partners."

Andrea let out a heavy sigh, and said, bluntly, "Zoe … the man's gay."

Her friend's head lashed back. "Wut? Then what was that kiss all about?"

Andrea shrugged. "I wish I knew … teasing, maybe … or maybe he just likes to toy with a woman's emotions … you know, to prove he has some kind of power with all that…." She searched for just the right word.

"Machismoness?" Zoe asked, quietly.

Andrea spat out her preferred word choice, "Brain and brawn." The man had definitely stolen her breath away, and she knew it had taken more than just good looks to set her heart to pounding, sending her head into a swoon.

Zoe shook her head. Determination settled on her face. "Andi … that man is definitely not gay!" she said with certainty.

Andrea fired back, "His socks say he is!"

Zoe pushed. "Andi, lots of people wear the rainbow in support of loved ones."

"Not with the word GAY running up the side of the leg!"

"Oh."

She spoke her next words strictly for her friend's percipience, "Whatever ... I don't pick up men in bars." she offered, resolutely.

Suddenly, Andrea's eyes filled with tears, and her words gushed from her mouth, "But ... oh gawd, Zoe ... you are so right ... I am w-r-e-t-c-h-e-d-l-y miserable with Shaun!"

Jolene had watched Andrea go to the powder room before sauntering over to the handsome stranger.

"Got a light?"

"No," the man answered, knowing exactly where this conversation was headed. He shot a glance towards the powder room. "I just gave up all my vices," he baited in a deep, throaty, through the teeth whisper, in imitation of a favorite actor he and his brother had perfected as young boys, and whose personality had now become a genuine part of his own persona.

Jolene rubbed the palm of her hand down the side of her purple, gauze-covered hip. With a confidence that had never failed her, she said, "God ... that sounds boring as hell... wouldn't you rather have some company for the evening ... maybe turn that frown around? She smiled, expectantly, at the gorgeous man, her mouth just shy of drooling.

Instead of an answer, the man impatiently motioned towards the group gathered in the lounge. "Who are all these people?" he asked, casually.

Jolene took her time lighting her own cigarette, took a puff and blew smoke into the air, then flicked the ashes to the floor. At last, she turned a contemptible glare on the group. "This crowd likes to stay anonymous ... they don't want anyone knowing that they drink all their meals."

"Who's the birthday girl?" he asked with a slight upwards tilt of the chin.

Another vile, bored expression crossed her face, and she answered in a flat-lined expression. "Now if I told you that ... I would have to kil...."

Impatiently, he interrupted, mid-sentence. "Got it." He sucked air as stale as the conversation. *Brantley Stone had always been especially fond of that time-worn expression,* he remembered. He stood, stuck a toothpick in his mouth, and threw some money on the table.

"You didn't answer my question," the woman taunted, still clinging to the possibility.

He stared the persistent seductress straight in the eye, seeing there a total lack of character. His answer came from his own pertinaciousness, "My answer is no."

On his way out, he harrumphed quietly, thinking that he should have used his grandfather's approach to aggressive women and shown her pictures, not of ten barefoot, hungry kids, but of ten, lazy deadheads shooting dope and throwing up three-day-old pizza in grandma's basement.

He stopped at the table laden with birthday cake, took notice of the lady's choice of drink, as well as her birthday gift, now unwrapped and lying in its gift box, face up, on different shades of crinkled, teal-colored tissue paper. The gift, itself, was a teal-colored coffee mug with the words *I Only Date Super Heroes* imprinted on the front in large, multi-colored lettering.

Interesting, he thought, with amused, smartass humor, *the woman likes teal.* Then Matthew J. McCormick walked out into the night, carrying away the largest chunk of double-layered, double-fudge cake from the table.

Outside the Lounge, Andrea had stood by, patiently listening to an exasperating, one-sided phone conversation between Zoe and her mother. "I'll go with you," she'd offered, in all seriousness.

"No, no ... go home and get some rest," Zoe had insisted, before rushing off to a pharmacy across town to pick up an expensive prescription refill, bringing an early end to their night out.

Andrea returned to work, but by late evening she'd found no satisfaction in her writing. She felt unreasonably moody and anxious to go home; but home to what?

Editor Rudd had called the death threat a non-event, but later, halted Andrea's drug series, temporarily. The police had traced the call to a throw-away cell phone with no leads. Even Andrea had begun to wonder if the threat had been a hoax. In the meantime Rudd had assigned her to a less controversial subject: *The effects of defunding the police.*

The young journalist, however, had the foresight to maintain her connections with her contacts, and continued researching and investigating—something she did without her editor's knowledge. And now, on this night of her birth, she found herself working late into the evening; the newsroom long abandoned, and completely forgotten by the rest of the staff.

CHAPTER **10**

At the pleasant sound of melodic whistling, she looked up. David Jennings strolled through the empty newsroom, returning after a football game. Her only conversation with the guy had been across the large conference table during their morning meetings. She knew little else about him. For some strange reason, her presence had not been requested during his job interview—something which still had her noodling.

He had slung his navy blue sport coat casually across his shoulder, and thinking himself alone in the newsroom, started to sing in a pleasant, baritone voice: "Working for the man both night and day, Rollin' ... Rollin' ... Rollin' down the river." Surprised to see Andrea, he walked to her door, and leaned in. "Hey, Birthday Girl." He laid a giant candy bar on her desk. "Heard you liked chocolate ... sorry I couldn't make your party. I hope all went well."

She grinned, "Thanks, David ... it did ... sorry you had to work." She shot a quick glance at the digital clock on her computer screen: 11 o'clock. He stepped up to her desk, his tie, loose, and just as crooked and wry as his grin. She looked him full in the face, judging him to be maybe two or three years younger than she, but a very good looking guy. "You're too young to know that song," she said, stoically.

"Well ... yeah ... so are you; but that doesn't mean we don't know it," he shot back, flippantly. I happen to like old music."

"As do I," she agreed.

"Any news on who made that threatening phone call?"

Andrea pursed her lips, and shook her head, negatively.

"Maybe it was old Randy, on a do-over across the Canadian border. Remember the actor who claimed someone was trying to kill him, and disappeared into Canada ... then was caught trying to re-enter the States at the Vermont border."

"Nah … he wouldn't bother me … I'm a fan. If he'd just acted like a flamboyant drug dealer … the feds might never have caught him," she lamented.

David's eyes opened wide. He turned his head, hiding his flushing face. Seeing drug information scattered across her desk, he asked, "So, what's up? I thought Rudd pulled you off your drug series after that death threat event."

"He did, but according to him … there was no event."

"No event meaning … no threat? So he's just sweeping it under the rug?"

"He says it never happened."

David's brows furrowed. His eyes dropped to the pamphlets. "So what's this?"

When she didn't answer, he tried a different tact. "Andi, I've been wondering … don't you have a home to go to … somebody waiting for you? You're here, working late almost every night."

The question stung. She gave him a hard look, and answered in rapid-fire succession. "Well … yeah David, I actually live in a small château … no, I don't have anyone waiting for me … and this," she pointed to the scattered literature across her desk, "is none your damned business."

Seeing immediate distress on his face, she quickly shot him an apologetic grin. Her voice softened. "Sorry, David … I've literally been marinated in caffeine since about four o'clock this morning."

He grinned back his apology, and his acceptance of her apology. "Then why are you still in this God-forsaken place … tonight of all nights?"

Andrea took note of his word choice: *God-forsaken*. That was exactly the way she would describe the present-day newspaper.

In devilment, Jennings lifted a newspaper from the stack on the corner of her desk and pretended to read. "It says, right here, that according to the latest *Forest Hills Daily News* poll, Andrea Daye spends way too much time on the job."

Andrea arched a brow, "It says that, huh?" She lowered her voice. "So why am I getting only pennies and promises when I cash my paycheck?"

They both laughed easily. Jennings ran his fingers through his short, dark hair. "Well, at least we knew, coming in, that we wouldn't get rich working as journalists … right?" He gave her an arresting grin.

She looked twice at the young man. There was something familiar in his manner, but she couldn't quite put a finger on it. "Dedicated people don't get rich, David," she said. "We're supposed to be so noble in our cause that we don't mind being permanently hungry."

David smiled, and his gaze leveled on the newspaper in hand. He suddenly dropped into a nearby chair, his eyes fixed on the picture and bold print caption. When he lifted his head, he asked, with concern, "What's this?" He nodded towards the three-year-old newspaper.

Andrea glanced casually at the dated picture of the war hero and his dog. "I'm doing a follow-up story—a where do old heroes go after they dismantle a surface-to-air missile compound … singlehandedly?"

His brow knitted. "Do you know this guy?" he asked, returning the paper to the stack.

"No … I have no idea who he is … have yet to read the article."

David rubbed his chin in serious contemplation, his expression remaining unchanged. "Andi, everyone left hours ago … why *are* you working so late?" Sometimes the direct approach worked best.

Andrea shrugged her shoulders and swiveled her neck trying to get out the kinks, "I'm not sure I know why myself, David." *Aside from not wanting to go home,* she thought. "I guess I just feel that I have 'miles to go before I sleep.'" She shot him a sheepish grin.

"I know that poem." He side-stepped the desk, and gently began to massage her neck from behind. "My big brother used to go around reciting it. Let's see, 'Stopping by the Woods on a Snowy Evening' by … Jack Frost."

"No," she chortled, "but you're partially right…it was Robert!"

David smacked his palm to his forehead. "Ah, that's right … Ole Rob—the Vermont Poet."

"Slept through junior high literature class, didn't you?" she teased.

"And Vermont history," he chuckled.

Her face softened. "Then allow me to finish your education … Frost was the first ever poet to be celebrated during his own lifetime," she offered. "He wrote that line way back in 1922, while living in Shaftsbury."

Since Andrea covered only hard news, David was surprised to find this softer side to the Assistant Editor. He liked it. It showed a different dimension to her personality—a lovely dimension.

His hands dropped, and he stepped away. "That's an awesome necklace … is it silver or white gold … I snored through Science class, as well."

Andrea's hand rose to her throat. She caressed the pendant. "It's gold …

it was a gift from my mother. She gave my younger sister one just like it." A tinge of melancholy shuttered the glint in her eyes. "We wear them all the time … it makes us feel close." She wouldn't apprise him of the fact that her sister and mother had both been buried in theirs. "Does that sound stupid?"

"Stupid?" David shook his head. "Nah … it sounds like you really loved your family. I know I love mine."

Loved. He'd said loved, past tense. She gave him a weak smile, wondering what he knew about her family. She swiveled her chair to face him. "So what's *your* favorite poem?"

David dropped back into the chair, liking the way she brought the conversation around to him. "I'm more into music than poetry, but I remember another favorite line of my brother's that I liked. It was a John Kennedy quote that he swears was actually gleaned from a dead white poet: 'What power corrupts, poetry cleanses.'"

Andrea shook her head and smiled, "That's one of my favorites, too. Where does your brother live?" she asked, starting to feel the weight of the day.

David sucked air, held it for a beat before pushing out his words. "I … don't know," he said, ruefully. His brow knotted with seriousness, and his eyes darted back to the dated newspaper. "I … think he's … dead."

"Dead? What makes you think that?"

The young sports editor shook his head in disillusionment, and his eyes lost their focus. "I think all the poetry went out of his life," he spat out hoarsely, sardonically.

Quickly realizing that the caustic nature of his comment demanded an explanation, he returned his gaze to the lovely woman, sitting poised and curious in front of him. He explained, "While he was away, serving his country in Afghanistan, his crazy wife decided to abort a full-term pregnancy—my brother's child … his son … my nephew, and she did it just to spite him for signing on for another tour of duty." He pulled down a heavy frown, "You know what they do with full-term fetuses."

"I do," she sighed, nodding.

Andrea shot him a saddened look, encouraging him to continue. "He never talked about it … never shared any of it with Mom and Dad, or any of the rest of the family, but becoming a father had been a really big deal to him."

David cleared his throat, and tears welled in Andrea's eyes.

"Early one Christmas morning, while he was home on leave, he met me in a large field covered with virgin snow ... we rolled giant snowballs for a snowman, a surprise for our mother ... had them loaded on the truck. We'd been laughing and joking ... having fun." David swallowed hard. "Then suddenly, he just stopped, and stared into the sunrise. He wished me a Merry Christmas ... said he had a gift for the country in need of a box and bow, and he took off ... I haven't seen him since."

Andrea grimaced, reaching over to touch his arm, commiseratively, a bond growing between the two. She awaited more details, but David's demeanor suddenly changed, and he fidgeted, aware that he was talking too much. "It's ... uh ... too complicated to go into, and it's getting late." He faked a yawn. "I've got a story to write, and I live all the way across town!"

Andrea leaned in towards the new man on the block. "I'll give you some advice, David ... look for an apartment a little closer to home."

Confusion clouded his face. "Oh, you mean *home,* as in the *Daily News.*"

"Yep ... you got it. A quarter of our paper is national and international news, but sports always gets about six pages ... filling those six pages is on you. Our readers are huge sports fans, and Rudd gives them whatever they want." She chuckled, softly. "He wouldn't think twice about cutting out the entire obituary column, all together, if he needed the space, especially for football or hockey. We'll have you covering so many events ... you'll pass yourself on the highway, comin' and goin' ... better keep your gas tank topped off."

"I can already see that," he chuckled in response. He offered, "The coach at the junior high was telling me about some young kid down in Boston, playing on a travelling hockey team ... they say he's one hell of an aggressive player for his age. I'm thinking about driving down and checking him out ... thought a story might inspire some of the local kids ... get 'em into sports ... keep 'em off drugs."

Andrea shot him a warm smile. She liked what she was hearing coming from this new sports editor. He sounded like a real go-getter. She smiled and offered, "Don't forget to turn in your gas mileage."

He gave her a quick head nod.

"Did you play, David?"

"Yeah, I did ... hence the broken nose." His hand shot to a diminutive bump on his nose, one she'd never noticed on his well-bred face. "I couldn't get enough of it ... I'd actually like to coach someday soon."

She gave him a big sisterly grin, and leaned back in her chair. "I can help you find an inexpensive apartment, if you'd like … help you get settled."

He acknowledged her with a nod. "I'll get back to you on that." He started to leave her office, but turned back to face her. "Oh … hey… Andrea … you know your friend, Zoe?

Andrea plopped her elbows on her desk and propped her chin up with her fists, eyes dancing. "Yeah … I know her," she teased.

"Is she married?"

David walked towards the door, glancing back over his shoulder at the lovely young woman sitting alone in her glass-wrapped office, surrounded by the empty newsroom. The lights had been dimmed, except for the one bright one directly above her head, shining down on her like a beacon. He studied her for a moment. She tried to hide it, but she was a sad lady, he could tell. She was hell on wheels in the newsroom, but after tonight's conversation he knew she had a softer, more gracious side, as well. He liked her. She had character, and that revelation, alone, would make his job a lot easier.

"Stay safe," he called out over his shoulder.

Andrea waved at his parting grin, then smiled, inwardly. Nice kid, she thought. She liked him; especially his wit. He seemed to have a maturity, too—a kind of wisdom she found lacking in a lot of young guys around Forest Hills. She wondered what might have nurtured that wisdom. A line of Ralph Waldo Emerson's came to mind: "Men are what their mothers made them." What would David's mother be like, she wondered?

As she shut down her computer, her mind kept streaming back to the Lounge, and her conversation with Zoe. Birthday, or not, there would be no celebration, or anything else waiting for her at the end of this day; nor would there be a handsome stranger.

On the way out, she stopped beside her desk, perusing the dated newspaper that had caught David's attention. She thought, *if he was interested, maybe her readers would be, too.*

She quickly grabbed a used manila envelope, stuffed the old newspaper inside, and wrote *Special* across the front, then shoved it into her desk drawer, knowing it would be weeks before she would have time to read it; but she would definitely do it, as time allowed. She wondered what might be the best way to track the guy down.

Andrea's cell phone chimed, lighting the car's interior. Immediately recognizing the number, she answered. "This is Andi."

"Oh, Andi ... thank goodness I got you," the harried voice said. "It's Lanie, here at the hospital. All of our beds are full tonight, and the stork just delivered a set of twins. The flu's hit our unit hard, and we're r-e-a-l-l-y shorthanded ... fact is ... I'm the only one working, and I'm not feeling well, myself. Is there any way you could give us a few hours tonight?"

Andrea hit the brakes, and quickly swung her car around, heading back down the driveway. "I'm on my way."

"Thank you, Andi—you're a life-saver."

CHAPTER 11

Andrea parked in the hospital parking lot then punched in the numbers to her own landline, leaving a message as to her whereabouts. Then she entered through the emergency doors, and rode the elevator up to the 5th floor where the sign on the door read: *NAS, Neonatal Abstinence Syndrome*—babies born into addiction.

She remembered facts from the articles she had written: the rate of babies being born with addictions had tripled in the last couple of years. Every hour, a drug dependent baby was brought into the world with an addiction to pain killers—often prescription pain killers; or the more serious drugs like cocaine or heroin because the mother had taken them all through her pregnancy. Cutting off drug use, cold turkey could cause the death of the infant; so new mothers were often put on methadone post birth—which is also addictive. Methadone helps the mother, but her baby, unfortunately, is allowed to enter into the world addicted to the drug, and struggles, seriously, the first couple of weeks following birth—often the infant dies from the addiction.

Andrea scrubbed up and donned a clean smock, then reported for duty.

"Thanks a million," Lanie said. "This gives me a chance to change diapers and clean them up. Bed Ten … a little boy … no name yet."

Andrea raised her eyebrows, hopefully, "Bed Four?" she asked, hopefully.

A grievous look settled on Lanie's face; she shook her head, ruefully. "He didn't make it."

With a heavy heart for the infants, Andrea entered the nursery filled with squalling babies. She padded past Bed Four, where another drug addicted baby now lay, writhing. She kept walking until she reached the last bed in the row. Carefully, she bent down and picked up the little, pink-skinned bundle, trembling and fretting inside the blue-trimmed receiving blanket. She carried him to a small, sound-proof room where a rocking chair, white and comfortably cushioned, awaited. Holding the warm, fretting bundle close to her body, she entered the room, and closed the door behind her.

An older woman was already seated, rocking another child—the twin. Andrea immediately recognized the woman from the high school, the Honor Society organizer who had called Andrea at the last minute, panic-stricken. She'd had a gymnasium full of rowdy students and visitors, but no keynote speaker. Now, she gave Andrea a huge, friendly grin. "Got a hold on you, too?" she asked, sleepy-eyed.

Delighted to see the woman again, Andrea switched off the bright, overhead light, allowing only the soft glow from a night light to permeate the room.

"Yeah ... I can't stand to see a child suffer," Andrea answered softly, emotion weighing on her words.

"Lanie tells me you're not only a journalist, but a registered nurse," the woman said between the stressful squalls of the babies, and the squeaking rocking chair.

"Yeah, my mother pushed me into nursing straight out of high school, but I quickly discovered that my natural talent was with writing; but I've kept my license current just to be prepared for whatever comes my way."

An amused chuckle rose from the spry, septuagenarian's belly, and she lifted her head in amusement, "You sound just like my grandson."

"What's your grandson do?" Andrea asked, genuinely interested, bouncing the wailing baby in her arms.

The woman's eyes saddened and worry dug a deep row of wrinkles across her forehead. "Well, to be quite honest, I haven't heard from him for a while," she said, regretfully, "but I think he's heavy into heroin."

Andrea's head dropped. "I'm so sorry," she whispered, empathically.

"The woman's eyes shot up as she woefully cursed her increasingly forgetful mind, "Oh, I didn't mean...." She suddenly cut off her flow of words.

With the child flailing in her arms, Andrea sat down in a wooden rocker—wooden rockers made the best comforting noise—and settled back. Running her hand under the infant's tiny tee-shirt, she began to pat and rub the baby's moist, fretful back with her bare hand—skin on skin contact, some called it. A tender smirk came to Andrea's face—*other people called it love,* she thought. "Tonight, little guy," she whispered, as she raised him to her shoulder and kissed his soft, sweet head, "your name is, Precious." The baby shook violently, writhing miserably in her arms. She began to pat his back and hum a time-honored lullaby. Soon, the world's youngest drug addict was asleep in her arms, and the exhausted journalist nodded off, mid-hum.

A gentle hand on her shoulder shook Andrea awake. Her bleary eyes looked up into Lanie's somber ones.

Andi ... he's gone."

"Gone?"

"The baby's dead."

CHAPTER 12

Still wiping her eyes and humming the same lullaby, grievously, Andrea fumbled for her house key. When she plunged the key into the lock, the door suddenly flew open.

Startled, she jumped back, her heart pounding in her chest. "Shaun!" she said breathlessly. "You startled me."

"It's about time you got home!" he scolded. "Where the hell have you been?" he bellowed as he loosened his tie and undid the top button of his shirt.

Aware that the first thing Shaun always did upon entering the house was to loosen his tie, Andrea felt certain he'd just beaten her home. Her voice remained calm, although she silently seethed at his comments. "I've been doing something humane, Shaun. Where else would I be? Sug knew where I was." She walked to the refrigerator and took out a carton of milk. "Where have *you* been for the last several days?"

He ignored her question. "There are rumors going around about you," he spat.

Her eyes narrowed into daggers, "There are *rumors* going around about you, bud."

His eyes narrowed, "Who was that piece of shit at the Writer's Block Lounge that everyone is flapping their gums about?"

A vision of the perfect man came to mind. Andrea wondered who had told Shaun. Jolene, she supposed.

She sucked in a deep breath and let it out, "It was my birthday, Shaun. A lot of people wished me Happy Birthday—which is more than I can say for you."

He yanked his tie off with force, and with the other hand grabbed her chin between his fingers and squeezed. "Well, you're *my* wife!"

He dropped his hand, but only to shove a chair into the table, in anger.

"I can't stay up all night waiting for you to come in like some damned, stray, alley cat." His voice reeked with hostility, and his breath with hard liquor. "I sent the help to bed hours ago … no need to keep the whole house up all night."

The help? Was he referring to the woman who had spent the bulk of her life caring for the people in this house? She spoke from her exhaustion, refusing to play his little game. "Shaun," she said with conviction rising in her voice, "I'm not your wife by any stretch of the imagination … I'm not your daughter, and I'm sure as hell over twenty-one. So you can just drop this little charade right now. I'll come and go whenever and wherever it is convenient to *me* … this is still *my* home, and still *my* life … and what's this crock about you having to wait up? The only time you're ever here for me is when you need a favor," she raised the glass to her lips, preparing to take a sip, "so what is it this time?"

The back of Shaun's hand across her face and mouth made a loud whopping sound, knocking the glass to the floor, where it shattered, instantly, its contents splattering across the floor. Shaun's cat, heretofore perched on top of the refrigerator, instantly leapt to the floor and pounced on the spilt milk. Forced to side-step the cat, Andrea fell into Shaun.

She heard a click, and felt the hard nose of a handgun against her ribcage as he pushed his angry face into hers. He hissed, in no uncertain terms, "It's whatever I say it is!"

Andrea's dazed, blurry eyes shot to a shadowy movement at the top of the stairway where Sugaraye stood, watching, fretfully wringing her hands.

Andrea's cheek seared with pain. She felt weak and her joints ached, but mostly, she was over-wrought from months of these emotionally draining scenes with this abusive man—a man she hated with a passion. She couldn't tolerate him on any level, and she certainly didn't want him in her house— but Shaun had simply refused to leave!

"You're driving me to the airport first thing tomorrow morning," he said in a voice commanding authority over all living creatures. "We'll leave at 5:30 sharp!" With these words he turned, and with heavy, pounding steps ascended the stairway to his bedroom. His cat followed, mewing at his heels.

When his bedroom door slammed shut, Andrea moaned, deeply and painfully, surprised at the sounds coming from her own body. She was so tired of fighting a war on this front. Benumbed, she cleaned up the broken glass, and switched off the light—on the whole damned, stinking situation.

Upstairs, she tapped lightly on Sug's door. When it opened a crack, she whispered, "Are you okay? Keep your door locked … we'll talk tomorrow."

Andrea's thoughts went to Sugaraye, or *"the help"* as Shaun had described her. The 75-year-old woman had been born to the owner of an old, maple syrup canning factory in the southern part of the state, and named after his beloved maple sugar trees. Even though maple sugar was considered the backbone of Vermont, her father had not been able to recover his losses following a fire that destroyed the sugarhouse and all the outer buildings, including the family home; and so, as a young teenage girl, Sugar had come to work as a live-in domestic for Andrea's grandparents. With a disposition as sweet as her name, they'd sent her off to college; but after a short, unsuccessful marriage, she'd willfully returned with a degree in hotel management never to leave the family's employ. In return, they considered her family.

Unfortunately, Sug had been diagnosed with fast-developing Alzheimer's disease a couple of months earlier, and the ravaging disease was rapidly attacking her memory. Soon, she would not recognize even Andrea. She would become child-like, requiring the care of a child.

Andrea had been in touch with Sug's sister, Rose, and at Rose's request, had made plans to send her to Toronto for the holidays, and possibly for the rest of her life. This saddened Andrea, for she too felt an enormous need to care for the one, who had cared for her and her entire family for as long as Andrea could remember. But she would respect Rose's request, knowing it would be best for Sug to connect with her own family before her mind failed completely—and she needed to be out of this house for her own safety and well-being.

Andrea showered quickly, and then searched for a book of inspirational quotes. She propped her plush, billowy pillow behind her back, then turned to a dog-eared page and read until her heart lightened, and her lids grew heavy. Finally, she switched out the lights.

Lying in darkness, she reviewed the events of the day, her work, her conversation with Shaun, David, the situation with David's brother, and the dear, sweet babies. Her anamnesis, however, was soon interrupted by a flicker of car lights. She listened as a single car door slammed shut. Who would be calling this close to morning? Inquisitively, she slipped from her bed and padded across the thick, plush Persian carpet, boldly looking out the window.

Immediately, she recognized the metallic, navy blue Hyundi, and the overly-dressed redhead exiting the car. "Jolene!" she gasped, disbelieving her own eyes. She shot a glance at the clock. What on earth would she be doing here at this time of night? She quickly answered her own question; Jolene was moonlighting. She snapped the blinds shut.

So Jolene was one of Shaun's women, just as Zoe had implied. Well, that would certainly explain a lot of things—things like the woman's expensive wardrobe, something she certainly couldn't afford on her salary as city editor. It also explained her contemptible attitude. Something nefarious was going on, for sure; but more importantly, this was a relationship that could have some very serious ramifications.

It was late, and Andrea decided to deal with it the following morning when her mind was fresh, and while Shaun was away. Being wide-awake, she walked to her large walk-in closet, finding a large box. With great ceremony, she began taking pictures off the shelves. She would be leaving this house soon and there would be, most likely, no time to pack. She knew she had to get away from Shaun, for her own safety. She'd also found that living with the ghosts and memories of her deceased family in every corner of the house was proving to be too emotionally draining.

She smiled at her own picture—a grungy twelve-year-old kid, sitting atop her first honey-colored horse. She had named her, Windy Foot, after the horse in her, all-time, favorite children's book *Sleigh Bells for Windy Foot* by Vermont author Frances M. Frost. She still remembered the picture on the front of the book.

She hesitated as she came to the one, and only, family portrait ever to be taken. Her family had always been too busy to have portraits done. She lovingly swiped dust from the frame, then wrapped it in bubble wrap. She would pack this picture, and then come back for the others at a later date.

She grabbed a picture of her younger sister from the shelf. It had been taken at the beginning of her sophomore year in high school. Dressed in her red volleyball uniform, her long, dark hair had been pulled around and arranged, becomingly, across one shoulder. Andrea studied the warm smile, large and friendly, and the expressive eyes with just a glint of mischievousness to them. The girl's image seemed to leap out of the frame … she looked so alive! Heather had been so full of love for those around her that it was hard to believe she was actually dead.

Hugging it to her chest, she sighed, grievously, "Dear sweet Heather … if only you could tell me what happened." Huge, hot tears welled up in her eyes and streamed down her cheeks, followed by deep, chest-heaving sobs.

At last, she wiped her eyes with trembling hands, having no energy left in her body. Doing that which had already been done, time and again, she ran through the list of people who'd had access to Heather just before her death. Long ago, she had narrowed it down to one person. She vowed to get the monster who had done this to her beloved, little sister. She packed the picture away with care; then stored the box in the closet for easy access.

Her hands came to rest on another smaller box. This one held her mother's belongings—her music. Andrea smiled through misty eyes as she sifted through the jewel cases filled with the music of saxophonist, Kenny G. Her mother had been a huge fan, always playing his happy, lilting songs on vacations, and attending his concerts whenever he came within a hundred miles of home. There in the box, as well, was Mom's beige, black-billed, Kenny G cap. She'd always worn the hat when she worked in her Garden of Many Roses, as she called it.

Andrea fingered the gold, jeweled saxophone pin attached to the cap, a birthday gift from Dad. She sighed, knowing that the pin had last been touched by her mother's hands. She had many fond memories of their road trips with this music playing softly in the background.

At last, she returned to bed, flipping through an advertiser featuring men's suits and shoes that had come with the Sunday paper. Her eyes settled on a guy somewhere in his 20's, modeling a high-priced suit. Somehow, he reminded her of David. Browsing through a page of western wear, she grew more unsettled by the minute, and tossed it to the floor. She turned off the light and snuggled deep into the cool, fresh linens. She closed her eyes and meditated on the words of Greek philosopher Epictetus: *When you have shut your doors, and darkened your room, remember never to say that you are alone, for you are not alone; but God is within….*

◄○►

A fresh, cool breeze nipped lightly at the ends of Andrea's hair, and a blissfully warm sun kissed her rosy cheeks as she stood at the end of a long, winding, tree-lined drive with a backdrop of misty, pristine mountains.

Dressed in tight-fitting jeans, and brown, hand-sanded Stetson boots, she slowly walked along the rustic, wooden fence row surrounding a shady grove. A proud palomino stallion pranced, impatiently, back and forth along the fence rail, eager to flee his restraints. Outside the large stable doors, lay a collection of rescued, once-orphaned dogs, sunning themselves, making no attempt to look like guard dogs.

Andrea stepped out of the bright sunlight, and into the cool, darkened stable. Her gaze immediately rose to the heavy, wooden beams, supporting the roof while creating a rustic atmosphere, strong and masculine. In contrast, her own femininity became more pronounced, and she felt comfortable within her womanhood. No gender confusion here, she chuckled.

She looked around at the neat stacks of dried, golden straw at the far end of the building. The scent of horses, the fragrance of sweet-smelling hay, and good quality leather all came together in one whiff in the distinctive essence of a stable. She saddled the mare that had been patiently standing tethered to the railing, and prepared to mount with great anticipation.

Her head shot up, when from the distance, came the insistent neigh of a horse, followed by the clippity-clop, clippity-clop of galloping hooves. She looked through the large swing-away doors to see a handsome stranger riding towards the stable.

"David!" *No, that's not David,* she thought. Why did she think it was David?

He was calling her name. "Andrea!" He was smiling, but his voice sounded angry. The horse's hooves grew louder and angrier on the hardened ground....

"Andrea!"

Suddenly, Andrea awoke with a start, her heart pounding wildly in her chest. She stirred, and looked around for the clopping sound and the handsome stranger. Slowly, reluctantly, and with great disappointment, she recognized her own room.

"Andrea, wake up!"

It was Shaun, rapping impatiently on her bedroom door—a door that had been bolted against him the night before ... and every night since their wedding ceremony.

"Andrea, you're late." he yelled gruffly from the other side of the door.

The four o'clock alarm sounded. Drowsily, she sat up and hit the off button. "Late?" She glared at the door in disbelief, but her nemesis was already gone. She could hear his footsteps descending the stairway, followed by the lighter, sassy clicking of a woman's heels. "Jolene!"

Shaken by the dream, and overwhelmed with frustration at Shaun, she heaved her pillow over her head and threw it fiercely at the door. She screamed, "What is your problem?" The pillow fell soundlessly, futilely, to the floor in a rumpled heap.

With little resolve, she threw her legs over the side of the bed. Her thoughts were unfocused, but her emotions had taken on a life of their own. With all her heart, and every fiber of her being, she longed to go back to her dream—to live!"

Once her mind had cleared, and the day's mission remembered, she went through her regular morning routine with little interest. She did, however, apply a little extra makeup to her bruised cheek, and lip gloss to her split lip. She piled her hair on top of her head, the way Shaun preferred it, pulling down swing bangs and a few side tendrils. She stepped into her sleek-fitting fuchsia dress that ended just above the knee; then slipped her arms into the gray, waist-length jacket. She glanced into the mirror, not seeing the stunning, young woman staring back. She reached, first, for the pair of heels Shaun preferred she wear; but quickly ditched them, and opted for gray leggings and gray boots with silver brads and trim. She selected her favorite chain necklace from her jewelry box, admiring the bold, but delicate pendant as she walked to the window. She pulled the curtain back for a better view of the early morning sky, realizing that nothing was going to brighten this morning.

From her second-story window she watched Shaun pull his Town Car around to the front entrance. Why he insisted on driving that big, old, black hearse everywhere was beyond her. She disliked driving large cars and wished he would just let her drive her old Honda.

She studied his face as he got out, and walked around the front of the car. His demeanor was as dark and tumultuous as the ominous sky, heavy and gray, threatening to unleash its fury on the world at any moment. When he slid in on the passenger's side, impatiently waiting for her, she heaved a heavy sigh, having grown so tired of his open hostility.

As she fussed, unsuccessfully, with the fastener on her necklace, she heard a blast from the car horn. "That man is going to be the death of me," she fumed. Opting to deal with the clasp later, she left it to dangle, temporarily, from her fingers. Having no time to switch-out her purse for something more complimentary to her outfit, she grabbed it and rushed downstairs to the kitchen.

On her way through the unlit kitchen, a sharp pain stabbed the pit of her stomach. She pulled open the refrigerator door and stared into the colorless light. Still clutching at the persistent pain, she took out a jug of orange juice.

"You got an ulcer, or are you just hungry?" a voice said from the darkened corner behind her.

CHAPTER 13

Andrea turned quickly to face her housekeeper. "Oh, Sug!" What are you doing up this early. Please, go back to bed."

"I'll go to bed after we've talked," Sug answered, resolutely. She stepped forward, taking the chain from Andrea's fingers, while admiring the younger woman's fuchsia-clad body. Her aging hands trembled as she placed the chain around the young woman's slender neck. *The lass would look good in a gunny sack,* she thought, fastening the clasp. "I'll bet you haven't eaten a thing in the last twenty-four hours, have you, child? I tried to leave you something last night, but Shaun ran me out of the kitchen before I could get it fixed." She huffed, "He seems dead set against you eating, for some no good reason."

Andrea smirked at the remark, "Nah, he's too self-centered to give me any consideration."

"Andrea sweetheart ... listen to me. These old hands," she lifted up her palms, and stared into them as though they displayed the past, "these old hands diapered your scrawny, little butt, and I love you like you were my own daughter. I loved your grandparents ... I loved your mother and father, and your dear little sister ... God bless their sweet souls. And I'll tell you right now ... it grieves me to see you living like this. I don't feel like I'm taking good care of you ... I feel like I've failed the family."

The woman's words grieved Andrea, but she didn't have time or the energy to deal with it just now.

The old woman read Andrea's seemingly diffident demeanor, and stiffened. Her voice grew stronger. "Andrea, I know exactly what's going on in this house. Why, in the world, don't you just leave that man? You're a beautiful young woman, and you're much too sweet a person to be treated so badly. You deserve better."

Andrea turned and grabbed the woman by her rigid shoulders. "Sug, I promise I'll leave just as soon as I have proof … money," she quickly corrected.

"You mean when Shaun returns your inheritance money, don't you?"

Andrea shook her head. "It's more complicated than that." She sighed at the round, sober face beneath hair as white and as fine as crystallized sugar. "Look Sug, this is not your problem, but I know things are seriously wrong in this house … and in the company, but I can't prove anything. Shaun's brought in an all new, inexperienced staff who knows nothing about pharmaceutical sales—and we're bleeding large amounts of money."

Sugar tucked her chin, listening as Andrea continued. "I know I've been grief-stricken too long, and probably need to see a shrink, but Sug … I do know the truth."

The woman pursed her lips. Wizened by age, and knowing it best not to speak the truth aloud, she offered, "Andrea, we both know the truth." She held Andrea's gaze. "Everything would be fixed in a minute if you would just get rid of that good-for-nothing husband!" Wrapped in the smugness of her candid remarks, she pulled a chair away from the ornate, highly polished table, and plopped into the seat. "There … I've said it!" Her arms flopped across her ample chest as she leaned back in the chair.

Andrea didn't hear the housekeeper's next words as details of the last several months whirred through her head. *And things aren't right at the News, either,* she thought, with growing apprehension.

"Have you gotten a look at some of those people he's bringing into this house?" Sug was asking. Andrea nodded. "They seem mighty strange to me, but you should see the mess they leave for me to clean up –they act like they've never lived in a house before or sat at a table to eat a meal."

"I'm sorry they make extra work for you, Sug."

"Ah." She waved away the apology. "You want to hear what he said when I complained about his friends? He told me I was just and old woman, dried up and useless … out of touch with what was really going on in the world. He said that *our* day was over. Ha! And when I tried to fly the Stars and Stripes on Veterans Day, he made me take it down. Andi … they don't even act like Americans."

Suddenly, Sugar had Andrea's full attention.

Another blast of the car horn filtered in from the driveway. Andrea bent down, and wrapped her arms around her friend in a warm bear hug, kissing the top of her lily-white head. "Stop worrying about me and go back to bed ... sleep all morning, because tonight I'm going to come home ... at a normal time ... and we're going to make popcorn, and fudge, and watch old movies ... Spencer Tracy and Kate Hepburn—Shaun's going away for a few weeks."

The old woman's hands came together for a single clap, and her face lit up, child-like.

Andrea smiled. Maybe Zoe had the right idea, after all; escaping this insane world for a few hours might not be such a bad idea. As she headed towards the door, she looked askance at the woman who had always been a part of her life. "Tonight, Sug ... don't forget!"

Guilt lay heavy on her heart as she walked to the car—towards the bane of her existence. *It is I, Sug, who has failed you,* she thought, wiping away a tear. She had been so deep into her own sorrow that she had not considered the toll it was taking on her dear friend. And Sugar was right—her life had become an absurdity. She vowed that not another month would pass before one of them, either she or Shaun, would be out of this house.

"Come on, come on," Shaun snapped, impatiently as Andrea slipped her slender body behind the wheel.

Tired of his bluster, she looked determinedly at her husband. "Shaun, don't you have someone on your massive payroll who could drive you to the airport? Or couldn't you simply drive yourself and park the car until you return? I'm really too busy for this."

"No!" he snapped. "No I don't."

"Then hire somebody!" she snapped back, heatedly, pushing down memories of the ugly scene from the night before. She maneuvered the car down the long driveway, past what had once been a professionally manicured lawn and garden, but now, to her distress, showed horrible signs of neglect. Before the accident, her mother had, lovingly, tended the roses and her father had carefully instructed the gardener on the placement of every plant and shrub on the property. They had loved their home.

The first thing Shaun had done after the wedding was to construct a twelve-foot high stone wall that completely surrounded the entire estate. At the end of the driveway, a heavy, electronically-controlled, cast-iron gate had been installed to separate the Fitzgerald property from the rest of the world. Shaun had carefully explained that its purpose was to keep out "undesirables." Andrea suppressed a laugh. In a day's time she saw a lot of people, but none as undesirable as those her husband brought home with him.

As they waited for the gate to open, Shaun turned down the sun visor, carefully studying his image in the mirror. Running a comb through his, expertly and expensively, trimmed hair, he reprimanded, "You wouldn't mind a little inconvenience once in a while if it wasn't for that silly job of yours … you sure as hell don't need the money."

Andrea could hold her tongue no longer. "Shaun, my job just happens to be very important to me … it's my career choice. I wish you could simply respect that fact," she answered, fervidly.

"Well, important or not, I want you to give it up!" His eyes flashed with virulence. "I only got you that job because you wouldn't stop wailing for that stupid family of yours."

Andrea felt as though a knife had been thrust into her heart at his obvious lie. Her face flushed and her throat tightened, indignantly, as a new supply of unshed tears burned hot behind her lashes; but she made a conscience decision to bury her feelings. Totally ignoring the reference to her family, she asked, "What do you mean by 'I got you the job'?" But by this time, Shaun had already dismissed their conversation and had busily spread his legal briefs across the console, creating a wall of indifference between himself and his beautiful wife.

As though apologizing for the uncomfortable silence, a heavy rain began to beat noisily against the windshield and continued for the remainder of the hour's drive to the airport. Andrea, however, felt relieved. She had no desire to converse with a man she loathed so completely.

As the wet blur of houses and telephone poles slipped silently by, Andrea reviewed the futility of her marriage. Shaun had become like a giant octopus, demanding constant control over her life. Each time she committed herself to a project outside the "Great Wall" he reached out a tentacle and yanked her back, placing undue demands upon her time; and yet, he made no effort to give her time, or attention, or any form of kindness, even after the deaths of her family members. During their funerals, he could only be counted present. Why Shaun, why? There had to be a reason for all of this absurdity.

At last they turned onto Airport Drive, and not a moment too soon.

Both the car and her clothes reeked of Shaun's incessant chain-smoking. She pulled the car up to the main entrance, and as though by destiny, a car pulled away, leaving the spot, conveniently vacant—an extremely rare occurrence. She eased the car into the space, satisfied with her flat-parking skills, but also taking note that, with all the heavy traffic, it would be extremely difficult to get out of, later.

Once inside, Shaun picked up his ticket and checked his luggage, then began walking briskly towards the terminal, swinging Andrea's umbrella at his side as though a club. Andrea followed, feeling demeaned, like a child trying to keep up with Daddy.

"I'll be in Mexico City for a few days."

She shot him a look of concern. "Mexico City is no longer a safe place for American businessmen, Shaun ... especially if your business is pharmaceuticals. They're averaging ten or more kidnappings a day."

Fitzgerald derisively shook off her warning, "From there I'm headed to Peru, South America ... for three weeks," he said flatly over his shoulder, as though it were none of her business.

"I wasn't aware that we purchased directly from Peru," she answered. "Isn't that the *new* cocaine capitol of the world?"

"Mexico City ... Peru ... Columbia," he snickered, "what difference does it make? It's all money ... your father made a fortune buying and selling drugs."

"*Legal* drugs," she shot back, heatedly, sarcastically—insinuatingly. "My father made a fortune selling *legal* drugs ... he saved people's lives." She paused a moment, then warned in a flat, business-like tone, "Shaun ... it's important that we guard the integrity of this company...."

He cut her words off, crassly, "I don't need, nor do I want your advice ... I'll call the morning of my return trip with my flight number and arrival time ... and, Andrea, I want you here, personally, to pick me up. Do you understand?"

Narcissistic behavior is not hard to understand, she thought; but instead, she said in a flat-lined tone, "Understood."

Shaun handed her the umbrella as he lit up a cigarette, eyeing her with acrimony. Studying her face, he rudely blew smoke in her direction; then he lifted his cell phone from the pocket of his black overcoat, and turned his back to her.

Once his call was finished, he started to walk away, but stopped and turned abruptly, snatching the umbrella from her hands. As he did so, his eyes roamed up and down her body, disapprovingly. "One other thing ... I'm not at all impressed by your appearance this morning. You look ... dowdy." Surprise etched across Andrea's face. "Someone with your limited appeal should be working harder to keep up with the competition!"

Andrea's body stiffened as she glowered at the man. "I'm not competing, Shaun!" Without another glance in his direction, she turned on her heels, and walked away.

From the observation tower, she watched the plane taxi to the runway—if only to know Shaun was actually leaving. "Competition, my foot," she groused. She knew she looked tired, but she also knew exactly how important a politician's wife could be during a major campaign. Shaun Fitzgerald was a political barracuda. It wouldn't do for his wife to look like an average working girl. He wanted her to have a Hollywood image with practiced smiles, and choreographed waves to fit into television sound bites and newspaper blurbs—glitz and glamour 24/7.

As the front wheels of the 737 rose from the ground on a rare lift-off and became airborne, she reached up, and yanked the elastic band out, freeing her hair to fall naturally across her shoulders. "Try not to get kidnapped," she hissed, her voice low, terse—and oozing sarcasm, as the plane quickly disappeared into the heavy, black rain clouds.

On the way out of the airport, she stopped to pick up a hot coffee and rushed to her car, more than aware that she was running late for work. Her ears still burned. "Dowdy," she hissed under her breath, "not in this outfit!"

She started the engine, turned on the windshield wipers, and signaled her intention to pull into the stream of heavy, fast-moving traffic. As she waited, watching through the side mirror for an opening, she found herself hypnotized by the slow, methodical blinking of the flashers, the splatter of raindrops and squeaky wipers swishing, seductively, across the windshield. She yawned, deeply, into her hand. She removed the lid from her coffee. Hot steam gushed into her face. Unable to get caffeine into her system fast enough, she blew into the cup, and took a tiny sip; then she pulled out into the rain-drenched street.

Tires screeched, and metal scraped against metal. Her car—Shaun's car—was getting rear-ended. Her body lurched forward with a jerk, before quickly snapping back in a whiplash effect, upending her hot drink.

Ultra-hot liquid seeped through to her chest and stomach before trickling through to the car seat, leaving steam to rise rapidly from the entire front of her dress. "Aaah ... hot ... hot!" she yelped, her staccato voice giving expression to her pain. As the liquid cooled, a brief flash of sarcasm surfaced. She unfastened her seatbelt, threw it aside and spoke with panache. "Shaun .... you have no idea how *hot* I am at this moment ... let me tell you ... I am *one hot lady!*"

Horns began to blast as she angrily batted away the empty cup from her lap and sprang from the car to assess the damage. A man, suddenly, stood at her side—the other driver. Through the heavy downpour, she glared at him, but for some reason, her usual, venomous tongue betrayed her with silence.

It wasn't his size, as he stood staring at the scrunched up metal of both cars, even though he had to be somewhere close to six-foot-four, with every inch looming large, or his rugged, taut jawline, his mouth sporting a moue that said, don't even think about messin' with me; nor was it his high-end, urban-styled clothing, unusual this far north. No, what unnerved Andrea the most about the man as he squared himself to face her, were his unreadable eyes, flashing like lightning, yet smoldering like hot coals on a cold, wintery night, scorching her in an uncompromising glare. She looked up and scowled back, watching raindrops trickle off his short, freshly trimmed hairstyle like beads of sweat, finally coming to rest in his knitted brows and neatly trimmed mustache.

Andrea stood before the angry man. The image of Shaun's angry face flashed across her mind. Suddenly, she felt sick—sick of dealing with angry people. She snapped, and began to lambast in an unprecedented rant, "Who in the hell gave you a license to drive ... the armored tank division of the U.S. military?

The man flicked the rain away from his thick lashes for a better look at the woman—a hotbed of anger with glowering eyes, and hair whipping wildly about her face, conjuring up, in his mind, strong images of Medusa. "That would be preferable to the death squad that licensed you!"

"You know, you've missed your calling, bud," she shouted, "you should be driving Humvees across the open desert ... with nothing but dust bunnies and camel dung to get in your way ... maybe a sand dune, or two, to help you get stopped." Even Andrea was surprised at the vitriol spewing from her mouth, like contaminated waters from a spout. She pushed past him, assessing the damages for herself.

His car had suffered the brunt of the collision; but her anger had taken root and wouldn't let go. She sizzled, remembering the lawyers waiting for her in Rudd's office, waiting to discuss one of their front page stories, with their demands of a total retraction. Raising her hot glare to meet his, she continued her assault. "You have totally ruined my day … and I'll probably lose my job because of it!"

He shook his head, disparagingly, "Not my problem."

Her lips pursed. "Well aren't you quite the egotistical ass."

The man's steely jaw clenched. He leveled his hot gaze on her, and spoke in a stubborn, flat voice, "Lady, I am more than damned sorry that you pulled out in front of me … and wrecked my agency's rental car."

Andrea's mouth dropped open with incredulity. Her eyes ran from the top of his wet head to the toes of his new, urban-style loafers. She pointed to her car with an exaggerated gesture, and shot his heated look right back at him. "Hey, jerk, my turn signal was flashing like a … like a trench-coated, sex pervert. I had just checked traffic before I pulled out … you were nowhere in sight, bud."

Appreciating the woman's quick wit, the thought crossed his mind that she might be fun to be around—fun if it wasn't for all that hot, burning anger.

He growled, "My name's not Bud, but I was there … and I had the right-of-way … if you'd wiped the mote from your eyes, you would have seen me." He looked up at the building. "The surveillance camera will show us what really happened."

"Surveillance camera?"

"Hell yes … efin' cameras are everywhere." He spoke words of anger, but his feelings of exasperation came, not from either wrecked vehicle, or from Andrea's wicked tongue, but from getting caught in an amateurish situation while tailing a criminal suspect—one who seriously needed to be taken down.

Having just returned from an intense week in Washington, D.C., testifying before the Foreign Affairs Committee, and taking care of some personal business, Matthew McCormick had retrieved his over-night bag and walked to the parking garage. When he looked up, he'd caught a glimpse of his worst nightmare, leaving the airport under a fuchsia-colored umbrella, a mite too small, proportionally, for his ample body size.

McCormick had watched the man cross the street, and climb into the passenger side of a sleek-looking, navy blue, Hyundai Elantra. He had followed in hot pursuit, got eyes on the license plate, and memorized the number; but suddenly, this big, old, black hearse of a car had pulled out in front of him. The Elantra had zipped down the ramp, and away through the drizzle and fast-moving traffic, but there had been no doubt, in McCormick's mind, as to who was getting away—Brantley Stone, a.k.a., Shaun Fitzgerald.

"We should call a cop," the sopping, but gorgeous woman was saying.

The man cocked a cynical brow. "Yeah ... this calls for someone with good, sound judgment and strong moral fortitude," he said, sardonically. Growing impatient with the whole untimely situation, he added, "Nah ... on second thought ... just give me your name and insurance information ... my people will handle it." He turned, letting his head droop as he headed towards his car, mumbling to himself, "I don't have time to argue with a crazy bitch ... in the middle of the street ... in the pouring rain ... over a damned dented fender in some *Festival of Fools* street production—there are more important things going on in the world...."

Andrea gasped, and McCormick stopped himself, recognizing his classic symptoms of PTSD (Post-Traumatic Stress Disorder) in its mildest form. He turned back to look at her. "You do have insurance, right?" Once he'd expressed his doubt, he could almost see the steam rise from her head as she felt the sting of his insult.

While Andrea reconsidered calling the police, realizing that processing the report would take forever, the man had the gull to snap her photo, multiple shots of both cars, as well as the *Yield to Oncoming Traffic* sign on his sophisticated, digital camera. With an eye to the time, she wrote her name, and that of her agent, on a leaf of her reporter's notepad, ripped it out, and, snarkily, handed it to the man; who, in turn, stood smirking, menacingly, while holding out his business card between his long, agile fingers. She felt it again, if only for an instant, that annoying flicker of familiarity that seemed to constantly haunt her, these days. "Do I know you? she asked, feeling somewhat daunted.

McCormick's stomach knotted. He said nothing, but widened his stance and stared at her with eyes wide open, preparing to lose his anonymity.

In a hurry to get to work, and escape this jerk's presence, Andrea snatched the card out of his hand, and apathetically, dropped it into her coat pocket. Turning, briskly, on her gray, booted heels, she walked towards her car, glancing guardedly over her shoulder. There, definitely, was something disquieting behind those dark, intimidating eyes. Then it came to her. She whipped around to face him. "I know who you are," she exclaimed, tauntingly, squaring her shoulders. "You're the pulchritudinous devil they used as a model for that new, male, robotic sex doll!"

Ire shot through McCormick like a speeding bullet—she'd found his weak spot. He glared at her, his look hot enough to melt the scrunched up metal on both cars. In a purely, knee-jerk reaction, he spouted, "I suppose *you* would know!"

Shocked at the insult, she climbed into her car, slammed the door shut in no uncertain terms, and sped away in the midst of honking horns and irate motorists, leaving the robotic, super-studded, glamour-puss standing alone in the rain.

"Hooyah!" McCormick growled as he stood in the pouring rain, watching her drive away. "That woman has embraced her inner bitch!"

With a mix of emotions coming to the surface, he walked to his car and pulled the door open. He had recognized her immediately, recalling the tender birthday kiss he'd laid on the lovely, young woman's lips at the Writer's Block Lounge just a few short days ago. Luckily, she hadn't actually recognized him this morning, in the foggy rain, without the beard, the ponytail, or smelly boots—and so he'd kept his mouth shut. He grimaced, readily admitting that his responses to her comments had been rude and over the top. *You can take the man out of the underworld, but you can't take the underworld out of the man,* he thought. But Christ … what had happened to *her* since that evening?

Something shimmering drew his eyes to the pavement. There, in the bubbling, pooling rainwater lay a shiny object. He bent low, scooped it up, and held it between his fingers, studying it—a chain necklace, beautifully crafted and extremely pricy. There was no doubt as to who its owner was; he had first seen it that day in the Lounge, fitting her perfectly, as though she had been born with it around her neck. The chain was the perfect length, the pendant the perfect size, made of a metal that complemented her skin tone perfectly. He dropped it into his pocket. He'd find a way to return it to her—as soon as he figured out who in the hell she was. He had been too discombobulated at seeing her again to get her license number.

Rain noisily splattered the hood and roof of his crumpled vehicle as he settled in behind the wheel, leaving the door standing wide-open. A long line of traffic waited impatiently behind him, horns blaring. Eager to learn her identity, McCormick quickly scanned the information on the soggy sheet of paper. With disbelieving eyes he read it a second time: *Andrea Daye, Forest Hills Daily News Assistant Editor and Special Reporter.*

Andrea Daye ... this is Andrea Daye?

His mind exploded. "Aw, for Chrissake!" he groaned, his chin dropping to his chest. This incredibly hot woman, this gorgeous, insanely crazy, wonderfully intelligent woman was Andrea Daye—journalist, Andrea Daye, the woman he'd been sent to investigate. Andrea Daye Fitzgerald—the wife of his archenemy!

CHAPTER 14

Only her deep-rooted respect for *News'* visitors prevented Andrea from taking one of the two available parking spaces in the front of the building as she pulled into the lot, windshield wipers flapping at full-force. She parked, instead, in the rear, leaving a fair distance to walk.

Digging under the front seat for an umbrella, she came up empty handed. "That's just great!" she hissed, ruefully remembering how Shaun had toted her umbrella all through the airport. Resentment towards the man filled her senses.

Numbed by the lack of sleep, the accident, and the hour's drive home from the airport through the heavy downpour, she sat. Her head dropped back as she listened to the rhythmic drumming against the rooftop, allowing her emotions to catch up to her frenzied life.

At last, she made a mad dash to the canteen door where, not protestors, but gushing water splashed from the awning, drenching her, gathering in puddles at her feet. David stood by the coffee machine, sipping from a paper cup, waiting, with concern for the tardy woman. "Wow!" He enthused, as she entered the building. "Girl … you've simply nailed that Casual Friday look."

"Shut up, David!" she hissed. *Why did everyone find it necessary to comment on her appearance this morning*? She ran her fingers through her soggy hair, "Some jerk just rear-ended Shaun's car."

"Bummer … he'll really be mad," The sports editor shuffled his feet, uncomfortably, never having witnessed Andrea so upset. "Seriously Andi, I was getting worried about you … you're never late." He looked at the exposed skin at the base of her throat. "Where's your necklace?"

Andrea's hand shot to the empty space below her collarbone. Sober dismay, wretched and disconsolate, crossed her face. "I've lost it," she whispered, grievously.

An ear-splitting squeal came across the public address system as it clicked on. A female voice droned, "Andrea Daye, you have a visitor in the lobby."

She threw her hands up in the air. "That's all I need … I'm already late for the meeting with Sue—to the Third Power." She had never been late to one of these lawyer-client meetings with Rudd.

"No worry … Jolene's not here."

"What? She's the sole reason they're here."

David took a quick, last gulp from his cup, and spoke decisively, as though suddenly being spurred on by some unseen entity, "Why don't I take your things to your office … I'll tell Rudd you're being held at gunpoint by a mad man." He tossed the empty cup into the trash can, and furtively grabbed her coat and bag.

Rolling her eyes at his cloak and dagger style, she grabbed his arm and squeezed it gently, in way of an apology for her earlier, harsh words. "I'm going to be ready to eat an elephant. Van you shake loose and join me … my treat?"

David winked in agreement, eying the coffee stain, huge and dark, down the front of her dress. As she walked to the front of the building, she chided herself for being so rude to the kid, who, unbeknownst to her, now followed—uninvited.

David's words proved to be more than prophetic. Andrea immediately recognized the tall, well-dressed gentleman in the dark suit and overcoat standing at the window with his back to her, staring out at the strong, gale-force winds whipping sheets of rain against the glass-wrapped building. She sucked in a breath. This was the same rogue who had plowed into her car at the airport only an hour, or so, earlier. The jerk had tucked a complimentary copy of Sunday's *Daily News* under his arm. *He followed me,* she thought, apprehensively, fear leaping to her throat.

She quickened her steps, and approached him from behind, stretching out her hand. "I'm Andrea Daye," she said, surprised at the scratchiness of her voice. "I'm over-due for an important meeting," she added, hoarsely, "but I can give you about ten minutes."

The man turned slowly, confidently, completely ignoring her cordial greeting. His dark eyes appraised her through her wet dress, deeply stained and clinging snuggly to her body. A gleam came to his eye. "Ten minutes should be long enough ... bots might require a while longer," he said with a slow, suggestive drawl and mocking lips.

She stood in stunned silence, blushing profusely, resenting his hot gaze and sexist innuendo.

Now that she was in the office, the whole shouting match seemed utterly absurd. Being the strongly conscionable person she was, feelings of contriteness began to gnaw at her conscience. Fact was, she couldn't recall if she had, actually, checked traffic before she'd pulled into the street.

The man took a step closer, "Ms. Daye?" a questioning look came into his eyes, as he raised his chin, and wrinkled his brow, as though trying to recall something important. "Isn't your name really ... Andrea *Fitzgerald?*" His question was suggestive, as though she had, somehow lied, or misled him. Andrea took immediate offense to the question. She didn't like being Mrs. Fitzgerald, and she preferred to never use that name.

For a long moment they stood staring, uncomfortably, into each other's unyielding eyes. Finally, she spoke without so much as trying to suppress her irritability. "Daye ... my maiden name is Daye, and the pseudonym I use when I write." Her lips formed a moue of disgruntlement.

"And Fitzgerald...?"

"Fitzgerald is my ... married name." She seriously resented having to make this clarification.

He looked at her with skepticism. "And you're married to....?" He hiked a brow as he checked her finger. She wore no ring, but the facts needed to come straight from her lips to his ears.

Her face flushed with embarrassment. Humiliation fluttered her lashes. "Shaun Fitzgerald," she admitted, weakly.

"Shaun Fitzgerald," the visitor repeated, slowly, shooting her a problematic glance. He raised his gaze, just long enough to look over her shoulder at the tall, cut, young man a short distance behind her. Standing silent, feet together, with her coat hanging across one arm and her tangerine purse dangling from the other, he looked to be a mismatched, personal valet.

The two men's eyes met and locked in a spark of recognition, exchanging serious, questioning glances. Just as quickly, they diverted their eyes away from one another, tamping down deep emotions.

Now her visitor spoke calmly and with great dignity, "Mrs. Fitzgerald, my name is Matthew J. McCormick." He bounced another quick glance off her valet. "Do you suppose we could find a quiet corner to talk … privately?" He nodded towards the noise and distraction of the crowded lobby.

Assuming the man wanted to further discuss the accident, Andrea said, "There's a conference room, just a couple of doors down this hallway." She led the way, her wet boots clicking against the tile flooring.

McCormick followed, thinking how hot she looked in her leggings and boots. He remembered how undeniably right she had felt in his arms for that brief moment at the Lounge a short time ago; but he knew, instinctively, that because of his changed appearance, and his hard-ass demeanor, she had yet to associate him with anything other than the accident—and the faux image of a devil sex doll. Chagrin rose and fell in his chest.

Andrea allowed him to enter the relatively small room, first; a room that stank from stale pipe and cigar smoke, and offered very little foot space; where several mismatched chairs were gathered around a long table, stained and marred by years of use and abuse. When she shut the door, the man seemed to fill up the space, creating a close, intimate atmosphere. She knew this would be uncomfortable, but it beat being humiliated in front of the entire newsroom staff. She turned to face the man towering, menacingly, over her.

He planted his feet, and squared his shoulders, shoving his trench coat back at the sides in one easy gesture. With hand resting, resolutely, on his slender hips, his dark, fiery eyes leveled in on Andrea.

"About the accident I…."

"I'm not here to discuss the accident," he offered.

It wasn't his ruggedly handsome features, his cut body, uncloaked, or the snark of authority in his speech pattern that caused her to almost hyperventilate; nor was it the holster strapped to his shoulder as though a permanent fixture, along with its protruding gun handle. No, what took Andrea's breath away was the knavish risibility dancing in the man's eyes like shimmering stars in a bleak, wintery sky.

"Mrs. Fitzgerald … I'm a special agent with the Federal Drug Enforcement Agency."

The color drained from Andrea's cheeks.

"We've been following your series of little stories on drug crime. Mrs. … may I call you Andrea?" The agent sorely regretted having no current credentials to show her, following a glitch at the printer's shop, allowing classified information to be printed on all his pieces of identification.

"Ms. Daye will suffice," she snapped derisively, sensing arrogance and glibness in the man's demeanor. "McCormick … I don't write fiction. My little stories, as you call them, are heavily researched, seriously composed, and seriously written articles, and editorials, representing the opinions of the editors and publishers of this newspaper; but yes, they are beginning to draw a lot of attention."

"I don't doubt it," he added, crassly, his eyelids shuttering, momentarily. He smiled woefully, his voice taking on a tone of condescension. "Mrs. Fitzgerald, if … and I say if … there is any truth to what you have been writing, you're making it sound as if you've stumbled upon a major drug-smuggling ring. In that world…." he added in all sincerity, "your kind of writing doesn't draw attention … it draws blades and bullets, and that could get very dangerous … for you."

Andrea's eyes widened and she took a quick step back, putting distance between them. "Are you threatening me?"

Surprised by her reaction, he noticed, for the first time, the swelling and discoloration on her left cheek, just below the eye. He also noted the recent split lip, and her futile attempt to cover it up, certain that it was no product of their fender-bender.

Wary of her state of mind, and suspecting the worse with the bruises, he eased up a bit. "No, of course it's not a threat … but isn't it possible that you just might be stretching the facts in order to … say … advance your career? You've been working for this rag, for what? … three years?" He raised both brows to emphasize his point. "And isn't it true that your own husband is running for political office against a very strong opponent, an incumbent, in fact, and has everything to gain from your articles?"

Andrea took immediate offense to the accusations. Her insides quaked and she could no longer think straight. This man was bothering her in ways she didn't understand.

He was saying, "We prefer to keep a low profile, Mrs. Fitzgerald, and would appreciate the opportunity to handle this investigation without your delightful, little exaggerations."

"Exaggerations?"

He shot her a winsome, but discrediting grin. "I need your list of sources, Mrs. Fitzgerald, and I need them … yesterday."

Andrea sucked air, glaring at the man's strong, ruggedly chiseled jaw and perfectly shaped nose, set on a tropically, tanned face. "You're just a reporter, he was saying, and frankly, you're in way over your head." His brows furrowed, "Simply put, Mrs. Fitzgerald … you're putting yourself in *harm's way.*"

Andrea watched each and every word roll through his firmly controlled lips, as though in slowed motion, before being clamped shut. A moment of doubt rose in her chest as Shaun's words came back to haunt her, echoing through her head as they had earlier that same morning: "I got you the job … because you were unhappy … I got you the job."

Drawing confidence from some untapped strength deep within, she quickly pulled herself together. Her eyes flashed with anger and she rapidly opened fire on the agent with all the vengeance of a mother bear fighting for the life of her cub. "McCormick … you can go to hell. My sources confide in me because they trust me … and they will remain anonymous, just as I promised … and just as the law allows."

She planted her feet, and took a deep breath, before adamantly continuing. "A year ago, this newspaper … no, me … Andrea Daye, contacted your office with the information you're asking for now. They refused to talk to me, saying that the agency preferred to conduct its own investigations, using information gleaned by their own agents."

Now it was McCormick's turn to look confused. He knew nothing of this connection—this two-way flow of information. Why not, he wondered.

"Well, I stepped aside … and I waited for my government to do its job. And while I waited, more and more of our young children died, right before my eyes: eleven, twelve, thirteen-year-olds—even BABIES!"

The words gushed from her mouth like rushing waters of a flash flood. "You're right … I am about to expose a major drug ring, no thanks to the feds. Not you, not the DEA, but this stupid little, *inexperienced* reporter! What does that say about the work you guys have been doing? While you pretty boys have been basking in the sun on some Orgie Island, on taxpayer money, these greedy drug dealers have been getting away with murder—the murder of our children—and prospering from it!"

With heated contempt, and honest anger, she took a step back, watching

THE OTHER SIDE OF FEAR

his jaw muscles flex and grow increasingly tense by the second. "My sources trust me to bring this carnage, this wholesale killing of American children, to the light of day, and into the public eye, and that's damned well what I'm going to do. If I hand this information over to you, you'll just bury it for another … what … two … three years?" She sucked in a deep breath, stretching her height to its limit. "How many kids will die during that length of time?" She lifted her chin, defiantly, and paused for a beat. "I certainly hope they won't be yours!"

The man winced, visibly.

Andrea walked to the door and spun around, looking him full in the face. "Your ten minutes are up, Special Agent Matthew J. McCormick." She smirked, taking her turn at being suggestive. "Was it good for you?"

The door slammed shut behind her.

"Sweet," he groused through gritted teeth, suddenly finding himself standing in the dark.

Once outside the building, McCormick walked with a fast-paced gait towards his car, totally oblivious to the rain pounding his head. Up until this moment, he had regarded Andrea as either an adrenaline-pumped, ambulance chaser, or a hack reporter, trying to help her husband win an election by making serious allegations against the opposing party; but now, he saw her as a strong force to be reckoned with. He did, however, take note of the metallic, navy blue Hyundai Elantra that had pulled in after him, and parked in the spot nearest the door. Doing a slow walk around the back bumper, he paused for a beat, matching the plate number with that of the car Brantley Stone had climbed into at the airport.

Finally sliding behind the wheel of his scrunched-up rental, he reached into his breast pocket, pulled out a high-tech tape recorder, and switched it off. As he started the engine and drove out of the parking lot, he whispered, "She gets it."

Seething, after meeting with the agent, Andrea tromped off to her office where she found her coat and purse lying across the chair, as promised. She fumed even more at finding several telephone messages, cluttering the front of her monitor. It was one of those little, daily annoyances that Jolene Jorgenson loved to perform, deliberately, just to goad Andrea. She picked up the first message, written in Jolene's scrawled penmanship, or lack of penmanship.

She slammed it down, just as David blew through the door. "Rudd just told me your meeting's been rescheduled for next week," he offered, setting a cup of steaming, hot coffee on her desk. Finding her in a state of perturbation, he grabbed her shoulders, and shook her, playfully. "Calm down girl ... you're going to stroke out."

Exasperation filled her eyes. "I can't help it David ... read this!"

Squinting, he tried to make out the juvenile scrawl. "I ... can't read it."

"Neither can I ... how in the hell am I supposed to respond to a message I can't even read?" David motioned towards the coffee then plunked himself down in her chair, making himself at home. He eyed the dress stains as she crossed the room to the filing cabinet. He swiveled around and propped his kicks on top of her desk as he looked through the glass, straight into the editor's office. "Rudd says he can't find good help these days."

Getting no response, he asked, "Andi, you didn't get hurt in that fender-bender this morning did you?"

She slammed the drawer shut, noisily. "Nah ... at least not physically," she said, her mind elsewhere. She turned around, catching him parked in her spot. Her eyes locked onto his wise-guy image in the glass. Holding his gaze, she shot him a big hand gesture, motioning him out of the chair with her thumb.

His feet dropped to the floor, but he took his sweet time swiveling the chair back around. At last he stood, tugging at the knees of his leggin' style khaki pants and the sides of his urban-cut blazer in an effort to stretch out his time with her. Eventually, both sides of the jacket were brought together, and buttoned, neatly.

"Oh, hey ... by the way," he said, nonchalantly, as he slowly straightened his tie. Andrea claimed her seat and flipped on the monitor, waiting for the other half of his sentence to drop.

"Who was that tanned, chiseled hunk you were talking to in the lobby?"

She considered his choice of words describing such a despicable character; and didn't she hear some kind of underlying emotion in David's voice? What was it ... jealousy towards the guy, perhaps? No, it was something much deeper. She slumped against the back of the chair, and echoed his words with dramatic flair. "Tanned, chiseled ... hunk?" She turned her head askance, holding the young sports editor in her gaze. "David ... you're not telling me you're gay ... are you?"

He locked eyes, and gave his head an incredulous shake to the side. "Girl … you might just want to clean the wet coffee dregs out of your gaydar pot." A disbelieving chuckle followed his quiet words of advice.

She breathed out a sigh, "Whatever," she said, readily dismissing the subject. Without taking her eyes off her monitor, she began to dish more details. "The guy's just a governmental, empty suit … but for some inane reason, he thinks he's *special* … and that there's something *special* about my writing that needs … investigating!" She blew out a hot breath as her rattled mind replayed the confrontation. "He's also the jackass who rear-ended my car," she added, heatedly, flipping her pen to the far side of the room.

David's brows shot up, finding amusement in her answer. "Whoa … you have had a morning." He cleared his throat, "Sounds like you don't hold federal agents in very high regard."

Andrea's eyes dropped. "Not at the moment," she answered with serious disdain.

David left her office shaking his head, and chortling. "Jackass," he repeated as a euphoric grin spread wide across his face. A monumental load had just been lifted from his shoulders on this wet, gloomy morning.

David shouldered his way through the heavy door of the hot, steamy locker room and into the cool, starless night following the trouncing of the local, high school varsity football team, and his one-on-one interview with the loosing coach. A string of surly, young players, loud and argumentative, rammed through the door behind him, and followed him out. Reliving the game's loss in loud, accusatory tones, they impatiently shoved their way past him, making it necessary to reign in his laptop and half-eaten bag of overly-salted popcorn as though he were a tottery, old man. They all piled into one car, and then with tires screeching, roared away, leaving David standing alone in the middle of the deserted parking lot.

The negative atmosphere worked its way into his bones, and the story of defeat he must write, yet that night, weighed heavily on his mind—no one wanted to read about losers. Beginning to feel the lateness of the hour, and the stress of his heavy workload, he dropped his head and shuffled across a fair distance of cracked concrete towards his old, beat-up, low-end Subaru. He reached for the door handle, wondering who he could call if the dang-thang didn't start. Before another thought could cross his mind, his face took a hard dive, splatting against the car's hardtop roof, his popcorn flying into the air and scattering across the hood of the car. His right arm was wrenched, unwillingly, behind his back.

"Spread'em," growled a commanding voice.

Recognizing the authoritative bark of law enforcement, David immediately spread his legs, and raised his left arm in compliance.

A voice of warning, softer but more chaffing, spoke into his right ear. "Never ... ever ... leave your six unguarded." Finally, his aggressor released his arm, and pushed away. Still, the voice taunted, but in a more amicable tone, "Good God, bro ... where'd you get those togs ... out of my Festival of Fools trunk ... or behind door number three of Fitzgerald's cedar-lined closet?"

When David threw a wary glance over his shoulder, he found himself staring into a face as familiar as his own, yet considerably changed and aged over a two-year absence. He swung around. "Matt!"

Hands shot forward for a civil handshake, but were quickly jerked back as the two men laughed in awkwardness at the situation. At last their shoulders collided in an emotional man hug.

"God ... I've missed you," David confessed, totally unabashed as his forehead dropped to the older, taller man's shoulder.

In Virginia the following morning, McCormick pulled out a copy of the Forest Hills Daily News while waiting for his boss to finish a lengthy phone conversation. He read the editorial written in defense of a man's right to his God-given masculinity, written by Andrea Daye. A wry grin lifted one corner of his mouth. *She gets it,* he thought, appreciatively.

Moments later, he sat across the desk from his superior officer, having related the story of the fender-bender with Shaun Fitzgerald's wife and how later, at the newspaper, she had verbally undressed him, leaving him standing alone in a dark, unfamiliar room, groping along the wall for the light switch. They laughed whole-heartedly.

"Now if she deliberately switched off that light, we could charge her with obstruction of jus…." the jovial chief offered.

"Nah," McCormick interrupted, waving off the assertion as he recalled the scene. "I'm certain she didn't realize she had left me standing in the dark."

He chuckled under his breath, thinking, *in more ways than one.* "But she did look like a half-drowned rat, dripping water all over the floor with these huge, dark, coffee stains running the full length of her dress ... front and back." He extended his arms in an exaggeration of the size of the coffee stains.

"But she was livid as hell, and I doubt she was even aware she was wet ... now that's a woman after my own heart!" he teased, regretting the comment before it was fully out of his mouth.

"Oh, yeah, I remember." Chief Straker shook a finger at McCormick in mocked seriousness. "You're the guy who claimed, during your interview, to like your women natural-looking. How did you put it ... earthy ... isn't that what you said?"

McCormick chuckled, "I said *real* ... I like for everything to be real." Again the two men laughed, robustly, before turning their thoughts to business.

"Matt, what does she know?" asked the chief, considerably more subdued.

McCormick sucked in his breath, forcing the grin from his face. He leveled his dark, serious eyes on the older man. "Chief, I think she knows just enough to get herself killed ... and there's a new wrinkle we haven't considered."

Not liking to be surprised, or bested, the chief rubbed his chin with impatience. "What's that?" he asked, gruffly.

McCormick locked eyes with his boss. "Miss Daye has been farming out her editorials to the New York Times, and the Boston Globe ... and she's, just recently, broken into national syndication."

"National syndication?" Straker exclaimed with alarm. "Don't you have to have a best-seller before you're granted that honor?"

"I'm sure you're right, but I'll check into it on my trip to New York."

"What's she write about?"

"The negative effects of the drug culture on American children."

The older man grimaced in disappointment. His eyes dropped to his desktop. "That's unfortunate ... that makes her a public figure ... people will be watching. Are her writings authentic, or just cover for her husband's illegal activities?"

McCormick answered, reticently, "Judging by the little I've read, they seem legit ... but I'll have to do a search for whatever else she's written." He pushed himself out of the chair, and rocked back and forth on his heels.

He remembered Andrea's strong fiery temper. He rarely saw such spunk in a woman, aside from politics, but he could only speculate as to how much she knew about her husband's terroristic activities. "She will, most certainly, continue writing her articles ... my brash comments got exactly the response we'd hoped to get. We should have no problems flushing out the opposition."

"Right, her harassers will be the people we want to watch," the chief agreed, a bit disinterestedly.

Straker continued his line of questioning, using the code name assigned to their number one most wanted—Brantley Stone, a.k.a. Shaun Fitzgerald, a.k.a. Kris Kringle. "Do you think she knows what Kringle is up to?"

McCormick didn't like the "also known as" acronym assigned to Fitzgerald. The abominable degenerate was the complete antithesis to the lovable, old guy, who had, for centuries, filled man's need for something good to believe in: a pure representation of unselfish giving.

McCormick rubbed his hand across his mouth, thoughtfully. "At this point, I have my doubts ... she seems totally guileless and innocent enough; but Mrs. Fitzgerald is a very intelligent woman and a damned good journalist, judging by the few articles I've read. If she knows anything about her husband's extra-curricular activities ... his atrocities, she's covering extremely well."

His boss scratched his silver-streaked head and studied the handsome, rugged features of his agent. "Matt, I'm going to level with you." His experienced, flinty eyes bore into the eyes of the younger man. "We have reports that suggest Andrea could be involved ... after all, she is his wife."

McCormick shook off the suggestion as he visualized Andrea's clear, soulful eyes and honest anger. "Anything's possible, but I'm not seeing it that way—I think she's made of stronger stuff," he countered dryly. At least he hoped she was.

"Well, keep an open mind," Straker cautioned. Suddenly, he stood up and slammed his notes to the desk. "How in the hell did Stone end up marrying someone with totally opposite views from his own?"

"It happens," McCormick offered, his voice going flat.

An ugly, black mood settled over McCormick as the chief continued along the same lines. He felt unsettled by what he was hearing. Who was making these allegations? What were they basing them on? And if someone else was working this case, why in the hell had he been pulled into the investigation? Based on his own evidence, he saw no reason to believe Andrea was personally involved in any of her husband's drug-running, or money laundering activities. The thought crossed his mind that he would have preferred to have met Andrea Daye under more favorable circumstances.

His supervisor read the doubt on his young agent's face, and heard the sound of it in his voice. Matt had proven himself to be one helluva good agent. He was solid, dedicated, analytical; but most of all, he was gutsy; and the man was brilliant at thinking on his feet. Finally, he said, "Okay Matt, here's the deal ... we're going to use Andrea to flush out our man; and just in case she's innocent, we're going to protect her at the same time...." He looked sagaciously over the rim of his glasses, "without making news headlines."

A problematic frown pulled down the sides of McCormick's mouth. "How do you propose we do that?"

The chief stared long and hard at his agent, "I'm assigning you to Mrs. Fitzgerald."

McCormick's heart bounced to the moon and back.

The chief continued, "Kringle knows we're closing in on him. He has to make his move soon. And when he does we're going to be around with a little surprise gift-wrapped package of our own. The FBI has loaned us a young agent, working under my purview. We've temporarily placed him at the *Forest Hills Daily News* with judicial approval for surveillance. He's a newbie, but he's good." McCormick showed no emotion. "He's already managed to slip a bug into both of the Fitzgerald's cars, and another one into her favorite purse. I think we've got some good leads." He handed a tape recording to McCormick. "Analyze everything we have recorded so far, and give me a written, hard-copy summary; but how you proceed in this case will be totally up to your own discretion. You've got eyes on ... you make the call."

The chief's eyes narrowed, "And Matt, keep in mind that Fitzgerald is on to you, as well—and he's got a score to settle."

McCormick's jaw hardened. He was already there in his own thinking—except, for one thing. "The maniac's not the only one with a score to settle," he hissed through gritted teeth.

Straker took notice of the festering resentment.

"You'll need to interrogate her at some point, but watch your back. Stone's been diagnosed as a schizophrenic sociopath, and I'm guessing he could be a really mean, jealous husband, as well."

Straker gave the venturesome agent another intense look, further assessing the young man's ability. On the plus side, McCormick was an outstanding operator, of the sort you didn't often find. He was extremely competent, a risk-taker. There was nothing he could not do, and he seemed to be afraid of nothing. McCormick's good looks and skill-sets were extremely well-suited for this assignment. He was driven, a widower with no children—and he was handsome as hell. He would be all over the Fitzgerald case in just a matter of hours.

Straker pulled his eyes away. On the downside, the chief knew he could not afford to underestimate this young agent. McCormick was a man of integrity. He had served his country with honors in the military; he was, in fact, the quintessential American soldier that presidents honored for valor, and balladeers commemorated in song. Should he lose this particular agent, the entire country would mourn his death—drawing attention to the agency. He tamped down the tinge of guilt that had begun to gnaw at him.

McCormick stood to leave, but Straker handed him a packet labeled *Drug Enforcement Initiatives*. "While you were away, we were given new rules. We now have to inform local authorities before we investigate or arrest drug dealers in their area."

McCormick grimaced. "Well that'll work ... until you meet up with a corrupt local sheriff ... and then you can kiss your ass goodbye."

The chief agreed, but settled, comfortably, into his chair. "By the way, Matt," "What do you plan to do, now that you're back in the states ... going back to Florida?"

"Nah," McCormick answered adamantly. "I'm done with that. I'm going back to the mountains. I had just framed and finished a new cabin and stable before I got tropicalized. I'm hoping my dad's been looking after things in my absence. If not ... I'll start all over."

"Have you talked to your family?"

Matt's face lit up. "I've been gone so long ... I figured I'd just show up and surprise them. I've accumulated several weeks of vacation time, so when I go home...." He paused, shooting his boss a dubious grin, "if you'll ever let me go home ... I want to stay awhile. My emotions are a bit tenuous at this point ... I've had so many different names and aliases. I'd just like to live my own life ... get a handle on who, the hell, I really am."

The chief glanced over the rim of his glasses, "There's no chance of you going to the dark side ... is there?"

McCormick felt his stomach clench at what sounded more like an invitation than a question; but he smirked, and rapidly shot back, "Hell no!"

His thoughts drifted back to his wilderness home, built by his own hands, with the help of his father and brothers. "I'm hoping we can wind up my part of this investigation in time to spend the holidays snowed in by a cozy fire, with nothing but good books, good music and maybe a hobby or two."

The chief, cooed, "What ... no women?" his voice rising in jest.

The young man's thoughts, naturally, went to the woman who had left him breathless, time and again—Andrea Daye Fitzgerald; but he astutely read his leader's veiled intentions: to plant the seed of discontent into a lonely man's mind. He cocked, what appeared to be clueless brow, and shoot him a humorous, wry grin. "Well now ... I might just have to reconsider that one."

"Good ... if any man deserves it, it's you, Matt." At last he lifted his hooded eyes to meet McCormick's. "I can't begin to tell you how much we appreciate you postponing your trip home to help us with this case. If we can hang in there and pull this thing off ... we'll all get a n-i-c-e long rest." His gaze dropped.

McCormick wondered, *what kind of rest are we talking about, and what exactly are we pulling off?* In a voice holding no conviction, he said, "After two years, bahss ... what's a few more weeks?"

The older man slid forward in his chair, and wrinkled his brow. He pressed his lips together. "Matt, I'm sorry to have to give you this assignment, but that under-cover investigation in Mexico last year, and then this latest roundup, has taken its toll on our personnel."

McCormick's jaw flexed, his eyes narrowed with anger. *Personnel,* he thought. He said, "What it took were five of our most experienced men—our finest. I watched four of my best buddies machine-gunned down, while I couldn't lift a finger to warn them." He raked stressful fingers through his hair, remembering the sting operation of a year ago.

An agent had been lost early in the investigation, which should have given them pause, but the operation had gone full speed ahead. Just when everything looked as though it was going as planned, after money and drugs had exchanged hands, a gunner unexpectedly turned, and opened fire on the four agents posing as drug merchants. Matt had been forced to watch, poker-faced, as bullets riddled the bodies of his four best friends.

He readily acknowledged that he was consumed with guilt and anger. Anger at whom, he really didn't know. "At times I feel like I'm to blame for their deaths ... since I instigated the sting. And after talking to Andrea Fitzgerald this morning, I feel like I'm responsible for the deaths of thousands of young children."

"Nonsense!" The chief frowned, taking note of the man's self-incrimination. McCormick had been under extreme levels of stress for a very long time; but he was a good man, a good soldier, and an excellent agent—the perfect man to have in the field at this particular time.

"Don't beat yourself up, Matt. We put our lives on the line every day ... and for what?" he said in a voice that sounded disillusioned. Straker gave the agent a hard look. "You had no way of knowing one of our own had gone bad. You were set up ... given false information."

McCormick winced, inwardly. *Yeah, the same kind of false information we're getting on Andrea Fitzgerald*, he thought.

The chief propped his elbows on his desk and leaned towards McCormick who had returned to his chair. "Agent McCormick ... it's not often that we can infiltrate the enemy at such high levels the way you did. You couldn't see it coming, and the only way you could have warned your buddies was to blow your own cover. You would have been killed, and all your work would have been for naught." The chief locked eyes with McCormick.

Fatigue settled on the agent's face. "I get it, but there's just one problem ... there are literally thousands of young punks all pumped up and eager to become the next head honcho ... each one more venomous, more evil than the one preceding him ... and we can't seem to stop them."

The chief read the impatience in McCormick's eyes. "But we will ... soon." They both stood up, and the chief gave McCormick a sympathetic slap on the shoulder. "Remember what Colonel Washington said to his Long Island Spymaster. "*It is a fine line that a trustworthy man walks who lives in the world of trickery....*"

This line, one that often got dropped on new recruits, was one of McCormick's favorites. He'd first gleaned it from history books as an 8th grade student under the vociferous tutelage of Mr. Greene. Since then he'd read in it numerous novels, and watched it played out on historical videos; but today the agent's blood ran cold as he picked up on his boss's disingenuous tone. McCormick finished what he considered to be the most important part of the message, "...*and still remain true to his cause.*"

The chief's eyes dropped, and he switched subjects. "I have to level with you, pretty boy ... you did get a damned nice tan while you were undercover."

McCormick winced. Not wanting his thoughts read, he turned his gaze to his tanned arms under rolled-up sleeves. Tamping down his sense of uneasiness, he raised guileful eyes, showing nothing but good humor. "It must be true ... you're the second person today to call it to my attention." He stood up, and walked through the door, but the pondering chief called him back into his office.

"I had one more question for you, Matt."

McCormick returned, closed the door behind him and sat down.

"This thing concerning this young island boy, being tethered to a donkey with government issued binocular straps... care to elaborate on that?"

A slow grin crossed McCormick's face, and then laughter gurgled up in his throat. "I came across the kid on my route home ... along with his daddy's base camp. I couldn't take the chance of someone following me, and doffing my head before I reported the location of the camp. The kid's okay ... right?"

Color drained, and lifelines, deep and serious, carved into the bosses cheeks and forehead. "You're referencing which camp?"

McCormick's jaw flexed and he gave the man an unsettled look, "You haven't read my report?"

The chief pulled down a serious frown, and gave his head a negative shake.

McCormick began to explain. "As soon as I got back to the States, I filed a full report on the camp. I included all the eye-popping details. The kid's daddy was meeting with our very own Brantley Stone. I gave the report a *high security clearance only* listing; but if you haven't seen it...." His voice trailed off with deep concern. Straker remained silent. McCormick gave him a nod and a promise, "I'll type it up again and hand-deliver it before I fly out of here tonight."

A grim look settled on both their faces. Disappearing reports were becoming a serious matter within the agency, and served as further evidence of enemies within their ranks—maybe even more than one. Both men realized that without the machete kid incident, the enemy camp might never have been exposed.

McCormick stood, and walked out the door, thinking, *so how did Straker know about the kid, but not the camp? They were in the same report.*

CHAPTER 15

McCormick stopped to grab a cup of coffee before heading back to his office to give the report first priority. Feeling certain that the second report would most likely disappear, as well, he retyped it; but before deleting to a level of non-recovery, he printed off two hardcopies. He sent one off to a camouflaged D.C. address; then personally hand-delivered the second copy to Chief Straker. Disquietude crept over him as he came to a realization that he was still working undercover, still living with the enemy, and still camping out in Hell.

He loosened his tie after a long grilling day, and plopped the cassette tape into the wall unit. He snatched up the remote and plunked down in the leather chair, stretching one long leg across the open desk drawer. He sipped coffee as he clicked on the tape that had actually started recording several days before he'd met Andrea.

He was drawn in by the pleasant sound of Andrea's voice. She spoke with a subtle, sensuous cadence, and a natural cheerful lilt—willingness towards buoyancy, his Grandfather would call it. She seemed to give great thought to each and every word that crossed her lips. Hearing mostly newspaper lingo and shoptalk convinced him that Andrea was the force that kept the newspaper functioning.

Finally, he heard music and background noise that sounded like the Writer's Block Lounge the night he'd been there—the night he had so brazenly, and unwittingly, smothered Brantley Stone's wife with a kiss that not only knocked his socks off, but all but melded the bold rainbow stripes together. *Ah, boy,* he thought. *That could have cost me my life … but worth every last gasping breath.* He smiled, audaciously.

Expecting to hear a lot of lame conversation marinated in alcohol and lengthy lapses, he forwarded the tape. The following conversation had taken place in the ladies' room, a dialogue between Andrea and her young friend.

When the young woman on the tape encouraged Andrea to leave her husband, the agent's leg dropped to the floor. He heard Shaun's name mentioned, and the younger voice saying, "Get rid of the jerk ... find your superhero ... start with the one out there." Now the agent sat at attention. The conversation had become more than interesting; it had become personal.

Andrea had replied in a distressed tone, "I don't pick up guys in bars, besides ... he's gay."

McCormick snorted. *The woman thinks I'm gay. Cool ... ready-made camouflage.*

Finally he heard Andrea admit, "But ... oh gawd, Zoe ... you are so right ... I am w-r-e-t-c-h-e-d-l-y miserable with Shaun!"

McCormick shot to his feet, pulled his gut in and his shoulders back, a paragon of masculinity—this was a game changer!

He started to fast-forward the tape past the sound of whaling babies, but upon hearing a voice that reminded him of his grandmother, he backed it up and listened to the late-night conversation at the hospital from the beginning. When he heard the words softly spoken, "Andrea, the baby is dead," his heart broke right along with Andrea's.

He switched off the recorder along with the light, and sat in darkened silence.

When he restarted the tape, it wasn't Andrea's lilted voice he heard or the chatter between friends; nor was it the logomachy, deciding which words best fit newspaper content and style. What McCormick heard next was the booming, braggadocio voice of the enemy.

He first listened to the heated discussion between Shaun and Andrea. The young woman was defending herself in regards to a kiss she'd gotten at the Writer's Block Lounge. She was holding her own, maintaining a semi-civil tongue—defending *him!*

Then, there it was—a thwacking sound, and the sound of shattering glass. McCormick shoved his chair back, and rushed to the wall unit to fine-tune the audio. He played the tape again, anxiously pacing back and forth across the floor, listening with rapt attention to every sound, every word—every nuance.

At hearing it a second time, McCormick felt certain that Fitzgerald had struck his wife; which would account for the bruised cheek and split lip he had witnessed, first hand, the following morning at the *News*; but there was another sound—a click—a metallic click. He played it again, his face turning to stone as he identified the sound—the safety release on a handgun.

"Son of a bitch!" *Fitzgerald had pulled a gun on his wife!*

The bastard was using and abusing Andrea—and McCormick knew him to be a lethal, cold-blooded killer. His mind filled with the searing image of his colleague's head exploding back on the island. Fitzgerald would kill again. He would kill Andrea in the blink of an eye—once she was of no use to him!

With acrimony aflame in his heart, McCormick stopped the tape. He chugged a swig of cold, bitter coffee, wishing for straight whisky. Guilt roiled in his gut. Andrea had been put in that position and taken the abuse because of his bodacious, smartass actions.

Now Shaun's voice returned with his usual blah-blah-blah as Andrea drove him to the airport. Then finally, "Someone with your limited appeal should work a little harder to keep up with the competition." Fitzgerald was saying.

It was hard enough to listen to anything Fitzgerald had to say, but for this reprehensible dope head to assail such a drop-dead gorgeous woman was nothing less than unconscionable, and should be a crime unto itself. No wonder she had been loaded for bear the morning he'd talked to her at the *News*, not to mention what he had later dumped on her.

Rudd had suggested that Andrea might not be willing to work with the Agency. Needing a guarantee that she would continue to write her articles, the chief and he had come up with the little speech he'd delivered that morning. He had set her up, deliberately antagonizing her, using her own quick temper against her. She had taken the bait, bought the pretext, and the plan had worked beautifully. But now McCormick regretted the duplicity, the danger, and the pain, his actions had brought upon this fine woman.

Beginning to understand, at least in part, why Andrea threw herself into her work, and why she was seemingly so hostile, McCormick wondered why a classy woman like Andrea—lovely, intelligent, sensitive, a woman both rich and rational—would marry someone like Fitzgerald; but he quickly chided himself for being cynical, remembering his own misguided mistake.

As he listened to the recorded, up close and personal, version of her car getting rear-ended at the airport, along with her expressions of coffee-splattered pain caused by the spill, his mood lightened, and he laughed out loud. He also laughed at her bantering soliloquy aimed at Shaun, describing exactly how *hot* she really was. Laughter sprang up from his belly in appreciation of her wit. He thought, jocosely, *It's not who you are that matters ... it's who you are when you're alone.*

Now, McCormick began to wonder how he could help this woman. Her situation was much too complicated to simply remove her from the danger; but he was obligated by duty to protect her. More importantly, he was obligated by soulful duty to ease her pain.

Recalling their rain-drenched shouting match, he remembered the shiny object he'd found lying in the street following their fender-bender. He dug deep into his pocket, producing the valuable piece of jewelry now enclosed in a small evidence bag. He took it out of the bag and strung it across the desk. He had intended to return it to her that same morning, but their conversation had taken them in a direction a world away from gallantry. Strangely, carrying the chain in his pocket had somehow made him feel stronger, more connected to Andrea.

The agent blew out a breath in frustration, fully realizing the mistake he was making by getting personally involved. He sank back into his chair, brooding. Andrea Fitzgerald was strictly off limits, especially now that he was permanently assigned to the case. From now on he would have to keep a tighter rein on his thoughts and emotions. This sort of thing could ruin a good career, or worse yet, jeopardize an agent's life—especially this agent's life.

Taking another long look at the chain, he blew out a determined breath, and dropped it into a full-sized manila envelope—Andrea needed her necklace.

He wrote no note of explanation, but simply sealed the flap, and addressed the envelope to Andrea Daye Fitzgerald, in care of the *Forest Hills Daily News*—away from the prying eyes of a jealous husband. Grimacing, he tossed the envelope into the out-going mail, fully aware of his actions, and what lay in the balance. He also was fully aware that he would, most likely, beat the mail plane back to Forest Hills.

He regained his focus, and typed his second report in great detail. Trusting no one, he printed two copies, sending one off to an anonymous address before walking the other to the chief's office to discuss his analysis of the tape. Only one other person had access to the report.

CHAPTER 16

The late October sky dawned fresh and bright the following morning in Forest Hills City Park. The musky smell of wet leaves and damp soil hung heavy in the air as the rising sun began to warm up the cool, crisp air. Planted on a wooden bench under a wide-spread oak, his legs comfortably sprawled out like tree-roots, McCormick watched the dew-moistened leaves of autumn flutter to the ground. He had shed his sweaty sweatshirt following his laps around the large, placid lake, and it hung loosely around his shoulders, drying out. Having this kind of free time was a rarity for the agent, and just knowing that extreme wintery weather would soon come blowing across the land at any time now, prodded him to thoroughly enjoy his Sunday morning, his freedom, and his large coffee.

His commercial flight from D.C. the previous night had been delayed in taking off, and so he had sat on the runway for hours, not arriving back in Forest Hills until the wee morning hours. Totally disturbed by all he'd heard on the tape, sleep wouldn't come. To his way of thinking, there was only one thing worse than getting stuck all night on a grounded commercial airliner in second class with a bunch of whiny passengers; that would be getting stuck in the stink of a cheap, stuffy hotel room. Not wanting to waste the morning, he had entered the park early enough to watch the stars fade and the sun to rise. His goal for the day was to get some exercise for his stiffening muscles, and soak up plenty of Vitamin D and fresh air, banking them towards those long, gray days of winter. After running two full laps around the lake, he'd sat down to peruse the Sunday morning paper with plans to run again later.

He had scanned the headline on an article about a young Boston hockey player, when a brisk breeze whipped across the park, fluttering the flimsy pages beyond readability. He folded the paper away, and switched to a hardcover book he'd picked up at the airport for his own private library.

When, at last, he raised his tired, heavy lids from the pages, a whole flock of brightly colored, hot air balloons was drifting, silently and lazily, across the clear, azure sky just above the treetops. On a distant hillside, a church bell tolled, calling its members to Sunday morning worship, its clarion call interrupted only by the loud honking of geese, announcing a sudden change in their flight pattern.

Going with the tranquility of the morning, and accepting it as a rare gift, McCormick comfortably leaned back, soaking up the warm rays and gentle breeze on his, yet to be shaven, face. Like the balloons, his eyes drifted lazily towards the walkway, his gaze settling on a young woman just entering the park and walking with quick-paced steps in his direction. She was slender, and even under the weight of her heavy backpack, he could tell she was unusually light on her feet.

The wind had whipped around to a different direction and was now tugging at the loose ends of her hair, and lazily lifting the corner of her light-weight skirt to reveal shapely legs. He watched her for a moment longer than he should have, liking the cadence with which she moved—no wasted energy, just a steady flow of easy motion. Her back was straight, her head erect. Her body had a beautiful contour, and she seemed to be greatly enjoying the day, as well. He could almost hear Louis (Satch'mo) Armstrong singing, *It's a Wonderful World.*

She was naturally sexy, he decided. The image from his youth flashed across his mind—yeah, she reminded him of that girl. He let his eyelids drop down like camera shutters, committing the vision to memory should he, one day, need to draw strength from some sweet memory.

As she came closer, he identified the colorful clump in her hand as a bouquet of flowers—red roses, to be exact. He zeroed in on her face.

Suddenly, he slumped low on the bench, and plunked his cap on his head, recognizing the owner of that womanly chi—Andrea Daye Fitzgerald. He yanked the bill down to further hide his eyes.

Certain that she would brand him a pervert for ogling women from a park bench, should she get a glimpse of him, he raised his book and opened it at nose level, continuing his surveillance over the top of the pages. When she left the walkway and disappeared through tall hedges, he rose from the bench.

There was no need to guess where she was going, or for what purpose—he knew.

He stashed his book in the crook of an upper limb and shadowed her into the local cemetery where he watched her walk along the neat rows of tombstones until coming to the end of her search. There, he watched her divide her bouquet, and lay fresh flowers on three separate graves. Finding a spot in the sun, she spread a bright, colorful blanket over the browning grass and russet leaves, and sat down with aplomb. Finally, she pulled out a box of fine, dark chocolates and began to munch, obviously savoring each delicious bite.

A soft chuckle gurgled in McCormick's throat. Not since witnessing a Day of the Dead celebration in Mexico City with his older brother, had he seen anyone liven up a cemetery in quite the same way. When she pulled a book out of her bag, a serious, contemplative look settled on the agent's face. He watched her begin to read in, what appeared to be a Holy Bible—the Book of Psalms, to be exact. McCormick dropped his head in solemnity, then turned and quietly walked away, giving her the gift of privacy.

With his tranquility evaporating with the morning mist, McCormick struggled to tamp down a sudden pall of loneliness. He didn't want to leave her; nor did he want to leave her sitting alone.

Ruing the circumstances that dictated his decisions, he returned to the lake to run several more laps. When he returned to the bench, wiping a profusion of sweat from his brow, Andrea was just leaving the park.

He sat for a moment, listening to the birds and the gentle breeze, rustling the leaves, now dried by the sun—and then he followed.

McCormick trailed Andrea's little gray Honda Civic out of town. When she turned onto a secondary road, he doffed his hat, rolled down his window and slowed, allowing her to put distance between the two cars. He followed, past fields of sunflowers, and honeybee farms, through a rustic covered bridge, and onto a paved road with badly patched potholes, ending at the Tell Family Orchard and Vineyard.

With the CD player blaring, *Honey, Honey,* from the first Mama Mia soundtrack, Andrea pulled into the gravel parking lot flush with cars, and drove to a spot between two SUVs near the back. She backed into the unlined space and inched her back bumper snug against the rustic, wooden rails. Rolling her window down a crack, she sat listening to the last measures of the song, before turning the player off with the engine. Still humming the tune, she got out, stretched her legs, and reached back inside for her purse. She slammed the door shut, and hit the key fob to secure the lock. When her eyes lifted, a hulking shadow stood between the two SUVs, trapping her between the fence and the two large vehicles.

"Mrs. Fitzgerald," he said, giving her an abbreviated courtesy nod as he cordially spoke his polite greeting.

Andrea's look of serenity immediately morphed into bitterness as she remembered their last conversation in the small conference room. She pursed her lips, and shot him a grievous, aggravated look. "McCormick." She glimpsed his faded jeans. "Dry cleaner got your suit?"

Undeterred, the hatless McCormick slowly raised his foot and rested it on the Honda's low-riding bumper, his forearm casually leaning into his thigh. He looked the embodiment of patient virtue as he dangled his own set of many keys from his long, agile fingers.

He studied the foliage with an unhurried gaze, truly appreciating the beauty and bounty of the golden, harvest season. Fall was at its magnificent peak, and the smell of smoke from burning leaves permeated the air, calling him home.

He glanced in her direction, arching a brow in question. "Are you out here all alone … in this wonderful world … on such a golden day?" He pulled his eyes away, and asked, "Where's hubby?" He looked around, as though searching for the man, fully expecting to find him. He turned, and looked her full-in-the face, still avoiding eye contact. When she didn't answer, his eyes widened with exaggerated surprise. "Not with you?" He paused and rubbed a hand downward, over his mouth and taut jaw line, shooting her a problematic glance.

He raised his chin. "So … how's that marital bliss thing working out for you?" His voice was quiet, but taunting.

"It's working out just fine," she spat back, just a little too quickly, to the agent's way of thinking. She raised her eyes in his direction, and squinted into the brightness of the mid-morning sun. "McCormick, are you *stalking* me … or did the cops just chase you off your park bench?"

The agent winced. She was sharp. Surprised by her vigilance, he took note of the need to step up his game.

When no retort came back at her, Andrea ordered, "Move out of my way, McCormick … my husband's waiting for me."

Fully aware of the lie, McCormick lowered his foot to the ground and slowly straightened his body, but remained firmly planted on the spot, deliberately blocking her path. He planted his hands, as though permanently, on his slender hips, and looked past her at the still waters of a nearby pond and the rolling, Rockwellian orchard scene beyond.

When, at last, he brought his eyes back to her, he shot her a weak, closed-mouth smile that quickly dissolved into cold austerity. His eyes narrowed and, at last, locked into Andrea's. He spoke, his voice a smooth, velvety whisper, "Let me know when you get tired of living that lie."

Giving her another polite half-nod, the light-footed agent walked off towards the winery, leaving Andrea speechless and feeling profoundly unsettled.

From the grape harbor, McCormick watched Andrea stop at an outdoor kiosk. Taking advantage of the long line in front of her, he jogged his wine purchase to his car, grabbed his cap, and returned to watch her order an apple cider slushy, which she sipped as she casually strolled along the orchard lane. When she disappeared into the trees where a trail began, and a sign pointed the way to the pumpkin patch, he felt more than certain that she was just killing time—not wanting to go home.

From a distance, he watched her board a tractor-drawn wagon loaded with fussy kids and fretting parents, heading for the patch a fair distance away. He studied the large, rolling field littered with multitudes of round, orange pumpkins. Seeing nothing to provide him cover, he decided to wait for her return.

He secured a warm, sunny spot beside a wooden fence where dry leaves had been raked into a pile, and heaped against a wooden fence. Seeing no sign of life behind the railing, no hollow horned *haedus kid* or *genus Ovis*, he sat down and leaned his back against a post.

Returning without a pumpkin, Andrea spied the exhausted agent right where he'd nodded off, with his cap pulled down over his eyes—and the goateed chins of multiple goats stretching their tongues through the fence, trying to remove his cap. She captured the charming, Rockwellian moment in its breathtakingly, beautiful setting on her Smartphone.

Not wanting to reveal her softer side, she stepped forward, and poked his foot with her boot. She spoke in a loud, sardonic tone, "Why am I not surprised to find you sleeping with the shaggy-haired goats, McCormick?"

The man's travel weary eyes shot wide open. Seeing only a dark shadow standing over him, he instantly leaped up, and simultaneously drew the gun from its holster.

With surprised, frightened eyes, Andrea took a frantic leap backwards and snapped, derisively, "Have you been sheep-dipped in delirium, or what?" She spread her arms, palms up. "I'm not armed … butt head!"

His dark eyes flashed as he backed away in obvious discombobulation.

She shot him an angry, taunting glare, "What? Did we get up on the wrong side of the goat herder's pen?" She spun around on her heels and walked away in a huff, leaving him no opportunity for explanations.

Irascibly, McCormick leaned against the fence, admonishing himself for not sleeping on the plane, and for having a frail, human body that demanded rest. He tried to ignore the high-pitched bleating, long and antagonizing, adding fuel to her sarcasm as she strolled down the grassy knoll and stopped on the wooded bridge crossing a stream.

Enjoying the brisk breeze and vivid fall colors, she suddenly heard, in the distance, the bleating sounds. She tossed a wicked glance over her shoulder. Her smartass grin spoke volumes as the wind carried her cloying treacle of laughter to McCormick's ears. A groan escaped his lips as he watched her meander, gleefully, along the winding path towards the lake—the breeze tugging at her hair and gently fluttering her skirt, along with McCormick's heart.

Once she reached the water's edge, McCormick pushed aside thoughts of his missed opportunity, and watched the gorgeous wife of Brantley Stone drop coins into a quarter pellet dispenser, feeding the hungry ducks and goldfish off the dock. Soon she struck up a conversation with three small children. Two were girls, the other a little towheaded boy, toting around a plastic, cinema popcorn bucket filled to the brim, not with popcorn, but with action adventure figures.

McCormick moved in closer, taking up a position behind a stack of straw bales.

In no time, Andrea had the kids laughing and giggling as she stooped down, lifted them up, one-by-one, helping them throw pressed pellets over the wooden railing and into the water. He watched her dig into her purse for coins, supplying the kids with more pellets. When a beautiful, white swan graced the water, gliding, serenely towards them, their attention was swept up in a spirit of fantasy and awe for several, long minutes.

McCormick seized the opportunity, to move, unnoticed, among the sprawled trunks of clump birch trees—close enough to hear their animated chatter.

At last, he watched them leave the pond area, climbing the hill together. Andrea led, while the parents brought up the rear, smiling and holding hands, obviously enjoying the short reprieve from entertaining their young. To their rear, a long procession of noisy, quacking ducks followed as they all laughed and giggled with delight.

The cortege passed in front of McCormick's blind. He watched as the two young girls raced to see which one got to hold Andrea's hand; but as they fussed with each other, Joey, the little boy, quietly sidled up beside the beautiful woman and without a word, slipped his tiny hand into hers. McCormick watched her gaze drop to the child with surprise. An appreciative smile, warm and tender, spread wide across her sensuous lips, and an inner glow radiated from her heart to her happy visage.

Like a reflection in a mirror, the same happy smile crossed the agent's lips, and her warm, loving glow quickly found its way to the bottom of his heart.

The older girl began to tell the story of *The Ugly Duckling*. Her captive audience listened attentively, asking questions along the way. McCormick watched the high-spirited scenario play out, finding himself in good humor as he did a loose foot-follow a short distance behind the ducks—hiding out in the open. Mrs. Fitzgerald was a natural with children, he realized. He wondered why she had no kids of her own.

The story ended at the pumpkin, gourd and chrysanthemum-laden entrance to the gift shop, where they all stopped to laugh and chat with the mechanical, talking tree. Finally, all but McCormick entered the shop.

As live, lively music spilled over from a sidewalk bistro, McCormick darted behind a John Deere tractor and a wagonload of giant pumpkins, peering through the shop's window through field glasses. He observed them all browsing the aisles, sampling the fudge, and homemade bread. He watched Andrea purchase a small bag of apples for herself, a larger one for the family, and caramel apples sprinkled with nuts and rainbow colors for the entire family of five.

Once outside, the girls still jabbered for Andrea's benefit, but the tag-a-long, little boy, grown tired and sullen, suddenly took a stand. He chided his sister, "Kieran, be quiet … it's my turn to talk." He pulled a black action figure from his bucket, and held it up for Andrea's inspection, telling her all about his favorite hero. "I've got the newer version … but I like this one better … he used to be a bad guy…." he said emphatically, "but now he's good." The bright-eyed child's voice dropped to a mere whisper, "He's complicated." Andrea dropped down to his level, raising her brows and giving the child the personal attention he so strongly desired. She asked him several questions about his hero action figure.

From his scrunched position behind the talking tree, McCormick both heard their conversation and watched as she cheerfully walked the family to the parking lot, and to their rusty, blue Subaru. She, laughingly, bid the family goodbye, giving them all an enthusiastically exaggerated wave as they started to drive away. The sound of her laughter tweaked McCormick's already glowing heart.

Gingerly, she walked through the clear, crisp air and golden sunshine towards her car, carrying apples, keys and a glow of exuberance. McCormick followed, his eye on her small handbag swinging rhythmically at her side. She'd enjoyed being with the children, immensely—he could read the happy radiance, still bright upon her cheeks.

In the parking lot, he stealthily, cut over one row, and followed not far behind, making his way back to his car, wondering how, in the hell, Brantley Stone had ever landed this lovely lady. *Something is seriously wrong with this picture,* he thought.

He also wondered if the young couple might possibly be one of Andrea's sources of drug information. He made a mental note of the car's make and model, and memorized the license number. Even as he did so, he could see the kids, still waving, gregariously, from the backseat until their car had completely disappeared from sight.

Now, a sudden heaviness stirred in the agent's chest, along with a tinge of self-contempt for what he was doing—and about to do.

—◄o►—

The generally slow-moving mail clerk stopped his squeaky cart outside Andrea's office the following morning, and quickly shoved his ample butt against her door, already ajar. Pronouncedly, he called out, "Mail call."

Deep into her own thoughts, Andrea looked up, startled.

Behind his thick, black glasses, and below the multi-colored hair, Deegan wore a look of complete bafflement. "Ms. Daye, is your name, really ... Andrea Fitzgerald?"

Taken aback by the question, Andrea gave him a noncommittal nod.

Having heard rumors of her death threat, the clerk's eyes widened with something akin to fear. In haste, he tossed a large, manila envelope on her desk, and then scurried out the door, in a rush to be anywhere but near Andrea Daye Fitzgerald.

Andrea watched the flummoxed, beefy young man in cargo shorts quickly disappear around the corner. "Nice socks," she offered, sardonically.

A sense of foreboding crept over the journalist as she glanced down at the conspicuous piece of mail. It was not without reason to believe this envelope could, might, or possibly did contain something that would cause her physical harm, something like anthrax, for one—fentanyl for another.

With a strong sense of dread, she summoned the courage to tear open the sealed flap. It appeared to be empty, but when she up-ended the package, and gave it a little shake, her beloved chain necklace fell out, and chinked atop her metal desk.

Feelings of elation flooded her soul as she immediately put the chain around her neck, and fastened it securely. She wondered who could have found it and returned it to her. Caressing the beloved pendant, she imagined that it possessed a new energy. She flipped the envelope face up. It bore no return address, but the pre-paid postal stamp came from a place in Virginia. She sat in stillness, mesmerized by the stamp. Who did she know in Virginia?

Finally, after great thought she spat out a name.

"McCormick!"

David, just leaving Rudd's office, thought he heard his name spoken, and looked up. Noticing the stunned look on Andrea's face, he stuck his head through the door left ajar by the mail clerk. "Did you say something to me?"

"No, I'm just talking to myself, again." she said, quietly.

Andrea fingered her necklace. David recognized it immediately, and enthused, "Oh great … you found your necklace."

She lifted her chin and gave him a dreamy-eyed look; but he sensed, immediately, that the look was not meant for him.

The car's interior was completely dark, except for the dimly-lit dashboard; but tonight the darkness felt mystically sweet—almost nourishing. Andrea rolled down the window in a quest for fresh air; allowing the cool breeze to hit her face. Tonight, she had an overwhelming need to be hidden, anonymous, even. Did the feeling stem from having her thoughts read daily by thousands of people, or was the death threat doing exactly what it was intended to do?

At 11:30, she was bone-tired and feeling the full force of her heavy work-load. The turnover rate at the News was extremely high. Sometimes Rudd would hire a new reporter, then fire him before a full week's work had been completed, forcing her to constantly be training and mentoring new, young reporters, editing their copy to save their skins—and their jobs. The burnout rate for a newsroom employee was estimated at around two years. Andrea had been working it for over three.

She recalled snippets of the late-night conversation she'd had with David, a while back. *Has the poetry completely gone out of my life,* she wondered, *just like David's older brother? What a horrible thing for a patriot to come home to, but why did David think he was dead?* She wondered what an older David might look like—minus the indiscernible bump. She chuckled as the image of her phantom warrior re-emerged in her mind.

In silence, she whizzed past houses where a warm glow shone out through the window panes. Upon closer inspection, she noticed front entrances decorated with cute, little straw-handed scarecrows, and porches lined with smiling jack-o-lanterns. An occasional white ghost, gossamery but friendly, hung from low-lying branches, fluttering hauntingly, in the gentle autumn breeze.

She imagined all the love in those homes as small children got tucked into beds and carried off to dreamland. By comparison, her life seemed so empty.

She readily admitted that she wanted more from life—needed more from life. She remembered the birthday kiss in the Lounge, both the gift and the giver—the kiss that had impacted her life in a major way ever since. Surely, life had more to offer than what she'd seen so far. She pondered that thought for the next several miles. Yeah, she longed for more of everything: romance, family, love. *McCormick was someone who could deliver on that score*, she thought, *if he wasn't gay or married—or such a hardass.*

She turned onto her own side road where lawns displayed, not whimsical scarecrows, but gray tombstones; skulls and crossbones. Instead of goofy pumpkin heads, lay severed appendages and dark, wraithlike depictions of suggestive torture and death. She slowed as she drove by one house in particular, remembering the young boy's Celebration of Life ceremony—well-attended by the community, but extremely short on anything celebratory.

Too soon, her lonely, unlit house came into view. Under the influence of ghoulish suggestion, and feeling, somehow, detached from reality, she thought it looked more like a haunted castle on a hill, rather than her home. She drove slowly through the wrought iron entrance, feeling strange, as though entering a Memorial Park.

It wasn't the full moon hanging over the gated property like low-hanging fruit that made her feel like a visitor; or the long, winding drive-way leading to the elegant Tudor-styled domicile with gorgeous landscaping and formal gardens; nor was it the stables, empty and eerily ghostly, over-looking a scenic, but brume-shrouded vista. No, on this night, it was the sum of it all that had her looking at it as though for the first time, the summation of her father's hard-won accomplishments and well-earned successes.

His roots were in these mountains and foothills. Having grown up a child of poverty, he had put himself through college, barely scraping by, while working as a lowly apprentice to a crotchety, old chemist until finding success through hard work and long hours. But he hadn't been satisfied to simply better himself; he had, instead, taken on the responsibility for his entire family, raising each and every one out of poverty.

Feeling moonstruck, she threw the car into park, and stepped out into the sepulchral night. She walked to a small grassy knoll and spun around, taking it all in, in sweeping, panoramic vision. She sucked in a deep breath, and spoke with awe, "Here lies the American Dream...." Gazing into the heavens, she suddenly cried out in remorsefulness, and slow, deliberate enunciation, "And I let ... a complete Neanderthal ... walk in ... and steal it all away!" Sobbing, her hands reached out as though to grasp the sky and pull it down. "Dad ... I am so sorry!"

Collapsing to her knees, she begged, "Oh, God, help me!"

CHAPTER 17

David stood in the doorway. He raised his eyebrows, and asked, "Going to lunch?"

Andrea checked her cell phone for the time, "Yeah, sure," she answered. "Zoe and I have plans already … want to join *us*?"

He answered, without hesitation as a very readable grin crossed his face. "Sure!"

She picked up her desk phone and punched in Zoe's number. Across the newsroom, a phone rang. Zoe picked up, and Andrea spoke. "You don't mind if Hockey Jock goes to lunch with us, do you?" she asked, shooting her wry grin at David.

Zoe looked into Andrea's glass-lined office. Seeing David there, she spoke with cattiness. "What's the matter … isn't *Jolene* eating lunch today?" she asked, unable to suppress her jealous feelings. She had learned about David's luncheon date with Jolene the week before.

Andrea laughed, knowing for a fact that her friend would jump at a chance to lunch with David. She had already come to the conclusion that David wasn't the rogue she'd been warned about; in fact, he seemed to be a person of real moral fortitude; but he didn't seem to have much of a personal life, at all. She, too, had wondered about his luncheon date with Jolene, but she figured she knew him well enough to know he saw nothing in that woman.

Andrea's eyes shot to the ceiling, then she slumped back into her chair. "Oh, gawd … I almost forgot." She added, quickly, "I have to pick up Shaun at the airport in ninety minutes … I'll have to grab a quick bite and run … darn!"

"Ooh," Zoe groaned over the phone, "do you have to? It seems like only yesterday that you told me he was leaving."

"Tell me about it … is *The Hut* okay with you guys? I'll call in our order, but Zoe … you'll have to ride with David." David looked across the newsroom at Zoe and they shot each other syrupy grins that said: *ain't that a shame.*

"Care to make this a Halloween Party?" David asked, as Zoe crossed the newsroom and sidled up beside him. "I have to work tonight."

"Aw, poor Davy," Zoe teased in a little-girl voice, "no chance to get candy corn in your widdle Trick-or-Treat bag?"

"No time to saran wrap your rusty, old pickup truck," he grumbled.

"You wouldn't dare!" Zoe screeched, forsaking her teasing, and finding her voice of wrath. "You're supposed to guard my gal…." She bounced a concealed smirk off Andrea, a look they both, clearly, understood.

They walked to the back of the building, together, laughing all the way. As they passed the antiquated wire service machine, Andrea's attention was drawn to a story just being printed out. She tugged on David's sleeve.

"Hey, just a minute guys. I need to read this Reutter's story." She started to read aloud. "An American airliner, Flight number … has crashed … in El Salvador … shortly after taking off from a Columbian airport." Her words slowed. "Twenty Americans were onboard…." Her voice faltered.

She stopped reading. "That's Shaun's flight," she whispered with a catch in her throat. She pulled his flight information from her coat pocket, confirming the flight number.

She gasped, "Shaun's plane has crashed!"

David and Zoe exchanged bewildered glances then hurriedly read the rest of the wire for themselves.

"I don't believe it," Andrea gushed, her face draining as she rolled back on her heels in lightheadedness. David instinctively curled his arms around her shoulders, leading her back to her office. Zoe followed, closing the door behind them. No one noticed the insipid grin on Jolene's face as she watched the little scenario unfold with vested interest from the copier.

Andrea asked, "How many survivors?"

Hating to be the bearer of bad news, Zoe tried to speak, but couldn't. She looked helplessly at David. The young sports editor ran a palm over his ashen forehead, and finally forced out the words. "Andi, there was an explosion midair … they don't know … they're pretty certain no one survived." He pulled a chair up close and sat down, pressing her trembling hands between his own. "Are you sure Shaun was on that plane?"

She nodded with certainty. "He called early this morning, before dawn, just as I was pulling out of the driveway. I wrote his flight number and arrival time on the back of this." She handed the card to David.

He read the information on the back of the card, written in Andrea's prim handwriting. Curiously, he flipped the card to the front side. Still reeling from news of the crash, a second startlement rolled over the sports editor as he read the bold, black lettering: *Lt. Colonel Matthew J. McCormick, U.S. Special Forces.*

Lt. Colonel?

David discreetly tucked the card into his pocket—and out of circulation. "Let's get to the airport. Airline personnel will know what's happened to Shaun before anyone else. I'll drive ... Zoe, come with us."

During the weeks following the crash, Andrea's emotions had been blown around like the dead, dry leaves outside her bedroom window. One minute she was relieved to be free of Shaun's manipulative control; the next, she'd have grievous thoughts for the lost lives of the other passengers.

Night after night she'd lain awake remembering Shaun and all the things he had said and done. What had caused him to change? Or, had he always had a dark side? Had he deliberately taken control of her dad's company; had he deliberately married her? If so, then there was only one word for it—*evil!* Had he kil....? She quickly shut down the unthinkable.

A feeling of vulnerability snaked through her. She had always taken control of her own life; but life had dumped on her, big time. She had so many questions with no answers swirling around in her mind. She was totally confused, yet unable to understand the cause of her confusion. Could Alzheimer's disease possibly be contagious, she wondered. After weeks of trying to forgive Shaun for his deficiencies, she'd finally come to an acceptance of one fact: *she had never loved, or even liked Shaun Fitzgerald. Truth was: she had despised him.*

And there was something not quite right about the plane crash. Events, conversations, and tiny details swirled around in her head like a whirlwind. At times she thought she would go insane.

Why had Shaun prearranged his own memorial service? Was it his own vane, egomaniacal personality; or had he experienced a premonition of his own death?

And what was his reason for buying a cabin and several acres of forested property in the mountains—a cabin she'd just learned about? Anyone who knew Shaun would also know he suffered from acrophobia, a fear of heights. No one with that particular malady would buy a vacation place in the mountains. Things just didn't add up. Some ominous fact sat perched at the edge of consciousness like a dark, foreboding storm cloud, refusing to be brought forward, and taking permanent residence, not in her mind, but in the pit of her stomach.

When her alarm exploded into a joyful exaltation of carillon bells, she groaned, and quieted it with a limpid hand. She'd lain awake through most of the darkest-before-dawn hours, awaiting a glimpse of the full Harvest moon.

Benumbed, she rolled over and buried her face in the pillow, letting the words of Alfred Lord Tennyson over-ride her thoughts:

> *This year I slept and woke in pain,*
> *I almost wish'd no more to wake,*
> *And that my hold on life would break*
> *Before I heard those bells again.*

Suddenly, she threw off the blanket, and sat up. "Hell … I'm not that far gone … yet," she said aloud, throwing her legs over the side of the bed. She stared, vacuously, through the window at the gray, overcast sky, and the stark tree limbs with a few stubborn, brown leaves still clinging to the branches. She wondered why it was that she could remember the words of an 18th century British Poet Laureate, but not what happened in her life three weeks ago.

A little sunshine wouldn't hurt her mood any, she thought, forcing herself to her feet. Maybe a trip to the Caribbean or the Virgin Islands would help. "Nah … they're too much in the news," she decided.

She trudged to the shower. As the streams of soft, warm water splashed over her face and body, her unanswered questions continued to invade her sense of peace.

Why had Shaun taken that trip to Peru, of all places? No one, not even the people who worked closest to him, had been able to explain the reason for the sudden trip—at least not to Andrea's satisfaction.

She dried off and slipped into a warm, fleecy robe and matching slippers then sat down at her dressing table and its full circle of lighting. In spite of the large, luminous bulbs, she was oblivious to the ghostly image staring back at her. Her usual bright eyes were dull and lifeless, without expression. Her skin was dry and feverish; her long, lustrous hair, usually worn like a crown of glory, fell limp across her shoulders.

Suddenly, she stopped and looked down at her trembling hands, noticing her unusually brittle, split nails. Over the last few weeks, her hands had become an obsession. Damn ... what was freaking her out about her hands?

She finished dressing, and then drove to work through the oppressive darkness.

Jolene, snarky as hell and overly dramatic, met her at the reception desk. "Andrea, you look terrible ... aren't you feeling well?" she asked, barely concealing her glee. Before Andrea could answer, she added, "You really should have stayed home ... the *News* can function quite well without you, ya know." Her words chirped with acerbity—hitting the assistant editor right smack between the eyes.

To hell with good work relationships, Andrea thought, and snapped back, "Assistant editors and senior reporters don't stay at home ... I have an important 9:30 deadline."

Jolene shot her a look of sheer vindictiveness.

Zoe, hearing the heated words spoken between the two women, walked up and took a stand beside Andrea, also noticing her friend's pallid, dry skin, and dark-ringed eyes. "Jolene doesn't understand the awesome responsibility of publishing the daily news ... daily," Zoe offered.

"For sure," Andrea added, flatly without taking her eyes off Jolene.

Jolene started to sound off, but Zoe pursed her lips, and shot the woman a look of warning that said, *back off.*

"You could work from home, you know!" Jolene spat, acrimoniously, hinting at something which neither of them understood.

Andrea's eyes roamed over Jolene's strange outfit. "What ... and miss your fashion statement of the day ... no way!"

A flustered Jolene turned on her heels, and with flippancy walked away.

Andrea's eyes followed her to the back of the room. Today the woman was dressed like Pocahontas on steroids. She wore dark brown pigtails with feathers and excessive glitter woven into the long, faux braids, and a headband across her forehead. Her feet were covered in something resembling seal-skin mukluks. In essence, Jolene was wearing a costume.

Andrea rubbed her hot, dry eyes, and then spoke softly to Zoe. "There's something very disturbing about that woman that goes far deeper than ignorance of journalism norms ... remind me to bring up the subject of appropriate newsroom attire at our next staff meeting ... I've had it with all these costumes being paraded around here in the guise of work clothes ... this is a place of business, not some Festival of Fools production ... for Chrissake."

Zoe gave her an assenting nod and went back to work. Andrea unlocked her door, turned on her computer, and sat for several minutes trying to focus on the monitor. She rubbed, absentmindedly, at her swollen ankles and glanced, listlessly, around the newsroom, half expecting to see David busy with the sports page. She saw only his replacement—someone who was only half the sports writer, half the editor, and a very small fraction of the friend David had been.

Remembering one of their last conversations, Andrea sank deeper into despair.

"What do you mean, you're leaving?" Andrea had questioned as she sat staring, disbelievingly, at the young man across the red tablecloth. Pizza scraps were heaped high on his plate and loud country music blared in the background. Zoe had excused herself to make a call regarding a young couple's wedding, and stood talking just outside the front door to insure reception.

For some reason, Andrea could not accept what David was saying to her.

His eyes went somber as they came to rest on his friend's disappointment. "It's time for me to move on ... I have another assign ... job."

"David, that's insane," she argued. "You've been here ... what? ... two, two and a half months? You're just now experienced enough to do your job ... and you're very good at it." She sighed wistfully. "David ... I have to level with you. Your friendship has become very important to me. You were a rock when Shaun...." For some reason, Andrea, could not speak of the accident or the memorial service. She could not say the words *when Shaun was killed, or when Shaun died.* Instead she sighed and threw him a woeful look. "Who will listen to me bitch about the unqualified people Rudd's hiring these days, or discuss my drug series? You're my sounding board ... my confidant."

For the first time, she realized how much like a brother David had become to her. He had joined them for Hero movie night at Zoe's, and when her mother had gone to bed, he had sat with his arm around Zoe; but they had all laughed and giggled like kids, drinking coolers and throwing puffs of popcorn into to each other's mouths. Later, they had gone to the ice rink, and he had given them both expert advice and professional skating tips.

Shortly after the plane crash, he had shown up at church with Zoe for a Sunday morning worship service. They had laughingly sandwiched her between the two of them on a middle pew in the large, but sparsely filled sanctuary.

Andrea thought back to that morning, remembering. All through a sermon based on the story of Zacchaeus, the wee little tax collector Jesus coaxed out of a sycamore tree so to stay at his house, she had felt eyes burning through the back of her head, hauntingly so. She'd figured her imagination was just conjuring up phantoms, again. *Surely not in church*, she'd thought, unable to throw off the feeling. During the closing prayer, curiosity had gotten the best of her, and she'd sneaked a peak over her shoulder, checking out the mostly empty pews in the back of the sanctuary. Only a small group of weather-withered seniors from assisted living sat behind her.

But then, she'd spied the top of a dark head, sitting two rows behind the feeble, white-haired ladies. The man's arms were dug deep into his thighs, and his shoulders were rounded forward. His head was bowed, his face cratered into his hands, giving the impression of a serious believer in heart-felt prayer.

Following the last amen, she'd stolen a second look, but the seat had gone vacant; she had however, gotten a glimpse of a shadowy figure passing through the dimly-lit vestibule, leaving the building through a side door. The shadow had long legs and wore a black, leather jacket.

Awe-struck, she'd whispered, under her breath. "McCormick."

Hearing the whisper, David had leaned in close, giving her his wide-eyed attention.

Trying to shove the memories aside, she clicked on the Letters to the Editor icon, but the memories kept surfacing. She'd asked, "David, you're not leaving *because* of me, are you?"

"I can't believe you would ask me that question." He'd leaned across the table and lowered his voice to a more intimate tone. "Andi, there's just no future for me here. I can't even begin to pay for my college education on what I'm making; and at this rate, I'll never be able to get married."

Married? Andrea had stared, intently, into David's handsome face, before dropping her eyes. "Ah, you're absolutely right … forgive me for being such a selfish oaf … you're probably right about the future," she'd added, slurping the last of her soda. "A lot of people think the printed word is dying, that newspapers are on borrowed time … or already dead."

Zoe had returned to the table at just that moment, and David had gallantly stood up. Andrea watched the two give each other huge smiles, warm and intimate. *So that's how it is,* she thought, hiding her joy behind her napkin.

They had said their good-bye's following an office party and promised to keep in touch. Almost a month had passed, but Andrea still hadn't heard a word from David. She had no idea where he was living, or working; nor did Zoe.

Now, Andrea had a news-breaking story to write about elections and mail-in ballots, but she struggled to focus on her work. Instead she found herself staring blankly at the fragmented sentences on the screen. Nothing would come together, and with extreme rarity, she was having trouble recalling the spelling of the simplest words.

"We're down!" someone yelled from the back of the room. Andrea watched her screen go black as the young reporters cursed in unison. Staring into a newsroom full of blank computer screens, Andrea groaned, realizing her antiquated news world had just exploded like an improvised, explosive device.

The new, green receptionist, fresh from the twitter world, tarried at Andrea's door. "What do they mean, 'we're down?' " she asked.

Andrea rubbed her forehead, impatiently and addressed the girl's question. "It means our server, our carrier—whatever—has stopped working. If you had anything on your monitor, it's probably lost." Once the girl was out of hearing distance, she said, with irony, "Or maybe our cloud with the silver lining just evaporated." She stepped out of the room. Her voice rose in volume as she spoke with authority to the rest of her staff. "Take a break."

Feeling certain that her work was deliberately being sabotaged, Andrea's feelings of hostility rose to the surface. As Zoe approached, she spoke indiscriminately. "This is happening all too often ... especially since Jolene came to work here."

Over-hearing Andrea's comment, rage registered on Jolene's face, and she quickly blew past her assistant editor. From her office, Andrea watched Pocahontas try to disappear into Rudd's glass-walled wigwam, where heavy smoke swirled to the ceiling like campfires of an indigenous people. She laughed, sardonically. "You can run, but you can't hide—not in this building."

Jolene glanced malevolently over her shoulder and through the glass.

Andrea checked her watch, anxiously aware of the minutes ticking away before deadline. Everything was out of control, upside down, and now she had another headache.

She opened her middle desk drawer, and took out a small bottle of coated aspirin. She couldn't remember bringing the bottle into the newsroom, but she was glad the pills were there when she needed them; she seemed to need them quite often the last couple of weeks.

She emptied two of the small orange tablets into her hand, returning the bottle to the middle drawer. Deciding to use the down time to get something to eat, she grabbed her purse, and walked back through the building to the water fountain. As she lifted the tablets to her mouth, one fell from her cupped hand. With dismay she watched the pill teeter into a crack between the old floorboards. She swallowed the remaining pill, grimacing at its, surprisingly, bitter taste.

In the canteen, she dug through her purse for coins, while exchanging greetings with two women from the advertising department. "How are you getting along, hon?" the one with orange-colored hair and a look that said she'd been around the block a few hundred times, or more asked. "Are you adjusting to ... ah...."

Andrea gave her a weak smile and spoke the word for her, "Widowhood?"

"Yes ... widowhood." She looked around at a gathering of young reporters. "I was just noticing all these young men."

I'll bet you were, Andrea thought, trying to avoid looking at the woman's large, high-riding cleavage above her shirt's plunging neckline. She dropped her eyes to the floor, unable to escape the sight of the woman's spindle legs below her very short, mini skirt. As the woman lit up a cigarette, blowing smoke indiscriminately in Andrea's direction, she braced herself for whatever might flow out of the woman's mouth next. "What ever happened to that ... David? Now that's one hot body."

Andrea looked up just in time to see Zoe coming to her rescue. In a reversal of roles, Andrea shot her friend a helpless look.

"David's gone!" Zoe yelled from across the room. She laughed, teasingly. "Fern, you have to stop harassing Andi ... she's only been a widow for a few weeks ... she's still in...." She bounced a knowing glance off Andrea, "in mourning ... besides, you're wasting your time with this one. Andi doesn't like showy exhibitionists ... she prefers quiet, self-assured men."

The sound that came from the woman's mouth was lewd and disrespectful, "Well, that's certainly not what she was married to, is it ... her husband knew how to have a good time."

Andrea cringed and diverted her gaze. She knew Zoe was trying to help, but being the butt of the women's jokes went beyond the pale. Relief flooded her senses when Fern's boss poked his head around the corner, harkening the woman back to work. Andrea watched her teeter away on three-inch heels, promising herself that she would never reach that level of desperation.

"Speaking of showy exhibitionists," Zoe said, downheartedly, "have you heard anything from David?"

"Not a word ... and I'm disappointed. I was sure he would keep in touch."

"Yeah, so was I."

"If I hear, anything, you'll be the first to know," Andrea promised. She paused a moment. "Zoe ... I just have this gut feeling that he'll show up, again, one day."

"I hope so ... I was really starting to like that guy—he had ...."

"Armor," Andrea offered, lightly touching her friend's shoulder.

"Yeah," Zoe whispered, wistfully, "shining armor."

Andrea turned, dropping coins into the coffee machine. She made her selection; then watched the black brew fill up the paper cup. "Just hang on to your faith, Zoe ... your knight will...."

Suddenly, Andrea's stomach lurched, and the walls began to swirl like the early morning leaves.

"Andi!" Zoe's voice sounded from a distance. "Are you okay?" Then, like the computer screens just moments earlier, everything faded to black.

—◁◯▷—

When Andrea's eyes fluttered open, they were immediately drawn to a warm, closed-lipped smile of an attractive, registered nurse, standing over the shoulder of an aging, white-haired, white-coated doctor. She vaguely recognized the guy checking her pulse, and staring down at her with great concern through thick-lensed glasses. "Well, now," he said, his chest puffing up proudly as though he'd just succeeded in some new medical experiment. He crowed, "Nurse Storm ... our Sleeping Beauty has awakened. The nurse, who was several years the doctor's younger, remained silent.

Completely disoriented, Andrea felt as though she were emerging from some hallucinatory, fairy tale. Her mouth felt dry and cottony, and as though it had been stuffed with bulbs of garlic. She couldn't remember eating anything made with garlic.

"Where am I?" She looked down at the blanket covering her body and realized the she was laying on a hospital gurney.

It was the nurse who spoke. "You're in the emergency room at Forest Hills Regional Hospital."

Finally putting a name to the doctor from year's past, Andrea wisecracked, "You've got the wrong fairy tale, doc." She tried to sit up. "I feel more like ... the beast." The tall, slender nurse quickly moved around to the far side of the bed, graciously pushing back the curtain as she moved. Again Andrea struggled to sit up, "What happened?"

The nurse, who appeared to be somewhere between fifty or fifty-five years old, with ribbons of salt and pepper hair twisted, attractively into a long, sophisticated French braid, leaned over the gurney and shoved against Andrea's shoulders, making her feel like a petulant child.

"Just lay back down," the doctor ordered, taking his own sweet time adjusting an intravenous needle in her arm. At last he answered her question. "You lost consciousness and banged your head on a table. We've bandaged you up and run some tests."

"Tests?" she questioned, totally bewildered.

"You're one of the lucky ones, Andrea ... you'll survive ... we should have a report back by late afternoon."

The old doctor looked into his young patient's eyes, remembering the girl she'd been in years past, when she and her family had spent their summers in the area. Many were the cuts and scrapes, bee stings and pulled muscles. Andrea had been quite the tomboy, as he recalled. It had been thirteen or fourteen years since he'd last seen her; and he marveled at her now. She had grown into one of the most beautiful women he had ever laid eyes on. It was quite obvious that she took after her mother, except Andrea was even prettier—and her mother had been a jaw-dropping knock-out.

He laid her hand and wrist across her tummy as though it were detached from the rest of her body. "Young lady ... we have another matter to discuss." He looked at her grimly. "Andrea your general condition is very poor. You're dehydrated, and you have a serious iron deficiency—your body is exhausted." He gave her a long, concerned look. "How old are you?"

Andrea shook her head. "I'm really getting old; but I'm surprised at you, Doctor Pierce ... you know you're not supposed to ask a lady her age," she chided, groggily, "but since it's you asking ... I just turned twenty-eight."

"You think that's old?" the doctor challenged. "Hell ... I can't even remember ever being twenty-eight," he laughed. Andrea heard the shakiness in his voice, and realized how much time had passed since she'd last seen him.

"Did you ever marry?"

"I'm a wi...widow," she answered, flatly, the term sticking in her throat, and sounding foreign to her own ears. The old doctor peered over the top rim of his glasses.

"Got any children at home?"

"No ch...." Andrea let the sentence drop.

The doctor removed his glasses and folded his arms across his chest. "My point is this ... if you don't stop and rest, young lady, your body is going to stop functioning on its own ... or you'll develop some sort of serious illness. You're much too young to have that happen."

She started to protest, "But ... I'm working on...."

"I know what you're working on," he interrupted. "I read your column, and it's an honorable thing you're doing, but this incident should tell you that it's time to give it a rest. Be nice to yourself for a change. Take a leave of absence, or better yet, take a vacation ... get away somewhere. Rudd can't expect you to work for a while after this—and I forbid it!"

Andrea tried to swallow the emotional lump in her throat. She said nothing.

"I'm going to keep you here for observation. We'll run more tests and build up your blood. We'll bring you three squares a day and a snack ... eat them. I'll release you once I see you improving. In the meantime, no visitors, no phone calls, and positively no newspapers! Understand?" Andrea pursed her lips, but remained silent, pertinaciousness filling her eyes.

The doctor hiked his eyebrows, and locked eyes with the nurse. "Understand, Nurse Storm?" Andrea raised her gaze in time to catch the serious, no-nonsense glint in the nurse's eye.

"Yes doctor," the nurse answered, firmly.

The doctor headed towards the door, mumbling. "At least one of you gets my point." He stopped at the door, and looked askance at the young woman, giving her a long look of appraisal, heartfelt and respectful. "It's good to see you again, Andi." He gave her a quick, serious wink, and then left the room with the nurse trailing close behind, leaving Andrea alone with her memories of a much earlier time.

Lying flat, and feeling as though she were on a slab in the morgue, she pushed herself into a sitting position, dangling her bare feet over the edge of the bed. For the first time since recovering consciousness, she became aware of her attire. A blue, cotton gown, several sizes too large, had been draped around her body. It drooped low in front, so low as to expose what needed to be covered, and with a constant need to be tugged up. A slit ran down the full length in back, with nothing to tie the two sides together, allowing her no modesty. Encircling her wrist was an identification bracelet made of tough, white plastic that would later have to be cut off. Soberly, she studied the ID—at *least it's not on my toe,* she thought, gratefully. She looked down and wiggled her toes just to confirm the fact that she was, indeed, alive. She caressed her necklace, surprised it hadn't been removed.

Once she'd been moved into a private room, Andrea tried to relax, but a continuous stream of cold air blew steadily over her bed. She had asked that it be turned off, and been told the blower was broken. A maintenance man would be sent in shortly, she'd been assured.

Hours later, the shivering patient tossed and turned. It wasn't just the vent, or the hard, lumpy mattress and too-thin of a blanket that kept her awake; nor was it the pillow beneath her head that may as well have been a rock for all the comfort it afforded her. No, she just couldn't shake off the bizarre events of the last several weeks, months, and even years.

Overtaken by exhaustion, she finally drifted into a light, troubled sleep.

Suddenly, a hinge squeaked, startling Andrea to wide-eyed attention.

Her eyes shot towards the door, and she watched it slowly creak open. In midnight murkiness, a shadowy figure stood lurking inside her room.

Except for the sliver of light shining through the window, the room was completely dark. Andrea's pulse quickened as she rose on one elbow, quickly taking stock of her defenseless position. Silently, her hand stretched out towards the small remote that controlled the bed, the TV, and the call button to the nurse's station. Using her nails, she pulled it within her reach. "Are you here to fix the heater?" she asked in a voice pitched higher than normal.

No answer came back. She quickly threw off the blanket, preparing to kick, bite or groin-punch in her own defense.

She heard no footfalls, but suddenly a presence stood beside her bed.

CHAPTER 18

Frantically, Andrea pushed the button on the remote, and out of desperation, pushed it a second time. To her chagrin, the TV quickly flickered on and off. She pushed a second button, and rode the squeaky bed down to a slow, grinding halt. Sensing that she was about to scream, her intruder stepped forward and clamped one hand over her nose and mouth. "Don't," he ordered, gruffly. He tapped her hand, and expertly flipped the remote into his own hand, as if by magic.

She thrashed beneath the vice-like grip, desperately trying to wiggle free of his hold. With frightful eyes, wide-open, she looked up in an effort to identify her assailant. Like heroines in the whodunit stories she'd read as a teen, she damned well, sure as hell, wasn't going to die without first getting a look at his face!

Seeing her IV connection about to fall away, the intruder ordered in a low, demanding voice, "Don't move … and stop playing around."

Andrea froze.

"And don't even think about screaming … I'm going to turn on the light … got it?"

Recognizing the rich, timbre in the man's voice, she nodded. "That's okay," she offered, her words muffling through his fingers. "I don't need a light … really … I know who you are."

In spite of her insistence, the man took two quick steps towards the bathroom and flipped the switch. In the sudden glare of florescent lighting, she saw, staring back at her, piercing, but unreadable eyes. She took in his taut, chiseled jawline, the blacks of his leather bomber jacket and his knit stocking hat. First she raised her head, then sat up, tugging at the gown's inadequacy. She felt chilled and vulnerable, but mostly she felt on despicable display as she shot daggers into the eyes of her uninvited guest.

Startled by both the woman's near nakedness, and the bright luminescence of her eyes, the man hurriedly tamped down his natural reaction to a beautiful woman. He squared his shoulders, and sucked in a nonexistent gut. From force of habit, he shot her a quick, informal salute. His healthy ego, with its penchant for humor, was evident in his strong, but roguish, grin. In a quiet tone, he offered, "Agent Matthew McCormick."

Andrea's only response was to further glare at him. Having never seen any form of identification, she still imagined this man to be a fraud, a poser— someone pretending to be someone he was not.

His heart sank at the sight of Andrea's bandaged head, and multiple slow IV drips into her arm. Cognizant of the trauma she'd just experienced, and aware that several weeks had passed since their endearing, little orchard chat, McCormick switched off the light, and stepped into the dim sliver of moonlight, taking care to keep a respectable distance. He removed his hat, giving her a better look at his friendly countenance. Getting no response, he asked in a tone somewhere between a dull whisper and a low growl, "Remember me ... Mrs. Fitzgerald?"

Andrea winced at being addressing as Mrs. Fitzgerald, and immediately felt chagrined, even in the face of this gregarious show of his, previously hidden, winsome personality. "Well ... well ... well. You claim to be McCormick, but you sure, as hell, don't look like him," she said, deliberately taunting, feigning disbelief. The McCormick I know has a full mustache ... you've got an itty-bitty one attached to a two-day-old Vandyke." Now her gaze settled on his head. "And what's this...." she razzed, choking back a chortle, "you're completely *bald*?"

His long lashes batted once, and his dark brows lifted in response to her brazen taunts. He ran his hand, slowly, across his shaved head, finding its smoothness in stark contrast to his normal head of healthy hair. "I've been assured, on numerous occasions, that bald is quite sexy," he offered in a jocular explanation for his hairless state.

"Oh yeah ... and where was that? ... on an all-male nudist beach?"

At the sound of voices outside the room, McCormick's steely eyes shot towards the open door with concernment. Leaving her side, he skulked quietly along the shadow-shrouded wall, checking the hallway. Finding that the overhead lights had been dimmed to nighttime lighting, and the night nurses settled in for the next hour, or so, he pushed the door shut, leaving it ajar just enough to allow for privacy without alerting some wandering gadabout.

Skepticism surfaced in Andrea's voice. "I don't know anything about you ... how do I know you're who you claim to be? Aren't you supposed to have some kind of identification—maybe a badge, or ... I'm just guessing here ... something with a *Special* in front of your name? What's happened to that ... did you get demoted ... or did you flush your *specialness down* with your hair?" She shot him a sassy wink.

McCormick's hand ran down the full length of his face, annoyed as a professional, yet totally entertained by her snarky sparring, and quick wit. His chin notched up with uncommon smugness. "I guess you'll just have to figure it out for yourself, Mrs. Fitzgerald ... I'm here with you."

Andrea bristled, feeling the indignity of her situation. She shoved back her long, thick hair in one angry swipe. Desisting with all banter, she doubled down on seriousness, "You scared the hell out of me, McCormick. "Why are you here?" she asked, her tone implying a threat of some kind, should he not come up with an acceptable answer. "You've brought me no flowers, so this must not be an empathy visit. Oh ... I get it," she snarked, irritably, "you're some kind of hospital pervert who gets off on flapping gowns and droopy asses... right?" She yanked at the neck of her gaping gown.

"Nah...." he answered in jest, his hands resting at belt-level, "you're getting me all mixed up with past presidents and movie moguls, but I'll tell you why I'm here once you've calmed down." Inconspicuously looking around, he spied her untouched tray on a dinner cart, and let out a heavy breath in disappointment. The patient blew out a breath, mocking him. McCormick took it as a good sign. He knew this wasn't going to be easy, but at least she was talking to him.

He drew a chair up close to the bed, though uninvited, and settled in, macho style, with his long legs spread wide as though planning to stay awhile. At last he leaned forward, and rested his forearms on his knees, his eyes briefly brushing across her partially-clad body. Quick to force his gaze onto something safer, he settled on her chain necklace, which had been returned to its rightful place around her neck, and nestled just above her cleavage. In the obscure lighting, the pendant seemed to be winking at him, teasing even. The corner of his mouth drew up in a slow, diminutive display of satisfaction; he'd done right by returning it to her.

When he lifted his gaze, he found Andrea's eyes locked into his—his quickly darted away.

Fully reading, and understanding the man's demeanor, Andrea questioned in a, somewhat, kinder voice, "Why are you here?"

McCormick rubbed a heavy hand across his mouth, dreading what he must say. He made an attempt to clear away the huskiness in his voice. "Believe it or not, Mrs. Fitzgerald ... I'm here to help you."

"Just drop the Fitzgerald crap, wouldya," she spat back, testily. "I have a very strong aversion to being called by that name!"

"Whatever," the agent said, flatly, his tone indifferent towards the wrath she was spewing. He recognized this classic symptom of poisoning—unusual irritability. Checking her left hand, and seeing no wedding band, he sucked in a satisfied breath—at least she wasn't wallowing in widowhood—another good sign.

He paused for a beat. "Is it okay if I call you Andrea?"

"Andi would be better," she offered.

The agent's empty stomach fluttered at his obvious progression. "Look, Andi," he said, "I know you don't like me much...."

The sound of her loathing breath invaded the darkness, but was quickly met head-on by his chortle, his hands shooting out to his side, in a defensive display. "Okay ... I get it ... you don't like me ... a lot, but I'm asking you to put all that vitriolic crap aside for now, and engage both sides of your brain ... can we at least agree on that much?"

"Crap?" she repeated with virulence. Enough was enough—she wanted him out of her room, and out of her life. Stubbornly, her hand inched towards the remote where he had, trustingly, laid it on the far side of the bed.

"I wouldn't do that if I were you," he warned, staidly as he reached across her body, and quickly snatched up the remote.

Andrea heard the growl in his voice, and saw his warning headshake; but she also glimpsed his laughing eyes and amused grin. The softness of his leather sleeve slid across her thigh, and she felt his warm, minty breath flit across her cheek like the gentle caress of a butterfly wing. Something long dormant stirred inside of her.

Resisting the agent's charm, as well as her own stirrings, she hissed, "I was simply going to raise my bed ... are you going to arrest me for that ... or am I already in your custody?"

"Babe, you're workin' on all counts." In a throaty grievance, he warned, "It's a felony to obstruct or lie to a federal agent."

"Yeah right," she snickered, bouncing a dubious glance off him. "I'll be sure to remember that … if I ever meet up with one."

Ignoring the insult, McCormick clicked the button on the remote, and the iron bed, groaning and whirring, returned to its maximum head tilt, a more comfortable position for his patient. Knowing no family member or visitor would be coming to her rescue, he snatched up her sad state of a pillow, and out of compassion, fluffed it up and propped it, comfortably, behind her head. He caught a glimpse of her goose bumps, and sensed her state of exhaustion. Her smooth, shapely legs were a whole other issue.

Deciding it best to go on defense, he gathered up the blanket she'd kicked to the foot of the bed, raised the tangled heap two feet into the air, and let it drop, unceremoniously, over her body. He raised a roguish brow, and in a tone lighter and more playful than before, teased, "You know … if you spend more than one night in solitary confinement … you get a free visit from the hospital clergy … you might want to dress for *that* occasion." He watched her doleful eyes roll to the ceiling.

While Andrea gratefully grabbed the blanket, and pulled it up to her chin, McCormick turned to refill her water cup from the small pitcher. A treacle of laughter sounded behind his back. "You're too good at this, McCormick."

"Y-e-a-h," he answered, ruefully. "I've had a lot of practice perfecting my bedside manner."

"I bet…," she sighed, studying his ruggedly handsome features in half-shadow, "with that classic profile … I'll just bet you have." She fell back against the pillow.

"Ah, be careful now … you're casting aspersions on someone you know nothing about." He handed her the cup and watched her drink.

When he returned to the chair, his heart was filled with heaviness, recalling his many visits to hospitals, and to the homes of widows and children of his fallen military brothers.

He tried to reassess his charge based on information gleaned from his investigation. Was she stubborn? Yes. Was she bitchy? Yes. Was she gorgeous? Hell yes. Totally distracted by that beauty, he shoved back in his chair, scraping loudly against the floor. Trying to regain his focus, he crossed to the window, studying the light drizzle that had begun to fall on the sidewalk below. His worried eyes, now haunted by the past, took in the quick flashes of lightning across the midnight sky. A storm was coming, but it was nothing compared to the one brewing inside McCormick as he remembered the many fine men who had been killed by this woman's husband—a formidable, cold-blooded killer of the worst kind. He knew he had to get control of this situation, or else—or else Andrea Daye Fitzgerald would soon be dead. The woman was totally clueless as to the dangers that lay in wait for her.

With renewed determination, he returned to her bedside and, once again, took a seat. "Andi something very serious has happened here," he said in all earnestness. "You've been poisoned," he leaned forward, "I'm quite sure it was no accident."

Andrea dropped her knees, and sat up straight, her gaping gown forgotten in her weariness. She stared at the man with astounding disbelief. "Poisoned?"

"Poisoned," he repeated, as lightning flashed across his shoulder. "You were lucky, but whoever is responsible, will try again; and believe me, the next time he won't leave the job half-finished."

Next time?

She shrugged her shoulders with incredulity, and challenged, "I don't believe that … Dr. Pierce would have told me if I had been poisoned."

"Should've, but didn't. He also neglected to report it to the proper authorities. Stop and think, Andi … your skin's dry and patchy due to dehydration … you're having stomach pains … your ankles are swollen … your mouth is dry with the taste of garlic…."

Both hands shot up in distress. "I get it!" she cried out, recognizing the symptoms. Without breath or motion, she sat in darkness, digesting the man's claim. Was he speaking the truth? Could she trust him? If she could only look into his eyes, read the lines on his face. Her father had always claimed that you could see a man's true character by looking deep into his eyes. Either a light shined from within, or they reflected a dead, dark soul. If only she could look into McCormick's eyes at this moment, she would know if he was telling her the truth—or not.

"I'm here to help you, Andi," he was saying, over a loud grumble of thunder. He wanted to reach for her hand, to give her a comforting hug, but he held back, remembering his responsibilities as a federal employee. "I can show you the lab reports ... someone is seriously trying to hurt you!" He paused for a beat, giving her time to absorb his message.

"And how do I know it's not you?" she charged, belligerently.

The agent pressed his lips together, disheartened, and gave his head a quarter-shake. "You'll just have to trust that it's not," he said in a low growl.

She responded with renewed acrimony, "Trust ... Special Agent ... Baldy ... is not in my vocabulary!"

A deafening clap of thunder, long and loud, punctuated her callous words, creating an awkward silence between the two. McCormick leaned into his thighs and cupped his hands. His eyes dropped, solemnly, to the floor, waiting out the intrusive rumbling as it rolled across the lugubrious sky. Once stillness returned, he raised his head, slowly, and spoke with tenderness, "Then I feel *very* sorry for you, Mrs. Fitzgerald."

As if by decree, a bright flash of lightning zigzagged across the pitch-black sky. It's brighter than normal candescence illuminated the room, giving them each a sudden, startled look into the face of the other.

When all went dark again, Andrea could see only the man's muscular frame in silhouette, but in that brief flash of light she'd seen enough. She had seen, on his taut face, genuine concern; and emanating from his eyes, came a fiery passion. His rigid body projected a steely strength of raw energy—a force that almost frightened her. But she had also seen something rarely found on the faces of men in this current culture—open-faced honesty, and unimpaired integrity.

At last she asked, "What do you want me to do?"

"Well ... for starters, you can get past the crazy idea that I'm here to kill you." He saw her face lift with a smile, exposing beautiful white teeth. "Andi, at this point ... I'm the best friend you've got in this whole, wide world ... and if you're really having doubts about me ... then put your trust in the agency—we're the good guys."

"I'm aware of tha...." she said, softly, her words eclipsed, again, by stormy rumble.

McCormick paused, sensing the need to play this one straight. "Andi, I'm going to tell you something that will probably blow your socks off, but

I want to be completely up-front and honest with you. Okay?" He watched her face for a reaction. He saw none. "Our conversation at the newspaper … that was all a ruse—I was just yankin' your chain."

"Yankin' my chain?" she repeated with confusion. "What are you talking about?" she asked impatiently, her emotions already shattered to hell.

"The agency needed a guarantee that you would continue writing your series for a while longer, so … we used … reverse psychology." McCormick began to explain. "We knew Rudd wanted to end the drug series, but we needed a little more time to watch the response coming from the general public. Rudd had told me on the phone that you were a bit of a bitch…."

"Bitch?" Andrea retorted, indignantly, remembering the same heated word coming from his mouth following their collision at the airport.

McCormick grimaced. "Excuse me, what I meant to say was that we knew you were a bit hot tempered and strong willed."

Another exasperated gasp escaped her lips.

The concerned agent jumped up, "Oh, come on now … we just used your weakness to our advantage."

"Weakness?"

"The people screaming for you to be fired were put under surveillance."

"F-i-r-e-d?"

With each word spoken, her voice become increasingly louder, until suddenly, some anonymous person in the hallway pulled the door shut.

The agent's flinty eyes shot towards the creaking hinge as the latch snicked shut. Aware that his words had only served to upset her, he asked, "Andi … you do understand what's on the line here, don't you? We're dealing with no one less than the devil … and your life and the lives of a lot of very good people are riding on the trust you have in me."

"Deceit and double-cross are not hard to understand. You've been using me … your stupid investigation has put *my* life in danger!"

McCormick winced at her sharp accusations, unable to deny them; but he needed to dissuade her from that kind of thinking. Fact was, she'd been in grave danger far longer than he had been around.

He squared his shoulders. His hands settled on his hips and his voice strengthened with determination, and prophetic caution, "Andi … you can hate me to hell and back; cuss me out … throw things at me … I don't care; just know that I'm your best hope … your only hope." He turned away, leaving his words to hang in the air. "But God ... whatever you do, he added humorously, please don't shoot me ... I hate, like hell, to get shot!" He walked away chuckling; but seriousness soon returned as he looked through the window at the abating storm.

He rubbed a hand across his shiny head, and began to pace the floor in deep thought. "Andi, we have to find the person who did this ... can you tell me how the poison was administered ... was it food poisoning?"

She watched him make another trip across the floor and back. In spite of everything else that had happened, her trust in this agent was, actually, growing. There was something reassuring in his deep, mellow voice and manner—a manner that was, frankly, melting her ironclad reserves. And hadn't he returned her precious necklace—even though he had yet to take credit or mention his good deed?

But, the man was an enigma. One minute he teased, almost flirting. The next minute he sounded dead serious. At times, she heard raw emotion in his voice; the next, he was gruff or aloof. It was like talking to two different people. Trouble was: she had to admit to a powerful attraction to him—to both of them.

At last she blurted out, "It wasn't food poisoning." "I haven't eaten since breakfast ... yesterday."

McCormick shook his head, seeing that she had such little regard for her own health. In a voice dripping with sarcasm he said, "You certainly take good care of yourself, don't you?" Too late, he remembered loss of appetite was also a symptom of this particular type of poisoning. He steeled himself for her returning salvo.

"McCormick ... how I care for myself is none of your damned, n-o-s-y business," she hissed in return.

He hid his smile, but both hands went up in mock surrender. "Okay ... you're right," he said through a blithesome chortle. "I readily admit my nosy culpability."

Vague and incoherent images flashed across her mind. "It had to be the coffee." She remembered her mouth being extremely dry, and not being able to force herself to drink. "No, I didn't drink any coffee."

At last it came to her, "The aspirin! I took a couple of low-dose aspirin tablets from my desk and went to the drinking fountain." She explained the aspirin situation.

"Had you taken any before?"

"Oh yeah," she answered, exasperated by the thought. "I've been having excruciating headaches, and a lot of body aches and pains. I've been taking five or six-a-day."

Five or six a day! McCormick jumped to his feet. "Where's this fountain located?" A building that size must have several, he reasoned.

"In the back hallway, near the distribution department ... next to the canteen," she spewed, excitement mounting—maybe she did have a partner, after all.

"Okay, we can use the pills as evidence when we go to court. Is the bottle still in your desk?"

"Yes."

The agent offered her the remote. She ignored it, but clutched his arm, instead. "What do you mean, go to court?"

The agent's eyes dropped to her slender fingers, desperately clinging to his leather sleeve, then lifted to meet hers. "The best way to get this kind of crime off the street is to prosecute as soon as we have enough evidence."

Her questioning eyes burrowed into his. "What's ... the worse way?"

His eyes settled on her lips as she spoke. Refraining from doing anything stupidly impulsive, he answered, "You don't want to know."

He dropped the remote on the bed. "Andi ... trust me. I'm not here to use you ... or kill you." His head dipped at the absurdity. "One of your nurses is an agent ... a damned good one—that's how I learned of your poisoning. She'll keep an eye on you tonight. I'll be back ... but try to get some sleep in the meantime."

Now the man gazed, unabashedly upon Andrea's frail, yet lovely body, only partially-covered by the thin blanket. He looked up, thinking the room felt cold, even in his jacket. "I know they don't serve gourmet food in this joint, but try to eat." His earnestness dropped to gut level as he spoke in an almost breathless whisper, "You've gotten really thin, kid ... I'm worried about you."

Andrea blushed. It had been a very long time since anyone had called her *kid*. Hot tears slid down her cheeks as his words of kindness melted her reserves. Not wanting the agent to know how very fragile she really was, she felt grateful that her tears were hidden by darkness.

"Is there anything I can get you while I'm out," he asked, once again considering her solitary situation.

"Yeah," she said, jokingly, "a wool blanket, and a pillow as advertised on TV … and how about a huge vat of chocolate fudge frosting, while you're at it?"

McCormick chuckled, softly. "Andi, I need to caution you about something. No one must know that I was here. Drug runners are like cockroaches … they crawl all over the place, but they get especially bold in the dark of night."

She sniffed and, childlike, used both hands to wipe away the tears. "Yeah, they're a lot like agents, aren't they?"

Grinning, McCormick returned the chair to the corner of the room; then lingered for a long, quiet moment beside her bed. When at last he spoke, his voice remained soft and soothing, but distant. "Andi … my condolences on the loss of your husband … I remember you saying, at the orchard, that you had a good marriage." McCormick's jaw flexed hard at his parting words—words deliberately meant to prick her veracity; but, boy-oh-boy, did he ever feel like a jackass as they tumbled out of his mouth. Without a backwards glance, he disappeared into the night.

Feeling as though he'd taken a part of her with him, Andrea laid staring into the darkness, her pillow beginning to feel more like a headstone. She regretted misleading McCormick about the state of her marriage.

Faint rumblings and weak flashes of lightning were all that remained of the stormy sky as McCormick drove directly to the *Forest Hills Daily News* building. He parked a distance away, and shucked down to his T-shirt. For several minutes, he crouched in the damp, darkened shadows near the back door of the distribution department. He felt more than grateful that Andrea had finally opened up to him, certain that she would've been signing her own death certificate, had she not. Now the words he'd spoken replayed in his mind. *I am her only hope.*

He heard the thumping presses come to an abrupt halt, and watched several long-haired workers saunter out of the building, and down the back steps. It wasn't their slumped shoulders or their lazy foot-shuffling in flip-flops across the loading dock that McCormick found offensive; nor was it their stuffing their mouths full of chaw from round tins of tobacco retrieved from little purse-like bags hanging from their shoulders or from the pockets of their pajama-style britches. With disdain, he watched matches light up faces, along with their marijuana cigarettes, now legal in this state. The smoke wafted through the air, reaching McCormick's nose. At least they're working, he reasoned.

From his crouched position, McCormick watched the men take advantage of the lull in the storm, and leave the dock to flop across the wet parking lot to an old, rusty, pickup truck. Cleaving to the sides and staring into the truck bed, they checked out something of interest, laughing perniciously while blowing smoke into the damp air. Grasping his moment of opportunity, McCormick dashed through the unlocked door.

CHAPTER 19

Like a fox, the experienced, light-footed agent slipped undetected through the press area, and down the darkened hallway towards the hub of the newspaper—the newsroom. Entering the large room, filled with rows of desks, he quickly fished a penlight from his pocket, and began checking the office doors. At last, shining light on a gold-plated placard, he was pleasantly impressed as he read: **Andrea Daye,** *Forest Hills Daily News Assistant Editor, Senior Reporter and Special Publications Editor*

A grin spread wide across his lips. *The lady stays busy,* he thought, and *maybe she really does hate her married name.*

Using his tool kit to pick the lock, he stepped inside. The substantial size of his body suddenly filled the room. Feeling awkward in the small office space he looked around, studying the out-dated technology and well-worn furniture. *Why would a beautiful, young woman work so hard grubbing for next to nothing pay at a job often dubbed the worst job in the world?*

He tried to make sense of her situation, as he searched the surface of her desk. Nothing. He opened the shallow, middle drawer and rummaged through a collection of pens and paper clips in total disarray. *Messy* desk ... *organized mind,* he remembered from his investigative training. When his hand came to rest on a small, gift-sized book, a rare copy of American Indian Poetry, he curiously pulled it from the drawer and shined his light on the cover. He smiled. He'd been apprised of the fact that Andrea enjoyed poetry.

He flipped through the book until coming to one dog-eared page. After perusing the poem, he turned to the front cover and read the inscription: *Happy Belated Birthday. Aren't you surprised? I actually remembered your birthday—even if it is several weeks late, and just when you thought I didn't care. I even remembered the title of the book you've been searching for—TRAILS.*

Wonderful theme … soon I will walk the trail, dear. I'll be with you, when it seems that I am not; and when I am not, you will swear that I am. Shaun.

What the hell kind of birthday message is that, McCormick wondered. To the experienced agent, it sounded more like a threat. Suddenly, he felt uncomfortable reading Andrea's personal messages; and he, sure as hell, didn't like reading something Fitzgerald had written to her. He remembered how thin and frail she'd looked less than an hour ago; her tears, glistening in the dark. Animosity towards her husband balled up inside him, and he snapped the book shut as a new emotion churned deep in his gut—one he preferred to leave unidentified.

From the second drawer, McCormick pulled out a picture of Andrea and Editor Martin Rudd being presented some kind of journalistic award. The beautiful young woman smiled happily at the camera, looking like a model in a glossy magazine ad. Her cheeks were tanned, and her lips were rosy—the antithesis of the woman he'd just left. In the picture Rudd was grinning from ear to ear; obviously happy at the awards she was raking in for his newspaper.

Modeling—that's what she could be doing instead of married to a scurrilous scumbag and writing about drug dealers.

McCormick opened the drawer marked Files, and began to flip through the many tabs and folders. One, in particular, drew his attention. He pulled it from the drawer. Inside the folder labeled *"Special"* laid the same manila envelope used to carry her necklace from Virginia to Forest Hills. Andrea's name and address were scrawled across the front in his own bold handwriting. He smiled, remembering his act of kindness.

What reason would she have to hang on to the envelope and consider it special, he wondered? He lifted the flap, and glanced inside, not at all surprised to find newspapers. Suddenly, the hardened agent rocked back on his heels, completely taken aback by what he'd stumbled upon. He slowly pulled out the contents, finding himself staring at a normally formatted front page of the *News,* except for one caveat—this particular issue had *his* picture above the fold, sleeping soundly on a bed of dry leaves at the Tell Orchard and Winery. He grimaced as he read the caption: *Leaf Peeper grown tired of his own company.*

He blew out a gust of hot, concerned breath. Wouldn't his boss love this little detail? Not only had she taken his picture, unbeknownst to him, but she

167

had plastered it all across the front page of the local newspaper. *Why would she do that,"* he wondered, grateful that his face had been mostly buried beneath his cap.

Feeling additional thickness, he pulled a second front page article from off the bottom. It too had a picture above the fold. His normally steady pulse quickened as he examined the paper, now yellowed with age. In jaw gaping disbelief, he stood staring at the image of a soldier—his image, three years earlier. Sweat popped on his forehead—his enemy's wife had managed to put the two pictures together!

Not knowing what to make of his find, he returned the envelope to its rightful place, and closed the drawer. He slammed the middle drawer shut with aggravated force. *Nothing!*

McCormick stood, rubbing his chin and staring down at Andrea's desktop, trying to imagine her hard at work there. His gaze lit on a playfully illustrated calendar with the saying: *Nothing so strong as gentleness, nothing so gentle as real strength.* The page being displayed was dated October 4th. Almost seven weeks had gone by since she'd last ripped off a page. *Interesting,* he thought, as he flipped through the remaining pages reaffirming her penchant towards buoyancy. *What monumental thing had occurred on her birthday that made her want to preserve the date as a remembrance?*

Finding no evidence of the pills, he began to question Andrea's story— and begrudgingly, the woman's innocence.

Now seeing everything through a shadow of doubt, he began to wonder if he had made a huge mistake by telling her about the undercover nurse.

In a fit of disgruntlement, he left the newsroom in search of the supposed *other* pill Andrea claimed to have dropped. *Supposed? Claimed?* His own thoughts surprised him now, but he justified them by remembering that he had been trained as a thinker, a doubter, a man of the law. Assessing possible erroneous information and dangerous situations was a vital part of his profession. He wanted to believe Andrea had nothing to do with Shaun's crimes, but as a man of training and expertise, McCormick needed proof— and he needed it now.

He located the water fountain in the back of the building, and immediately spotted the little orange tablet sandwiched between the cracks of the old, wooden planks—just where Andrea said it would be. His black mood lifted.

He pulled his blade from under his pants leg, but his first attempt to retrieve the tablet failed as vulgar voices filtered into the building. Now considerably more subdued, the printing crew streamed into the hallway. McCormick darted into the darkened ladies room to wait them out.

With the return of silence, McCormick returned to the hallway and pried the pill loose. He straightened, and dropped the coated tablet into a small evidence bag, then slipped the bag into his jean's pocket. From the darkened basement stairs, loomed a shadowy figure, watching his every move.

Early the next morning, Andrea awakened to a bustle of activity in her room. She was quick to notice that an extra blanket had been added to her bed, adding tremendously to her comfort. She grinned, suspiciously, at the can of fudge frosting placed on her breakfast cart. A young nurse's aide accompanied her down the hallway to a shower stall. Later she was brought back to the room where her cold breakfast sat, unappetizingly, on the bed stand. Remembering her promise to McCormick to pick up weight, she forced down the bland egg, and cold, greasy toast. As she sipped the last of the orange juice, a registered nurse appeared in the doorway pushing a wheelchair in front of her.

"Good morning, Mrs. Fitzgerald." Andrea recognized Nurse Storm from the day before. "I'm your nurse for the day … most people just call me Stormy."

"Please, call me Andi … I abhor being called Mrs. Fitzgerald."

Andrea saw the questioning look on Stormy's face, and raised her hands in defense of her own statement. "Don't ask," she cautioned with a warning smile.

"Okay, dear … whatever," Stormy lobbed an understanding smile back to her patient. "We're going downstairs for a routine chest x-ray this morning."

"O-k-a-y," Andrea murmured under her breath, feeling a loss of control over her own life. As she sat down in the ironclad chair, she studied the nurse fussing with the foot guards. She seemed like a very nice, no nonsense type of person. Even at her age, she displayed strength, grace and beauty, and her voice was low and measured, soothing even. She had an ageless quality, tough and intelligent, but very kind and pleasant, and she seemed to have an unassuming acceptance of Andrea's situation. As a patient, that pleased Andrea tremendously, but today, her nurse seemed preoccupied, and her demeanor seemed more somber than the day before.

Together they boarded the elevator and rode to the ground floor. As their route took them past the emergency room, Andrea could see immediately that something serious was astir. Nurses bustled in and out of the room in preparation for an incoming patient.

Suddenly, the doors burst open with a loud thud, and a couple of EMTs rushed in, pushing a stretcher between them. Under the blanket, lay a male accident victim. The man's head was wrapped in blood-soaked bandages. The color of his clothing was barely distinguishable, being heavily soiled with both dirt and blood, indicating multiple wounds. Andrea tried not to look, but her reporter's curiosity prevailed.

An emergency room nurse removed the man's jacket and cut open his bloody shirt. Another nurse hastily stuck an IV needle into a vein. A doctor connected him to a heart monitor, while issuing orders to prepare for immediate surgery.

Stormy gasped and fell back on her heels. Her hand flew to her mouth. "Oh my god!" she whispered in shock as she grasped the reality of the situation. And then as a way of explanation to Andrea, she offered, "I know this man. He's my ... he's a ... wonderful friend." Stormy looked at the young man again, and then turned her head away, unable to watch. Andrea heard the distress in her voice and thought it an odd reaction for someone who must see this kind of thing every day.

"What do you think happened to him?" Andrea asked in a whisper.

Stormy sniffed back a tear, then tried to conceal the fact that she was, indeed, dabbing at her eyes. "I heard someone say they were bringing in a young man who had been hit by sniper fire on the highway last night." Her voice sounded hollow, then wispy. "This must be the boy ... they found his wrecked car under a pile of heavy brush about an hour ago. They had to cut him out of the vehicle ... someone had gone to a lot of trouble to slow up his rescue."

Andrea leaned forward and peered through the emergency room doors standing ajar. She dismissed the vague feeling of recognition gnawing at her subconscious, but there was definitely something about the man that beckoned her in a spiritual sense.

Expressing concern, she questioned the nurse. "It looks serious, doesn't it?"

"Oh yes ... life threatening ... he's lost a lot of blood." Stormy's voice choked with emotion. Then, surprisingly, the nurse asked quietly, "Andi, do you pray?"

Andrea was startled by the question, but her nurse was obviously upset. So without completely understanding Stormy's relationship to the man, or knowing who he was, she promised, "Yes ... I'll pray." She dropped her head and began her prayer in silence, even before her answer left her lips.

"Okay, let's get him to surgery," the doctor ordered, but when his staff failed to move fast enough, he barked out his orders in no uncertain terms. "Let's move it people ... this man's life is slipping away!"

Watching the man being whisked down the hallway and into an elevator, Andrea continued her silent prayer for his recovery. Stormy kicked away the brakes on the wheelchair and pushed it down the corridor, a new heaviness slowing her footsteps.

The sounds of sirens and flashing red lights had filled the early morning sky as the accident victim floated in and out of consciousness. Engulfed in pain, he groaned as EMTs pulled him from the twisted wreckage of his rental, lifted him onto a stretcher too short for his long body, and carried him to a waiting ambulance. At one point he thought he saw the face of his little brother, but when he looked again, he was gone. *Hallucinating,* he reasoned.

Inside, he deliriously assessed the contents of the lifesaving vehicle: oxygen tanks, heart monitor, IVs, banda.... Everything faded to black. When he drifted back into consciousness, it was to the sound of desperation in a doctor's voice, barking out orders for his staff to prepare for surgery. "Let's move it ... this man's life is slipping away!"

In his delirium, he wondered, *whose surgery ... whose life?*

He looked around the room. With his vision blurred and painful, he thought he saw the face of Nurse Storm. He gave her a squinty-eyed look, past doctors and nurses. Yes, it was Stormy. Good, he thought, as a rush of relief swept through him. He had worked many times with this woman, and knew her to be one of the best in the business—tough as nails, sometimes crabby, but always top-notch. His body relaxed, knowing that she had his back.

Again a siege of pain convulsed his body, and his mind began to swim in a sea of darkness. "Clear!" a voice barked at the long end of a dark tunnel.

An electrical jolt hit his body, and his mind returned to drift in shimmering, teal-blue water, amid gently rolling waves of pain. He swam towards the light.

At last, his eyes fluttered open. His blurry gaze rested on the iron configuration of a wheelchair through an open door, and the lovely young woman sitting there.

Andrea!

Panic stricken, he tried to sit up, but two nurses, one on each side, quickly shoved his shoulders to the gurney. *What is she doing here, for Chrissake, they'll kill her; I'm supposed to be protecting her!* At last his body began to fight against his multiple injuries—Matthew J. McCormick had reason to live.

McCormick awoke with a start. He raised his head, and suspiciously eyed tubes connecting him to a guy on the gurney next to him. "What in the hell are you doing here," he asked, gruffly.

"Shut the hell up…." the guy responded in kind. "I'm saving your life."

A grin came to McCormick's lips, and he let his head fall back on the pillow. "Thanks David," he offered, groggily. "Where's Andrea?"

"She's safe … who did this to you, Matt?"

"Kringle."

"Kris Kringle is dead … he died in a plane crash."

McCormick sucked air, and rasped through head bandages and gritted teeth, "He's not dead!"

CHAPTER 20

Stormy knocked on Room 308, pushed the door open, and motioned towards the wheelchair. "Girl, we're really going to miss you."

Andrea looked at the chair in disbelief, "Hey ... what's with the chariot? I don't need it, I'm an able-bodied adult ... the doc just told me so this morning."

"Hospital policy," the nurse explained. "All patients get a ticket to ride when they leave our care."

"You're kidding!" A week had passed, and then another. Each day Andrea had grown just a little stronger, but she couldn't help but notice that the opposite had been happening to Stormy. Each day her nurse looked more exhausted, more heavy-laden. Andrea was beginning to feel concern for the woman.

With reluctance, she climbed into the chair. "I'm sure there are other patients in this building who need your care a lot more than I do this morning. It seems like a waste of valuable resources to me ... I don't even know why I'm still here."

Stormy turned her head as a sly grin tickled her lips, and the chair began to clatter and clang as she slowly pushed Andrea towards the door. "Don't you worry about the other patients; I'm *your* nurse until you leave this building."

For a reason, unbeknownst to Andrea, a group of young nurses had gathered just outside her door. Stormy patiently pushed the chair through the gaggle of young women. Once through, she turned to face them, speaking in a stern, authoritative manner, "Ladies ... the gentleman in Room 310 gets his healing from sleep ... and meds; not from giggling girls. I'm sure you have *other* patients who need care?" They blushed, collectively, then quickly scattered.

As they waited for the elevator, Andrea asked, "Stormy, I've noticed that you work really long hours … don't you have a family?"

The nurse gave out a low chortle that sounded more like a groan. "Oh, yeah … I've got family. I've brought five children into this world. All but the youngest have moved on … in one way or another." She sighed deeply, and a sound of ruefulness pulled down the tone of her voice, "You know, Andi … when you're a mother with young children, your hair turns gray with worry over every little bump and bruise those kids get; and then when they grow up, damned if they don't, deliberately, go out and put themselves in harm's way."

"Drugs or military?" Andrea asked, trying not to sound nosey.

"Yeah," the nurse sighed, deliberately evasive, as she impatiently pushed the elevator button.

When the door opened, a young man stepped into the hallway, walking with a fast-paced, authoritative clip. Andrea couldn't see his face, but something about his manner seemed familiar.

She gasped, "David!"

The young man's steps hesitated ever-so-slightly, but kept walking as though not hearing her. From the end of the hallway, she could hear the young nurses whispering and giggling as though he were some kind of heart-throb celebrity. He disappeared into the room next to hers.

Feeling rebuffed, she said to Stormy, "That's strange … I could have sworn that guy was a friend of mine."

"Nice looking kid," Stormy said, her face lighting up, "but I wouldn't think a thing of it, sweetheart," she soothed, after seeing the look of disappointment on Andrea's face. "I've seen him around here a few times … I think he's been donating blood." She pushed Andrea into the elevator, clicking her tongue, humorously. "I'm always mistaking strangers for people I know." She pushed the button to the ground floor. "I once walked up to my older brother on the street and gave him a great, big, old bear-hug. You can imagine how embarrassed I was when I discovered he wasn't my brother, at all." She chuckled lightly, "It took me twenty minutes just to get rid of the guy … he wanted to move in with me! Can you imagine?"

A cab waited at the curb. Nurse Storm guided the chair down the ramp, then helped Andrea to her feet, while the driver put her flowers and numerous gifts in the trunk, including the mysterious pillow that had been mailed to her in a box.

"Andi," the nurse said, pleasantly airy, as she helped her patient into the backseat, "promise me you'll follow the doctor's orders and take care of yourself. You're an excellent patient and we all love you to death, but sweetheart … we don't ever want to see you around here again … under these circumstances." As she spoke their eyes locked in shared secrecy. Andrea had known from the beginning that Stormy was the agent assigned to protect her.

"I guess I can thank my lucky stars you were here when I needed you." Andrea's voice was husky with emotion. Stormy reached over and fastened her seat belt. The two women hugged each other, warmly. As the nurse backed out of the open car door, she answered, flatly, "You can give all your thanks to Matthew McCormick." Without further explanation, she slammed the door shut, and waved as the cab pulled away.

Confusion cluttered Andrea's mind as she gazed back through the window at the slowly disappearing figure. *McCormick,* she thought. *Why had Stormy suggested she thank Matt McCormick? What had that man ever done for her?*

One week later, as Andrea pulled her car in front of the airport terminal, a feeling of unrest swept over her. *Gloomy November,* she thought, as she walked around to the passenger door. Finally, she recognized what was bothering her. It was here that she had last seen Shaun before his departure to Peru, not to mention her fender-bender with that crazy McCormick. She wondered why she had not heard from him. As she unlatched her seatbelt and exited the car, she looked around and over her shoulder, halfway expecting him to be there. He wasn't, and for some reason, life seemed empty without his presence.

Now, she was losing Sugar. *God,* she thought. *People are dropping out of my life like flies.* She was, however, determined to stay on top of her emotions. Besides, this trip was different. This time she was doing what she knew was in Sug's best interest.

Andrea opened the door, and offered her hand, helping the aging woman out of the car and into the building. Sug had good days and bad days—this was a bad day. On the elevator, she clung tightly to Andrea's arm, completely intimidated by the situation. In year's past, it had been Sug who had driven Andrea to the airport as she flew back and forth to nursing school; but today, the older woman acted as though she had no will of her own.

At the gate, she handed Sug's boarding pass to the flight attendant, then stepped aside to allow other passengers to board the plane while they waited for a second attendant to accompany the elderly woman to her seat.

When at last the attendant appeared, Andrea tarried with an aching heart, not wanting to let go. Finally, she gathered the old woman's hands gently into her own and kissed her soft, pink cheek as aging, gauzy eyes stared back at her. With great difficulty she tried to put her own sorrow aside, to make her voice sound as airy and enthusiastic as possible. "Sugar, this is a wonderful day. I feel so happy that, at last, you'll be seeing Rose and her daughters … I know how you've missed them."

Sugar grabbed Andrea's hands and squeezed them tightly. "Thank you, dear, for understanding my loneliness."

She's not dressed warm enough, Andrea thought, removing the woolen, fuchsia scarf from around her own throat, and placing it around the older woman's neck. "Sugaraye … I've put my number into your new cell phone. If for any reason, you don't like it there, or feel uncomfortable, give me a call … you can come back home to me. Understand?"

The old woman smiled and the two exchanged hugs. "Thank you for understanding my loneliness," Sugar repeated again.

Andrea's throat closed with emotion as a moment of awareness hit her. Constant repetition was common among Alzheimer's patients—looping, it was called. Andrea had studied up on the disease when Sug was first diagnosed, and now she was experiencing its devastation first hand. She had a gut feeling that Sug would never be coming back to her.

The attendant indicated that it was time to leave. "Okay, remember … Rose will meet you as soon as you step off the plane," Andrea reminded her for the fifth time.

Sug grabbed the attendant's arm and, together they entered the boarding chute, but she stopped to throw Andrea a promise over her shoulder, "I'll fix your favorite breakfast in the morn."

Andrea's hand flew to her mouth, and she sighed, sadly. Already Sug had forgotten where she would be the following morning.

All doors closed behind them, and soon a woman's voice came over the loud speaker, "Flight 1574 is now departing from gate 5 in Terminal A." Andrea waited, watching through the large window as the plane backed away from the terminal and taxied to the runway. When it lifted off into dark, threatening clouds, she turned away and wiped tears from her eyes. Sugar and sweetness had gone out of her life forever—on this Thanksgiving Day.

She turned, searching for a familiar face—whose face exactly, she didn't know. It was way past midnight, and the airport felt cold and lonely even in the midst of holiday travelers. *Yeah, Sug,* she thought sadly. *It's not at all hard for me to understand your loneliness.*

On her way home, Andrea sat numbly at a stop light in Forest Hills, waiting for it to change to green. Her thoughts had returned to Matt McCormick, but by now her feelings of loss and loneliness had turned to anger. Why had he not returned to check on her, or rather, report to her? Three whole weeks had passed since their conversation in her darkened hospital room. Why hadn't he contacted her? She wondered if he had found the pill. Had it been tampered with? Who would have put it in her desk? She had so many unanswered questions.

She hit the steering wheel hard with the palm of her hand. "Damn you, McCormick!"

Curiously, she looked down Main Street in the direction of Shaun's office. There had been no time to go through it—a job she certainly didn't relish. In the meantime, Shaun's junior partner, Wade Duncan had made an effort to merge Shaun's workload with his own. It should have been a major job, except for one thing: *Shaun had never had a workload, she was finding out.*

Wade had been sympathetic and willing to help her when she called from her hospital room. She had requested he look into the arrangements her father had made for Sugar's retirement.

"Andrea, I'll be happy to help you anyway I can," he had offered. "Unfortunately, I have a very heavy court schedule; but, I'll have my secretary look into the matter as soon as she can find the top of her desk."

Having worked summers in that office as a college student, Andrea was well aware of the heavy work load the secretary experienced from time to time. Still, she felt put off. She'd tried not to push, but weeks had passed and she was growing increasingly uneasy about Sug's financial future—and she was, after all, Wade's boss.

In a flash of inspiration, she flipped on her turn signal and drove in the direction of the office. She would look for the papers herself. She was still familiar with office procedures; she knew where all the keys were kept—and it was, after all, her property, now.

Parking in the rear lot, she entered the building through the back door— the door her father had always used. Shrouded in early morning darkness, the building had a creepy, ominous feel, one she'd never noticed before. Shaun's office was in the front, at the other end of the long hallway. The sound of her boots, clicking against the hard flooring, echoed the building's haunting emptiness.

She could almost smell Shaun's expensive brand of cologne as she stepped into his office. It appeared as though he had just stepped out for coffee. Nothing had been changed, no dust had gathered on the top of the desk, even though the room had been locked for weeks.

She sniffed. Damn ... she did smell Shaun's cologne! A cold chill ran up her spine as she became increasingly uncomfortable. Wade must be working out of this office, she reasoned. She flipped through the manila folders lying on top of the filing cabinets. *This is eerie,* she thought. Everything looked untouched, and laid out in that same peculiar way her dad would want it to be, ready for the next day. Andrea took a couple of steps towards the desk, and then stopped in her tracks at the rustle of paper beneath her feet.

Reaching down, she picked up the half-sheeted legal memo. It was addressed to Shaun's private secretary, who was no longer on the payroll. Andrea examined the signature closely. Her pulse quickened. Not only was it in Shaun's own handwriting, but it had been dated just the day before.

"That's odd," she whispered, feeling unnerved by the sound of her own voice in the large, empty room. Instinctively, she shot a glance over her shoulder, reassuring herself that she was alone. She looked at the memo again—it didn't look old.

Another shiver ran up her spine, and she chided herself for being so rattled.

"You're just spooked," she reasoned aloud. That note was probably stuck in last year's case file. Maybe it just fell out, or perhaps Wade has just now brought the

Shaun's case to trial; but that couldn't be—Shaun had no cases.

A thorough search found a file with provisions for Sugar's generous retirement benefits. She closed the drawer and started to leave when something lying on the desk drew her attention. Her mouth gaped as she picked up the packet of papers which included a deed. She identified it as belonging to mountain property Shaun had bought, and Wade had just recently spoken to her about, just before…. This was property *she* now owned. Why hadn't she been informed at the time of the purchase? Why hadn't these papers been put in a safe, or at least filed away? And why hadn't she been included in the purchase? She would call Wade tomorrow, first thing, and find out what the hell was going on.

CHAPTER 21

Andrea read the location on the deed, Red Springs, in the Northeast Kingdom of the Green Mountains. "Sounds Christmassy," she clipped, whimsically. She crossed the hallway to what had been her dad's legal library and pulled a map of Vermont out of the drawer. Vaguely familiar with the area, she quickly located the exact location of the cabin.

As she studied the map, with its many lakes and streams, a faint memory began to flutter to life in her mind's eye. The cabin described was about ten miles west of a lovely, little tourist village—on the wilderness side of town. One summer, when she was a young teen, her family had camped in a primitive campground near a very large lake, on the other side of town—also a wilderness area. It had been late May, and everything had felt fresh and new. She had caught a glimpse of the picturesque lake from a scenic overlook, and she'd longed to hike the seldom used trail—actually a simple footpath—that had been blazed through the forest, leading to town. She remembered the trail as being an extremely long one.

Her best friend Natalie, had vacationed with them, and the two girls had been hiking all up and down the many rugged trails for several days. Then Nat became ill, and Andrea's parents had driven the fussing, feverish girl home, leaving Andrea to fend for herself for the day. Even at the young age of fifteen, she was already an experienced hiker and skilled woodsman, having camped out and hiked the Green Mountain trails her entire life. Her parents, reluctantly, gave her permission to tackle one of the lower trails during their absence. Andrea chose the footpath.

After hiking for several hours, it had started to rain, and her wet, heavy backpack had begun to rub her shoulders raw. Still determined to make it to her final destination, she had kept walking towards the footbridge that crossed the wide creek. Once she got to the bridge, a sign would point her in the direction of the rustic village at the end of the trail—Red Springs. Once there, she was to go to the restaurant, get something to eat, and wait for her parents on their late return trip through town.

She'd come upon the bridge; but a sudden roar had filled the air, and the ground had begun to vibrate beneath her feet. She'd quickly recognized the signs of a massive amount of water moving rapidly downstream—and straight at her. With haste, she pulled herself and her backpack up into the highest branches of a tall willow tree and sat perched, obscured from sight. In no time, the water had begun to swirl around the trunk of the tree, and from her vantage point, she could only watch the devastation as the rushing waters quickly rose. In horror, she watched the swift, churning water lift the little, weathered, bridge and carry it downstream.

Exhausted, starved, and scared, she was trapped in the tree. As the long, boring minutes ticked away, she had tried singing above the gurgling sound of the gushing water, and reciting poetry to keep her spirits high.

By dusk, her perch had become increasingly uncomfortable, and as the thought of approaching darkness permeated her thoughts, she had begun to lose her bravados. If she could make it till morning, her father would send out a search and rescue party; but as fears began to surface of the harm that could befall a fifteen-year-old girl overnight in the middle of a wilderness, she had turned her mind to scripture, prayers, and once again, song.

Suddenly, from out of the murky, raging waters popped a head, followed by the deeply tanned body of a teenaged boy. Shirtless and wearing loose, low-riding, khaki cargo shorts over his slender hips, he grabbed hold of a small branch, shook the water from his hair like a dog, and pulled his weight up onto the first sturdy limb. With bare feet and little effort, he climbed towards her on long, brawny legs.

He climbed up close, positioned himself across from her, and straddled the limb with his dripping, muscular legs. He sat awhile, catching his breath. The fact that he didn't know what to make of her was evident in his smoldering, questioning eyes as he propped his back against the tree trunk, and sat mutely staring at her.

At last he smiled, flashing his bright, pearly whites. "Hey, kid ... whatcha doing?" he asked, as though finding a girl perched in a tree in the wilds of Vermont during a flashflood was an ordinary, every-day occurrence, "You out here alone?" She didn't answer.

"I heard you singing ... you've got a beautiful voice." He smiled again.

Deciding that he meant her no harm, Andrea explained her predicament.

"Don't worry ... this happens all the time," he said. "I'll getcha across the creek ... soon as the water goes down a bit... people around here call me McCreek for good reason. I'll just use standard Boy Scout fare: ropes, knots, and pulleys."

They sat chatting in random conversation, never fully identifying themselves to each other. She got a sense of his age when he gave her advice on what high school courses to take; encouraging her to push herself academically. She told him that she wanted to be a writer, and he encouraged her to read everything she could get her hands on, especially the classics.

She had asked a follow-up question. "What do *you* want to be?"

He had grimaced, "I like to paint, but that's just hobby stuff. I'm really into football, but I expect that will change, drastically, once I'm out of the Academy. My dad tells me that life is what you make of it ... I want to make my life count for something. I intend to be ready for anything that comes my way...." He paused and dropped his head, "The only thing I don't want to be is a doctor."

Andrea leaned forward, "What's the Acad...." Suddenly, the willow wept, dropping water on them. They laughed heartily, as they playfully splashed the downfall into each other's faces.

At last the water had stopped rising and he climbed down from the tree, yelling back at her over his shoulder, "I'll be right back ... Scouts Honor." For several long minutes, Andrea had sat, holding her breath in awe, watching him swim back and forth across the dangerously dark, churning water, dodging floating debris and downed tree limbs. Intrigued by his actions, she waited as he adroitly devised a rope contraption, then tied it to the trunks of trees on both sides of the creek.

Her eyes had grown heavy as she waited. Suddenly, she was asleep, losing all sense of her body. The next thing she knew, she was freefalling into the raging, swollen creek below. Hitting the water hard, she tried to scream, but that only produced mouthfuls of dirty water. Her arms and legs flailed, but the amount of floating debris wouldn't allow her to swim. She was going under, losing the battle, unable to stay afloat in the turbulent, muddy onslaught.

Suddenly, from the water beneath her, something lunged at her like a shark at the smell of blood. She could feel herself being pushed through strong undercurrents to the surface, and then carried, and shoved onto a tree limb. Jumping onto the limb with her, the young man threw her across his lap, and held her in his arms while she spewed up brown water and vomit. This mountain boy had saved her life!

When she had recovered enough to be left alone, he tied her to the tree with a length of rope and a terse comment. "Don't go anywhere!" She watched him attach a type of bucket to another rope that, finally, allowed them both to skim across the top of the swiftly flowing water to the safety of the higher bank.

Once across the creek, he had made sure she was alright, then further offered to walk with her to the end of the trail, and to the safety of her father. When he lifted her backpack, offering to carry it for her, he had groaned at its heaviness. "Dang, what have you got in this thing?" he'd teased.

"My books," she had answered, demurely.

He turned his head to the side, and cocked a questioning eyebrow, giving her a teasing, dubious look, he peaked into the bag. Lifting out a heavy tome, he strained to read the title in the disappearing light. "*Homer's Odyssey*, he read aloud. Pulling a second book from the bag, *Greek and Roman Mythology*, he laughed, jocosely. "I'd say you're well on your way to that writing career." He had shot her a wry grin that seemed to glow, even in the obscure light.

There had been no moon, nor stars, that night to light the dark pathway as they walked among the sounds of croaking frogs and crickets, all chirping out their mating calls. The constant dripping of rain from the overhanging branches prevented their clothes from drying. When the sky further darkened, and the wolves began to howl, she admitted to being just a little frightened. Her charming hero had put his strong arm around her, as they continued down the trail, laughing and singing together, and sharing thoughts about their mothers. Andrea vented about her mother always wanting to live vicariously through her young daughter, wanting to make decisions for her, and never understanding who that daughter really was, inside.

Her young rescuer had complained that his mother thought of him as her personal lump of clay, to be molded and shaped into anything she desired—never understanding that he had already *been shaped, baked and glazed in the mountain wilderness*. He complained that his mother had thought he and his younger brother were growing up too wild and brash, and had tried to ship them off to a fancy prep school; but his dad had put a stop to that, assuring her that the world would knock the cockiness out of them soon enough. Now, the young man thought she was being too harsh with his younger siblings. In the middle of it all, the two teens had bonded.

As the temperature dropped, and another thunderstorm hit the mountain, they took shelter from the cold rain and fierce bolts of lightning under a den of bushy, scrub Cedar. Watching her shiver, he teased, amid a crack of lightning, "I'd give you the shirt off my back … if I had one." He smiled and opened his arms to her. "We'll use what we've got."

At the storm's conclusion, and by the time they reached trail's end, they had become more than friends.

After meeting up with her dad, hugging and explaining only her adventure of getting caught in the flashflood, she had turned to thank her young hero, but he was gone.

Deep disappointment had filled her young heart, as she stood staring at the rustic, weathered sign missing half its letters, pointing the way to Mc… Creek Campsite, the trail completely swallowed up by utter darkness and the sound of chirping crickets.

Realizing that she didn't even know his name or where he lived, she had cried, grievously, into her pillow all night.

Believing that she, too, was sick, her parent's had driven the second fussy, teenager home the following morning, never to return to the same area.

Andrea smiled gently at the bittersweet memory. In the years that followed, she had always regretted not being able to thank him for his show of bravery—for saving her life. He had been more than cute, and loads of fun, and very intelligent. In spite of everything, she had felt completely safe in his presence—and she had never shared her experience with another soul.

She also remembered that for months, maybe even years following the adventure, she would often climb to the top of a tree and just sit, remembering, and swooning over the young man—actually she was still swooning, she realized.

As a young adult, she had often wondered where he might be on his pathway through life—wondering if he had actually been prepared for *anything*. A tender smile crossed her lips once more, and then she dismissed the memory.

Now the names on the map were hard to read as Andrea looked through misty eyes. Although an autumn vacation hot spot, the bulk of the tourist went farther south, but by this time of the year the threat of snow and cold temperatures would have driven away all but the heartiest Flatlanders, and only a handful of local residents would be seen wandering the tree-lined streets.

She folded the map, and started to put it back in the drawer, but stopped herself. This was as good a time as any to check out the property, she decided. She would probably sell it eventually, and it would be good business to know what she was putting on the market. Besides, her curiosity had been piqued. Why had Shaun bought such a place? The act was totally out of character for him. She grimaced at her word choice: *character*—Shaun had no character!

Realizing she would be traveling all alone, she began to have second thoughts. But wouldn't she be alone no matter where she went? Wasn't she always alone? The philosophical words of Epictetus came to memory, "but you are not alone, but God is within…"

She would go.

"This is just butt-head stupid," the patient groused.

"It's hospital policy," Nurse Storm argued, feeling a sense of exasperation at the convalesced young man. Aware of his humiliation, and against his loud protest, she wheeled her long-legged patient through the hospital doors and down to the curb where a beat-up, old jeep sat parked on the street. Not waiting for the wheels to stop turning, her patient spread his legs, and impatiently leaped out of the chair, walking himself to the jeep. She opened the driver's side door, and stepped back, staying near, yet not too close behind him. "Watch out for the bird dirt … swallows got into the barn," she warned as he opened the door. Still weak from his injuries, he lifted his manly body into the rusty vehicle, and slid behind the wheel, as his steely eyes roamed the street, checking for signs of danger. Stormy made sure he got situated comfortably, before handing him the set of keys.

He eyed them. "Why don't we know what happened to my satphone?" he asked, grave concern darkening his face. Why had no one seen fit to brief him of this detail? He fastened his seatbelt with a loud click, and adjusted the rearview mirror—totally ignoring his image.

"It's been recovered," Stormy offered, matter-of-factly. "Someone found it at the crash site, and turned it in to headquarters—right after they used it to report your accident. The agency has promised to replace it with a newer model sometime early next week."

He arched a dubious brow, and started the engine. "It takes four weeks to replace a damned phone?" Suspecting that the woman knew more, the young man's brows knotted, and he grimaced. "So what do they say I'm supposed to do without it in the meantime?"

Looking stern, with no show of emotion, the woman paused before relaying the message. "Punt," she finally answered. "They want you to punt." His face turned sharply towards her, recognizing the insult. "Stay in touch," she added, "I'll see what *I* can do." He turned his angry eyes away, and once again surveilled their surroundings.

Stormy's expression hardened. "Listen up, McCormick."

He took his sweet time finishing his surveillance, then brought his eyes back to her, pushing back against her unrelenting coldness. Her eyes held no glint, no humor, and certainly no sympathy. She looked tired, and he noticed that she was beginning to show some age. With clenched jaw and pursed lips, he returned her look in kind, but hung on to her every word. "Don't you dare come back into this building in that condition, ever again! We don't want your kind in here … do you hear me?"

He tried to stare her down, but she wouldn't flinch. Damn, he had forgotten how strong-willed she could be; but he had gotten her message loud and clear.

She slammed his door shut with unnecessary force—if only to accentuate her point.

He gave her a quick head nod, and then, solely for her benefit, pulled away from the curb with a loud roar and a screech of the tires. He glanced back at her image through the rearview mirror, admiring the woman's courage and strength. She was still standing, glued to the spot, hands on hips, watching him drive away. As he turned the corner, and pulled out into the heavy Friday morning traffic, he threw back his head, unable to suppress his sniggers and cachinnations any longer. "Hell … Delta Force would have loved that woman," he said aloud.

CHAPTER 22

Andrea used her Smartphone to call the realtor used for the real-estate purchase. After receiving directions to the cabin, she searched the classified ad section of the newspaper. She needed a companion—a dog. If she was going to stay in the wilderness, it would be wise to have a dog, both for companionship and protection. Besides, she was sick of her own company.

Astounded by the prices listed for a pedigreed dog, she finally called the animal rescue center in Red Springs, and was told they had the perfect dog for her: a beautiful gray and white, 5-year-old male, blue-eyed Siberian husky. He'd been found, exhausted and starving, walking along the highway. He was an exceptional dog, she had been told, except for one thing—he didn't like noise or loud voices. *No problem there, she thought. Her life was nothing but quiet.*

Huskies were known for their wondering ways, needing lots of room to roam, which eliminated a lot of would-be owners. This dog had been at the rescue center longer than most. He had worn a collar and tags bearing his name, and a phone number; but the landline had been disconnected for non-payment; so, naturally, he was assumed to be abandoned. With Andrea he would have a home, and plenty of room to roam.

There was also a bonus for taking this dog. The head of the center had assured Andrea that the dog had been professionally trained—probably as a guard dog or a service dog, he had said.

A search of Shaun's room produced a key to the cabin, and at sunrise on Saturday, Andrea filled a bag with fresh fruit, threw a suitcase, a box of books, magazines, and newspapers, and enough groceries to tide her over for a week into the back seat. Her well-worn hiking boots, she tossed into the trunk.

Her landline was ringing when she reentered the house. Her answering machine identified the number as coming from the Boston Globe, so she took the call in the kitchen. Another call had come in from a newspaper syndication firm and had gone directly to voicemail. She listened to the message and returned that call as well. When the phone rang a third time, this time from a well-known book publisher, Andrea just let it ring. Whatever it was, it would just have to wait.

She had taken care of business from her hospital bed, and now she felt happy that things were falling into place like standing dominos.

From the doorframe of Andrea's upstairs bedroom, Matt McCormick stood listening to the precise clip of Andrea's professional voice on the phone. Satisfied that she'd be detained awhile longer, he rounded her bed. He'd been in the house all night, trying to make up for the time lost in the hospital.

He found it interesting that the Fitzgeralds had lived out of separate bedrooms, having already searched Shaun's room extensively while Andrea slept.

Now he checked out the large stack of hardback books on the floor beside her bed. *The lady is a reader,* he thought, dauntingly surprised at the authors: Kyle Mills, David Baldacci, Raymond Khoury and Christopher Reich. He'd read them all, and knew them to be hard-hitting novelist of international intrigue. *Impressive,* he thought. He also glimpsed a copy of *The Complete Works of Ralph Waldo Emerson.*

The lady likes big books; he chuckled with amusement as he lifted the humongous, green tome off the floor for closer inspection.

He was surprised to find, lying beneath the heavy tome, Mat Best's, *Thank You For My Service,* an irreverent look at life in the military. He picked up the #1 NYT Best Seller, totally chagrined by what lay beneath.

In total astonishment, he glared down at a newspaper advertiser bearing his own image—his magnificent image in an effing urban suit!

"And that's why you stay tenacious, bad-assed and detached," he whispered, totally vexed.

McCormick restacked the books, and returned to the door, listening, unable to make much sense of the one-sided conversation. While the call held her attention, he thoroughly searched her dresser, one drawer at a time, starting at the bottom. When he finally opened the top drawer, he was surprised to find a colorful array of brand spanking new Victoria Secret gowns and undergarments—a bridal trousseau, all very neatly folded, and all unworn with the original price tags still attached. He studied the tags, and whistled under his breath at the pricy items.

Tucked beneath a lacy, white gown, fit for a princess's bride, lay a Dillinger handgun, small but fully-loaded. He returned to bedside, and lifted a pillow—pepper spray. *This is one tightly-wound lady,* he thought. At the sound of Andrea's feet treading up the stairs, McCormick dashed into the walk-in.

With her mind cluttered with details, Andrea entered her room, and walked past her dresser, absentmindedly, shoving the top drawer shut. The phone calls had excited her, but she'd still take a few days in the mountains, and then come back refreshed to deal with the more important issues. Her illness, her lengthy hospital stay, and settling Sug's financial affairs had left her drained, but now she planned to simply follow her doctor's orders and rest.

She stepped into the closet and retrieved the box containing her mother's cap and CDs, anxious to get on the road. She stood at her dresser, setting the cap on her head, threading her ponytail through the hole in the back. She studied her reflection in the mirror, and then smiled at the image. She liked what she saw. Color was coming back into her cheeks. "Life will be good again, Andi," she promised herself, aloud, starting to feel the freedom widowhood. She decided to take the CDs with her; after all, what was a Daye trip without Kenny?

When she returned the box, a faint rustling sound caused her to pause, thinking she saw movement behind her hanging clothes. She stood still for a second, but at hearing nothing more, she breathed out, thinking the noise was only her imagination. Still, she shuddered. During the night, she'd thought she'd seen a shadow in the hallway, and she had definitely heard noises coming from Shaun's room; but she'd been unable to summon the courage, or the desire, to enter his room in the dark of night. Living here, alone, in her parent's big, rambling house was starting to get just a little too spooky.

She walked to the bed and straightened the pillows, then went to the bathroom to gather toiletries. When she returned, she found the closet door ajar and cool air blowing in through an open bedroom window. *Someone's been here.*

She dashed to the third floor, her dad's office, where windows looked out in all directions, providing a panoramic view of the property. She spied a tall, jean-clad man with short, dark hair and athletic build. She watched him skirt along the lower, outside stone wall of her house, and then nonchalantly sprint across the lawn, and down the hilly drive towards the stable.

"McCormick!" With mixed emotions, she watched him disappear into the shrubs. Why had he been skulking around her bedroom, or her abandoned stables? If he'd had a question, why not ring the doorbell? Weren't they supposed to be partners? What had he been looking for?

A part of her felt worried; but another part felt hurt that he hadn't bothered to talk to her in person—or to report back to her. Woefully, she shook her head at her fragile feelings. "Oh g-a-w-d … am I ever an emotional mess!"

McCormick's actions were puzzling, alright; but just as puzzling—why wasn't she afraid of him? She supposed her circle of urban friends might think him a bit of a rogue, possibly dangerous; but for some reason, those characteristics only served to awaken Andrea's senses. She'd always liked adventure, and McCormick seemed like a guy who had seen a lifetime of adventure. He was more than movie star handsome, yet his demeanor oozed down-to-earth realism. He was definitely of the real world—there was not an ounce of pretense about the man.

She decided to just leave. This house had totally lost its beloved ambience and her security had seriously been compromised in spite of Shaun's elaborate security system. She smirked. She'd have to give McCormick the credit for that one.

Once in the car, she popped Kenny's "Silhouette" into the deck and stashed his other CDs in the middle console. She fast-forwarded the disc to the third song, and headed for the mountains, surrounded by the sounds of, "I'll Be Alright."

McCormick had pulled his jeep away from the curb just in time to avoid being spotted as Andrea drove down the long, winding drive-way. By the time she pulled out into the street, he had plopped a black Stetson on his head as camouflage, and circled around behind her little gray Honda. Watching the stoplights ahead, he trailed her, staying two car-lengths behind. When she turned left at a service station, he pulled into the one on the right, and pulled up beside a payphone, surprised to find one still in existence. Using a pre-paid phone card, he circumvented her caller ID and listened to the messages on her answering machine. *Interesting,* he thought.

Andrea filled her tank, checked the oil and air pressure in her tires, then pulled back onto the street. McCormick followed her out of town for several miles, all the while wishing she'd slow down. Wondering where she was headed, he sorely longed to follow her to her final destination; but that was not possible. He figured she would be safe as long as she was away from home—long enough for him to take a few days to heal—per his doctor's orders. She hadn't packed enough to be gone more than a few days, or a week at the most. He guessed that she had gone shopping in Boston. Wasn't that what most young women did—go to the malls? In the meantime the Agency would pick up her whereabouts, via the GPS device he'd attached to her older car. Other agencies would assist with shadowing her every move.

When he reached the sign that read Green Mountains, he slowed down and gave Andrea's little car a playful, half-hearted salute, then turned off the highway to take the scenic, back roads home—his reward for staying alive another day.

Maneuvering the narrow roads and curves, his mind kept going back to what he'd learned at the Fitzgerald residence: the happy couple hadn't shared a bed. But more importantly, in searching Fitzgerald's bedroom, McCormick had discovered an internet feed to Andrea's newsroom computer, and evidence that the man himself had been sabotaging Andrea's articles for months.

Certain that Shaun Fitzgerald was alive—and certain that he was the one who had shot his body all to hell—McCormick had made the decision to stick as close to Andrea as possible. It would only be a matter of time until Fitzgerald came back for her—for reasons that had nothing to do with love.

He'd been caught off guard and trapped inside Andrea's closet when her alarm had sounded at the crack of dawn. From his concealed nook, he had heard Andrea slip from her bed, and offer an emotional, heart-felt prayer for Stormy's *friend* who had been shot and seriously injured. Then she'd prayed for Stormy's strength. For Stormy's family, she asked that they be saved from the drug culture. A weak, wry grin had crossed his lips, as her caring gesture both touched and warmed his heart in an unimaginable way.

Once awake, she'd taken a long, hot shower, singing her way through every splish-splash of water out the shower head. She had the voice of an angel—a very serious, no-nonsense angel.

The little jeep rounded a curve and headed into the golden sunrise. Two years was a long time to be away from his responsibilities, and McCormick had scheduled back-to-back major banking appointments, along with other business, more personal, but timely. As his jeep followed the curvy flow of the rocky riverbed, he began to experience more than a little homesickness. He lowered the window, listening to the gurgling water, longing to plunge into its cool, mountain sweetness, ruefully aware that it would most likely be daybreak the next morning before he reached his cabin, especially if he stopped to see Nicole.

PART II

CHAPTER 23

The miles passed by quickly as Andrea drove by corn shocks, stubbles and barren fields. Everyone, it seemed, had a red barn. She reveled in the quaint split-rail fences, churches with white steeples, and apple and pumpkin stands bathed in a cool, golden sunshine; but seeing grape arbors white with frost, she soon realized that she was definitely on the down side of the season. Most of the deciduous trees had lost their leaves, leaving only the stark naked trunks and limbs amongst the dark evergreens. What leaves remained were of a dull, brown color. Everything had taken on an ephemeral, temporary feel, just waiting for the bottom to drop out of the temperature gauge, and for the snow to start to fall.

Suddenly, her head jerked up, and she realized that she was no longer driving into the sun, but away from the mountains. She had completely missed her turn-off. Feeling frustration, she hit the brakes and veered onto the shoulder where she consulted her map. Yep, she'd overshot her turnoff by several miles. Making a wide U-turn on the highway, she drove back five miles to the road that headed into the mountains and to Red Springs. She smiled as she rolled down her window, refreshingly inundated by the joyful splash and gurgle of the rushing mountain streams.

Late that afternoon, in Red Springs, Andrea rented a temporary postal box, and advised the local officials of her intention to stay awhile, in case of an emergency; and then she stopped by the animal rescue center, and picked up the dog known by the name on his collar: Tracker. It seemed unoriginal, but she saw no reason not to go with that name.

The gray, Siberian husky was beautiful, but showed indifference towards his new owner, as though expecting someone else. Andrea had read that this variety of dog was very sociable, but would only take orders from one person, accepting only one master. Still, she had taken an immediate liking to

Tracker. She felt it a noble deed to rescue the dog and give him a loving home. They would need time to bond, she realized as she drove towards the cabin with her new friend in the back seat. She only hoped he hadn't been abused.

At long last, she pulled off the two-lane highway and onto a narrow, gravel road that went up, disappearing into a thick forest. She stopped, letting the engine idle as she read the sign. To Tracker she said, "It says Grandma Burns Road ... but it doesn't look like much of a road." She downshifted, and slowly followed what amounted to a meandering dirt trail along a beautiful, gurgling, rocky stream. She marveled at the way her little car handled the incline, hugging the curves on what little gravel had been spread on the road. She really did love this car. When the road dead-ended, her jaw dropped as she rolled to a stop in front of a most charming L-frame cabin.

Nestled in a grove of pine trees, the cozy, little cabin sat on a hidden cove, snugly overlooking an impressive-sized lake surrounded by a forest of pine trees, dense and dark, their image reflecting off the shimmering water below. At the far end of the lake, a ridge of rugged mountain peaks jutted out of the water and stretched towards the sky. She smiled. This state had it all.

By the looks of the peeled-bark logs, hunter green roof, and huge stone fireplace running up the side, she judged the cabin to be relatively new, perhaps ten to twelve years old, at the most.

To the front and side of the cabin, stood a gigantic oak tree, guarding this lovely, private corner of the world like a seasoned sentry. Surprised that it had survived so long at this high altitude, Andrea appreciatively studied the tree for a long moment. At last, she gazed out across the large, placid lake. Checking her map, she was surprised to find the large, body of water didn't appear on the map.

She opened her car door, and planted a tangerine, sandaled foot on the ground, and leaned blissfully against the open door. In delight, she watched swallows swoop gracefully over the shimmering water, as the pungent scent of pine found its way to her nostrils. She smiled inwardly, gazing at the gorgeous scenery stretched out before her. This had to be one of the most beautiful, tranquil spots in all of Vermont.

A chill wind suddenly kicked up. Andrea shivered as she unloaded the car, her feet wet from the damp pine needles. Acorns crackled and popped beneath her feet as she walked to the front porch.

She kicked away a pile of wayward, brown leaves blown against the cabin and used her key to unlock the solid, wooden door. She read the plaque bearing the cabin's name: *Little Bear.* She laughed at the fanciful woodcarving of a rascally bear cub etched into the bottom panel of the impressive piece of art.

"Wipe your feet," she chimed to Tracker as she opened the door to a cozy, but guest-accommodating foyer. Happy to have Tracker's company, she squeezed his new, stuffed Mallard play toy, making it quack like a duck, then tossed it across the floor. She followed the beautiful dog, blue-eyed and silver-haired, into the cabin. Like a playful puppy, he immediately bit into the toy, creating the woodland sounds for himself. She smiled.

She sucked in a surprised breath. Her eyes drank in the cabin's interior. Beautiful, pinewood floors glistened. The cathedral ceiling, rustic log walls and floor-to-ceiling fireplace screamed: Andi you're home! In the middle of the living room, a stairway led to a balcony and loft bedroom overlooking the first floor.

The décor was elegantly simple. Over the floor-to-ceiling native stone fireplace, hung a single, acrylic painting of a bear cub on a background of snow-covered boulders. A heavily cushioned chair and loveseat with matching red upholstery, bearing the images of bear cubs, were attractively arranged around the fireplace. Floor-to-ceiling windows, large and wide, covered the wall facing the lake, allowing a wide panoramic view of the water from anywhere in the cabin. And from the lake, Andrea surmised, one would be able to see the entire contents of the cabin, for there were no drapes or shades on any of the windows.

The kitchen was complete with a mud room, a coat rack, and a sturdy back door with small panes of glass to let in the light. She crossed to the deck off the far end of the cabin. The lovely, built-in bench was the ideal place to sit and view the lake. This cabin was a dream home, a fantasy hide-a-way for whoever had built it—a place utterly befitting its beautiful, natural setting.

Not until she'd unpacked, putting everything in its place, and she'd laid claim to the cabin, did the awestricken, young woman stop to gaze through the window at the breathtaking view of the shimmering lake with its rugged, stark cliffs, and deep, dark pines.

Shivering again, she bolted the door. She searched for a source of heat but found only the fireplace. She looked for electrical outlets, but found none. Thankfully, the cabin had a full tank of propane gas in the kitchen, and a bathroom with a shower, at least.

A quick excursion into the bathroom uncovered a bit of troubling truth as she washed her hands. There was no hot water. "That's strange," she said aloud as she looked around for a towel, "all this charm, but few comforts." This was going to be rustic living at its best. Something inside her welcomed the challenge.

In search of a towel, she opened the narrow closet door and was surprisingly hit in the face by a man's winter-heavy, shirt swinging from a high rustic hook. She gave it a closer look. Its large, plaid flannel squares of bold, red berry and hunter green smacked of Christmas. It also suggested a man of the outdoors with great strength and masculinity—way too macho to be anything Shaun would ever wear. Its broad shoulders and tapered waist told her it belonged to a man with slender hips. He was tall, judging by the length. The two missing buttons suggested that it had been hurriedly ripped from his body, and haphazardly tossed into the closet from a bit of a distance. Her gaze scanned the floor, settling on one of the missing buttons. *Wow,* she thought as she picked up the button and dropped it into the shirt's pocket, *wouldn't she love to know who'd been bedecked in that bolt of Christmas Cheer.*

Downstairs, she put water on for tea, and then built a small fire from the kindling, left stacked on the hearth. She walked off the deck, surprised to find the stack of firewood greatly diminished. She made a mental note to find someone in town with a wood splitter, or someone who could chop wood. She would check for additional blankets in the morning, as well.

Carrying in a couple of logs, she carefully placed them on the already smoldering heap. When the larger logs ignited, Andrea was delighted by the cheerful snapping and crackling of the open fire. Suddenly, the room filled with smoke. "Oh, my god ... the damper!" She rushed to the hearth and flipped open the rustic lever that allowed the smoke to rise up the chimney.

She bolted the door. The snow was late coming in this year, but it was coming, she had been advised in town. The area normally received between 60 to 100 inches of snow each winter. She hoped it would hold off until she could get some more food in the house, and poke around the lake area.

Finally settling into the comfortable, high-backed chair, she sipped tea from a black mug she'd found in the cabinet, and allowed herself to become mesmerized by the high leaping flames reflecting off the rafters above. She gazed out the window, at the lengthening shadows on the lake, watching the setting sun disappear behind the mountain. "Absolutely gorgeous," she breathed.

The hour was getting late, and the fire burned low in the hearth. A sleepy-eyed Andrea rose and stretched; then banked the hot coals. They reminded her of Matt McCormick's eyes as he'd stood at the window of her hospital room while lightning flashed all around him. What was it about that man that left her feeling unsettled? She wondered if she should try to get in touch with him, maybe call the agency. She decided in the negative.

At last she doused the flickering candle and ascended the stairs to the loft, smiling at the silver moon, large and round, shining through the windows and skylights. Its beam fell across the steps, guiding her footsteps up the stairs.

She snuggled deep into the bed, a nice comfortable full size, with a little extra length at the foot. She pulled the lovely quilt up under her chin. Unfortunately, it had a musty odor. The two feather pillows were all fluffy and white, sans cases. Sheets would top her list of purchases when she went into town in the morning; but the fresh bed linens would be the only luxury she would allow herself. She was on an adventure, she decided.

She yawned sleepily, and closed her heavy lids, focusing on the night sounds. All was quiet, except for the small tree branch tapping playfully against the windowpane, as a friendly breeze whistled softly through the whispering pines, swaying and singing in the wind. *Lovely,* she thought. Downstairs by the hearth, Tracker gave out a little, plaintive whine. Somewhere off in the distance, a twin-engine plane whined, but it was soon gone.

The last thing she heard before falling asleep was the distant howling of coyotes, and the forlorn wail of a loon, late in beginning its annual migration from the lake to the Atlantic coastline. The coyotes, she figured, were just teasing Tracker. She remembered that Vermont coyotes were larger than normal because of cross-breeding with wolves. She wondered if there were any bears in the area.

She slipped deeper into the quilt, soon drifting into a light, peaceful sleep.

Suddenly, something stirred beside her bed, arousing her to wakefulness. Her heart quickened, and her thoughts raced back to McCormick. Raising her head off the pillow, she cocked an eye, and looked around. She filled with mild disappointment, realizing that it was only Tracker stretching out, claiming the spot beside her bed. Her last thought before dropping off a second time was awareness that McCormick was nowhere near Red Springs.

Thank God.

When Andrea awakened again, it was not to the wind or to yipping canids, but to the early chirp of a cardinal. She lay snuggled under the cozy, warm quilt, studying the grey, pre-dawn light reflected across the timbers and beams in the loft, deciding that whoever built this cabin was a master wood craftsman.

Feeling inspired by all the hard work that had gone into the cabin, she quickly dressed, then walked out into the cool, golden morning. From the porch, she could see the sun just rising, casting crimson, gold, and gray reflections across the sky. So new was the day that the cloud cap had not yet lifted from the mountain top at the end of the lake, and a veil of morning mist stretched out endlessly across the water. A covey of quail winged their way across the water against a backdrop of proud, naked trees silhouetted against the sunrise.

When she stepped off the porch for a better look at the lake, something hit the ground with a soft thud near her foot. Bending down, she picked up an acorn from the rich aromatic soil. Hearing the chatter of rodents, Andrea gazed up into the giant oak tree. A squirrel ran back and forth across a limb, its jaws stuffed full of acorns. Suddenly, it took a huge leap from his limb to the one far below. Andrea sucked in her breath, fearing he wouldn't bridge the distance; but he landed safely, and then sat, complacently, staring back at her.

"Oh, hi there," she greeted, delightedly, her frosty breath spiraling upwards in the cool air. Tracker jumped up, ran to the tree, sniffing and prancing around its entire circumference. He gave out a loud bark, and shot Andrea an expectant look. Unable to get her full attention, he plopped to the ground with vigilance, his head and feet facing the tree.

Baffled by the dog's behavior, she walked towards the tree, popping acorns with each step. She breathed in the musky smell of decaying wood and foliage beneath, noting the tree's sturdiness, its huge round trunk, countless, but sparsely placed limbs, and a few remaining dry leaves. It was huge, and she guessed it to be well over 400 years old, judging by its trunk, height and crown spread. She loved this tree!

She wondered why she didn't feel dwarfed by the giant. In an insightful moment she realized that she felt comfortable around strong, sturdy things. Somehow, she too, felt stronger because of their strength.

Two more squirrels scampered across the ground, across the porch and behind Tracker. As though in full animation, they jumped up, mid-air, and bounced off each other's paws. Andrea's mouth flew open. "I didn't know you could do that," she said, in amazement. They shot her a quick, leery-eyed look, and then, in cartoon fashion, skittered up the tree. She laughed as their claws dug deep, noisily obliterating the bark on the way up the tree. Tracker didn't budge from his spot, but looked expectantly back and forth between the woman and the tree.

More squirrels appeared. "Oh, Tracker!" she squealed. We have a family!

Happily, she stretched her arms skyward, basking in the sun's glorious warmth as it caressed her skin. For the first time in months, she felt alive. She was at one with the earth—at peace with her soul.

CHAPTER 24

At 5 a.m., a weary McCormick pulled his jeep into the driveway. At 5:02 he heard the first chirp of a cardinal as he pulled up the *For Sale* sign by its stake and tossed it aside with indignation. He'd made it home just in the nick of time. He stepped into the stable, breathing in the strong smells: horses and straw. In the tack room, he breathed in the quality leather saddles halters and reins, hanging from arms and pegs on the wall. His shoulders relaxed, and a deep sigh of relief escaped his lips. For once, there was no need to tamp down his emotions. *God, it's good to be home again*, he acknowledged.

He plopped a can of Folgers down on his long-abandoned desk, his heart yearning to romp with the mischievous pup that had once sat at his feet, but he quickly realized that time and circumstances would not allow for that possibility. He did, however, revel in his strong affection for the chow hound.

Suddenly, a noise shattered the silence. "What the….?" Seeing a light, he peered around the doorframe with caution, and a smooth, covert move. There, stacking bales of straw neatly against the back wall was a tall, distinguished-looking, older gentleman dressed in snug-fitting jeans, a red plaid shirt and barn boots. For a long moment, McCormick stood and watched, feeling respect for the old guy. He still looked strong as a stallion; but now there was a slight stoop to his shoulders, and his hair had grayed, considerably. McCormick stood, mute, filling his heart and senses with the scene.

At last, he stepped out of the shadows and into the light. He spread his legs into a wide military stance, hands on hips, and in a loud, flinty voice called out, "Hey … Old Man! Stop and take a rest … I'll make us some coffee."

The old guy slowly straightened his back, raising a bale of straw waist-high. He stopped, and slowly turned his head askance, looking directly at McCormick. Suddenly, he let go of the bale, and brushed the chaff from his eyes, as though he'd seen a ghost. He took another look towards the voice.

Making recognition, his knees buckled, and he collapsed in an emotional heap onto the top row of bales. Quick, sudden sobs began to rack his chest.

With head down, and lips pursed with compassion, McCormick turned on his heels and retraced his steps to the tack room, where he put coffee on to brew.

McCormick wasn't comfortable with these kinds of emotional displays, but he certainly understood where this one came from. The outburst had been years in the making, a clumpy slump made from experience and knowledge, love and loss, and of joy and sorrow; still Matt knew the old guy felt the same way he did about wearing your heart on your sleeve, and right about now, he figured the old man would be feeling shame for his weakness. He just worried more, and felt things deeper than most folks. He seemed to have a greater understanding of things lost, and a premonition about what was to come. Matt didn't always understand it, but he respected it. McCormick was smart enough to give him some space. Besides, most of the guys he knew would just go out and get drunk or high—this guy would drop to his knees and pray.

At last, he poured the hot, steaming coffee into two heavy, earthen mugs and slowly approached the old man, still sitting with his head in his hands.

"Dad?" he said tenderly.

The older man raised his head, his eyes blurred with tears.

Matt offered him a steaming mug. He took it into his rough, weather-worn hands, held it like a treasure, staring down into the hot liquid as though solace could be found there. Finally, he lifted his eyes, staring into empty space.

"I thought you were dead, son." The rasp of raw emotion was in his voice.

"I figured as much." Matt's own voice crackled with emotion as he sat on the bale next to him. They both took time to sip the coffee.

After a pause, Matt offered, "It's been hard for everybody … have you talked to Mom?"

"Oh … no," He shook his head, pertinaciously, and let out an exasperated breath. "She won't talk to me while she's working… says it's too dangerous."

"She's right … you know our enemy," the younger McCormick answered, his voice going guttural. The family had always honored the practice of going off the family grid and maintaining silence while working undercover, so nothing or no one could follow them home. Matt took another sip, counting himself extremely blessed to be having this talk with his dad—to still be alive. For a long moment, he just sat, basking in his father's presence.

After a while, Matt asked, "Where's he buried?"

The older McCormick dropped his head, "Red Springs Cemetery … his decision … it was on his *If I Die* sheet." Suddenly, the man's voice got stronger. "Matt I want you to know how very proud he was of you."

With downcast eyes and a heavy heart, the younger McCormick shook his head. "I can't talk about it, Dad."

They both sipped coffee.

McCormick offered, "No need to worry about Mom … she's okay … just exhausted, and missing everyone like crazy; she should be home today. She doesn't know I've come back to Red Springs." It seemed strange to Matt, that he would be the one bringing this information to his dad. "I'll give you fair warning, though," he cocked a brow, and grinned, "she's as badass ever."

The old man grinned, proudly, appreciatively. "What brought you back, son?"

"My investigation…." McCormick would spare him the details of his gunshot wounds. "I've been undercover until just recently."

The older McCormick gave an understanding nod.

"They're giving me a few days to recuperate, but that could end at any time, depending on how things play out here. Stormy can fill you in on the details. I'll have to make every minute count towards my investigation."

Matt stood up, and then helped his dad off the straw bale. They locked eyes, holding on to the moment. Then Matt pulled his father to him in a big, bear hug. "I missed you Old Man!" He shook his head and laughed, a deep sense of gratitude flooding his heart. "It's still okay to call you Old Man, right?"

The steely-eyed man gave his son a wizened grin, "Sure thing."

McCormick stood, set his mug on the straw to shake hands. "I've got work to do," he explained. He nodded towards the surrounding stable. "Thanks for staying with all of this." He clapped his free hand on top of the one whose blood flowed through his own veins. "I'll be in the area …we'll square things."

"Do what you have to do, son. We can talk about that later … I've got your back."

Matt started to walk away, then stopped, and turned to face the older man. "Dad … you still carry a gun?"

The man shook his head, indicating that he didn't.

McCormick paused for a long moment, thinking.

"Carry one.

―◄◦►―

In the stillness of daybreak, McCormick parked his jeep in the graveled access road of Red Springs Cemetery, antically renamed *Boot Hill* by he, and his brothers as kids. As he looked out over the hallowed, timeworn burial ground, a long-forgotten memory surfaced. The local, young scouts had brought their BB guns up here to take target practice under the leadership of his older brother. In spite of his insistence that they show respect for the dearly departed, one kid, notorious for his acts against authority, had mocked the dead by running, ram shod, across the graves, shooting the epitaphs right off the tombstones, including the one belonging to Matt's grandfather, a highly decorated veteran. The sheer act of insubordination and destruction of property had gnawed at the insides of both he and his brother for years.

In that moment, with the first blush of the sun revealing veils of vivid crimson stretched out across the horizon, McCormick took a solemn oath.

He reached for the black Stetson riding in the passenger's seat, put it on, and tipped the brim towards his right eye, positioning it just so. Soberly, he walked to the top of the ridge through the early morning mist, through layers of russet leaves in various stages of decay. Regretting missing the peak season of fall color here on this scenic ridge, the words of English poet, John Donne came from out of nowhere—something about always being autumn in Heaven.

He ambled among the tombstones, and mostly naked trees, all shrouded by the heavy, gauzy brume. At last, he came to a halt before a tall, impressive stone. He slowly removed the hat, and solemnly bowed his head, saying a silent prayer for the brother who now lay buried beneath his native soil, the tragic scene of a year ago replaying through a mind manacled by the past. Besides being an awesome brother, Clint had been an integral part of the sting operation—the one that had gone sideways. Answering his younger brother's call for help, he had been one of the four agents whittled down before his very eyes. Someone—inside the Agency—had betrayed them.

McCormick sucked in a deep breath, and stood, heart-naked, in his brother's presence. With jaw clenched and eyes burning like hot coals, he spoke with tenderness, "I'm glad you made it home, bro ... I've wished a thousand times that it could have been me instead of you." His throat closed up with wadded grief, his tone modulated, "But Clint, I promise you one thing ... and I swear it to God ... Stone will never step foot on your grave." His frosty breath spiraled in the cold December air.

A sudden breeze rustled the branches, and the last leaves of autumn fell to the ground, covering the gravesite as though in blanket. Through bleary eyes, he took in the slanted rays of early morning sunlight, filtering through the trees and foggy haze, playfully dappling his brother's grave in shimmering flecks of gold. A tear dropped, and weak smile tugged at the corners of his mouth. Lifting his eyes, he spoke to his creator. "Always lighting a lamp in the darkness, aren't you?" Then, his eyes settled on something that shook him to the very core of his being.

Beside his brother's tombstone stood a similar stone of black granite. The inscription read: *Matthew Justice McCormick, 1989-2019.*

"What the hell?"

CHAPTER 2 5

Andrea ate a light breakfast, then slipped into a pair of snug-fitting jeans and a black, turtleneck sweater. She diligently brushed her hair to a lustrous shine and pulled it into a ponytail before donning her Kenny G cap. Both the cap and the spirited, saxophone music, had become her symbol of hope for the future. Today, she noticed a new look to her eyes: they were brighter, more lucid. She smiled at the image in the mirror, seeing shades of her mother looking back. *Yeah,* she thought, *Mom would have really liked the cap idea.*

Her new companion lay asleep on the floor. "Tracker," she called softly.

He yawned and stretched out his front paws, making no effort to get up.

"Come on lazy bones, she persisted, "let's go for a walk … I want to walk through the mist before it lifts."

At the mention of a walk, the dog's ears pricked up, and he jumped to attention beside her, wagging his tail and whining in anticipation.

"Ho! So you know that word, do you?" she teased, rubbing his ears. She grabbed her hiking boots and carried them outside to the front porch. Rays of golden sunshine hit her face, and she reveled in the joy of the fresh, new morning. The air felt crisp, and a gentle breeze toyed with the tendrils of hair around her cap. It was going to be a beautiful day. She laced up her boots like a pro, while laughing at the squirrel family at play.

The ten-mile trek to town would be cold. She guessed it would take her somewhere around four hours, if she leisurely strolled the rugged distance. That should put her in town by early afternoon. She grabbed her vest, and slipped a cartridge of pepper spray into the inside pocket—just in case.

She found, not far from the cabin's back door, the start of a footpath, wide enough, and level enough to jog. It was, obviously, a well-established trail, once routinely trod upon and trampled down by some wanderlust soul, but not recently. A smile spread wide across her face as her boots rustled through musky, dry leaves on the sun-dappled path. She relished the gurgle and splash of the rippling brook, running alongside the unfamiliar trail inviting her to go "light-heartedly into the woodlands," as Frost had written.

When the trail suddenly took a sharp turn through a forest of pine trees and boulders near the head of the lake, she took a deep, full breath and filled her senses with the fresh scent of damp needles that lay beneath the tall, stately trees; the trunks, she recalled, of the kind once used for masts in patriot ships during the American Revolution.

She walked on, finally stopping in a copse of smaller trees and red-leafed underbrush, the very shrub from which Red Springs had been named. There, she was surprised to find a second cabin, larger and more isolated, a rustic up-scale version of her own. Her eyes followed the path going forward, noting that it veered off, and meandered around the tall boulders, linking the two properties together; both sharing the same awesome view of the large, shimmering lake.

Dreamy-eyed, Andrea settled her gaze on the scenic pasture beyond the stable, where long-legged yearlings grazed, leisurely, on dried autumnal grasses. She smiled, reminiscently. She'd been here before, months before—in her dreams. Accepting the lovely setting as a gift, she leaned against the split-rail fencing, basking, euphorically, in the warm, golden sunlight. This was her chimera—the dream that had never come true.

Over-come by curiosity, she climbed through the fence for just one quick look through the stable window. Tracker followed, excitedly, sniffing around the door. Peeking through the glass, Andrea admired the large, well-equipped, well organized tack room and office area. She sniffed the air, detecting a dry, scorched odor. "Oh, no," she groaned, pushing her nose to the glass, cupping her eyes to block out the sun. "Someone's left the coffeemaker on." She walked to a second window, seeing a row of stalls and a stable full of straw. "Fire hazard," she said, alertly, to the dog. Before she could get the barn door open, Tracker blew through her legs, sniffing and prancing around as though on a hunt. "H-e-l-l-o!" she shouted. No answer came back. "I don't think anyone's here," she whispered to herself. She hit the off switch on the pot, and lifted the empty, brackish carafe off the burner and into the sink.

"Tracker," she called, in annoyance, tracking the wandering dog past the stalls, through an unlocked door, and into a garage-like space with drywalls and heavy gym equipment in one corner. A high-speed mountain bike hung on the wall, and an extreme, heavy-duty motorcycle stood leaning on its sturdy kickstand. Tracker sniffed the bike. Parked in a stall of its own, sat a sports car of an undeterminable make and model beneath a canvas of desert camouflage design. An unidentifiable, oddly-shaped mystery vehicle sat in the stall beside it. Hanging above it all, was a tarp-covered canoe, suspended from the rafters by ropes and pulleys. A very large heavy-metal, gun-safe, wrapped in a chain with heavy-duty locks sat against the wall. "Wow ... this is the home of one very serious dude," she said aloud. "Why does the word TOXIC come to mind?" The dog whined. "Tracker, let's get out of here ... before we get shot for trespassing."

She climbed back through the fence, but stood, mesmerized, her dream replaying like a video. From out of nowhere, came a rush of wings, and the loud honking of geese, lifting her out of her reverie, and her strong sense of déjà vu. The heavy-bodied birds flew directly overhead in precise V formation, their calls echoing above the tall pines, then fading, hauntingly, into oblivion. Feeling the sun's warmth go with them, Andrea gave the scene one last look of appreciation. "Only in my dreams," she whispered, striking a course towards town.

A chilling breeze whipped up, blowing swirling dust, dross and woodsy debris through the air just as the trail came to an end on the far side of the village, near the post office.

The town clock struck one. Andrea commanded Tracker to wait outside while she mailed a letter to Sugar, letting her friend know she was in Red Springs. She watched with pleasure as her dog sat, obediently guarding the door, as though trained. She couldn't exactly call him loyal, but she liked the respect he had begun to show her; but first and foremost, Andrea liked having him to talk to, someone with whom to share her life.

She gazed up at the postal building. It was old, a dinosaur, a survivor of a by-gone era. When she'd first arrived in town the previous day, she had been in too big of a rush to appreciate all that the building represented; but today, her senses were alive, sharpened by the invigorating hike.

She tugged open the door, and as though walking through a time portal, entered what had once been a vital part of history. She noticed the large dome lights suspended from the high ceiling, the extensive detailing of the tall windows, and the beautiful, elaborate wood molding around the ceiling.

The inner chamber was cold and mostly empty. It felt haunted by an aura of unworthiness recently ushered in by the new era of technology and social media. *Everything feels haunted these days,* she thought, pushing down the feeling.

She started to walk towards the metal boxes with old-style lock and key access, her hiking boots squeaking, as though in agony, across the gray, marble flooring. She cringed and slowed her steps, so as not to annoy the patron by the window; the one with his head drooped, reading a piece of mail.

She went straight for her box, tossing only a casual glimpse at the guy. He appeared to be a local, judging by his manner of dress; he too, wore a pocketed, khaki hunting vest with the collar turned up, obscuring his facial features. Unlike her greenhorn vest, his had seen years of wear.

Andrea took the key from her pocket. Knowing she'd be away from Forest Hills for a while, she'd routed time-sensitive papers needing her immediate signature to this address; but having just rented it the day before, she expected no mail. Her transactions were usually done online; but she would check the box, if only for the novelty of the experience.

A voice echoed across the open space. "I don't suppose you'd know the price of a first class stamp these days ... I've been gone awhile ... I'm bettin' Uncle Sam has raised the price two or three times by now."

Hearing mellowness resonating from an, otherwise virile voice caused Andrea to freeze. A silence, long and deafening, hung in the air of the tomb-like chamber.

Still aggrieved by his visit to his brother's grave, and feeling both smote and gutted by finding his own tombstone, he immediately grew suspicious of the lingering silence—being home didn't equate to being out of danger. He dropped coins back into his pocket, and slipped his mail inside his vest, letting his fingers tighten, covertly, around the handle of his Glock as he shot a quick, flinty-eyed glance over his shoulder, glimpsing a woman. He turned, cautiously, to face the communication-challenged patron. His face lifted in both surprise, and wariness.

For an endless moment, his gaze locked into hers. At last, his hand fell to the wayside, and he spoke exasperated words through a gush of hot breath. "Mrs. Fitzgerald ... what, in the hell, are you doing in Red Springs?" His unenthused voice rang ragged to his own ears.

Andrea gazed at the poster boy for masculinity. It wasn't his golden tan, faded somewhat, but golden just the same, that made her legs want to buckle, or his new hairstyle: dark, short-clipped, and punked-up in front with gel; nor was it the days' worth of stubble, defining his strong, resolute chin. No, the thing fueling her sudden diffidence was the grievous cloud that darkened his demeanor, and the keen expression of guardedness she'd never seen him wear.

He walked towards her, taking long strides across the floor. Her eyes locked onto his worn, leather boots and denim jeans, faded and holey. *Gawd, this man's larger than life,* she thought; but despite his knitted brows and sullen mood, he looked at home in his own skin. Even in her state of perturbation, Andrea recognized the look for what it was: quiet confidence. *The kind of confidence created by repeated success.* She thought she caught a whiff of leather, the pleasant scent finding her soft spot—her weak spot.

She swam, for a second in the bottomless depths of his dark, dusky eyes, until suddenly coming to her senses. Flashes of their last conversation rushed to mind. In his late-night visit to her hospital room, this man—this jerk—had promised to help her; but to her knowledge he had done absolutely nothing ... zero ... nada. He had disappeared for three, almost four solid weeks, seemingly forgetting all about her—and his promise to protect her. His absence had left her feeling betrayed, and even more frightened than ever. Then strangely, just the day before, this dirtbag had summoned the gall to surface. She'd caught him on-the-run after breaking into her home—the slob was even wearing the same gray shirt. First, he had pleaded for her trust; then he had abused it, pure and simple. She glared at him in frustration, feeling the depths of her disappointment clear to the bone. There was no way she could afford to be vulnerable around this man. What she wanted, needed the most was someone to believe in, someone to trust; not a guardian of her galaxy, like Zoe, but an armed guardian of her heart. Her face flushed with anger—anger being, by far, her safest emotion.

"McCormick," she spat, her voice free-falling with disgruntlement.

Catching the glint of averseness in her eye, McCormick took a step closer, planted his feet, and crossed his arms across his chest. Menacingly, he stared down at her, and asked, drily, "Why are you here? ... vacationing with friends? Or did you and *Bot* drive up by yourselves?"

Loathing flashed in her eyes. She hissed, "*You* are an incorrigible degenerate!" Her hand flew up in an effort to slap him hard across his smug, smirking mouth, but his forearm shot up briskly to block the blow.

Dark, smoldering eyes narrowed in on hers. "You're the one who introduced the subject of sex toys into our scintillating conversations, Mrs. Fitzgerald," he growled. "Why are you here?"

Andrea felt herself start to melt under his molten stare. Whether his sour mood stemmed from anger at her, she could only guess; but there was, definitely, something working on the guy today. He seemed more wary, more somber—and much more contemptuous than ever before. Her breath escaped, hot and heavy. "McCormick ... I'll go any damned place I want ... but I sure as hell wouldn't be in Red Springs if I'd known *you* were going to be here ... *trust me*." Her words came out fast, furious and snarky as hell, and she glared at him with eyes ablaze. "Why are *you* here? I certainly hope you're not *investigating* me," she said, petulantly. "That would be a shameful waste of taxpayer dollars....." She shoved her key in the lock, "Heaven knows they've already wasted enough on you!" She gave the key a twist, but the lock wouldn't turn. She cursed in frustration.

Deciding to make use of this unexpected opportunity to get inside her head, McCormick stepped towards the box. Returning her rudeness with feigned arrogance, he brushed her aside with his hip. "Yeah, lady ... and you're right smack dab in the middle of my worthlessness." Deliberately dropping a bomb of facticity, he added, "My sole *fuckin'* purpose in life is to follow you wherever you go ... to save you from yourself!" As he jiggled the key in the lock, he watched for her reaction. When she threw off his comment, thinking it a joke, he grinned to himself, completely satisfied with her benign reaction; but he continued to feed her surliness. "Actually, the truth is ... I've missed your hysterical, hard-assed hyperbole and your raunchy potty-mouth."

Andrea stood back, and planted her hands on her hips. "You know what, McCormick ... that sounds like a perfect description of you ... you are so full of yourself."

The box opened instantly. McCormick reached in and pulled out a political brochure, glossy and tri-folded, addressed to Occupant. Recognizing one of her husband's otiose brochures, he handed it to her, feigning disinterest, hoping she wouldn't take notice of it. She didn't.

"Why are you here?" she asked.

Staying close to the verity of the situation, he offered, "For your *exclusive* information ... I've been out of the country for a couple of years; but I've come back ... just to be insulted by you, *Mrs. Fitzgerald.*" His gaze dropped to her pouty mouth, remembering his photo plastered across the front page of *her* newspaper, and the model-perfect image of his younger self in a suit ad lying beside her bed. He leaned close, his voice dropping to a whisper, "Make sure that information gets front page coverage, wouldya ... above the fold ... with maybe a couple of interesting little side bars ... I'll getcha my résumé ... and one of those bald, but beautiful, beach photos of my stunning, classic profile."

Her breath caught in her throat—*he's still reading my stuff.* She bounced a glance off him, and snarked, "So ... you're telling me ... what exactly ... that you can read?"

As he leaned away, her eyes caught a glimpse of the gun butt under his left shoulder, protruding from the holster in a foreboding way. She tried to divert her eyes, but that only increased her uneasiness.

She forced the issue. "So what's with the gun?" she asked. "Are you afraid you'll be attacked by incoming airmail ... or by some psycho, mammoth moose stampeding down the cobbled streets of the Kingdom?" Both her hands shot up as guns from imaginary holsters, mockingly shooting towards the street.

McCormick winced at the sound of her twisted, negative opinion of him. With impatience, he looked around the room, "Looks like they've done some remodeling ... where in the hell did they put out-going mail?"

Deliberately virulent, she chided, "Aw, you have been gone a long time ... these days, it's called Social Media: you know, Gmail, Facebook, Twitter, Snapchat ... for those who don't want to be held accountable for anything ... but if you're still stuck in the muck of yesterday's snail-mail, its right under the sign marked Out-Going Mail." Pointing in the direction of the mail slot, she shook her head, and feigned a laugh. "Oh, those rascally feds ... they just love to *yank your chain* ... don't they?"

Sharp, stealthy eyes locked into hers, seizing the moment. He yawped, "Mrs. Fitzgerald...."

Her head ticked up in instantaneous ire. She couldn't afford vulnerability, but neither could she afford to be intimidated. She slammed the metal door shut with force, creating a loud, clanking noise that turned the large, empty room into an echo chamber. Shooting him a warning glance, she hissed, "McCormick … I have repeatedly asked you not to call me by that name." She tried to pull the key from the lock; it wouldn't budge.

"Ah hell, Andrea … you've asked me repeatedly not to call you by your *n-a-m-e* … that makes no sense. If I hated *my* legal name … the one on my birth certificate, the one on my driver's license, could you come up with a better way to identify me?" He plastered an incredulous grin on his face, fully aware that he was inviting a salvo of returning insults.

Andrea met his eye, and feigned an accommodating, happy face. "Well s-u-r-e I could … let me think … investigator … McCormick." Her eyes roamed around the room then quickly came back to him, wide-eyed. "Wouldn't the name Sleazy Special Shamus address your particular style of duplicitous badassery?"

Without warning, McCormick stepped forward, snapped up her wrist with his left hand, and locked eyes. His lip curled, and his voice lowered to a deep growl. "I think *you, Mrs. Fitzgerald,* have been dancin' with the devil … but now you're having to face the leaping, fiery flames of hell … alone."

Seeing, by her expression, that he'd hit a perfect bulls eye, he added, egregiously, "What do you have to say … Mrs. Fitzgerald?"

Andrea struggled to take control of what was left of her shattered dignity. Both attracted and repelled by the smug, smooth-talking agent, she dropped a hot glance to his vice-like grip. She spat out in a slow, deliberate whisper, "Don't *ever* do that again." He loosened his grip, and she yanked her arm loose. "I have *nothing* to say to you, McCormick … because I have done *nothing* wrong!"

Refusing further involvement with this man, Andrea straightened, shoring up her own display of quiet confidence. Her voice dropped to the same low octave, adversarial but cunning. "McCormick, it's been real, chatting with both you … and your toxic masculinity … but I don't have time to waste on either one of you." She swiveled on her booted heels.

McCormick's eyes gleamed with satisfaction as she walked away, rattled. People made mistakes when they got agitated. In pure devilment, he growled, "Have a good day … *Mrs.* Fitzgerald," deliberately accentuating her title. "It's been *bitchin'*."

A hairball of lividness caught in Andrea's throat. Her eyes blurred, but her boots continued the long, humiliating squish across the marble floor. She thought, *if Hell were, in any way, conquerable, McCormick would be the agent of evil to do it!*

He watched the door swing shut behind her, chuffed that she hadn't switched off the lights, as she'd done in the past. From out of the back room, the aged Postmaster suddenly appeared, snapped his suspenders in place and leaned over the counter, chortling, "McCormick … you sure as hell have a way with women."

"Yup," he yawped, pulling her key from the lock, "I've had a lot of practice."

Outside the post office, Tracker greeted Andrea enthusiastically, aggressively sniffing her hands and clothing as though on to something. She rubbed behind his ears, trying to calm her new hiking buddy, while her own ears burned with red, hot emotion.

Making her way across the quaint, little street in the direction of the bank, she tried to justify her rude behavior. She couldn't. She had acted like a child, and she knew it. "Where's all this coarse language coming from?" she asked, aloud. "I don't cuss!" One thing she knew for sure: there was no room in her life for a man—definitely not this man. She simply was too fragile.

Andrea entered the town's only bank, and managed to pull up a civil smile for the teller while she cashed her traveler's checks, pushing down her serious financial concerns. Following Shaun's death, her bank cards had all been frozen, and her assets tied up in the estate until everything could get legally straightened out. That would take months, maybe even years. She blew out her breath—the winter promised to be long and lean if she didn't get back to work.

As she slipped the money into her pocket, her fingers curled around a letter. "Aw shss…." She had forgotten to mail her letter to Sug. This meant doubling back to the post office. With downcast eyes, she bounded through the double wooden doors.

Just outside the door, a man sat, squatting on his haunches, patting and talking to Tracker in warm, mellow tones. In return, Tracker was, greedily, licking the man's face with affection. Andrea collided, full-force, into both. The guy instantly shot up. Strong hands grabbed her firmly by the shoulders, breaking her fall.

"I'm sor…." Andrea looked up into the dark, disquieting eyes of Matthew McCormick. "Sor … I," she stuttered, thoroughly embarrassed. "I forgot to mail…."

He clutched her tightly, long after she had recovered her balance. His demeanor was unreadable as he nodded his head towards Tracker, who in turn, looked at Andrea, apathetically. "If this fur ball is your animal, you might consider trading up for a seeing-eye dog."

Rudely backing out of his hold, she spat, "McCormick, go back to Hell!" She looked fondly at the canine, and patted his head. "This dog is the best friend I have in the *whole, wide world!*"

McCormick leveled his eyes, "Am I supposed to be surprised?"

He turned and stepped away, but Tracker whined, and danced around his legs, trying to follow him. He knelt, acknowledging the attention-seeking animal. "Stay with *Mrs. Fitzgerald,*" he said in a low, commanding voice, nodding towards Andrea as the dog licked his hand with adoration.

Andrea threw up her hands in frustration; then turned to retrace her steps to the post office. At the corner, she tossed a curious glance back over her shoulder, and for a long moment, watched the exasperating ass walk with a loose, confidant gait in the opposite direction. Not only was her dog following, nipping at his heels, but a young, beguiling woman was sneaking up from behind.

She was beautiful. Long, dark professional curls cascaded down her back as she, playfully, danced behind McCormick's back, waiting to surprise him. At her tap on his shoulder, he turned around. His face instantly lit up with recognition, and something Andrea couldn't read—love, maybe. Flashing his pearly whites, he smiled wider and sexier than anything Andrea had ever witnessed. When he picked her up and swung her around, Andrea's breath caught in her throat. When she planted a possessive kiss on his cheek, leaving imprints of dark red lipstick, Andrea's heart sank to a sick, gut level. She watched the two disappear, arm-in-arm, around the corner of the building, laughing and talking in rapid-fire discussion, each endeared with the other. She watched her dog trot behind the two lovebirds, his tail wagging with fawning adulation. Andrea struggled with full-fledged, identified jealousy. *Well now … there's a classic example of dancing with the devil … if I ever saw one,* she thought.

The vacuous postal building was without patrons, and it felt almost alien without McCormick. *Why do I always feel betrayed and abandoned by that guy?*

She dropped her letter through the mail slot, and listened as it slid down the chute, hitting the bottom of an empty container. Her life felt as empty as the mail receptacle, and she almost wished for McCormick's presence; but these feelings were ridiculous. Matt McCormick was certainly not a part of her life, nor was she a part of his, and never would be. She wasn't at the center of anyone's life, or of anything—except misery. She made herself a promise: *from this day forward, she would decide who came into her life, and who didn't.* Her experience with Shaun had been a hard, well-learned lesson, one she wasn't about to repeat; and this thing with McCormick—there was no *thing*.

CHAPTER 26

Slowly roaming the sidewalks, she realized that the autumn tourist season was over. The walkways and quaint, little shops were still lined with chrysanthemums, but long dried and faded. Earlier, before the frost, there would have been a variety of gorgeous color: pumpkin, lavender and crimson. She wished she could have witnessed their brilliance, realizing, for the first time, how much of the good life she'd missed.

Most of the shops were closed, but she decided to browse the few that remained open. It would be nice to find something special to personalize her cabin. Then she would get a bite to eat at one of the two local restaurants before the long walk home.

She found an inviting shop, and pulled the door open. The sweet, melodic strings of a door harp sounded above her head, and the heavenly aroma of freshly brewed, spiced cider teased her nostrils. Somewhere in the background the sweet, spirited lilt of a hammered dulcimer played softly.

She smiled, and her spirits lifted immediately as she made her way past boxes of apples, jars of homemade apple butter, maple syrup and honey lining the front of the shop. She, cheerfully, browsed the row of pewter pitchers, clay figurines, wooden paintings, and ruffle-lined baskets. Another aisle was lined with country quilts, stuffed pillows and embroidery items. She selected a cross-stitch sampler that read: "Happiness is Homemade," then climbed a small flight of stairs to the second story.

Delighted to find a charming Christmas boutique, Andrea was infused with a sudden surge of yuletide spirit. Inundated by the soft strings of a Christmas CD playing in the background, and breathing in cedar-scented potpourri, her reaction to the merchandise became joyfully child-like. She admired a selection of colorful, woven throws tastefully displayed next to an antique rocker sitting beside a colonial-style hearth. Drawing her favor was a colorful, life-sized image of a steely-eyed Kris Kringle, cloaked in a handsome floor-length robe in rich shades of red with the Christkindl, the Christ-child, standing at his side. Excitement towards the holiday mounted inside her, a joy that, for the last several years, had lain in abeyance.

Spread open wide across a coffee table, in kaleidoscopic colors, laid a beautifully bound picture book; its glossy pages describing the Old World Santa. Accompanying the book was a plate of pressed, butter cookies, along with a handwritten note, in a most elegant calligraphy, encouraging shoppers: *Please sit and rest a spell. Good marketing,* Andrea thought.

She sat, thumbing through the book giving the icon's country, and historical origin, dating all the way back to his pre-Christian ancestry. Surprisingly, Kris Kringle's distinctive characteristics, kindness and benevolence, had been attributed to the mythological, sky-riding gods who ruled the earth, Odin, Saturn, and Thor, who rode his chariot drawn by a team of goats.

In turning the page, she was reminded of a darker side to the old gent. She read the description of how he not only brought gifts for the good, little children, but brandished rods and switches to the naughty. She had, somehow, forgotten this dirty, little detail. She replaced the book, grabbed a cookie, and moved on, determined to do her own research on the subject.

She sighed as she was reminded of how much she loved Christmas, especially the trees. She thoroughly appreciated the stunning ornaments, the blinking lights, and the warm ambiance of the professionally decorated trees.

On the next aisle, she smiled at the German nutcrackers, nativity scenes, and small, lighted villages. She approached a table displaying the entire collection of figurines from Charles Dickens', *Christmas Carol.* Her gaze fell on Ebenezer Scrooge. Suddenly, her warm feelings turned to ice as thoughts of Shaun filled her mind. Now she tried to push away memories of the last couple of holidays—difficult holiday's, shrouded in a gaudy display of wealth, but devoid of any real meaning: a complete mockery of Christmas with no family, no love, and no Christkindl.

A clatter behind the wall brought her out of her anamnesis, and her eyes were drawn to a beautiful display of Christmas paintings. A wooden sign, hand carved and gorgeous, proclaimed that they'd all been painted by local artists.

Her eyes went, immediately, to a painting simply titled, *"Geniture."* The painting had been given a subtitle: *"Babe in a Manger."* Her trained, artistic eye immediately recognized the artist's talent as exceptional. The painting was of a Palomino mare. Her new-born foal stood on wobbly legs at her side. Fresh straw covered the stable floor, and a simple wreath hung on the rough-hewn door. Through a window, one could see snow-covered mountaintops and pine forest, shrouded in a frosty mist. Andrea thought they resembled the mountains she'd seen from her cabin window early that morning. Both mother and babe were bathed in the first rays of early-morning light.

With eyes agog, she studied the painting, feeling as though she, too, was standing in the stable, at one with the animals—a living part of the painting. The animals looked so real as to leap right off the canvas. She could smell the flaxen straw, reach out and touch the rustic roughness of the wooden stall, feel the chill dampness of the morning mist upon the fragrant trees and pine cones. She laughed aloud as she sensed the wobble in the newborn's legs, sharing, fully, in the mother's joy. She basked in the warm, golden shimmer of love and joy being cast upon the world. She stood back, feeling as though she'd been, mystically, caught up in a dream. This was no mere painting—this was an experience.

Andrea wanted to applaud the artist, to shout *Bravo* to his talent, to his theme. Her gaze settled on a patch of early morning sky just outside the stable window, surprised to find there, just a hint of a face—a weathered, age-wizened face: the face of God, watching over the foal. It had been painted with a touch so light and delicate that she could barely see the paint hidden behind the frosty mist, but it was there—a mere wisp of a suggestive thought. Chills shot through her body as she studied the ethereal quality of the painting, the image plucking at every heartstring in her body.

She caressed the rustically carved frame—a precious work of art in its own right.

She had to have this painting!

She looked around for the shopkeeper, suddenly aware of the absence. "Hello," she called out. Finally, she spied a woman in a back room. Her back was turned, but there was no mistaking who she was—McCormick's lady friend. She was laughing and talking, animatedly, to someone. Was it McCormick? It was.

Feeling faint from hunger and humiliation, she promised herself that she would come back for the painting at a more convenient time. With that whopping price tag, and the streets devoid of shoppers, she was certain it would stay put until she could make it back to stake a claim on the gift she would give herself.

Suddenly, she stopped short, as she was first hit with the realization that she would be alone at Christmas—completely alone. Hot tears surfaced on her lashes, threatening to escape as heavy sobs. Quickly discarding the sampler, she rushed out a side door exit, leaving the bewildered shopkeeper gaping, and frenetic wind chimes jangling, wildly, behind her.

With bleary eyes and ladened feet, Andrea blindly descended the steps into a cold, wind-driven rain. Not until she was a full block away, did she allow herself to take shelter under the weather-beaten roof of a buffet restaurant, where she had, years ago, waited for her dad. Today, due to Covid-19, it was closed and boarded up.

She was cold, wet, and miserable, and her empty stomach grumbled, mercilessly; but, as if that wasn't bad enough, Tracker had pranced off to Hell with McCormick. She eyed a wooden bench, weathered and damp, and sat, waiting, hoping her dog would, eventually, come looking for her. She leaned back, kicked her feet out, and pulled her cap down over her eyes, McCormick style. "Cue the music, Kenny," she mocked, chortling through tears.

Twenty minutes later, as she sat shivering in her wet clothing, the spirited dog came trotting around the corner of the building, carrying a piece of left-over steak. "Well, I'm glad at least one of us is not starving," she snarked. "Where'd you get that?" She sniffed the damp air. Smelling hickory smoke, she followed her nose.

CHAPTER 27

The town clock struck three. Outside the Mountain Inn, with an ancient gristmill as its facade, Andrea turned to her dog, "Okay … it's your turn to wait for me." She instructed him to stay under the cedar-shingled awning as she entered through the double, wooden entrance, barely noticing the gaily decorated doors, both bearing holly and pine bough wreaths. Breathing in the scent of centuries-old wood, smoke and freshly baked bread, she was immediately welcomed by the warmth and quaintness of the rusticated building. She ogled the walls and high ceilings constructed of huge, pine beams, and large windows that looked out upon peak after peak of mountain beauty. She eyed the gigantic millstone on display, thinking how hard the early Vermonters had worked for their daily bread. The term *work ethic* came to mind.

A sign above the open swing doors, leading to the dining area read: *Ye Olden Mill*. The large room was filled with heavy pine-wood furniture, sitting obtrusively on a bare wooden floor. Rich red cloths draped the tables, bringing the story of the legendary Kris Kringle to mind. The same red graced the window valances. The finishing touches were functional, coal-oil lanterns adorned with fresh greenery, berried holly and little red bows. She would have found them charming, had it not been for her diminished energy level, and the hungry grumbling of her stomach.

Several minutes passed as she stood, wet and shivering, waiting to be seated by an absent hostess. Miserably, she thought, *this trip to Red Springs isn't working out*. She'd hoped to find peace and contentment, but so far, she'd found nothing but frustration and emptiness. The red in the curtains reminded her of David's favorite red shirt, and the many lunches she'd shared with him—and where was David, anyway? Why hadn't she heard from him? Suddenly, she felt desolated—abandoned by everyone.

Scanning the sea of tables in the large, dimly-lit dining area, her disheartened eyes were drawn to the crackling fire in a gigantic hearth, with its heavy mantel aglow with candles and adorned with aromatic, pine-scented garland, morning fresh from the forest. Suddenly, she froze.

Through the dimmed lighting, Andrea spotted the profile of a person sitting fireside, and silhouetted by the flickering flames. Was it McCormick? The man's long, straight back and muscular shoulders were covered in the same gunmetal gray the agent had worn earlier. Her eyes shot to a peg on the barn wood coatrack where McCormick's khaki vest hung, in obvious view.

Suddenly, this third meeting became more than humiliating. He's probably meeting the shopkeeper, she reasoned, catching an unexpected glimpse at herself in the smoky haze of the antique mirror. She sucked in her breath, "Oh, gawd ... I need a glam squad," she groused, using the expression bantered about by TV anchors, and spoofed by newsprint competitors. Craving invisibility, she had just made up her mind to slip out the door when she realized that McCormick was already on his feet, walking in her direction. His expression was innocuous, but still Andrea detected his smartass smirk, lurking just behind his laughing eyes as he approached her in the foyer.

Taking special notice of her soggy appearance, he addressed her with reservation. "Mrs. Fitzgerald," he offered, his hands resting on his hips. "You'll be happy to know that I've checked my gun at the desk ... why don't we call a temporary truce?"

Andrea hesitated, her eyes thought-filled. "We can try, Sp ... Matt," she said through gritted teeth, "but only if you promise to call me Andi. I really do hate being called by that *other* name. Frankly, if you insist on using it ... I'm going to be mentally ill."

The corner of his mouth lifted, along with an amused brow. "Going to be?" he shot back quickly.

She shot him a sassy smirk that needed no interpretation.

After a moment, McCormick's pursed lips and heaving breath signaled that he'd just made a tough decision. "You look cold ... why don't you join me by the fire? It looks like the rain has set in for a while...." He checked the dining room, "and it seems we have the place to ourselves ... in case you find it necessary to yell at me."

"I don't want to intrude," Andrea said flatly, ignoring the barb.

"Believe me, you're not intruding … I don't enjoy eating alone."

Andrea leveled her eyes on the man. So, he's not meeting the shopkeeper after all, she thought, hiding her surprise. With reluctance, she accepted his invitation.

She shimmied out of the heavy, water-logged layer of vest, and watched him hang it on a peg next to his. When he turned around, a smirk rode his face. "I'm pretty certain you won't need that canister of pepper spray," he said, risibility flashing in his eyes. "The meat here is all served post mortem."

Her mouth gaped open, speechless. How did he know she had pepper spray? He led the way to his table, all the while thinking that this wasn't the best idea for an agent.

Andrea followed, thinking the jerk had multiple personalities—one of them had been to charm school – the other had been privately tutored in Hell.

He seated her in the captain's chair, nearest the fire. When he was satisfied that she was comfortable, he sat down across from her.

"I have a question for you, McCormick. Are you this raw and brutish with your … felons?" she asked, determined not to let him get to her.

"I am … if I'm doing it right," he offered, shooting her a sportive wink.

"Good cop, bad cop … minus the good cop?"

"Something like that," he grinned, thinking that bad cop was sometimes his best defense. Innocent lives were often at stake, as in this case.

She reached for a menu. "I highly recommend the corn chowder and Orchard Bread," he offered, casually. "It's excellent."

The waitress came, bringing two mugs and a pot of fresh coffee. McCormick poured while she took Andrea's order. When the pleasant, older lady turned to McCormick, Andrea was surprised to watch her lay a gentle hand on his broad, gray shoulder, giving him a warm, familiar greeting. "Sir … I am overjoyed to see that you've made it back to us safe and sound," she offered, in genuine approbation."

The agent responded with a warm smile, a wholesome wink and a nod of gratitude.

Andrea took a sip from the heavy, white mug; then raised serious eyes to meet his. After witnessing the woman's deep show of regard, she felt a need to sweeten her tone. "I'm sorry if I was so … earlier…."

He opened his mouth to speak, but waved away her apology, instead.

She asked, "So … are you still on the case?"

Hesitation caught in the agent's throat. "If you're asking if I'm on your case in regards to your sources, the answer is no ... I'm not." Matt answered quickly, thinking of himself on sick leave, and officially off-grid. "I was just filling in during a short-term personnel exchange ... it was always meant to be a temporary assignment," he said, his tone dismissive. He glanced up, giving her a steady look while trying to come up with something more credible to offer her, "and of course, you're no longer writing your column."

Aware that he was being slightly misleading, McCormick felt he had no choice. Andrea wouldn't tolerate his hanging around if she knew he was investigating *her*. Deep down, he was hoping it was just a matter of time before he was pulled off the case, and someone else brought in to do the official investigation; if not ... he would have to clear the air.

Andrea took in the total of their conversations. "Wait a minute ... in the post office you said you had just returned ... and the waitress just mentioned that you'd been here before. Does that mean you live around here?" she questioned, surprised at the possibility.

McCormick strove to take back what had already been said. With shrewd duplicity, he offered, "I haven't been up this way for a long while ... getting back was number one on my ... bucket list."

Andrea caught the glint in his eye as he quickly clamped his mouth shut before saying more than he should. She frowned and shot him a challenging look, "Bucket Lists are for people at the end of their lives."

His smile, weakened. "One never knows," he offered.

His words fell shroud-like over Andrea's feeble attempt to shore up her own emotions. "That's a rather fatalistic view for such a young man," she challenged.

"Yeah, well ... to be quite honest ... I don't actually have a bucket list, per se—mine is more *a things to get done before I die,* kind of list."

"Just as fatalistic," she exclaimed.

Having no reply, he asked, "Where are you staying?"

"I'm on Grandma Burns Road." Her eyes dropped, missing McCormick's frown and furrowed brows of concern. "It's beautifully serene up there," she continued, "I think the flatlanders have left for the winter, and taken all the locals with them."

"That's why I like it here," he offered, drily. He took a sip of coffee, thinking; then with slow deliberation he set his mug on the table. "Andi, are you, by any chance, in that little log cabin at the end of the Grandma Burns?"

"Yes … Little Bear Cabin," she said smiling, her voice trilling with delight.

McCormick quickly diverted his eyes, concealing his shock. *Like the collision that took place between the two land masses at the end of the Ordovician Period, 466 million years ago, creating the Green Mountains, his two worlds had just collided in a cataclysmically dangerous and possibly deadly way!*

Oblivious to the agent's inner turmoil, Andrea smiled with contentment, "Oh McCormick … you should see it. It's the perfect little cabin … a perfect hide-a-way. The builder knew exactly what he was doing," she added, cheerfully. "And the location has to be one of the most serene, scenic spots in Vermont."

Wholesome self-regard skimmed across McCormick's face; but quickly dissolved into magnanimity.

"I do have to admit … it's a little on the rustic side," she offered.

"Isn't that the whole idea of a cabin?"

She shot him a teasing smirk, and added, "The road could use some gravel … but I'm all for adventure … you know, living life in the real."

She caught his slow grin, but missed the deep concern as his eyes dropped to his mug. "How did you happen to come by that particular cabin?"

"My husband bought it," she clipped, nonchalantly.

McCormick's pulse quickened and his breathing came to a halt. This little game, which had obviously been weaponized against him, had gone on for too long. He quickly tamped down any show of misgivings. Instead, he raised his cup and took another slow sip, quietly observing the woman in her state of dampness. Soon, a spark flashed in his dark eyes. "You need to find yourself an umbrella."

"Look who's talking," she quipped as memories surfaced. "The first time I met you…." She glanced up, and grinned, puckishly, remembering his water-drenched appearance, "I thought I'd won the prize for dragging the mysterious sea monster out of the deep, glacial Lac Memphremagog; remember—the pouring rain … your dark, formidable demeanor?"

The unsmiling McCormick rubbed a slow palm down the full length of his face, considering her analogy. The pitch-dark legendary sea serpent, she referenced, inhabited the lower twenty mile stretch of the long, narrow lake shared by Quebec/Vermont. The Indians had refused to swim or bathe in the eerie waters.

He shot her a steely-eyed look. It was time to clear the air, time to level with the woman in regards to who he really was; but he needed to play it straight, to have no misunderstandings between the two of them—for both professional and personal reasons.

His head drew back, slowly, and his hands encircled his coffee mug for reinforcement as he eyed the mesmerizing woman across the table. "Correction," he said, through clenched teeth. "The first time we met was … actually… on your birthday … at the Writer's Block Lounge … you've even commemorated the day with a page on your desk calendar." He sucked in his breath and held it, watching for a reaction to his bold statement.

Puzzlement claimed her face. She shook her head, "No, it was … at the airp…." Her mouth clapped shut, as she shot him a confused, questioning look. He gave her a mildly abashed, closed-mouth smile, as she slowly let the reality of that day permeate her thoughts.

"My birthday?" she questioned, her brows knitting.

He gave her a half nod.

"In the Lounge?"

"Writer's Block … to be exact." He watched her eyes fill with memories.

Suddenly, high color rose to her cheeks, and she spoke in the firm whisper of reason, "The hug … the kiss."

He cocked a brow and his eyes locked into hers, "The beard, the man tail … the dark," he said, raggedly, without humor as he, too, remembered the exact moment the sensuous, emotional bolt of fate had shot through him, melding his destiny to this troubled, young woman. He had done nothing to stop it, and so he sat, wearing his heart—not on his sleeve, but over his entire body.

"That was you?" She queried, her eyes skeptically searching his face.

Seeing her lost in the memory of their impassioned kiss, he asserted, audaciously, "That was *you*!" She searched the depths of his dark unwavering eyes, realizing, with certainty, that he was speaking the truth.

Flames in the hearth leapt and crackled as hearts pounded in both their chests, both remembering how their bodies had flamed to life, lips scorching lips in a most hot-blooded, passionate kiss, a kiss that now had them both, desperately, trying to quell their blushes.

At last, Andrea exhaled a hot breath, "Well, Agent McCormick, I'm … I'm totally speechless."

"It's about time," he teased, softly, without a smile.

He watched her try to get control of the situation by removing her hat, and fussing with stubborn strands of hair that had gone astray; then finally, giving up and completely removing the band from her wet ponytail, letting the hair fall to her shoulders—to the man's delight.

When her hand rose to her necklace, both sets of eyes dropped in silence.

Feeling the need to apologize for his behavior, McCormick offered, "I'd just returned from a miss… a rather stressful two years…." He stopped there, understanding that this wasn't the time for a lengthy discussion. "You might say I was pumped on adrenaline, high on life … and bold in my audaciousness."

After hiding her feelings behind a long sip of coffee, Andrea finally peeked over the rim. "So you're expressing regret?"

Seeing misdoubt, McCormick leveled his eyes, and locked into hers. "Regret is not in my vocabulary," he said.

She shot him a wan, closed-mouth smile, trying to swallow the emotion that had swelled her throat. "So … where do we go from here?"

McCormick's gaze was unrelenting as his imagination took wings. He knew exactly where *he* wanted to go from here—if only the circumstances were different; but recognizing the innocence of her question, as well as the folly of his thoughts, he leaned in and grinned, roguishly lifting his eyebrows. "Do you suppose we could just be friends for a while—I'm really starting to feel beat up?"

Lost in each other's gaze, they both flinched with startlement when a young waitress suddenly appeared beside their table. Andrea looked up. At first glance she could tell the gorgeous, young girl was only about seventeen, but like the older waitress, she was dressed in colonial-period clothing. Her hair was pulled back in a messy bun, and topped with a white bonnet, fresh and lacey. At closer range, Andrea could see the dress had been hastily, and temporarily, pinned on the sides to snuggly fit the young, under-developed body.

Color drained from McCormick's face when the girl suddenly shrilled in recognition. "Matt!" She shrieked, "Oh my gawd ... I can't believe it's you!" The biggest, warmest, happiest smile Andrea had ever seen glowed in the girl's dancing eyes and fresh, dewy complexion. She was stunned, even further, as the young lass suddenly plopped onto McCormick's lap, and threw both arms around his shoulders, giving him a tremendously warm hug. Only when her bonnet fell to the floor, and long, auburn, waist-length tresses fell across her shoulders, did McCormick make positive identification. She cooed, "I've missed you so-o-o-o much!" Tossing both legs across his lap, in the way of a young child, she buried her face in his neck. "I thought you were...."

"Cadaverous?" he said, obtusely, finishing her sentence. Andrea watched as McCormick slid an arm around her tiny waistline, and lovingly ran his hand down the full length of her shiny tresses. "Little Miss Precocious," he laughed, appreciatively. "What in the world are you do...?"

Andrea sat, impatiently, studying both their faces. It was quite obvious that McCormick was totally spellbound, unable to take his eyes off this gregarious, young maiden. At twenty-eight, she suddenly felt like an old crone ... like a wet blanket—like an, unwelcomed, third party.

In time, McCormick shot a glance across the table. Staring back at him were clouds of a gathering storm. He quickly rose to his feet, letting the little miss drop to hers; but the girl quickly pushed him back into the chair. The chattering of her youthful voice suddenly deepened, as she exclaimed, "Matt ... everybody... and I mean everybody ... is asking about you." Then, gazing at him with the understanding of a seventeen year old, she gushed, "Gawd ... you've gotten o-l-d."

The young girl planted a heart-felt kiss on his cheek, then left, just as she'd arrived—as though floating through air. McCormick stood, watching her go, stunned and slack-jawed. When he shook his head in appreciation, Andrea could tell his mind had fluttered away. *So he likes them young,* Andrea thought, miserably.

He made an attempt to explain, to downplay, "Hero's welcome."

"Hero worship ... don't you mean?"

"I mean she hasn't seen me in a long while," he said, his eyes agog, and his mouth in a sheepish grin.

Oh barf! Andrea groaned inwardly, thinking she could chalk up another personality to his long list of psycho behaviors. She tried to find a word to fit this particular one—deviant came to mind. *This… this charlatan, this lounge lizard must hit on every female he meets,* she thought.

Experiencing emotional whip-lash, and feeling her mood sink to a new all-time low, Andrea pushed her chair back. She stood to her full height beside him. "Excuse me, Special Agent McCormick, but I really don't want to be here," she said simply, her voice low and composed, yet power-packed with hostility. "It's quite obvious that you're a salacious, wanton flirt, of one sort or another, and I have no interest, what-so-ever, in competing for your attention against some hip-wiggling, almost breast–jiggling, hood-winking, under aged, teenaged *skank*." Andrea looked him straight in the eye and spat, "From here on out, Romeo … you can *gift* your kisses to anyone else but me!" At that, she tossed her crumpled napkin on to the table, and turned to leave.

Raw anger rose and flashed in McCormick's eyes, "Andi, sit down!" he growled. He looked into her cold, unrelenting eyes. "This isn't what it looks like … I can't explain it right now, but please sit down." He looked around to see if they were being watched. They were still the only patrons in the dining room. "She's always like that with me … with men," he corrected.

"No," Andrea said, her voice soft, yet heated. "She's like that with dirty, old men who allow her to be like that!"

McCormick grabbed her wrist. "Andi … this is not what it looks like." The lines in his forehead deepened. "Why are you so angry?" The rugged McCormick towered, menacingly, over her, his fiery eyes glaring down at her; his flushed face frowning with full-blown anger.

Andrea shot the look right back at him. "I'm angry at you for not holding true to your promise … for not coming back to the hospital to che … to report to me. I was there for *two effing weeks!*" She spat out the words with heated fury.

"You're angry with me? … I don't understand," he said, relieved to see her true feelings rise to the surface.

Her eyes dropped to her wrist, throbbing from being clasped so tightly; he immediately released his grip, and she walked to her chair, totally impervious to anything he might have to say.

"You promised … in the hospital … that you would get back to me the following morning." Andrea raised her hands, palms up, her voice rising with them. "I never heard from you again ... not until we," she put the next word in air quotes, *bumped* into each other at the post office this morning."

Finally, a hint of understanding flickered across McCormick's face, and he plopped, unceremoniously, into the chair across from her. At that exact same moment, Andrea's gaze fell on a deep, purple wound on the side of the man's forehead, near the hairline, made more prominent by his flushed face and punked up hair. She surmised it to be a recent wound, judging by the color.

Suddenly, the pieces came together in Andrea's mind: the head wound, McCormick's disappearance, Stormy's friend. Her hand shot to her mouth. "My gawd ... it was you. *You* were the one who got shot ... I didn't know."

"And you the nosy journalist!" McCormick clipped, unsmiling, looking a bit chagrined. Muscles worked his jawline as he worked to shut down a fresh infusion of adrenaline. He frowned at her from across the table. "The shooting made front page headlines in your own newspaper ... didn't you save a copy?" he asked, sardonically.

Not understanding the root of his sarcasm, Andrea let out her breath in a loud whoosh. "Matt, Dr. Pierce wouldn't allow a newspaper anywhere near my room. I'm sorry ... I didn't realize ... I just didn't know." She looked across the table at the handsome devil with the ability to attract obsequious women to him like hummingbirds to nectar. "Enough about me ... are you okay?"

His lips pursed, and he nodded, affirmatively.

She thought, *I prayed for this guy, day and night; I prayed for his recovery, not even knowing who he was.*

McCormick read sincerity in her demeanor. Finally, he shoved his chair back, and returned the look. "Look Andi," he said, "I'm the one who's sorry. You're right ... I did let you down, big time, but let me explain." He related everything that had happened at the newspaper that night. Andrea listened in awe.

"I had found the pill and made it back to my car without incident. I was driving along that deserted stretch of highway on my way back to the hospital." He wouldn't tell her that he had been returning to stand guard at her bedside. "Suddenly, a car gained speed, pulling up beside me, and this lame brained, loggerheaded, jackass leaned out the back window and started shooting ... Chicago gangsta style. My car flipped over the guardrail as soon as I took the hit. Luckily for me, the bullet just grazed my head, but there was a lot of blood," he paused, "and … I took a couple of other solid hits. The wreckage must've looked a lot worse than it was, because when they came back to finish me off," he paused, "Well … I guess they thought I was already dead."

Once again McCormick chided himself for taking the bullets. He'd been thinking of Andrea as he drove away from the newspaper that night, feeling gratified that her story had checked out; but rattled to find his picture plastered across the front page of a recent issue.

"You don't think it was anyone from the *Daily News*, do you?" she was asking.

"No," The agent's eyes flashed like lightning; and his next words came out hot and heavy. "I know who it was." He offered no further explanation.

"The aspirin bottle had already gone missing from your desk drawer … and when I came out of surgery, the pill was gone from my pocket. I'm afraid we have no proof of how you were poisoned other than the lab report."

Also troubling, had been her reason for having, and holding on to, a three-year-old newspaper accounting of his time in Afghanistan. His thinking had been clouded by the possibility that she, along with her husband, were stalking him. Had his mind been clear that night, he would have certainly noticed the suspicious car gaining speed in the rearview mirror, and taken defensive action. Now, as he remembered his ancient suit advertisement lying beside her bed, he lifted his gaze in suspicion. "Andi … why are you up here—alone."

Stunned by his story, she answered in a tone, totally bereft of feelings, "McCormick … I'm always alone."

The younger waitress returned, carrying napkins, the older one brought wine; but this time Andrea had Matt's full attention. She smiled up at the girl. "Thank you," she said sincerely, watching the napkin get set before her. She totally missed the little wink Matt gave the blushing, young miss.

The older waitress set her tray on the table behind Andrea, fishing a camera out of her apron. "How would the two of you like to take part in our Frame of Fame?" She pointed to a super-sized picture frame, and the collage of photos populating the wall space. "We truly value our customers," she said in answer to Andrea's questioning look. "Especially those brave souls who make it this far north during the winter months."

McCormick chuckled, "My brave soul is already up there."

The waitress looked at Andrea, "Ma'am?"

Andrea grinned, coyly, at McCormick, "Sure, why not ... as long as Matt's in it with me ... evidence," she taunted, laughingly. They smiled at the camera, and the waitress snapped the shot. She handed Andrea a pen and a form to fill out. "We'll send you a copy of the photo."

"Great!" Andrea enthused, signing the form. She didn't see the waitress retrieve her tray; nor did she see her lay the camera in its place.

"Where were we?" McCormick asked, seemingly mollified.

Once the wait-staff was out of earshot, Andrea continued. "My physical condition had deteriorated to the point that my doctor ordered me to take sick-leave following a couple of weeks in the hospital."

McCormick shook his head in understanding.

"I've sent my housekeeper off to be with her family; she's in an advanced stage of Alzheimer's disease, and the estate is looming larger than life ... way too many ghosts ... and shadows."

She paused, expecting McCormick to jump in with an explanation as to why he had been inside her house. Instead, he only gazed at her, his eyes glowing dark and golden, remembering how he'd found the woman sleeping alone, in a king-sized bed, in the middle of a huge, rambling, three-story house.

She continued, "I knew that if I wanted to recover, I would have to get away."

She paused and dropped her head, "Forgive me for rattling on."

"No problem," he razzed, glibly, "Your rattles don't scare me."

She related the rest of the story about how she came to know about the cabin. "And that's how I ended up here ... I think I've decided to stay awhile."

Deep concern crossed McCormick's face, "You can't ... I mean ... the winters get really brutal up here."

"I know. I've thought about that. I spent a lot of time hiking these mountains as a kid ... we even snow camped up here, once. I was never responsible for supplies, but I think I have everything I need, except for a few groceries.

"You say you didn't know your husband owned this property? How is that possible?" The agent's gaze dropped to his wine, watching it slush around inside the glass, not wanting Andrea to see the hotbed of concern brewing in his eyes.

Her cheeks flushed hot at being questioned about Shaun. She stammered, "Shaun and I were not ... close," she admitted. "He was a complex person...."

The agent's ears were pricked. "How long were you married?"

"Not long, but it seemed like a thousand years, at the time."

"I'll bet," Matt said earnestly, remembering their conversations from the tape he'd listened to a couple of months earlier.

Determined to change the subject, to move on, she asked, "Are you and Stormy close friends?"

Surprised at the mention of Stormy, his mouth curved up in a slow, mischievous grin, "Yeah, I guess you could say that ... I've known her for several years now—she's a pretty good woman ... and a damned good nurse."

"She's a beautiful woman," Andrea added.

A thoughtful look crossed his face. "I've never looked at her quite like that, but yeah, I can see why people might have that thought." Andrea studied him, thinking his answer a bit strange. *Why wouldn't he recognize a beautiful woman?*

Thunder suddenly rattled the windows as the ingratiating waitress quietly refilled their glasses then left. McCormick lifted his glass in a gallant gesture, his face reflecting high spirits, "A toast ... to stormy ... weather."

The cheerful tinkling of crystal meeting crystal was music to Andrea's ears. Her heart lightened as she realized she was actually enjoying talking to McCormick. He gave her space to think, to speak her own mind, without pushing or trying to manipulate the conversation, or trying to put words into her mouth.

The corner of his mouth inched up, once more. "Andi ... I'd like to see...." Suddenly, a soundless reverberation came from somewhere on his body, catching even McCormick by surprise.

Puzzlement rode McCormick's face as he pulled a sophisticated, high-tech phone from his shirt pocket—a satphone. He stared at it, never having seen it before, and having no idea how it had gotten there. He quickly checked to see who was calling. Throwing a rueful glance across the table, he said, "Excuse me ... I have to take this ... it shouldn't take long."

He walked out a side door where a wooden porch stretched out the full length of the building. Andrea's eyes followed, watching him through the window as he talked and paced, using persuasive, conversational hand gestures. She couldn't help but notice that every gesture was strong and forceful. McCormick was every inch the man—one would think—he certainly brought out the woman in her.

Using the secure satphone the young waitress had dropped into his pocket, McCormick explained to his boss in Virginia that he was with the Widow Fitzgerald, and that she was staying in his old, abandoned cabin on the same property as the one he'd built more recently.

"I don't like the sounds of this, Matt, her being in that cabin," the chief was saying, all-the-while surreptitiously tamping down his exuberance, "but I'm sure it's just a coincidence."

McCormick didn't believe in coincidences. From his own experiences and professional training, it looked, to him, as though the enemy knew exactly where he was, had a lock on him, and were closing ranks. He guessed they were using Andrea as bait, with or without her knowledge.

"We may have to get rid of her, as well," the chief was saying.

A sick lump hit the pit of McCormick's stomach as he listened to the inane argument from the other end of the line. He took a long, hard look through the window at the woman who had all but spit in his face, trying to avoid him at every turn. He shook his head in defiance. "I think you're wrong, boss ... there's no way she's playing me. I don't think Andrea knows anything about her husband's depravity ... I'd stake my reputation on it!"

A low growl came over the line. "I'd rather you didn't have to do that, Matt; but you're there, and I'm not. You make the call ... but keep an open mind."

"I say we let it play out awhile longer," McCormick offered. If she's guilty, I'll know it—I'll sense it."

"So be it, then," answered the chief, "but keep this in mind ... at some point you're gonna have to interrogate her under oath ... the sooner, the better."

McCormick's hot blood ran cold.

"I know you're officially off-grid, McCormick, but you're the only agent we've got in the area ... and I need for you to check out that small plane crash last night in the National Forest," the chief continued, "I'll get you the coordinates and have a team ready to go as soon as you give me the word."

"I'll check it out," he assured his boss, sounding less than enthusiastic.

Hearing the splatter of rain in one ear, and the drone of his boss's voice reviewing drug enforcement initiatives in the other, McCormick turned his gaze on Andrea—and the opportunity that had just presented itself.

CHAPTER 28

Gazing beyond the red curtains, waiting for McCormick to complete his call, Andrea watched the heavy rain splattering over the clogged guttering of a nearby building. In the distance, a steep, slope of evergreen trees surrounded the swift-running mountain stream as it cascaded over a rocky cliff, pooled, then flowed through the meadow covered with wildflowers, their droopy, little heads now deadened by a hard frost. The musical stream meandered through town, under bridges and walkways, finally sidling up beside the old mill where Andrea sat appreciating its natural flow; but she also found it impossible to keep her eyes off McCormick as his long, sexy legs paced back and forth across the rustic, rough-hewn porch.

When, at last, she took notice of the white puffs of frozen mist being released into the air each time McCormick spoke, the obvious hit her. The temperature had dropped, dramatically. Walking the ten miles home would be challenging; walking home without getting soaked would be impossible—getting soaked to the bone by a cold, hard rain without getting pneumonia would be improbable. She grimaced.

When, at last, McCormick returned to the table, his mood had soured, and he looked troubled as he eyed her, soberly. "You walked into town." He was guessing of course, but it seemed as though he were reading her mind.

"I did."

Hearing regret in her voice, he said with a surprising softness, "Then gather your things … I'll drive you home."

Casting a doubting eye, she countered, "I've got my 'fur ball' with me … and I need to pick up a handful of groceries before I return to the cabin."

"Fur Ball can ride in the back … store's just around the corner," he offered.

As they walked towards the door, Andrea didn't notice McCormick dropping the satphone on the table, trading it for the waitress's camera; nor did she see him flip the hospitable, older woman a droll thumbs-up. Had she seen the quick, loving kiss he blew the young girl as he retrieved his gun and holster from the counter, she would have been livid; but she didn't see. She was busy grabbing the complimentary mint and book of matches, while her mind worked to coin a phrase for this new, foe-friendly, kiss-christened relationship.

She had known all along that McCormick had been toying with her, trying to convince her that he was an everyman kind of guy. Far from average, McCormick was actually very well-spoken, without accent of any kind. She guessed he'd spent a lot of time in the Halls of Ivy; but he wasn't as pompous as she'd first imagined him to be, which pleased her immensely.

Once outside, impatience sounded in the man's voice, and his words rang out in a sharp, fast-clipped, military fashion, unlike the congenial tone he'd used inside the restaurant. "I need to make an official side trip ... how do you feel about taking a ride through the National Forest? We've had a report of some unusual activity in the area ... I've been asked to check it out before I retire." Reading her dubious demeanor, he added, "You'll really enjoy the beautiful, pristine vistas up there...." He motioned to the misty mountaintop, "they're awesome," he added, trying to sell the idea. His head dropped his feet shuffled, before shooting her a wry grin. "Think you can trust me that long?"

"Retire? Andrea asked, ignoring the jab. "Are you leaving the agency?"

"Temporarily ... the bahss says I need a vacation," McCormick looked at her askance, to see if she was buying, not a pre-text, but his lie. Fact of the matter was, he had just been assigned to further, and fully, investigate Andrea Daye Fitzgerald, as well as provide protection against any known or unknown enemy. He needed an excuse to be hanging loose; but in McCormick's mind, this whole thing was getting entirely too complicated, too uncomfortable, too hinky for words. "I'll meet you back here in fifteen minutes," he said, tamping down a strong distrust of his boss, his cryptic orders, and his own rueful feelings towards this whole, unprecedented assignment.

Andrea purchased a few supplies, and then retraced her steps to the restaurant. She stood outside, waiting under the over-hanging window boxes, emptied of their withered, fall blooms and vines, and now decorated early for the holidays.

It wasn't long before McCormick rattled up in his rusty, old army jeep with wipers screeching across the windshield. Stepping to the curb, Andrea threw a backwards glance at the time-forgotten gristmill and restaurant, appreciating the historical value of the rusticated facade. Her gaze rose to a second story window where the young waitress stood soberly eyeing both she and McCormick through the glass. "He's too old for you, sweetheart," she whispered, feeling a little bit sorry for the young maiden. Matt McCormick was every woman's dream. He was intelligent, handsome—ruggedly handsome—and sexy. Yeah … he was definitely sexy. And yet, he seemed totally unaffected by his good looks, his unusual masculinity—his charm— all the things that would make him desirable to women.

McCormick slipped a new, inexpensive cell phone into his vest pocket, then hopped out, leaving the engine idling. Andrea blushed as he rounded the front of the jeep, feeling more than silly for her own schoolgirl crush. As he grabbed her grocery bag, she could tell his mood was dour, made visible by his flexing jaw, and knitted eyebrows.

He opened the passenger door and let an exuberant Tracker into the back, then turned to her. "Ready?" he questioned, giving her a crooked grin.

She breathed a silent sigh of relief. Thank God he wasn't angry at her. She caught one last, brief glimpse of the young waitress over her shoulder, then lifted a black Stetson from the passenger seat, climbed in, and sat with the ample-sized hat balanced across her knees.

McCormick climbed behind the wheel. His gaze immediately dropped to the hat. "That's my brother's," he growled, broodingly, lifting the hat from her knees. Andrea noticed the respectful way he handled the brim, laying it gently on the foot-well behind his seat.

"Does your brother live around here?" she asked, spritely, with genuine interest.

McCormick rubbed a heavy hand across his mouth, then shot his passenger a wily, yet steely-eyed look, "Yeah … I guess you could say he's become a permanent resident."

He stole a look at her as he shifted gears and hit the gas. "Are you okay?" he asked. "You look a little flushed."

—◁○▷—

The narrow gravel road through the National Forest was filled with rugged ruts and potholes, awakening Andrea's journalist instincts. "Matt, I've been reading social media accounts suggesting the Northeast Kingdom is just a lot of hype and myth, a state of mind ... that there's really nothing special here. Is there any truth to that ... or is there really something magical about this place?"

He shot her a slightly affronted look, remembering how he'd hungered and thirsted for this place, while actually living in Paradise.

"Hell yes, this country's special, but in order to find the magic you've got to understand the concept of appreciation. Before you can fully appreciate the coziness of a cabin, you have to live in a house of sticks, so to speak—*or in a grotto,* he thought. And it all depends on what your interests and goals are ... everyone has to live their own reality ... their own dream ... walk their own trail." He sneaked a glance at her in his peripheral vision.

The jeep hit a hole, jolting Andrea out of both her seat and her comfort zone.

"Not everyone is meant to live this simple, backwoods lifestyle, he continued. "What snowboarder would willingly move to the Arabian Desert ... or bikini-clad sunbather to the frozen tundra? If you like throngs of people, big Broadway productions, or standing, for hours, with the drunks on Times Square," he shot her a teasing wink, "you're probably not going to be happy hiking up the spine of the Green Mountains, smelling bear stink, or scraping mud and muck off your boots. He bounced a wry grin off the woman trying to regain her equilibrium. If one doesn't like it here, they might consider moving on. He stared straight ahead. "Either that, or start taking Vitamin D$_3$ gels, and an oath to start looking for the awesomeness that surrounds them."

"My gawd, McCormick ... I didn't know you could string that many words together."

"Too verbose?" he grinned, down shifting the gears. "Then in the words of my dear, ole grandpappy: *'get your head outta your ass, suck in that gut and lift that chin ... cause life is what you make it.'"*

CHAPTER 29

McCormick pulled the jeep off the road, to a spot overlooking a mountainside of dense, coniferous forest. The view was breathtaking. The rain had stopped, momentarily, allowing a profusion of golden sunlight to streak down through the white, wispy clouds, dappling the ground with patches of light, creating a misty, fairy tale illusion to the forest.

They left the jeep, and for several minutes stood gazing with pleasure at the awe-inspiring scenery. Andrea breathed in the fresh, fragrant scent, feeling her spirits soar.

McCormick breathed deep, taking it all in. "If that's not special, then I don't know what is," he said in a whisper. He sidled up beside her, placed a hand on her left shoulder; with his right hand, pointed to a spot across the deep, river valley. "That's where we're headed."

Once back on the road, they soon entered a grove of taller, darker pine. Immediately, Andrea's intense study of Greek mythology came to mind. She turned to Matt who sat poised behind the steering wheel, quietly preoccupied, but looking like a Greek god in his own right as his jean-clad legs stretched out to the gas pedal. Damn … he did have sexy legs, she confirmed.

"Trees, trees, so many trees … 'I think that I shall never see….' "

McCormick finished the line in a burly voice, "A poem as lovely as a tree."

She gave him an appreciative smile, pleasantly surprised by his input. "Joyce Kilmer," she offered, leaning forward a bit, but still taking in the view. "My au pair often recited it to me."

McCormick grinned, wryly. "I had an au pair growing up…." he shot her a sideways glance, "we called her Grandma."

"Funny," she laughed. "Did you know that people once believed that the tree was sacred, especially the oak tree? They held ceremonies to honor them." Her words flowed, naturally.

McCormick looked to the right, and then swiveled his head to check the left side, looking for a particular side road. "Yeah ... I think I heard that somewhere."

"But...." She shot the agent a teasing look. "Do you know how the pine tree came into existence?" Andrea's eyes glistened, mischievously.

He grinned. "Why do I think I'm about to find out?"

The English major needed no further encouragement. She offered, "The pine forest and glades, according to Greek Mythology, were the homes of nymphs, dryads and gods. Pitys was the little nymph who took care of the forest, but she just happened to be a very naughty, little girl who liked big masculine, macho guys, like her lover Bjoreas, the god of the north wind." She grinned, casting a questioning look at the driver. "Anything sounding familiar here?"

She continued. "Pitys was also an unfaithful little flirt, spreading her charms around with both Pan and the brutish Bjoreas." She bounced a side glance off McCormick. He appeared to be listening, so she continued. "One day the jealous and suspicious Bjoreas asked Pitys why she'd been spending so much time hanging around the pastures where Pan and the shepherds tended their flocks. Well, unfortunately, the truth came out, a big brouhaha followed. The angry Bjoreas picked Pitys up and threw her against a rock ledge. As you can imagine, the minute she hit the rock she was toast ... or rather instantly transformed into a pine tree.... Andrea spread her hands wide to indicate the trees, "and voila! Now we have this whole, huge, amazing forest."

She bounced another look off McCormick. His head was tilted back slightly, looking straight ahead. "Serves the bitch right!" he said with narrowing eyes. The muscles in his jaw twitched, and Andrea watched unstated pain flicker across his face.

Taken aback by his sudden black mood, she continued. "Some cultures even believed that nymphs lived in the pine trees—and some cultures believed the trees actually were nymphs themselves. They believed you were killing a nymph if you cut down a tree."

McCormick's eyes scanned the road. "Keep going ... I'm listening."

"Some Greek mythology claims that gods made their entrances and exits from one world to another by climbing up and down the trees."

"Was that the big gods, or the lesser gods?" he asked, with a smirk.

Andrea laughed, "That was 8th grade Literature, G-man ... you studied it." Andrea punched his arm, playfully.

He flinched.

She quickly withdrew her fist, "What?"

"Bullet wound," he hissed.

"Sorry ... didn't know."

"It doesn't end there," she said, continuing to pour forth her knowledge. "In this country they believed then, as they do now, that if you carve a face in a pinewood branch, it will bring you good luck. They call it Spirit Wood."

"Good luck?" His eyes narrowed, and his head tilted to the side with emotion. "Try telling that story to those old cowboys buried in pine boxes up on Boot Hill."

She laughed, and looked at the man. He wasn't laughing, and his face had turned to stone.

"Okay, a smart guy like you has to know that, in olden days, pine cones were regarded as symbols of fertility. They had phallic meaning."

The air suddenly filled with a gentle burst of laughter, as the agent shot her a quick, guarded look, recognizing a possible attempt to seduce; but she relaxed, feeling comfortable with his reaction—he had made no obscene comment, nor had he used the occasion to his advantage to make a pass. Her senses told her she was safe in this guy's company. Besides, his contagious laughter made her laugh, which was not an easy task, these days.

Suddenly, McCormick pulled to the side of the road, under a shady tree. He rolled his window down a crack, turned off the engine, and removed the keys from the ignition. He pulled his gun from its holster, checking, should there be a need. He turned to face her. "Okay Pitys ... here's the deal." his words shot out in rapid-fire succession. "I'm going to take a little hike up through that Spiritwood forest." He pointed to the trees through the passenger window. You can go with me, or you can stay here ... your call.

"I'll go," she answered immediately, needing no time to think.

"Better leave your dog in the jeep ... he might get caught in an illegal trap. We have to walk fast and silent ... if we come across anyone, let me do the talking. If we have trouble...." he locked eyes and held out the keys to the jeep, "forget the pepper spray and run like hell."

She sat staring blankly at the keys, stunned that he was suggesting she leave without him.

"Got it?"

When she didn't answer, he gave her a hard, flinty look. "Got it?"

She snatched the keys from his hand, "Got it!"

The rain had stopped, but a cold mist hit their faces as they stepped out of the jeep. When they entered the timberline, a colder, crispier air nipped at their noses with the pungent, musky scent of pine needles and damp, mossy soil, stirring up memories in both their minds. They began their fast-paced hike through the forest. Andrea stirred with excitement as she walked through the tall, wet pines turned magical by the silvery mist. It had been years since she had been hiking in the way she was today, and she dearly loved every minute of it.

When they came to an old, beaten trail, McCormick stopped. With curiosity, Andrea scouted around the old signpost. Its top half had recently been broken over, and now hung, dangling towards the ground with the letters reading upside down. She read, "*Trail 9*".

McCormick studied the broken post; saw the black paint residue left by the vehicle that had sideswiped it. To Andrea, he explained. "This is an old fire trail. At one time there was a lookout tower at the end of it. It's no longer in use, now that they have more sophisticated methods for detecting fires." Watching her face for a reaction, he said, "This trail ends where your property begins."

She looked puzzled, "Are you saying that I can walk out my back door and end up here?"

"More or less ... it would take a while," McCormick offered, flatly. "It's at least five miles long, and it's pretty well grown over, at this point." He dropped to his haunches, checking the treads of freshly laid tire tracks. *Law enforcement*, he deduced. Intrigued by this detail, he pulled a small, sophisticated camera from his vest pocket, and snapped pictures of both the sign and the tread.

Andrea eyed his camera, choking off a chortle, "Oh hey ... your camera is just like the one the waitress used to snap our picture."

"Oh yeah?" McCormick said, dryly. "What a coincidence."

Without a glance in her direction, he stood up, and started to walk away. "Follow me ... keep your mouth shut ... and stay in my footsteps," he warned as he rounded the sign, and trudged off into the woods at a slower, more cautious pace.

Andrea breathed out a sigh of relief at the slowed pace, and followed. Earlier, she had found it necessary to speed up her natural gait in order to keep up with the long-legged McCormick, pushing her diminished stamina to the max. The air turned much cooler as they crossed a lengthy, swinging bridge, spanning a deep, dark ravine; then walked into a deeper, darker forest. McCormick lifted his eyes, staring into the woods.

He saw it, in the tree: a black cat, dead and hanging by the neck—an ominous warning to unwelcomed intruders. Before Andrea could get a glimpse, he grabbed her elbow, guiding her away from the ugly scene.

Totally oblivious to the cat, Andrea's eyes followed a sudden dash of movement, and fixed on a tiny chipmunk sitting on a rotted limb. As they drew closer, the small, striped-back rodent chirped and flicked his reddish-brown tail, watching them. "Ooh, how adorable." she gushed, instantly dropping to her knees, temporarily forgetting their mission.

McCormick stopped. His flinty eyes scoured the surrounding trees in all directions before his troubled gaze settled, not on the chipmunk, but on the enraptured, young woman.

"Andi...."

She raised her eyes to encompass the man, the treetops, and the dark, looming sky behind the two. He found himself caught, guard down. Her smile, her dazzling effulgence, so casually tossed over her shoulder, had the same effect on him as being hit by a ray of pure, golden sunlight. Glowing from within, her rosy cheeks shone from the exertion of their invigorating hike, and a delightful, joyful gleam softened her eyes. He'd only seen the look once before; and never had it been aimed in his direction.

He smiled back, but quickly dropped his eyes, realizing how vulnerable he was to this lady's charm without her so much as trying. When he raised his head again, seriousness had settled across his face, and his voice took on a more somber tone, "Andi ... there's something you need to know...."

Suddenly, a loud snap of a twig shattered the silence.

Andrea stood, the glow fading from her cheeks as she watched the muscles in McCormick's jaw grow tense, and his eyes turn razor sharp. "That was no chipmunk," she whispered.

"Animals don't usually step on twigs or branches," he said tersely. She sensed a fire igniting inside him. Surprisingly, he stepped forward, and lowered his lips to within an inch of hers, his hot breath searing her cheeks. "In a demanding whisper, he said, "Quick … throw your arms around my neck."

"Wut?" she asked in disbelief, thinking he had been about to kiss her.

"Just do it," he demanded.

Apathetically, she flung stiff arms around his neck with all the zeal of one being asked to bathe in raw maple syrup.

He groused under his hot breath in feigned disappointment, "Aw come on now … I'm not feeling the love here … babe."

Intending humor, she bantered back, "I'm not your babe … and I don't consort with the enemy."

Wary that she had chosen that particular phrase, he grabbed her roughly around the waist with one arm, lifted her off the ground, and did a quick half spin, putting his body between the woman and any possible danger, while freeing up his gun in the veiled action. With no time to take cover, they stood in silence, and vulnerability, waiting for some unknown danger to come charging out of the trees. Andrea started to speak, to move away.

"Don't." McCormick said in a rough whisper, reining her in. Suddenly, two surly men stepped from behind a fragrant, wide-spread cedar tree. McCormick turned to face them, suppressing a snigger.

It wasn't their tattered, camouflage clothing, ill-fitting and dirty, that bothered the ex-warrior, or their sand-colored boots, sized wrong, and designed to be worn in the dry desert. No, it was their bodies, too flabby and out of shape to have ever served in the military. Figuring they'd picked up their desert wear at an Army surplus store, McCormick was put off by these slobs pretending to be military, dishonoring every real soldier who had ever worn the uniform.

The younger one wore a mask, but the older one wore a long, gray beard, scraggly and hanging longer than his jacket, revealing only his hardened eyes. McCormick could tell, by the smell, that these two jokers had been living in the woods for a very long time. Out of the side of his mouth, he wise-cracked to Andrea, "I sure as hell hope these aren't the wood nymphs you were talking about? They smell like putrefied gnomes that just fell off the rotten gourd truck."

"Shut up!" growled the old codger with the long beard, as he stepped forward, aiming the barrel of a sawed-off shotgun at McCormick's chest. "This is private property, he said through teeth, rotted and blackened by years of neglect, tobacco, and drug use. "Git the hell out of here … or you'll be made dead!" He shoved what remained of the shortened barrel into McCormick's ribs, pushing him backwards.

It's private property, all right, McCormick thought. *It's just not your private property.* Recognizing the men as amateurs, he shoved the gun barrel away before it could explode in his chest; but explode it did.

McCormick gaped at the hole and splintered bark on the tree behind him. Feigning a local, backwoods accent, he yelled with insulted incredulity, "F - - k … you almost kilt me!"

The masked man pulled a pistol from his belt, and quickly stepped forward. When McCormick didn't cower to the threat, he began to wave it in Andrea's face, in warning. She tried to bat it away, "Don't wave that thing in my…."

McCormick quickly stepped forward, cutting off her words. "Hey listen, man … me and my bitch … just lookin' for a roll in the pine needles … that's all," he assured them.

Andrea's face reddened from the perceived insult. She shot McCormick a look, shocked, and glowing hot. The long-bearded gunman lowered the shotgun and approached her, stroking her cheek and hair. Spitefully, he grabbed a hank of long, loose hair and jerked her head back for closer inspection. "This one's about as purdy as I've ever seen … how'd you ever git so purdy, little miss?" he asked, lecherously.

She gasped, turning her face away from his stinking breath. McCormick's breath still carried the scent of sweet, fruity wine; this man's breath smelled like rotting road-kill.

"Let her be," McCormick bellowed, anger widening his eyes.

The younger man stepped forward, drew his gun and, purposefully, placed it in the space between McCormick's eyes.

Without so much as a flinch or an eye bat, McCormick glared back.

Andrea gasped. "Matt … your gu…."

In an effort to distract from what Andrea was, unthinkingly, trying to say, McCormick looked his antagonist square in the eye. He pushed ominous words past clenched teeth, "Go ahead and do it … if you think you have the balls!"

The old gnome turned away from Andrea, and rushed to the aid of the younger man. Once again, he plunged the shortened gun barrel deep into

McCormick's ribcage, shoving him backwards. McCormick doubled over, pain riveting throughout his body. The old guy had hit a rib, for sure, still he groaned louder than necessary, and fell to the ground, deliberately playing the wimp. Luckily, the gunman had just missed discovering his shoulder holster.

Now, gnome the younger gave him a hard kick to the ribs, then stepped away.

As McCormick lay on the ground, writhing in pain—some of it real—he looked off into the woods, finding what he'd come searching for. A few yards left of a mammoth boulder, surrounded by burned-off undergrowth, and positioned with its tail in the air with its nose down, sat the downed plane; but the only thing McCormick could do, at this point, was memorize the tail numbers. He'd have to come back, without Andrea, to get a closer look.

Feigning pain, he staggered up on one knee, his shoulders slouching in the way of a broken man, his deportment so unnatural to McCormick that Andrea thought he must have practiced it in front of a mirror. He threw his hands in the air. "Okay ... okay ... we're goin' ... you can have the whole effin' forest for all I care ... this frigid bitch ain't worth gettin' kilt over." He gave the dumbstruck woman a hard shove in the direction of the trail, yelling back over his shoulder to the bumpkins in disgust, "There ain't nothin' in here, don'tcha know, but fuckin', stupid trees!" To Andrea, he whispered, hoarsely, "Go ... go ... go!"

They made a hasty retreat through the stupid trees.

Once they reached the bridge overlooking a vast expanse of valley, Andrea stopped, and whipped around, turning explosive eyes on the agent. With breath jagged from their hasty retreat, she screeched, apoplectically, "Looking for a roll in the pine needles ... not worth getting' kilt over .... frigid bitch ... how dare you, McCormick ... you almost got me raped!"

Rejecting her assumption, he shouted back, "No ... *you* almost got us killed!"

Andrea shot him a look bordering on hysterical.

"Just calm down," he cautioned. "These dope heads aren't conscious enough to pull off anything but their own stupidity; but you need to rearrange your priorities, lady. Lesson number one: when you're working with the underworld, life precedes honor ... got it?"

"I don't work with the underworld, "she hissed, indignantly.

McCormick moved closer, his eyes narrowing. "Lesson number two: if you can get a guy thinking about his penis, his mind will turn to mush."

She looked at him disparagingly. "Where did you get that bit of advice … from your visits to Orgy Island, or one of the graphic novels on your must-read, bucket list?"

"You know what I'm talking about," he said pithily, giving her a brusque, impatient look. "I couldn't let those strung out, schizophrenic zombies know I'm DEA; they would have killed us both in an instant. I was just trying to divert their attention away from me…."

Exasperation gushed out with her breath. "Well, aren't you a fine, self-serving son-of-a-bitch?"

He breathed out, disparagingly, through his nose, and shot her a chastening frown. Patting his holster, he gushed, "Well, duh … sweetheart … I was the self-serving, son-of-a-bitch packin' heat … the only thing you're packing is a righteous attitude … and hot, pent-up anger!"

She turned, and stomped ahead, leaving him standing alone with his lips pursed, and his hands planted, unyieldingly, on his hips. He groused to her back, "Aw … jeez … where's all this indignation coming from? With your hot body, I'm guessing you've been around more than your *fair share* of lascivious men." The agent wasn't merely being crass; he was fishing, using serious bait.

The silver bullet of seething outrage she shot in his direction could have "kilt" a man, he thought, facetiously; but it had just given him volumes of information: *hubby must not have been master of his own domain*. The corner of his mouth hitched up in a roguish grin. He followed.

This time, she didn't wait for him, but charged, ahead, across the swinging bridge. At last, she slowed, turned around, panting, heavily. "Matt, who are these people?"

Suddenly remembering that she was still recovering from being poisoned, he crossed the bridge, quickly closing the space between them. He brought them both to a halt, giving them time to breath. Seeing her tear-stained face, he thought, *somewhere along the line, this lady's heart has been broken—big time*. He sat on a downed tree trunk, stalling, and began to roll up his sleeves.

As he rolled the first cuff, Andrea stared at his newly exposed forearm, seeing there the dark, iniquitous tattoos she'd first observed in the Writer's

Block Lounge, a lifetime ago. Their existence had completely escaped her mind during lunch, as they'd chatted across the table. Believing the man to be blowing off her question, she asked louder, more pertinaciously, "Who are they?"

"It's a long story...." he said, checking the trail behind them. He turned the second cuff, raising his eyes to meet hers. "But since you're the frickin' story lady ... I'll tell you." He stood, and stepped away from the tree, ducking low-lying branches. "Fact is ... criminals plant illicit marijuana gardens every year on government property ... this one included. They're worth millions of dollars."

"I'm aware of that," she answered, her breathing quieting.

He wouldn't discuss the fact that they also used the forest as drop zones for killer drugs; nor would he tell her that they, most likely, worked for her husband.

He looked around, in surveillance, gently nudging her towards the trail. "Let's get out of here."

Once at the jeep, McCormick arched a brow, "Keys?" She flipped them across the hood.

He ordered the excited Tracker into the back seat, and they jumped in. He started the engine, and popped the clutch, tearing out with a screech of tires and a spray of gravel.

As he burned rubber, a look of pure joy came to his face. He laughed, full-heartedly, and glanced at her in askance, "My mother would skin me alive if she knew I drove like this."

"I didn't know psychotic robots had mothers," she said, snarkily.

Her comment brought an amused glint to McCormick's eye, and a chortle to his throat. "Mother ... believe it or not ... would appreciate that little zinger," he said, with amusement.

"Yeah ... I'll bet she thinks you're a *real* doll," she droned.

McCormick swallowed his response.

Once on the road, he offered, "We'll let'em think they've scared the living hell out of us."

"And for some reason, you think they didn't?" Andrea shuddered as she thought about what might have been, had the stupid goons actually shot McCormick!

He chuckled, lightly, before continuing to enlighten her. "These guys, Andi, are just amateurs … probably local boys … working for somebody a whole lot smarter and a whole lot meaner than they are … I'll get a team out here to clear'em out." He turned his head, studying the aggrieved woman. "Andi, you do know that I would never let anything happen to you?" He locked eyes with her as he laid his 9 mm Glock on the dashboard; then, expressly for her benefit, let his blade slide down his arm, and gently laid it next to his gun.

Andrea eyed the weapons; then turned her head away, soberly.

As he shifted gears, McCormick realized he had erred twice this afternoon. Once when he invited her to have lunch, and once when he brought her along; but what in the was an agent supposed to do when your boss gives you orders to investigate and protect. That's exactly what Chief Straker had done.

He continued, "It's too late in the year for a marijuana crop, so this has to be something else, something bigger." He wouldn't tell her about the downed plane. "Since our national culture has become so accepting of marijuana, the drug dealers have moved on to greener pastures. Cocaine's been around for a long while, but now heroin, fentanyl and all kinds of killer crap from South America and China are the big moneymakers."

Andrea nodded her head, in seriousness, "I'm aware of that."

Hearing the earnestness in her voice, McCormick turned his face to her, "Sounds crazier than that Greek myth stuff you were spouting, doesn't it?"

Her attentive eyes clung to his. He could tell she was hanging on to his every word, and after spending so much time alone, he was enjoying her company immensely—even with all the vitriolic shrapnel she shot his way. "We've got this particular bunch already tied to a money-laundering scheme. We're about ready to shut them down, along with the banking offic…."

Humph … mistake number three, he suddenly realized, remembering that Andrea wasn't just any woman, but Brantley Stone's wife. He clamped his mouth shut and backed off his words, becoming conspicuously quiet.

Perplexed by the man's sudden mood swing, Andrea let out a frustrated sigh—multiple personality, number 666, she thought to herself.

She looked at the brooding McCormick, and questioned, emphatically, "So what's wrong?"

McCormick—angry at Andrea for no other reason than being Stone's wife—snarled, "Nothing I can tell *you* about."

She squealed, "What have *I* done?"

He'd never intended to sound rude, but having no explanation, he began to brood.

As they rode the next several miles in silence, Andrea sulked, her ears burning with anger and confusion. After a while she began to follow the changes in the cloud formations. Like her tumultuous feelings, thunderheads loomed dark and heavy as they bore down from the sky, until, finally, the angry clouds burst open and rain poured down in sheets.

"It rains a lot here, doesn't it?" She addressed her question to the open air.

"It's usually snow by now," McCormick answered, not fully committed to the conversation.

There was another long silence, before he spoke again. Then, from out of nowhere, he offered, "I'm sure you're more than aware that the American Indians in the Southwest ate pine nuts for food."

Andrea answered, listlessly, "Right." *Was he trying to recapture their earlier camaraderie?*

Craving normal conversation, McCormick continued, knowledgably, "Actually, the pine tree is much older than the time of classical Greece ... it dates back to the age of the dinosaurs."

She didn't know that, but she said, "R-i-g-h-t," her voice dull. In her own dour moodiness, she gazed out the passenger window imagining mythological sky-riding gods. She droned, mindlessly, "And I know the truth about Kris Kringle, too; but do spare me the dirty details, will ya ... I enjoy a little mythos in my life!"

Suddenly, McCormick's foot hit the brakes, full force. Andrea's body lunged forward, then back, as the jeep fishtailed before coming to a halt sideways of the road. With brows knotted with untold alarm, he turned dark, fiery eyes on her.

"What?" She yelled, wild-eyed, her heart trying to thump its way out of her chest. Completely mystified by the man's actions, she chided herself for being stupid enough to climb into a vehicle, and ride into the woods with such a questionable character. Summoning her courage, she added, irascibly, "Didn't your mother explain all of that stuff to you ... before you went off to build your house of sticks?"

The look on McCormick's face was of a rougher nature than any she had ever seen there. For a long moment, the jeep sat idling, noisily, in the middle of the road. Finally, out of utter frustration, he banged a palm hard against the steering wheel, then sat in silence, thinking.

Andrea sat in silence, sulking.

At last he spoke, without so much as a glimpse in her direction. Trying to keep his voice under control, he said, emphatically, "Andi, you've made a lot of noise about whether or not you can trust *me*. It just so happens that trust is a matter of life or death for me, and very possibly for you ... now I've got a question for you."

Completely clueless, she heard herself saying, "Okay ... ask."

McCormick's jaw tensed; his eyes locked into hers.

"Are we ... or are we not ... playing on the same team?"

"Sure," she said, flippantly, and much too quickly, to McCormick's chagrin.

He asked, doggedly, "Sure what? Does that mean I can trust you ... explicitly?"

The intensity of his words alarmed her. Her answer came out soft and simple, "Yes."

Still not sure of her sincerity, he shot her a long, hot look, then threw the gears into neutral. He took his foot off the brake. They sat shoulder to shoulder, watching and listening to the wipers screech and swipe across the glass as rain hit the windshield like large pebbles. Soon their hot, heavy breaths fogged up the windows, making it impossible to see out. The silence within the claustrophobic jeep became deafening. Andrea could almost hear the wheels turning in the tormented man's head.

It was Andrea's gentle voice that finally broke the silence, "You know Matt ... I don't have a clue as to what's going on in your mind ... or in your life; and I know I haven't always shown you my better angels, but I'm not a raging maniac, either. I'm normally quite sane, and ... I like to think ... a really good person ... you can trust me."

Taking note of her use of the term *better angels*—a term used by recovering drug addicts—he let his eyes rest, momentarily, on her kissable lips. At last he blew out his breath, and let his shoulders fall back against the seat, seemingly satisfied with her answer. But he was utterly exhausted; whether from working undercover, from his injuries, or this beautiful, maniacal lady sitting beside him, he really didn't know. All he knew was that he had to find a way off this man-made cliff of disaster.

He leaned forward, and with the back of his hand, swiped the fog from the inside of the windshield. Andrea watched the move as if in slow motion, marking the time and the place. As he rubbed, he spoke, "I'll bet you didn't know that Pinocchio was made of pine, did you?"

"Pinocch…?" She stared at the man in disbelief, catching the mischievous glint in his eye. Suddenly, they both burst into hysterical guffaws of laughter.

Once the snickering and sniggering had run its course, she laid a gentle hand on the man's arm, where the tattoos came to an end. "Matt … I'm sorry … I don't understand what's got you so upset," she said, softly.

His gaze dropped to her fingertips, feeling the gentleness of her touch. When he raised his head and looked into her eyes, he found there nothing but genuine concern. Giving her a weak, apologetic smile, he laid his hand on her knee in a benign, peaceful gesture, but said nothing.

When, at last, he stomped the clutch and shifted gears, Andrea caught a glimpse of the agent's austere profile, as well as the distant, worried look that had crept back into his eyes.

No, she didn't understand him at all.

CHAPTER 30

Under the best of circumstances, Grandma Burns Road was only a rutted, unimproved, dirt access road that followed the creek bed to Andrea's cabin. As they began the assent up the treacherous mountain road, McCormick turned his full attention to his driving, and to the engine whining with stress.

He down-shifted, and suddenly, the jeep jolted and slipped sideways towards the creek, then stalled in the deep mud. He tried to drive forward. The back tires spun, exasperatingly. In haste, he turned, hooked his arm across the back of Andrea's seat, looking over his shoulder at the jeep's swerving rear axle. "Aw, hell," he groused, casting an enervated grin in her direction. "It's not even mud season."

From the rain-splattered passenger window, Andrea got a terrifying view of the murky waters rushing downstream. It was hard to believe that this angry, churning water was the same delightful little creek bed that had so charmed her on her hike into town.

Once more he downshifted, and hit the gas pedal. Still no luck, Matt quickly unclipped his seatbelt, and reached across her lap, grabbing his stocking cap from the glove box. He tugged it down over his ears, and jumped out to assess the damage. What he found was serious enough to quell the most stalwart of hearts—all four wheels were buried up to the axel in thick, dark mud!

Returning to the side of the jeep, he shouted through the open window. "Andi, this doesn't look good, but let's give it a try. Get behind the wheel," he directed over the swishing of the windshield wipers. "At my signal, hit the gas … give it all it's got—I'll push." A wry grin played across his lips, and his eyes met hers. "Just be sure you're not in reverse." As he yelled, a crack of lightning split the dark, tumultuous sky, followed by an earth-shattering clap of thunder, loud and low.

Andrea rolled her eyes, drolly, then quickly slipped behind the wheel. Through the rearview mirror she watched McCormick step behind the jeep. At his signal, she pushed her foot against the accelerator. The engine leaped and labored in agony, but made no progress. Again Matt yelled the signal. Andrea hit the gas pedal a second time. The tires began to spin and smoke. She gasped as she felt the rear of the jeep slide sideways towards the creek.

"Whoa!" a harried McCormick yelled, his finger cutting across his throat.

With mud splatters covering his face, McCormick walked to the driver's side of the jeep, pushing down his deep concern. He shouted above the storm's clatter. "This isn't working … it's going to take a tow truck and wench to pull it out."

A sober Andrea studied the man, as the rain pelted his head and face, washing away only a fraction of the splatters. Even in the pouring rain, his head in a stocking cap, and his face blackened with mud, Matt McCormick had the air of a gentleman. His back was straight, his demeanor poised. He looked comfortable in his own skin no matter where he was, or what he was doing. He had a rare kind of dignity.

Suddenly, the churning waters at the side of the jeep parted, and a huge bull moose raised its heavily-antlered head, and brayed, crudely, gutturally, into the air. In the back seat, Tracker began to dance and scratch persistently at the window. The beast stood up in the shoulder-high rapids, his hairy dewlap hanging and dripping water below his chin. Both Matt and Andrea watched as its huge form, dark and lumbering, wandered to the bank of the raging creek.

As the moose did a fast trot into the forest, they looked at each other, remembering the taunting moose joke she'd cracked at the post office earlier that day. Both, instantly, broke into laughter. Matt laughed the loudest, "Crazy twig-eater! He's been fattening up on aquatic plants at the bottom of the creek … helps him get through the frigid winters."

Suddenly, a fiery bolt of ear-piercing, lightning cracked and struck a nearby tree, splintering the limbs and trunk into a thousand tiny, glowing chards. Matt felt the electrically charged air, and saw the fear rise on Andrea's face as she tried to calm the whining Tracker. He could tell she'd never been this close to a lightning bolt—or maybe she had.

Whichever, he felt the urgency to get her out of the jeep. The wheels were just inches away from the cliff's edge, and the jeep had begun a slow, sideways slide. Any sudden jolt and Andrea, Tracker and the jeep would tumble hopelessly into the raging ravine.

In haste, he opened the driver's side door. "Hey Andi," he yelled, nodding towards the smoldering tree. "Don't let that little fireworks display worry you," he said. "That's just Thor, the god of thunder, quietly slipping out of this world and into another—must've dropped his damned, heavy hammer, though." His eyes danced, as he looked, encouragingly, at Andrea, offering her his hand. "Come on out here ... and enjoy life in the real."

"I've never seen anything like this," she admitted honestly, her face growing pale, her words getting lost in another low rumble.

Nor have I, thought McCormick, feigning calmness, while encouraging her to latch on to him.

As Andrea grabbed his hand, something began to gnaw at her subconscious—a noise. Somewhere in the distance she could hear a rumbling sound, a kind of muted roar. "What's that noise?"

Matt quickly cocked an ear and listened, immediately identifying the sound. "Flash flood!" he yelled over the roar of the raging waters. "We've got to get out of here...now! This whole area will be under water. We'll leave the jeep and walk to your cabin." His steely eyes locked into Andrea's. "Trust me enough to hoof it through the forest?" He felt an obligation to warn her. "It'll be dangerous." Again the sky exploded like fireworks on the Fourth of July.

She gave him a challenging look. "If a damned twig-eater can do it, I can do it!" she enthused, over the rush of water. She started to reach for the grocery bag, but stopped short, and grabbed instead, a couple of cans of dog food from the bag, and shoved them into her pockets. McCormick noticed her act of kindness towards the dog, but he also noticed the rocking of the jeep. Holding his breath, he forced his hand up her arm, and yanked her out, into ankle-deep mud. At the same time he yelled, "Tracker, let's go home!" An excited, whining Tracker bounded over Andrea's head, and immediately took off in the wrong direction.

A grievous look crossed McCormick's face, and he, instinctively, put his thumb and finger to his mouth, giving out a loud, shrill whistle, "This way fur-ball!" he yelled, waving his arm in the opposite direction. Andrea watched the action with bewilderment, looking first to McCormick then to Tracker, then back to McCormick who was already charging up the side of the cliff, his hand out-stretched, animatedly, towards her. Tracker quickly followed.

Continuous lightning lit up the dark, tumultuous sky. When at last they reached a safe height and distance, they stopped for a breather. The jeep began to squeak and squawk, behind them. Andrea turned just in time to watch it tumble into the rapidly rising water, hitting the foaming deluge with a loud clank and desolate groan, like a sinking ship at sea.

"My God!" she shrieked, her heart pounding wildly, "Your brother's hat!"

Stunned by her thoughtful nature, McCormick reached out, and pulled her to him, protectively burying her face in his chest. Rivulets of rain streamed down his mud-streaked face, obscuring the lone, hot drop trickling down from his lashes. "It's okay, Andi," he consoled, "he won't be needed it anytime soon."

With heads bent low to protect their faces from the cold, biting rain, the fed and the journalist trampled through the slushy, water-logged forest. Strong, sturdy trees bent like twigs in the face of the wind, their limbs swaying and screeching against each other in hair-raising, gooseflesh-boosting sounds, creepy and unworldly. Andrea sidled up closer to McCormick. Tracker flanked his other side. When a limb crackled loudly and broke from a tree, McCormick's arm, foot, body and soul shot out in front of the startled, wild-eyed woman as it crashed at their feet. He pulled her closer, and followed the creek bed upstream. After an hour of sludging through wild growth of wet foliage, their legs became sodden and heavy, and their uphill pace slowed, considerably. Andrea stopped in her tracks. "Matt, my coffee's worked its way through."

Instantly getting her delicately stated message, McCormick nodded, and turned his back, giving her privacy as she rounded a nearby shrub. Suddenly, the muddy earth beneath her feet, caved. She gave out a loud, startled cry as she slipped head-first, on her back, into the gorge. Terrified, she reached out with her foot, managing to wedge the toe of her boot under a tree root, just in the nick of time, preventing a further slide of her body, full-force, into the roaring, raging water.

"Matt!" she yelled, trying to get a look around. She glimpsed the muddy gorge, splashing and gurgling just below her head. She squeezed her eyes shut. "Matt, I'm in serious trouble here!" Her voice faded to a distressed whimper, "M-a-c."

McCormick tore off his hat and vest, running to the edge of the cliff. He looked straight down at Andrea, hanging, precariously, upside-down on the steep precipice, her head just above water level.

"Andi, don't look down, and whatever you do, don't move!" he ordered as he quickly braced himself against a scrub shrub.

"*Now* you tell me, G-man," she whined, trying not to feel dizzy.

Even as McCormick's mind worked out a way to save her, he had to shake his head in amusement. With her life on the line, and just inches away from drowning, Andrea still retained her strong sense of humor. *She's a survivor,* he thought, *and she would have made a good warrior—or a good warrior's wife.* With his feet wrapped around, and intentionally entangled in a shrub, and in danger of falling into the deep abyss, as well, McCormick lowered himself down the cliff, stretching out to his full body-length. He stretched out his hands, ready to grab hold of her legs, coming up just inches shy of being able to give her a firm hold. Even if he could reach her feet, he wouldn't be able to get them both back up the cliff—not with recovering gunshot wounds, but he had to get her off this cliff before they both passed out.

"Andi?" his voice rose in question. "How do you feel?"

Dizzy and fighting back impending nausea, Andrea answered in a weak, fraught voice, "With my fingers."

Just as she was about to retch up her orchard bread and free-range chicken, he asked, "Andi, do you know how to do a sit-up?"

"McCormick, if you ask me one more stupid question, I'm going to shoot you dead with your own gun!" she said in rapid-fire succession, while totally feigning anger.

Without giving her time to say another word, he continued. "Listen carefully … this'll be easy, if you choose to make it so." Rain pelted hard against his face and head. "When I grab your ankles, I want you to do a big strong sit-up, and thrust your upper body up from the waist … grab onto my head, my ears, anything … crawl onto my shoulders. Then grab my belt, put your feet into my armpits, like stirrups on a saddle, and crawl up the length of my body to safety. "Got it?"

"I think you've got me confused with your teenybopper girlfriend, McCormick!" she groused. Suddenly, the root loosened and she bounced down another couple of inches.

McCormick grimaced. If they didn't get this done STAT, as his mother would say, they never would. "You can do this, Andi," he yelled impatiently, his voice coarsening with concern, he reached down and grabbed hold of her hiking boots, all the while praying that she had laced them too tight to be pulled off. "On the count of three: one … two … three!"

With a tug, and a loud grunt, Andrea thrust her arms and upper torso forward and upward, grabbing McCormick around his head and neck. He gave her legs a slow boost up. In desperation, she grabbed a double-fisted handful of his shirt, popping the buttons loose from his belly, exposing a recent slow-healing bullet wound. Finally, she reached for the buckle of his thick, leather belt, and grabbed a hold as he slowly let go of her ankles.

When she reached for the hem of his jeans, she froze, awestricken— beneath the man's pants leg, laid a sheathed blade, strapped securely to the shin of a skin-colored, tatted-up, *prosthetic* leg!

McCormick has an artificial leg?

Feeling the immense heat emanating from the man's body, she sucked in quick gasps of breath, and then shouted impishly over her shoulder, "Hey, McCormick … is it good for you?"

Dangling, up-side-down, from the side of the cliff, and in immediate danger of falling into the gorge himself, a huge grin spread wide across the agent's reddened face as he struggled to bear up beneath both their weights.

None too soon, she reached up and grabbed hold of an over-hanging branch. He did a quick tailspin with his body, and she planted her foot firmly on his butt, and shoved off, finally pulling herself up. She collapsed onto the bank.

Seeing McCormick entangled in roots and vines, she pushed herself up from the safety of the mossy forest floor, and returned to the side of the cliff. The water was rising. She watched, in awe, as he used his hands to walk his way back up the side of the rock. When he finally looked up, she offered him a helping hand. He grabbed it; but not fully trusting her strength or stamina, he lunged forward, knocking her backwards, quickly finding himself facedown, in a most uncompromising position between the woman's legs.

To prevent his sliding backwards, Andrea grabbed him, wrapping her arms and legs around his torso. Like a first responder, he quickly slipped his hands beneath her shoulders, pushed up on his knees, lifting them both away from the danger of the cliff's crumbling edge.

Finally sensing safety, guffaws of relief, and laughter-smothered grouses shot from their mouths. For a brief moment, McCormick lay, gazing down into her mirthful lips, and shimmering, ocean-deep eyes; she into his dancing flecks of golden risibility—each seeing a flash of a kindred spirit in the other.

McCormick rose up on one elbow, blithely watching the rain pelt her face. He gave his head an astounded shake. "I have to flat-out tell ya," he said, breathing, heavily, "I've been chased by a lot of crazy, aggressive women," he teased through a wiseass grin, "but nothing has e-v-e-r come close to this!"

Choking back a laugh, Andrea immediately untangled her arms and legs, and shoved against his shoulders. "Get off me, Sleuthhound," she ordered, gruffly, a mirthful grin playing across her lips. McCormick took note of her amusement as he helped her off the ground.

Feeling extremely grateful that they had both survived the ordeal, unscathed, the jubilant Andrea, once again, stepped a little too close to the edge of the cliff. McCormick rudely jerked her to safety. "Lady," he groused in disbelief, as lightning flashed, and rain splashed across his face. "Something tells me you attract danger like flies to a pile of dung."

Her eyes flashed. "Aw ... I'll bet you say that to all the ewes."

His head dipped and he shot her a baiting, goading look. "I just saved your life ... you might consider using that acerbic mouth of yours to say thank you," he offered, helping her off the ground.

She leaned into her knees, and snuffled in a couple of deep breaths; she then straightened, lifted her sweater and wiped the mud from her face, exposing her taut midsection. "Thank you, Special Agent Matthew J. McCormick, for allowing me walk all over you."

She took a long, sober look at the man who had just rescued her, sizing him up. This guy was extremely well-trained and well-disciplined. She asked, seriously, "How'd you ever come up with a crazy stunt like that?"

With a playful flutter of the eyebrows, he offered in a suggestive, sexy drawl, "Well ... this isn't exactly my first cliff."

Andrea suppressed a laugh, but planted her hands on her hips. "Just answer the question, smartass."

McCormick grabbed his hat from the bushes, and slapped it across his upper thigh. In a deeper than normal voice, he answered, "Delta Force, ma'am—two tours in Afghanistan."

She remembered reading the nickname given to Delta Force: *Gang of Pirates.* Dead panning, she answered, "I should have known."

As they continued their hike through the deluge in silence, Andrea recalled the research she had once done on Delta Force: military, Army; created in the late '70's to combat what was happening in Iran. She remembered Delta Force consisted of small, autonomous teams with special skills for direct action, and unnoticed counter-terrorism. They were capable of conducting clandestine missions, including hostage rescues, and raids. She knew that the secretive, elite Special Education Group (SOG) of the CIA, and the DEA heavily recruited operators from Delta Force, because they were, simply put, this country's finest—of course that opinion was seriously contested by the Marines and Navy Seals. Whatever, she reasoned ... their competition kept them sharp and the country safe.

When, at last, they reached the porch of the cold, dark cabin, both were drenched to the bone. Andrea was exhausted from the ten-mile hike into town, as well as their little episode in the National Forest. Her harrowing ordeal of hanging, head-over-heels, over a rushing gorge had her completely discombobulated. She had been frightened of what Mother Nature had wrought.

McCormick, on the other hand, was more concerned about what the guiding source of nature was gearing up for, next. He reached the door first, but halted, waiting for her to produce a key.

"It's not locked," she offered, panting heavily.

As he twisted the doorknob, he glared back over his shoulder. "Start locking it," he said, gruffly, as though an order.

A look of obstinacy crossed her face, and he quickly added. "A black bear might try to get in ... they don't always hibernate, and when they get hungry, they start scavenging. ... one can get inside and screw the lid off a peanut butter jar before you can say scat." He saw the look of doubt on her face. "This area is full of them ... and they're always hungry." Studying the little bear carving on the door, McCormick grimaced before shoving it open—hungry, black bears were the least of his worries.

A sharp crack of lightning ripped through the evening sky, its bright bolt striking near the front of the cabin, lighting up the foyer. Grateful they hadn't tarried on the porch, Andrea fell to her knees and kissed the wooden planks with great ceremony; then she collapsed to her stomach and lay in an exhausted, rumpled heap. She made no effort to pull herself up, while McCormick stood holding the door open for Tracker. He, too, was bushed and relieved to be out of nature's fury; but he didn't feel as secure in their relative safety as Andrea. Even though he wished it different, there were things he had not yet shared with her—things he *could not* share with the wife of Brantley Stone.

CHAPTER 31

At last the whimpering, fainthearted dog came cannonballing through the open space, pulling up short at Andrea's form. He stood over her, sniffing, and vigorously shaking rainwater from his coat. She covered her head with her hands, but the excited dog, repeatedly and aggressively, tried to bat them away with his wet paws while snuffling and licking her face as she lay face-down on the floor.

McCormick breathed out a soft, amused chuckle as he pushed against the wind and blowing rain to shut the door. He admired her spunk; especially when he took into account everything she'd been through in the last few minutes, the last few months—the last few years.

"What is it with this animal?" she called from the floor, her words muffled by the wrestling. She went up on an elbow, ruffling the dog's throat, before pushing him away.

"He thinks you're secondary to his alpha male."

"Well, don't you all?" she teased, resting her chin on her hands, watching the dog sniff his way to the cold, dead fireplace. There, he let go of a sneeze and scratched at the oval hearthrug, before settling down. She groaned, "It's looking more and more like I've adopted a psycho dog."

McCormick chuckled. "I wouldn't go too hard on him." He thought, *Babe … you ain't seen nothin' yet.*

Andrea groaned, as she sat up, legs akimbo, looking at McCormick, dauntingly, through the darkness. Her head throbbed, and her legs felt as heavy as barbells, her feet as wide, and as webbed, as those of a duck. "Oh, Matt," she bewailed, unlacing one of her hiking boots, "I can't believe what just happened to your jeep?"

A lamentable chuckle shot out of the man. "Yeah, but one more can of dog food, and you and Tracker were going to be food for the fish."

"We were that close?"

"Y-e-a-h," he offered, his voice a serious, low growl, "you were."

"Yikes," she whispered in response to the danger they had faced. "And that gorge … did you get a good look at all that raging water?" She grunted, tugging hard on her boot, finally popping it off. She loosened the strings on the second boot.

McCormick took two quick steps forward. "Yeah, I saw it…." he said, bending down on one knee, quickly pulling the second boot off her foot, "but I'm pretty damned sure I got a better look at it than you did." He stood, and teasingly, tossed the boot back at her belly. Lightning flashed as she lay it aside and removed her heavy, but cute, pink socks, exposing long, straight toes, painted toenails, and slender ankles. McCormick quickly crossed to the fireplace.

"Where's your kerosene lantern?"

"Hum-m-m … I haven't come across a lantern," she offered, seeing his look of concern as his hand groped along the top of the mantle, knocking over a picture frame. He quickly set it back up. A devilish smirk flitted across her lips as she slipped her feet into a pair of fur-lined moccasins. "But I did pick up a beeswax candle at a quaint, little roadside shack," she deliberately baited.

In cover of darkness, McCormick rolled his eyes towards the ceiling. In a voice sounding the same concern as when he'd first opened the unlocked door, he advised, "Get one—yesterday."

She peeled off her sodden vest, hanging it on a peg in the mudroom, next to the kitchen door. "Ahhh, boy!" she grimaced, "This is gonna take days to dry out."

At last, she faced McCormick standing in front of the lifeless hearth. "Coffee, hot chocolate, or tea?" she asked.

Looking askance, he asked, "Got any orange juice?"

"Yeah, actually, I picked up a jug at the market; but it's gone out for a long, leisurely, swim," she answered, ruefully.

With lightning flashing in the windows behind him, McCormick's large frame turned and walked towards her in silhouette. "Then I'll take hot chocolate," he answered, shucking his vest. It had been two years since he'd sipped hot chocolate, and he needed the extra energy. "I don't suppose you have any marshmallows?" he teased, fully understanding her scant food supply.

"Are you kidding," she laughed. "Matt, I don't even have electricity, let alone amenities of any kind.

Andrea took his vest, and hung it next to hers in the mudroom, noticing the sizable difference, while McCormick went to the sink, washed his hands and splashed cold water on his muddy face. Unsuccessful in his mission to find a towel in the dark, he stepped away, and wiped his face on his shirtsleeve.

With amusement, he watched her feed her dog, upending the last of a small bag of food in the dark. He grimaced as the hungry dog began to chomp, noisily, on the hard nuggets, knowing that huskies had a quick digestive system and preferred a softer diet. He watched her wash her hands, dry them on a paper towel, then lift the lid off the teakettle. As she turned to fill it with water, a streak of sharp, white lightning flashed through the window over the sink, lighting up her face. She looked cold, and her cheeks were wind-blistered, but beautiful.

He returned to the hearth and started a small fire. The room instantly fluttered to life, and smoke began to roil. He flipped open the damper, then added larger logs. As a word of caution, he offered, "Andi, you'll need to close this damper when there's no fire … otherwise, all your heat will go up the chimney; and keep the safety screen in place … a draft coming down the chimney or through the kitchen door will scatter the ashes onto the floor."

How did he know? She wondered, as the fire lit up the room.

After quickly eyeing the cozy, little cabin with appreciation, McCormick's gaze returned to Andrea. When she stretched up to reach the top shelf of the cabinet for mugs, he quickly moved to her side.

"I'll get that," he said with light consternation. Andrea stepped aside as he easily reached the two mugs. She noticed his eyes glued to them as he handed them down.

She glimpsed one of the mugs, "Looks like somebody around here went to West Point … and these cabinets must have been built for the giant Cadet."

McCormick grimaced. "That's what I was just noticing."

As she washed the mugs, Matt took a better look around, his gaze stopping at the loveseat and winged-backed chair—a reading chair. "This really is a nice place … nicely furnished … did your husband do it?" He was fishing.

Andrea was not surprised by the question. "No … Shaun bought the cabin in early October, but I seriously doubt that he furnished it ... he had no interest in quality of life matters."

Uneasiness crept through McCormick's mind, pushing out the sweet tender thoughts he'd been nurturing these last hours. *How had Shaun gotten access to this cabin?*

His eyes dropped to the floor, as he remembered the *For Sale* sign that had been placed at the entrance to his driveway—the one he had pulled up by the stake, and discarded in disgust. Thanks to Stormy, he'd been apprised of the fact that his property had been put up for sale with everyone thinking him dead. McCormick was more than aware of how the criminal mind worked, taking advantage of property placed on the market and often left uninhabited, and untended. The question was: did Fitzgerald know who really owned this property? The answer to that question mattered—it mattered a lot.

"I only learned of it after Shaun's plane crash," Andrea offered, "just a couple of days ago ... actually."

In McCormick's head, a dull alarm sounded on two levels: how had Fitzgerald come by the property, and why didn't Andrea ever use the word death or died?

When he looked up, she was still talking. He studied her movements in the dim flicker of firelight. "When I decided to come up here, I thought I would be walking into a dilapidated, old fishing cabin with cobwebs hanging from the ceiling. Instead, I found this gorgeous place ... virtually spotless. There are jars of food, and some canned goods over there." She pointed to the cupboard behind the dog bowls. "The peanut butter's almost past the expiration date. The only thing I've found neglected is the wood pile."

Matt walked to the cupboard and pushed both Tracker and his bowls to the side. He opened the small wooden door and took out a can of beef stew. Carrying it to the firelight, he checked the expiration date. It was a relatively new can. Covering his nosiness, he held up the can and said, "This is still safe to eat."

With trepidation building in his mind, the agent asked, "So this was Shaun's cabin ... not yours ... did he come here often?" McCormick wanted to know more about Shaun Fitzgerald, both from an agent's point of view, as well as a man's.

Why so many questions, Andrea thought, feeling annoyed. She turned to speak to the tall, shadowy figure in sharper tones. "Hey, Matt, could you please lay off the interrogation stuff? I've been in Little Bear Cabin for less than twenty-four hours, and I've only known about it for just over two days ... that's the full extent of my knowledge...." Her voice rose with frustration, "There could be bats in the belfry, bodies under the floorboards, or women in the lake, for all I know ... and as for Shaun ... he traveled all the time. I don't have a clue as to where he went, or when ... or why!"

McCormick stiffened, not liking the images she was projecting onto the property; and as far as Fitzgerald's travels, he knew the exact route, as well as his reasons—and he also knew that Andrea wasn't being completely forthcoming with him. A sense of foreboding darkened his demeanor.

Andrea felt the atmosphere grow tense. She sweetened her tone. "Matt, I honestly don't understand why he bought a place like this—your guess is as good as mine." She offered, "Truth is, Shaun had a fear of heights ... he struggled with flying, and as far as I know, he'd never been to the mountains." Her thought-filled eyes dropped to her hands.

McCormick looked out the rain-streaked window, his brows knotting at what he knew to be a false statement. He recalled the birthday message her husband had written in her book of Indian poetry: *'Soon I will walk the trail ... I'll be with you when it seems that I am not; and when I am not, it will seem as though I am.'*

"Maybe he had a premonition...." he said; but he thought, *or he had a plan.*

Trying to cover his rankled feelings, but still pushing, McCormick asked, "Do you have a deed to the property?"

Andrea considered his rancorous tone, but bit her tongue, carefully measuring out the cocoa mix. "Sure." She popped the lid on the container, and put it back in the cabinet before answering, further. "I found it in the dark of night ... lying out in the open on Shaun's desk." She slammed the cabinet door shut with a loud, unnecessary thud. "I locked it in the company vault."

Again, McCormick grimaced, as he realized the implication of her actions, and what it meant for him. He was determined to look at that deed, certain that he was being set up, with her being used as bait; but the big question was: *did Andrea know about it?* Looking for reasons to hang around, he spoke up quickly. "Do you have a plan for restocking the woodpile?"

She sighed audibly. McCormick really was on a mission, she realized.

"Well, yes. I made a couple of calls before I went to the post office this morning. I got the name of a local man ... John Donahue. Unfortunately, when I called his office I was told he was in Burlington, attending some kind of sheriff's convention."

McCormick pulled down a frown, mumbling something unintelligible. "Andi, be careful around that guy." That's what he said. What he wanted to say was that John Donahue was a dishonest scoundrel with a badge, and had never developed anything above his gun belt ... his sister could attest to that fact. The thought of Andrea meeting up with this guy was mind-blowing.

McCormick's relationship with Sheriff John Donahue had been contentious for years. His mind seared with memories of the guy from his high school football days. The wide receiver had been caught taking huge bribes from opposing team members, and then betting against his home team. To insure the opposing team's win, he would deliberately fumble the dead-on passes McCormick threw to him during a game. He said, "Andi ... you've probably met some of these redneck, mountain boys. Trust me ... you don't want that one up here."

"Thanks for the heads-up," she answered gratefully, not wanting to go further into that particular discussion—she was already quite wary of mountain boys. "But, I don't think there's anyone else in the village to help me. If that's the case, I'll have to go back to Forrest Hills ... I can't live without heat."

The conversation had turned negative and Andrea was beginning to feel chilled and edgy as she poured hot water into mugs. Matt picked up on her fragile mood and leaned his elbows congenially onto the countertop oasis, stirring the chocolate powder. "Why don't you let me worry about restocking your firewood," he offered in a caring, neighborly way. "You're not ready to go back home yet, are you?"

"No ... not by a long shot ... I just got here," she said, aware that, earlier McCormick had been of a different opinion, as had she.

"Then it's a done deal, "McCormick said, grinning in a neighborly way, deliberately ending the discussion on an upbeat note. *Investigate and protect,* he thought, sardonically. He was chomping at the bit to get a look at that deed, but if she went back home, it would be increasingly difficult to protect her. Besides, he was enjoying having her here in familiar territory, and he was more than happy to be home, on any terms, after two long years away. He would play along with their little game—for a while.

269

CHAPTER 32

McCormick grabbed the steaming hot mugs, put them on a tray, and carried it to the table at fireside. Andrea graciously offered her guest the chair nearest the heat. McCormick, stifling his amusement at the hospitable, yet farcical, vignette being played out, made himself very much at home. She leaned forward, handing him a mug, and a conspiratorial wink. "We'll just pretend we have marshmallows," she whispered before dropping to the hearth rug. In weariness, they sat in peaceful silence, sipping their drinks and letting their aching muscles soak up the heat. Tracker stretched out, well-fed and lazy, at their feet.

For the first time since entering the cabin, Andrea noticed Matt's mud-splattered boots and wet pant legs. She jumped up. "You know, Matt, we were both soaking wet the first time we met, but we don't have to stay that way forever."

Something in her words stirred a feeling of de 'jay vu within McCormick.

She grabbed the tray, heading for the kitchen. "Please take off your boots and get comfortable." From behind the kitchen island, she watched as he pulled off the first boot, revealing a durable, hiking sock, black and gray, of a style made by a local manufacturer—and accented by a Beretta tucked into an ankle holster. She breathed out a droll, but silent, sigh of relief.

Aware that he was being scrutinized, and feeling a bit conspicuous, he said, "You better get out of your own wet clothes … you, sure as hell, don't need a case of hypothermia."

"Don't worry," she called over her shoulder as she turned the gas on under the teakettle. "I'm in great shape," she lied.

Matt's head quickly swiveled towards the fire, hiding his arched brow, and nurturing a roguish grin. He tugged off his second boot and set them together, next to the fire.

Andrea prepared a plate of fresh fruit and cheese, then quickly disappeared to the loft. Without ceremony, she pulled the cold, wet denim down over her shivering, thighs. Truth was, she was chilled to the bone, but she didn't dare worry McCormick. He had been through enough for one day. She actually felt concern for the man. She slipped into a pair of old, IU sweats, souvenirs from her college days. Shivering in the cold loft, she grabbed the quilt off the bed, eager to return to the warmth of the fire.

At the top of the stair railing, she paused, taking in the whole of the hearth scene. Suddenly, her heart swelled. It wasn't the charming little cabin, the scenic lake, or the silhouetted, hazy mountain peaks just outside her window that fed her appreciativeness; nor was it the burning logs in the cozy, native stone fireplace, casting lively shadows upon the walls, and bathing the room in a soft, golden glow. No, what filled her heart, making it feel ready to burst was the man sitting by the fire, his back bent forward at his slender waist, elbows on knees, gazing pensively into the flickering fire. She found it strange, but everything in the cabin seemed to compliment this man's persona; and every log and stick of furniture seemed to do him justice as he made himself at home. His mere presence filled the cabin.

He's an enigma, she thought. In just one day, he had brought her to the heights and depths of her emotions; snatched her from death, and a deep, watery grave; thrust her into the arms of gun-toting thugs, only to save her, making her feel safe, while healing her self-doubt; and he'd literally walked off with her dog. And then, in the middle of it all, he had lifted the veil, and revealed himself to be the benefactor of her all-time most precious birthday gift: the most sensuous kiss she could ever imagine possible.

She sucked in a deep, wistful breath, having no clue as to what was in her future, or even if she had a future; but McCormick was helping to raise her expectations. She would count herself lucky to have someone as fine as Matthew McCormick in it—the man seemed larger than life.

In the flickering firelight, his dark eyes, chiseled jawline, and rugged demeanor appeared softened by the dancing flames, giving him a more youthful look. Seeing him in that light caused something to stir deep inside of her. She stood in silence a moment longer, studying the man, watching him casually drop his hand over the side of the chair arm, to caress Tracker behind the ears in a most endearing way. It was touching, extremely touching, actually. A wistful smile crossed her lips.

She appeared, unsmiling, beside McCormick's chair. He lifted his weary gaze, askance. Trying for a heart-felt whisper, she said, "Thanks for saving my life." But her weathered words came out in a raspy croak.

The stone-faced, McCormick searched the depths of her eyes, holding her gaze for a long moment in serious contemplation. Suddenly his eyes flashed like lightning. "Which time?" he asked in a low, husky whisper, his mischievous, wry grin begging to be set free.

Striving to withstand the onslaught of this guy's understated charm, Andrea quickly thrust the quilt into his lap. "Take this," she offered. "Get out of those wet clothes and wrap this around you … it's all I have to offer," she said, apologetically, as she turned to walk away.

Hesitating for a beat, and taking full account of everything the woman had to offer, McCormick looked away.

Sensing his reluctance, she turned, and quickly set about correcting an, earlier, gross exaggeration. "Hey, smartass … just for the record … I have no intention of adding you to my wanton list of many men. You can sit around in soggy clothes all night watching all your metal turn to ferric oxide; or you can change in the loft … whatever yanks your rusty chain," she chortled, dismissively.

McCormick's first response came from his manly man, *This woman is entertaining as hell,* he thought. Then uneasiness followed his snigger, and his breathing stopped mid-breath—she had just invited him to stay the night. *They're using her as bait—and I'm swallowing the whole frickin, wiggly worm,* he thought with no small amount of chagrin.

More than eager to get out of his wet jeans, he accepted her offer, and mounted the steps, two at a time. An adoring Tracker followed, nipping at the frayed threads of his wet jeans. Andrea watched them tromp up the steps together, shaking her head in befuddlement at their instant bonding. It took a while in coming, but, at last, an amused grin claimed her mouth.

McCormick, finally, descended the steps, still wearing his ripped shirt, with his shoulder holster tucked neatly in place, and carrying both pairs of wet jeans, his and hers; but she gawked, incredulously at the something wrapped around the lower part of his body and between the man's legs, resembling a ghostly kilt. The whole thing was fastened securely in front by complicated knots.

Andrea identified the sheet as one she'd never seen before—she had no sheets. Her lips pursed, and she asked, "Where did you get that?"

McCormick's grin widened, "I stumbled onto a hidden linen closet built into the loft wall."

She gave him a dismissive, improbable stare. "Yeah … right." She asked, "Where'd you learn to tie knots like that?"

His eyes bounced off handiwork he'd learned as a kid; but remembering his military training, he thought, *these things are nothing … you should see what I can do underwater with my hands tied together behind my back while someone tries to end my life.* He said, "These are here in case you get frisky, again … like you did at the Writer's Block Lounge … and then again this afternoon."

Her eyes dropped to his holster. She sniped, "What are you planning to shoot tonight … raindrops?"

He grinned, handing her the musty-smelling quilt. "And whiskers on kittens," he teased, trying to lighten the mood.

She sank to the floor, leaning lethargically against the love seat while he shook out both pairs of jeans just inches away from her. Hanging them near the fire, he couldn't help but take notice of her hair, mostly dried and shining, lustrously, in the flickering firelight. She looked frazzled, but there was new life in her eyes, and her cheeks glowed rosy from the wind, rain, and the exertion of their demanding afternoon. He sucked in his breath, too aware of the new softness she wore demurely over her entire being. He wished, like everything, that he'd met Andrea under different circumstances.

When he returned to the chair, he grabbed his mug, and lifted a more controlled gaze towards the woman. In a gesture quickly becoming familiar, McCormick raised the mug into the air. "A toast," he offered. Grinning, she raised hers to meet his. "To stormy nights, cozy fires, and excellent conversation with one of the most beautiful, intriguing—strong-headed, foul-mouthed, dangerously bitchy women I have ever met."

Andrea laughed, but had no rebuttal to his teasing comment. Still chafing from his crude accusation in the forest, she shot him a derisive glare, and turned the disparaging comment back on him. She taunted, "Women … huh? I'll bet *you've* had more than *your* fair share."

Surprise etched across his face, not expecting the conversation to flow in his direction. "Not as many as you might think," he added quickly, suddenly sober.

Most of the women he'd met in the last two years, either talked incessantly about themselves, were hyper-sensitive or were into drugs or other women.

Andrea's eyes held a quizzical look as she seized the made-to-order opportunity. She stood up and grabbed a small tape recorder off the mantel. "Hey G-man ... mind if I ask you some questions? I'm thinking about writing a story about guys like you. You know ... hero or no hero ... there's always a story." She held up the battery-operated recorder for his inspection.

McCormick lowered his eyes. A feeling of trepidation crept over him. A very short time ago, he had dangled, precariously, by his bloody fingertips from a slimy precipice, while dodging bullets from a next-generation rifle in the hands of this woman's husband, but he agreed to the interview. He gave her fair warning, "Ask what you want, but I may not answer every question."

"Fair enough," she said, shooting him a bold, competitive look. Menacingly, she held his gaze as she flipped on the recorder.

When opportunity knocks, McCormick thought, watching her lay the recorder on the table beside his chair, and feeling rather chuffed with the opportunity to do some fact gathering of his own. "Do you write for any other publishing entities other than the *News?"* he asked, nonchalantly.

Feeling too exhausted to go into the details, she answered, "Uh ... no."

McCormick's gaze dropped to his nails. *Uh ... wrong answer,* he thought.

Assuming her demeanor as a professional journalist, Andrea asked, "Special Agent Matthew McCormick ... what were you like as a kid?"

He smirked at the featherweight question, "Smart-assed and too wild ... according to my mother."

Giving him an impish grin, she taunted, "So you haven't changed at all."

"Not one bit." He grinned, wryly.

She tilted her head to the side, studying him for a moment. "That stunt you pulled ... getting me off the cliff ... how were you able to do that?"

He sniggered, "Practice ... lots and lots of practice." He saw the question in her eyes, and added, "When you practice something often enough ... it becomes second nature."

"So you've done a lot of that kind of thing?"

"My fair share." The corner of his mouth hiked up, but he let the subject drop.

Suddenly feeling invigorated by his modesty, she looked at him straight-on, and asked, "So Sherlock, what exactly does it mean when just one corner of your mouth curls up?"

He shot her a dubious look, and another sample of the wry grin she'd referenced. "It means I'm having two or more conflicting thoughts, simultaneously. One is honorable … but there's a good chance the other one comes from a much baser nature."

She sat staring at him for a long moment. "So you're a baser kind of guy?"

He tactfully turned his eyes away. "Sometimes," he grunted.

She grabbed his mug and tossed an over-the-shoulder glance, audacious and unintentionally sexy, in his direction. Mischievousness played across her lips. "Yeah, that's just what I thought—multiple personalities."

McCormick's hands shot up in protest, but fell futilely to his side. Had it been anyone other than his enemy's wife asking, he might have answered more honestly—he might have told her that he'd been trained to go deeper, to have baser thoughts, to think like the enemy. Still, she'd nailed him. He shot her a sample of his abashed grin.

Ok, she thought, victoriously, as she hastily refilled his mug. *She'd disarmed him; now on to the more serious stuff.* She delivered the mug back into his hands, and dropped, cross-legged, to the floor, continuing her questioning from the hearth rug. "McCormick, I'm aware that, like you, an increasing number of government agents come from a military background. After putting your life on the line on the battlefield for your country, why come home and continue to put yourself in harm's way?" Why continue to risk your life?" She raised her gaze for an additional comment. "Mothers want to know."

McCormick was surprised by the depth of the question. He shook his head, and shot from the hip. "I don't know … I suppose all the usual things: duty, honor … love of country … love of family…." He shot her a wide grin, and his eyes danced, tauntingly. "Isn't that what they all say?"

Austerity settled on his face as he searched for an appropriate answer. Truth was, he hadn't given it much thought, as of late. The simple act of staying alive had taken most of his thought process. When her probing eyes met his, certainty preceded his words. "Being in the military changed my perspective on a lot of issues. I've heard it said that we're trained to kill bad guys and break things, but all I'm after is a safer world for the people I love.

Somebody's got to fight the battles...." His eyes burrowed into hers, "it might as well be me."

"Is it worth the danger, the risk ... the sacrifice?"

McCormick's mind quickly streamed over the long list of lives he'd saved both at home and abroad. "Hell yes," he answered, forcefully.

She nodded her understanding. "But don't you ever experience fear?"

"Yeah, sure ... but fear is just a state of mind ... you have to get beyond that ... to the other side of fear." Their eyes locked, and he held her gaze, trying to assess her depth meter. He slid forward in his chair, and leaned into his thighs. With the clear preciseness of a storyteller, he began: *"Fate whispered to the soldier, 'You cannot withstand this coming storm.' And the warrior whispered back...."*

An excited Andrea suddenly rose to her knees and instantaneously came back at him with precision and gravitas matching his own, *"I am the storm!"*

In unison, they called out the author whose words they'd quoted, "Nelson Demille!" she said.

"Brad Thor!" he said. Both being right, they laughingly smacked hands in a rapid, high-five gesture.

McCormick grinned with satisfaction—she got it.

Andrea plopped back down and added, "So you like the danger?"

He lifted his brows, playfully. "I like the adrenaline rush I get when I stop some lowlife from destroying decent, hardworking people's lives." A haunted look came to his eyes. "Sometimes adrenaline, brought on by fear, is the only thing we have working for us."

Seeing her surprised reaction, he offered, "The job's become a big challenge, requiring constant training. Andi, we have enemies on multiple fronts, all growing in technology and sophistication ... and the rules keep changing." He paused before continuing. "Every time I strap on a gun ... I'm chancing, not only my life on that day, but possibly my life for the next twenty years, or so."

Her eyebrows bunched, "Are you talking about going to jail for shooting the wrong person?"

"Nah ... I'm talking about having a split second to make the right decision, and follow through with the right action, while weapons of every make, model and caliber are being shot at my ass."

Andrea stared at him in silence—and awe.

McCormick addressed the silence. "These days, you not only have to be faster than a speeding bullet, as the saying goes ... but you also have to know how to dodge a barrage of speeding bullets ... and if you're gonna fight crime today, you better have the physical fitness and training of a soldier, the legal knowledge and tenacity of a lawyer ... and the intel capability of a rapid-fire super computer."

"Yeah, I've been reading about the advances the military's making in turning humans into computers."

"Next Generation Cyborg Soldiers," McCormick offered. "They connect computer technology to the human brain to facilitate data delivery ... use the human skeletal system as sound conduits."

Andrea shook her head and winced, "Sorry ... I just haven't wrapped by mind around that one yet."

"It's the future," he offered, dropping the subject.

Andrea quickly organized her thoughts. She asked, "What kind of person goes into your line of work?"

A savvy expression settled in his eyes, but he held his glib tongue, as he seriously searched for the best answer to her question, knowing his words would most likely end up in quotes in one of her articles. Finally, "The job requires a tough-minded, self-disciplined son-of-a-bitch."

Surprise flickered across Andrea's face.

"I'm just being honest here," he assured her. "Whether he's military or law enforcement, he has to be made of strong fiber, have the right training, and the right skill set...."

He paused and ran a hand across his mouth and chin, "But ... I'll level with you ... it's also just as important to have a tough-minded, self-reliant partner at home to normalize life ... someone who understands, and respects, and strongly supports the kind of work you do ... whether you're at home or away on a mission. It's crucial to have someone capable of maintaining her own individuality and autonomy while he's away, and still love and respect the SOB when he comes marching home."

"Is that hard to come by?" she asked, genuinely interested.

A gloomy pall settled over McCormick. "Damned hard ... almost impossible," he answered, his mind flashing back to his Taskforce days. He remembered the high rate of divorce, the broken families ... the suicides, and attempted suicides caused by the stress of missions, too long, too hard, and too many. "You need someone who can understand, accept and be able to handle your darker side ... especially coming off a mission."

The experienced journalists didn't miss a beat. "Do *you* have someone like that at home?"

Andrea held her breath, watching the man's face turn to stone, before a slow ruefulness cut across his jawline. A pregnant pause precluded his answer. His voice lowered an octave.

"No."

Her gaze dropped to his left hand. She'd never seen a ring on his finger, and he was extremely closed mouth, keeping details of his private life close to the vest. But she got it. This gorgeous, hunk of man, obviously, had been seriously wounded; not by a weapon of war, but by a woman. She wondered what sorrows lay hidden there, what secrets—*McCormick definitely had secrets,* she thought.

"Kids?" The standard question flew out of her mouth as though winged, surprising, embarrassing Andrea.

McCormick's lips pursed and the lines around his mouth deepened; but soon firelight and risibility shined from his eyes. "None ... that I know about," he answered, audaciously.

A flash of suppressed jealousy, hot and wicked, leapt inside of Andrea. She quickly turned her head away, and shifted uncomfortably on the rug. She decided not to push on that front. She would, instead, redirect her questioning. What difference did it make to her if he was married, or had kids—or lovers?

"The money's pretty good ... isn't it?" She asked quietly, with nonchalance.

"It's not about the money...." he said, decisively, "but all about making a difference." His last words came out as a mere whisper.

She considered his answer, and popped a plump, purple grape into her mouth, studying her intriguing visitor. "Hey, Mac...." she said at last, taking time to chew, and swallow. "I've been wondering something." Now she scratched her neck and looked at him, straight on. "What's up with all the different hairstyles? Every time I see you, you look different ... what's up with that ... is your mother a hairdresser?"

Taking note of yet another reference to his mother, McCormick's amused chortle rose from deep within his chest. He took a slow swig from his mug before answering. "It's camouflage," he said, simply. "I don't want to be easily recognizable, so I'm constantly changing my look ... trying to blend in with the surrounding environment and culture." Playing on words from their creek side adventure, he wisecracked, "Why don't we just say ... that Thor isn't the only one slipping in and out of different worlds, these days." He shot her a cagey wink.

Instantly getting the joke, Andrea's face lit up, and she laughed unguardedly, appreciating his ability to use humor and quick wit to turn a phrase.

"Makes sense," she said, satisfied with his answer. "Is that also the reason you wear that brand of distressed jeans with bling on all the pockets?" He winced at the word bling. She nodded towards his pair of worn, but pricy jeans drying by the fire. With sober eyes fixed on the agent, she leaned towards him, and asked, in all seriousness, "What exactly are they camouflaging?"

Blindsided by her jaw-dropping question, his head snapped back. Raucous, but good-natured laughter spewed from his throat. He leaned forward and shot the inquisitive journalist a derisive, squinty-eyed glare. "Truth is, sweetheart ... I'm just trying to cover my ass ... any way I can," he answered, irreverently.

Andrea shot back with an irrepressible grin. "So ... in which country did your get that badass tan?"

McCormick's head dropped back, and he laughed. "Not for publication," he answered, getting a firsthand look at the dynamic, badass journalist Rudd had talked about. He had to admit that Ms. Daye was a good interviewer. She knew all the right buttons to push, but he wouldn't tell her that the expensive bling, as she called it, were actually called brads, and their purpose, hopefully, was to help him blend in with the Mexican and South American drug culture which had rapidly invaded the country. On a personal level, he hated the bling, but somewhere in the back of his mind, he had halfway hoped they might deflect a bullet or two along the way; but why was she so interested in what he wore on his ass?

Now Andrea eyed the wild, dark tattoos running from his ankles on both legs, all the way up—she suddenly realized—to the back of his neck. Undeterred, the reporter nodded towards his prosthetic leg, instead, and asked, bluntly. "Did you get that in Afghanistan?"

Having anticipated her next question, McCormick looked down at his legs, his eyes still filled with laughter; his face crinkled with humor at how far sideways this interview had gone. He asked, "Are you referring to the leg, the tats, or the blades?"

"The leg," she clarified, suddenly disconcerted by the audacity of her own bold question. She turned her eyes away, feeling embarrassed, not wanting to be rude.

McCormick sucked in his breath. He gave his head a slight shake to the side, his eyes growing serious. "Nah ... I returned from duty, hale and hardy ... with full body intact," his voice dropped to his chest, "and very gratefully so, I might add." Sensing the earnestness of her question, he continued in a softer tone. "I got caught...." Suddenly, finding his emotions impossible to swallow, his voice stalled, leaving his words to hang in the air as the whole ordeal came back to him in vivid detail. Andrea sat, expressionless, waiting.

At last, the words slowly rolled off his tongue. "I got caught ... in a drug dealer's submachine gun spray ... just outside of Ciudad Juarez, Mexico."

Surprise flooded her mind and heart. "Bummer," she said with true feelings, catching the quick, contemptuous baser look, cold and lethal, that instantaneously marched across a face already reddened by windburn. She recognized the area he spoke of as one of the most dangerous places in the world.

McCormick decided to stop with that simple explanation. He couldn't, and wouldn't, tell her that while he had lain in a pool of his own blood and shattered bones, his older brother had lay before him, riddled by bullets—dying; nor would he tell her how he'd buried him in a dry, shallow grave of impermanence under the hot, Mexican sun. As for the ugly tattoos, they would eventually wear away—a fact she need not know.

A crack of lightning suddenly shattered the quiet atmosphere. Deafening rolls of thunder shook the ground, and windows began to rattle, explosively, unnerving the journalist. *Drug dealers ... submachine gun* spray ... *Ciudad Juarez, Mexico,"* she thought, dropping her eyes, and taking a sip of a drink gone to scum. Now her gaze raked over his blades and tattoos. Not exactly MS13, but the tats did resemble those of Shaun's friends—the ones he had insisted on bringing home with him—extremely dark with wild, bold colors, and foreboding symbols of death. A premonitory thought surfaced: it was dark, and they were alone in the middle of nowhere—shouldn't she be afraid of this man? An icy shudder travelled through her body.

McCormick noticed the slight tremor to Andrea's hands. Was she frightened by the lightning, or had he just scared the living hell out of her? He rose, stepped to the hearth, and stoked the fire in silence.

She studied the man's, otherwise, august form. Other than wearing gross, indelible marks, toting an arsenal of lethal weapons strapped to his body, and having multiple personalities, this man seemed like a genuine, squared-away dude—most of the time. She loved his realness, his brand of humor—humor gleaned from truth and knowledge. At times, when he looked at her, a golden flicker of gentleness settled in his eyes—a look so warm as to burn a hole clear through her heart. She threw off the uneasiness.

McCormick turned, and shot her an apologetic grin.

There it is again, she thought. Struck by a sudden feeling of light-headedness, and fully understanding the cause, she fought to cover up her physical attraction, quickly asking, "So … you were in Delta Force?" *Yet another reason to feel alarmed,* she thought as the question trickled from her lips.

He gave her a quick noncommittal nod. "Yeah … for a short while…." he said, modestly, "Before I became a Navy Seal."

Navy Seal: sea, air and land, Navy maritime … special operations forces—a very elite group of warriors. She leveled a skeptical gaze at him, not sure if she believed his claim. She laughed, and with nonchalance, recited the Seal slogan she'd read in Mark Greaney's **Gray Man** series, "Stay low, go first, kill first, die last…."

He gave her an amused head nod, but said nothing.

Playing devil's advocate, Andrea challenged, "Matt, I've often wondered … what makes a soldier, or someone in law enforcement different from … any deranged killer?"

McCormick's pleasant demeanor quickly faded, to be replaced by a hot, flinty-eyed stare. She felt scorched by this different kind of heat, and with rare timidity, froze, immediately regretting the question.

When at last he spoke, the clarity of his reasoned response surprised her. "That's a good question … I'm glad you asked. The one thing separating a soldier or a law enforcement officer from a killer … deranged, or otherwise … is the reason for the kill." He raised his mug, as though to drink.

Andrea hastily shrugged off his answer. Her eyes flashed. "Soccer moms don't want to read about killing…."

McCormick's head shot up, wondering which subject bothered her the most: killing or soccer moms. Leaning forward, he lopped off her sentence. "Soccer moms are a valuable, national asset ... but they don't put their lives on the line for their country," he said, facetiously pushing his words out with his breath.

He stood up. "Andi ... we don't deliberately set out, gun in hand, to kill someone ... we fight to protect the lives of our citizens...." He started to pace. "We have serious enemies ... both in this country and abroad ... all on a mission to destroy our people, and our whole way of life ... and that includes Mom, and every kid on the soccer field. This war is being fought, not with bullets, but with division and drugs. They're poisoning our kids, in hopes of destroying our country ... our culture. In a phrase, they're selling death ... death in a plastic bag." He heard the gasp, and saw the uptick to her chin.

Andrea's ears flamed—she'd just been schooled! *So why couldn't she wipe the silly grin off her face?*

She dropped the professional façade, and her voice softened. Absent the driven reporter, she asked, "Matt ... were you ... you seem rather cavalier about your leg ... weren't you totally devastated by the loss?"

Sensing her sincerity, his head dipped, and his stomach clenched. Since the tragedy, no one had dared ask such a bold, personal question of him—to get that close. He dropped back into his seat and spoke words of heartfelt honesty, words he'd never spoken to another living soul. "Of course ... I try to make good use of whatever I've got ... but, Andi, the damnedest thing is...." he rubbed a hard hand across his mouth, "I still feel responsible for the loss." Seeing her questioning eye, he added, "towards my foot ... my leg ... even my toes." He sucked in a deep breath, letting it out with a shake of the head, and a rueful snigger. "A good soldier always takes care of his feet."

Andrea sat, stunned by his answer. This guy actually felt guilt for losing the limb entrusted to him; entrusted to him by whom ... his god ... his mother? As they sat in the deadened silence of the moment, a huge chunk of Andrea's heart melted away.

When he turned to stoke the fire, her eyes followed his every move. She studied his broad shoulders, and straight back. She eyed his prosthetic as he laid a log on the fire, replaced the screen, and returned the poker to the rack as though having done it a million times. The only *for sure* thing she knew about this guy was that he was, hands down, the most charming, charismatic, sincere man she'd ever met. Speaking to his backside, and referring to the prosthetic, she said, "It looks very sophisticated."

With the task finished, he turned, and sat down on the raised hearth. He leaned in to his wide-spread thighs, his prosthetic in full view. "Waterproof and comes with an app for different types of motion … the sleeve hides the inner workings."

She openly studied his leg; then, she too, leaned forward, "You'll have to explain that to me sometime in more detail … I haven't had much luck getting information."

He shot her a dubious look. "You've researched prosthetics?"

"Yeah … I've tried to nail down a price tag."

Simultaneously, McCormick felt both impressed and apprehensive. Supposedly, she had only learned of *his* prosthesis just a few, short hours ago when he'd rescued her from the raging waters, while putting his own life—and limb—on the line; but why had she been researching artificial limbs—it wasn't exactly a high priority item on most young women's shopping list.

"I'll getcha some information," he offered, before returning to his chair, and falling into silence.

Andrea bounced a glance off him, surprised at his answer.

With the mood somber, and the fire burning low, throwing off less heat and light, Andrea rose and moved closer to the smoldering, red hot coals, quietly fixing her eyes on the, peacefully, hissing logs. The only sound in the room, other than the occasional pop and sizzle of wood turning to ash came from Tracker's gentle snoring. With eyes still glued to the glowing embers, she asked in a quiet tone, "McCormick … are you a man of faith?"

Another heartfelt question. The agent stood up, and slowly walked to the window, staring out at the dark, tumultuous sky. His enemy's wife had just asked him one question too many. In the diabolical worlds he slipped in and out of, it just happened to be the one piece of information that, if put in the wrong hands, would lose him his head!

Misinterpreting McCormick's silence, Andrea assumed, wrongly, that he considered her question trivial. She straightened her back, and stood up, eager to change the subject. "Oh, Matt … let me tell you about the most wonderful experience I had today." Her voice ran rich with enthusiasm as she slipped down to the rug.

He settled back in the chair, all looks of torment faded from his countenance before Andrea could catch a glimpse. Grateful to move the conversation away from himself, he offered in an encouraging tone, "Fire away." He wondered when she'd found time to do anything. She had walked ten miles into town that morning, met him for a late lunch, and had been mostly in his presence ever since.

"I picked out my Christmas present today … well, I didn't actually buy it, but I'm going to, just as soon as I get to town again … I really shouldn't pay that much … my money is all tied up in the estate, but I don't have anyone to spend Christmas with this year, so I figured…."

An unreadable expression flickered across McCormick's face. Andrea suddenly realized that she had been babbling on about her personal life. Surely the man was bored stiff, being trapped inside her cabin all this time. She continued, considerably more subdued, "You know how, ever so often, you find something that just feels like it belongs in your life … like it was predestined to be yours … something that conveys the essence of your very being?"

McCormick was in no way a shopper, but he shot her an admiring glance, then dropped his head and smiled, inwardly. Yes, he could relate to that feeling.

"That's the effect this painting had on me today," Andrea continued. "It's the statement of my life … I mean, where I am right now."

"I didn't realize you were interested in art." he said, pleased at the revelation. He sat back in his chair, feeling his appreciation for Andrea grow deeper by the minute. "Where did you find this rare treasure?"

"It's in the loft at the Holly Shoppe."

McCormick covered his surprise by sipping the thick dregs of chocolate from the bottom of his mug before responding. "I'm impressed … some of those paintings are done by this country's finest."

"I know … I recognized some of the names." She enthused, "I plan to return to the shop as soon as possible and talk to the owner."

"Have you met her?" he asked, feeling mild trepidation trickle up his spine.

"No, but I've seen her." Andrea paused, "She's lovely." Andrea dropped her eyes as she remembered the gregarious greeting McCormick had given the gorgeous woman on the sidewalk that very morning. As she spoke of her, a warm, appreciative glint filled Matt's eyes.

"Nicole is probably the classiest woman you'll meet in Red Springs" he said, dismissively.

Suddenly, the fit of jealousy Andrea had easily shoved aside, earlier in the day, became a much greater nuisance; but she was growing increasingly impatient with herself. Over the last few years, she had learned to bury her emotions, but now these invidious feelings of jealously kept popping up—this overwhelming feeling of possessiveness, feelings she'd always considered a weakness. Besides, what rhyme or reason did she have to feel possessive of Matt McCormick?

"Tell me more about your painting," he was saying.

Andrea moved closer, turning her back to the fire. "Okay," she said, shooting the agent a green-eyed, doubtful look. "But are you sure you're interested in art … I don't want to bore you to death with my drivel."

McCormick grinned and dropped his eyes, along with his voice. "Trust me … there are worse ways to die."

He assured Andrea of his interest in art, all-the-while marveling at her renewed surge of energy. She looked beautiful as she stammered and rambled … her enthusiastic spirit shining from her eyes. Her face glowed merrily, and her speech turned lively. She was like a different person, McCormick thought, a whirlwind spinning from some unseen, inner force. Andrea Fitzgerald was a lot of woman, he was finding out.

"The painting is called … now get this… *'Geniture',*" Her lips caressed the name as it slid past her lips. "It's another word for Nativity … first used in the 15th Century … the artist's name is Will Remington."

An icy chill ran up McCormick's back. Goose bumps popped on his forearm. He was speechless. Slowly, he leaned forward in his chair, not knowing quite how to respond, but feeling a strong need to stay truthful. Finally, "I've … seen the painting," he offered, cautiously, his voice husky with emotion. Yes, of course he had seen the painting—he had painted it! His answer was not a lie.

Everything he'd considered mere hobbies, were the things that had kept him sane during those years working amongst the lowest denominator of society as an undercover agent, waiting for the enemy to surface, waiting for his leg to heal, wishing, all-the-while, that he could grow a new one. The painting had become his obsession. He had painted others, but to him, they were just worthless seascapes of terns and gulls. But *'Geniture'* had come alive in his mind, and he had used a technique bringing realness, light, and unbelievable life to the canvas. Geniture was his camouflage word for Birth of a Colt, Birth of Christ, Nativity,

New Beginnings—*but in essence, in McCormick's heart, the scene represented the joyful birth of a son that had never actually taken place in reality.* Venting his grief on canvas had been a life-saving, cathartic experience.

The package had been bulky to carry, for sure, and it had slowed him down considerably. Truth was, he had risked his life in order to bring the painting home; and he had cautiously shipped it all around the country from gallery to gallery before allowing it to come home to Red Springs. He had a vested interest in where it found a home.

CHAPTER 33

McCormick looked into Andrea's soulful, as she asked if he knew the artist. He swallowed hard, and nodded that he did, trying his best to remain honest in all his responses. "Can you ... tell me anything about Remington ... what's he like?"

There was no escaping her questions. A feeling of stress crept over him, and he found his normally glib tongue in an unprecedented stammer. He rubbed his hand slowly across his mouth. "Well ... yeah ... I've known him for years; but I ... don't feel like I know him very well ... at times." Andrea didn't understand what he meant, but she sat eagerly awaiting more information. "One thing I can tell you is that he uses a pseudonym ... Will Remington is not his real name."

"A pseudonym ... really?" She leaned forward, "Can you tell me his real name?"

"Nah ... if I told you that...."

"I know ... I know," she interrupted, jokingly. "If you told me ... you would have to kill me."

McCormick's heart plummeted to his stomach as Straker's guileless suggestion regarding Andrea's involvement in her husband's crime came to him like a wraith on a dark, stormy night; but he said, "I'll tell you what ... I'll let him know you're asking about him ... if he wants to disclose his identity, he'll reveal himself."

"Deal. Tell me more about this ... Remington...." A twinkle came to her eye, and an impish grin played at the corners of her mouth. "I think I'm in love!"

In love. The simple act of breathing was becoming impossible for McCormick. *Is it even possible to feel jealousy towards yourself,* he wondered.

McCormick racked his brain for something to share with Andrea in regards to Will Remington. Finally, "I suppose he's just a regular joe … he works out of the country a lot." He paused for a seemingly long time, and then offered, "He's a widower … over two years now."

"How did his wife die?"

McCormick felt the cabin close in around him, not wanting to go down that emotional rabbit hole. He quickly stood, checking the progress of his drying jeans. When his answer finally came, his back was still to Andrea. "She drowned."

Andrea sighed sympathetically, sincerely feeling the artist's loss. "That's tough … has he always lived around here?"

He turned slowly, giving her a patient grin. His voice dropped, and he spoke with disdain, "Yeah … he's just another local, redneck, Green Mountain boy."

Andrea had listened intently to McCormick's every word. Now, she sat in silence, remembering the painting, knowing that it would be emblazoned on her memory, forever. Slowly digesting this newly acquired information, she said with great thought, "I think the painting shows that Remington is ready to give up the pain and get on with his life. That aspect … that freshness, that new beginning … is exactly what drew me to the painting … there's such an ambience … an ethereal glow about it." She turned her misty eyes on McCormick, and whispered, "Quite frankly, Matt, that painting moves me to tears." Silent, twin tears slid down her cheeks.

Sharing the same perspective of the painting, Matt tried to clear his own throbbing throat. Andrea, without any awareness, understood him in ways he didn't understand himself. Suddenly, he was standing beside the exhausted woman, pulling her off the drafty floor. He looked into her tear-stained face, and sensing her vulnerability, tenderly rubbed his hands along the curves of her shoulders.

Just as quickly, he came to a halt, gave her shoulders a brusque pat, and lightly kissed the top of her head as though she were a sister. He took a step back. "I think a great many things move you to tears, Mrs. Fitzgerald."

Changing the subject, he said, "If you're really wanting to meet a local artist, Farah is awesome … she'll give you an interview, a tour of her gallery, or spend the entire day with you … she'll even teach you to paint, if you have the time. He thought for a moment. "If you see her … give her my best."

Taking the name to memory, Andrea whispered, drowsily, "Farah … Matthew J. McCormick sends you his best." Suddenly, the wicked tongue of jealousy smacked both her cheeks. *His best what,* she thought, remembering from a Google name search that Farah meant Joy. She asked, "Does Farah have a last name?"

"If she wants you to have more information…."

Andrea cut off his words, "I know … she'll reveal herself to me."

He chuckled. "Her studio is downtown, near the stoplight."

McCormick suddenly swallowed his chuckle, and groaned, inwardly. These two women meeting could create problems for him. *Oh hell … any woman Andrea might meet in Red Springs would be problematic for him.*

His concerns would have deepened, had it not been for the earsplitting bolt of lightning, shooting down from low-lying clouds, illuminating the entire cabin. Andrea gasped, and Tracker fretfully jumped up and nosed his way between the man's legs. "Here we go again," McCormick groused. Sounding as though the sky was a crumble, a continuous stream of loud rolling thunder, rumbled ominously just over their heads.

Alarmed at the sound, and totally unraveled by the day, Andrea flew to McCormick, fighting Tracker for the space surrounding the man. She wrapped her arms around him, clutching him in a way that took him by surprise. His hands shot up, and away from her body as she clung tightly to his waist. When she finally glanced up, her eyes held an out-of-body, dreamy-eyed expression, before they batted shut.

McCormick smiled wryly at the woman who had literally fallen asleep on her feet. *Battle fatigue,* he reasoned, taking in her sleepy-eyed look. But soon he felt the warmth emanating from her body. Memories of the Writer's Block Lounge surfaced, and he dropped his arms to encompass her shoulders, to keep her steady on her feet, he told himself. He gazed upon the somnolence of a face still stained by tears. His roguish grin morphed into one of simple endearment. In his own drowsy, out-of-body experience, he gently thumbed away the moisture beneath her eyes, then bent down and gently kissed each closed lid. For a fleeting second, his nose brushed against her long, locks of hair, carrying the scent of fresh, mountain rain.

Something powerful stirred, and he pulled her snuggling body closer.

Her lids flew open, suddenly, and McCormick quickly pushed away. In his effort to escape the egg-on-his-face moment, he first stumbled over the whining Tracker, and then backed into the chair, upending it to the floor. In a blustery effort, he righted it, then busied himself at the hearth.

With cheeks aflame, Andrea gaped at the normally self-assured man, now surprising in his clumsiness, and totally distressed by his own masculinity. In haste, she turned away and picked up the dirty mugs, marching them, double-time, to the kitchen, as though washing dishes was the most important thing in her life.

When she returned several minutes later, her emotions were in check. She said, "You're right, Matt ... I do cry at everything." She laughed nervously, trying to gloss over what had just happened. "You should have seen me in the Holly Shoppe earlier today."

Matt *had* seen her in the Christmas shop. At least he had seen her leave in an utter state of turmoil, and it had not been difficult to read her mind. He had followed, discovered her sitting on a weathered, wood-splintered bench, brushing away the tears. His heart had filled with compassion. Andrea was a woman alone, completely alone, through no fault or design of her own, and she was just now coming to terms with that reality.

When lightning, once again, lit the room, McCormick glimpsed her red cheeks and frightened eyes. Was she afraid of the storm—or of him? "Maybe I should go," he offered, softly.

Her eyes shot up, and locked into his, pleadingly. "No ... please stay."

McCormick gave the knots around his waist a reassuring tug, and then wearing a look of determination to do the job set before him, and to do it well, he turned to face Andrea. "Tell me more about yourself, Andi."

She shrugged her shoulders. "I never discuss my personal life." She sat back down on the rug, rubbing Tracker behind the ears. *Truth was, she couldn't talk about her personal life without breaking down in sobs.*

"Okay ... we won't talk about you ... tell me about your ... husband." He walked to the hearth, bracing himself against the mantel. With that movement, he knocked over the picture frame for the second time that night. He grabbed it, and set it right. In the flickering light, he studied the picture of Andrea's family: Mom, Dad, Andrea and Heather. His eyes froze on

Heather's image, studying her face, seeing something familiar; but a sudden alarm sounded in his head, stealing away all other thoughts—Andrea was the only one in the picture still alive!

He brushed a glowing cinder back into the bed of dying coals, and then turned around; but the lovely young woman lay slumped, and asleep, in an exhausted heap on the floor. Her snoring dog, lay snuggled up beside her, nose nestled against the warmth of her body. The agent smiled. *Lucky dog,* he thought.

He lifted his gaze to the loft, thinking he might carry her up to bed, where they both could get some rest; but he immediately dismissed the thought, knowing that action would explode like an IED. Instead, he stooped down, scooped the young woman into his arms, and carried her to the loveseat, careful not to wake her. He gently laid her head on the pillow, then draped the quilt over her body. Tracker stirred; Andrea did not.

McCormick jerked awake; annoyed that he'd dozed off. The hour was late, and a shiver ran down his spine. *The temperature's dropped,* he thought, as he turned his concerned, heavy lids towards his first priority.

Seeing that Andrea was sleeping soundly, he stood and stretched out his sore, aching back. *Gawd, I feel like such an old man,* he thought, stoking the fire, and adding another log to the heap.

He dropped to the rug, and stretched out his lengthy body between the hearth and the loveseat. He'd been trained to sleep anywhere, in all conditions, but tonight sleep evaded him. Memories and raw emotion flooded his mind as he laid, hands behind his head, staring up at the huge, wooden cross-timbers of the ceiling.

Finally embracing his sleeplessness, he rallied, intending to put his time to better use. Freeing the sheet around his waist, he pulled on his damp jeans, and like a caged animal, paced the cabin. He walked to the window and braced one arm against the frame, the other settling on his hip. Drowsily, he stared out at the soggy earth. The storm had passed, but a wind-driven rain still streaked the glass. He considered looking for his jeep, but dismissed the idea, knowing there could be no rescue until the water receded.

He tried to glimpse the gloomy sky through the glass, but saw, instead, his own depleted image reflected back at him. Also reflected were the flickering flames of a warm, cozy fire, and the image of the sexiest woman he'd ever met, asleep on the loveseat. Tamping down the vision's lure, his bleary eyes gazed across the swollen lake.

Suddenly, he froze. He blinked sleep deprived eyes; then zeroed in on a point of light, bobbing and jiggling beyond the choppy water. *What the hell,* he thought. With nerves already raw, he grabbed his boots and walked in socked feet across the floor to the mud room. Once dressed, he checked his weapons and slipped, soundlessly, out the back. Walking away, he could hear Tracker's faint whimpering from behind the closed door.

Through pelting rain and pitch black darkness, the light-footed McCormick jogged along the familiar trail as it snaked around the lake, remembering every twist and turn. He'd run this trail a thousand times; often with his brother. When he came upon a Ford all-terrain vehicle, he slowed to a walk.

With eyes alert, he looked around, and quickly spotted the backside of a dark figure, sitting atop a boulder facing the water. He stopped to calm his breathing.

The man, decked out in rain gear and surrounded by a medium-sized cooler, a large coffee thermos, and a Coleman lantern, was using a pair of binoculars to spy on the cozy, little cabin across the lake—Andrea's cabin. McCormick's jaw clenched. *How'd he get up here?* The front road would still be flooded. He must've come up through the national forest, using the old, abandoned fire trail—the same trail he and Andrea had inspected the day before. The man had the necessary wheels to do it. With resoluteness, he circled the vehicle, stopping to study a long scratch mark along the passenger side. The driver would've needed daylight to maneuver through the obstacle course of downed tree limbs and new growth, which meant....

"He's been up here for hours," McCormick hissed through his teeth.

. With silent steps, the former Special Forces warrior approached the man from behind, slipping within inches of his old high school wide receiver. When he broke the silence, his words came out in a low-pitched, military grunt, "Donahue ... I see you haven't changed any since high school."

Startled, but immediately recognizing the voice from the past, Sheriff Donahue stood up, and slowly rounded the boulder. He faced his former quarterback with a smirk.

"Well ... what do ya know ... Matthew McCormick!"

The men stood glaring at each other, eye to eye, through heavy drops of rain.

With a tremor of apprehension, the sheriff asked, "What are you doing up here?"

McCormick shot him an amused, but problematic look, "My property ... my lake...." With eyes turning to flint, he nodded towards the building across the way. "My cabin ... I've come home to clean house."

Rain beat down through the over-hanging trees as the sheriff sized up his unwanted intruder. "Hell man, I heard you were dead ... or went rogue," he said, his voice dripping with impertinence through a thick wad of chewing tobacco.

McCormick ran his fingers through his short, wet hair. "Nah ... you need to find yourself a more reliable source ... I went DEA." Now, the taunt of incredulousness crept into McCormick's voice. "Actually ... that's why I'm here, Donahue ... to see you. According to the rules of the new drug enforcement initiative program, I'm obligated to inform you ... Sheriff ... that I'm working this area. I'm investigating yesterday's plane crash over here on government property. Hell of a thing, though ... seems there were no survivors—or fatalities ... looks like the damn thang just loaded itself up with illegal drugs, and flew in all by itself." He looked the sheriff straight in the eye. "You know anything about that?"

The sheriff' shook his head, but his lips twitched with amateur smugness.

Accurately identifying the twitch playing across the man's surly mouth as a *tell,* McCormick thought, *the guilty always rat themselves out,* Now the agent shot the sheriff an authoritative glare. "That's top secret information, on a need to know basis only ... consider your department informed ... and sworn to silence."

Unable to hide his aggrievement at having feds nosing around his territory, the sheriff's mouth puckered and he spit out a long stream of dark, tobacco juice. He sniggered, "The fucking hell, you say ... from where I'm sittin', it looks like you're playing house ... with that newspaper lady."

McCormick's chin slowly lifted in exasperation. "Now there you go again, Donnie ... fumbling a perfectly good pass."

McCormick watched a shit-assed grin spread across lips still dripping with chaw, his insult rolling off the sheriff's back faster than raindrops off his long, black, reversible rain slicker.

Donahue jerked his head back and sniggered. His eyes locked into McCormick's. "Hell, man ... you're getting to be about as pretty as she is ... you know who she is, don't you? That's ole Brantley Stone's wife...." His eyes went lifeless, his voice went guttural, "And you're a fuckin' dead man."

How did Donahue know that Andrea was Brantley Stone's wife? Andrea didn't even know she was Stone's wife; and the *name she never used was Fitzgerald.* Already knowing the answer to his question, McCormick asked, "Has ole Brantley come home?"

"Naw ... I ain't seen him in years."

McCormick ignored the lie.

Donahue continued, incapable of stopping himself, "I don't suppose you'd have that pretty, little lady's cell phone number, would ya ... I'd love to whisper...."

Perceiving a sick enemy, McCormick immediately pinned him with a steely glare; then took a quick step forward, grabbed both hands full of raincoat and orange liner, and lifted the dumbfounded man several inches off the ground, and up against the trunk of the nearest white pine. Anger gurgled, deep in his throat, "Donahue ... I suggest you get your sorry ass off this mountain ... if I ever see you up here again for any reason, other than official business, I'll put a bullet clear through your thick ... stupid ... skull." He let the man fall, unceremoniously, to the ground.

The sheriff, laboriously, pushed himself out of the mud, and countered, "You're threatening a law enforcement officer?"

Cold, solid conviction settled into McCormick's hardened jawline, and he shot fire into the eyes of the charged, but never convicted, rapist. With his voice resonating deep inside his chest, the agent growled, "Y-e-a-h ... I am!

He'll be back, the agent thought as he pulled his shirt up over his head and broad shoulders, then stripped off anything not fully water-proof. With his hand resting on his holstered weapon, McCormick had stood watching as the corrupt sheriff started the engine to his ATV, flipped on his bright beams and drove off, deliberately spinning the wheels, splattering mud and wild animal muck behind him. McCormick's flinty-eyed stare had followed the taillights as they slowly jiggled and bounced along the rugged, back trail, until they completely disappeared into the night.

Now, in the way of island pelicans, McCormick dove deep into the voluminous, freshwater lake, keeping track of his time below the surface of the cold, underwater currents. Finally breaking the surface, he treaded water; then flipped to his back, allowing the hard pelting rain to pummel face and body. *"I'm home,"* he thought, acknowledging the surrealism of the moment.

Taking full advantage of the circumstances, McCormick swam leisurely half-way across the lake towards the distant shore, and back again, before jogging back to the cabin, fully aware that he was being watched and followed.

Once at the back door, he froze in place. From out of the cold, rainy night came a deep, guttural sound. Without turning around, he spoke to the darkness, "Nice surveillance and foot-follow ... but you screwed up big time by not wearing deodorant. Out for a wet-night stroll and a little nocturnal noshing, are ya?" He stepped into the kitchen, screwed the lid off a peanut butter jar, and returned to the deck to throw a long pass, quarterback style, into the darkness. Rising out of the blackberry bushes, came a bear of considerable size, and smell, on hind legs, to catch the jar.

"Now go to bed, will ya ... before you end up a hearth rug in some rustic bed and breakfast," McCormick warned. The bear growled, as though understanding; then dropped to the ground and lumbered off into the wilderness, carrying the jar between his lock-tight jaws.

Tracker greeted McCormick at the door, but he mostly ignored his friend, and immediately crossed the room to the warmth of the fire, while being reassured of Andrea's relative safety. She looked as though she hadn't moved a muscle since he'd left. The corner of his mouth inched up. In sleep, she appeared an innocent, totally unaware of the multiple dangers surrounding her.

He turned and stoked the fire, thinking. This cabin sat on a very large piece of McCormick property. Fitzgerald must have known it was vacant. Of course, Andrea's deed was a forgery, pure and simple. Did they think he was dead, or were they setting him up—coming after him; but how'd they know he would return to the mountain—to this cabin? One thing he knew for sure: *Fitzgerald's henchmen were definitely here, and they were using Andrea, whether she knew it or not.*

CHAPTER 34

McCormick walked quietly to the kitchen, filled a glass with water, and leaned his back against the sink, sipping, his eyes resting on the loveseat. He wondered what Andrea would have to say if she knew she was sleeping, not in Fitzgerald's cabin, but in his. What would she say if she knew he had built it with his own hands, and abandoned it, following a flash flood that had all but washed it away over three years ago?

He'd learned a lot about this lady through his investigation. He knew that, not only did she write articles about the damage the drug culture was doing to the nation's youth, but she was actually working to counteract its devastation. After a full day of work, she often worked the night shift at the hospital, caring for addicted babies, alongside the little, ole white-haired grannies. She was a Big Sister to young members of the same organization, and to kids who had lost their parents to drugs, by death or incarceration. She'd even bought coats and clothing for many of the abandoned kids, and paid their school expenses when funds dipped low.

Just recently, she'd set up anonymous funding for the wife of a fallen law enforcement officer, killed by drug-dealers. McCormick thought he understood why she'd made a huge charitable donation to a Children's Christmas Fund—she, obviously, had a heart for children; but her more than healthy donation to the Wounded Warrior Fund still had him noodling. Other than an act of patriotism or human kindness, that one, made as recently as early October, still had him stumped.

He'd learned from a reliable source that she often sang solos on special occasions at her Protestant church, getting top billing ... although her attendance had dropped off considerably during the last few months; but she'd rallied enough to serve turkey and homemade, blackberry cobbler to a throng of hungry homeless on Thanksgiving Day—all on the heels of her own life-threatening ordeal with poisoning. He had to hand it to her—she had heart.

So far, McCormick's investigation had turned up nothing that could tie Andrea to anything criminal; she had been travelling a completely different path from that of her husband. His investigation had proven one thing, though: it had proven her to be an intelligent, driven young woman, highly educated and extremely talented. Her friends loved her dearly, her colleagues respected her, and her enemies were, normally, wary enough to not cross her.

He also had learned another valuable detail. Very early in the investigation, he had realized that the two of them had been living parallel lives, fighting for the same cause—except from totally opposite ends. Feelings of high regard and deep respect for the woman rose in his chest. He admired Andrea, and for some strange reason, just knowing this lovely woman made him want to be a better man. In Andrea, McCormick had found *his* hero.

He drew in his breath, and let it out, slowly. Unfortunately, there was a troubling, dark side to Andrea Daye Fitzgerald, a side fueling his need to, earlier, ransack her luggage in search of her gun; he'd come up empty handed.

He thought through the information he'd gleaned over the last few months. She had been described as kind and fun, but socially reserved. He suppressed a chortle—the Andi he knew was anything but reserved. The woman had been taunting him, throwing herself at him since the first day they'd met, giving him that hot, sultry look, hot and sexy one minute, then doing a three-sixty and coming at him like a wounded bear. Earlier that same evening he'd suspected she'd been trying to seduce him, to compromise him, to get him thrown off the case; but she hadn't played that hand— she'd actually been quite companionable. *Yeah, Andrea Daye Fitzgerald,* he thought, *you are a sure-fire enigma.*

Tracker followed as he walked from door to door, checking all the locks and bolts. His plan was to keep a vigil until morning. Then he would get answers to his questions. Finally, his security check ended back at the loveseat, where he stood studying the sleeping woman: the woman with the habit of rising at the break of dawn, praying for daily guidance, giving thanks at the end of a very long work day—and weeping silent tears in the wee, dark hours between.

He took the liberty of tucking the quilt under her chin—his grandmother's hand-stitched quilt given to him when he'd first moved into the cabin. A tender, abbreviated smile crossed his lips as he gently brushed a strand of hair away from her eyes, before turning away.

He removed his weapon from its holster, and placed it on the end table beside the reading chair; a chair that had once belonged to his grandfather. His heavy breath escaped through his nose as he settled back, almost smelling the smolder of cigarettes, and hearing the old codger's seasoned voice warning him to watch his six. *Miss you, Gramps,* he thought.

Watching the ex-warrior stand down, Tracker did a slow belly-crawl across the floor, and then stood on all-fours, sniffing the gun on the table. He whimpered, grievously, and laid his head across McCormick's knee in commiseration. Literally reading the dog's mind, he whispered, "It's okay soldier ... our enemy has retreated ... temporarily." The exhausted McCormick stroked his pal's head, consolatorarily, until drifting into a light, troubled sleep.

A metallic click and the cold, hard barrel of his own loaded Glock, being shoved against the side of his forehead, brought McCormick to a state of awareness. Images of his most immediate adversaries flashed across his mind: Sheriff Donahue and the stinking meth-heads in the forest. When he lifted his lids, he found himself staring into formidable eyes, cold and unyielding.

"Aw, hell," he muttered, drowsily, his hands griping the sides of the upholstered chair arms. "Does this mean my interview has come to an unsatisfactory conclusion, Mrs. Fitzgerald ... or have you simply lost your fuckin' mind?"

Andrea fought to balance the surprisingly heavy weapon between her quavering fingers. She hissed, "McCormick ... first, you break into my house in Forest Hills ... and rummage through my closets without any explanation, whatsoever; and then you come in here and prowl around this cabin like you own the place. I'm just sending you a message, bud." Adding more pressure to the barrel, she issued a pugnacious warning, "Don't ... tread ... on ... me!"

McCormick leveled his gaze, looking into eyes now exquisitely alive in the flicker of firelight. He raised both hands in seriousness and total abidance.

"Got it," he offered, drily.

Then in one well-practiced motion, he kicked the legs out from under the unsuspecting woman, wresting the gun from her double-fisted grip. He flipped her into his lap, instantaneously pinning her arms against her body. "Don't," he whispered gruffly as she struggled to wrangle loose.

Once she'd come to grips with the inanity of her actions, and the tug-of-war had ceased, she fell back, lifeless, against the man's chest. McCormick, abruptly, stood up, standing her on her own two feet. He loosened his arm-lock, and gave her a brusque shove forward as he would any common perp. With his voice plummeting to his chest, he said, wearily, "In case you've forgotten the rules of the game we're playing, Mrs. Fitzgerald ... I'm still the good guy ... you have nothing to fear...." He turned away, but his next words came out in a gush of hot breath, "....at least not from me." He holstered his weapon. "Now go back to sleep ... before one of us ... gets our fuckin' head blown off ... and the other one spends life in prison for killing an officer of the law."

His harsh words, and the abhorrent images they stirred up in Andrea's mind, shocked her; but the only shot fired was her repugnant glare as she plopped onto the loveseat, where she petulantly pulled the quilt up over her head. McCormick heard her low, terse grumbles coming from beneath the quilt, "You didn't have to go out in the rain ... don'tcha know ... you could've used the bathroom in the loft."

McCormick cocked his head, and grimaced at her misguided inference. "Crazy woman," he muttered under his breath as he warily settled back into the chair. Eventually, he drifted back to sleep, thinking, *this never happened.*

Andrea awakened, thinking about the Remington painting. She wondered if the artists could possibly be the kid who climbed into that tree, all those many years ago—he had mentioned his love of painting; but for all she knew, he could have been a painter of lines on parking spaces, or animal faces on zoo patrons. The smell of freshly brewed coffee and sizzling bacon, further stirred her to wakefulness. She stretched and yawned, thinking it a pleasant way to start the morning.

She sat up, massaging her stiff neck muscles. The rain had stopped and the sun sparkled through the windows, dappling the floor where Tracker lay, not in dreamy contentment, but as though listening, and understanding each word spoken by McCormick who stood at the stove, cracking eggs into a skillet as his formidable voice barked instructions to someone over his cheap, throw-away phone. Andrea relished the domestic normalcy of the morning.

"Why hasn't this thing been shut down," he was asking, audaciously, "people are dying, families are being destroyed … and I'm not buying the excuses … and where in the hell is *my* backup?" He paused, listened, then responded, "Either the Eagles, Devils or Knights … they're all first-rate."

At seeing Andrea astir, McCormick spoke three more words into the phone, "Finalize the details." Then the phone call came to a quick end.

McCormick turned away from the stove, his hands settling authoritatively on his hips, sending a no nonsense message. He held Andrea's gaze in cold austerity, deciding whether she be friendly or unfriendly. At last he shot her an upward nod, and said cheerfully, "Mornin' Songbird."

She shot him a discomfited glance. McCormick had obviously done some research sometime during the night, and knew that "Songbird" was the name of one of Kenny G's all-time greatest hits.

Dismissing his comment, she rose from the couch, and stretched high for something imagined. She bent at the waist, her fingertips gracefully sweeping across the floor, and then back up towards the rafters, stretching out her sore back. She completed the warm-up exercise, and then shot him a slightly plaintive grin. "You know, Matt, I have to level with you … Kenny G was my mother's favorite life-affirming artist, but my taste in music runs more along the lines of Dierks Bentley."

"Dierks Bentley?" A surprised McCormick lifted a brow in recognition of the artist. "I Hold On?"

She shook her head.

Grinning, slightly, he guessed again, "Drunk on a Plane?"

"No … those are golden oldies," she grinned, watching him crack another egg into the skillet. She shook her head again. *"Riser,"* she said, naming her favorite song. McCormick's chin ticked up, but he squelched his smile.

She walked to the hearth, and held her hands to the fire. With a tinge of solemnity, she offered, "That song has been my metronome for getting through all these horrible days."

Her revelation made McCormick feel closer, more in tune with her. "That one's been around at least a couple of years, hasn't it?"

"Yeah ... but I've had a couple of years' worth of horrible days," she chuckled.

He gave his head a half-shake. "I'm a little behind the times when it comes to my music collection." Already knowing the answer, he asked, "Are you a ballerina?"

She immediately deflected his question, "No-o-o ... that was my mother's dream ... not mine," she said, her words falling flat. "Mom had been a world-class ballerina before I came along, and she wanted me ... no, she demanded that I follow in her footsteps; but, unfortunately, all her vicarious ballet performances came to a screeching halt when I, fortunately, fell out of a four-hundred-year-old tree." She laughed, puckishly.

McCormick took note of her downcast tone inflection whenever she spoke of her mother, and its under-lying emotion: the dark side of love. He shot her a skeptical glance, his head aslant, "Fortunately?" he asked.

"Oh yeah ... I'd much rather work my mind than my toes," she offered over her shoulder as she walked to the window and leaned against the sill, admiring the old oak tree and the rain-freshened woodlands.

McCormick studied her for a moment, before posing his next question, knowing the answer to it, as well. "You a member of American Forest ... or something?"

"That and the Green Mountain Club. I spent one entire summer as a Big Tree Hunter, measuring four and five hundred-year-old trees." Embarrassment rose to her cheeks. "I even camped out in one for weeks, trying to prevent it from being cut down ...but then I fell out of it, and severely fractured my ankle." She put her hands on her hips, and leaned back to stretch out the kinks. "Gawd ... my entire body feels like rough, tree bark."

"Yeah ... hanging upside-down while you're shootin' off your mouth will do that," he said, drily. A mischievous glint came to his eye. "I could spray you down with natural menthol and tea tree oil, if you'd like...." He turned, and flipped an egg with expertise before again raising his eyes from the skillet. "Or I could give you a full-body rub," he added, waiting, tauntingly, for her reaction.

"Like hell you could!" she said through soft, low cackles of laughter.

He gave her a mocking grin. And then added, "To be honest, I'm feeling like an old piece of petrified wood, myself."

She turned her face back to the window, concealing the fact that she found her houseguest anything but old or petrified—experienced, maybe, but not old. In spite of his head injury, he was strong, robust, and sexy. Gawd yes, he was sexy with his shirt unbuttoned down to the fourth buttonhole, giving her a peek at the thatch of thick, dark chest hair. She blushed, and turned away. "How old are you, anyway?"

He carried plates and silverware to the table and grunted with a degree of surliness, "Older than you."

"How do you know?" she asked, throwing the question over her shoulder.

He bounced a knavish glance back at her. "Just do."

She guessed him to be somewhere around her age, but his actions and mannerisms seemed a bit older, and he seemed to be an extraordinarily mature person. She credited it to his fast and furious lifestyle. She liked it, cognizant of the fact that she had been aged by life.

A chill ran up her spine, and she stepped towards the fire. "What's the temperature in here? It feels like winter in Murmansk."

"Try the cold at 29,000 feet … in blizzard conditions."

"Twenty-nine thousand feet … that would put you on … Mt. Everest. You've climbed Mt. Everest?"

McCormick, modestly, let the question hang in the air. "I'll have to hustle to get you a couple of ricks of wood before the snow flies." More than aware of the uncomfortable dampness of his own clothing, he too, had become unaccustomed to the drops in temperature after two years on a tropical island.

Andrea watched him drain the bacon between two sheets of paper toweling. She asked, "Why did you learn to cook?"

"Why?" He lowered the pitch of his voice, and grunted, "The military, ma'am, teaches self-reliance in all things."

He took a pan of perfectly browned toast from the oven and set it on the table; then tossed her an inviting look across the room. "Come join me … I don't like to eat alone." He watched her hesitate, hold back, keeping her distance. Jokingly, his hands shot out to the sides, palms up for reassurance, "Hey, I'm not carrying … but believe me … today I'm t-r-e-a-d-i-n' lightly."

Her hands shot out in mimicry. "Ditto," she answered, softly, blushingly apologetic.

He pulled a chair from the table, and motioned to it. In a rare offering of personal information, he answered her question, "Actually, I learned to cook at an early age because I had a slew of hungry, younger siblings."

"You come from a large family?"

His shoulders shrugged, indifferently. "I suppose you could say that … if you're using current day birth statistics."

Ruefulness crossed her face as she sat in the chair. "I always wanted a big family." She sized up the abundance of food, and lifted one eyebrow. With sleepy-eyed impishness, she gushed, "You know … I l-o-v-e a man who knows how to feed himself."

Something between a snicker and a grouse gurgled deep in McCormick's throat, and he shot back, just a little too quickly, "I think you must be in love with every guy you know."

She rolled her eyes upward, "Only the ones I respect," she said with conviction.

McCormick lifted a brow. "You referring to the ones you do … or don't shoot?"

Her lips pursed.

He continued to tease. "Does your respect include the really old ones … like that old geezer, artist guy?"

She gasped, and a look of delusion over-rode her smile. She clutched her chest. "Remington's old?" she asked with genuine concern and a problematic edge to her voice. "You didn't tell me he was … old."

"Hell yes, he's old … I know for a fact that he's in pain a lot of the time … I've heard him groaning of a mornin', about this joint, and that joint creaking or gummin' up if he didn't get enough sleep." He said grumpily, "And I know for a fact that some mornings, the old guy can barely move around at all," he raised an observant eye in her direction, "truth is, he uses a crutch at times … and you wouldn't believe the shit he goes through just to protect his feet." He passed her the plate of bacon.

She looked at him, quizzically, mouth agape, her voice rising with disbelief. "So he's a tender-footed old geezer?" she asked, comedically.

"You could say that."

Sensing that McCormick was putting her on about something, she offered, "Doesn't matter … you can tell by his painting that he has a r-e-a-l-l-y big heart." But she thought, *if Remington is old, then he couldn't be the kid who saved my life.* She leaned her elbows on the table, and cupped her chin in disappointment. She said, flippantly, "Any man who can paint like Remington still has a red hot fire burning deep in his belly!"

Finding her clueless assessment of him amusing, McCormick kicked back in his chair, and chuckled deeply. Relief flooded his heart at the return of Andrea's sense of humor. Although she was still drowsy, he was finding her cheerful banter, laid-back and totally unarmed manner, enticing—and dangerously inviting.

Andrea studied the man across the table. She could almost swoon at the sound of his voice. It was strong, but with a wholesome quality, projecting intelligence, knowledge, and high self-esteem. There was no sign of an accent or drawl, yet his words came out deliberately measured, giving them life and depth. It also projected a quality of inherent joyfulness, and casual self-regard. It could be playful at times—even sensual.

Putting butter to toast, and remembering the events of the previous day, she asked, "Where do you think your jeep ended up?" Before he could answer, she grimaced, and added, "I can only imagine what those people cleaning up the riverbeds are going to think once they come across that hunk of junk."

"Aw, be nice." McCormick's hand covered his heart, feigning hurt feelings. He looked up and caught her eye. She boldly met his gaze, but his quickly darted away. Coming face to face with Andrea in the middle of a dark, stormy night was one thing; but in the bright light of morning, this hero's knees easily buckled. Doubt seeped into his mind. What made him think a woman like Andrea would give a guy like him a second look? His gaze dropped to his leg.

"I'll have to locate that 'hunk of junk' this morning," he offered, sliding another egg onto her plate.

"Gawd … it screeched like a sinking battleship." She dropped her eyes, remembering how kind and protective McCormick had been as they watched it slide off the cliff, and how, awesomely, protective he had been when she had buried her face in his chest, weeping and scared out of her wits; and then later as they trekked through the storm, guiding her footsteps away from potential dangers—twice saving her life. With gratitude, she added strawberry jam to the toast, and laid three of the four slices on his plate.

Watching coffee splash into her mug, Andrea became aware of McCormick's pleasant, accommodating grin. He was actually enjoying pouring her coffee. She offered, jovially, "The net says that drinking coffee, not only puts hair on your chest, but also lengthens longevity."

His eyebrow arched, and his eyes flashed. "Hell ... if there's any truth to that, I'm damned near immortal." He returned the pot to the stove, then sat, sipping, peering over the rim of a brown mug with the lettering: Man, Myth, Legend. His eyes locked onto the tiny, brown mole strategically placed at the high point of Andrea's collarbone, as though deliberately placed there by a playful God. "Remind me to check out the progress of that hair thing a little later," he said, jocosely.

In unguarded banter, she offered, "Well, it certainly seems to have worked for you." Her taunting gaze brushed over McCormick's open-neck shirt.

They laughed—both fully understanding their quips to be nothing more than good-natured teasing; but an unsettled look suddenly parked on McCormick's tired, strained face. He rubbed the bristles under his chin with the back of his hand. He hadn't shaved, and he smelled of the lake. He checked his watch.

"Matt, about last night...." she began.

"Last night?" McCormick gave Andrea a furtive look, uncertain of what she was referring to. Was it her felonious assault on the life of a federal agent? He remembered his own misdeeds: his flagrant threat against the life of a fellow law-enforcement officer, his illegal feeding of a nuisance bear, and his shamefaced, inappropriate reaction to her hot body pressed against his. Any, or all of the three could still get him into trouble. His eyes locked onto her full, luscious lips, lips that rendered him totally incapable of looking away. "We don't have to talk about it."

As he ate, he could sense her eyes upon him, but for some strange reason, he didn't mind getting caught in her crosshairs this morning. He looked up and gave her a knavish wink, before his jovial smile disappeared.

At last, he wiped his mouth with his napkin, sat back, and squared his shoulders. His voice took on a more serious tone as he offered, "Andi, I'm scheduled to go back to the hospital this morning ... for a cheek-up ... then I'm on to headquart ... another assignment." He couldn't tell her that, on her behalf, he would fly to D.C., from D.C. to Miami, from Miami to South America, and then back to the Islands. To Andrea, he said, "If all goes well ... I'll only be gone a couple of weeks."

"Weeks?" she gasped. He watched her stiffen, noticeably "And, if things don't go well?"

His countenance darkened, but no answer followed.

Reading the silence, Andrea rose from the table. *He's not coming back,* she reasoned.

He watched her struggle to hide her disappointment without success. Whether she admitted it, or not, she had started to put her trust in him; but it was no longer just about the trust. He had watched her respond, time and again, to his masculinity, rescuing his own libido from its deep, watery abyss.

This agent had seen the dark side of life, the dark side of death, and the dark side of the human heart. Who knew what tomorrow might bring—if he even had a tomorrow left to live? *If things go sideways,* he thought with sharpened acuity, *I won't be coming back at all!* In a moment of soul-searching, the young man, who had put his life on the line for his country, time and time again without regret, was suddenly stricken with a puissant thirst for life.

He studied her reaction a moment longer, then pushed away from the table.

When she turned around, he was there, surprisingly pulling her into the warmth of his strong, caring arms.

Thinking herself a widow—bound to no man—she shot him an accepting smile, and lifted her lips to welcome his. He kissed her passionately, deepening the kiss, demanding more. Her long, tamped-down passion flared, hungrily, rising up to match this larger than life paragon.

Sensing no resistance, McCormick scooped her into his arms, and carried her to the stairs, mounting the first two steps to the loft. As his foot hit the third step, a thought hit him like a jagged bolt of lightning. The haunting image of a bloodstained face appeared before his eyes, stone cold and covered in hot, Mexican dirt—the image of his brother, now lying in the ground up on Boot Hill.

An inrush of dishonor flooded the Good Soldier's senses. His brother was dead, rotting beneath the leaves and between the tree roots; and here he was—about to bed his killer's wife. Once again, his boss's words reverberated through his head: *they're using her as bait.*

Andrea felt the jolt as McCormick suddenly came to a halt on the fourth riser. Slowly, he reversed his steps, reached the landing, turned, and set her feet firmly on the floor. Laying his hands subtly on her shoulders, he spoke with ragged, breath, "Andi ... we can't do this ... I'm invest...." Ruefully, his hands slid down a length of her arm, then back to her shoulders. "This isn't meant to be."

She fell silent as the embarrassment and the absurdity of the situation hit the pit of her stomach. McCormick fell silent, as well, hoping she would accept his advances as a mistake, and welcome his sudden change of mind—he prayed that she would. Finally, hearing no response, he offered, "Andi, there are things you don't know about me ... things I can't explain...."

She let out a grievous sigh. "What things?"

Ignoring her question, McCormick's voice dropped to a throaty whisper, "Andi, I'm a serious guy ... on a serious mission ... I live a dangerous life. I need ... a relationship built on trust, and strength—not weakness."

Her eyes fixed on his head wound. "You think I'm wea...."

Sensing the need to further explain and stall, the agent said, "Before I cross that line, I need to know that we can trust each other unequivocally, beyond a shadow of a doubt. I have to know that we have each other's loyalty and long-term best interest at heart—that we have each other's back ..." his voice crackled, "and ... as a man ... I have to earn your respect." His hands fell to the wayside. "I don't think we're there yet." Deep regret flashed in his eyes.

Her eyes clouded with confusion as she searched the depths of his, hoping to find a bit of the humor he'd displayed earlier; or if nothing else, the glow of tenderness she'd witnessed the night before. Instead, she found only a deep, dark abyss; wilder than yesterday's raging flood waters, in eyes rapidly growing cold.

"So ... in essence, you're saying ... what? ... that your mind just went to mush?"

McCormick's head dipped, abashedly. He raised his gaze to encompass the room, aching for a means of escape. "You could say that."

Suddenly feeling debased, Andrea moved away, revealing a face of unmasked devastation. She had assured him, just the day before, that he could trust her; and here, just hours later, he had no confidence in that trust. Yeah ... because of her senseless insecurities, she had stupidly pulled a gun on him! "You think I'm weak," she said, as though making a profound statement.

Suddenly, the air came alive with pulsating, high-spirited, Reggae music as McCormick's throw-away phone jangled out its factory-set ring-tone. He grimaced at the timing, pulled the annoyance from his pocket, and immediately muted the sound, something an undistracted McCormick would've done hours earlier. He checked the caller ID. "I have to take this," he said, resignedly.

He took the call; then made several more from the deck outside. After some time, he finally stowed the phone and reentered the cabin. He closed the door, slowly, behind him, and warily approached the distraught woman.

He longed to wrap his arms around her shoulders; but Andrea, already wrapped in self-conflagration, pulled away. Stubbornly, he stood planted at her side. He spoke, quietly, "Andi ... I have to go ... I have no choice, but I'm concerned about you being up here all alone."

"I'll be alright," she answered, showing no emotion.

It wasn't only the fact that he'd hurt her deeply that concerned the agent, for he had, or that she'd hit bottom, having no will to fight; nor was it the fact that she hadn't the strength to be left alone in the woods, in the world—alone in life. No, it was knowing what sicko Donahue would do if he knew she was here alone. Not wanting to frighten her, he decided to use humor as a caution. He pointed to the door. "Andi, on the other side of that door are a lot of wolves in sheep's clothing ... I'm afraid I'll come back and find you with that painter guy, that old Remington fart."

"Yeah ... well...." She gave out a heartless, little laugh, "It's the young wolves dressed as old goats that scares the living hell out of me," she said with sarcastic saccharinity.

A sober McCormick raised his eyebrows, plaintively, and leveled his eyes, "Are you referring to me?"

She gave him a smug look, "If it quacks like a duck...."

Suddenly seeing himself through her eyes, McCormick pursed his lips, shut his eyes, and slowly nodded. He shot her a glance of apologia, and added, "Okay ... I get the clichés ... but I'm concerned for your safety. Are you sure you want to stay up here? There's another weather front moving in ... it'll be snow." Beset by worry, his voice suddenly took on an authoritative tone. "Gather your things and I'll take you home...."

Andrea sucked in her breath. He was casting her off, giving her the grand kiss-off speech, while, sickeningly, being a gentleman to the very end. She cut him off, rudely "What could possibly happen to me, McCormick?"

Pointing fingers to herself, she said, "I'm safe ... I'm well ... I'll be all right ... besides, who, in the hell, put you in charge of Andrea Daye Fitzgerald?"

McCormick's shuffled his feet, and a frown tugged down the corners of his mouth. He knew he was risking losing her; but he couldn't explain himself—not yet; there were other, more serious risks to consider.

"Stop worrying about me," she snapped, sudden bitterness rising to her throat. "Just go to your new assignment ... you don't owe me a damned thing, McCormick ... and *I* sure as hell don't need a crazy, inked up, one-legged, bullet-riddled, geeky, sleuthing, gun-toting G-man as a babysitter!"

The light went out of McCormick's eyes.

Silence, loud and awkward, hung in the air; its chill seeping into Andrea's bones as she witnessed the man leave his body—to morph into someone she didn't know. His chin shot forward in resoluteness, and his voice took on a new terseness. "Then have it your way ... Mrs. Fitzgerald."

He thrust his hand deep into his pocket, and pulled out the key to her rented, postal box. He let it drop, with a thud, to the table.

Andrea's hot glare dropped to the key.

McCormick, not wanting her to pick up on his reluctance to leave, or to know that her acidic words had wounded him, turned and reached for his twice-sodden vest. In an impersonal tone, clipped and chilled, he offered, "Your wood should last awhile longer—if you ration it. If it runs out ... burn the furniture."

Already feeling his abandonment, she lashed out at his back, "Yeah, I'll just do that," she sniggered, bitterly. "But don't worry about me ... I'll just sit here ... roasting imaginary marshmallows over a table-leg fire ... overdosing on java and watching the hair g-r-o-w on my chest ... unto perpetuity!" She sucked air. "Sorry you'll miss all the action, Special Agent Matthew McCormick."

"We live or die by our decisions," he said, drily, impersonally.

A doleful whimper came from Tracker. McCormick dropped to his haunches, ruffled the dog's noggin with one hand, and stroked his rump with the other, giving the canine a silent goodbye—lest he not return. "Wish I could take you with me, pal," he said, in a barely audible whisper. Seeming to understand the unstated, the dog whined grievously, wagging his tail, halfheartedly, his chin drooping, sadly, to the floor.

Jealousy towards the man's inexplicably, close relationship with her dog rose in Andrea's chest, and she hissed, "Yeah, it'd be just like you to abscond with my dog!"

Ignoring her comment, McCormick spoke in a low growl, "Take care of the bitch."

Andrea's head jerked up, and she tsked, snarkily, "You … are totally gender confused … Tracker's a male dog."

She didn't see the sharp glint in the agent's eyes as he stood, resolute. "My comment was meant for the dog … and it was used in its psychologic form!"

In one swift movement, Andrea snapped up the postal box key, and hurled it at the man's head. In one swift movement, McCormick caught the flying projectile with one hand, and hurled it back at her with force.

As the key dangerously skipped across the table, their pained eyes met and held, each seeing the torment registered on the face of the other—each having a painful insight into the hopelessness of their situation.

McCormick pulled his eyes away, and walked to the door. Grabbing hold of the knob, he paused. His head dropped. He wished like hell that he could explain himself. Finally, with renewed determination, he squared his shoulders and stiffened his back. His voice dropped to a deep, military grunt.

"Bolt this door!"

CHAPTER 35

Three weeks later, a small unmarked Cessna 208, modified for precision skydiving, creaked and groaned across the tumultuous sky above a specified area of South America's Peruvian rainforest. Perusing a local travel guide, the plane's only passenger chuckled as he read the pamphlet, touting the dangers that lay before him: *"Called the Lungs of the Planet, with twenty percent of Earth's oxygen being produced here, the rainforest is the home of many creatures, but mostly those that live nowhere else in the world: flesh eating piranhas, rabid, blood-sucking bats, as well as the Blue Poison Arrow frog, which carries enough poison in its body to kill a hundred men. The forest also supports the growth of many different types of flora, including 200-foot trees, giant ferns, human entangling vines, and, of course, the famous Corpse Flower."*

Laying the brochure aside, he chuckled, again, stood and buckled his parachute. As the plane drew near his point of departure, Matt McCormick prepared to jump, to dive down through the tree canopy, now being pelted by heavy rain. Had he been in the States, this night would break every rule in the US Parachutes Association rulebook. McCormick was prepared to night jump, in hazardous weather, without a lighted altimeter; and he was doing it without a drop zone staff, should something go wrong. He was, however, dressed in a lightweight dry suit similar to that of a diver as extra protection for his prosthetic leg. The night-vision goggles, hanging around his neck, would be useless, considering the charged lightning bolts crackling all around him. Even the simple act of being in the plane on this night, for this mission, was tantamount to a death wish; but the small crew had voted, unanimously, to fly with McCormick.

It had been three, long years since he had jumped from a plane. Never having jumped with his prosthesis, McCormick had spent the previous week practice jumping with the Black Knights, a team of highly skilled skydivers.

At last the pilot signaled to the jump pilot. The jump pilot signaled the jump master, who opened the side door to the plane; then turned to shoot McCormick a challenging grin. With a wave of the hand, he gesticulated to the desolate blackness outside the plane, while reciting a time-honored, Seal team mantra, "The only easy day was yesterday ... right Mac?" he offered, puckishly.

McCormick shot the man a smartass grin, his eyes sweeping over the ancient aircraft. "I'm just hoping the rivets in this piece of crap metal hold together until I'm out of here," he said in good-natured bandying, eliciting a grin and an assenting nod in return.

Now, all humor left the jumpmaster's face, and the nod he gave the now-austere diver was for permission to jump. McCormick threw out his rucksack, then, in quick succession, a second bundle. As he followed them out the door, a broad grin crossed his face, and with undue haste, his body started to free-fall through the tumultuous, night sky, all-the-while being chased by the ancient, but admonishing, canned voice of Bitchin' Betty: "Danger ... danger ... danger!"

Lightning flashed, and McCormick's skin and eyebrows prickled in the electrically charged air. His chute opened, and he flicked on his mag light, shooting a quick beam up through his parachute canopy to ensure himself that it had opened correctly. Satisfied, he immediately killed the light.

As he soared, earthbound, visions of Andrea flashed through his mind, making his heart race, even as he licked his wounds over her caustic remarks. How had she described him? *Oh, yeah, she'd referred to him as a crazy, inked up, one-legged, bullet-riddled, geeky, sleuthing, gun-toting G-man!"* He groaned and chuckled all at once. At least she was accurate, if not kind; but just the same, her words had cut him to the quick; and what was the thing with Tracker? Could she have possibly been jealous of the dog?

He quickly suppressed his thoughts, preparing for the earth to go black. Someone with credibility had reported Brantley Stone as being in this rain forest, and a fly-over by a small drone had confirmed his presence. This jump was for Andrea's life, and the endangered lives of thousands of American children.

Soon, the ground rose up to meet him. With precision, he landed on the spot he'd marked on his map weeks earlier.

Swiftly getting to his feet, McCormick discarded his parachute canopy, and dropped to his knees. He wiped away the rain; then smeared dark heavy camouflage grease over his face, before recovering his possessions.

With his rucksack on his back and dragging his bundle, he began tromping through the thick, heavy foliage. As he walked, his mind started to grind away. Getting into this place had been a cinch, but getting out would be an entirely different matter—getting out alive would be almost impossible.

He'd been here once before. On that trip, he'd learned that the property had been armed with men and guns—mercenaries, all experienced in warfare, and specifically trained to kill with no compunction against taking a human life. He'd also learned, on that trip, that every type of booby-trap imaginable had been set-in-place against unfriendly visitors. McCormick grunted, derisively, under his breath—he was about as unfriendly a visitor as they would ever get.

He made his way through the forest, his face hot and sweltering beneath the grease. Soon, the monkeys in the trees, swinging from limb to limb, sensed his presence, and began their incessant screeching and chattering. To avoid getting tangled up with them, he crouched low to the ground, working his way around the huge leaves and fronds, all dripping, profusely, with heavy rain. When a salvo of monkey poop shot through the air, McCormick quickly ducked under the broadleaf shrubs. He remembered his most recent research. Supposedly, the monkey's practice of throwing their own feces proved the intelligence of the animal. As a wad of the stuff landed nearby, he grinned, inconceivably, seriously doubting the intelligence of the data collectors.

A drenching rain had fallen for seven consecutive days, severely swelling the tributary McCormick needed to cross. He began to swim the distance, keeping an eye out for crocs and piranhas. When at last he waded out of the water, dripping—God only knew what—he raised his head and looked around, not at all surprised to be staring at the backside of a fortressed compound. Aware that the front gate would be heavily guarded, McCormick had chosen to attack from the rear, where entry was merely deemed impossible. His mission was to get into the compound, and clone the hard drives containing Stone's data; but his main goal was to destroy the connection to his rogue satellite feed. *All in a day's work,* he thought, facetiously.

He eyed the property, and the tall, metal fencing topped with layers of coiled barbed wire. Razor wire had been recently added to the area, enclosing three large airplane hangars, housing for staff and computer equipment, a building for packaging and distribution, and a drop zone for illegal drugs from other countries. McCormick studied the wire, trying to decide whether or not it held an electrical charge. He clicked his tongue, and gave his head a negative shake. "Ah, Shaun … there goes your property value, right down the drain … people just don't think prison fencing is that sexy, anymore!"

At the sound of his voice, something rustled, and rubbed against the tree bark in front of him. With both anticipation and caution, McCormick slowly pulled back on a large, green leaf, finding himself face-to-face with the yellow eyes, evil and lidless, of Brantley Stone's cuddly, prized pet— Hero. The large, semi-aquatic snake had slithered out of the water, and lay wrapped around a low-hanging tree limb. Its head dangled and joggled, and his bright, glaring eyes fixed on the agent as though trying to hypnotize him. As he captured the monster's image on his knock-off, smartphone camera, McCormick wondered why the giant, man-squeezing, man-eating, anaconda had not been added to the brochure's list of life-threatening inhabitants.

Like the angels that once guarded Eden, Hero, guarded the back entrance to the hangar area, next to the fence McCormick needed to access. He knew he could handle the fence—no problem; but this huge, evil monster was another matter. He focused on the limbless creature before him, the seriousness of his mission suddenly hitting him in the gut. The words of American poet, Carl Sandburg, came to mind: *Valor is a gift. Those having it never know for sure…if they will have it when the next test comes.* McCormick breathed a prayer that his courage would be there when he needed it the most.

From memory, he pulled an image of a smiling Andrea, glowing in the bright, autumn sunlight, holding the hand of a wee lad who had already figured out what to value most in life. In that moment of reckoning, he promised himself that he would put that image to canvas—and he would, humorously, add a long stream of noisy, quacking, clichéd ducks.

He studied the long, flicking tongue, aware of the special heat sensors surrounding the mouth used to locate prey; but McCormick had no concern for the mouth—at least not yet. This particular snake was without venom, but over the last two years, numerous horror stories had surfaced about *the boss's* infamous reptile, and the many men it had, at Stone's behest, squeezed to unconsciousness—and then eaten alive! According to legend, this serpent could swallow bites as large as a donkey. McCormick sucked in a full, deep breath to quell his roiling stomach. If his mission failed tonight, the insides of this demon could, very well, be his final resting place.

In true McCormick style, he had eagerly looked forward to meeting Hero, the serpent named after Stone's product line, and he was more than eager to bring an end to the man's depravity. Now, he took a long, contemplative look at the serpent, "Hey there, Hero ... whatcha doing?" he said aloud.

Knowing a reptile that size couldn't stay long in the tree, McCormick backed off, as the largest snake he'd ever laid eyes on, began to uncoil from the limb.

He dropped to his knees, knowing that Hero could move faster in water than on ground. Opening his rucksack, he dug deep into the bag. Once he'd found what he was after, the former Navy Seal, experienced and well-trained in warfare, got busy—clearing the way to the building.

At last the man grabbed his knees, and sucked air, his labored breathing coming in large gasps and gulps; but the exhausted McCormick had emerged as the true hero. He straightened, and got to work cutting through the heavy fencing, and the multiple strands of barbed wire. Once he had an opening large enough to enter, he crawled through and under the cover of darkness, worked his way towards the nearest and most isolated hangar. There, he tried to open the heavily rusted door, not at all surprised to find it locked.

Hugging the outside wall, and extremely wary of booby-traps, he walked around to the side of the building; and found, to his astonishment, an open window. He smiled at his answer to prayer. He propped his bags along the outside wall, and in Hero fashion, slithered his long body through the small window frame. The putrid combination of fuel, oil, and fresh paint made him almost retch. Silently, he slipped around stolen planes, waiting to be reassembled, repaired, and repainted.

A low murmur of voices came from somewhere in the back. His pulse quickened when, over the din of loud, pelting rain against the metal roof, he recognized the voice giving instructions—Brantley Stone, a.k.a., Shaun Fitzgerald, a.k.a., Kris Kringle! The SOB was, indeed, alive!

With mind whirling, McCormick cautiously advanced towards the faint light shining from an office window, too dirty to see through. He took a position within hearing distance, and crouched low in the oil-blackened shadows. He listened, as though his life depended on it—it did!

He could hear Stone giving general flight instructions to José, his pilot, and occasionally throwing out a comment to a third person in the room— someone named, David. Suddenly, his ears pricked up, at the sound of his own name being bantered about in a long flow of profaned rhetoric. He grinned with jocosity, happy to have so rattled his enemy; but at the mention of Andrea's name, and the McCormick family, his jaw clinched and set to stone. His blood ran cold.

Suddenly, something moved among the cannibalized planes. He held his breath, watching from the corner of his eye, not daring to move his head. At last, a pair of yellow, glowing eyes glared back at him from ten feet away. Unable to tell if it was another reptile or something worse, McCormick pulled his gun from its holster, leveled it on the eyes, and froze as the *something* started to move out of the shadows in his direction. A twitch of his nose, and McCormick instantly knew what was approaching. He quickly stifled a sneeze and holstered his gun.

A long-haired, white cat approached, reticently at first, then padded bravely across the oily floor, its tail curled high in the air, and proud-looking, as he pranced about as though royalty. McCormick got a better look at its ghoulish face and watched as it advanced to a spot of dappled light in front of him, sat down and began to preen. There was definitely nothing cute or cuddly about this animal. Instead, it reminded him of Charles Dickens's depiction of death.

McCormick recognized the cat as Stone's—the cat he carried around with him almost everywhere he went. In spite of its ghostly face, the cat was harmless, he reasoned—his allergy to the cat, however, was not.

McCormick fought off another sneeze, and then let out his breath slowly, focusing on the sound of abomination that was Stone's voice.

"David, you're my man," Stone was saying. "I want you riding shotgun with me; if anyone comes near us, blow 'em away—I don't care who it is. I've got two or three days-worth of work to do on the island, then we'll fly on to Boston from there. Once in Red Springs, we'll take over the territories from those stupid, hick amateurs. We'll meet up with Donahue, canvas the area, and make our final plan once we know where everyone is situated. Jennings ... make sure we have all-terrain vehicles, and are ready to roll, when I get there."

"Leave Andrea alone ... I have special plans for her. We'll concentrate on the others, but our main target is McCormick … we've got to get rid of that guy—the bastard's got nine lives. We'll load up and fly out of Lima at sunset."

McCormick chided himself for being too late to catch more of the details, but at least he knew a storm was brewing—and he had better get out in front of it.

A door hinge creaked, announcing the men's intended departure from the office. McCormick quickly stole away to a far, dark corner.

Stone exited first, his head a swivel as he strutted through the hangar with bold impudence. When fresh air hit his hot, sweaty face, his eyes shot towards the open window. "Jennings," he bellowed to a man dressed in gray coveralls, his harsh voice, grievous and accusatory. "Why is that window open?"

Jennings immediately stuck his head out the door, and answered, apologetically, "The fumes got too strong … I'll close it."

McCormick's chin suddenly shot up, and an extra shot of adrenaline coursed through his body as he watched the young man exit the office and start to move towards the window. Suddenly, Stone's hand shot out, grabbed the kid's arm, and roughly twisted it behind his back. When he shoved the hardnosed muzzle of his 9 mm pistol under the kid's chin, everything went quiet. McCormick drew his gun. The sound of rain beat hard against the metal roof, adding tension to the already abominable situation. Fitzgerald shoved the gun under the kid's chin, suggesting that he might just blow his head off.

From the darkened corner, McCormick leveled his gun on Stone/Fitzgerald's head, watching the scene unfold before him. He calmed his breathing, certain that he could drop the man in a nanosecond, before the man could squeeze off a shot. Knowing that all hell would break loose should that happen; he prayed that this inimical confrontation would escalate no further.

Fortunately for everyone involved, Fitzgerald begrudgingly lowered his gun. With eyes glaring, he hissed, "Lock up, Jennings—everything!" With brute force, he shoved the young man away from him, holstering his gun.

McCormick breathed a silent sigh of relief; but there was no stopping the white, hot anger scorching his chest. He considered taking down both Fitzgerald and the pilot, but quickly reasoned that it would do no good to take out just a couple of these miscreants; he was here to gather facts—evidence of their atrocities. He needed to hack the computer systems and learn the names of Fitzgerald's contacts and connections, to learn their methods in order to shut down the entire operation. It wasn't enough to merely shut down one; he had to prevent others from emerging.

Fitzgerald raised the hangar door, and then swaggered out of the building, cursing the heavy rainfall. Seemingly frozen to the spot he stood upon, the pilot hesitated a long moment, preferring not to follow his overwrought boss; but in time, he turned, and reluctantly followed in Fitzgerald's slushy footsteps.

Once they were gone, the kid pulled the office door shut; then, just as the pilot had done earlier, he stopped in his tracks. He looked around, guardedly, as though sensing something—or someone.

McCormick's gun dropped to his side as feelings of both relief and exasperation, simultaneously, flooded his senses. He wanted to speak to this guy they called Jennings, to warn him to get the hell out of here; but he knew it wasn't in the other's best interest. The kid was too green, too inexperienced. Fitzgerald would know, read it on his face—smell it on him. An agonizing sense of déjà vu flooded his soul. He'd been in this position before, a year ago. His troubled eyes fixed on the young man—*what in the hell was his kid brother doing here?*

Suddenly, the cat was at his feet, scratching and clawing his boot. A loud purr followed, as the vexatious creature started rubbing against McCormick's long, black leg, in a most friendly manner. He started to sneeze, but quickly clamped a hand over his nose and mouth, cursing under his breath—the damned cat was giving away his position!

All at once, McCormick heard a crack of gunfire, and a bullet whizzed by his ear, pinging off the metal wall beside him. Another bullet ricocheted off the metal; he had felt the breeze from the bullet as it blew by his ear. *Go low,* he thought, ducking down. A third shot rang out. McCormick clutched his shoulder.

"Hold up!" Jennings shouted to the shooter, the returning pilot. "You're shooting at Stone's cat!"

"Gringo ... in umbra," the pilot grunted with a snarl, and a thick accent as rain water dripped off his clothes and onto the oil-soaked floor.

"Nah, you're just spooked ... it's the damned cat. You kill Stone's cat, José, and you're a dead man for sure!" Jennings spat out the warning with vehemence, his tone threatening.

The pilot harrumphed in a gush of profanity, and McCormick watched him leave, disappearing into the white, heavy deluge of rainfall. Then he watched Jennings stare off into the direction of the open window, hold it in his sites for a long moment—and then, deliberately, decide to leave it open.

Whistling a seasonal tune, the young man stepped out of the hangar and lowered the rusty door to the ground. Once the latch locked down, he slowly walked away from the building in an air of nonchalance, acting as though everything were perfectly normal.

McCormick let out a sigh of relief, and in darkness, finally holstered his weapon. Blood oozed between his fingers from the shoulder wound. Realizing that his time had just been shortened by the bullet, he moved swiftly towards the office door and turned the knob. A wide grin shot across his sweat-lined lip as he discovered the door, unlocked.

"Gutsy kid," he whispered.

At sunrise, Brantley Stone, aka Shaun Fitzgerald, rose to face a morning full of chaos. He first discovered one of his over-night guards in a coma, and his vehicle missing. Then he discovered that every tire on the compound had been slashed. Around noon, as everyone chowed down in the mess hall, his technology building suddenly exploded into a huge, orange fireball, destroying, not only his computer lab but his entire data base. Also completely destroyed in the explosion was Stone's private, clandestine satellite feed.

Last, but not least, he discovered, just behind the hangar, his pet anaconda raised, stretched, and tethered to the fencing in several places, just below the razor wire. His mouth had been taped shut, and an artificial Christmas wreath placed around his neck. Red and green glitter glue had been spray painted down its entire length, and a large silver bell hung from the very tip of its tail, making the 550-pound creature look like cheap garland.

Stone was livid, but he could place the blame on no one within the compound. They had all been gathered in the mess hall gobbling down thirty boxes of Chicago-style pizza that had just arrived by plane—compliments of an anonymous donor. At the time of the explosion, Jennings had sat at the end of a long table, yukking it up with Stone's security goons.

That evening, Stone's private jet taxied down the Lima runway and lifted off into the sublimable, tangerine sky, heading for the islands. In the luggage hold, Stone's Dickensian cat slept soundly on fluffy pillows inside a cage. Sprawled out beside him, on suitcases filled with contraband headed for the Puerto Rican airport, was Matthew J. McCormick, stifling sneezes and swallowing pain-killers, while making plans to send in a team with a larger glob of C4 Explosive Compound. Nothing in Stone's prison-fenced operation would be allowed to stand for long. McCormick tapped the medical adhesive bandage covering his shoulder wound, assuring himself that the copying device was indeed taped inside. A mirthful grin played across his lips as he nodded off.

CHAPTER 36

Andrea had carried her breakfast coffee to the deck, studying the direction of the wind, and watching what she perceived to be snow clouds moving in. Taking heed of the weather predictions in the Old Farmer's Almanac, as well as McCormick's dire warnings, she'd driven into town for a few supplies, finding the place a bustle with harried, last-minute shoppers. She'd stopped at the post office, and had been pleasantly surprised to find a package from Sug, bringing relief to the concern she'd felt in regards to her dear friend. Ye Olden Mill had made good on their promise, and sent her a copy of the photo taken for their Wall of Fame. She shot a quick glance at the photo and smiled, before sticking it in her purse.

Last but not least, McCormick had, surprisingly, stayed true to his word and sent, from San Diego, California, her information on high-tech prostheses. No note had accompanied the information, and it had sat in her postal box for over two solid weeks while she rested, er, brooded in isolation at the cabin.

Having the photo, somehow, eased her loneliness; still, she felt the man's presence, or rather his absence, everywhere. She casually glanced over her shoulder, longing to see his laughing eyes. She could almost hear his voice whispering her name, as she checked out every bald head, Vandyke, or two-day-old chin stubble she passed, wondering if it might be McCormick in camouflage. She wondered which disguise was the real Matt McCormick. It didn't matter; she liked them all.

She remembered their last heated words at the cabin, and gave out a loud, rueful groan. The door had barely slammed shut behind him, before she'd been forced to admit the truth: she had been a first-class bitch. She whole-heartedly regretted her stupid, hurtful words, having no idea as to what had possessed her to say such horrible things. And now, today, her greatest fear was that she might never see the man again—to apologize.

Now, she found herself standing at the side entrance to the Holly Shoppe, more anxious than ever to claim the painting, and take it home—to cherish; for she had also received, in the mail that morning, a very substantial royalty check for a published work. She mounted the steps and pushed down on the latch, wondering if Will Remington was really an old man, as McCormick had suggested. The door wouldn't budge. She peeked through the small panes of glass, hoping they had simply forgotten to unlock it. In haste, she skipped down the steps and rounded the front of the building.

She groaned at seeing the *Closed for the Season* sign hanging on the door; but all was not lost. The track-lighting was on, and she could see someone moving around inside. She twisted the door handle. Surprisingly, it opened.

Excitedly, she walked into the shop. The chimes had been removed from their jangling place above the door, but a sweet, agreeable musical arrangement played softly in the background—a Josh Groban Christmas carol.

The smell of paint was in the air, over-riding the lingering spicy scent of autumn. She was immediately greeted by an older gentleman. He was actually very handsome for his age: tall and slender, about sixty, maybe older. His hair had turned almost entirely gray. He was dressed in painter's coveralls, with splatterings of several different paint colors.

The man's eyes were razor sharp, but his mouth suggested warm friendliness.

"What can I do for you on this fine morning?" he called out, cheerfully. As he walked towards Andrea, she could see a few deep wrinkles, but otherwise, he was in good physical condition; not exactly cut, but with a flat tummy, and trim jaw line. He had been whistling along with the music as she'd entered. Strangely, something about his manner reminded her of David. And then she saw it: a gun holster tucked under his armpit. Inside her head, she screamed: *Does everyone in this town carry a gun?*

She said, instead, "Yes, I'm interested in purchasing a painting I saw here a few weeks ago." She smiled briefly, using a no-nonsense, straight-forward business approach. "I think Nicole is the person I need to speak to."

"I'm sorry miss," he apologized. "Nicole closes the shop and takes her vacation at this time every year. She and Matt flew out of here over three weeks ago."

"Matt?" She raised her eyebrows in question.

"McCormick," the man added, as though she should know exactly to whom he was referring. He chuckled, "Those two kids don't get much time with each other, so they like to travel together whenever their schedules allow ... it's a good time to catch up and strengthen their relationship." He breathed out a low chuckle. "The girls just love him to death."

Relationship ... girls? Andrea's body went numb, and her heart sank into dismal despair. Well, that certainly explained some of McCormick's strange behavior, didn't it? Rage quietly rose up inside her. *Yeah, McCormick,* she thought, bitterly. You *were right ... we have to trust each other ... and no, we're not there ... yet!*

To the older gentleman, she struggled to say, "I see," as her throat constricted with raw emotion. But Andrea did not see; she did not see at all. In the last few years, there had been very little she had desired, but today, she wanted that painting in the worst way. Now the shop was closed, and the owner had flown off to the land of sand and sun, taking her very own, almost, lover with her.

Andrea looked at the man with cold determination. "Is there any way you could help me?" she questioned, a resurgence of hope rising in her chest."

"Maybe ... which painting did you want to purchase?" he asked.

"Geniture ... Will Remington is the artist." She looked at him hopefully, "Are you ... by any chance ... Mr. Remington?"

The man looked at her with surprised eyes. He shook his head humbly, chuckling as he began flipping through a stack of paper orders and receipts. "Oh no-o-o-o ... Will Remington is much taller, much smarter, and much better looking than I could ever hope to be." His eyes settled on one paper in particular, and he pulled it out of the stack for a closer look. His mouth drooped. "I'm sorry, Miss ... that painting has been pulled off the market ... by the artist himself ... just a few weeks ago." "Hmmm," he said as puzzlement settled on his face. "This even looks like *his* handwriting."

A sense of loss took hold of Andrea. She asked, "Is there a phone number ... an email address, a fax, or some other way I can reach him?"

The man shook his head, "No, Mr. Remington is off gri ... out of the country right now ... can't be reached." Clearly reading the disappointment in her demeanor, he waited patiently while she dug through her purse in search of her cell-phone, preparing to exchange information. Finding it uncharged, she laid it on the counter in frustration, and rummaged through her bag, finally producing a *Forest Hills Daily News* business card.

She quickly scribbled her cellphone number on the back. "*If ...* the artist returns, could you please give him my number? I really would like to have that painting, and I'm willing to pay top dollar."

"If what I'm hearing about that painting is accurate, ma'am ... top dollar is going to cost you a great deal of money."

She handed him the card and looked him straight in the eye. "And worth every penny," she said, smiling. "I'm just asking for the opportunity to buy it ... if I can't be reached by phone, I'm staying in Little Bear cabin at the end of Grandma Burns Road ... he can find me there."

The man's eyes dropped to the card, and his smile faded. "Little Bear Cabin," he repeated, his tone suggesting doubt. He lifted his head, giving her a scrutinizing look. "I hear that cabin's a mite drafty ... you'll be needing one of those Christmas throws over there on the table ... half price ... quality weave on both sides, and guaranteed, one hundred percent, to keep you warm."

"I'll take one," she said, without turning her head to look at the display.

"Which design would you like?"

With the Remington painting foremost in her mind, Andrea shot a bothered, half-glance at the table. "It doesn't matter...." she answered, "the one with the most red will do."

He bagged a colorful throw of his own choice, while studying her with suspicious eyes.

He took her cash and handed back her change. "Have a good day, miss," he offered, half-heartedly, as he excused himself from her presence and walked to the back room.

Andrea stood staring at the now empty space where he had stood. "Thanks a lot," she answered, mocking his sudden disingenuousness, as well as his quick departure. She left the shop wondering what the heck had just happened—totally annoyed by the absence of door chimes.

Andrea turned the old guy's words over in her mind as she walked away from the town's only stoplight. Huge, fluffy snowflakes had begun to drift, silently, to the ground. *Matt and Nicole... travel together ... strengthens their relationship. They're a couple,* she thought, feeling as though her heart had flat lined and been entombed in her gut.

In the three weeks McCormick had been gone, she had been sick with worry. The disappointment of not being able to buy the painting was nothing compared to the tortuous thought of his being hurt, or with another woman, or possibly even worse—married! Her heart would not allow her mind to go there for fear that they both might shatter completely. The feeling of impending doom surfaced again; and the depths of her loneliness and despair almost frightened her—no, they did frighten her.

Feeling the need to walk, she strolled past houses built during a much simpler time—a completely different era, actually. Once upon a time—just a few weeks ago—she had been totally charmed by the lovely Rockwellian atmosphere of this tourist village. Now Christmas decorations and soft, amber lighting shone out from candled windows, sending a message of love and hope to a world that had sorely abandoned the message; a world of hardened hearts, disbelieving and condescending in nature. She looked around and blew out a discouraged breath.

Once upon a time, she would have been completely charmed by the lovely evergreens, their soft, white lights peeking out from beneath a thin layer of snow, the gossamer image lending a sense of enchantment to an area otherwise forgotten by time. Suddenly, in the street already dimmed by twilight, a light flickered, and the antiquated lamppost above her head came to life. Andrea lifted her gaze and spun around, taking in the full panoramic view of the sky and her surroundings. A snowflake fluttered against her cheek like the gentle wings of a butterfly. She closed her eyes as a melancholic memory passed through her heart like a warm phantom breeze. "McCormick," she whispered.

Andrea stopped and looked around, suddenly realizing how far she'd walked. Shadowed by the mountain, the town was already near darkness. She shivered and peered ahead at the snow-covered walkway, breathing in the mountain air, whitened by frozen mist. Her eyes fixed upon a shadowy figure—a woman, an old woman. At first glance it looked as though she had just wondered out of the yellowed pages of a Dickens novel. She was thin, and dressed in a long skirt. As she walked, the fresh layer of snow tugged at the hem of her garment, causing it to swish and sway, revealing boots and leggings underneath. Her long, straight, whitish-gray hair hung to her waist, completely covering the back of a heavily textured jacket of a drab and lifeless color, the likes of which Andrea had never seen before. She carried a cane and a crocheted basket. Andrea caught herself craning her neck to look, wishing Zoe could be here to get a gander at this specter from the past—she would've loved it.

Now, the woman turned and looked towards Andrea, appearing to be stopped, and waiting for her to catch up.

As she cautiously approached the woman, Andrea could see that it wasn't hair covering the woman's head and shoulders, but a hijab, the traditional covering of a Muslim woman. The woman suddenly reached out a gnarled hand to clutch Andrea's. Andrea dropped her eyes to the misshapen fingers, cold and bony. Alarmed, she looked into the withered face, surprised to find there, a kindly look, a warm, friendly glow shining from the woman's eyes. "My dear young woman ... I feel a need to warn you ... I'm Farah. Child, these streets are not safe for a pretty, young thing like you ... twilight has been stolen by the evil-minded. Once the sun goes down, it's best to get inside and lock your doors. These streets are no longer safe."

A feeling of shock and unease travelled through Andrea. She was aware of the nocturnal unrest of the inner-cities from New York to California; but, good-grief, she was standing in the middle of Red Springs, Vermont—it should be one of the safest places in the world. "How sad," she answered. "I love to walk in the twilight."

The old woman squeezed her hand and nodded her head, ruefully. "As do I ... but heed my warning dear ... the world has changed." The aged woman dropped her hand, and walked away, her long skirt swishing behind her.

Yes, it's changed ... and it can just change back, Andrea thought, deploringly, as she walked a block farther. *Wait ... Farah.* She stopped in her tracks. *Wasn't that the woman McCormick had asked her to pass along his greeting?* She quickly turned, intending to go after the woman, but she was already out of sight. Not only was Farah not in sight, but not a single other person could be seen on the abandoned street. She headed back to the center of town, wondering what a man like McCormick could possibly have in common with this woman.

CHAPTER 37

"Andrea…Andrea Fitzgerald!" A male voice, gruff and grating, was calling out her name. Shivers traveled up her spine as she turned to face the voice. A large man on crutches, tall and muscular, in a sheriff's uniform, was approaching her from across the street. A pistol rode high on each hip, and a shoulder holster was tucked under his armpit. It was quite a sight to behold. If it was possible to swagger while hobbling on crutches, this man was doing it.

Zoe's father had been a county sheriff. He'd told his daughter that a lawman's swagger was caused by the bulk of his gun riding on his hips, rather than from a swelled ego. Andrea doubted that she could apply that same logic to this man.

"You probably don't remember me, Mrs. Fitzgerald," he was saying as he approached Andrea. I was a friend of your father … John Donahue is my name. I'm the County Sheriff. Your father and I used to hunt the high country together. We bagged some really big game—black bear, to be precise. The spine of the Green Mountains is just chocked full of them. One year, your dad took down a male, 300-pounder."

"How do you know me?" she asked, a sense of foreboding rising up in her.

"I read your column, and I recognized you from your picture. My staff told me a drop-dead, gorgeous woman was in the area … I figured it had to be you."

Andrea doubted his claim, thinking the *News* didn't get distributed east of the mountain. Looking into the man's shifty eyes, and noting his crass comment, she wished she'd brought Tracker along.

She searched her memory. The name did sound familiar; but there was something unsettling about this man. She glanced over her shoulder, half-hoping to see McCormick lurking somewhere in the shadows.

"Yes, my father was fond of sharing his hunting expedition stories with me. Frankly, he always wanted a son … I wasn't," she whispered, as though revealing a secret.

He pushed her comment aside. "Yeah, we sure did drag in the big ones."

Andrea's cautious gaze settled on the hard lines of his thirty-something face. In face reading terms, he looked more mercenary than sheriff.

"Of course I've climbed the ladder of success since those days. Hell, back then, I was just the local part-time dog catcher, working as a trail guide on the side to pick up a little gambling money. I guess you could call me a-jack-of-all-trades. I've done it all." He laughed. "Hell, I became sheriff by default … no one else wanted the job … all this nasty drug stuff … you know? Why don't you follow me on back to my office? We can have a private one-on-one talk."

Casting an eye to the abandoned street, Andrea cringed at the thought of being alone with this man, but he was the law, so she followed him up a flight of stairs, one laborious step at a time.

"I apologize for being so gimpy," he wheezed. "This is my first day back on the job since I broke my leg in three places. It's brought me to a complete halt. I can't walk, can't drive my car; but the worst thing is, I can't sleep. This damned thing gets in my way." He tapped the full leg-cast lightly with his crutch. "Have to keep it propped up all the time." His breathing was heavy. "I've been waitin' for a good snow base, so I can get around these mountains on my snowmobile."

Andrea recognized his easy-walking, shock-proof, snowmobile boot with a Thinsulate lining on his one good foot. She'd searched through the catalogues, looking for new snow gear, and had idly come across the men's pages, wondering what kind of boot Matt wore.

"What's your ride?" she asked, feigning interest.

"Polaris," he answered quickly, proudly. "They're the best for this kind of terrain."

At last they reached the landing and Donahue pushed his office door open with his crutch. The otherwise powerful man plopped into a well-cushioned chair behind his desk, and let both crutches fall aside, clattering to the floor. "Push that damned door shut, would ya?"

Reluctantly, Andrea closed the door, immediately feeling like a fly stuck to sticky paper, as she sat down in the unlit office. Her eyes swept the small, cluttered space, coming to rest on a pile of skin-flick magazines scattered across a table beside his desk. *Oh, very professional, sheriff,* she thought, confirming her first impression of the man.

"What are you doing here in the mountains … this time of the year … all by yourself?" He questioned.

Andrea didn't want to be here, and she sure as hell didn't want to answer this man's questions. "Resting … I'm just resting." She tried to force a smile as she grew, increasingly, uncomfortable.

Finally, Donahue gave her a stern look, long and hard. "Mrs. Fitzgerald, I wanted to ask you what you know about the investigation?" he said, still huffing from his climb up the steps.

"What investigation?" she asked, totally clueless.

"The DEA investigation. About three weeks ago, a small plane belonging to your husband … excuse me, your late husband … crashed in the National Forest which is only a couple of miles from your cabin."

This was the first Andrea had heard of a plane crash. She sat speechless as Donahue annoyingly tapped a pencil on his desk, playing the important sheriff role to the hilt. "We know that large quantities of cocaine were found in the wreckage. The feds have launched a full investigation of what, they think, could link Shaun Fitzgerald to drug-smuggling in South America." He paused, trying to read her reaction to his news. Andrea, still feeling the numbing effect from her earlier shock in the Christmas shop, sat listening, stoically.

"What do you mean, trace it to Shaun. He's dea…." she stopped mid-sentence.

"That's right … he's dead. But the ring is still active and somebody has to be the leader." He saw the objectionable look on her face. "Shit! I personally never did like, that Fitzgerald, and I never understood why your father did business with him." He gazed at her over the top of his glasses, "But, then of course, you married the guy, didn't you?"

She had already decided, upon first sight, that she didn't like this sheriff. With a little weight loss, he wouldn't be a bad looking man, but he had a seamy, smarmy manner about him, and his hungry coyote look made her feel like prey.

"How did you know Shaun?"

"Your father brought him up here a couple of times, but the young stud wasn't interested in hunting. He spent all his time tracking down the little hotties ... you know, the hot little college girls working in the shops during the summer." He grinned through yellow, tobacco-stained teeth.

Andrea stiffened, trying to ignore his lewd comments. She guessed him to be heavy into porn. She remembered where she had heard his name before, and that Matt had warned her to stay away from him. Had Matt also told her he was a law-enforcement officer? She couldn't remember, but for some reason hearing his name, began to dredge up remembrances of long-forgotten details.

"Why are you telling me this?" she questioned.

"Well, I just wanted to warn you ... this thing could get really ugly for you."

Andrea looked at Donahue with cold, piercing eyes, "What are you saying?"

"Well, it's obvious ... you're Fitzgerald's woman, and you're in this thing up to your pretty little neck. Most broads know when their husbands are involved in something illegal, and I won't even mention your father's involvement."

Andrea's head reeled. Somehow hearing her father's name linked to Shaun and drug-smuggling left her completely disoriented. Mortified, she jumped to her feet. "Are you suggesting that my father was involved in a drug-smuggling ring with Shaun Fitzgerald, and now *I* am implicated, and being investigated, as a member or leader of that ring?" Hysteria sounded in her voice.

"Yes, ma'am, that's exactly what I'm saying ... and I'm supposing the title on that plane that crashed in the National Forest three weeks ago would have already been transferred over to you, and in your possession."

Andrea dropped her eyes to the floor, her face burning with anger and disbelief. Something was seriously wrong here. Her father would never become involved in anything illegal, most of all illegal drugs. The whole driving force of his life had been to help people, not hurt them, and he certainly would never befriend a man like Donahue—he was a church deacon, for God's sake.

She hesitated, afraid to ask her next question; but feeling certain she already knew the answer. "Do you know who is handling the investigation of the Widow Fitzgerald?" She held her breath.

Donahue smiled, cunningly, extremely pleased at her question. The seeds of doubt he was deliberately planting were taking root. "No, I can't say that I know his name," a moue of churlishness parked on his mouth, belying his spoken words, "but I'm told they've assigned a brilliant, young man to the case …I understand he's one of the best … honors and degrees out his ass … a killer of a detective with a computer for a brain … so I'm told."

Andrea showed no emotion. "I also hear," the sheriff continued, "he comes on like a real likeable guy, but I understand he's a sly dog, for sure." His seamy eyes locked into Andrea's. He sniggered, "I'm told he's an extremely handsome devil … with a slew of young women he visits in the area … if you follow my drift."

Andrea sat, silent. The air in the room was fetid, and she couldn't breathe. With shaky legs she rose from her chair, walked to the window and stared at the slow stream of traffic creeping along the snow-covered street, below.

A horrible, wrenching tightened her gut. She was still trying to deny her broken heart over McCormick flying off with a beautiful woman; but, at least that was simple to understand. McCormick was obviously a player, a cad, and she'd been snowed, but now this sheriff had dropped another bombshell.

It was pretty obvious that McCormick wasn't the agent working the case, she reasoned. The sheriff's description didn't fit the man—not with his look-of-the-day hair, his irreverence, and those horrible, grotesque tats. He was an educated man, for sure; but he was also unpretentious. It was ridiculous to think McCormick might have all those honors, and multiple degrees. Actually, the only parts of Donahue's description she could ascribe to McCormick were his handsome looks and the ladies' man insinuation. Under her breath, she mocked the old guy in the shop—*the girls just love him to death*.

Andrea studied Donahue. There was something about this guy that didn't add up, either. She immediately decided that he definitely could not be trusted. And why was he telling her these things? Was he trying to frighten her, or could it possibly be an effort to keep her from cooperating with law enforcement? Somehow, she had to clear her father's name, as well as her own, but was there anyone, in this world, she could trust? She really wished she could talk to David.

"Of course, I could make this all go away…." Donahue was saying, smugly.

Well of course you could, Andrea thought, knowing exactly where this was headed, and of course she would have nothing to do with it; but his words triggered an idea. If reverse psychology and *mush* would work for McCormick, perhaps it could work for her. She turned to face the sheriff, cordially extending her hand to him as she chose her words carefully. She would say exactly what the man wanted to hear.

"Sheriff Donahue ... I do apologize ... this has all caught me by surprise. I didn't know a thing about any silly, ole investigation. How can I thank you for taking me into your confidence? I'm so lucky to have such a good friend right here in Red Springs ... and believe me, I'm not the kind to forget a favor when the time is right." She paused, coyly, her stomach doing a sickening flip at the sound of her own voice. This was a dangerous game she was playing, but she figured that his broken leg would stall his activities until she was safely away from Red Springs.

She gently patted the leg cast blocking her exit from the room. "You take care of yourself now, you hear?"

He asked, robustly, "So you're planning to stick around for a while?"

She pretended to give his comments deep consideration. "Well now ... I believe my father would want me to get to know his good friends, don't you?" She turned to leave, "And I would enjoy hearing more about your hunting expeditions ... Dad was really very modest." She paused, pretending to be in deep thought. Suddenly, her face lit up with feigned excitement. "Oh, I've just had a wonderful idea ... perhaps I can help you compile your stories ... I could even ghost-write a book for you. Of course ... I'd give you full credit." She shot him a sexy, little wink—the kind McCormick had given her.

Donahue's eyes glazed over as he fantasized about his name on a book jacket.

Andrea glanced anxiously towards the window. "I've got to get back to the cabin, but I can count on seeing you the next time I'm in town, can't I?" She swallowed hard, recognizing the lump in her throat to be her swallowed pride.

"That's a hell yes!" the sheriff answered with enthusiasm as he pushed himself out of his chair, trying to suck in his ample gut. He walked her to the landing. "I can't get around to your cabin with this leg, but my door is always open ... maybe you could come by my apartment, instead. I'm just over here on Bear Wallow Trail ... Apartment 3C." Donahue was all but licking his chops.

Andrea lifted large expressive eyes to meet the sheriff's. "That would be my pleasure," she lied.

The sheriff's excitement mounted as he watched Andrea descend the wooden staircase. He scratched his scraggly beard, his eyes lusting after the beautiful young woman—she was playing his game.

His game. It was like hunting deer; sitting high in a blind, watching a helpless doe wonder in and out of range of his deadly arrow. His orders had been to eliminate Andrea Fitzgerald in the near future, at Stone's behest, and here she was, making it so easy; but maybe if he waited awhile, he could have it all—the girl, the book, and a large cache for killing the girl.

"Mrs. Fitzgerald," he called out from the top of the stairs. "Why don't you just stay in town tonight?

Andrea stiffened. "Wonderful idea ... but I've got a hungry, vicious, killer dog at home, and I've already been gone too long.

Trying to persuade her to change her plans, he offered, "I've been notified that a New York cop-killer has been seen in this area. He's a real handsome dude ... likes to tell unsuspecting women that he's a ... get this ... DEA agent. He's armed, wounded and dangerous. Thought you'd want to know ... in case somebody comes a knockin'."

"Thanks, Sheriff ... I appreciate the heads up," she shouted over her shoulder as another ill-boding chill ran up her spine.

After a beat, his brusque voice called out once more from the top of the stairs. "Mrs. Fitzgerald!" Andrea stopped between steps, and turned around, looking him full in the face, fully understanding that his goal was to scare her, to keep her in town. "The weather service has issued a blizzard warning. Be careful not to get snowed in up there." She watched the man's facial features morph into luridness, menacing and predatory. "You don't want to *die* in these mountains."

Die. Goose bumps popped on Andrea's arms, and fear clutched her heart. *Oh my God ... it's him!*

She recognized that deep, gravelly voice—the voice on the phone at the *Forest Hills Daily News*, threatening her life if she didn't stop writing her articles.

"I'll be bringing a load of wood up your way," he was promising.

She stared into the man's eyes, seeing not as much as a flicker of light in them. What she saw instead, was someone quite capable of inflicting deadly harm. She nodded her head in acknowledgment, and waved, feigning a pleasant parting, then walked out into the storm—totally terrified.

Damn, damn and triple damn, Andrea thought, shivering as her feet took careful steps on the slippery, snow-covered walkway, backtracking the three, long blocks to her car. *I'm being investigated!*

As she walked, her faith in herself began to plummet. How could she have been so stupid as to marry someone like Shaun Fitzgerald? A gust of strong, frigid air blew ice crystals, cold and pelting, into her eyes as though reading her thoughts and tossing her an insult. Blinded temporarily by the wind-driven snow, she stopped, and pulled her light-weight jacket up to her chin, instinctively knowing her chills came, not from the elements, but from her conversation with Donahue.

With her face numbed by the cold, and her mind streaming all the stupid failures of her entire life, she murmured, "Well, Agent Who-so-ever-you-are ... you'll find me quite guilty of three things: making a list of sexy, current-day actors, looking dowdy—and being a world-class fool!" She buried her chin in her collar.

Her mind whirled. If some human computer was doing the investigation, then who in the hell was McCormick? Was he the impersonator? Had their meetings been by accident, or by design? She thought about each and every meeting. She thought about the kiss in the Lounge, and that morning in the cabin. Had he been stalking her all this time? She blushed and shuddered all at once.

She looked down the street full of idle men; a dying street, decimated by years of exorbitant taxes and the contagious pandemic. Shuttered shops with vile, contemptible graffiti scribbled on the outer walls now looked like some Sci-fi, end-of-the-world movie. *Farah was right—the street wasn't safe.*

Finding the library housed in what had once been a cozy, little cottage, and still open, Andrea dashed to the door. She came to a quick halt at the sign in bold print: **Must wear mask.** She dug through her pockets, and eventually came up with a mask. She fastened it behind her ears. Seeing no one, she slipped, unnoticed, into a computer carrel, where she logged on, and searched for a toll-free-number. Immediately finding what she needed, she logged off, and approached an elderly librarian who had suddenly materialized behind the counter.

Without looking up, the frail, stoop-shouldered woman, spoke, "Y-e-s?"

"It's important that I make a call," Andrea said to the woman's back, "to a toll-free-number ... but, unfortunately, my cell phone has died."

The woman slowly turned and lifted her chin, shooting Andrea a no-nonsense look, scrutinizing and skeptical. "Lucky cell phone," she droned, pulling her mask up to her nose.

Andrea volleyed back, using her friendliest voice. "Would it be possible for me to make the call from here?"

In the same boring monotone the woman answered, "Only patrons are allowed to use our phones ... never seen you before ... doubt you've got a library car...."

Cutting the persnickety woman's words short, Andrea challenged, "Look ... this is a tax-payer funded phone, and I am a taxpayer ... this could be a matter of life or death for me."

The elderly woman tucked her chin under, indignantly. "Well then ... maybe I should just call the sheriff," she said, in pure waggishness.

Andrea shot the librarian a look powerful enough to ricochet off the walls.

Seeing the look, the vexed book specialist threw her shoulders back as though she'd been slapped; but making no bones about her annoyance, she acquiesced. Her words muffled through the mask, "If you must." She plunked an antiquated dial phone on the countertop. "Better make it quick ... it's about closing time."

Where's all that neighborly, Vermonter courtesy, Andrea wondered, begrudgingly? "Thank-you," she said, pushing words of common, everyday politeness out of her mouth. She dialed the toll-free number with her index finger, totally unaccustomed to a rotary dial.

A young, energetic, male voice came over the line. "Drug Enforcement Agency ... how may I help you?"

Andrea sucked in her breath. "I need to speak to Special Agent Matthew J. McCormick ... it's urgent."

"One moment."

Andrea glanced up, catching the nosey librarian watching her every move, her evil-eyes shooting warning glances towards the clock on the wall.

Andrea turned her back to the woman's snooping eyes. She waited. Finally, after the passing of several minutes, the robust voice returned to the line. "I'm sorry ma'am, but we have no one by that name."

Andrea's heart dropped to her stomach. "Are you certain?"

"Yes, ma'am," he said, definitively.

Oh God, Andrea thought, grievously, *McCormick is the imposter!* She hung up the receiver, and handed the bulky phone case back to the old woman. "Thank-you," she whispered, drily. She turned, and started towards the door.

"Urgent, huh?" groused the chafing, old woman. "So that's what your generation of young ladies is calling it, is it?" Her crotchety, old voice grew in intensity. "Sweetie … let me give you some advice … every female in this Kingdom would dearly l-o-v-e to speak to Matthew J. McCormick … and it's always urgent. What makes you think you're so urgently special?"

Andrea froze, feeling every last ounce of energy and certitude ebb away. *Gawd*, she thought, as the woman's words shrouded her mind, *everyone in this town is as old as Methuselah and armed to the gills with a killer weapon!* She glared back at the sulking, old hag, unsophisticated and aging by the minute. In a muzzy, out-of-body experience, and in a manner completely out of character for the journalist, she raised her hand in anger, and extended her middle finger at the nosey, old crone.

She flew to the front entry, tugging on the solid oak door. It wouldn't budge. She tugged, harder.

"Told you it was closing time," the old librarian cackled in a sing-songy voice. "Can't get out … security door locks down at o-dark-thirty," she droned, pointing to the darkness outside the window.

"How do I get out?"

"Guess you'll have to escape through the back door."

Andrea glared at the Draconian old woman as she rushed towards the back of the building and out the unlocked door. She, angrily, yanked off the suffocating mask. Like flags a furl, the wind slapped her hair against her face as she ran down the darkened alley to her car.

As she cleared the accumulated snow from the windshield, her thoughts raced back to all her conversations with McCormick. *"No one by that name,"* she repeated. Hot tears began to roll down her icy cheeks as she cupped her hands and blew hot breath into her numb fingers, remembering their tender, fireside chats. She walked to the rear window and swiped a hand across the accumulation of snow. "Yeah, McCormick ... you were right...." she said aloud, "a lot of things make me cry ... but nobody does it better than you!"

Suddenly, something thumped hard against her back, causing her head to bobble, and her feet to slip on the ice. Her first thought went to Donahue as she leaned against the car; her second, to the old librarian, but when she struggled to turn around, snow-encrusted paws hit the back of her shoulders, pushing her ear-down onto the snow-blanketed trunk. Her fears dissipated as she felt a lick, wet and warm, across her mouth. "Tracker!" she blurted out, pushing down her surprise visitor. "How ... what are you doing here?" He greedily licked her hands and rubbed against her jean-clad legs, tail wagging. She had been mistaken to think a dog, with the instincts of a wolf, would stay alone at the cabin while she shopped for supplies. Sibes liked activity, and they liked people, she remembered from her reading as she wiped a handful of snow across her mouth; but how had he gotten out?

She subdued the dog with a treat from her pocket; and, with urgency, retrieved her snow-buried purse from the gutter. Unlocking the door, she let the wet dog into the back seat, feeling extreme relief to have his company. She climbed behind the wheel, and hastily slammed the door shut, quickly hitting the switch on the door panel. With rapt attention, she listened to the sound of each and every door locking down. At the sound of the last one, she let out her hot breath in relief.

The engine was cold. It churned and labored on the first turn of the key, but wouldn't start. She gave it a second try, and a third. "Come on, for God's sake," she urged, through chattering teeth, bemoaning the fact that she had never found time to get the car winterized. She imagined the disaster it would be, should she get stuck here in town with that rakish sheriff on the prowl. She tried again. At last the engine fired. Fighting back tears of relief, she backed into the street, giving the car no time to warm up.

Visibility was at near zero, and snow had already accumulated on the road atop a layer of black ice. Happy to be in the car with Tracker, relief consumed her; but just as quickly, a shudder of foreboding besieged her entire body—she was in big trouble.

Her mind reeled with worry. Why would anyone want to investigate her ... an investigative reporter ... of all people? How was she supposed to know who to trust—what was real, and what was not? She didn't know anything about a plane, or drugs—not really. Everything she knew came from research. She was just a stupid reporter—McCormick had said as much, himself. His words haunted her, angered her.

Soon, she was on the road that followed the ridge with nothing but deep ravines on either side. As she struggled to keep the car between the obscured lines, she was struck by a thought. McCormick was a fraud, an imposter—that was a given; but why had he not returned? Had something happened to him, or had she driven him away forever. And how, and when, would she meet this new computer for a brain, this Boy Wonder—the one with degrees out his ass?

The old wiper blades labored nosily, only partially removing the heavy onslaught of fresh snow. "Tracker babe," she whispered, as her knuckles whitened around the steering wheel. "I'm afraid you're going to wish you had stayed at home."

Suddenly, the inside of the windshield turned white with fog as the defroster failed to keep up with the conditions. Andrea groaned aloud to the cold, car. Seeing no place to pull over, she started to panic. Rolling down the window to see the road, she whispered, "God help us."

She began to swipe at the thickening haze with the back of her fingers, suddenly seeing in them, an image of McCormick's hand as he had wiped at the jeep's fogged up windshield in the National Forest. Her little Honda started to fishtail. Correcting the steering, she thought, Oh *God, I wish he were driving!*

Sensing Andrea's panic, Tracker began to whine and pace back and forth in commiseration. Immediately, a solution popped into her head, and she quickly turned off the heat. She switched on the air-conditioner, trying to even out the differences in temperature between the car's interior and the air outside.

"Yes!" she yelled, ecstatically, as the windshield began to clear, Now shivering in the frigid air, she rolled up her window, then quickly lowered the back one halfway so Tracker could hang his head outside, bringing an end to his pacing.

With crisis solved, Andrea turned her thoughts back to the investigation. She didn't know how she would handle it, or if she would have any control. Of course, she was innocent. As with the cabin, she'd had no idea Shaun had bought a plane. She was facing extremely serious charges, charges that could land her in prison for a very long time. She knew it was in her best interest to handle the investigation well. She thought about the sheriff's insinuation that Shaun had been involved in drug smuggling in South America. *Oh, boy,* she thought, *was that one ever lame and insane—or was it?*

At last she reached her own road. Her head throbbed and her eyes blurred from the tedious trek over the treacherous, mountain road. She was more than aware of the danger of sliding off into the same deep abyss that had almost claimed her life, just a few short weeks ago.

As she guided her Honda towards the cabin, a huge, heavy-bodied bird flew over the car's hood, and took roost in the oak tree. "Vultures!" she moaned, her mood darkening even further. Tracker began to pace in the back seat. As the cabin drew nearer, he stood on all-fours with his ears pricked forward and a growl in his throat.

She parked as close as possible to the cabin, out of the cold, blowing wind; but it still left her a distance to walk. She grabbed one of her two grocery bags, and a large bag of dog food from the car, deciding to leave several items behind for a second trip, including a gallon jug of orange juice. She walked along the foot-path, thinking that if the road drifted shut, she would have to walk the ten miles to the highway, and hopefully thumb a ride—not exactly the safest thing in the world for a woman to do.

Snow crunched beneath her boots and her breathing came in gasps, her white, frosty breath spiraling high above her head. The tips of her ears grew numb from the cold, and she became uncomfortably aware of the metal hoops, large and frigid, in her pierced ears.

Suddenly, Tracker stopped in his tracks and turned his nose towards the oak tree. His ears pricked up, and his neck ruffled. A low growl rumbled deep in his throat.

"What is it big guy?" she questioned as her eyes skimmed the shrouded area. "What do you see?"

At the far side of the clearing, near the salt block, two deer stood in silhouette, their heads held high in alertness. An owl, just awakened, fluttered in a nearby tree, flapped his wings, and flew away. The deer quickly turned, then leaped into the tree line, their white tails disappearing into the darkened forest. Unease seeped into Andrea's mind as an unnatural hush fell over the clearing.

A sound, a faint popping sound came from somewhere under the oak tree. She took a step towards the tree. Although leafless, its huge branches spread wide, leaving the area beneath the tree bare and snowless. Something or someone had stepped on an acorn. Through waning light and flakes large enough, and icy enough to be heard, the image of Shaun Fitzgerald suddenly appeared before her!

CHAPTER 38

Andrea stood motionless, her heart threatening to stop its beating. *It can't be,* she reasoned. She blinked away wind-driven flakes, coming fast and furious. She called out, weakly, "Shaun?" From a distance, Tracker gave out a rare bark, and shot towards the tree.

She looked again, this time seeing nothing but the outline of the naked tree against an opaque skyline. Darkness swallowed any possibility of finding tracks.

With dumbstruck numbness, she trod over the ice-covered walkway, unlocked the heavy door, shoving it open with her hip. She encouraged Tracker to enter quickly, while she eyed the ever darkening tree line. She followed the dog's thumping tail in, and with ferocity, slammed the door shut, and quickly bolted it behind her. She felt exceedingly grateful that she'd heeded McCormick's warning to lock the door. Suddenly, her body stiffened, and she froze in place. *How had Tracker managed to get out a bolted door?*

Her heart began to race, again. "Calm down," she ordered herself. Something came to mind, spooking her further. She had written about people who claimed to have seen images of their dead spouses ... apparitions. She'd always thought that sightings of that kind could easily be explained. But now, Andrea found herself shaken to the core by her own experience— explained or unexplained.

Her hands began to shake, uncontrollably. She glared at them. Why was she so preoccupied with her hands? She fretted. "I'm freakin' losing my mind here," she screeched aloud.

Dragging a chair to the door, she hastily braced it under the knob, and then stood flat against the darkened shadows of the wall, studying the exposed windows, wishing like hell, that she had drapes to pull shut.

341

Becoming aware of her snow-packed boots, her eyes dropped to the floor in front of her. She gasped and grabbed her stomach—the floor was already wet with large-sized boot tracks.

"Shaun," she whispered, with horror. *He would have the cabin's second key—were he alive!*

From the kitchen window, she nervously checked the area around the tree, before crossing the dark, unlit floor to inspect the locks on the double doors that opened onto the deck. She scanned the frosty clearing. No deer; but something was out there—she could feel it.

She shoved her nose against the window, peering across the deck through the disappearing twilight at the barely visible salt block. For the first time, she wondered who had placed it in the clearing. She was dead certain it hadn't been there on her first day at the cabin.

Something moved on the deck. Her breathing halted as her eyes shot towards a dark shadow. *Shaun!* Suddenly, the shadow rose straight up in front of her, looming large and threatening, startling her into a state of panic. A strong stench hit her nose, just as two dark eyes glared at her through the glass. She screamed, and quickly darted away from the doors, feeling the tingle of fright shoot straight to her toes.

Staring at her through the glass, stood the largest black bear she'd ever seen in her life. Transfixed by fear, she stared back, taking in the large bulk, aware of the large crease running down the middle of its mammoth head, indicating a bear of accumulated age and enormous size. Two paws the size of dinner plates leaned against the window pane. Tracker rushed forward, and bared his teeth, growling ferociously; but then he backed away in a weird way, and sat on his back haunches, appearing to smile in recognition of the wild animal.

At last, the humongous visitor, sluggishly, dropped to all fours, and lumbered away, seemingly with purpose, leaving paw smears, wet and dirty, on the glass.

"Bears are supposed to hibernate!" Andrea screeched, before remembering McCormick's detailed explanation as to why they didn't.

The hour was late. Andrea's nerves were raw as she lay in bed, listening to the wind whistle around the cabin—a cabin cold, damp, and pitch black. It swished through the pines, making whispering sounds, eerie and haunting.

At times, she could swear she heard the voices of men, making her skin crawl. When coyotes commenced their baneful howling, she buried her head beneath her pillow.

Her mind dwelt on what she thought she'd seen, earlier. If she had to choose between seeing Shaun, or an apparition, she would readily choose the apparition. She sorely regretted not remembering to pack her pistol.

What she did remember was the coal oil lantern she'd, at last, picked up in town. It was still in her car, along with a large can of coal oil, and a new propane gas tank, along with some other purchases to make her life more bearable. No way, was she was going back outside to get them out of the trunk—not tonight!

Having a strong need to take control of something, anything, she sat up and neatly folded a part of the musty-smelling quilt away from her nose. As though blind, her fingers groped along the top of the nightstand in search of the almost depleted book of paper matches she'd picked up at the Mountain Inn restaurant weeks ago. She grabbed the unread mail she'd picked up earlier in the day and spread it across her lap. Estimating only about an hour's worth of tallow left on the candle, she struck a match and lit the wick; but the stubby, paper match burned too hot and too fast, searing her fingers. Totally stunned, Andrea could only watch as the match dropped to the papers in her lap, and caught fire. The old, dry threads of the quilt ignited, quickly devouring the cloth, along with a number of empty food wrappers. The flames leapt high, licking her face. She tried to scream, but the sound was muffled by the Hostess Ding-dong she'd just shoved into her mouth.

Tracker suddenly appeared in the doorframe. Finding the woman in a blaze of fear and panic, he instantly sprung to the bed and quickly dragged the burning mass onto the floor. Finally coming to her senses, the benumbed women grabbed her pillow, and started to beat out the hot, licking flames.

At last, they both collapsed to the floor, exhausted but keeping a keen eye on the smoldering heap in front of them. She let her muscles relax, remembering, too late, her purchase of kitchen matches still in the car. Tracker let out another rare bark, and a reemergence of flames shot up from the pile. Aghast, she jumped up and began battling the burning heap with what little was left of her pillow, stomping her feet until every last spark was dead—and the entire cabin stank from the putrid smell of singed feathers.

Sighing deeply, she plopped down on the exposed mattress, and leaned back against the wooden headboard, hugging her knees. *A dog had saved her life!* In darkness, she sat for several long minutes, sans blanket or pillow, listening to the wooden beams creak and groan like a ship at sea. Finally, she dropped to the floor in front of the dog, and butted her head up against his. Looking, gratefully, into his eyes, she cooed. "Tracker ... you're my hero ... thanks for saving my life ... got it?" she asked, farcically, feeling as though she were speaking to a human. The dog slowly staggered to his feet, shot her a hindmost glance indicating the end of a successful mission, and began to trot down the steps.

Downstairs, the windows rattled and a blustery wind howled down the chimney. She imagined the ashes and smoldering, hot coals being scattered across the room, as McCormick had warned they might. She got up and walked to the top of the stairs, checking it out, assuring herself that everything was securely contained behind the safety screen.

On the landing, she tarried, frozen in time. The vision she saw at the hearth was no phantom, or apparition, but a warm memory—the memory of Matthew J. McCormick, now long gone. She could still see his image as he had sat before the blazing fire, muscles tense, looking as though he were about to pounce. She smiled, thinking cognitively: Why were moments never of importance until they became a treasured memory?

She had recognized the immediate bond between her dog and the agent that night as Tracker had, adoringly, lain beside his chair.

Now, the dog lay by the abandoned hearth, himself looking abandoned and lonely, with one eye open, his tail curled around his nose, waiting for some special person to enter through the door. Knowing that huskies only took to one person, she wondered who his old owner might have been. "He must have been one helluva master," she said aloud. She knew this breed of dog preferred the cold; but still, she felt sorry for him in this dark, dreary cabin tonight. She called to him, "It's okay, boy ... go back to sleep—I promise not to burn the furniture."

She sighed, and started to return to bed, but the swaying branches outside the frosty downstairs windows drew her attention as their shadows swayed back and forth across the cabin floor. It wasn't fear, or the cold, that suddenly made her shudder, nor was it the draft coming from under the kitchen door. No, it was the gnawing sense of total isolation creeping into her bones. She was alone, not only in this cabin, but in the cold, dark world beyond. Andrea wrapped her arms around herself—trying to shore up her emotions.

The wind whistled under the kitchen door. Finally growing impatient with the draftiness, Andrea grabbed the stub of flickering light and slipped down the cold stairway. Hastily, she snatched up a dated, local newspaper beside the chair, yet unread, and began folding and stuffing its pages between the cracks in the door, using all but the inside page. That particular page, she kept, thinking she'd read the *Around Town* column—that ought to put her to sleep in no time.

In the kitchen, she walked to the cabinet, thinking a cup of hot chocolate would be just what she needed to calm her nerves, but she was running low on propane gas; she'd need to save what was left for her morning morsels. She longed to soak in a hot bath, but she had no hot water—hell, she didn't even have a tub.

Wistfully, she accepted the fact that the cabin—to her deep regret—was no longer a peaceful haven, and there was no earthly reason for her to stick around any longer. Begrudgingly, she made the decision to return to Forest Hills the following morning, if she could get her small, low-built Honda through the snow—and if she hadn't frozen to death by morning's grey light.

She walked to the frosted window over the sink, finding there, the Wall of Fame photo she'd hastily tucked into a loose pane. She held the candle higher, shining light on the agent's image. She was surprised to find such a bright, open smile on McCormick's, seemingly, happy face. With caution, she went up on her toes and peeked outside through the frosted pane and the blowing snow, barely able to see the outline of the lake. She suddenly dropped back on her heels as an alarm sounded in her head—the road was already snowed shut!

With ceremony, she placed the last birch log on the fire, then dropped to the rug beside Tracker, watching it burn slowly, beautifully. Soon, she came to a second realization—she would probably never see McCormick again. The man was either snuggled up in a soft, warm bed with a beautiful woman, arrested by the police—or dead. Her mind and emotions drifted with that last thought.

The acrid smell of ashes brought her back to the present. Cold cinders sifted through the bottom of the grate, leaving, only a few red coals where the log had once burned brightly.

When she finally returned to bed, her feet felt like chunks of ice, and she would have willingly traded her fortune for the brand new Christmas throw, still in the car. Going for it was out of the question. She reached for the newspaper, and started to read by what light was left of the candle, readily admitting that she hated gossip columns.

Suddenly, she bolted straight up in bed, reading aloud: *"The Red Spring's grapevine has it that Red Spring's former star quarterback and war hero, Matt McCormick, has been seen back on local streets after a long absence. Rumor also has it that the war hero, turned federal agent, is investigating the recent plane crash in the National Forest … and does anyone know who that dark-haired beauty was with him? Around Town is dying to know. Welcome home Matt— Susan and Charlotte still love you!"*

Star quarterback? War hero? Susan and Charlotte?

She checked the three-week-old dateline. Experiencing a labyrinth of emotions, she wadded the newspaper into a small, tight ball and threw it angrily at the wall. On impact, the wall began to rattle, and a chain behind the logs began to creep and crawl. Suddenly a hidden door panel creaked open, revealing a closet—a built-in linen closet.

In disbelief she sat up and stared, wide-eyed, at the large, recessed area as her baffled mind tried to make sense of the conundrum. How had McCormick known of its existence? Rolling out of bed to shove the door shut, she first noticed a winter-heavy flannel shirt casually tossed onto a shelf: a size 2X, tall, fitted waist. She hadn't noticed before, but the shirt had obviously been moved, she now realized, from the hook in the bathroom closet to this hidden closet. She stared at the many large coils and cables running up and down, and around the entire insides of the closet. *Damn— this space once held sophisticated, technical equipment,* she realized.

She plopped back down on the side of the bed, glaring at the gaping hole in the wall. *Cables meant electricity.* Her eyes locked on to electrical outlets. Like a rocket, she shot off the bed. She began to pace. "And the only place with electricity in this whole frickin' cabin is this frickin' hidden closet?" As though in tantrum, she sucked outrage in with her breath, and hurled the red and hunter-green plaid garment back into the closet. She bellowed, "And McCormick knew about it!"

She blew out the candle in exasperation, splashing the remaining melted tallow across the nightstand. She groaned in delirium. *If a light was needed tonight, she'd have to light up the whole freakin' tabletop,* she thought, plopping back into bed. She remembered Donahue's conjecture that *she* owned the small plane that had crashed in the National Forest. "So that means," her breath caught in her throat, "that means that *I'm* at the heart of McCormick's investigation!"

She stretched her body out on top of the mattress as though dead. The baneful howling started again. This time Andrea felt certain the sound came, not from a coyote or wolf hybrid, but straight from the hounds of hell. Fear and paranoia took hold. Not until she had stuffed her ears with Mp3 ear buds, and Tracker had snuggled up beside her, did she finally fall into a light, troubled sleep, listening to the original Josh Daniel's version of "Jealous."

CHAPTER 39

He parked his all-terrain vehicle behind a thicket of snow-packed brambles; close, but out of sight. In pre-dawn darkness, his footsteps crunched across the frozen snow as he approached the cabin amid the forlorn sounds of a hooting owl, just returning to roost from its night-long hunting. He took steps around her car, completely buried by snow, and swiped away the heavy accumulation on the passenger's side. He peeked furtively through the ice-encrusted window, seeing a few scattered groceries on the back seat, as well as a plastic-wrapped blanket, of some sort, sticking out of a familiar-looking shopping bag. He squared himself, then stopped in his tracks and looked up—no smoke rose from the chimney; her fire had died out.

Inside the cabin, Tracker's head rose with guarded alertness. A low, menacing growl gurgled deep in his throat, awakening the sleeping woman beside him with a start. Warily, she lifted her drowsy head to see what had the dog's attention. The cabin felt abnormally cold, and was eerily quiet, tomb-like. According to her watch, it was 4:30 in the morning. A shudder of foreboding swept through her at the mournful hoot of an owl.

He stepped to the door, and rapped loudly; then waited.

The knock shook Andrea to the core. Fearful images of Shaun popped into her mind. She remembered Donahue's warning about the imposter, his lies; then she remembered Donahue and his vow to deliver firewood. A deep innate fear clutched her chest. She was totally defenseless.

Her bare feet hit the cold floorboards as she rose from the bed, and peeked through the hoary window pane. The sky was pitch black, but she could tell that several more inches of snow had fallen overnight, clinging heavily and illuminating every tree branch. Her eyes swept to the front of the house, and her heart dropped to her stomach. A man of considerable size stood on the porch.

A few more minutes passed, but no one came to the door. He looked for signs of life inside the cabin; he saw none. He rapped a second time, louder and more demanding.

Tracker whined, and started towards the door, but Andrea grabbed him by the collar, and yanked him back. Again, she looked out. The man's face was shadowed in pre-dawn darkness; but he carried something white—birch logs, maybe. She held her breath, considering his height and build. Was it Donahue? She looked again.

"McCormick!"

Her first emotion was extreme elation, but as she slipped down the cold, dark stairway in bare feet, her sense of euphoria quickly dissipated. Memories of her findings the previous night flooded her mind. "Too little, too late," she hissed under her breath. She debated whether or not to let him in.

By the time she reached the door, she was livid, and shivering in the extreme frigidness of the cabin. She removed the chair from under the door knob, and unlocked the bolts, finally understanding why someone might need so many different locks.

Hearing the snitch of the last lock, McCormick shoved against the door. A shower of folded newspapers rained down around his head and feet as he entered the dark cabin. Entering with him was a long blast of cold air, ice crystals, and a whiff of woodsy, masculine cologne.

He took two steps inside the door and stopped short. "Sorry to wake you so early, but I was wor…concerned about your wood supply." His non-committal eyes, cold and impersonal, darted immediately to the cold, dead hearth, noting that she had failed to close the damper.

"Yeah, sure," she spat crossly. "I'll just bet you were concerned," she countered, somehow managing to sound both cross and indifferent. "Why in the hell are you here?"

He sucked air, disappointed by the hostility she breathed so early in the morning. He had hoped she would have put aside her pride, accepted the fact that her life had gone sideways, and started to reason things out a little more rationally.

He turned his head askance, eying the folded newspapers, the straight-back, kitchen chair beside the door, and a large opened bag of birdseed leaning against the cabinet. *She was resourceful; he'd give her that much,* he thought. He took in her bedraggled appearance, her dark-rimmed eyes—the putrid stench in the air.

"Still a little *bitchy*, are we?" he asked, scowling, deliberately projecting more devil than imp. He walked towards the hearth, noticing that she had pulled the upholstered chair to the window. Multiple books and newspapers were scattered and piled about—just as he had done in years past. She'd obviously been hard at work during his absence.

He dropped the wood, unceremoniously, where he stood—at a distance from the hearth. "Did we get up on the wrong side of the bed this morning?"

"*We* did not!" She snapped angrily, catching his double entendre, and feeling appalled by his nerve.

He removed his hat, and tossed it into the winged-back chair; then ran his fingers through his hair, noticing that the only lighting in the cabin came from the illumination reflecting off the snow, and filtering in through the tall, wide windows. Through the gauzy light, he eyed her jeans, hanging wet and limp across the fire screen in front of the cold, dead ashes of the hearth; her coat had been thrown over the back of a kitchen chair and moved to the hearth—*she'd spent time outside sometime in the last few hours.*

A disquieted feeling swept through the man. "So what's going on?" he asked, his speech brusque and impatient.

To Andrea, his two-day old stubble looked unusually ominous, but his hair had been recently trimmed, and now stood casually tufted into a neat, new and very becoming style. Andrea shook her head in amazement. She stepped between the man and the fireplace, forcing him to look directly at her. "I have just learned, Agent Matthew McCormick ... that the DEA ... you ... to be precise, are not only investigating the drug dealers I write about, but me ... *me!*" Her hands rose to point to herself. "Why on earth, would you be investigating me? I don't know anything about a stupid plane!"

McCormick winced at her remarks, calling to mind the illegal fleet of planes her husband had assembled in South America, and loaded to the gills with contraband, their pointy, little noses stuffed to the hilt with heroin; and Fitzgerald—very much alive—was at this moment, using them to deliver his illegal cargo to the states. But he stood silent—wanting to speak, knowing he couldn't.

She shoved her hands down to her sides, and with daggers for eyes, shot him a heated look, "You lied to me!"

He looked at her in bewilderment.

"That might be acceptable behavior in the circles you run in," she continued, "but to me, a man is no better than a pile of shit if he can't be trusted!" She turned her back to him, refusing to look at his handsome face. She was angry and the distraction was unwelcomed. Even in the pre-dawn light he looked darker, more tanned, more roguishly handsome than the last time she'd seen him? She guessed he'd spent the last three weeks on a warm, sandy beach, while she shivered in the cold, rationing firewood, and swooning—like a damned idiot!

She hurled her words over her shoulder, "Why didn't you tell me you were some ... Boy Wonder ... some egg-headed, intellectual g-e-e-k?"

He frowned, and thrust his chin upward in question. *How did she know about the investigation?* He grabbed her shoulder and spun her around to face him. "Andrea, I didn't lie to you. When we discussed whether or not I was on the case, I'd just returned from the hospital. We talked at the restaurant."

He waited for her reply, but she only glared at him. He continued, "I got a phone call that day at the restaurant ... from headquarters. They gave me two days at home before they wanted me in Washington to give congressional testimony on another matter. That was Day One...." He dropped his hands and took quick steps to the foot of the stairs. "Day Two was right here ... on this very spot ... remember?"

Andrea remembered, alright. She scowled as the scene replayed in her mind. She wanted to believe McCormick, but he had disappointed her too many times. She was through being played a sucker—through being snowed.

Lines deepened in his forehead, giving expression to his, more than deep, concern. He had not lied to her, nor had he been completely honest. That day in the restaurant over three weeks ago, Straker had doubled down on his assignment to investigate Andrea. In truth, he had started to tell her about the investigation that very day, while she had chummed up to the chipmunk in the National Forest, before they had been so rudely interrupted by the long-bearded garden gnomes. She was in no state of mind to deal with that now, but it was something that definitely would need to be addressed, later.

He considered the situation at hand. In order to know about this investigation, one would need top security clearance, and here Andrea—a woman snowbound in a cabin with no phone, no electricity, nor internet service was giving him details of the case. That certainly didn't bode well for him, or for her.

"Andi ... how did *you* find out about this investigation," he asked, caustically.

"I can't tell *you*," she snapped, churlishly, too embarrassed to tell him that she had learned it from psycho Donahue.

"For Christ-sake, Andi!" he exclaimed, cupping a fretted hand to his forehead and turning away, his patience totally depleted. Ordinarily, he admired her spunk, but today he was bone-tired from his trip to and from Peru, and he had new disturbing information, deadly information—information he couldn't share with the wife of Shaun Fitzgerald. Tormented by that thought, he spun around. "Andrea, this is extremely important ... your life is in danger!"

"Oh yeah ... right," she challenged, cynically, dropping back on her heels and crossing her arms. "How many times have I heard that line?" she spat disbelievingly. "I'm not writing for the *News,* Inspector Columbo ... so why should my life be in danger?"

He raked all ten fingers through his hair in total frustration; then spoke with unusual gruffness, his words bellowing out in an uncharacteristic manner. "Andi ... spare me the theatrics ... how did you find out about the investigation?"

When she turned her back to him and refused to answer, he reached for her.

She quickly spun away. "Don't ... touch ... me!" she hissed through gritted teeth, meeting his peck of gruffness with a bushel of her own.

She turned stubborn eyes on the agent. "You have done nothing but lie to me since the day we met ... I didn't invite you into my life...." she jabbed a finger towards the door, "and I want you out of my house!"

It wasn't her anger that had McCormick totally frustrated, nor was it the fact that he'd just been ordered out of his own house; it was, instead, the need to get control of this situation before all hell broke loose. Not only were both of their lives in danger, but the lives of his family members, as well. Driven by this deep concern, he took a quick step forward, cupped her face with both hands, and locked eyes. He considered kissing her.

"Let go of me, you ... you Bjoreas ... I'm not Nicole!"

Nicole? He shot her a bewildered look, his hands hopelessly dropping to his side. Weariness crept into his voice. "I have no idea as to what mythos might be dancing through your head ... but you go ahead and believe whatever you want, Mrs. Fitzgerald."

"We have to trust each other," she goaded as she rushed to the foyer, "we're not there yet ... remember?" She threw open the door and yelled, "Out!"

With pursed lips, he took a step towards the door, but his manly pride and conviction quickly surfaced—it was time for a little more tough love. Like Phoenix rising from the ashes, he turned flaming eyes on the angry woman. His jaw hardened, and his chin jutted upwards. Exacting words shot out of his mouth with force and rapidity as his deep, booming voice rumbled like thunder through the early morning opaqueness. "Mrs. Fitzgerald ... I've got a *news flash* for you ... I'm not the object of your wrath! You're angry at life ... your life, and I'm not saying that I blame you ... but it's a life that's going to be all fucked up forever, unless you get that anger under control and talk to me!"

"Screw you, McCormick," she hissed, dismissively.

He stepped closer, tauntingly close, "Ah, come on Fitzgerald ... is that really your best shot? That tired, old line's older than Will Remington's paints ... I figured a nationally syndicated columnist, such as yourself, would have something a little fresher, a little more creative to hurl at me ... considering you harbored enough animus to put a gun to my head."

Andrea sucked in her breath, and shot his fiery, insolence right back at him. She sneered and chortled all at once, "You think you know me so well, but you don't know anything!"

McCormick gave her a long, hard look. He straightened his back and shoulders. "Actually ... I do know you, Mrs. Fitzgerald." He fortified his stance, and with smugness and aplomb started reeling off his findings, making it personal. "I have personally read every single gerund, metaphor and transitive verb of your controversial editorials expounding the hazards of illegal drugs." He took steps forward, forcing her backwards.

"Controversial?" A shiver ran through her, and her brows knotted with confusion. Her feet shuffled towards the backside of the loveseat.

McCormick noticed the move, but tossed her a dismissive glance. "And I have discovered that you, Mrs. Fitzgerald, have been living a life of wanton duplicity."

Andrea watched as incomprehensible words escaped through teeth as white as the falling snow. "Of wanton what?" she screeched through the dim morning light.

"Duplicity," he repeated, his tone turning accusatory. "And incidentally, Mrs. Fitzgerald … it's not me, but you who is the liar. While you've been working for old, bourbon-headed Rudd, you've also been writing for the *Boston Globe*, using a fictitious name."

"It's called a pseudonym," she said, drily.

"But one of your biggest offenses is the fact that your columns have gone into national syndication, and now run in newspapers all over the country."

Andrea stood glaring with disdain at the man, too shocked to speak.

"And as a direct result of my super sleuthing," he continued, "I've learned that in order to become a syndicated columnist, you usually have to have written a book … a Best Seller, to be exact."

He paused as an expression of deep thought seized his demeanor. Suddenly, he raised his palm, and comedically conked himself on the forehead. He chortled, "Oh, wait … damned if you don't … hot off the press, as a matter of fact."

Andrea glared at the agent. *How did he know? She'd gotten notification, only yesterday, of her book's place on the Best Sellers List*—by snail mail. She breathed out a distressed sigh. "So where's the crime … Inspector Clouseau?"

"Three weeks ago you told me you wrote only for the *News*. Now, the way I see it … you either write with the expeditiousness and velocity of a speeding bullet … or you, flat-out, lied to me … Mrs. Fitzgerald—that's not only a lie … that's a felony."

Andrea's eyes widened. *Who would have thought that the minutia of her boring, little life would become such a big, frickin' deal?*

McCormick shot her a plaintive look, showing more than an inkling of emotional frustration. "The real crime, Andi…." he said, planting his hands on his hips, and letting his now humorless gaze rest on her face for a beat, "occurred … when you failed to share your good news with *me* … *we* could have celebrated your success," he offered with benignancy.

Her eyes flashed, and she howled, sarcastically, "In your dreams!"

Enough of the abuse, he thought, and stepped forward with austerity. "Mrs. Fitzgerald … there is one more question I'd like for you to answer … and then I'll get the hell out of your life."

A pause, tense and pregnant, fell between them, as they both considered the emptiness of a life without the other. He stepped closer. "My *stalking,* as you like to call it, has revealed the fact that you have an immense love for children, and yet for some reason, you have none of your own." His brows furrowed with genuine concern. "Why is that?"

Anguish, deep and painful, flickered across Andrea's stunned face— anguish that turned, unfortunately, to hot, molten insolence. Seeing the change of expression on the woman's face, McCormick groaned inwardly. He walked to the window and looked out into the storm. Letting his soul absorb the harsh wintry scene, he embraced his inner SOB. He slowly turned around, capturing Andrea's gaze in soberness. "In your thousand-year marriage to the Devil Incarnate ... was he not man enough to get the job done ... or did he just not want any h-e-i-r-s to the kingdom?"

Time stood still as Andrea felt the last protective leaf callously ripped from her fragile heart. Friendly or unfriendly, this man had just struck a fatal blow. Her eyes flashed. "Fuck you, McCormick," she screamed, wrath pouring from every fiber of her being.

With a saddened heart, the agent swept down, plucked his hat out of the chair, and rose to lock stubborn eyes. "In *your* dreams ... sweetheart," he growled. Without another glance in her direction, he stalked out of the cabin, as though never to return.

Shuddering, more from the man's harsh words than from the cold, and with his question hammering against her skull, Andrea quickly built a fire, using the wood he had carried in—and for some insane reason, dropped in the middle of the living room floor. She watched the flames slowly ignite; then sat back and let her eyes wander aimlessly over the cabin walls. For the past two years, the logs of her life had been nothing but pain, grief, and disappointment—with extreme loneliness as the only chinking. Angry? Hell yes, she was angry, but what right did he have to come in here in the middle of the night and preach to her?

Her eyes shot to the top of the stairs, where Tracker stood, whimpering, lacking the courage to descend the steps. She called to him and, with empathy, walked him to the kitchen door. She gave him a love pat, and let him out; then she climbed the stairs, numbly bracing herself for an icy cold shower. Her heart felt as heavy as the snow weighting down the branches outside the huge windows, offering her an intimate view of the first blush of dawn, through a gray horizon and whiteout conditions. It was the perfect depiction of her cold, lifeless heart. What was the word McCormick had used with the gnomes? Oh, yeah ... frigid.

Andrea showered, dried off on her one and only towel, now wet and smelly from overuse, and shoved her toes into her fur-lined slippers

Suddenly, the buzzing sound of a chainsaw pierced the air outside the cabin. Hiding behind the towel, she walked to the loft window and stared down at McCormick, seeing the blade bite into the rough bark of a limb—a limb felled from her graceful, old tree.

Her coat and jeans were still wet from the day before. She remembered the man-sized, winter-weight shirt she'd found in the hidden closet and grabbed it as a last ditch effort.

Throwing the holey, singed quilt around her shoulders, she thundered down the stairs, and flew out the door, with no thought of pulling it shut.

From the corner of his eye, McCormick saw the angry woman unexpectedly, explode like a cannonball out of the cabin, and appear at his side. "What in the hell do you think you're doing?" she yelled over the persistent buzz, and spewing flecks of sawdust.

His eyes widened as he perspicaciously looked the fuming woman over from head to toe through his brown aviators, and the first gray light of dawn. "I thought you'd need a bigger flame ... for all those imaginary marshmallows you're always talking about roasting," he taunted, snidely, over the buzz and burr of the menacing, circuitous cycle of biting chain.

"Not from this tree!" she shouted, authoritatively, her brows arching and eyes flashing daggers.

Momentarily backing away from his cutting, he thrust his chin up, stubbornly. "Why not?" he asked, his hot breath spiraling.

"Because this is *my* property, and *I* don't want this tree defaced!"

McCormick's face flushed from a rich, golden tan to a deep, crimson ire as he pulled the hungry blade away from the rounded limb. In sheer frustration, and pure toxic masculinity, he ripped off his shades, and flung them, with force, against the base of the mighty oak.

CHAPTER **4 0**

With determination riding his body like an immotile glacier, McCormick took a giant step forward, planted his feet and looked at Andrea with eyes as cold, and as piercing as the chainsaw's biting edge. Through the thick, snowy downfall, he spoke with righteous indignation. "Mrs. Fitzgerald ... I think it's about time you woke up and smelled the coffee ... I've looked, but I don't see any wood nymphs dancing around this tree; and I'm not a hundred percent sure, but I'm guessing there are no spirits living in it, either ... nor are there any Spiritwood faces carved into its trunk...." His face jerked up, "but lady ... just in case you haven't noticed, we're standing in the middle of nowhere ... smack dab in the middle of an extreme fuckin' blizzard. You're black, not only on wood, but on food, and all the Wrath of Hell is about to descend on us; but by God ... you'll be the first to know if my nose starts to grow longer because of all the fuckin' lies I've told you!"

Andrea glared at the man. His snide remarks referencing earlier, lighter times, cut her to the quick—times she had savored and cherished—and now she hated him for it. "Wrath of Hell," she snarled, dismissively.

McCormick heard her chiding remark of unrestrained indignation, but saw the huge tears welling up in the woman's eyes.

He turned, and as he took strident steps towards the tree to retrieve his glasses, he had to admit what he'd been trying to ignore: Andrea wasn't herself. Sure, she could be bitchy, but she could also take it; for some reason, that wasn't happening today. Something unnerving must have happened to fuel this kind of hysteria. He sucked cold air, as the thought occurred to him that her actions almost smacked of PTSD. *Maybe that's exactly what it is: Post Traumatic Stress Disorder; actually, she had experienced a lot of trauma over a very short time,* he thought. Deciding to back off for now and give her some space, he tamped down his own rankled spirit, realizing that his own terse responses hadn't exactly been stellar in nature.

"Alright ... alright," he said, feigning impatience. He tossed an exaggerated nod at the oak. "Keep your effing tree ... I'll cut deeper in the woods..." He checked his watch—time was of the essence. This woman's husband was just hours behind him: a man with half his mind blown away by drug use, and the other half possessed by pure evil.

Remembering that he had yet to contact his boss for reinforcements—and to place security around each of his own family members, he was in a hurry to get to the wood-cutting. He swept down and retrieved his tinted lenses, then stopped to train his narrowed eyes on Andrea—on her state of dress. His mind seared with images of Donahue's obsessive binoculars across the lake, and the shotgun-toting, numbskulls who had already shown way too much interest in the gorgeous woman, and were now camped in the woods just a few klicks away. He was certain that, once the snowstorm ended, any or all of them would be sniffing around the cabin looking for food, shelter, and anyone could guess what else.

As McCormick continued to think like the enemy, the ugly truth surfaced. He knew Stone's demented thinking would run along those same lines. Weighing the evidence, he was certain he knew which way that would go.

The least he could do was warn her. He stood steadfast, as harsh, wind-driven snow pelted his unsmiling face. He trained his sober eyes on the pugnacious woman, noticing, for the first time, her singed eyebrows, wondering why she hadn't retreated to the cabin. "Mrs. Fitzgerald...." He lowered his voice to a confidential tone, "if you don't take care, you're going to find yourself with a houseful of company you didn't invite, having chats about things that don't interest you, and being forced to do things, you sure as hell, don't want to do ... or maybe something even w-o-r-s-e."

Andrea knew, intuitively, that he was insinuating rape; yet still she challenged, churlishly, dangerously, "Well, at least I know ... McCormick ... the w-o-r-s-e won't come from you ... given your proclivity for sheep and goats!"

McCormick tamped down a chortle. He had to admit, Andrea certainly knew how to deliver a gut punch.

Seeing sudden movement in his peripheral vision, he looked past the fuming woman, to the furry-tailed rodent, scampering from the tree into the cabin through the gaping door. *Ah, hell,* he thought, *that won't end well.*

In the woods, Tracker got a whiff of something with a tail, and tracked it into a hole under a rotted tree stump. When the hissing animal turned out to be a skunk, he got sprayed royally, and began to react to the smell of burning, putrid n-butyl mercaptan by regressing to a flashback episode from his earlier years in Afghanistan. With eyes blinded by the stink bomb, and hearing the sound of angry voices echoing through the trees, Tracker's PTSD kicked into gear. He immediately assumed his master was under attack and ran towards their voices.

McCormick started to stalk off, saw in hand. Suddenly the dog bounded out of the woods, seeing only images of heavy, befouled cloth wrapped around a human form, he began to growl.

McCormick quickly turned to warn Andrea, "War Dog!"

"How do *you* know?"

"Just do," he clipped.

Now the edges of the quilt fluttered, wildly, in the blizzard winds. Tracker's instincts and training came to the forefront, and he responded by doing that, which he had been trained to do in years past—attack. Andrea screamed as he snarled, and rose up on hind legs, knocking her to the ground with his powerful, ice-encrusted paws. Reeking from the smell of skunk, and blinded by fear, the delirious canine ferociously tore into the blackened, fowl-smelling burn hole—snarling, tugging, trying to rip the quilt from her body. She started to scream.

From his own gruesome memories of war, McCormick knew what visions of horror streamed through the dog's head. He feared the worst—that Tracker might take a bite out of the woman's exposed thigh as he had been trained to do. "Andi, don't scream," he cautioned from a calm exterior, developed through years of rigorous training and nightmarish, war-time experience. "Don't move ... and don't look him in the eye—it only emboldens him."

More frightened by the threat of nudity than by the dog, Andrea futilely tugged at the disappearing quilt as it was quickly pulled away from her, leaving her totally stunned, and face-down in the snow.

McCormick lunged forward, trying to land on the dog's back, knowing that a distraught animal could sometimes be calmed by covering its body with your own. He landed on his mark, but the delirious canine suddenly flipped over, snapping and growling viciously through bared teeth.

The former warrior instantly righted himself, and barked out a loud, military command, sharp enough and gruff enough to startle even Andrea. "Halt!"

Instantly, the dog dropped to the ground.

McCormick grabbed the collar, and sidled the snarling canine. His heels dug into the frozen ground as he tugged back against the straining animal, calf-roping style. He winced at the strong, putrid odor, but peppered the distraught animal with words of kindness. "Good work, soldier ... good boy!" He offered soothing, empathetic tones, deliberately drawing the dog's attention away from Andrea.

While McCormick focused on the dog, Andrea pushed herself out of the snow, and ran to the tree. With knees about to buckle in humiliation, she hoisted herself up to a low-hanging branch. Leaping higher, she shimmied up to a limb of a larger size, stopped, and pressed her back against the trunk. Heated by red, hot embarrassment and the heart-pounding presence of danger, she clung to the rough bark with cold, stiff fingers, totally transfixed by fear.

Suddenly, the cock-sure dog broke the hold McCormick had on his collar. Andrea stood motionless as the spirited dog sniffed around the foul-smelling quilt then abandoned it to nose around the base of the tree. At last he sniffed his way to the deck, completely oblivious to the fact that he had become weaponized in this hostile human conflict.

Once the dog had been calmed, the bemused McCormick stood, grinning wryly, holding up his grandmother's quilt as though a prize. Finding Andrea gone, he dropped the wet, smelly, coverlet where he stood, and followed slivers and scraps of a recognizable, bright-colored cloth, scattered across the ground like breadcrumbs through the forest, leading straight to the tree.

Expressions of unexpected joy battled for a position on McCormick's face as he glanced up through snow-flocked branches, catching a glimpse of Andrea's lithe and lovely body; not au naturel as he had feared, but exotically sexy in his very own red and green plaid—her hot, sexy legs, bringing it home and making it personal beneath the shredded remains of his favorite shirt. Unable to pull his eyes away, the war between man and agent was being fought in full battle mode.

With his hot gaze upon her, Andrea could only glare down at the man while battling the wind for control of the billowing, over-sized shirttail in an attempt to cover her starkness.

McCormick spread his feet in a wide military stance, unzipped his Generation 3 jacket, and shoved it back at the sides. He planted his hands firmly on his hips. A snigger rose in his throat, but seeing her embarrassment, he dropped his gaze. "Okay," he said, oozing a ton of roguish charm, "so you've proven me wrong ... there really are wood nymphs in this tree."

When the wind threatened to whip the shirt above her head, McCormick quickly dropped his gaze with gentlemanly embarrassment, finding there, her fur-lined moccasins frozen to the ground. He kicked them loose with the toe of his boot, and shook out the ice and snow. He spoke with great concern, "Mrs. Fitzgerald ... you're exhausted ... and we're both in danger of frost bite and hypothermia ... you need to get inside, STAT, wrap up in a blanket, and take a long, winter's nap by the fire." Streaming through the alpha male's head, was a better way to warm up a woman, but age, experience and possible liability helped him tamp down the thought. Instead, he extended his hand in kindness, showing his willingness to help her down.

Searching for a way out of the tree, Andrea quickly realized there was no path to climb down; the branches were spaced too far apart. "There's no way down," she yelled with fainthearted exasperation.

Not at all surprised by her dilemma, McCormick said, calmly, "It's okay ... I've got your back ... just walk out on that limb, turn and drop ... I'll catch."

"And how do I *know* you'll catch?"

McCormick's chest burned with consternation. He growled, "Zacchaeus, come down out of that tree!"

"Zacchaeus?" Andrea asked, somewhat surprised, "You know Zacchaeus?"

"Yeah, I know him." A pause ensued before he spoke again, this time using a softer, but more definitive voice. "His house guest is a good friend of mine."

"His house guest ... a good friend?" A broad grin broke across her face.

It wasn't the squirrel-like chattering of her teeth that fed her courage to walk out on that limb and look down, nor was it the loss of feeling in her fingers and toes. It was, instead, their shared faith that helped her turn her backside to the man; but even then, her resolve faltered. With the shirttail billowing like a flag on the 4th of July, she shouted, "McCormick ... if you dare crack one single, droopy ass joke, I'm going to *drop* dead ...right here ... right now!"

McCormick fought back a snigger, but encouraged, "Stop being so critical of yourself ... and just drop into a huge, imaginary vat of decadent, fudge frosting."

And so she did. Closing her eyes, she let herself free-fall, trustingly into the only thing better than fudge frosting—the open arms of Matthew J. McCormick.

Taking one quick step forward, McCormick caught her with ease, just as he had done those many times for his younger siblings.

The roguish grin still played across his lips as he lowered her feet into the slippers—a grin that would've brought a blush to her cheeks had she seen it; or a bullet to his head, had her husband. With that thought in mind, he quickly shucked his jacket, and draped it around the gaping shirt with the missing buttons. Remembering that women succumbed to hypothermia quicker than men, he took the liberty of tugging the fronts of the jacket together. Reading her embarrassment, he asked in the way of a distraction, "So what do ya think ... am I'm getting any closer to deserving my paycheck?"

Andrea looked up in confusion, burrowing deeper into the jacket's warmth; and then, in complete silence, her entire body crumpled into a heap at his feet.

By his own admission, McCormick was no doctor; but neither was he completely lacking in medical knowledge. As a former warrior, he had voluntarily added Seal Medic to his skill set, and had relied on this training to save many lives. He immediately dropped to his haunches, checking Andrea's pulse. Finding it weak, he scooped her out of the snow and slogged, post-haste, across the knee-deep snow to the loft. He searched for something other than his coat to warm her body. What he found brought him to the brink of humiliation: all the tight knots he'd jokingly tied into the sheet, still remained, just as he had tied them weeks ago, rendering the sheet totally worthless for practical use.

Use whatever resource you have available, he remembered from intense training. Clattering down the stairs in two leaps, he stopped just long enough to throw a log on the fire; then, totally without pelage, dashed to the car through white-out blizzard conditions to retrieve the blanket he'd seen in her car.

Returning to the cabin, he ripped open the zippered plastic, ignoring its elegant packaging. What he did notice was its Wintertec label. He shook out the thick folds, and the full-sized image of an Old World Kris Kringle spread out across Andrea's blue-tinged body. Feeling somewhat chagrined, he gazed upwards. "Well of course," he groused. With hands on hips, he stood observing his patient, aware of each shallow breath she was not taking. They had lingered outside too long, and now her body was incapable of producing heat fast enough.

When his own chin began to quiver, and he felt his vitals take a nosedive from slogging around in cold, wet clothing, he did the very thing he'd sworn he'd never do. Without a second thought, McCormick tugged off his boots, and dutifully stripped down to his famous brand of underwear. Boasted to be "Best" for men in their ads, the underwear was, laughingly, guaranteed to solve problems. Going with the irony of the situation, McCormick whispered, "Let's see you solve this problem."

With his teeth chattering, and with visions, not of sugarplums, but of the probability of lawsuits dancing through his head, he quickly grabbed Andrea, blanket and all, in one swoop and headed down the stairs. Using his foot to drag the loveseat closer to the fire, he then plopped himself into the seat, pulling her close, as one would a sick child, and covering them both from head to toe with the blanket. Tracker watched the two from the floor, and then, dutifully, piled on, adding his body heat to the heap. Grateful for the dog's training and company, McCormick cooed, softly, "Good soldier." One crazy war dog was better than none for what was ominously shaping up as a three-dog life.

Sometime later, a precious, toasty sigh came from beneath the blanket, but instead of waking, Andrea only turned, and nestled deeper into the warmth, closer to the woodsy scent of cologne.

Once her breathing had normalized, and his own vitality had returned, McCormick carefully rose. He stretched her out comfortably on the loveseat, watching her fall back into a deep, peaceful sleep.

Satisfied that she would be alright once rested, he donned his clothes and retrieved his jacket. He guzzled a quick glass of milk, long past its expiration date, and working its way towards buttermilk. He stopped to check her pulse, one last time. With a rueful glance over his shoulder, he willed himself away—they were in dire need of firewood.

CHAPTER 41

Unable to get the woman off his mind, McCormick cut the last limb into hearth-sized logs. Like the fiery glob of volcanic mass, smoldering deep below Vermont's crusty surface, Andrea was hot in so many ways. But his investigative probing had taken a surprising turn. For months, he'd studied the open hostility aflame in her eyes. However this morning, for the first time, he'd heard a tone of hopelessness in her voice. He'd immediately recognized it for what it was—*a tell*. At last, he'd hit the bottom of a very deep, emotional well; and he sensed, not only a deep cover-up of something, but a dark, nefarious one, at that. Ordinarily, at this juncture in an investigation, a triumphant feeling would have sated his senses, as he watched his poison-dart arrow hit a bull's eye at the very core of her being—but not today. This woman needed his professional help.

He brushed the sawdust from his troubled brow. Having not slept in over forty-eight hours, his arms ached and his ears rang from the buzz and burr of the saw. His stomach and shoulder clamored for attention, but both would have to ruck up, and go unattended a while longer. He had only a very short window of time to get into Andrea's head before the enemy arrived.

He was convinced that his smartass comments, and the audacity of his lifesaving technique, had just destroyed any chance of a relationship with Andrea—friend or foe. Eventually, she would figure out what had just happened, on the heels of his being, quite heatedly, thrown out of the cabin. It was pretty much a given that she would sue him for sexual harassment, or accuse him of nonsexual assault—either way, he was, leeringly, guilty; but he had to get into her mind, before it all erupted into a molten mass of tragedy.

He gathered up an armload of logs, and started walking towards the cabin. He thought, *Gawd, I'd rather go another round with Hero, than use the only option left.*

Tracker had appeared, but run off chasing adventure, leaving McCormick to trudge back to the cabin alone with his hunger and dour mood clinging to him like saw dust to his jacket. As he approached the old, oak tree he chased away a flock of wild turkeys, first thinking them ugly vultures as they scratched, and gobbled up acorns from beneath the frozen snow.

He looked around for signs of the old, hungry bear that annually foraged the woods, feeding all winter on the tree's profusion of acorns. He shoved over a large pile of frozen scat, belonging to the six-foot, three-hundred-pounder, and fondly spoke the name he'd given it years ago while they were both young cubs, "Belly-dragger!" His gaze followed the bear's tracks away from the snow-flocked tree.

He stared up into the huge branches, his mind and heart burning with memories. He sucked in a deep, emotional breath. Andrea wasn't the only one to feel sentiment for this old, dry bark of a tree; nor was Andrea's heart the only one shrouded by loss.

And it hadn't been by accident that he'd built on this serene, scenic spot. His brother, Clint, and he had played for hours at a time in these same branches as kids on their grandparent's property. They had been Hawkeye fighting off the British; Eastwood in search of punks. They had tied ropes to the wide, spread-out branches, and jumped from limb to limb, pretending to be Batman and Robin in hot pursuit of evil—Skywalker and Solo, using the force. A neighbor kid had often hung around and played with them, always taking the role of the evil enemy. "You can't catch me, *Pretty Boy*," he had a habit of saying, to Matt's chagrin.

McCormick forced a smile at the memories; but wondered what Andrea found so enchanting about this tree? Why had she defended it so rigorously?

Suddenly seized by a boyish curiosity, he circled the tree's base. The cabin side of the trunk looked normal, but on the backside, he found, to his disgruntlement, a large, gaping hole, starting out the size of a bushel basket just above his head, then diminishing in size towards the ground. The bottom four feet of the trunk was hollow, but with the bark still intact. He looked at the hole with puzzlement, thinking it an unusual way for a tree to rot.

Dropping the wood, he peeked inside the dark hole—something glossy winked back at him. Inquisitively, he pulled his small Maglite from his pocket and shined it around the inside of the trunk. The tree had been purposely and meticulously hollowed out by router. He shoved his head in farther for a better look, and in so doing, scraped the side of his face on the rough, protrusive bark surrounding the hole. Blood and pain went unattended as his light bounced off a very large pile of bagged-in-plastic packages, small and tan, filling the deep space. He groaned, and settled back on his heels in astonishment, instantly recognizing his find. The term used for both cocaine and heroin hissed through his teeth. "Snow!" He'd just discovered a very large stash of heroin. He picked up a couple of the bags. One of them had been ripped open. "That can't be good," he speculated.

He pulled out a couple of dark, opaque packages, quickly tossing them back on the heap—black-tar heroin! A different kind of white package drew his attention. He reached for it, held it in his bare hands, studying its texture and composition. A deep groan escaped his lips, and his heart took a sick leap to the pit of his stomach. he immediately dropped the package to the ground as though it were the plague: fentanyl—the drug that kills on contact! He let the package lie, and thoroughly snow-washed his hands.

Frozen in both body and spirit, he shot a fiery eye towards the cabin. Did Andrea know about this? God … he hoped not. It would almost certainly implicate her, along with Shaun and the other drug dealers, possibly getting them all the death penalty. McCormick sucked cold air into his lungs—and if Andrea knew anything about the contraband stashed in this tree, he was duty-bound to arrest her.

He gave the scat an angry kick in utter frustration as another thought crossed his mind. Legally, the tree was on his property—and that implicated him!

McCormick's heart and chin hung heavier than a twig-eater's dewlap as he stepped up to the cabin door—a door still bearing the image of the rascally bear cub he'd hand-carved while still an idealistic, young kid. Quietly, he stacked the arm-load of wood along the outside wall. Barely able to breathe, and with great reluctance, he tapped lightly on the door.

"I could use some coffee," he said, his voice resonating from somewhere deep down in his chest as the door opened a crack.

Reluctantly, Andrea widened the opening and stepped away. He entered cautiously, but not without first noticing that her blue tinge was completely gone. He also noticed that her face had been freshly scrubbed, and a little make-up applied with additional eyebrows penciled in.

Unaware of his ghastly appearance, he tried, unsuccessfully, to meet her eyes, but she was, he noticed, still wearing her embarrassment. She was also dressed in black leggings, an active-wear jacket, loosely unzipped at the neck, and ballerina-style slippers. Was she okay? Yeah, she was more than okay; but he was certain she didn't know all that had happened to her. Her hair had dried, and been brushed to a smooth, healthy shine and pulled back into a ponytail. She'd either been dancing, or working out, he surmised—and crying.

McCormick sucked in a deep breath, and hesitatingly closed the door behind him. He slowly slipped out of his jacket, and wearily dropped into a seat facing the door.

Andrea couldn't help but stare at his frozen, weather-ravaged face. His glowing tan had turned ashen; his eyebrows, long lashes and stubble on his chin were completely white with frost and snow. Strangely, he reminded her of the image in the painting she loved so much: the barely discernable face of God, hidden in the early morning mist, watching over, guarding the foal. Once again, chills shot through her body.

"You brought in my new Christmas throw?" she questioned, dubiously.

"I did," he answered, without expression or explanation.

Spotting blood on the side of his cheek, she dampened her last paper towel, and tossed it to him.

Tracker had found his way home ahead of McCormick, and now ran between the man's wide-spread legs, whining and licking his hands. The foul smell of skunk had beaten him to the cabin, as well. McCormick pushed back his chair and rubbed the dog's ears, ruffling up his throat hairs; then addressing only the canine, he spoke in a slightly scolding tone. "You just had to go chasing tail, didn't you?" The animal laid his head on the man's knee, whining as though apologizing, but McCormick ordered him away.

To Andrea, the scene seemed a tad perplexing.

McCormick lifted his head, shooting Andrea a mildly astonished grin. "I'm surprised you let him in."

"I didn't," she groused, "he let himself in … the back door was unloc…." Her voice trailed off in obvious discomfiture.

Andrea filled a mug with freshly brewed coffee, and set it before him, breathing in the scent of cold air, sawdust and sweat with just a trace of cologne, as she did so. The stirring, manly scent caused her to pause, momentarily, in her tracks. With hands trembling, she filled her own mug, but not without first splashing some of its contents across the table. She sopped up the spill with the potholder.

As she returned the carafe to the counter, she looked askance at the man. There was no denying his work ethic. She set a pan of warm, butter-basted, homemade, yeast rolls on the table, careful to keep a safe distance. She answered his questioning stare. "It's the last of my staples … my cupboard is officially bare."

McCormick took a final dab at the blood on his cheek, wiping away all traces.

Andrea pointed to his shoulder, "Um … there's a spot there on your shirt," she said, tapping her own shoulder.

McCormick took a quick swipe at his shirt, knowing the blood hadn't come from his facial scrape. He asked, "So … how are you today … besides bitch…." Correcting himself, he shot her an appreciative glance, clicked his tongue, and added, "….incredibly lovely?"

She frowned, ignoring him, at first; but then, deciding his reaction to her most embarrassing moment was acceptably comedic, she reluctantly returned his grin—she couldn't seem to stop herself. "I suppose now, you have something to share with your grandchildren," she said with a barbed voice. She grabbed her mug, and slid into the chair across from the slowly thawing, frost-covered creature.

He took a sip of coffee, and grinned, nodding towards her jacket, "You're wearing my favorite color this morning."

She glanced down at her sleeve, and frowned in disbelief, "Fuchsia?"

His eyes sparkled, "No … coffee. I've seen you wear it … a lot."

Her eyes dropped to the front of her freshly stained jacket. She groaned, and turned her eyes away.

McCormick shoved his chair back to a more comfortable position. "S-o-o-o … besides *me* being a complete SOB, what's going on?" he asked.

CHAPTER 42

What's going on? Andrea hesitated to reply. *What's not going on,* she thought. Finally, she offered, "I didn't sleep well … last night."

He teased, "That's obvious … I was sure I'd walked into a cave full of bats out of hell, earlier." He smiled apologetically for his part in the little drama, but the smile quickly faded and he looked deep into her eyes, searching. With a ragged voice, he asked in all sincerity, "Andi … what's wrong?"

She eyed him contemplatively. "Something happened after I returned from town yesterday. I'm still trying to reason it away." She tried to shake off Shaun's ghostly image, trying to convince herself that there was no way that he could still be alive. His plane had crashed and burned—exploded, actually. He had been declared legally dead, and they had buried his few remains in a funereal ceremony. She had stood over his grave, watching the vaulted casket lowered into the ground. And just as she had done for her sister and both her parents, she had written his lengthy, biographical account for the obituary columns—end of story.

Suddenly, she felt overwhelmed with humiliation, not wanting to discuss the matter, further. McCormick already thought of her as crazy.

Accurately reading her complex emotions, he slowly picked up his mug, and took a sip, swallowing, the hot liquid soothing his aching throat. "Why don't you talk about it … it'll make you feel better."

"You'll just think I've lost my mind…." she whispered, dejectedly.

His eyebrows arched up, and he held them comedically high. "What mind?" he whispered gently, teasingly, giving her a playful grin.

To Andrea, the gentleness of his words sounded forgiving—almost loving.

Once the frost melted from his face, Andrea noticed how gaunt and exhausted he looked. A distant, forlorn look was in his eyes. She wondered what he'd actually been doing for the past three weeks. He, obviously, hadn't been frolicking on a sandy beach.

Finally, she shrugged and slowly let out her breath, "Okay … I," she stammered, "I thought I saw Shaun yesterday."

The bottom of McCormick's coffee mug hit the table. His back stiffened, and he leaned forward. "What do you mean … *saw him* … where?"

Surprised by the intensity of his eyes, she suddenly felt silly, wondering why he was taking this so seriously. She tried to minimize the incident. "Relax. I know it's just my imagination; I'm really not crazy…." She gave out a nervous, little chortle, "I don't think."

Recognizing how tightly wound she'd become, McCormick tried to mask his deep concern. He tipped back in his chair, and lazily stretched his arms out, casually locking his fingers behind his head. He smiled, nonchalantly. "Just tell me what you *think* you saw." He gave her a quick, impish wink.

Responding to his laid-back demeanor, she began to relate the events of the previous evening, of thinking that she had seen Shaun; but sooner than later, she became aware of the sharp glint in McCormick's eye, and saw through his counter-measure tactics. She balked. "Look … I've been under a lot of stress for a very long time. I'm bothering you with things that are really unimportant. Let's just drop it." Her heavy eyes fluttered as she tried to bat away her own doubt. She gazed through the window, settling aimlessly on the old, stately upper branches of the oak tree.

McCormick's eyes followed hers to the tree, sorely disappointed that she still didn't trust him. She'd trusted him enough to drop out of a tree and into his arms, but she wouldn't trust him with this. He thought, *it must be something earth shattering … at least to Andrea.* He feigned a yawn, and let his chair legs drop to the floor. He would switch subjects.

His eyes began to dance with risibility as he raised the mug to his lips; then without taking a sip, quickly lowered it to the table. He shot her a look of taunting dubiousness, cocking his head towards the oak. "I'm surprised to see you all gaga over that tree … I thought you were in love with ole Will Remington."

Grateful for the change in subjects, gentle and unexpected peals of laughter trickled through her lips. Her defenses fell to the wayside, and she began to confide in him. "Mac … I do, dearly, love these beautiful, old, graceful trees … I tear up every time a single limb is lost."

McCormick's head dipped, and he grinned, audaciously, "Yeah … I've kind of noticed."

Appreciating his humorous, glossed-over response to her earlier abusive rant, she glanced, once more, at the old oak, standing naked in the cold, blowing wind, but strong, like tempered steel. "I haven't measured it, but I'm certain this particular tree has been here since before the founding of our nation … the Revolutionary War … or the Green Mountain Boys. It's at least four, maybe five, hundred years old … it should be listed with the National Register of Big Trees … who knows what all has happened in its branches, or in the shade of that wonderful, old tree."

Tamping down his own memories, McCormick nodded his agreement. "So-o-o … you really *are* into trees," he acknowledged." The tree had been listed with the registry for years, and although he couldn't add his two cents at the moment, he appreciated talking to someone with knowledge on the subject.

He watched her lips curl up into a gentle smile, warm and charming, one he had never seen before, as she confided, "My dad always claimed I had sap, instead of blood, coursing through my veins."

McCormick chuckled, softly and smiled, gently, "Your dad was right."

Kindred spirits sat admiring the broad branches of the bark-covered witness to history as she casually explained her love of trees, beginning with her childhood tree-house built in a 300-year-old oak. She explained how it had been hewn to make way for a new ski resort, its demise crushing her tender, young heart. When she'd learned the trunk had been halved, preserved, and used as pillars to the new ski lodge, her obsession with trees had been born; and her family had begun their annual pilgrimage to the forested Green Mountains as an offer of appeasement.

Familiar with both the resort and its pillars, McCormick sat basking in her warm companionship, wishing like hell, that he could postpone the inevitable.

Seeing Andrea shiver, he quickly rose from the table and crossed to the hearth. As he threw a couple of large, slow-burning logs on the fire, he reviewed everything she'd told him. He'd watched her every grimace and eye-bat, and he was certain she knew nothing of the multi-million dollar stash in the hollow tree just outside her door; nor did he believe that she had any connection to its being there. Unfortunately, her very presence in this cabin under these circumstances suggested otherwise.

He wrinkled his nose as the same putrescent odor as the blackened quilt hit his nostrils. He turned and grimaced. "You been cooking wild turkeys in here, or what? I smell … what is that? Roasted feathers?"

"Y-e-p, that's it … except it's not wild turkey …it's goose.

"You cooked your goose." he said, deadpanning.

She laughed, and explained the burnt feathers smell.

McCormick shook his head at her bizarre story, and returned the poker to the rack. "Gawd," he said teasingly. "I leave for a few days, and the whole place goes up in a freaking stink bomb."

Andrea's demeanor turned serious, and she lifted guarded eyes to meet his. "I didn't think you were coming back."

McCormick met her gaze, but let her words hang in the air.

"I have to level with you, Matt … those are not the only things stinking things up around here." Elucidating on her experiences in town the previous day, Andrea led with her strange visit to the Christmas Village Shoppe. Reticently, she repeated, word for word, her conversation with the old guy, expressing her exasperation that the artists had pulled his painting off the market.

McCormick pulled his eyes away, offering no comment.

Then she told him about meeting his old friend, Farah, on the sidewalk, describing her strange behavior. Finally, she told him of meeting the sheriff. She immediately identified Sheriff Donahue as the voice who had threatened her life via the phone conversation several weeks earlier at the *News*.

McCormick's feet shuffled, restlessly, under the table. "Tell me about the phone call.

Andrea explained the death threat she'd received at the newspaper several weeks earlier. McCormick wondered why the agency hadn't apprised him of this event.

Reluctantly, she told him of Sheriff Donahue's recent warning about the armed, wounded, and extremely dangerous, cop-killer passing himself off locally as a federal agent, as well as a rogue of a lady's man.

McCormick shoved back from the table, chagrined, finally understanding why his cred-pack had taken so long to catch up with him. He had been double-crossed, set up, his authority undermined; but even worse, doubt about his integrity had been seeded into Andrea's thinking, leaving him with no recourse, or way to prove otherwise. In his world, reputation was everything; his enemy was cunning in their wide-scale corruption, and this could very well prove to be his waterloo. But on the positive side, this latest information explained Andrea's distrust of him, and let her off the hook on a number of counts.

When Andrea finally got to the gist of her conversation with Sheriff Donahue, she blushed as she included the part where she had stupidly tried to play the man.

McCormick turned his head askance, and his brows furrowed; duskiness settled into his eyes. He asked, reticently, "Is that something you're in the habit of doing?"

"Lead a man on? Hell no ... I'm a complete amateur; but I've been studying your moves, McCormick." She winked at him, sassily.

McCormick grimaced, dubiously.

Trying to suck courage in with each breath, Andrea continued, "While I was in town, I called your headquarters from the library ... I asked to speak to you." She exhaled through her nose. "I was told there is no Special Agent Matthew J. McCormick."

The agent remained mute for a beat, and then asked, "Why were you calling?"

Andrea looked him straight in the eye. "Verification of employment," she answered, honestly, fully aware of the insult imbedded within her answer. McCormick's head tilted to the side, his frustration showing through his normally complacent veneer. She offered, "I also wanted your opinion of Sheriff Donahue." *And I was scared stiff,* she thought *....and I longed to hear your voice ... to feel safe in your presence,* she remembered, dropping her eyes.

At last, with detail, and great dramatic flair, she shared the negative experience she'd had with the crotchety, old librarian.

McCormick clung to her words as though having a vested interest. He could easily understand why his agency had denied his existence— an undercover agent on their payroll. The old guy in the shop needed no explanation—he was just covering McCormick's butt; but as for the librarian, he had no way of explaining her strange behavior. He'd check it out, though. He couldn't have locals interfering with an official investigation—nor did his honor need defending.

CHAPTER 43

Andrea rose from the table and dashed to the reading chair. Out of a thick tome, she pulled the crinkled newspaper column touting McCormick's investigation of the downed plane in the National Forest, three weeks earlier. "And then ... I came across this." She thrust the article into his hands.

First, McCormick eyed the mysteriously crumpled paper; and then his mind seared as he read the column.

"Donahue informed me that a plane loaded with illegal drugs had crashed somewhere nearby on my first night here... and that it was registered in *Shaun's name*, of all people...." she paused and took in a deep breath, "which, he claims, is synonymous with *Shaun's widow*." She put his words in air-quotes, and groused, dryly. "He said the crash was being investigated by some war hero with degrees out his ass...." She quickly corrected her speech. "He said some computer-for-a-brain agent ... was investigating *me!*"

With fear and panic riding high on her face, she finally told of seeing Shaun's apparition outside the cabin, and explained how utterly distraught she had been ever since.

McCormick's eyes flashed with anger, almost frightening Andrea; but when she told him of nearly being frightened to death by the humongous, trophy-sized bear, the corner of McCormick's mouth shot up in a roguish grin.

At last, she fell into silence. McCormick asked, "Other than you thinking you saw Shaun's ghost last night, and the fact that he was a complete shitstorm while the two of you were married, why are you so afraid of him now?"

Andrea found McCormick's bluntness and strong language, coupled with his negative opinion of Shaun, a bit off-putting, but she had no dissenting opinion. Her eyes dropped to her hands as she struggled for words. Finally, she looked at the man sitting across from her, and answered his question. "I'm afraid of what Shaun might do to the people I love," she answered, ambiguously.

Might do, McCormick thought. *Not had done, but might do—maybe she did have doubts about her husband's demise; and who were the people she loved? Her family was all dead.*

McCormick's steely, unyielding eyes narrowed in on Andrea. "Is this the first time you've seen him since...."

Her drawn-on eyebrows hiked up. "Since ... he d-i-e-d?" she blurted in exasperation. "Yes."

Died. There it was. To the agent's relief, she'd finally said the word that had been absent from her discourse for weeks—and she'd said it in a tone of healthy skepticism. The corner of his mouth lifted in a satisfied grin, and he cocked a comedic brow. His tone became teasingly taunting, playful even. "Had you been...." he paused, trying to shape his intrusive questions into more delicate phrasing, "....drinking hard cider, smoking ... pine cones, snorting birch ashes off your compact mirror?" Both corners of his mouth shot up to meet in the middle for a full, ear-to-ear grin.

She laughed, sassily, instantly getting his point. "No ... I don't do any of those things." She smirked, and asked, "How did you get to be such a smartass?"

Without missing a beat, he laughed, boastfully, "Lots and lots of practice."

She studied him for a long moment. Finally, "You have a sexy laugh," she offered.

Caught off guard by her observation, his answer came back soft, serious and unsmiling, "So do you."

They sat in quiet comradery as the fire popped and crackled in the hearth, each basking in a rich appreciation of the other—each easily reading the other's mind.

After a while, McCormick's tone turned contemplative. "Andi, I've been wondering ... what was your life like while you were married to Shaun?"

Andrea shrugged, lifted her eyes, letting them wonder around the room. When she brought her gaze back to the sober-eyed McCormick, she was shocked to find that the tender sound of his voice didn't match up to the hardened expression on his face. His brows were knotted, and his jaw muscles flexed with intensity. His eyes were dark and narrowed, and he seemed to be pleading with her in a way she didn't understand.

Astute enough to realize that the tension was of a different nature from that of a couple of hours ago, she dropped her eyes to her coffee mug. When McCormick made no effort to fill the silence, she began to speak in a voice wispy with emotion, sharing with him, in confidentiality, her never-before-told story.

"Matt ... living with Shaun was a freakin' 24-7 nightmare ... I had lost everything, and everybody I had ever loved...." Her heart plunged to her stomach, and she covered her eyes with her hands. Tears, large and anguished, streamed down both cheeks.

McCormick winced, sensing the depths of her pain. *No one could fake tears of that nature,* he thought.

She used dispirited words, painting a picture of loss, loneliness, and verbal abuse, ending with the bombshell news that she was ready to give up—to give up on life! "Matt ... I've simply come to the end of myself ... I have nothing left to live for."

As McCormick glimpsed into her troubled soul, heaviness invaded his own heart. He leaned forward, and spoke slowly, responding in all sincerity, "Then tie a knot in your ass, and hang on to your faith, Andi." *I'm here,* he wanted to say.

Without hesitation he doubled down on the day's mission. Already knowing the answer, and knowing it would help her to talk about it, express it, get it out, he asked, gently, "How did you lose your parents?"

Andrea took a deep breath, swallowed hard, and explained her parent's belated anniversary trip to Hawaii. "They had been devastated by Heather's death, and it was taking its toll on their marriage." She explained, "My dad was working all the time, and Mom was lonely ... their personal grief was so devastating that they could no longer be there for each other."

"Meaning...." McCormick offered, "no one was there for you."

Feeling, somehow, diminished by the truth, Andrea dropped her teary-eyed gaze, but she continued to describe the head-on collision, which resulted in their deaths. "The other driver was miraculously thrown clear of the crash."

"Do you remember the driver's name?"

Andrea shook her head, having no recall.

McCormick let everything hang in the air for a moment, asking at last, "When and how did Shaun come into the picture?"

Andrea let out a deep sigh. "I met Shaun my first year of college," she began. "My mother had pushed me into nursing, and I must admit ... I wasn't exactly the happiest camper on campus—I'd always wanted to be a writer, so I was constantly looking for diversions. I had no interest in nursing, or in Shaun. He was an upperclassman, and I would see him around campus ... I remember he was in one of my science classes ... we worked on a lab together. He was older, had spent time in the military, and seemed to have a solid interest in pharmaceuticals. He was always asking me questions about my dad's business."

"Did you date?"

"Never, but it certainly wasn't from his lack of trying."

"So he pursued you?"

"You could call it that. He later went to law school, and passed the bar. He worked awhile at some kind of job in Washington D.C. for a couple years, and then one day he decided to look me up ... even came to work for my father's pharmaceutical company as a corporate lawyer."

Targeting, McCormick noted.

"But they had some kind of serious misunderstanding ... I never knew the details, but after a while my father decided he didn't want him in the company. He talked about firing him, but I guess he changed his mind...." she sucked in a deep breath and blew it out with her words, "or Dad ran out of time."

McCormick caught the flicker of sudden awareness that ran across her face.

"But Shaun was reliable, always there, rain or shine. It wasn't until after Heather...."

She rose from the table and quickly crossed the room, turning her face to the window, and to the dark sky.

Even with her back to him, McCormick sensed the stress mounting inside her, and saw her pain reflected in the glass. He pushed away from the table, and approached her from behind. He laid a gentle hand on her shoulders, giving it a quick squeeze. Already knowing the answer, he asked, "Who is Heather?" His soft, soothing tone flowed with tenderness.

Andrea couldn't breathe, and the words stuck in her throat. Hot, unshed tears, filled her eyes. She turned quickly, and in an emotional, raspy voice, blurted, "Your question should be … who *was* Heather? She was my younger sister … she was seventeen-years-old with everything to live for. She died … of a drug overdose…." Andrea wanted to scream, but she controlled her voice. "Except … Heather did not, and would never do drugs." Her head dipped, before bobbing back up. With a low wispiness, she offered, "I … found her body."

He gave her a moment, leaving his hand on her shoulder, then asked, "Had she ever talked to you about having problems?"

He saw her face redden, and her expression turn livid. "Oh, yeah," she whispered, plaintively. "Heather had complained about Shaun … getting too friendly … however, that last day, he had offered to take her to see the latest Avenger movie … for some insane reason, she agreed to go."

There she'd said it. She had spoken words that had been locked inside her mind and heart since that tragic Saturday night, too afraid to speak aloud. She continued to relate every detail she could remember; then dropped her eyes, sniffing back the onslaught of tears. "There was a gap in our ages, but my sister and I were very close," she added, in painful anguish. "In many ways I was like her mother." She covered her face with her hands.

When all her tears had, at last, been shed, she gently pushed away, feeling embarrassed by all the emotion. *Why was it coming out now, in front of this man, of all people, after years of being suppressed?*

"I'm sorry, Matt," she sniffed, as they both returned to the table. "I've had this all bottled up … I don't know why it's all coming out now."

McCormick lips pursed, realizing that she was crying because she'd lost someone near and dear to her, and the death still remained unresolved in her mind. The fact that she had just placed her trust in his hands became secondary to her grief. "Loving someone is not a crime, Andi," he offered, consolingly.

McCormick gave her time to recover, then asked with compassion, "What happened after your parents' accident?"

"After my parents' died, I was completely alone and suddenly faced with control of a very large, prestigious company and estate." She explained how unprepared and overwhelmed she had been, how Shaun—the more than willing attorney—had come to her rescue, and eventually taken control of her father's company.

Wrested control, McCormick thought.

"I agreed to marry him."

McCormick's ears pricked up, and his back flopped against the back of his chair, his face a blank stare. *She agreed to marry him—that smacked of a business deal.*

Andrea didn't see the grim expression that shrouded his countenance. "Shaun took advantage of my grief, and my money. He moved into my parent's home, and took control of the company."

The agent immediately connected the dots, thinking, *he took control of the company* and *turned it into a fentanyl distribution center. The deadly drug would be smuggled into Canada where the poison would then be pressed into pills and sold back by the legitimate drug industry as pill packs.*

"He took control of my finances," Andrea was saying. "I was too grief-stricken to think in terms of money at the time."

"He took control of your money?"

"My inheritance ... he called it a loan ... after the fact."

She swiped at a tear; then lowered her voice to a mere, agonized whisper, "but I soon realized, that I had made the biggest mistake of my life. At first I trusted him—he was there, helping, doing; but eventually, I pulled myself together enough to realize that the ledger columns weren't adding up, and that he was letting all our stellar staff members go ... anyone with working knowledge of a pharmaceutical company ... anyone who could give me help or guidance. He tried to cut me off from the business, from my friends, and activities; but the strangest thing he did was to turn our home into some kind of sanctuary for ... for...."

A deadly spark of seriousness ignited in McCormick's eyes. "Men with tatted up arms and legs ... like mine," McCormick offered, biting his tongue, knowing he shouldn't coax answers through her well-guarded lips.

Andrea turned a serious eye to McCormick's forearms, to his bold tattoos. Her voice weakened, and her courage began to wane. "Yes ... unfortunately, by the time I figured all that out, it was too late—he had become too powerful for me to fight alone."

McCormick's mind wondered back: it was midnight, moonbeams shone through the windows of the uninhabited stable—his blind. He'd watched the house, hoping to catch Fitzgerald at home. Instead, it was Andrea who'd pulled into the driveway. Through diaphanous webs of a spider, spun across cracked and begrimed windowpanes, he'd watched her get out of her car, alone and unusually sullen. Under the huge harvest moon, she'd cried out, attempting to bring down the sky in an expression of loss and loneliness. At the time, he'd thought it melodramatic, even a bit crazy—moonstruck, perhaps. But when she'd dropped to her knees, crying out in prayer, he'd wanted to go to her. Instead, he'd turned away, bleary-eyed; not from the dusty stacks of wheat-flaxen straw, or the litter of wayward kittens, but from glimpsing into the heart of a kindred spirit, ensnared in the same intricate, lethal webbing of his own diabolical enemy.

"And this all happened over what period of time?" he asked.

"Six months."

"You were married for only six months?"

"Actually ... less than six months." She wouldn't reveal the fact that she had suspected her husband of being a part of the very drug culture that had killed her sister; nor would she admit to the fact that she thought her husband may have had something to do with her parent's death, and she certainly wouldn't share the fact that she thought her husband could possibly still be alive. Her strong intuitive feelings were no more than that—mere hunches. Shaun's ghostly image had been the closest she'd come to proof of any kind. At last, she let out an exhausted breath, long, hot and heavy. She lifted her gaze to encompass the whole man. Story time was over.

But the persistent McCormick wasn't about to let a suspect off the hook that easily. In a casual tone he asked, "Did you ever work with Shaun on any of his projects ... did he discuss or involve you in his business dealings or foreign travels in any way?"

"No ... Shaun wouldn't even look at me—unless he had to. The only time he discussed anything with me was that final flight." She sniggered, cynically. "For that trip he was profusely forthcoming with his travel plans ... and opinions."

McCormick hated the question he must ask next, for fear of the answer that might come back at him; but needing to get a direct answer in her own words, he charged forward. "Andi...." He paused to run a reluctant hand across his weathered mouth. "Was there ... physical abuse?"

A high-pitched laugh escaped her lips as she tried to throw off his probing question. This was the humiliating part. She had always considered herself too snarky, too savvy, too bitchy even, to ever get caught in an abusive trap, but she answered him honestly. "There was some … mostly just jabs and slaps, pushes and shoves … but even those were intensifying in nature."

"Did he ever threaten your life, or pull a gun on you?"

A long pause preceded her answer. "No."

Disappointed by this equivocation, McCormick scraped back his chair and stood, abruptly.

Andrea paused, seemingly to reassess the situation. "The emotional abuse started on day one," she continued, "it was horrific…." She lifted her pain-filled gaze, locking into his sober one, getting lost in their infinite depth, "and yes, he threatened me, continuously … and pulled a gun on several occasions," she corrected.

McCormick began to pace the floor. His next question was spoken with a clipped tongue, conveying doubt at what she was saying. "Did you go to the police?"

Hearing the tone of skepticism come from his mouth was like having a dagger thrust deep into her heart. She looked at him through watery eyes, and then quickly pulled her eyes away, instantly knowing what he must be thinking: that any sane person would have run to the police. She hadn't, but with good reason.

Finally, "No … I didn't go to the police. I was too frightened of what Shaun might do."

There it was again … what Shaun *might do*? McCormick pursed his lips, but treaded lightly, a multitude of questions flooding his mind.

He thoughtfully rested his hands on his hips. Finally, his chin notched up and he asked slowly, "Might do to whom?"

McCormick kicked her words around in his mind another few minutes, evaluating their impact upon his investigation. Andrea had, unfortunately, paled and declined to answer his last question, leaving him with no recourse but to put her under oath; and leaving him thinking there might be another guy in the picture.

McCormick was an investigator, not a lawyer, but the obvious question that remained in his mind was not *if* she was innocent, but could he prove her innocence to the satisfaction of the demanding Chief Straker, who was hell-bent on tying Andrea to Fitzgerald's crimes. Leery of Straker's motivations, McCormick was hell-bent on finding the truth.

He put on a pot of coffee, all-the-while eyeing the smiling couple in the Wall of Fame photo stuck in the window pane above the sink. As the aroma of freshly brewed coffee permeated the cabin, masking the offensive odors, he asked, surprisingly, "Do you need the bathroom?"

Questioning the question, she shook her head.

He poured them each a cup; then moved a chair away from the table, to a space behind her, where his voice could be picked up by his sophisticated, microcassette recorder, but far enough away that he would be out of Andrea's line of vision. A video cam would have been preferable, but under the circumstances, a recorder would suffice.

Now, his voice rang out, deep and gravelly, but hollow sounding as he approached Andrea with his back ramrod straight. His, here-to-fore, easy-going demeanor turned to pertinaciousness as he offered, "Mrs. Fitzgerald ... I once tried to explain to you that I was a serious guy ... on a serious mission." The formality in his voice caused her chin to jut up, to lock into his cold, flinty eyes. She nodded. "*This* is my mission ... and *this* is me at my most serious," he explained. She shot him a bewildered, suspicious look, as dreadful visions, dark and alarming, flashed through her mind.

Numbly, McCormick tossed a black, pocketsize packet on the table in front of her. He flipped it open, revealing his photo ID and a shield, identifying him as a serious, special federal investigator. He began, "Mrs. Fitzgerald ... Sheriff Donahue was absolutely right ... your husband was a known terrorist, and there are quite a few people willing to testify that you were his accomplice. He took in a deep breath and blew it out through his nose. "At the moment, I'm inclined to agree with them."

Tearing his eyes away from her shell-shocked expression, he glared out the window at the huge oak, being brutally savaged by snow and blizzard winds, its trunk chocked full of dangerous, killer drugs. The tree had been used as a temporary hold en route to innocent young children, and would have, most likely, brought about their deaths had they been delivered. He turned to face Andrea, and with grave severity, challenged, "Prove me wrong, Mrs. Fitzgerald."

McCormick had delivered his pretext, the great lie—a little bit of truth, and a whole lot of fabrication. "Mrs. Fitzgerald ... I also need to remind you that lying to a federal agent is a felony ... prosecutable by law."

Pulling the small recorder from his pocket, he clicked it on and spoke words with the full authority of the U.S. government behind him. "I am Matthew J. McCormick, DEA Special Investigator. This is an official interrogation of Andrea Daye Fitzgerald, wife of Brantley Stone, aka Shaun Fitzgerald, aka Kris Kringle ... on this ... 24th day of December in the Northeast Kingdom of Vermont." He checked his watch. "The time is 8:45 a.m." Avoiding her glaring eyes, he laid the recorder on the table in front of her; then took the seat behind her.

"Please state your name and occupation."

CHAPTER 44

Disheartened, and in utter shock, Andrea's hand flew to her lips to hide the quivering, as she grasped, at least in part, the seriousness of her situation. Ruefully, she realized that Donahue had been right on a second point—her special investigator was a sly dog. Facing a dangerous imposter would've been preferable to this, she agonized; but what could she do now but answer his questions? "Andrea Day Fitzgerald … I'm Assistant Editor for the Forest Hills Daily News."

"Do I have your permission to record this interrogation?" McCormick asked, his strong, authoritative voice coming at her from behind.

A dazed Andrea closed her eyes and nodded her head.

"Please speak all your answers … loud and clear," the agent instructed, sternly.

"Yes…." she answered with greater force and volume, as humiliation settled into her soul, "you have my permission to record this … interrogation."

Andrea sat stoically, as Special Investigator Matthew J. McCormick asked each and every question a second time; doubling-down, and quadrupling the number of additional, in-depth questions. He waited patiently, and attentively, for each and every response.

When the lengthy interrogation was over, McCormick returned his chair to the table, and turned off the recorder. "You're free to go to the bathroom," he stated, dryly.

Tossing a hardened glare in his direction, she rushed towards the stairs, sniping irascibly over her shoulder, "I'll be right back for the waterboarding … don't you dare start without me."

The austere agent breathed out a heavy sigh, and sat down at the table, waiting, contemplatively, for her return.

While away, Andrea reviewed the agent's questions and the nature of his questions, letting them stream through her head. When she returned, she spoke with conviction. "So this investigation is not really about me, but about Shaun."

McCormick's chin jutted up. A saddened look was in his eye. "Shaun Fitzgerald ... and his wife," he answered.

"So you're accusing me of being Shaun's partner in crime? That's absurd!"

"It's hard to tell what really goes on inside a marriage." His hand rose to his breast pocket, and he drew out four photos. "Maybe this will give us a fresh perspective." He tossed the first one down on the table in front of her. It was a shot taken two years earlier by a security camera in the theatre parking lot—the day her sister had died. Heather was caught on camera leaving the theatre through the front doors. She was being followed by a familiar looking man, but it was hard to identify him from the rough-grained photo. The time stamp indicated a much earlier time than when the movie had actually let out.

McCormick threw down the second photo. There was no mistaking the man's identity in this one. Heather was being harassed and shoved into a car by Shaun Fitzgerald. A look of terror was on the young girl's face. McCormick's eyes dropped to the table as a low groan escaped Andrea's lips.

The next photo came from Google Maps, Street View, taken by a roving satellite. It showed Shaun Fitzgerald's car leaving the Daye estate just seconds before Andrea's Honda pulled into the driveway. Two hours had elapsed between photos—from the time they'd left the theater to the time Shaun had driven away from the house. These three pictures justified her worst fears, leaving no question as to Shaun's involvement in her sister's death.

Stubbornly tenacious, McCormick slid into the chair next to Andrea. Hating himself for what he was about to do—not as an investigator, but as a man—he laid out the fourth photo, deliberately keeping his thumb over the time stamp. This photo showed the same man, with a different woman, Shaun and Jolene Jorgenson—surreptitiously engaged in compromising, sexual activity—in Andrea's very own, teal-colored, king-sized bed. Balloons and bottles of pricey, celebratory champagne cluttered the nightstands.

McCormick breathed out, softly. "Andi ... this photo gives you just cause for divorce."

Divorce, she thought, totally discombobulated, *Shaun's dead....*

"How did you get these," she rasped, lifting her misty scowl askance to scorch him.

With eyes dropping, he answered, somberly, "Once a sleazy shamus … always a sleazy shamus." He quickly gathered up the photos, and stuck them back into his pocket as evidence.

Understanding the mindset of criminal minds, and how they often give themselves away by their celebrations, McCormick had earlier placed hidden cameras in strategic areas throughout Andrea's home—but that was a shouting match for another day.

McCormick topped off both their mugs, carrying his, restlessly, to the window amid a leaden silence. A black mood settled into his bones as he studied the frozen lake. His ears burned, aware that Andrea was mad as hell at him; little did she know of the agony he had suffered for his role in this investigation.

He mulled over her detailed answers to his barrage of aggressive questions. He believed every word of her story, and he had just witnessed, too close and too personal, the destructive force of a drug culture upon the lives of ordinary people. A family, simply trying to live a quality life, had been decimated. Furthermore, Andrea's situation served to magnify and solidify his reason, and the necessity, of his chosen profession. Grievously, innocent people were being mortally wounded on this bloody battlefield.

Sullenly, he watched snow drift deeply into the cracks and crevices of the deck. He considered Andrea's depth and compassion, as well as her ability to bring him back among the living. Setting aside his personal feelings, at this point, was impossible; and he, sure as hell, didn't need orders from headquarters telling him to protect this woman. He rubbed a slow hand across the day's fresh growth of facial hair. In that one cataclysmic moment, his mind, heart, body and soul suddenly converged and began functioning as one. In that moment, he knew that he could have no life without Andrea. Right or wrong, it didn't matter. He would sacrifice his job, his reputation, and yes, even his life to protect her.

Benumbed, and exhausted by the grilling, Andrea dried her eyes and tried to pull herself together. Without an upwards glance, she rose from the table and walked towards the hearth, stooping to pick up the remaining logs McCormick had dropped to the floor earlier that morning—for some insane reason.

She stacked the wood on the hearthstone then walked to the double doors overlooking the deck, strangely remembering all the winter fun she'd had playing in the snow as a kid. Today, winter had become her enemy, an obstacle to her means of escape. In a momentary lull in the blizzardly winds, an Oriole called out from the top of a tall, white pine, his sharp, metallic call summoning the rest of nature. She watched it shyly swoop down, peck hungrily at the seeds, gulping them down while its feathers ruffled in the stiff, bitter wind. A couple of squirrels had joined them, hungrily stuffing their jaws with the large black and white-striped, sunflower seeds she'd put out earlier that morning. She knelt down for a closer look. A tender smile crossed her pallid lips as they stared back at her through the glass, as though saying thanks.

She straightened, and took notice of the man staring pensively out the window with his back to her, obviously brooding. He was dressed all in black: turtleneck shirt, a little too thin for the weather, sleek fitting dri pants, and black boots—tactical boots. He seemed different; but what was she seeing now, that she had not noticed before?

The little boy she'd met in the orchard several weeks earlier came to mind. It wasn't the little guy's need to talk or his affection towards her; nor was it his bucketful of questions. No, what brought Joey to mind was McCormick's stance. He reminded her of the child's action figure, the black one—feet spread apart, muscles flexed, broad-shouldered, and back straight as a rod. She almost laughed at herself for not making the comparison sooner; but then, she slowly realized what was actually before her eyes. A shudder shot through her body.

Alpha male personality ... multiple weapons ... Black Ops attire! Why had she not noticed this before? She took another look at his shoulder holster, and another strapped to his back. She knew that, if she searched, she'd find multiple blades strapped to the insides of the man's arms and calves. She watched him check his watch in frustration—his black tactical watch. She sucked in a deep breath and held it, realizing that there was much more to this man than she had ever dared to imagine.

While Andrea had studied wind-ruffled feathers, the restless McCormick studied the feathering frost buildup on the windows, indicating the drop in temperature. He'd pondered the thought of Andrea living in the cabin without heat, hot water or electricity—alone. She was black on food. He considered the weather, the firewood cut, but still in the woods. He remembered the mindless, long-bearded dope heads with sawed-off shotguns, just a short distance away. He considered the depraved Sheriff Donahue, possibly watching her every move, having already threatened her life. He considered the trophy-sized bear with a super-sized craving for peanut butter and birdseed; and now Andrea, claiming to have seen the mere haunting image of her depraved and demented husband—too scared to admit that she had seen the real deal—or too mad and confused to believe she'd seen him at all.

McCormick dragged a heavy hand across his mouth, a hand still carrying the scent of tree sap and sawdust. He wished like hell that he could warn her, to tell her the truth, to explain that her no-good, murderous husband was coming for her—for them. He wanted to prepare her for what was sure to happen next. It felt cruel to keep her in the dark.

McCormick's gaze fixed on the blowing, drifting snow across the harsh, wintry terrain, knowing that Fitzgerald was out there—waiting; but waiting for what reason? As he stood thinking, feisty wisps of snow, swirled, somewhat merrily, past the window, reminding him of the TV Christmas animations he'd watched as a child. He remembered the wreath he'd hung around Hero's neck as a deliberate taunt, and it came to him—*Fitzgerald was waiting for Christmas!*

His mind ignited. He had to get Andrea out of this cabin. He turned brusquely. "Andi, why don't you stay with me for a few days?"

Surprised at the suddenness of his proposal, she wasn't sure how to respond, what to think or how to feel. She'd never fully recovered from the man's abrupt about-face on the stairway—committing himself, then reneging on the play; nor had she recovered from the grudge she'd nursed for the past three weeks. Both heartaches surfaced along with her strong, stubborn streak. *What kind of a guy does that,* she groused, inwardly; *and for what reason?* And now, she had to add to that ash heap of emotional pain, his snooping, and the humiliation of his invasive, in-depth interrogation. Gawd ... he couldn't have dug any deeper if he'd been mining granite.

"No way," she answered, totally disregarding his suggestion.

His voice came back with a biting edge, "Why not?"

With impudence, she spat back, "Because, McCormick ... I really don't want to know you."

Disappointment settled hard on his face, as a fierce gust of wind whistled, shrilly, down the chimney, and around the corners of the cabin. "Don't want to know me ... or afraid to know me?" he said, having caught the fleeting shadow of distrust in her eyes. "You still don't trust me," he breathed out, flatly.

"Why should I?" She asked, her eyes deliberately brushing across his ominous, operative-style clothing.

His eyes dropped down to assess his black attire. He'd been in the same clothes for only God knew how long. He'd even forgotten how he was dressed; but now, he became cognizant of the sinister image he was projecting.

Andrea was unable to read the intense, labyrinthine expressions that flickered across the man's face. Finally, he looked at her, purposefully, "My job is ... multifaceted," he said, his voice gruff; but he almost carried off a weak, smartass grin.

Raising a questioning brow, she asked in a wizened tone, "Don't you mean *complicated* ... your life is effing complicated?"

He leveled serious, fiery eyes on her—*she had figured him out!*

His voice faltered, "Andi ... are you ... *afraid* of me?"

Suddenly, the wind strengthened, blowing hard against the logs, moaning around the eaves as though in human misery, silencing all within the cabin.

At last, "Hell no ... I'm not afraid of you," she snipped, her voice gaining strength. "Your suggestion just caught me by surprise ... I thought you were *investigating* me."

He nodded, but momentarily pulled his eyes away. "I'm pretty certain the investigation has been brought to a satisfactory conclusion."

With her mind blurring with confusion, she returned to her seat at the table. *If the investigation has been concluded satisfactorily, then why is he still here?* All she wanted, at this point, was to be left alone, to take a nap—for the rest of her life!

A chagrined McCormick studied the woods beyond the lake. He wished, like hell, that he'd been able to record Andrea's conversation with the corrupt, no-account Sheriff. She had an extensive vocabulary, a sense of delivery, and a command of the English language—the sheriff didn't.

As he searched for answers to their dilemma, his eye caught the orange flutter of an oriole, flitting from tree to tree—late for the big migratory party in the tropics. A dash of the same color drew his attention at lakeside. His eyes narrowed, and he zeroed in on the stirring—to a hungry, red fox sitting atop a snow-covered boulder watching a Snowshoe hare try, frantically, to burrow deep into the snow. Suddenly, just as the taut, burnt-orange body leapt high into the air, and its quick, black paws pounced upon his furry victim, McCormick's answer came to him.

With eyes still glued on the kill, McCormick tilted his head back and asked, "Andi ... were you carrying a purse when you talked to Donahue?"

She lowered her lids, along with her mug, thinking.

"Sure."

He looked at her askance, "The orange one?"

What was with this guy, she crabbed, tilting her head to the side, giving him a mulish look.

Impatience shot through the agent, and he doubled-down on the question in a more pressing tone. "Was it the orange one?"

"It's called tangerine ... but yes."

"Where is it now?"

"Right here ... but, personally, Mac ... I think something in a size 2x, leather knapsack would better accessorize your cloak and dagger style ... just saying."

Ignoring her smartass acerbity, but reveling in her quick-wittedness, he asked, "Where was it early this morning ... when I first got here?"

"In the closet ... in the *linen* closet," she snarked, with a touch of sarcasm, "you know ... the one with all the *electrical* outlets. I brought it down following your proctological interrogation. It was up there the whole time you were out ... chucking wood."

Though her words were meant to rankle, they affected McCormick like a strong sedative. He heaved a sigh of relief, eyeing the purse hanging on the back of her chair. He turned his gaze back to the window, sated with the knowledge that Donahue's conversation had, indeed, been recorded; but, luckily, their pre-dawn shouting match had not.

Unable to pull her eyes away, Andrea studied his silent form standing strong and resolute. Guided by the heartbreak of rejection, and thinking this was the last time she would ever see the man, she goaded, "Hey, Mac ... I never did finish *my* interrogation ... it's *my* turn with the questions."

He shot her a wary, over-the-shoulder glance.

"Why are you still here?" she asked, boldly, "and why, in the hell, are you so conflicted? I really don't know." The words shot out of her mouth. "Are you married or single ... gay or straight? Which rainbow spectrum box do *you* check?" Turning palms up, she suddenly spoke with empathy, giving him the benefit of doubt. "Have you been injured ... what?"

McCormick's jaw clenched shut as he immediately grasped the crux of her question—she sure as hell wasn't asking about the bullet he'd taken to the head, nor the deep chasm running straight through his throbbing shoulder. A strained silence passed between them as Andrea's impatient eyes bore into the man.

He turned abruptly, just in time to witness the raw emotion flooding her visage; and he got it. *She did have feelings for him—but she had just drawn the proverbial line in the sand. He knew he had to answer, to act—or lose her forever.* His jaw hardened. He would most certainly answer her questions, but not while Fitzgerald was still at large—and not while the bugging device placed in her purse was picking up, and recording, every footfall and word spoken, sending it straight to Straker via satellite.

He had to devise a plan around the situation. He couldn't just put the purse back in the closet; the long silence would draw Straker's suspicion. He ran a slow hand over stubble, thinking, but every solution came with down-sided complications.

He widened his stance and faced the distraught woman, shooting her his most flinty-eyed, manly man look, crafting an answer for the benefit of both Andrea and the recording device. His voice dropped to its most virile, testosterone-driven tone. "Mrs. Fitzgerald." He spoke her name with deliberate precision, letting it hang in the air to make a statement of its own. "I understand why you're upset, and I'm going to be absolutely straight with you in the days ahead—but the only thing you need to concern yourself with, at this moment, is the fact that I'm working ... working to keep your world safe from ... from those who might want to cause you harm ... Mrs. Fitzgerald."

Andrea batted her eyes shut, considering his answer: *Mrs. Fitzgerald ... absolutely straight ... working ... keep you safe ... might cause you harm ... Mrs. Fitzgerald.* She blew out an exasperated breath. There it was again—Mrs. Fitzgerald. Hadn't they gotten past that stupid game ... why did he insist on calling her...? Suddenly, understanding permeated her, here-to-fore, muddled thinking. She slapped her hands across her eyes. Was McCormick trying to tell her that she was still Mrs. Fitzgerald … that Shaun might try to harm her—*as he had the rest of her family?* She cradled her head in her hands and fell into silence, *God … had he been trying to tell her this all along? But Shaun was dead … wasn't he?* Suddenly, every suspicion she'd ever had about Shaun Fitzgerald coagulated in her mind.

She rose from the table on shaky legs, and walked to the coatroom, mindlessly staring out through the small panes of glass at the wintry world, outside. Her misty gaze came to rest on a timid doe standing a short distance away, seeking shelter from the wind behind a frozen, snow-covered thicket of blackberry bushes. Innocence and vulnerability were evident in the big, dark eyes and frail, slender body as she drew closer to the cabin.

With strong feelings of affinity towards the deer, Andrea dropped her gaze to her trembling hands. *Shaun's hands had trembled every single time he boarded a plane,* she remembered; *except for that last day at the airport. On that trip he had been unusually calm.*

So his hands hadn't shaken … so what?

Suddenly, her spine tingled with realization. At long last, details began to fall into place. Shaun's hands hadn't trembled … *because he knew he wasn't going to get on that plane!* Andrea took a full, deep breath; a*nd … if he hadn't boarded the plane … then he wouldn't be dead … would he?*

A shivering sense of foreboding raked through her body. McCormick's presence suddenly became clear—Shaun was not only alive, as she had suspected, but according to the agent, he might cause her harm. Could she believe that?

Yes … she could!

Her insides quaked, and an involuntary groan, more mournful than the wind, escaped her lips. Color drained from her face. Frightened eyes blurred as she shot a cold, hard look at the real, live action-figure at the window. *McCormick was here to arrest Shaun.*

She took another look at the man dressed head-to-toe, not just in black, but in weapons, his woeful eyes upon her. *No … McCormick was here to take Shaun down!*

Their eyes locked in deadened silence and raw emotion. Numbed by the reality of the moment, she quickly dropped her eyes and turned away to hide her shattered emotions.

Certain that Andrea had gotten his message, the fleet-footed McCormick crossed the room and stood silently behind her. Sensing the cold shudder of fright running through her, he wrapped his arms around her shoulders, and tenderly pulled her close in an effort to share his own inner strength.

Feeling, the very essence of his ethereal soul wrapped tightly around her like a protective shield, she closed her eyes and let her head drop back, muting the sound of her own lamenting agony.

"Trust me," McCormick whispered softly, lovingly, nuzzling her ear.

Giving up the fight, she fell back into his rock solid body; as he silently tightened his embrace, holding her, gently rocking her trembling body in the safety of his strong, protective arms.

CHAPTER 45

The decision to leave Andrea alone in the cabin was a tortuous one to make; but it was imperative that McCormick find a way to communicate with his agency. After considering the bulls-eye he wore on his back, and the fierceness of the blizzard, he finally accepted the tormenting truth: Andrea was safer in the cabin than with him. Not knowing how large of a goon squad Fitzgerald would bring with him, he had tried calling headquarters on his throw-away, but got a *no service* message, and Andrea said she'd lost her phone. He figured the tower had been disabled; whether by the blizzard or by deliberate, human intervention, he could only guess. Either way, it didn't bode well for him.

It was imperative that he get to a landline in Red Springs; but he was also aware of the dangers of using an unsecure line to call. He would need to devise a code that could be easily understood, while being picked up by every wiretap, satellite snoop system, and rogue cell phone tower in the world—or by someone on the inside working against him.

McCormick was already mad as hell at his boss on several levels. The fact that he had never gotten him a satellite replacement phone would be the first issue addressed on the other side of this thing. Three times now, he had worked without any method of communication. This was no accident of omission, but a deliberate act.

After giving Andrea explicit instructions to hide in the wall closet that not only sported electrical outlets, but also a hidden exit from the cabin, should things go sideways, he carefully planned out the dialogue, and a few key words, to convey the message that Shaun Fitzgerald was alive and well, and had appeared at the cabin. He took his cue from his boss—and the enemy's wife.

Trained to drive in adverse conditions, McCormick still found the mountain roads nearly impassable. The highway was a glaze of black ice and snow, and it had been closed to thru traffic. As McCormick guided his new all-terrain jeep straight down the center line, he hoped the same conditions would slow Fitzgerald down, as well.

The trip had taken longer than usual, but at last he arrived in Red Springs without spinning, skidding off, or slamming into a 12-point buck, or a full-antlered, bull moose along the way.

After picking the lock to Nicole's apartment above the shop, he made the call from her landline. As he impatiently waited for it to go through the many security switches, he raided her frozen bread and opened a crunchy peanut butter jar, suddenly realizing how much he'd missed her these last two years. He guzzled part of a warm soft drink, and wondered about Andrea's left-field comment about Nicole. Where in the hell had that remark come from?

Finally, a tired, craggy voice answered, "Top Dog."

"Red Rover, here ... listen up. Kris Kringle has arrived. He's on the roof and ready to drop his bag of toys down the chimney. If you want your surprises, you better get here before dark. Pretty sure he's got those shiny, plastic-wrapped toys you've been looking for."

"How do you know these things?"

"A young woman spotted his little, round belly." A long silence hung in the air. Speaking to the silence, McCormick said, "You know, this fairy tale is really getting old ... I think I should tell her the truth ... she's having a hard time believing the fantasy."

"Red Rover, back off on that," the voice barked. "We still don't know if she's naughty or nice."

The dialogue was cute and trite, but the subject matter was of the utmost importance. McCormick was getting pushback from his supervisor, something he wasn't accustomed to, and he was steadily growing impatient. He didn't have time to waste. "Look," he said into the phone, his voice taking on a surliness that bordered on insubordination. "I'm telling you, she's *not* on the naughty list ... I'd bet my life on it!"

"Well ... that sure would be a big loss of sugar cookies if you're wrong."

McCormick pursed his lips in anger. "She knows I'm *the* elf," he added, with deep concern in his voice.

"How in the hell did she find that out?"

"Compliments of our local dogcatcher ... old Kris is euthanizing the whole litter."

There was a long, pregnant pause; then finally, "Okay, understood ... that corresponds with info from another elf. We'll throw the dogcatcher a bone, and send in the flying reindeer by dawn's early light."

McCormick blew hostility out with his breath. "ASAP!" he snapped. "You're running out of time if you want anything from Kringle's knapsack."

"Okay ... but you better wrap up this package tonight, and put a big bow on it. We just got our Cheer Fund slashed, again. It's time to blow out the wicks on those two candles."

McCormick froze, thinking he hadn't heard right. "Repeat," he croaked into the phone.

Chief Straker repeated his order in harsher terms, "Snuff them *both* out!"

Both? "You can't mean both," McCormick countered.

"That's exactly what I mean, McCormick ... follow orders!" The line went dead.

McCormick slammed the phone down in disbelief. He had just been ordered to eliminate Brantley Stone, a.k.a. Shaun Fitzgerald—and his *wife*—and the asshole had spoken his name over an unsecured line!"

As a member of Delta Force, the U.S Navy Seals, and later Special Operations, his ardent training, long and rigid, had placed him among England's SAS, Israel's Special Forces and various other foreign ops groups, the best the world had to offer, all conducting clandestine missions all over the world, including multiple hostage raids and rescues. Sometimes innocent civilians died; but never had they deliberately been ordered to end the life of an innocent.

As the troubled agent pulled his snowmobile out of its storage space in Nicole's garage, he went over the data in his head, looking for flaws in his thinking. He had proven that Stone/Fitzgerald was alive, and operating as a drug kingpin—the head of one of the largest U.S. drug-trafficking, and money-laundering schemes this nation had ever seen. Already known to be responsible for the deaths of an elite military unit, the man had also infiltrated a large pharmaceutical plant, and taken custody of a very large estate, murdering the owner, his wife, and teenaged daughter. He had taken the heir hostage, and somehow, coerced her into marriage. When law enforcement had gotten too close, the man had faked his own death to escape arrest.

McCormick, working in South America, had gotten his hands on titles and tail numbers of multiple aircraft being used in Fitzgerald's venture, including stolen, private jets. The man had been pulling in sensitive, governmental information from a rogue satellite feed, as well. Already guilty of murdering agents, police officers, and several of his own men, the maniac had orchestrated an attack on a U.S. military operation, and a foreign train station; and now he was making it personal, planning a hit on McCormick's very own family. McCormick prayed that his younger brother hadn't already been added to the statistics.

Filling the tank with fuel, he wondered: *how had it been possible for one man to usurp so much power in such a short amount of time?* He mulled over one last detail he'd learned from his Peruvian fact-finding mission—proof that Fitzgerald had a partner-in-crime—one with high rank and very deep pockets.

He held his breath, as he prepared to start a snowmobile that hadn't run in over two winters. When it started on the third try, he breathed a sigh of relief, and let the engine idle awhile to warm up.

As he waited, his troubled mind traveled back to Andrea. He turned quickly and flung open the doors to a built-in utility closet, and searched through a box of old clothes, hoping to find a pair of jeans left behind on a much earlier visit. Bingo. He changed out of his dri-pants and into a pair of faded-out Levis, all tattered and musty-smelling, but totally minus any bling—jeans that had gone bouldering. But, as was his lot in life, he found no gloves.

Certain he knew the identity of Fitzgerald's partner-in-crime, McCormick slipped on his helmet, and shoved off into the blinding snowstorm. In an effort to steel his soul, he reminded himself to remain calm. He had been trained in perseverance and self-reliance in all things.

With the gray, dusky sky to her back, Andrea sat in the reading chair by the window. Struggling to get her wondering mind off the danger, she reread the final lines of *The Old Man and the Sea,* and then thoughtfully set the book aside. She could cross the title off her long list of books to read or reread—her own bucket list, of sorts. "What was the theme of the book," she asked herself, playfully, as though still in junior high. "Never give up," she shouted aloud, chuckling under her breath at the answer her classmates had given the teacher for every book they ever read. She sniggered, and threw off the cozy, Christmas throw. She stretched and yawned, analyzing Hemingway's often-debated writing style.

She had changed into her black turtleneck sweater, jeans and boots, but still a chill had crept into her bones. She stepped over Tracker, who had lain at her feet as she read. Mortified by his actions earlier in the day, she had deliberately ignored the smelly beast.

For the hundredth time since McCormick had left, she paced from window to window, peeking out into the mounting snow. Seeing no fresh tracks—man or beast—she let out a sigh of relief.

Noticing the evening shadows stretching across the cabin floor, she struck the last of her book matches, and cautiously held it to the wick of her new lantern. Earlier that morning, as the gung ho McCormick had, undauntedly, left the cabin, wading silently through thigh-deep snow, she'd remembered her lantern purchase. While he was still in sight, she'd made a mad dash to her car, bringing the lantern and the jug of frozen, orange juice into the cabin. Pre-filled with coal-oil, the lantern now flickered alive with flames. The juice would take a couple of days to thaw, and she had forgotten to grab the kitchen matches.

Sporting her musical ear buds, she walked to the kitchen and turned the flames on under the kettle, hoping there would be enough propane to heat water for her late afternoon tea. As she dashed to the bathroom in the loft, the persistent whining of an approaching snowmobile went unheard. Neither did she hear the burbling exhaust pipes as they came to a halt beside the cabin. Dancing to the music in her ear, she returned to the hearth and removed the security screen, preparing to lay another log on the fire.

Tracker stood facing the door, but Andrea didn't hear his low, throaty growl.

When a loud banging came at the door, her heart leaped with joy, "Matt's back!" she chirped, enthusiastically, to the dog.

Relieved that the nerve-racking solitude had finally come to an end, she ran to the door, and twisted the locks to allow his entry. Suddenly, the door burst open and four men rudely pushed their way into the cabin.

A tune by American Authors tickled her eardrums, just as a young man backhanded her across the mouth, splitting her lip and drawing blood. The lively notes of "*The Best Day of My Life,*" flowed through her buds as another man grabbed her roughly from behind, clamping his hand painfully over her mouth. A hard, sharp object bruised her ribcage. Her feet were, suddenly, kicked out from under her, and she was dragged by her hair, kicking and screaming across the floor. Through terror-filled eyes, she watched a timid Tracker skulk up the steps to the loft. Angrily, she yanked the buds from her ears, and screamed inside her head, *where's the ferocious war dog when I need him?*

At last, she was unceremoniously dumped on the loveseat. Panic stricken, she believed her worst nightmares, and McCormick's dire warnings had become a reality. Peering through strands of hair covering her face, Andrea's eyes settled on the man shouldering a fur-lined backpack. "Shaun!" she gasped in horror, as blood trickled down her chin from her busted lip.

He looked different, dressed in heavy snow bibs and snowmobile boots; but there was no mistaking his identity. Normally smooth shaven, his face hadn't been touched by a razor for days, and his hair hadn't been trimmed, or washed with shampoo for quite some time.

Andrea searched his face. His eyes, wild with deep, dark circles, darted furtively around the cabin, suggesting wickedness. This was certainly no apparition! She remembered McCormick's name for him: the Devil Incarnate—the devil in human form.

Anger surfaced and consumed her. "I knew you were alive!" She spat out the words. It was true. Ever since the crash that supposedly killed him, Andrea had *felt* that Shaun was, somehow, still alive.

Her eyes watered and her head throbbed, still she turned to boldly face her tormentor. For the first time, she looked at the second man, Sheriff John Donahue, who up to this point had remained surprisingly quiet. He stood with his crutch propped under his armpit, freeing both hands to better aim his rifle at her. He laughed, loathsomely, quickly poking the barrel of his gun under her chin, pushing it upwards. "I'll bet Daddy didn't explain to you about this kind of gun, did he?" He patted the stock of a very sophisticated, extreme rifle. "One of these babies can turn a sweet little girl's head into a million fragmented pieces in a split second."

Andrea glared at Donahue, surmising that he had finally gotten the snow base he needed for his little joyride. Her obstinacy surfaced. "Does this mean we're not going to be working together on your book?" she asked, feigning disappointment.

Fitzgerald's head immediately swiveled towards the sheriff, and he shot him a look of questioning hostility. Donahue returned his boss's foul glare with one of ambiguity. He lowered the gun, and hobbled, nervously, around the cabin, his crutch in one hand and the automatic assault rifle in the other. The third man checked the loft. The fourth man stood behind Andrea, out of her line of vision.

Her patience quickly dissipated, giving way to unguarded rage. "You were never a friend of my father's," she hissed to Donahue. "My father didn't make friends with lechers!"

Donahue quickly hobbled back to her, shoved her to the floor, then raised his crutch above his head, preparing to whack her across the face; but the fourth man quickly stepped between them, intervening. "That's my job, Donahue!" he growled.

With head turned aside, he made a great show of offering Andrea a hand up. She took it, gratefully; but once she was balanced on both feet, the man reared his hand back, smacking her hard across the face.

Losing her balance, the surprised journalists slid to the floor in pain—and total shock.

McCormick killed the engine to his Polaris, and removed his helmet. For the last half-hour, he had been following snowmobile tracks through the fresh snow, beginning at the sheriff's office, and leading to Trail 9. Not wanting to tip Fitzgerald off by the noise of his ride, he had feverishly set off on foot with one major setback. Deep in the South American rainforest, he had gathered a treasure-trove of damning evidence against Fitzgerald, but getting that information had come at a very high price. The bullet hole in his shoulder was now ripped open, in spite of the treatment he had received at a Boston clinic the day before. Now his lungs ached from the exertion and sub-zero temperatures.

His skirmish with Tracker, and his wood-cutting venture earlier in the day, were partly to blame; but the high-speed snowmobile chase through the rugged terrain had finished the job. Snatching Andrea out of the tree probably hadn't helped either. He knew the wound was bleeding profusely, and sucking in air, which, in turn, would endanger his lung. Judging by the increasing difficulty of each breath, he figured the lung might already be damaged. He was losing strength, which meant that he would seriously have to ruck-up—to get extremely tough and uncompromising in order to get through this challenging situation.

Now, the tracks were more difficult to follow as they filled in quickly with drifting snow, but McCormick was certain they led directly to the front of Andrea's cabin.

Darkness fell as quickly and as silently as the large flakes. Through the scattered pines, he could see a dull light shining through a window. Moving several feet to his right, he leaned against a birch tree to catch his breath; but his rest was short-lived. Even from this distance, he could tell the front door stood ajar. Andrea, he reasoned, would never leave it open during such a devastating snowstorm. His steely eyes narrowed, spotting two snowmobiles parked in the thicket of berry bushes he'd planted years ago as an additional food supply for Belly-dragger.

A horrifying image filled his mind. Fear, unequal to any he had ever experienced, mounted up inside him. Andi was in danger, and he feared for her life; but he quickly sloughed off the negative thoughts, preferring a more pleasant image of the young woman's, exquisite face and beautiful body. In his mind's eye, he saw her sitting quietly beside the flickering fireside, demurely asking, "McCormick, are you a man of faith?"

In a much belated answer to her question, he growled, definitively, "I am!" Now a new fire ignited from deep within, and a renewed surge of adrenaline began to pulse through his body. With quiet confidence, he shoved himself away from the tree, and proceeded to the cabin ... slogging through thigh-deep snow to rescue the woman he loved more than life itself.

As he closed in on the cabin, McCormick was able to view the men through the large window. He watched them prance about like proud peacocks, brandishing their firearms like clubs. He quickly recognized three of them: Fitzgerald, Donahue, and the corrupt, hardened pilot who had most recently aerated his shoulder. The muscles in his jaw flexed. He had witnessed, firsthand, the depraved animal natures of all three men—all cold-blooded killers, ruthless and evil in their dealings. This was the same band that had killed his older brother, and shattered his own leg into tiny shards of bone. These were the monsters who had driven bullets into his arm, into his shoulder, and into his head.

McCormick sucked in a deep breath, his thoughts driven by

determination. *Death would reign in this cabin tonight! Whether it be me or thee, depends entirely upon my skill—and the grace of God; but I have to set the conditions—to get inside that cabin!* Once he entered, he would have only seconds to get control of the situation.

He took a second longer to study the action through the window. With conflicted emotions, he recognized a fourth man—David Jennings. Andi was nowhere in sight!

Andrea raised her head off the floor, trying to sit up. Suddenly, from the deep, dark recesses of her mind a forgotten memory surfaced. Fortunately, the terror she felt wasn't mirrored in her eyes. She spoke her mind. "The man driving the pickup truck that killed my parents was named John Donahue," she blurted out brashly, surprising even herself by her accusation.

"Shut up!" Shaun yelled. "Jennings, check the window."

Jennings? For the first time since they had charged into the cabin, Andrea got a good look at the fourth man. Her eyes widened with shock as she studied what little of the man's face could be seen—*David!* She was looking straight into the face of David Jennings, the former sports writer for the *Forest Hills Daily News*. His beard had grown to almost touch his collarbone; his dark, scraggly, shoulder-length hair was buried beneath a hunter's-orange, stocking cap. She opened her mouth to speak, but he quickly cut her off with a deadly glare.

Andrea thought her heart could sink no lower. So David had left the newspaper for this: more money and a life of crime? Heartsick, she raised her hand to her already swollen cheek. These men were for real; not imaginations, not apparitions, but demons.

Jennings looked out the kitchen window; saw a shadow crossing from the tree line to the cabin. Recognizing the man's build and gait, he remained silent.

Outside, McCormick blew into his cold, stiff fingers; then slowly, mounted the steps to the porch. He trod lightly across the wooden planks, the accumulation of drifted snow absorbing each footfall. Suddenly, the warrior-turned-lawman charged unexpectedly through the front door, appearing larger than life in a huge, kickass way.

"Matt!" Andrea blurted out in anguish.

One glimpse at Andrea, and McCormick's heart leapt with joy. She was alive! He held her gaze for a beat. The return look she gave him spoke volumes. He looked at the four men, cussed coarsely, feigning surprise.

All four men trained their guns on the federal agent.

David lunged at McCormick, pinning him, roughly, against the wall, all-the-while wondering why the man had not entered with guns ablaze.

"Well … well … well. Would you look at who we have here," Shaun enthused loudly, his smile twisted. He lowered his pack to the floor, and added with mocking disdain, "A real … live … celebrated war hero."

Andrea's eyes clouded with confusion at Shaun's recognition of Matt.

"You don't see many around these parts." Fitzgerald looked straight at Matt, addressing his next comment to him. "They don't usually live long enough to be celebrated … do they, McCormick?" He chortled, pugnaciously.

CHAPTER 46

Andrea's jaw dropped in muddled bewilderment at Shaun's insolent words. Why was he doing this? Why was he expressing such vehemence towards someone he didn't even know—surely it wasn't because she'd kissed the man.

Fitzgerald laid a hand across his heart in exaggerated reverence. "I'm honored that the agency would send such a high-profile representative after me. He smiled, buffoonishly, and shambled backwards, gasping for air. "This is … my childhood fantasy come to life." With a sick grin, he barked to Jennings, "Search him."

Ignoring his training, David commenced the search at McCormick's ankles, not at all surprised to find a commando knife, sheathed and fastened to the man's shin; he was, however, totally shocked to discover a prosthetic—an artificial limb—at the ankle of McCormick's frayed jeans. Without expression, he continued working his way up the pant leg, finding nothing. As he slipped his hands under McCormick's jacket, he ignored the pancake holster attached to his back. Sliding on up towards his armpits, his finger's made contact with Matt's gun and shoulder holster—and then he quickly discovered Matt's blood-soaked shirt. At that point, the two men's eyes met and locked with deadly seriousness.

At last, David stepped back and announced. "He's clean."

The stakes were running high in this game, and Jennings knew his act had to be convincing. Without warning, he heavy-handedly cuffed McCormick across the jaw, and shoved him towards Andrea, now standing horrified beside the loveseat.

"Jennings, stand watch," Shaun said. "Make sure our hero here, is alone."

As David reluctantly stepped out of the cabin, Shaun moved towards Andrea and roughly grabbed a thatch of hair, pulling her forward. He said to Andrea, "Honey, I want to introduce you to one really i-m-p-o-r-t-a-n-t dude. This is the bastard who's been trying to mess up all my superb plans for a bright and prosperous future, but it looks like you've already met the hero of the undercover world." He laughed, but his eyes glared at McCormick with a vengeful stare.

McCormick shot him a taunting, badass glare back, but said nothing.

"The two of you have worked so hard to unravel my plans, and I believe such diligence should be rewarded. So, I've decided to explain it all to you in detail … before you die."

Andrea gasped. No movie, or printed word, nor work of art could ever capture the surrealism of this moment as it threatened to overwhelm her. Although totally confused by what Shaun was saying, she knew at gut level that he was not joking—he fully intended to kill them. He had exhibited unstable behavior for the past several months, and it would be easy to think him insane; but something told her that he was in full control of his faculties—Shaun was simply evil.

Her chest heaved heavily, and her throat closed into a tight knot; but behind her, she could feel McCormick's presence, his hot, steady breath on the nape of her neck. Wasn't he at all frightened, as she was?

"I have to hand it to you, McCormick," Shaun was saying, "You did a really good job on this cabin. I want to thank you for accommodating my plans, and hosting this little party—your lake, your property, your cabin, as you say … and now,,, you."

A stunned, perplexed look traveled across Andrea's face. She shot a questioning look at McCormick.

Fitzgerald continued. "I knew the cabin would lure Andrea up here, and I knew a nosey fed would soon follow her scent." He pulled a chair away from the table, and sprawled his legs around the seat. His forehead rested, momentarily, on his arms. Finally, he lifted his chin, and like a bad boy coming clean, he spoke, ruefully. "Andrea, I have something to confess to you … I do hope you can find it in your heart to forgive me."

Andrea bristled. Shaun was mocking her faith. Like the chipmunk that had dared to cross her pre-dawn courtyard, she felt trapped and pawed by the tormenting cat while the mad man cheered with exuberance. Things had not gone well for the chipmunk.

"You know, Andrea, your little sister was a really cute kid, wasn't she? … so dynamic and full of life; she was very much like you … too much like you, actually: adventurous … inquisitive … noisy. Getting her turned on to drugs was so easy … of course she only did it once, which just happened to be enough." He sniggered, balefully at his own baneful act. "You do understand what I'm saying here, don't you?"

Andrea gasped in horror—she had just been clawed, decapitated, and disemboweled.

"You bastard!" McCormick hissed under his breath, while laying a supportive hand, firm and reassuring, on the small of Andrea's back, hoping she wouldn't lose control of her fiery temper. His move went undetected by his captors.

"And Officer Donahue here, took care of dull, old Mom and Dad; didn't you, officer?" He winked at Donahue. "But of course, you have astutely figured all that out for yourselves, haven't you?" He glared at McCormick.

Andrea's cheeks burned like fire as she licked blood from her throbbing, split lip, feeling the swelling begin. She kept silent, but inside, she seethed with a white, hot rage. "You know, it's a funny thing about your father, though. I realized, one day, that owning a pharmaceutical company had benefits that dear, old dad wasn't using to his full advantage."

He turned, conversationally, to McCormick as though passing information on to an old friend. "Mac … did you know that the pharmaceutical industry started right here in Vermont?"

McCormick ignored his comment.

"I explained to him how financially rewarding it could be, for us all, if we simply merged the legal drug business with the illegal trade. After all, the one major drawback I have in dealing in illegal drugs is in the distribution— getting the merchandise to the public. What better way than through a legitimate, and well respected, drug manufacturing company? Drugs in … drugs out … how simple could it be … and if we could get doctors to prescribe it…. Ah," he said, dejectedly, "already been done." A sagacious, cunning look crossed his face. "Simple, but Daddy wasn't buying any of it." Shaun shook his head sympathetically. "Well, nice folks not only finish last … sometimes they don't finish at all." He laughed at his own cleverness, but it was a bitter, menacing laugh. His loathsome eyes fixed on McCormick, and then traveled back to Andrea, away from the agent's badass stare. "I'll bet you don't remember who suggested the folks go to Hawaii?"

Andrea gave her head an angry shake.

"It was me!" he said, gleefully, childlike, like a person deranged. "I needed a way to explain my expanded income and unusual trips and purchases to the IRS. Your daddy's company was the perfect cover. After I took over, I just fired anyone who knew anything about the company and replaced them with my own people."

Fitzgerald stood up, and began to pace. "And the banks ... ah, yes, the banks. They are so computerized, these days, and accommodating. Believe it or not, I can sit in my office—excuse me, Daddy's office—and fax my *income* into just about any overseas account I want. I just keep moving the money around from country to country. After a few strategic moves, it's almost impossible for the feds to trace. Isn't that right, McCormick? And I don't have to pay taxes on any of that drug money I'm dragging in ... crime is so easy these days!"

"And as for you, Andrea," Shaun continued. "I thought I could keep you around as cover for all my other activities. You were just so sweet and innocent. Your friends all thought I was a h-e-r-o for coming to your rescue after all your ... what shall we call them ... t-r-a-g-e-d-i-e-s?" An evil laugh gurgled up in his throat.

Suddenly, his voice turned angry. "But you just wouldn't leave well enough alone. You had to start snooping around and writing those fuckin' articles about things that were none of your fuckin' business."

He grabbed Andrea roughly by the jaw, squeezing it hard between his fingers. He glared at her nose-to-nose, as blood from her lip ran down her chin. "The pills were a little present from me too, darlin'." He hissed, wickedly, certain that she understood him.

Andrea swallowed hard, and glared back, all-the-while feeling the gentle pressure of McCormick's fingers, lightly massaging the small of her back. She wished he would fight back. Wretchedly, she dismissed the thought. What could one man do against four guns?

Monitoring her breathing, McCormick wished he could spare Andrea all this ugliness, but Fitzgerald was spilling his guts. McCormick wouldn't disrupt the flow. Before Andrea could heal, or put her full trust in him, she needed to hear Shaun's confession.

"Of course, I had Jolene's help with that one," Shaun was saying. "You see, like so many other young people these days, Jolene didn't like living in poverty; she has a weakness for beautiful clothes, and all that expensive stuff you girls like so much. She agreed to work as city editor, if I would make nice, little deposits into her checking account each week. In fact, Jolene even spent nights in our home, right under your fuckin' nose." He rolled his eyes to the ceiling and laughed. "Ha! Some investigative reporter you are!"

"I've always known," Andrea said, monotonically. "I just didn't fuckin' c-a-r-e!"

McCormick caught a glimpse of her profile. This might explain why she had gotten so angry at him at the restaurant. He guessed Fitzgerald had a habit of rubbing her nose in his infidelities—just as Lauren had done with him. When Shaun, at last, let go of her chin, her blood was on his hand, but McCormick breathed easier.

"Jolene's job at the paper was to control Rudd, and Rudd's was to control you. Of course, Rudd doesn't do anything very well, so I had to resort to the pills."

"So Rudd was working for you?" McCormick asked.

Shaun stood up and kicked the chair away. "Nah ... Rudd is just a damned, old, useful idiot."

Suddenly, the loud, angry hiss of a cat startled everyone. Upon hearing the agent's voice, the snowy apparition clawed and scrambled its way out of the top of Fitzgerald's backpack, jumped to the floor and ran straight towards McCormick, purring loudly, and affectionately rubbing against his leg.

Fitzgerald turned abruptly to his foe, inflamed irritation flickering wildly in his eyes. He hissed, "What difference does it make to you, McCormick? You're going to be fuckin' dead." He raised the butt of his rifle, and smashed it hard against the side of McCormick's head. Andrea fell back, gasping in horror.

Work through the pain, McCormick told himself as he straightened his body. Once again, this vexatious cat had jeopardized his life. He sensed Shaun's jealousy and growing impatience with his own game. Shaking off his wooziness, McCormick saw the cat's sudden appearance as a missed opportunity. He knew he had to make his move soon, or it would be too late. He needed another distraction—any kind of distraction.

Shaun skirted the room, examining the structure of the cabin's ceiling, walls, and hearth. At last he walked towards the door. Greed and malice sounded in his voice, "Well, I hate to leave the party early, but I've got a lot of money to make—billions actually. Once the two of you are out of my way, I'm going to be one of the richest men in the world ... there's no one else to stop me!"

McCormick considered his words: *No one else to stop me.*

Fitzgerald turned his focus to his wife. "Andrea, I had special plans for you, but I've just fuckin' run out of time. Donahue raised his gun as if on cue, aiming at both Andrea and McCormick.

Shaun reached for the doorknob. "Kill 'em!" he ordered, gruffly.

Before Shaun could get out the door, Donahue stopped him, asking for clarification of his orders. Strangely, the three abductors huddled together, whispering to each other, temporarily taking their eyes off their hostages.

Andrea's eyes glazed over as she stood waiting, but the agent lifted his towards the ceiling, hearing a distant, high-pitched whine of a helicopter passing high above the cabin. It was soon gone, but the sweet sound of the gently, whirring blades was music to the ex-warrior's ears.

Andrea sat, head bowed, quietly reciting the Lord's Prayer, when she heard McCormick's husky voice, calm and laid-back, spoken in the spirit of casual, everyday conversation, "Oh, hey … Bran. Be sure to give my best to Hero … would ya?" he offered, mockingly, his voice dripping with cockiness. An audacious display of courage was planted on a face dripping blood.

At the sound of McCormick's voice, Fitzgerald turned, and shot an intolerant look over his shoulder.

"We got to know each other really well a couple of nights ago," McCormick continued, boldly. "He's a little shy around *real, celebrated* heroes … but we actually got to be good buds … I'm bettin' he had one hell of a hangover the next mornin', though!"

Fully understanding the implication of McCormick's words, Fitzgerald, spun around, and shot daggers at his enemy. Just as he'd suspected—McCormick had been the one who had wrought destruction on his Peruvian compound.

Andrea started to move. She hadn't the foggiest idea what McCormick was referring to, why he had called him Bran, or who Hero was. The only thing she understood, for sure, was that she was looking down the barrel of an extreme rifle as Donahue stepped up and shoved his gun in her face.

Shaun's confession and sordid details had confirmed her unspoken suspicions of the past several months, but it was all going to end here—the man who killed her mother, father, and sister would end her life as well.

Fitzgerald's mouth tugged up in a grin; not the good-natured grin, charming and jocular, that so often played across McCormick's lips, but the fiendish pronouncement of yet another attempt at evil. A low, wicked laugh roiled from his chest as he clutched his gun, checking the magazine, joyful at the priceless opportunity presented to him—McCormick's admission of guilt. His face darkened, and he raised his pistol to shoulder level, taking aim at the agent's head. "I'll see you in Hell … Pretty Boy!"

Oozing both, blood and confidence, the agent shook his head to the side as he shot Fitzgerald a cock-sure grin. "Sorry pal … I'm … not goin' that direction."

Andrea gazed laudably, though wistfully, at the agent. In anguish, and in pride, she thought, *Quiet confidence.* In that moment, she found herself in that altered state, the state McCormick had once referred to as *the other side of fear.*

Her own will to life had ended with the death of her family; but what kept her grounded in reality was no longer a simple mug of coffee, or mindless chattering to herself, but rather her deep concern for McCormick. He was here because of her, an innocent victim of Shaun's depravity. She had, unknowingly and unwittingly, led him here. She couldn't, she wouldn't let him die. Emboldened by the agent's flippant comment, she heard herself saying, "Shaun, you can't kill me now!"

Fitzgerald trained his icy stare on the woman, just as a frigid wind blew in through the open door, matching the cold exasperation on the man's face. Having grown accustomed to the dead eyes of a killer, she lifted her chin with insolence to meet Fitzgerald's stare. "I'm the living heir to the Kingdom," she said, tauntingly, "I've made no will … everything will go to the state." She let her comment hang in the air, then sniggered, audaciously "You can't inherit, Shaun … you're already dead and buried … remember?" Her deliberate, bitchy laugh chilled Shaun's thinking.

McCormick's senses quickened, and his muscles grew taut. He thought, *Bless her little, bitchy heart!*

Meanwhile, going unnoticed was the damage being done by the wind as it blew through the cabin, exciting the flames in the unscreened, unattended fireplace, scattering the hot coals onto the hardwood floor, where they lay smoldering, unnoticed.

For a long moment, Fitzgerald stood mute. Finally, the realization that Andrea was right manifested itself on his face. He leaned his rifle against the door and holstered his gun. Following their boss's lead, Donahue lowered his rifle. The pilot, who had taken a liking to Andrea, gave out a grateful sigh of relief and lowered his weapon.

"Wow, some lawyer you are," she hissed with utter contempt. "I'll bet you're not even a real lawyer, are you?"

McCormick shifted his weight and deliberately planted his hand possessively, around Andrea's shoulder, gently pulling her to him, both for effect and protection. "No babe ... he's a lawyer, all right. He worked a couple of years for the DEA, prosecuting drug dealers; but it didn't take him long to decide he would rather have a piece of the action. He went to the dark side, Sweetheart ... and ratted out our own agents ... even his closest friend."

Babe? Sweetheart? Fitzgerald stood in a frozen rage, unable to move as he witnessed, with his own eyes—his own angry, jealous eyes—the handsome McCormick with his arm wrapped smugly around *his* wife. Matthew J. McCormick—the man who was, and always had been, everything he was not. His face reddened, and veins popped on his neck.

Accurately reading the jealous rage, McCormick recognized his moment of opportunity. *One shot, one kill, no luck, all skill,* he thought, finishing the slogan Andrea had begun weeks earlier. He pulled her closer, and put his lips to her ear. Fitzgerald saw it as a kiss; but in reality, McCormick whispered, "Down!"

What happened next, transpired in a matter of seconds. In one rapid movement, McCormick's leg shot out, kicking Sheriff Donahue's legs, crutch and rifle out from under him with force. He moved towards Fitzgerald, and his other leg shot out, causing the man to drop his gun and lose his equilibrium. Shoving Andrea to the floor, McCormick dropped his knee to her shoulder, holding her down as he drew his Glock from his open jacket with his free hand, surprising both Andrea and his oppressors.

Recovering his gun, Fitzgerald fired the first shot; then quickly moved from the door to the opposite end of the room. McCormick dropped and hovered over Andrea, as the bullet whizzed over their heads. The second shot came from the pilot. McCormick moved to the side, as the bullet burrowed deep into the wall.

Donahue fumbled to control his crutch, his cast, and his hefty weight, while trying to regain his balance. Finally, he awkwardly pulled the gun from his holster and fired off a wild shot in their direction.

Frightened, Andrea started to raise her head. "Stay down!" McCormick growled. He stepped away and fired two shots—one shot at Sheriff Donahue and one at the pilot. Both men fell to the floor with a bullet between the eyes, leaving Fitzgerald standing alone in wild-eyed, unprotected bafflement.

Striving to keep his momentum going, and knowing the man's reaction time to be slow, McCormick rushed his enemy, preparing to drop-kick him to the floor.

Suddenly, a look of consternation darkened the agent's face. Something was holding his feet to the floor. He looked down and stopped short. The white, silky-haired body of Stone's cat had entwined itself around both McCormick's feet and ankles. Its entire body vibrated with every purr, as the head and furry tail rubbed against McCormick's leg. The agent tamped down the mounting urge to kick the cat through the glass window; instead, he fought to free himself of its sharp, clinging claws.

Stone snickered wickedly, taking up a position behind the chair by the window, while taking wild shots at both the agent and Andrea.

Suddenly, the totally unexpected happened. From out of the rafters came a squirrel's loud chitter, and a flash of bushy tail flying through the air, landing on the cat's back. The two animals tore into each other, scratching, clawing and rolling around the floor. Fur balls flew in every direction amidst their vociferate caterwauling. Taking advantage of this unprecedented opportunity, McCormick hustled back towards Andrea. A shot rang out, as he dove across the floor, and threw himself on top of her, putting his life and limb on the line for her.

All hell had broken loose so fast and so furious, that Andrea couldn't tell who was winning. With the breath completely knocked out of her, and feeling the full weight of McCormick's body, she lay, flattened, unable to move. A trickle of blood splattered her cheek—blood from the silent, lifeless agent. *He was hit—was he dead?* She waited, trying to get a handle on her emotions. Only fear held back the tears.

Silence, long and dreadful, prevailed.

From her suffocating position, she could hear grunts and shuffling noises coming from the living room. At the sound of scraping chair legs, she opened one eye in time to see the chair bump into the table, and the kerosene lantern teeter, its flame flickering wildly. She gasped as it fell to the floor with a thwacking sound. Glass shattered in every direction, and coal oil splashed across the floor, where glowing embers lay smoldering. Instantly, they burst into flames.

Unexpectedly, the kitchen window shattered, and a burst of rapid rifle fire poured in from outside the cabin. Bullets whizzed over the tops of their heads, traveling through the living room, plugging the loveseat and Christmas throw full of holes. Doors to the deck on the far side of the cabin shattered, completely.

At the first sound of cover shots, McCormick suddenly sprang to life and quickly rolled off Andrea's back, who opened one eye to watch him roll another two times across the floor to better position himself, landing belly-down, his pistol gripped, firmly, between both hands. She was daunted by his courage and selfless determination as he fired two shots towards the chair. One shot came back at him, the bullet burrowing deep into the wooden floor less than an inch from his head.

Stone went for the stairway and started to climb, shooting back over his shoulder. Suddenly from out of nowhere, a crazed war dog appeared on the top landing in a ready-to-leap crouch. With teeth gnashing, his wolf-like eyes glowered red in the leaping flames. A continuous growl, ferocious and threatening, gurgled deep in his throat.

Trapped between McCormick and his dog, Stone's eyes furtively shot around the room. He lifted his gun, and trained it, not on McCormick or the ferocious canine, but on Andrea.

Sensing the movement, more than seeing it, McCormick leaped to his feet, did two, rapid, forward somersaults across the blazing floor, stood and returned to the two-handed pistol grip. He fired off two shots in rapid-fire succession as he walked, confidently, towards his enemy.

A deadly silence fell over the cabin. Only the sounds of the loose, crackling flames as they snaked across the wooden flooring could be heard. Andrea feared that everyone might be dead.

"You okay bro?" came a concerned voice from outside the shattered window. Andrea recognized David's voice.

"Yeah," the agent answered in a less than convincing tone.

Andrea lifted her head as McCormick moved to quickly check Stone's

413

pulse, insuring himself that his enemy would never rise up to fight again. He took a step towards the body, then stopped in his tracks and turned away. With smoke rising, he grabbed the Christmas throw off the chair. "Merry Christmas," he said, his raspy voice, forlorn and careworn, as he slowly draped the throw over Stone's body. He returned to check the other two intruders.

Satisfied that the enemy was no longer a threat, he turned, and dropped to his haunches beside the woman he had taken an oath to protect. Carefully choosing professional words for professional reasons, he asked, "Mrs. Fitzgerald ... are you hurt?"

Andrea looked into McCormick's austere face "No ... I'm not hurt."

He thought she looked fragile as he offered her his hand. She stood, taking a quick glance around. On the floor, a short distance from Matt, laid the bodies of Sheriff Donahue and the pilot.

Flames leaped, and smoke roiled in from the living room. At the bottom of the stairwell, a third man lay dead. "Oh, my gawd!" she whispered, suddenly feeling faint. McCormick would have warned her not to look, but in his heart he knew that her nightmare would never be over until she knew, for certain, that her attackers were dead.

"Mrs. Fitzgerald," he said, "Your abductors are dead ... are you sure you're not hurt?"

"I'm okay," she uttered, her throat closing up with emotion.

McCormick sensed that Andrea's tender, compassionate heart and high regard for human life might have kicked into gear, threatening to over-shadow the reality of the day. He walked her over to Donahue's body. "Mrs. Fitzgerald ... can you identify this man?" he asked, in a low, gentle tone.

She gaped at the body, giving no answer. Concerned that she was going into shock, McCormick questioned in a louder, more compelling voice, "Is this the man you know as Sheriff Donahue?"

"Yes," she said, weakly.

"Is this the man who called you at the Daily News and threatened to kill you if you continued to write your newspaper articles?"

"Yes."

"Can he kill you now?"

"No."

He walked her to the body of the pilot, and asked, "Have you ever seen this man before?"

Andrea stared numbly at the rounded face and belly, and fully-tatted arms, short and chubby. She turned her head away, and answered in a mere whisper, "Yes ... that's José ... he's been to my house."

"Did you invite him?" McCormick asked, his voice turning to hoarfrost.

"No ... my hus ... Shaun would occasionally bring him home with him at the end of the day."

"What's his last name?"

"I was never given a last name."

A grimace came to McCormick's face as he walked her over to the third body. He paused, momentarily, not sure if he was even ready for this. He lifted the bullet-riddled throw. "Mrs. Fitzgerald, can you identify this man as that of your husband, Shaun Fitzgerald?"

She glared at the body with its head completely severed from its shoulders. Suddenly, she more than found her voice. She pointed to the lifeless form, and with acrimony cried out, "That ... Agent McCormick ... is the source of all my anger!"

"Is this your husband?" he asked in a clipped voice.

"Yes ... that's Shaun Fitzgerald!"

"Is he dead?"

"Yes," she affirmed, her voice suddenly going weak.

A new vitality came into McCormick's voice, "Mrs. Fitzgerald ... are you one hundred percent sure he's dead?"

Andrea glared at McCormick as though he were crazy, then at the lifeless eyes staring back at her from the floor—cold and dead. Trembling, she answered, "Yes!"

"Can he hurt anyone you love?"

"No!"

McCormick reached inside his jacket, flipped off the technical device, and pulled her close, regretting every harsh word he'd spoken to the woman. Lowering his head, he whispered, "Andi ... it's over."

She breathed out a hot breath and leaned in to him as a wave of calmness rolled through her body.

David, standing on the deck, looked in through the shattered window and raised an eyebrow in question. McCormick gave him a serious nod over Andrea's head.

"Andi."

She turned her burning, smoke-filled eyes towards David's voice. His Glock was pointed upwards, and a semi-automatic rifle was slung across the shoulder of his load-bearing vest. To Andrea, the whole scene seemed like something to be viewed on a wide screen from a comfortable theater seat, sharing a bag of buttered popcorn with someone donned in serious armor. In Zoe's words: *the whole thing was just too, damned frightening!*

Lifting her chin, McCormick asked, ruefully, "Are you sure you're okay?"

"Yeah," she answered, "totally confused … but okay."

CHAPTER 47

David stepped up beside them, and spoke with compassion, "Andi … I'm sorry things had to happen this way."

Unable to speak, she acknowledged him with a head nod, and started to cough as dark plumes of smoke rose, and flames, fanned by the wind, leapt higher.

"Let's get out of here," McCormick said. He took her elbow and gently guided her through the smoke, now swirling across the floor. Walking through shards of glass, they simultaneously, stepped over Shaun's body, thus fulfilling McCormick's graveside promise to his older brother.

Outside, Andrea embraced the cold as Matt led her through a crowd of congregating law enforcement officers. All had arrived too late to help, but now they strained for a glimpse of Brantley Stone's wife. Her swollen lips throbbed and bled, her cheeks flamed red, both from the hard slap she'd received, and the embarrassment of being the center of attention. Andrea blanched with abashment as someone snapped a picture, hoping to sell it to the media. She had become *newsworthy*.

Noticing her embarrassment, McCormick approached the man and tore the camera out of his hands. "Get the hell out of here!" he growled, angrily. The man quickly disappeared.

He steered her towards a new all-terrain jeep parked nearby, of the type used only by the military. He opened the door, and tossed the camera in the back. Facing her, he offered, "Climb in here … no one will bother you." McCormick's voice was soothing, but his eyes and demeanor were hard, preoccupied. "Get comfortable … this may take a while."

Andrea could hear the engine running, and she immediately felt the warm air blowing from the heater. She groaned, as she slid behind the wheel, her bruised body already beginning to stiffen.

McCormick shut the door, giving her a hard, but caring look through the glass. *What must she be thinking of me by now,* he thought? His head dropped as he turned away, and walked a short distance in the direction of the burning cabin just as the three bodies were being carried outside.

A young female agent-in-training loped over to meet him. "Get this woman a blanket and some hot coffee, STAT!" he ordered, borrowing his mother's term.

"Yes sir," came the immediate answer.

When the white cat ran towards him, he growled in exasperation, "And get this damned, fuckin' cat out of here before I shoot its fuckin' head off!"

"Yes *sir!*"

A weak smile crossed Andrea's swollen lips, as she witnessed McCormick's execution of his *multifaceted* job, fully cognizant of the respect he was getting from the gaggle of agents.

In the next moment, someone brought Andrea a blanket and a cup of coffee, while someone else quickly scooped up the obstinate cat, yowling and ghostly, like something out of a horror movie with one addendum: missing thatches of hair. "Better lock down that attack squirrel as evidence," McCormick advised David, "in case someone gets a craving for roasted, cocaine rodent."

"No one will believe this," he grunted as he walked away.

Andrea pulled the blanket around her shoulders and collapsed against the back of the seat, her burning eyes never losing sight of McCormick. She raised the cup to her lips, sorely in need of comfort; but before she could take a sip, a loud whooshing sound filled the air. Everyone moved back, as red, hot flames erupted from the cabin's roof.

Remembering that Tracker had run upstairs earlier to escape the loud, harsh voices, she opened the door and set one foot out of the jeep. "Tracker!" she yelled, frantically. McCormick's head swiveled towards her with concernment as he stood talking to a large group of men. She yelled a second time, hoping the dog had gone into the woods.

No Tracker. Heartbroken, she stood beside the door, watching the roof start to cave in upon itself, shooting hot ashes and flaming debris her way. Concerned, now, for her own safety, she was startled to see the crazed dog come crashing through the collapsing, loft window, bounce off the front porch roof, and blindly run towards the sound of her voice. Carrying the singed, rogue squirrel between his teeth, he dropped it at her feet. She slid into the seat, and the wet, hairy mass of smelly dog followed, jumped across her lap and into the seat beside her.

"Aw, Tracker, are you all right?" she cooed as he plunked a singed paw against her chest and licked her face. Wrapping arms around the smelly beast, she gave him the biggest, most loving hug ever, finally forgiving him for creating her, all-time, most embarrassing moment.

She rolled down the window, as a grave-faced McCormick returned to the side of the jeep and pronounced the squirrel dead. Together, they watched officers drag out bag after bag of plastic-wrapped packages from the tree's hollow center.

"What's all that stuff?" she asked, in a voice oozing innocence. Before getting an answer, she connected the dots. Her voice went wispy, "Oh my gawd ... its cocaine, isn't it?"

McCormick studied her face and demeanor for a beat; then finally lifted his chin in a self-justifying manner. "No," he paused. "It's heroin." His eyes locked into to hers, "and fentanyl ... Shaun's been air-dropping tons of the stuff into your mythological Spirit Wood Forest at night. They were using Trail 9 to get it out of the woods, and into the surrounding cities. When one of their small planes crashed, a short distance from here, they got the idea to hide whatever they salvaged, but since you were occupying the cabin—their drop zone—they hid what they could in the hollowed-out tree."

McCormick would wait until later to explain how her husband had also deliberately tried to set him up, to implicate him in the crime, using his property in an effort to incriminate, frame and defame him.

David hesitantly approached the jeep, picked up the charred squirrel and spoke. "Matt, the coroner is here, and air ambulance just landed ... they've got a gunshot specialist on board ... better let'em take a look at that shoulder."

"Shoulder?" Andrea threw a questioning look at David, before turning piercing eyes on Matt.

McCormick said he would, but didn't move.

As the attendants came with body bags for the deceased, Andrea slipped down from the warmth of the jeep and faced the cold, biting wind. Not a word was spoken as Shaun's body was carried off and loaded into a wagon. Unlike the paying of respects to the honorably fallen, this silence was an expression of loathing towards a man who had brought death and destruction to so many innocent lives.

Suddenly, the quietude was shattered by a loud, deafening explosion on the back side of the cabin. Aghast, they all turned to look at the orange plumes of hot, fiery debris shooting high into the air. Bothered by the noise, Tracker whined and danced in the back seat, rocking the jeep.

Matt let out his exasperated breath, "Aw, hell, Andi ... your car just exploded ... damn, what'd you have in that thing?"

"Propane...." Andrea answered, "and coal oil...." she shot them both a sheepish grin, "and kitchen matches," she added, breaking into a snickered laugh.

Both men joined her, laughing heartily; but David remembered how she loved her old car, and quickly slipped his arm around her. "Sorry," he said with sympathy. McCormick's head dropped as a twinge of jealousy wormed its way through his heart. He longed to hold her, to give her a sense of security; but this was neither the time nor the place—he had work to do.

A sheriff from a neighboring county had arrived, and a corroborating statement taken from everyone involved in the shooting. Now, as duty agents departed with the evidence, the muted thumping of sound-suppressed, rotary blades, whipping through the cold air, reached their ears, then visualized as a black, next-generation helicopter. Matt and David shot each other hard, knowing glances, as it swooped overhead, quietly swung around, then set down in the clearing a short distance from the blazing cabin.

McCormick eyed the high-tech, radar-suppressed chopper, watching his hypothesis materialize before his very eyes.

Now he shot Andrea a concerned look. Reaching into the jeep, he turned off the engine, and warned, "Andi ... it's of the utmost importance that you stay out of sight. Get back into the jeep ... lock the doors, and stay low." He pocketed the keys.

David shot Matt a glance of concernment, "Any chance this thing could go sideways?"

"Every chance," McCormick growled. "Want out?"

David shot him a killer look.

McCormick grinned, appreciatively. "Then let's put a bow on this thing," he said through clenched teeth.

Earlier that morning, as the runners of his snowmobile had sluiced through the heavy snow on his return trip from Red Springs, he'd looked around, realizing that everything was too quiet. Under normal operating procedure, law enforcement should have been crawling all over this mountain. As the miles had slipped by, McCormick's thinking had crystallized, and he had figured it out, suddenly realizing what was actually at play. Criminals always had a way of telling you exactly what they were up to—this time was no different.

Chief Straker, himself, had gone to the dark side. He'd partnered with Stone, worked with him, covering Stone's tracks. But Stone had been compromised, and was now worthless to him. So, Straker had begun orchestrating an illegal takeover from his government-run office. His plan was to seize control of Stone's assets; but in order for that to work, he had to remove both Stone and Andrea from the picture.

Matt had first been tipped off by Straker's General Washington quote: "*It is a fine line that a trustworthy man must walk who lives in this world of trickery....*" He had wondered, at the time, why Straker hadn't bothered to finish the quote—now he knew. *Straker had not remained true to his cause.*

Accepting the fact that there would be no backup, McCormick had quickly made a U-turn in the middle of the snowy highway, and followed his tracks back to Nicole's apartment—where he had made a second and a third phone call: one to his retired Colonel, and one to his dad.

Now, as the helicopter doors opened, the mantel of authority descended on McCormick like a dove, beginning at the top of his head and shoulders and settling, stalwartly, into his tactical boots. Confidence rode in his posture as he approached the next generation chopper with gravitas—along with his war dog.

Inside the chopper, Straker gave his twelve men their orders upon landing. "Don't do anything until I give the order."

When the passengers disembarked, McCormick met, and pulled aside, the official-looking, silver-headed gentleman—Chief Straker. He quickly recognized the aggregation of men following at the chief's heels; not as the agents they pretended to be, but as trained mercenaries—professional killers. The two men shook hands, and then went into a serious, lengthy discussion.

Inside the Jeep, Andrea could hear just enough of the conversation to know that something was going seriously wrong. When the rotor blades ceased their whirring, the men's voices grew clearer, and she could hear McCormick making serious allegations against the older man. She lowered the blanket, and pulled herself up, just enough to view the action.

She heard the names Fitzgerald and Stone bantered about; then someone by the name of Clint. The body language on each man grew angrier, more tense as each struggled to make his point.

"Agent, I gave you explicit orders to get rid of her," she heard the older man say in a loud, authoritative voice.

McCormick spat back in a slow, deliberate voice. "It's not my job to kill innocent people ... I'm not one of your assassins."

Not liking the conversation, Andrea wandered who they were referring to?

Straker bellowed back. "Andrea's innocent only if I say she's innocent!"

Andrea gasped. *McCormick's defending me, and this man, this Straker is outraged that I'm still alive!* "Oh, my God!" she whispered as the bottom fell out of her stomach. *Does that mean....*

Planting his hands firmly on his slender hips, McCormick leaned into the man's face, and spoke truth to power. "And who made you judge, jury, and fuckin' executioner?" he charged.

Straker pulled in his chin, and bellowed, "You're a dead man, McCormick!"

"My God ... my God ... my God!" Andrea gushed, her breath spiraling white inside the frigid jeep. This man had just threatened Matt's life, and he was backed up by an army of thugs! She watched David inconspicuously saunter over, unbutton his coat, and stand beside Matt. They were seriously outnumbered; but the two young, lionhearted men stood with shoulders squared, their weight balanced between their wide-spread legs. Like gunslingers of the Old West, their hands hung loose and ready for action, their eyes never off the enemy.

Straker grinned perniciously, and reached for his gun. Without warning, McCormick's arm shot out, and instantly dropped the man to the ground. He relieved him of his weapons, then yelled out an order to the supposed agents. "Put this man under arrest for narco-terrorism, shipping contraband across national borders, money laundering, selling sensitive information to the nation's enemy, using government facilities and resources to conduct criminal activity, the premeditated murder and attempted murder of his own federal agents ... and the attempted, cold-blooded murder of an innocent civilian!"

Murmurings traveled through the cluster of imposters. No one offered to move. Having no authority and fearing the consequences of going against the powerful Chief Straker, the men stood mute. Finally, David stepped forward, flashing his gun in one hand and his FBI creds in the other. Eyeing the gang of surly, disgruntled men, McCormick stepped forward, and drew his Glock. David holstered his gun; and dragged the man out of the snow and onto his knees. Taking plasticuffs from his jacket pocket, he wrapped them around the man's one wrist in an attempt to arrest him.

Straker, aging but savvy, had travelled much the same career path as McCormick. He, too, was a trained weapon, and now he was enraged at the turn of events. Aware that McCormick had gathered enough evidence on him to send him to life in prison, or possibly to the chair, he lunged at David, wresting the gun out of the young man's holster. In desperation, he aimed the gun at Matt.

Everything was happening at a dizzying speed. Andrea strained to see through the obscure light, and accumulated snow on the windshield. The cabin fire was waning, but still very much ablaze, casting the men as dancing shadows. A shot rang out in the dark. "Matt," she screamed, watching McCormick's tall, dark form buckle, and fall to the ground, his gun falling a fair distance from his body. He lay unresponsive in the snow.

Tracker lunged at Straker, grabbing his thigh with angry gnashing teeth. A second shot rang out, and Tracker dropped to the ground.

Andrea's hot, anxious breath fogged over the window. She wiped it with the ball of her fist, and frantically pushed her nose hard against the pane.

Just as Stone had done two nights before in Peru, Straker thrust the gun under David's chin. Fully expecting the maneuver to work for him, he started yelling orders to his men, using David as a hostage, should someone besides McCormick be around to challenge him.

From the ground, one eye popped opened, quietly assessing the situation through thick, dark lashes, locating his gun in his peripheral vision. With only the dull, flickering glow from the burning cabin for light, McCormick read the courageous glint in his brother's eye.

Not a single muscle could be seen twitching or moving, as the former warrior silently slid his concealed blade into his waiting fingers. With lightning speed, and one smooth motion, he sat up, and sliced the darkness with his knife, past David's ear, delivering it deep into the chest of Chief Straker.

As the once-honorable Straker gasped, and crumpled towards the ground, David leaned in, and without missing a beat, retrieved his gun from the man's withering hand. When his body hit the ground, David crouched beside him, checking for a pulse; he found none.

McCormick quickly scrambled to his feet, and recovered his gun. Straker's men began to grumble and mill around, immediately sensing their own fate. They reached for their guns and tried to escape into the woods.

Suddenly, from out of the beautifully snow-flocked trees, and popping up from waist-high snow drifts, came a horde of heavily armed, white-faced soldiers—all members of the local search and rescue team, and all former members of the old man's former Taskforce Unit.

Andrea sat, benumbed, inside the jeep, watching, with mouth agape and eyes agog.

Dressed in white camouflage, the aged warriors looked more like hunched-back, phantom fighters from some 50's, sci-fi, made for TV movie. Bent and wrinkled, but trained and experienced, they took chase after the imposters.

McCormick took advantage of the opportunity to scoop his dog out of the snow, and rush him to the Medi-helicopter. He was met by the harried pilot/attendant standing beside the chopper. "Sir … the doctor wants to take a look at your injuries," he advised over the whine of the engine and the whipping rotor blades. McCormick gave his head a no-nonsense shake, and dropped the dog into the man's arms. "The hell with me," he shouted above the din, "Save my dog … he's been shot!" He quickly handed off the whimpering animal and returned to the fight.

It wasn't long before everyone was rounded up at gunpoint or accounted for—except for one man who remained at large. A frenzied hunt was on for him.

Andrea dropped back in the seat, breathing out a deep sigh of relief. Suddenly, a loud thud hit the driver's side door, and the angry face of a mercenary hit-man appeared in the frosted window. With nose flattened against the glass, the thug glared into the jeep, making immediate eye contact with the frightened woman. She gasped; then froze, holding her breath. Raising his gun, he leveled it at a spot between her eyes and squeezed the trigger.

The bullet pinged against the window, but glanced off the bullet-proof glass. He tugged at the door handle. Andrea's heart seized up with fear as she realized that in all the heart-thumping excitement, she had never, actually, locked the door!

Unable to locate the lock in the waning light, she grabbed for the handle in hopes of rendering it useless; but still the latch released, and the iced-up hinges creaked open.

Andrea knew, in a heartbeat, that she was a dead woman.

The perpetrator reached in, the icy fingers of death encircling her throat. Suddenly, from 20 feet away, a gun resounded. Andrea's eyes shot towards the crack of gunfire From out of nowhere, the silhouette of a man appeared, silently gliding towards the jeep, as though a phantom. His Glock was locked between his hands, the barrel still aglow. It flashed a second time at closer range, and the hands around her throat released, and the body of would be killer her crumpled into the snow.

Catching the flinty-eyed flash of the gunman's eye, Andrea let out a loud sigh of relief.

"McCormick!"

Her hands shot to her throat. *Damn ... the man had saved her life yet again!* Tears of gratitude rolled down her cheeks.

With lips pursed, bloody and mute, McCormick opened the door, reached in, locked down the jeep, and slammed the door shut with force. Andrea watched him stalk off—she could tell he was pissed. Tonight, the man dressed in an aviator jacket was the second dead body to be dropped at her door.

Someone switched on the outside helicopter lights, and McCormick took photos of the crime scene. Totally ignoring Andrea, he snapped shots of the dead man. Soon everyone was either handcuffed, or placed in body bags and carried to the Chinook waiting in the clearing. The last to be loaded was the body of Chief Straker.

Once his body was on board, the aged taskforce leader, mean and lean, approached McCormick, and saluted the younger man. "Sir ... you wouldn't, by chance, have any of your mother's sugar cookies strapped on you, somewhere ... would ya? I've completely bottomed out."

Still in fighting mode, wearing the emotionless armor of a badass warrior, McCormick looked away, hiding the glint in his eye, thinking that a good soldier always carried power bars and at least one bottle of water on his body. At last his face cracked, and a snigger escaped his lips. "Yup," he teased, "dropping out of a tree like bird turd will do that every time." He watched as a hint of a grin creased the old guy's wrinkled, white mouth.

McCormick nodded towards the burning cabin as he fished through his jacket pocket. "If I had any cookies, they'd be toast by now ... but I'll tell you what ... I will personally bake up a batch ... just for you and your men." He plunked a wrapped fruit and nut bar into the old guy's hand. Suddenly, his eyes flashed like flint, "Speaking of my mother...."

"Relax," the older man consoled. "She's safe ... we'll leave a couple of our guys on her roof overnight, just to be on the safe side."

McCormick smiled his gratitude. He nodded towards Straker's sophisticated chopper. "You got anybody savvy enough to fly that black devil out of here?" he asked. "I'm pretty damned sure I just shot the pilot," he added in a thin voice.

"Oh, y-e-a-h," the man chuckled. "They're all over there, as we speak, fighting over who's gonna get the pleasure ride." The two men laughed, appreciatively, at the diverse skill-sets of the geriatric unit. *You can take a man out of the war, but you can never take the warrior out of the man,* McCormick thought, more than grateful.

Studying McCormick's battered face, the old guy offered, "This storm's got our unit out in full force, so we'll be taking off. We're camped just over the ridge tonight, if you want to join us for a beer and a wild hand of poker ... or a wild night of search and rescue." The man paused, mid-sentence, and lowered his lids into a squint. He leaned in closer. "Dude ... did you get shot with a BB gun ... or am I looking at ... an ear piercing?"

McCormick groused, "Aw, hell ... the only hole I'm concerned about is this one runnin' all the way through my shoulder." McCormick unzipped his jacket, exposing his blood-soaked shirt. He touched the wound, and his fingers came back blood red. "I'm hoping you can get that big, old, ugly goose out of here before I bleed out!" he said with a smartass grin. "Hey ... thanks for delivering my new jeep ... it saved, at least, one very important life, tonight."

"Hell of a mission, son ... even if it did take you two years to git her done."

Again, the man saluted McCormick out of sheer respect, and walked away.

In the jeep, Andrea tried to calm her frenetic burst of energy, watching the two men talk, but unable to hear their conversation. She watched the elderly man, looking as though he'd been dipped in white chocolate, grab McCormick's hand and shake it enthusiastically. Andrea recognized him as the old guy from the Christmas shop. "I guess this explains his reason to carry," she spouted to herself.

Knowing that Andrea was cold, but safely locked in the jeep, the concerned McCormick approached David. He grabbed his hand and shook it. "You okay, bro?" he asked.

"Yeah, just plenty embarrassed," David answered, abashedly.

"Shake it off," McCormick offered with kindness. "Every mission's a learning experience." Now, he spoke with great respect, "You're a brave man, David Jennings."

David shot him an appreciative grin, then asked with concern, "How's that shoulder?"

McCormick gazed into the outer darkness. "N-o-t good," he said.

David studied his brother's face, handsome as the devil, but bloody as hell. He, too, looked off into the distance, momentarily. Straight-faced, he jibed, good-naturedly, "I suppose you know that those are my jeans you're wearing."

"Oh yeah?" McCormick's eyes flashed, "I thought they seemed a little tight...." he slapped his little brother on the shoulder, "in the crotch."

David's chin rose, investigative style, and he quickly bantered back, "Ya know, bro ... that sounds a lot like the words of a jealous lover."

"Nah," McCormick answered as they watched both helicopters take to the sky. "I'm just the dragon slayer," he added, ruefully. He turned abruptly, and stomped off towards the jeep, towards Andrea. David followed close behind. "You got my back on this one?" McCormick asked, gruffly, over his shoulder.

The younger man groaned, "Hell no ... I'm not *that* brave."

Using his key and a scowl, McCormick unlocked the driver's side door. He looked at the woman, and in complete frustration, raked all ten fingers through his hair. He barked, "Do you have a death wish, or just some kind of aversion to being locked up? Gawd ... you scared the Bjoreas out of me!"

Seeing the ravages of war upon the warrior's body, she shot back, "Well it's about time something in this weapon's riddled, mercenary infested, rusticated arboretum scared you … and I'm absolutely euphoric to be the one to do it!"

Ignoring her vitriolic speech, McCormick feigned a scowl as he gently took hold of her chin, turning it to the side for a closer look at her reddened neck and swollen, painful-looking mouth. "You need an ice pack."

Without missing a beat she groused through chattering teeth, "I don't need a frickin' ice pack—I'm already frigid … remember?"

McCormick cocked his head, and lifted his brow at the silently smirking David. The scowl instantly transformed into a crooked grin. "She's obviously in shock … and probably not in her right mind," McCormick said in jest, "but at least she's still breathing … fire."

Once Andrea was squared away and sipping hot chocolate with marshmallows in the cockpit, McCormick approached the medi-copter. "How's my dog?" he asked the attendant, showing great concern.

"He'll live," the attendant answered, unwavering. You can take him home tonight … just keep the wound clean." He took a quick peak at the fresh blood coming from McCormick's shoulder, and offered, grimly. "But you … I'm not so sure about." He lost no time in shoving Matt inside to look at his head wounds, and to stop the bleeding from his shoulder.

Like the walking dead, McCormick tromped up the steps into the helicopter, and lifted his swollen gaze to the bullet wound specialist on board. His jaw dropped as he stared into the sharpest, flintiest eyes of any doctor he'd ever seen—Stormy. As her aggrieved eyes leveled on him, he shot her an abashed grin, badass but war-weary.

"I'm b-a-c-k!" he teased.

CHAPTER 48

Time ticked away as Andrea huddled close to David, beating her upper arms, and stomping her feet in the frozen snow, talking in hushed, but caring, tones about Matt's accumulated injuries. Tracker guarded the door. With her back to the ambulance, she asked, "David ... who are you ... really?"

A voice growled from behind her, "He's David ... FBI...." McCormick's feet clattered down the steps as he deplaned. They both turned to witness the man with battle wounds and frontline injuries. His ribs were wrapped, his shoulder heavily bandaged, his arm in a sling. Multiple butterfly bandages surrounded his eye. He took a couple of steps forward and slapped David on the shoulder, "And the best ever agent I've had the pleasure to work with."

"FBI?" Andrea questioned, startled by the revelation. "Wait a minute, let me get this straight. When you worked at the *News,* were you sports writer or agent?"

"Uh, huh," David chuckled, in the affirmative, "but bullets pay a lot more than words," he answered, tongue-in-cheek, his cold breath spiraling.

They joked with the attendant who quickly transformed into the co-pilot, with Stormy as his pilot.

Andrea's mouth gaped open, and she gasped, "Stormy's licensed to fly?"

Both men nodded in good-natured bandying, David cracked, "Yeah, she learned to fly by test-piloting surveillance drones." As the copter lifted into the air, the pilot-doctors waved back at McCormick & Gang, leaving Andrea standing in the middle of nowhere, between the two men.

Feeling as awkward as hell, McCormick wondered what you say to a woman after she's just witnessed you end the lives of five men, her husband included. It was Andrea who broke the uncomfortable silence.

"Who were you investigating, David?"

David's face reddened, and he quickly bounced a questioning glance off McCormick, now nodding his permission to disclose the truth.

"You."

"Me?" Andrea raised her hands in protest, but David quickly explained.

"The agencies had been tracking Shaun for about a year and a half. Matt had done most of the investigation, but we really had no idea as to how you fit into the picture, then a report came from a questionable source. The crackpot identified you as being one of Fitzgerald's gang … so they put me on it, and I became a sports writer." He grinned. "And then Matt came home."

Feeling embarrassed for having her name linked to Shaun's, and Shaun's crime, Andrea sucked in her breath, and let it out slowly. "I see," she said, softly. She felt humiliated, but quickly pushed her feelings aside. She figured both men had only been doing their jobs. "How did you guys end up working together? I thought the FBI and DEA hated each other?"

The two men looked at each other and laughed.

"Only in theory," McCormick offered. "In practice, there's no greater love … David stuck by me today like a brother." Matt's eyes shimmered, and David turned his face away.

"By the way, bro," David said, addressing McCormick with humor in his voice. "I hope that little box I felt in your left, breast pocket when I frisked you, is a tape recorder … and I hope it was turned on."

More than familiar with the tape recorder, Andrea shot McCormick a savvy grin. He winked, and slipped his hand inside his jacket, producing the infamous, micro-cassette recorder. "Yep, after I talked to Straker this morning, I figured backup might not get here, so I decided I better come prepared for battle."

He flipped the ON button, and let the tape play out just long enough to hear Andrea's question at the cabin about the pharmaceutical company going to the state if Fitzgerald killed her. Then he quickly flipped it off again. "Straker's on here, too," he said, solely for David's benefit.

Looking admirably at Andrea, David said, "Andi, that question to Fitzgerald was ingenious."

Seriousness replaced the humor in McCormick's eyes, and his voice lowered. "It saved our lives."

Soft laughter spewed from her lips, "Guys, to be honest, I didn't know if there was any truth to what I was saying, or not … I just knew I didn't want to die."

McCormick shot her a long, soul-searching look; then blew out a silent, thankful breath in relief.

Speaking from her cluelessness, she asked, "Where'd that crazy squirrel come from?"

They both looked at McCormick.

"You mean the mysterious, sky-riding cocaine rodent?" McCormick chortled,

"I'm thinking it was the work of the gods."

McCormick had handed over proof of Chief Straker's corruption to the proper authorities upon his return from South America the day before; and this night had proven Andrea's innocence—she was free to go. But, where was she to go? The cabin was completely in flames, and burning to the ground before her very eyes. Her car was a smoldering hunk of junk. Shaken and unnerved, she dreaded returning to a house that had become a monumental shrine to Shaun Fitzgerald, a house haunted by the ghosts of her beloved family members—all of whom were now deceased.

Now everyone was gone, even David, as she sat alone in the jeep, feeling completely depleted, her mind going blank. She pulled the blanket tighter around her shoulders, staring mindlessly at the flames as they finally ceased their leaping. When Matt appeared at the door, she slipped into the passenger seat, and closed her eyes. He slid behind the wheel, and started the engine.

He saw her shiver, and cranked up the heat to full blast. Her face had gone pale, and he saw signs of extreme stress and fatigue etched around her eyes and mouth. "Andi, we'll find you a place to stay tonight. We can put you up at the motel in town, if they're open…." He shot her a serious glance, askance, "or my offer still stands." There was no teasing, no gleam in his eyes, no merriment in his voice. "We can leave whenever you're ready."

Andrea opened her eyes, scanning a wider view of the smoldering rubble. The fire had melted the snow on the surrounding trees; but now, the moisture had begun to freeze onto the limbs, or drip to form icicles. Away from the heat, a subtle snow still fell from the sky. She looked towards the sturdy oak, now standing alone as though abandoned. "Would you mind if I ... first say good-by?" she asked, stammering, and looking relatively embarrassed in the waning glow of the smoldering fire.

"Take your time," he said, offering no resistance. *She really is a very loving woman,* he thought.

He too, got out, and stood beside the jeep for a while, watching her walk off towards the tree; but soon he impatiently tugged the shoulder sling up and over his head, and let it drop into the pile of mounting snow. He followed loosely. When she reached the tree, he stopped, giving her privacy, while still standing within earshot.

No squirrels were visible, but still, she spoke to them. "Hey, guys, thanks for hanging out with me ... and Tracker ... for being our family." She paused for a deep breath. "It's been a really rough night ... but I think everything's going to be all right ... now." She stepped closer to the tree, and lovingly ran her fingers across its rough bark, then stepped back to look at its full height. "You're beautiful," she whispered, then quipped, "even if your branches are spaced too far apart." She paused; then spoke lamentably, with a catch in her breath, "I guess we all got snowed tonight ... didn't we?"

She stood in silence for a long moment. When she turned around, Matt was at her side, his head bowed with emotion of his own.

They settled into the jeep, sitting side by side in silence, soaking up the heat, and watching the cabin turn into ashes, each caught up in their own sense of loss.

At last, Matt asked, "Where to?"

"Home," she said simply.

CHAPTER 49

It was well past mid-night. Exhausted, her emotions in tatters, Andrea entered Matt's cabin.

"Welcome to my Nerd Cave," he said, stone-faced, his voice flat and without humor, or emotion, as she stepped into the considerably large entryway. Tracker followed her in, readily making himself at home.

Sensing her unease, McCormick studied her soot-blackened face, and became cognizant of his own grimy appearance. "Why don't you take a long, hot bath?" he suggested. "It'll make you feel better—warm you up." Then he offered, "I'll rustle up some grub, and find you something warm to put on."

Andrea took his advice, then returned to the living room, feeling somewhat refreshed. She sat on the plush cushions of a smartly designed leather couch, as she waited for him to shower, in danger of nodding off. Matt had built a roaring fire and spread out a feast of fruit, crackers and cheese, along with a bottle of rosé wine bearing the Tell Vineyard label—her favorite.

She pulled Matt's over-sized, gray woolen shirt tightly around her, the one he'd laid out for her. His masculine scent clung to the fabric. Aware that the man had a reason for everything he did, she wondered why he had chosen this particular shirt—the one he had been wearing when he pulled her from the watery abyss.

Now, returning from the shower, he wore the same gray, athletic cut tee shirt he'd worn the first time they'd met—over a pair of black lounge pants. He poured her a glass of wine, and handed it to her. "This'll help settle the nerves, a bit. You've been through a lot today."

She accepted the glass gratefully, appreciating his clean, wet hair and waterlogged appearance. Tilting her head to the side, she smiled and said,

"Hey ... you know what? ... you're not half bad looking when you're not dripping blood."

"Ya think?" A grin flickered across his face.

"Where did you get all this food?" she asked.

"The old man's church ladies sent it over by sleigh. They found out about the fire."

She took a deep breath, and blew it out slowly.

Surprised to learn that Matt lived in the cabin she had so admired on her walk into town a few weeks earlier, Andrea looked around the charming room. There was a striking resemblance to her cabin, except this one was much bigger, better, lovelier with a higher cathedral ceiling—and it came with heat, electricity and hot water—and it had a tub. The stone used to build the fireplace was of a superior quality.

"You built this cabin, as well?" she asked.

He nodded his head, modestly.

Her eyes darted around the room, finally locking on to a spot above the heavy, rustic mantel. Not believing her smoke-bleary eyes, she leaned forward, seeing a painting, perfectly hung, above the fireplace. It looked as though it had been painted with this one spot in mind. "Where did you get that painting?" she asked, bluntly.

Matt smiled, hesitantly, shooting a look of satisfaction towards the painting. "I got it for a friend ... it was a real steal." In truth, it had been a steal, for he had literally, walked into Nicole's shop, removed it from the display wall. He'd settle with her later.

Disappointment washed over Andrea. "M-a-t-t," she said, incredibly, "that's the painting I was telling you about."

"Are you sure ... how can you tell it's the same painting?" he asked, deferentially.

Her eyes burrowed into his. "I can see the face of love in the morning mist," she explained.

McCormick's head dropped, and he grinned to himself. She'd nailed it. His head lifted. "Forget about that ole painting ... I prefer pictures with people in them ... like that one over there on the bookshelf." He was trying to hide it, but his voice was ladened with weariness.

Andrea looked past a serious-looking desk, a serious reading chair and lamp, and gazed at the rows and rows of leather-bound classics and various other tomes, realizing, for the first time, that Matt was a reader. She spotted a family portrait. Setting her glass on the table, she stood, and took the picture from the shelf, carrying it to the couch for a closer look.

The picture featured seven people: a mother, a father, four grown children, and a young teenaged girl. Andrea's eyes widened, her mouth went agape. "This can't be your family," she countered, skeptically.

He shot her a circumspective glance, and laughed, hoarsely. "What makes you think I would claim these people if we weren't really related? The picture's a little dated … it was done a couple of years ago."

Andrea set the portrait in her lap, and looked up at the fire, and then at Matt. "I don't believe this!" She picked it up again and studied the faces. She recognized all but one. Matt was standing on the back row, looking proud and tall next to a handsome, older brother. A younger brother stood on the other side. He too, was handsome. All three wore bodacious, smartass grins. "Wait a minute … that's David! David Jennings is your *brother*?" she exclaimed, her voice rising, as she momentarily forgot everything that had happened earlier that day.

"Yep … except his name is David McCormick."

"Of course."

A beautiful, sophisticated, young woman stood on the other side of Matt's older brother. "That's Nicole … Nicole is your *sister*?" Andrea put her hand to her forehead, blushing at her earlier misconception of Matt and Nicole. "Matt, this is too incredible for words … I'm so sorry I accused you of.…"

He waved her off. "I figured you'd probably seen us in town." A furtive grin crossed his lips as he, like David, recognized jealousy's green-eyed monster where ever it popped up.

Andrea, sheepishly, studied the other members of the family. Matt's father was the older gentleman she had spoken to at the Holly Shop, and the guy dipped in white chocolate at the crime scene, but Andrea was most surprised by Matt's mother. "Stormy is your *mother*?" She squealed, as she shot off the couch.

"Yeah, her real name is Serenity; my brothers and I renamed her—but she's really a saint."

"She sure is," Andrea agreed. "This is just too unbelievable!" She sat back down, and stared at the cute, little girl, sporting obvious braces on her teeth. "What is her name?"

"Melissa, but we call her Missy around here … you met her at the restaurant." Andrea's mouth fell agape. Matt laughed as he topped off their wine glasses. "Imagine my surprise when I returned to the States after working undercover for two, long years."

"You worked undercover?"

Matt nodded, noncommittally. He was enjoying this little disclosure, immensely. He had wanted to share this information with Andrea, earlier, but circumstances wouldn't allow it. Tonight, he was trying to divert her attention away from the day's tragedy. He knew this incredible revelation would stave off her loneliness, and give her a better sense of the supportive people around her.

Andrea focused in on the handsome older brother. She tapped the picture. "Tell me about this one … does he belong to the hat?"

Matt's face went taut. He leaned forward, and set his wine glass on the table. He slid forward in his chair, and with slow deliberation rubbed his hand over his mouth, and chin. His forearms rested firmly on his knees. "That's my older brother, Clint. He was DEA, as well…."

"Was?"

Matt nodded. "I followed him into Delta Force and then, later, into the Agency."

McCormick searched her face. Should he say more? He decided to live by the McCormick family code, and get all the secrets out of the way.

"Andi," he paused for a very long moment, unable to speak or look at her; instead, he focused his eyes, steadfastly, on his clinched fists. Giving her warning, he said, "You don't want to hear this…." He took in a deep breath, and let it out slowly, through his nose. In a tone, bereft on so many levels, he said, "Brantley Stone, a.k.a. Shaun Fitzgerald killed my brother, Clint—in cold blood."

Andrea's face went ashen. McCormick decided to disclose everything. "And he was the one who deliberately shattered my leg with automatic rifle fire … that same day. It was a sting operation—my brother and I were both working undercover, but from opposite sides."

A look of grief cloaked her face. Dark, hollow eyes stared back at him, completely frozen with shock. Looking into the very fires of hell, and grasping the full significance of his revelation, Andrea quickly buried her face in her hands and began to sob, uncontrollably.

McCormick rose from the chair, walked to the back of the couch, and laid a hand, momentarily on her shoulder; then sensing a need for privacy, on both their parts, he walked away.

In deep anguish, he braced his arms against the refrigerator, and hung his head. He, too, was overcome with emotion, and nothing in all his elite education or badass training had ever prepared him to face this kind of pain and turmoil.

Tracker rose from his cozy spot by the fire, and found them both in a state of grief. Not knowing which one to go to first, he lay down on a spot somewhere in- between and covered his face with his tail.

When McCormick returned several minutes later, she had dried her eyes—his were still moist.

"Matt, I'm so sorry," she whispered.

"It's not your fault, Andi ... and we don't have to talk about it ever again."

Much later, Matt continued his revelation with a renewed lilt to his voice as he paced around the room, reacquainting himself with his own home. "Every time I looked up, there was a family member watching out for me, or helping me with my job."

"How was that possible?"

Matt took the picture from Andrea's hands, and set it on the table, then settled into the seat beside her. "My father was in the military—Army to be exact. He took a bullet in the leg, and that's how my parents met. She was his nurse. After they got married, and living in Washington, she wanted to work for the FBI; but they weren't hiring many women at that time, and they turned her down. Four kids and one Doctor of Medicine degree later, she was hired as an agent. My dad went on to work as a member of Special Forces, with missions all over the world.

A look of surprise came to Andrea's face, "Your dad was a snake eater?"

McCormick grinned, appreciating her knowledge of the subject. "Yeah, he was—but the old man has PTSD."

Andrea nodded her understanding. She'd written articles on the subject.

"He's retired from all of that now, but he still works as an ordained minister, and he heads up the local search and rescue team."

"So that explains why he was dropping out of trees," she stated. Another look of surprise showed on her face. "You're a preacher's brat…." she teased, "raised in the church?"

McCormick gave her a half nod.

Andrea sat, marveling at what she was hearing.

"Dad preaches love and forgiveness." A grievous look crossed his face. He spoke to the air. "Forgiving an enemy is an extremely hard thing to do," he opined. As though to himself, he said, "Sometimes, forgiving yourself is even harder."

"My mother served in the military, then as a nurse-practitioner for several years until she realized that she could be a much greater help to the community by becoming a physician. This local area was in dire need of a doctor, and no one else was stepping up. She maintains her own medical practice, but still tries to assist all of the agencies whenever it's possible."

"And that's why she was in the ambulance tonight?"

McCormick nodded, "Yeah … can you believe it … while I was AWOL, she became a freakin' bullet wound specialists." He paused for a long moment, shaking his head. "I have to tell you, though; she was mad as hell at me when she learned about my leg—a whole year after the fact. I think she's still pissed at me for not coming home."

Andrea caught the look of frustration as he took a gulp of wine and sat his glass down. He leaned over and cut a large chunk of Vermont's favorite cheddar cheese, placed it on a napkin and shoved it in her direction. Then he shoveled a large piece of chocolate cake on a plate, and held it out to her between his two hands as though it were a love offering. Andrea thought it a beautiful, kindly gesture, one that gave her insight into the man's heart.

She accepted the food gratefully, realizing for the first time that she had not eaten since the night before.

"I'd been working undercover and hadn't been in touch with the folks for two years … for security reasons—theirs and mine. When I returned, I discovered my little brother working as a sportswriter for some rag."

"Hey, be nice!" Andrea retorted. McCormick tried to give her a mischievous wink, but the skin and muscles around his eye had stiffened.

"Did you know he had become an agent?"

"Didn't have a clue … the first I saw of him was that day with you, in the lobby of the newspaper. He was standing right behind you."

A puzzled look crossed Andrea's face; then she groaned. "Umph … I remember that day only too well," she recalled, covering her face with her hands.

"I ambushed him one night in the high school parking lot after a varsity football game, but it was a short conversation. I had a flight back to D.C."

McCormick paused. "By the way … I'll give you a heads up … David is totally distraught over what he did to you tonight … hurting you that way."

"I'll live," she conceded, reluctantly.

Judging by her tone, McCormick guessed she just might be harboring a grudge towards David. Moving closer, he scooped up both her hands in his. "Andi, you'll live—because of what David did tonight. He took on the role of a brutish thug in order to save both our lives … his life was on the line, as well."

She shrugged her shoulders, trying to shake off her negativity. "The whole thing just … I don't know … hurt my feelings, I guess."

McCormick pursed his lips. "You guys have worked together … you're close, I understand that. You can still trust him … he's a great guy. Tonight he was just acting out the role assigned to him. He's still the David you know … and love." He studied her for tells of deeper feelings for David. He saw none.

McCormick touched his sore jaw, in jest. "If it makes you feel any better … he hurt my feelings too … thank God. Things could've gotten a whole lot uglier for all of us." He reached for his wine glass and took another sip, wondering if he should go on.

"What happened to you after you talked to David in the parking lot," she asked.

The corner of his mouth ticked up, ever-so-slightly. *She was interested.* "He contacted my mother, and I eventually met her one evening, face-to-face, at the hospital. I'm told that when she learned I was alive, but unable to come home, she took it upon herself to kill two birds with one stone. The Agency was investigating a couple of doctors for possible Medicare fraud, so my mother volunteered to take a job as a temporary nurse, and at the same time get a chance to visit her prodigal son. And then, of course, after I got shot she became my doctor, my nurse and my guardian angel."

McCormick sniggered, trying to shut down the memory of his most embarrassing moment with his mother. Unable to tamp down his exuberance, he stood, cupping his hand to his forehead. The snickers quickly turned into deep, throaty chortles. He looked at Andrea, his face flushed, glowing with radiant energy. "Let me tell you something ... there's nothing quite like trying to look and feel like a macho, badass Special Agent, while your own mother is standing guard over you...." he tried to swallow a guffaw, "with a blade tucked into her cleavage, a Beretta stuck into her support hose, and a syringe clamped between her teeth." Finally, he erupted into a side-splitting, full-fledged belly laugh, leaving him gasping for air.

Still enmeshed in shock, Andrea watched and listened with rich appreciation, unable to reach the same level of euphoria, but thoroughly treasuring its sound. This was a side of Matt's personality she'd never witnessed, and she dearly loved hearing his joyous laughter. She smiled. "Well, that explains why she was looking so exhausted at the end of my hospital stay." Andrea shook her head, and raised her eyebrows in disbelief. "Incredible."

Wiping his eyes, he offered, "Andi, I'll bet you weren't even aware that our hospital rooms were right next door to each other, or that we added an extra week to your hospital stay so we could keep an eye on you?"

She threw him a deferential look. "I knew young nurses were always congregating around my door ... and I knew they, sure as hell, weren't there for me."

"I figured it would blow your mind." Suddenly, their eyes locked, and they chimed in unison, "What mind?" Now they both guffawed at their private little joke.

McCormick continued, "Nicole told me that Mom took my absence really hard ... they all thought I was dead after not hearing from me for so long, and of course they'd just lost Clint. They had put my property up for sale, and started to empty out my personal effects, which explains why you're wearing that smelly shirt ... but I'd found myself in a really hard spot. All my phone numbers, e-mails, and social media were being spied on. I had no other choice but to just drop off the face of the earth." He took a bite out of a huge piece of chocolate cake, recognizing his own mother's cooking, regretting the pain he had caused her ... his family. He would try to make it up to them.

"Missy was totally freaked out, at the restaurant, when she saw me. All she'd been told was that she needed to meet a big, tall guy and sneak him a satphone. Not only did she not know I'd returned, but she didn't even know if I was dead or alive." His eyes twinkled, "and of course—she's never been trained in the fine art of clandestine exercises."

He looked at her near-empty glass, "Would you like some milk?"

Andrea shook her head, and as Matt went to the kitchen to pour a glass for himself, Andrea realized that she needed to have a follow-up conversation with Missy—to apologize. "And all this time, I thought I was all alone in the world," she said to his back.

As he returned with milk in hand, a glazed look came into her eyes—a moment of epiphany. "Matt, I can't believe how much you know about me. It sure saves me the trouble of having to explain my crazy life; but I'm afraid no one, but you, will ever be able to understand me in the future—or believe me, for that matter." She threw out the comment in despair.

McCormick grew pensively quiet, his dark eyes searching the depths of both their souls. He stood up brusquely, removed the screen, and poked at the fire.

Almost afraid to ask, she said, "Which is Nicole, FBI or DEA?"

"Neither." She prefers a much more sophisticated lifestyle—her words, not mine." McCormick tried to use descriptions that couldn't, or wouldn't be used against him in later conversations once he was free to divulge the truth—that Nicole was actually CIA. "She enjoys the sun and the urban setting ... she travels." He replaced the screen, and turned to face her again. "She never lets us forget that she thinks we're all a bunch of knuckle-dragging, bottom-feeders." He smiled, "Still, she returns to the mountains every summer."

He sat down beside her, weariness setting in. The lack of sleep, and pain in his shoulder and throbbing head had begun to dull his thinking. Suddenly drowsy, he laid his head back, sinking deeper into cushions and suspended consciousness. In an out of body experience, he replied, "and ... she makes a very large commission every time she sells one of my paintings."

Andrea jumped on his casual, or meant to be casual, comment. "Your paintings ... you're an artist?"

His eyes popped open, and the weary agent jerked to attention. He had, unintentionally, let his secret slip and Andrea had been quick to pick up on it, giving him no choice but to confess.

He cleared his throat. "Would you believe … a very embarrassed, Will Remington?"

"Will Remington!" She jumped to her feet. "Are you saying … that you painted that picture…." she pointed to the beloved painting hanging above the mantel, "that you're the old fart?"

Matt nodded modestly, a slight blush coming to his, already weather-beaten face. He grumped, "I am."

"My God!"

Figuring that he was, once again, yanking her chain, she asked, "Does everything and everybody around here belong to you?"

McCormick heard the challenge in her voice, and took a deep breath. He had seen this one coming. He reached for her hand, pulling her into his lap. "No." He locked into her eyes. His words came from his heart. "This painting belongs to you, Andi. After you explained what it meant to you, I pulled it off the market … I couldn't let you *buy* it." He paused, thinking that his very own heart and soul—his blood and guts—were in that painting. "No, this is my gift to you, Andi … I don't know another single person who would appreciate it in the spirit it was painted," he shook his head, "not like you do."

"Matt, I'm, totally, flabbergasted by everything that's happened tonight. I'm in total shock on so many levels … I don't even know how to respond."

"There's no need to respond … I just thought it important that you know you're among people who care about you…." At last, McCormick gave in to his impulses and cradled her in his arms.

As the fire crackled and the flames leaped high behind the screen, Andrea nestled closer, laying her head on his shoulder.

His cheek dropped to the top of her head. "Andi … every year … for a long time to come … you're going to look back on this day, and remember all the nightmarish things Shaun said and did to you and your family—and mine. I know it will take time, but I hope that soon you'll be able to forget that he ever existed, or that these atrocities ever happened. I want you to remember it, only as the day this badass, smart mouth agent gave you your painting."

A lump formed in Andrea's throat, and hot tears filled her eyes. Never had she known such a loving, kind man. "I love you, Matt," she whispered, drowsily, her voice soft, raspy, "but I suppose you already know that, too, don't you?"

Matt's laugh was deep, but guileless as he brushed back her hair, and tenderly kissed her ear. "I might've noticed micro-expression or two along the way, but there's no rush to talk about it, Andi. You need time to get over everything that's happened." He ran his hand down the back of her head, and then tightened his arms around her.

I love you, too, McCormick thought with an aching heart. He would've liked nothing better than to believe that one day soon, after the healing process had taken place, that they could have a life together; but he realized the chance of that actually happening were slim and none. He figured Andi was still in shock, and that what he was hearing tonight was her exhaustion talking. She was saying things she wouldn't remember come morning; and tonight he figured she was—once again—confusing gratitude for love, as she had with Fitzgerald.

As the fire burned low, he began to think through all the angles. Tonight, she had witnessed him kill five men. How could she even stand to look at him … to be in the same room with him—to be in his arms? He thought, by dawn's early light, she will have started to grieve for who-knows-what—the squirrel, most-likely; she'd be scared stiff of him, and leave the mountain hating him for the nosy job he'd done investigating her—and then he would never see her again.

There was also a second angle—his angle. Could he ever really fully accept, and respect a woman who had been married to Brantley Stone—the man who had brought so much harm to his own family, physically and emotionally—could he trust himself to always be fair to her?

What an emotional mess, he thought. A single tear welled up in his eye, and trickled down his battered, wind-blistered, unshaven face; but he knew one thing for sure—Brantley Stone, a.k.a. Shaun Fitzgerald, would neither end, nor destroy, another single life; McCormick knew his own contentment would have to lie somewhere within that reality.

Andrea felt McCormick's chest heave, sensing his turmoil. She stirred. With red, blurry eyes, she studied the man's face. His eyes had gone vacant, pulling down his handsome, full mouth into grimness. She reached up and pulled down his chin. "Please don't leave me," she whispered.

Too exhausted to resist, he laid his head back, and sunk into the cushion. He closed his eyes, while Andrea gently outlined his hairline scar with the gentle tip of her finger.

Slowly, and with immense feeling, she wrapped her arms around his neck. "Special Agent Matthew McCormick … thank you for saving my life," she whispered, hoarsely.

"Which time?" he added, soberly. He wanted to laugh, to say something smart-assed, but his heart had settled into heaviness.

She scrunched down into his lap, resting her head on his chest, stretching her arm across his taut stomach. "Where did you get that shirt?" she asked, drowsily.

McCormick's eyes dropped to the lettering on the grimy, gray t-shirt: *Pain is just weakness leaving the body.* "I skinned it off a drunken Marine … I liked the saying," he grunted.

Mesmerized by the flickering flames, Andrea realized she was unable to get enough of this man. She longed to crawl up under that shirt, to live as a part of him. Suddenly, she sighed deeply. "Mac," her voice sounded weak, as the numbing, anesthetic effect of shock began to wear away. "I feel like an old, worn out toy on Christmas morning."

McCormick pulled her closer. "I know the feeling."

A tap came at the door. It was past three in the morning, and Andrea's eyes shot open, awakened from the sleep of the dead. She imagined the smell of freshly baked cookies as she lay motionless on the couch, afraid to breathe, unsure of her location. A pillow had been placed under her head, and a woolen blanket thrown over her body. She listened as the bolts and locks were tripped, and the door opened.

She heard Matt's voice. "Yo … Davy," he said as David came in out of the cold, dark night, stomping packed snow from his boots.

"I saw your lights, and I didn't want the night to slip away without touching base with you … are you alright … you look like shit." As his brother gave him a nod, David caught a glimpse of Andrea Fitzgerald asleep on the couch. His eyebrows shot up in question.

Ignoring his brother's probing eyes, Matt asked, "Tying up loose ends?"

David nodded, affirmatively. "Yeah, I've been in the air most of the night … got'em all behind bars: Jolene, lawyer … banker."

"The butcher … the baker … the candlestick maker," Matt added, sober-faced, reciting the line from a riddle they'd both been taught as young kids.

"Matt, I thought you'd need to know…." David looked askance at Andrea and lowered his voice. The only words she heard of their sparse conversation were: found him in the basement … cord … electrical company cut him down … glad … wasn't Andi who found…."

She heard Matt ask in a hushed whisper, "Suicide?"

"Murder … no way he could have … himself…."

McCormick ruefully added a sixth name to his long list of kills, "Because he'd talked to me…."

"Heck of a thing with *your* boss … what first put you on to him?"

McCormick shot his brother a hard, flinty look, and answered through clenched teeth, "He called me *Pretty Boy*."

David raised his chin in percipience, "Just like Bran had always done."

"Yep." McCormick's chin jutted up, "He even used the same, stupid tone inflection—it told me they'd probably been in contact with each other … that, and the fact that Straker was the only one who knew I was returning to the mountains. When he showed up in the field tonight, I knew for certain that he'd set Bran and me up, figuring we'd do him the favor of killing each other off."

David looked at a baking sheet full of freshly baked cookies on the stove; another one lay ready to pop into the oven. His eyes dropped to the table, seeing Matt's many bills, and late notices scattered across the top. Not even heroes escaped the reality of the obscene cost-of-living. "Why are you still up?"

"Concussion … and adrenaline's still pumping."

"Adrenaline or testosterone?" David teased. When no answer came from Matt, he added, "Bro, you really hauled ass tonight."

Matt slapped his hand across David's shoulder, in a show of appreciation, but said nothing.

David kept talking, "Talked to the fire marshal; he'll be in touch." Matt nodded his tired, gaunt head.

"Recovered your snowmobile … put it in the stable for the night. Temp's well below zero."

"Thanks pal." He delivered another appreciative slap to his brother's shoulder. "Sit down and have a cup of cocoa with me. I just made some, but be warned, there's no marshmallows."

"That's okay," David answered, relieved that his brother was talking. "I need to drop a couple of pounds ... have to look good for the ladies, ya know."

Matt shot him a questioning glance, askance. "You smell like wood smoke," he charged.

"So do you," David shot back, chuckling.

From the couch, Andrea could hear the clatter of cups and the scraping of chair legs, homey sounds. She would have liked to have joined them, but realized that the brothers needed time to catch up, to give each other support, and in Matt's case, time to heal. Through slit lids, she watched David draw a book from an inside coat pocket. The book jacket was bright and shiny, with the exception of the edges—they had been singed. "I pulled this out of the fire. I thought Andi might want to keep it. Looks like a first copy, or something ... it might make a nice Christmas surprise."

Matt nodded. "Davy, to be honest ... I'd completely forgotten about the holiday until yesterday morning ... I don't have gifts for the family."

"Don't feel bad ... neither do I; your being back home is gift enough ... trust me." His face waxed serious, as he handed the book to his older brother. Matt took it, read the title, *Suffer the Little Children,* By Andrea Daye Fitzgerald, PhD. McCormick laid it gently on the table, gazed upon it for a moment, and then shoved it back to David.

"I'm sure she'd rather get it from you than from me." Matt grinned at his younger brother.

David pulled Andrea's small tangerine purse from beneath his jacket and handed it to Matt. "I was able to save this as well."

Matt nodded. "That's evidence ... the work you did on this purse simplifies our job, Davy. Everything's been recorded in D.C. ... and that includes Donahue's conversation with Andrea."

A blank look crossed David's face.

"I'll explain later," McCormick offered.

Believing Andrea to be asleep, David gave Matt a long, serious look. "Did you know she wears a cross," he asked. "She told me it was the last gift her mother gave her."

McCormick gave his brother a quick head nod, "Yeah, I've noticed it a

446

couple of times." Matt's weary mind flashed back to Andrea's chain necklace with the look of delicate lace—the one he'd carried around in his pocket for over two weeks before mailing it back to Andrea—the one that had winked at him from her hospital bed; and the one she'd clutched tight in her fist every time her sister's name crossed her lips.

"I'll bet that didn't set well with Stone," David opined.

Matt nodded his agreement. "Yeah, her relationship with Fitzgerald was unbelievably complicated—and dangerous."

"Matt, I'm sorry things had to go down the way they did."

"Yeah, well, me too. I'm just happy you were there, David. You saved our asses, you know. If one of the others had done that search in the cabin...." He paused. "I hated for Andrea to have to listen to all that garbage, but she needed to hear it, to know the truth; and we needed the evidence to clear *her*."

"Is she alright?"

"She's exhausted and a bit disoriented ... I don't think she's ever fully realized how much trouble she was in. She has a lot to digest, but she seems to be accepting everything okay. We don't want to overwhelm her regarding Bran's activities, so we'll read her in slowly." Matt took a sip from his mug, while stealing a glance at Andrea, then set it back down, "But ... I'm not at all sure how she'll feel when the sun comes up, and she finds herself here ... with the man who killed her husband." He paused and let out a deep breath. "I was hoping to avoid this particular can of worms—I didn't want to be the gun who took out Fitzgerald." He raised his weary eyebrows, and his eyes filled with regret.

It was pretty obvious to David that the two of them had bonded, but he also understood the shadow enemy of that bond, as well as the force that could destroy it all. *Would Andrea be able to love the man who had killed her husband?* He could also see the situation from Matt's perspective.

He took a long, inquisitive look at the brother, who at a very young age had bit into the Delta Force mantra: *Impossible is not in my vocabulary!* Tonight, he had lived the adage; but in spite of his huge success, he seemed empty, emotionally wrung out; and his deep, hollow voice reflected it all. David had only seen his brother in this state one other time. That was when his son had been, not born, but aborted—destroyed. It had nearly killed Matt; but why was he so moody, so dark tonight? He had almost single-handedly brought down two of the country's most dangerous international, narco terrorist. He would soon be summoned to the White House, awarded and celebrated—again. Why wasn't *he* celebrating?

Seeing signs of both love and hopelessness, David offered, "I get it, bro; but I'm curious ... how did all of *this* happen?" He gestured towards Andrea, lying on the couch in an agent's cabin. "You've always been the *strictly by the book* kind of guy; and in my last conversation with Andrea, she ... well...." David tipped back his chair, scratched his chin, and gave his brother a taunting grin, "she pretty well hated you!"

Matt's head dropped. When he raised his eyes to meet David's, they held a dreamy-eyed luminance. "I don't know ... it just happened." A diminutive grin skittered across his mouth at the irony of the situation.

David tamped down the joy he felt; this wasn't the time to let it show—things could still easily go sideways. "Mom wants to cook us all a big turkey dinner tomorrow or as soon as Andrea's rested. We were afraid you'd taken her back to Forest Hills." David nodded towards the couch. "She took everything okay, though; don't you think ... especially that part about her sister?"

"Yeah, she did ... she's a strong woman, but I think she suspected something like that all along. She just never had any proof."

"It's possible ... heck of a thing to live with, though."

David stirred his drink, and a prolonged silence hung in the air. Finally, he looked at his brother in all earnestness, "How long have you had that leg, bro?"

"About a year ... same day Clint...."

"So you were there when...."

McCormick gave him a brief head nod.

"What hap....?"

McCormick choked up, and cut him off. "I can't talk about it, Davy."

David's throat tightened. He scratched his beard, trying to hide the pain he carried for both his older brothers. He was every inch the man, but now his voice faltered, and he slipped into the role of a younger brother. "You know, Matt ... I have to confess: this was the very first assignment that put real fear in my gut. For the last two weeks, I've been running around scared stiff of my own shadow." The tenor of David's voice rose. "I ... failed ... as an agent; I couldn't make my contacts, nobody was where they were supposed to be, and Brantley—that son-of-a-bitch—was eliminating anybody and everybody he no longer needed!"

McCormick blew out his hot breath. "Davy, I'm only going to say this one more time, so take ownership: without you ... Andrea and I would have been *eliminated*. You were there when it counted the most ... and little brother, hear me; when you took that job with Fitzgerald—you rode straight into Hell."

David slowly nodded. "Yeah ... I'd only been with him a short time, but I was quickly finding that out."

Matt studied David's face. "How'd you manage to get that close to Fitzgerald? You didn't have to kill anybody, did you?"

A nervous laugh caught in David's throat, "Nah ... I didn't even know who I was working for, then one day I found myself riding shotgun for the sleazebag. I'd been talking myself up to Jolene Jorgenson," he locked eyes with his older brother, "your tip on her was spot on. I convinced her that the feds were coming, locked and loaded, and that Fitzgerald needed to beef up his security. I told her that after I'd fulfilled my military duty, I went to the agency, but got fired for insubordination—but I knew all the agents—and that I was just the experienced gun he needed." Matt scratched his neck to cover mixed emotions.

"I knew all along that I was a throw-away, that Fitzgerald would leave no witnesses ... including me. I'd put on my Big Boy pants, prayed up, and was ready to die."

A profusion of tears rolled down Andrea's face as she listened from the couch.

Her friend's countenance lifted. "But, Matt, I have to admit....I was euphoric ... absolutely euphoric ... when you walked into that cabin tonight. David's face lit up, irradiating heartfelt gratitude and brotherly love.

Matt nodded in serious agreement. Shooting his little brother a secretive, operative look, he lowered his voice to a confidential tone. "I was *euphoric*, little brother, when you came to my crash site to finish me off, but left me alive ... and when you left that Peruvian office door unlocked ... and that window wide open."

"So, that *was* you ... I ... just had a feeling." David shot his brother a joyful grin as both men rose and leaned across the table for a high-five.

Matt groused, "Feeling, you say ... hell, you could've smelled me after the kind of night I'd had ... swimming across swollen, crocodile infested streams, dodging projectiles of monkey shit—staring into the cunning eyes of Hell's very own serpent ... I'd almost shit my britches at that point."

David laughed, incredulously. "How did you manage to get all twenty-one feet of that son-of-a-gun tethered to the fence?"

McCormick, his voice raspy, used a term he knew David would appreciate, "I went prepared for battle, bro!"

"Why didn't you just kill it?"

"I wanted proof ... everything well preserved for forensic evidence...." he snickered, "and I wanted to leave Fitzgerald unnerved ... a shot across the bow; besides, you know what they call people who kill snakes."

The brothers locked eyes and, laughingly, answered in unison, "Stupid!" Once again they went up for a high-five.

Deciding his brother deserved a better explanation, he raked both hands through his hair in post-mission stress, eager to forget the nightmarish episode. He offered, "I used Ketamine ... intramuscular injection ... it took a ton of the stuff ... once he took a liking to this hot, sexy body, giving me one of those long, mesmerizing, come-hither looks, I threw my rucksack over his head, and grabbed him by the tail ... that stopped him from wrapping me up in his big, ole, sweet embrace."

Visualizing the danger his brother had faced, David asked, "How'd you get him up that high?"

McCormick blew out a hot breath, "Just standard Boy Scout fare, Davy—ropes, knots and pulleys—and long, lock-tight bands."

On the couch, Andrea's hot, liquid eyes flew open and she gazed, blurry-eyed, into the smoldering fire. *Serpent ... ropes, knots ... pulleys?*

"How'd you get into the compound?" David was asking, toning down his feelings of jubilation as he picked up on Matt's more somber mood.

"I jumped out of a rickety, old Cesena 208 about to pop its riveting. I was wearing a frogman suit, in the middle of an electrical storm ... with Bitchin' Betty chewin' my ass ... and nobody looking up."

David smiled to himself, feeling a rich appreciation for his brother's tenacity on the job, and his panache for unintended humor. "How'd you get back home?" he asked.

A mischievous glint came into McCormick's eyes, "I rode back with you, bro!"

David's jaw dropped. "What ... on Fitzgerald's private jet?"

"Yup ... no reason not to ... we were all headed for Bean Town."

David shook his head, "Incredible!" They both guffawed at Matt's brazen stunt.

"Where did you learn all those Ninja moves you used tonight?"

Again, the corner of Matt's mouth shot up, "Same place you did, kid: *Teenaged Mutant Ninja Turtles* ... before I moved on to the more serious, ancient Japanese art of stealth and espionage."

"I hope Andrea feels up to coming to dinner tomorrow. Mom's really excited about seeing her again, but she'll understand if she's not ready."

The image of the young woman standing between the licking flames of the cabin and the snow-flocked tree, heaping beatitudes upon the tree and unseen squirrels ensconced within the limbs, her *family,* had stuck in McCormick's craw, or better defined, heart and soul. Now he sucked in a deep breath, and let it out slowly. "I'll do my best to get her there," he promised. "We're both pretty beat up, but she needs to be surrounded by her friends, right now."

Recognizing his brother's beneficent spirit, David reached into a final pocket and drew out a photo. "This flew out of the cabin while I was busy blowing out the windows." He handed Matt the Wall of Fame photo. "I thought Andi might like it to remember you by."

A scowl settled on McCormick's face as he laid it on the table, crossed his arms, and eyed the photo as though a thing to treasure.

Deciding that he had a firm understanding of the situation, David leaned forward, and offered, "Matt ... you do realize that they didn't *really* have a *marriage,* Shaun and Andi?"

"Yeah, she said a couple of things that led me to believe they didn't have a very good marriage."

"No ... Matt ... I mean, they really didn't have a *marriage*—she was considering having it annulled."

"Annulled?" Matt thought through David's comment. He knew one could have a marriage annulled if it had never been consummated, among other things. Now he looked at his brother as though athirst. "She told you that?"

David nodded his head, slowly, meaningfully.

"They never...."

David shook his head, his eyes dancing, jocundly, his mouth forming a moue of mirthful negativity.

McCormick slowly rubbed the palm of his hand back and forth across his dry, chapped mouth, seriously contemplating David's words. Then he looked straight-forward at his young virile, brother, cut in every way, and just a few years his younger. "Bro, do we have a problem here ... I mean ... it sounds like the two of you ... am I buttin' into your territory?"

Astonished, David reared back in his chair and laughed uproariously. "No ... no," he said, shaking his head, "we're just friends ... she's way out of my league, and pay-grade; but I will say one thing, Matt ... you're a damned lucky cuss." David's eyes crinkled and a clever grin crossed his mouth.

On the couch, Andrea smiled, realizing that it was the first time she had ever heard the good-natured David actually laugh out loud, so unrestrained.

Matt borrowed his brother's Satellite phone to call Washington, and then David left the same way he had come—in the dark; but before he closed the door, he turned to Matt and asked, "Hey, Matt ... it's Christmas ... are we gonna do it?"

Matt rubbed his chin and thought for a moment, "No reason not to."

David grinned, "Five o'clock?"

Matt grinned back. "Five o'clock ... meet you there."

David cheerfully closed the door behind him.

Andrea clutched her necklace and looked fondly at the McCormick family photo. They were the bravest people she had ever met, and the kindest—but they sure did love their secrets. Then her eyes came to rest on the painting above the mantel—her painting. She was learning, hourly, just how *special* Matt McCormick was, and just knowing that he had painted it, made it that much more precious. Suddenly, she felt a new surge of hope, and a fresh new thirst for life—with Matt. She sucked in a deep, happy breath—and yes, she did smell cookies!

Matt's face was taut as he entered the room and tenderly pulled the blanket up over Andrea's shoulders. He had talked to Washington, using David's phone. After describing and explaining what went down with Fitzgerald, and then with Straker, he then explained his situation with Andrea. When the other end of the line went silent, McCormick offered to tender his resignation, but his superior refused to accept it. Instead, he congratulated him, and gave him a new assignment. Ending his conversation, Matt had answered, "Yes sir … yes Mr. President … thank you, sir … and a Merry Christmas to you."

He sat down in the chair beside the couch. Should Andrea awaken, frightened, in the dark of night—he would be there.

When another loud rap came at the door, Andrea jumped. This time when Matt opened it, his father entered. Like David, he stomped the snow from his boots and then gave Matt a big bear hug, proudly pounding on his arms, forgetting Matt's wounded shoulder. "Merry Christmas, son!" Matt returned the hug and the greeting. "I just wanted to let you know that I've hitched Windy Foot up to the sleigh, just in case you two want to go for a sleigh ride."

Matt gave his dad a grin, "I heard the bells, and thought they belonged to Kris Kring…." Trapped somewhere between childhood fantasy and adult reality, Matt quickly cut off his words.

Andrea's eyes popped wide open, needing assurance that she was not dreaming. She heard Matt's voice, saying, "I'll have to check with Andi first, to see if she's up to it, but I think it's a great idea. Why don't you ride with us … I know how much you love the sleigh."

"No, no," his father answered, selflessly. "I'll have plenty of time for that later. David tells me, you two kids have a lot to talk about … but I'll race you to the turkey and dressing."

"I hope Mom doesn't expect us to dress for dinner; dirty, smoky jeans are the only things Andi and I have to wear … my closets have been emptied out."

"Yeah, well … we don't care if you smell like a smoked ham butt, or if your ass is shot full of bullet holes, just be there—for your mother's sake."

PART III

CHAPTER 50

At first light, Matt had slipped out the door, excusing himself to feed the horses and to take care of some unfinished business. Having no coat, Andrea stayed behind to leisurely sip her coffee by the fire. Neither had been able to sleep, and so they'd rallied around each other in the kitchen. In benumbed silence, they'd whiled away the darkest-before-dawn hours by baking a second and third batch of cookies, both having a need to stay busy. Understanding why Matt had left, untouched, those cut in the image of Kris Kringle, she took it upon herself to ice them, and to add a few frolicsome, decorative touches, turning them, not into Santas, but into caricatures of gnomes, like the ones they'd faced in the forest.

Grown silent from his reflections on the preceding day, McCormick returned and showered. He gratefully came to the conclusion that Andrea harbored no malevolence, no desire to blow his head off this morning. Instead of a shouting match, they sipped coffee and made small talk. He shot appreciative glances her way for her efforts with the cookies, sardonically, biting the heads off of more than a few gnomes.

It hadn't taken much effort to talk Andrea into a sleigh ride. When she joined him outside, he smiled and said. "We missed celebrating Thanksgiving, but that doesn't mean we can't still go over the river and through the woods."

Not exactly chipper, but in a decent mood, Andrea asked, "How far over the river?" She shot an appreciative look at the colorful, blinking twinkle lights skillfully strung around the sleigh.

"It's not far, just a little over fifteen miles … just long enough to clear the smoke out of our lungs without turning us into popsicles." She watched as Matt patted Windy's neck, the horse responding by nickering out a greeting. Andrea thought the horse had a familiar look, but she batted away the thought—everything seemed familiar these days. He checked the bridle, bit, and reins, then stroked the long face, and soft, velvety nostrils. "Did you miss me, sweetheart," he asked.

Andrea, foolishly started to answer, then quickly realized his question had been addressed to the horse. Windy, bobbed her head up and down, vigorously in the affirmative. A hint of a smile broke out across Andrea's bruised lips.

An appreciative grin came to McCormick's face, as well, as he walked towards her and stood beside the sleigh, looking around for Tracker. Finally, he gave a two-fingered whistle and the dog came running, jumping energetically into the back of the sleigh as though he had been doing this his whole life.

McCormick nodded towards the dog, "I wish I felt as well as he does," he offered as he gave Andrea a lift up. Once she was seated, he handed her a black, medium-weight jacket. "I'm afraid it smells a bit like the stable." She studied it for a moment, putting her nose to the fabric. The stable smell permeated every fiber. She smiled furtively, and slipped it on.

McCormick tucked blankets carefully around her back and neck, and threw one over her knees aware that she still wasn't dressed suitably for the weather. When he had settled into the seat beside her, he cracked the reins and yelled, loudly, "Yo, Windy!"

The horse took off with a jerk, setting the harness bells off in a merry jingle, knocking Andrea back against the seat. She felt spellbound as the chilled air hit her face and the pure joy of riding in a one-horse, open sleigh tickled her Christmas fantasy. With a broad, but painful, smile plastered across her face, she sat back and enjoyed the ride as Windy kicked up the neck-high snow. They glided up one rise and down another, past snowy landscapes, split-rail fences, and different variations of pine groves.

When they slowed, Andrea scooted closer for warmth, and slipped her arm through his. She asked the question that wouldn't leave her mind. "Matt ... I know Farah is a local artist, but who is she to you—I get the feeling there's more to the story."

He chuckled at her observation. "Farah's a rare jewel ... I call her the *light* of my life ... she's my mentor. Actually, she taught me to paint in the Luminism style you like so well. She's won all kinds of awards and she's made a fortune from her paintings."

The smile left his lips, and he searched her eyes, "She's also Brantley Stone's grandmother ... she raised him." Disbelief flooded Andrea's eyes, and she batted them shut. "When she found out how he was making his living, she disowned him ... and completely cut him out of her will ... a considerably large will."

"You knew him before?" she asked, eyes widening.

McCormick gave no answer, but suddenly stood up, snapped the reins and yelled, "Go, Windy Go!"

As the road followed the creek bed, they slid past a charming, covered bridge, with fresh garland and a gigantic Christmas wreath adorning the entrance; but instead of crossing that bridge, they glided further down a hillock and across a rustic, open-air bridge, not much wider than a bridle trail, which quickly put them in the company of a hulking, heavily-antlered moose. Tracker began to dance and growl in the back seat as they dashed through a deep snowdrift, splashing slush high over the moose's heavily matted back. As though a prank, Tracker's strong, ever-present skunk odor floated over the back seat, Windy broke wind, and the stench from the wild moose all co-mingled in the nostrils of the sleighing riders. When they rounded a sharp, snowy bend, McCormick returned to his seat amid trickles of light-hearted laughter.

After much gasping and gagging, Andrea asked, laughingly, "Do you suppose that's the same twig-eater from the creek bed?"

McCormick shot her a wry grin, and jokingly shouted into the wind. "Naw ... I think that's the one you conjured up in the post office ... you know ... the one you hoped would stampede down the cobbled streets of Red Springs," referring back to her moose comments, weeks earlier.

"Andrea laughed. "I'm just glad you're not *carrying*,"

McCormick shot her a concerned look—he was carrying, as always, just nothing she could see.

At a scenic over-look, Matt reined in to a slow, easy cadence. Like a metronome, the hollow, measured clip clop of horse's hooves, proved haunting as they slowly traveled the desolate, country road, plodding through virgin snow. They breathed in the cold, frozen mist hanging over the mountain, and shrouding the valley floor in a most gauzy, mystical way. Shifting even closer to each other on the wooden bench, they spoke in whispered tones as bright, red Cardinals flitted in and out of white birch trees. Their heads swiveled as a small herd of deer appeared at the tree line, nuzzling snow and hoarfrost off the dormant grass, pulling it up by the roots. Suddenly feeling left out, Tracker whined, plaintively, from the back seat, and stuck his nose under their arms, seemingly content to stay that way—forever.

As the sleigh approached a copse of tall Hemlock and Frazier Fir, Andrea grew quiet, her breathing silenced by the beauty. Beneath the high-reaching trees, stood an elegant white church, its blue roof overlooking the pristine valley below like something straight out of a Thomas Kinkade painting. Multi-colored, stained-glass windows, and an elegant, proud steeple, gave it a look of solemnity—touched by God. They both grew quiet as the sleigh passed by the church. H*ushed, like a prayer in a troubled world,* she thought, noticing the signboard in front listing Rev. John McCormick as pastor.

McCormick usually let his thinking guide his actions, but today his heart had taken the lead. He could sense a level of turmoil in the woman, figuring Andrea's faith was battling the reality of the morning. Whatever … at this very moment, he felt that he could not stand to live another day, another minute, without Andrea's respect; and right now, that respect—in his mind—was hanging by a spindly, single thread. He shot her a rare, obscure look, his voice laden with emotion. "Andi…." he swallowed hard, "I really regret that you were a witness to all that carnage last night. I know you've made several references to the fact that I carry a gun … I need to know … is that really a concern for you?"

Andrea gave him a long, hard look. "Carry a gun…." she repeated, letting the words fall flat, "multiple knives … C4 explosives … pretexts and interrogations," she added, raising her eyebrows. "McCormick, aren't you really asking me if I mind that you're a trained killer?" He shot her a discomfited grimace. She continued, "I know what the D-boys are trained to do, and I know that the Taskforce, DEA, FBI and CIA all feast on those skills. Last night, I watched you in action. McCormick, you're no Boy Scout … no amateur neophyte."

Windy began to follow the ridge. McCormick heard, as though amplified, the loud squawk of a blue jay, the muffled clop-clopping of the horse's hooves plodding through the mounting snow, and Tracker's gentle, devoted panting; but he'd heard no answer to his question.

He, skillfully, guided the horse and sleigh off road, into a very old stand of hardwood forest, where a canopy of huge white limbs hung heavy over the narrow lane, creating a feeling of intimacy—which at that very moment was a mite too uncomfortable for McCormick. Clumps of snow dropped, rudely, from low-hanging limbs onto the sleigh as they slowly passed beneath them as though sharing his uneasiness. He sucked the frigid air into his lungs, trying to shore himself up, figuring that just like the snow on the branches, he was about to get dumped.

Suddenly, a huge black bear, shaggy and odiferous lumbered across their path and stopped in the middle of the lane. He pulled back on the reins, cooing softly, "Whoa." The dark, creature stood frozen in place, staring at the slow-approaching horse and sleigh, waiting for something to catch up to her.

Tracker immediately jumped to his feet, giving out a threatening growl. "Stand down!" McCormick commanded in a low whisper over his shoulder. "That's Belly-dragger's ladylove … with last year's cubs."

The dog obeyed. Andrea eyed both man and dog with skepticism.

Once the runners had come to a halt, the agent reached under his seat for his rifle, just to be on the safe side. Soon, a small, round head with cute, little ears and coal-button eyes peeked out of the underbrush, followed by another. Finally two clubby, little bodies loped across the roadway, catching up with mama, who gave the sleigh one last disdainful look, before all three disappeared into the forest.

A hush fell over the woodland. Matt returned the rifle, and turned his eyes on Andrea. "Maybe I should to ask my question another way … is there a problem … with me being the one who took

McCormick's head drooped Shaun down?"

Her face filled with wistfulness. "Matt, I'm more concerned about *you*.…" You're always referencing Hell … aren't you the least bit afraid you'll go to Hell for all the men you've killed?" she asked, earnestly.

, momentarily. Windy whinnied, and an impatient twitch ran across her shoulders, setting the bells a jingle. Taking a couple of impatient steps, she dragged the sleigh forward another couple of feet before being reined in. With an anguished grimace, McCormick spoke words straight from the heart. "Andi … watching a man die at your own hands … is its own private hell ... it's something that haunts your sleep for the rest of your life ... but in today's world, it's kill or be killed," he said simply. "The fight has come home ... you've witness that, up close and personal. We have to protect our loved ones...." He eyes stared, unfocused into the forest. "I offer no apology for what I do."

He tilted his head back, and in silence, took in the beauty of the season. Finally, he sucked in a deep breath, and blew it out through his nose. "Andi ... to be honest, I've wrestled with this very question for over a decade...." He locked eyes, "I'm just hoping to get to Heaven based on all the beautiful souls I've saved ... from the men I've sent to Hell."

Andrea sat, silenced. McCormick's statement was a powerful one. She remembered how wonderful it had been to have the love of her parents, and her sister's lively companionship—a family. She remembered the sweet innocence of the babies in the NAS unit at the hospital; how they trembled violently, and cried, non-stop, in their addiction. She remembered the dear, precious ones who hadn't survived. She also remembered all the abandoned children, left alone in the world after their mothers had over-dosed on drugs, or their fathers were sent to prison. She remembered the neighbor boy, and that handsome face in the McCormick family portrait—Matt's own brother. Shaun had ended his life, as well, while she and Matt, and David had been next on his long *To Do* list.

She remembered how she'd once thought of Matt's body as super-hero perfect; but because of Shaun, it was now riddled with bullet holes, while missing one of his precious, sexy legs. Did it bother her that Matt had strapped on a gun to put an end to this reign of terror? Did it bother her that ridding the country of hate-mongering terrorists was his life's calling?

She remembered Shaun, and at last shook her head, in answer, "No Matt ... there's no problem ... and there's no need to ever ask either question again."

Suddenly, with majestic clarity, the chromatically tuned bells in the steeple began to peal out its message on Christmas morn. McCormick closed his eyes, listening with deep satisfaction. A smile rode his lips as he first heard the joyful, carillon sound echo over the mountain top and across the misty valley. He remembered what a struggle it had been, helping the old man set the bells in place—before he'd gone searching for Stone.

CHAPTER 51

When the sleigh pulled up to the rustic, two-story house, Missy was hanging out the upstairs window, waving large with one arm and holding a small, sweater-clad Yorkshire Terrier in the other. A smile, reaching from ear to ear, was planted on her face. The kid had her brother's smile, Andrea noticed. David and Zoe were just arriving, carrying in food and drinks from the car. Why was Zoe here? She wondered, totally surprised, but extremely happy to see her friend. She was wearing her hair loose, in a new style, cascading down her back, and she was dressed up; but David still wore his jeans from the night before, was unshaven and looked like he had been up all night. Thank goodness for that, Andrea sighed, looking down at her own disheveled appearance.

The guys made a big display of greeting each other, shaking hands and grinning, bodaciously, at each other, while the girls hugged. In whispered tones not heard by the others, David asked, "How's the shoulder?"

"Painful."

"Drink water."

"Y-e-a-h ... right."

"Oh, Andrea," Zoe sympathized, "I've heard all about what happened. Are you okay?"

"Andrea gave her a faint smile, "I will be," she answered, feeling certain that Zoe hadn't heard *the entire* story—not from tight-lipped David. Neither woman mentioned what had happened to their boss.

With a slight flush to his face, David introduced Zoe to Matt. Andrea realized how good it felt to be with her friends, again, as Matt and David teased each other about their unshaven faces, with David promising to get his shaggy hair cut ASAP.

Now, David shot Matt a worried look. "I have no idea where Grams is ...

she was supposed to be following Zoe and me, but they closed the highway right behind us."

A pensive look came to Matt's face. "Well ... she just may have to fly in on the *Christmas Goose* ... I think it's still in the area. Hand me your satphone."

Dad and Mom came to the elaborately decorated door, graced with fresh, green wreaths, and adorned with long sprigs of spruce and holly. The pungent smell of cedar filled the air as everybody hugged their excited greetings. Holding her breath, Andrea watched with vested interest as Matt gave his mother a kiss on the cheek, then hugged her to his chest, his arms completely enveloping her svelte body for several long seconds before letting go. "I love you Mom," he said in a voice, deep and raspy. "It's good to be home."

Andrea smiled as the older woman looked long, into her son's handsome, tired face, now weathered and beaten. "I love you, son ... welcome home," she said in all earnestness, vigorously returning the hug.

Touching, Andrea thought, swiping away a tear.

Matt moved on, shaking hands with his dad. When it was David's turn, Andrea watched him bend down and whisper something in his mother's ear, nodding towards Matt. She nodded, and then shot Matt a no-nonsense look before returning her younger son's hugs.

To enter the house, everyone had to walk past a skinny, freshly made, six-foot tall snowman, obviously moved from its original spot of creation. It came complete with a long, French-braided wig, surgery cap, face mask, and lab coat. Hanging around its neck was a child's pink stethoscope. Hands and fingers had been sculpted into the snowman's arms, and held an extremely large hypodermic needle with a sign which read in bold, red and green letters: *So you want to be a warrior, do ya?*

Seeing it for the first time, and taken aback, Stormy turned to study her pristine, snow covered lawn. It was just the way she liked it on Christmas morning—untouched.

"Where in the world did that thing come from?" She queried. As the snowman instantly became the hot conversation topic, everyone took turns guessing who had delivered the work of art to the porch. No one seemed to know. "Matt ... David?" she asked. "How in the world did you two find time to be up to your shenanigans?"

They both feigned innocence, struggling to keep straight faces, and to tamp down their joyful delight, knowing that they had just given their mother three priceless Christmas gifts—the snow doctor, her pristine lawn, and the return, of a least two, of her bodacious, fearless boys.

Passing through the front doors, Andrea breathed in the rich, pungent smell of cedar boughs. It was a smell she would forever associate with happiness.

Stormy invited Andrea into her home with a huge, accepting hug. "Andi ... welcome to our humble abode." She immediately recognized Matt's jacket. "Wow, my son's West Point jacket ... I haven't seen that in years."

Matt jumped in, tauntingly, "Yeah, I know it makes you see red, so I've kept it hidden away."

Stormy put her hand to her nose. "Yes, and I don't need to guess where."

Everybody laughed. Stormy turned to Andrea, showing concern for the young woman, cold and windblown from the sleigh ride. She grabbed both of Andrea's hands in her own. "Oh, sweetheart, your face is wind burned, and your hands are like blocks of ice ... oh, and that sweet, beautiful mouth." She turned to Matt and playfully scolded in her motherly voice. "Matt! What have you done to this child?" She looked conspiratorially at Andrea. "He used to think it was so funny to go gallivanting all up and down this mountainside."

Matt burst out laughing, "No, Ma ... I've grown up a little since then." He gave Andrea a sly, playful wink. Stormy quickly turned to face her son, pointing a determined finger at him. "I'll see you ... funny guy...." She reached up and gave his ear lobe a hard yank, "and what's left of that perfect body I gave you at birth, after dinner—in my office!"

He shot Andrea a quick glance. "And she calls *me* the smart mouth."

Matt's next comment was directed over his shoulder to his little brother. In a voice just loud enough to be heard by all, Matt hissed in a reprehensible tone, "Tattletale!" For some reason, David found the comment extremely hilarious and burst out laughing.

Remembering the wallop David had given him in the cabin the previous night, he let the kid in him come to the surface. Clutching his jaw in a comedic gesture, and in the grievous, whining tone of a wronged sibling, he sang out, "Ma, Davy tried to break my j-a-w!"

David immediately picked up on the playful accusation, responding with an even deeper, richer belly-laugh. "Ma," he whined in rebuttal, his voice child-like. "Matt's been throwing combat knives at me ... again."

Matt, David and Andrea were the only ones to laugh at the private joke.

In good humor, Matt collected their coats and walked away with his arms loaded. Stormy turned and pleasantly addressed her visitors. "I'm in the kitchen getting ready to put the pies in the oven; come on in and warm up by the fire ... we can enjoy each other's company without these guys guffawing at every word out of our mouths. We've all been through a harrowing ordeal, and we need to be with each other." Andrea noticed that Stormy pretended to be distracted by her sons' joking, but she could tell that her friend relished every utterance and peal of laughter out of her sons' mouths.

Now Stormy turned to Zoe, who had been hanging back, listening to the banter. She offered, "Zoe, I'm Stormy to most people. I don't know why they insist on calling me by that name ... David has told me so much about you." Andrea shot Zoe a curious grin. "Come on in and join Andi and me in the kitchen?" At the sound of the Yorkie's constant yapping on the second floor, Stormy stepped to the foot of the stairs and yelled, "Missy, put that yapper in a doggie bag, and come wash up. I need you in the kitchen."

Andrea marveled at the woman, aware that she was in the presence of a woman in full control of her circumstances.

They left the large foyer, and Stormy guided them through a living room the size of a barn. One whole wall was completely taken by a beautiful stone fireplace, where a large, cheerful fire crackled and popped. Every dark corner glowed with flickering candlelight, feeding warmth and life into the room. A very large floor-to-ceiling window covered the entire outside wall, revealing the white-blanketed lawn, a huge, silvery lake, and an undisturbed snow-covered valley of evergreen forest. On the far end of the room, a raised platform had been added—a stage.

A second stairway, fully decorated with fresh garland, ascended only to the loft and balcony area. In the nook at the foot of the stairs stood an extremely tall, rustically decorated Christmas tree. In awe, Andrea gazed upon the gorgeous star shining down from the top of the tree with ethereality. Not in all her many shopping trips to the city, had she ever seen a star so magnificent.

Stormy explained the mammoth-sized room with a high cathedral ceiling, "When we first moved here, John didn't have a church, so he, and all three boys, built this big house and we held services here for several years." She laughed, "It really came in handy as our family got older—and taller." Andrea imagined Matt growing up in this stunning, rough-hewn home. "Later, of course, they built the church...." She looked at Andrea, "You passed by it ... on your way in."

"Your family built that gorgeous church?"

She smiled. "Yes ... my boys," she offered, proudly.

The women proceeded to the kitchen, where another crackling fire burned in a cheerful hearth. Sitting at a worktable with her head down was a woman with salt and pepper hair, filling, what else, salt and pepper shakers. When she raised her head, a surprised Andrea gasped.

Recognizing Andrea, the woman shot her a look of indignation, and groused, puckishly, "You probably ought to count all your fingers, dearie. I think you let one fly away back at the library!"

Andrea stood, staring at the old hag, astounded.

Suddenly, the back door flew open, and an elderly gentleman backed into the room, carrying an armload of firewood. His slightly-stooped shoulders were covered in a bold, berry and hunter green plaid shirt. "Coming through," he chimed, cheerfully.

Stormy sighed, grievously, and picked up a potholder in each hand, preparing to take a casserole from the oven. "Wade ... lay that wood down, and come gag our little sister, would you; then come say hello to our beautiful guests."

When Wade stood up, he was neither elderly, nor stoop-shouldered, but tall and robust. He looked at his sister. "Katherine ... have you been popping off at the mouth again?" She cocked an irritable brow in response."

He looked at the two young women. "Don't mind her ... she's breathed in too much dust from all those old, decaying library pages ... probably swallowed a few bookworms in the process ... it's addled her brain, somewhat;" he grinned, "but her biggest problem is the role she plays at the local theatre ... it's an Agatha Christy production they put on annually for Leaf-peepers ... she's been doing it now for five years ... and she likes to stay in character."

Katherine stood, straightened her shoulders and stepped away from the table, a refined woman. She poked her brother playfully in the tummy, "Stop telling all my secrets, you old fool." When they turned to greet the two young women, bright smiles were on both their faces.

Suddenly, the loud rotor blades of a low flying helicopter shattered the peace. It banked and then hovered, momentarily, over the house. The deafening sound of the twirling blades, beating through the frosty air, made conversation impossible. They all rushed to the window to watch the big bird gently set down on the lawn.

"Well, there goes my pristine lawn," Stormy lamented, throwing up her hands.

"What's going on ... what's happening?" Fear sounded in Missy's voice as her feet trampled down the stairs.

Stormy stretched a calming arm out towards her daughter, her voice rising above the racket. "Come watch, sweetheart ... this is one for the memory books. Grams got stuck in the snow, so Matt sent a helicopter after her."

From the window, the women all watched as Matt and David waded through the knee-deep snow towards the big, gray chopper, their heavy, white breaths spiraling in the bitter cold. They watched Matt shake hands with the pilot and hand him a very large tin of Christmas cookies, a tin with the image of a stone-faced Kris Kringle on the lid. This prompted raucous laughter from all three men.

Suddenly, the side-door slid open, and a woman dressed in tight-fitting jeans, fashion boots and a red coat with a foxy, fur-trimmed hood pulled over her head stepped to the door. Matt and David turned their backs to the chopper, and allowed the woman to grab ahold of their necks, and ride their backs to the ground. Once her boots were in the snow, they all laughed and joked with excitement.

Katherine turned away from the window, throwing off the scene with her hand. Back in character, she groused, "Ah ... she's always been such a show-off."

Matt turned towards the house and gave a two-fingered whistle. Two men on the roof threw down tactical repelling ropes with grappling hooks attached to the ends, and shimmied down the side of the house. With rifles slung across their shoulders, and heavy packs on their backs, the men ran towards the helicopter, and jumped on board.

At last, everyone stepped away, McCormick signaled the pilot, and the chopper rose straight up, disappearing over the trees.

Soon, Matt walked into the kitchen with his arm around a familiar-looking, white-haired lady; he carried her coat while she clutched him around the waist.

"Awesome entrance, Grandma," Missy yelled. She hugged the woman, then walked to the sink to help her mother with the salad preparations.

Matt gave Andrea a mirthful wink, then walked straight to his Uncle Wade, giving the retired Air Force pilot, a firm, respectful handshake and a warm man hug.

"Been flying?" his uncle asked.

"Nah," Matt answered ruefully. "I've been knee deep in mud and shi….," he bounced a glance off his grandmother, "scat … but we need to get our runway open again … I'll be flying back and forth to DC for a while…." He shot a jovial look at his mother, "and, in case you haven't' heard, Mom … we've all been invited back to the Oval Office. He looked at his uncle, "Naturally, the girls will all want to go shopping first."

Andrea looked at Matt in cluelessness.

Concern crossed Matt's face. "I do still have a plane, don't I?"

Everyone laughed but Andrea and Zoe.

Uncle Wade shot Matt a proud grin. "You do … but you'll need to get that eye taken care of, and your license up to date … I'll worry about the runway." He laid his hand on McCormick's shoulder. "Actually, truth-be-told, I could use a little bump in income."

"You got it," Matt answered in an austere, professional manner.

He turned and lovingly wrapped his arms around the crotchety Katherine. "Aunt Kat … I see you're still doing the thespian *thang*," he said, teasingly.

She straightened. "Yes, Matty dear … but I've never played a character as daunting as the one you've played for the last two years," she answered, sincerely, using her own spritely persona and chipper voice. "Come back to us, Matt, and play King Arthur."

McCormick, smiled, somewhat abashed. He lowered his voice to a military grunt, and spoke humbly from his chest. "I've already got a role bigger than I can handle."

Andrea stood, silenced by what she was hearing. *Matt was a pilot and a thespian?*

Now everyone clustered around Matt's grandmother. She sighed loudly, "Oh, boy! I never thought I would ever have to be rescued by helicopter. My car got stuck coming through the pass. Just as I was speaking to my god, preparing to freeze to death, that big, ole' whirly bird came out of nowhere, and sat down on the road, right smack in front of me. I don't know how they knew I was there, but I certainly am grateful."

Matt grinned, "I'd heard rumors, Grams ... that if you fed it homemade sugar cookies, it would transform into the Christmas Goose."

He turned to Andi and Zoe, "I'd like to introduce you both to my grandmother, my dad's mother." Andrea could tell that he was very fond of the woman. "She calls herself Mrs. McCormick, or Mac, depending on her mood; but around here, she's Grams or Granny. I'm sure she would feel honored if you wanted to call her by any one of those names. Just be warned—if you call her *Hey You*, and ask her to bring you a cold drink, she'll throw her 20-pound tome of the *Complete Works of Charles Dickens* at you..." he looked up, mystified, "or at least that's what always happens to me." He grinned at his grandmother. "Those wicked boots carry a mean wallop, too." Everyone was in stitches with laughter.

Granny turned to Andrea. "When he's not a comedian, my grandson is a marvelous, fantastic, blessed young man, who looks just like his grandfather." she said with an edge—her voice carrying a kind of possessive warning.

She's got his back, Andrea thought, somewhat bemused.

"He's a bit of a bookworm, though, just like his grandfather, so anything that gets him to crawl out from between those dusty pages is alright by me."

"Amen to that," Aunt Kat offered.

Andrea smiled, thinking the older woman didn't fully understand the nature of Matt's work. She wondered how Grams felt about mammoth bears, humongous snakes and cocaine-riddled rodents.

Delighted to see the humorous side to the older woman, everyone laughed, and Gram's face immediately softened into a friendly smile. She grabbed both Andrea's hands and squeezed them, tightly. "Andrea you probably don't remember me, but I'm the lady who dragged you, kickin' and screamin', to address the National Honor Society—right after I threatened to sue the pants off that good-for-nothing Marty Rudd for being a no-show."

David locked eyes with Matt, thinking his grandmother shouldn't be speaking ill of the dead. Matt read his thoughts, and gave his head a cogent half-shake. Andrea read both their minds.

Following Matt's lead, she feigned ignorance and laughed, "I had no time to prepare … my speech was fifty percent impromptu and fifty percent bluff."

Grams offered, "Sweetheart, your speech one hundred percent better than the one Rudd would have given."

Surprised, Matt's mouth hung agape. "Wait a minute," he questioned, with a hint of satisfaction in his voice. "You two already know each other?" They both nodded.

"Yep … we're best buds." Andrea grabbed Granny, and held her like an old friend, hugging, and rocking back and forth, mimicking their many hours together rocking addicted babies in the wee hours of the night. Finally dispensing with the humor, the older woman grabbed both Andrea's hands in her own, and held her in her gaze for a long moment, giving her a look of sympathy that Andrea understood, immediately.

Matt said, "That's awesome … but, Grams, let's expound a little more on that word *bookworm*." Now, mimicking his grandmother, he feigned a stern expression. "Don't you have better words in your vocabulary *rucksack* to describe a dude like me? "Wouldn't crazy, inked up, one-legged, bullet-riddled, geeky, sleuthing, gun-toting, G-man babysitter better describe me."

David had entered the room and joined into the conversation. "How about words like West Point Cadet, Delta Force, Navy Seals, B.A. in Criminal Justice, Masters in Science and Defense Analysis; or here's a new one for you," his voice rose in tenor, "how about PhD in Criminal Justice?"

Embarrassed by the sudden attention, McCormick gave his head a half-shake and sniggered. "The learned man knows that he is ignorant," he droned, bypassing David's praise.

John Donne, Andrea pleasingly thought to herself.

"PhD?" Grams repeated excitedly, clapping her hands together and dropping her coat to the floor in the process. Hopefulness shone from her face as she looked at Matt and asked breathlessly, "Matt … you've finished your dissertation?"

"Yup … I'd already taken the exams before I went AWOL," he said, bending down to pick up his grandmother's coat and hanging it on a chair back, "I finished it, while my leg was healing," he answered. "I took the orals just a few weeks ago. A little shyness showed through his confident armor as he locked eyes with Andrea, giving her a slow, modest grin. "I just turned the marathon into a sprint," he explained, aware that he and Andrea were the only ones in the room to truly understand his reversal of the well-worn adage. She grinned back.

A sense of pride in his accomplishment filled her heart, and she spoke up. "McCormick, you should have shared your success with me … we could've celebrated your success!"

Recognizing his own words coming back at him, McCormick's head shot up and their eyes locked for a long, tense moment. Finally realizing that her words held promise rather than animus, he gave her a warm smile.

Now McCormick spoke to everyone in the room. "This whole family can accept the credit for my success; but Grams here, is the one I have to blame for my badass, bookworm lifestyle." He looked at his grandmother in askance, not wanting to miss her reaction. The image of a strong disciplinarian returned to her face.

Matt laughed softly, and turned to Andrea and Zoe, offering an explanation. "My grandmother's a High School English teacher."

"Retiring English teacher," she corrected. This is my last year."

"It's about time." David added, and Missy nodded her head in agreement.

Matt sat down on a high stool. Missy came up beside him, slung her arms around his neck like a young child. Ecstatic to have her big brother back, she laid her head on his shoulder, in a sisterly way. He smiled at the young girl, and lovingly curled his arm around her waist. Looking on, Andrea thought it was a sweet and tender moment, realizing the girl would have been a very young child when Matt went off to war. "Grams taught us all to read by the age of four," McCormick explained, "and supplied us with enough books to fill the Library of Congress."

"That's right," Aunt Kat agreed.

He raised his eyes and shot his mother a taunting look, "This was while Mom was away … studying to be a nurse practitioner and getting friendly with all the cadavers … she was on a first name basis with all of them." Everybody laughed. "Dad wasn't overly concerned about any of it, until she came home one weekend, complaining about his hands being too *warm*."

Having lived through it, David roared with laughter, and Matt's eyes twinkled with merriment. Then he lowered his head, and his voice took on a more respectful tone. "Excuse me, what I really meant to say, was that Grams made serious students of us while Mom was away learning how to save *my* life...." He raised his eyes to meet his mother's flinty ones, "for which I am eternally grateful."

Stormy turned her head, flicking away a tear.

Matt continued, "Grandma kept us in line; and believe me, n-o-b-o-d-y crossed Granny! Isn't that right, Davy?"

"For sure!" David gave a jovial nod and everybody laughed again, appreciating the humor—including his grandmother.

Suddenly, the door flew open. "Who wants Orchard Bread?" chimed a cheerful female voice. Andrea turned to see the older waitress from Ye Olden Mill restaurant.

Uncle Wade rushed to help his wife. "I was getting worried about you," he exclaimed.

"I just wanted to be sure I'd baked enough," she answered, light-heartedly.

As the kitchen began to buzz with activity, Matt stood up from the stool, and winked at Andrea and David. He gave Missy a hug and a big kiss on the forehead. "Thanks for the cleaning job, Sis ... I really appreciated coming home to a clean cabin." He grabbed his grandmother's coat from the chair, and left the kitchen.

Grams looped her arm through David's. "Zoe, let me give you the lowdown on *this* handsome dude."

CHAPTER 52

The Old Man had been standing just outside the kitchen door, listening to the laughter—the magical sound that could not be heard during Matt's absence. When his son passed through the door, he playfully snagged him by the arm and walked him to the coat closet, waiting patiently as he hung his grandmother's coat on a wooden hanger. Then he led him into his study, to the hearth where a warm fire popped and crackled, seemingly to say, *Welcome Home!*

"How are you son," he asked in a tender voice.

McCormick had requested this meeting, needing the opportunity to thank his father for his help, and to show his respect.

"Dad ... I wanted to tell you thanks for activating the unit ... David, Andi and I wouldn't be here without your help."

"Forget the unit ... how's your soul?" The Reverend asked, as he placed a mug of steaming hot coffee into his son's hands. They sat down in opposite chairs, facing each other in front of the cozy fire. The human soul was his dad's favorite topic, so Matt had seen this one coming. He gratefully, took a slow sip from his mug, and then answered with the same earnestness his dad had used to ask the question. "I want to say all is well with my soul, but...."

The old man could tell something was eating away at his son, "I know ... so what's the problem?" he asked, kindly.

McCormick locked eyes with his dad. "You know I have a problem?"

"Of course ... I've known you for a long time ... I've never seen you this troubled." Matt had always been a pretty open kid, so whatever this problem was, he figured it must be a real humdinger.

Matt rubbed his hand down his itchy, three-day-old stubble. "I'll be honest with you ... I've just killed five men...." He dropped his head. "Dad ... I've killed Bran ... and Donnie." His dad nodded his understanding.

"You killed them in the line of duty?"

"I did."

"They started shooting first?"

"They did."

"You saved innocent lives?"

Matt's hot breath pushed out his answer, "Many."

"You've asked for forgiveness?"

"I have," Matt answered, in all seriousness.

"Then it sounds like you need to forgive yourself, son. God doesn't have trouble with forgiveness … neither should you."

McCormick took a deep, full breath and let it out. "The other thing is … after we talked at the stable yesterday morning, I went up to pay my respects to Clint, but like Ebenezer Scrooge, I found myself staring at my own tombstone … into my own grave."

His father nodded his head, knowingly, but pursed his lips, trying to formulate an explanation. Finally, "Son … when we recovered your brother's body on an anonymous tip…." he paused and rubbed his hands up and down his thighs, "we found an extra boot alongside him in the shallow grave."

A serious frown pulled down the corners of McCormick's mouth. "A boot," his chin shot up, "a boot … with my foot still in it," he added, dryly.

The Reverend nodded, solemnly. "There was so much blood … we thought … we thought both our boys had been killed." He blew hot air through his nose. "Straker ran the DNA … he confirmed your death."

Straker. McCormick dropped his head, blowing out a hot breath.

His dad topped off their cups, then sat back, giving his son time to emotionally process the information.

Matt sat in silence, then with his voice going raspy, said at last, "That … brings some closure."

"I'm assuming you're the one who gave us the tip."

"I am."

The fire crackled as they sat, both dealing with the deep stir of emotions. Finally, "I'm hoping my family can forgive me for going AWOL. I know Mom's really hurt and angry with me for not coming home, but the truth is, Dad … losing my leg was the key to my success. That's what helped me work my way inside. Our enemy has been defeated because I didn't come running home, but stayed to dig for information. And when it came time for my escape, no one thought a one-legged, smart-ass crooner would have reason to scale a sheer cliff to freedom and safety ... but I did."

His father chuckled, "Well son, they didn't know you'd started bouldering at Smugglers' Notch before you could walk, or that you were a trained and experienced mountain climber; nor did they know that you had fought in extreme mountain war combat."

Matt pursed smiling lips, appreciating the fact that his dad knew him so well. He paused, and took a deep breath. "Dad, Andrea ... and a lot of other very good people ... are alive today because I stayed with it long enough to find out who was really running things."

His father's mouth jutted up in a semi-wry grin. "Are you saying this mission was worth sacrificing an arm and a leg?" His gaze went to his son's shoulder.

"Hopefully just the leg ... but yeah ... that's exactly what I'm saying. I would've easily given my life for this one.

The two men sat in silence.

Finally, "Dad, I've heard it said that war is where the Christian is truly tested, and I agree; but this was worse than war. This undercover job, living with the enemy, was one of the toughest things I've ever done. I couldn't be true to my faith ... I couldn't be true to myself. I was playing a role—living a lie; but the faith I had in a higher being ... knowing that there's a better way to live, helped get me through it all. When things really got tough, I remembered the words to all the old hymns, and all those sermons I squirmed through as a kid ... those were the very things that kept me going. I remembered hearing the one predicting that the world would become as decadent as Sodom and Gomorrah." Matt took in a gulp of air, "Dad, we're there—we're worse. What we did last night—stopping Stone and Straker—that was just a drop in the bucket, there's so many more out there, just like them. We're in a fight for our lives, for the survival of our country, and for our entire civilization, except this time ... we're all living with the enemy."

Knowing that Matt had degrees in world history, the Reverend nodded his head, listening respectfully. Moisture formed in his eyes as his son continued. "I can't deny that God was with me every step of the way ... neither can I deny that it was you, Dad—your influence, your parenting—that saved my life, over and over again."

The battle-tested, older McCormick raised his eyes to the ceiling, trying to bat away the tears. "I was just the messenger."

McCormick gave his head a shake, and chuckled, softly. "I'll have to apologize ahead of time for my salty language." He snickered, "It's really bad."

"Get your heart right, son … the rest will take care of itself."

The comment reminded Matt why he loved his dad so much. His patience and understanding knew no bounds.

He set his mug on the table in front of him, "Dad, this is not to be shared yet—the timing's not right … it'll be announced publicly soon. As you well know, I've just been on loan to the agency from Special Forces. Our units are overwhelmed by the sheer number of missions they're asked to respond to … they want me back. I've been asked to head up a new International Taskforce. It will include all the U.S. agencies, hopefully with a number of allies from around the world. They're willing to set me up with an underground command center nearby, so I can communicate without having to fly back and forth to Washington every time there's a threat. It'll be dangerous … but it has to be done."

The old man filled his lungs with air; then breathed out a long, sorrowful breath. His wrinkles sunk deep with a whole new line of seriousness. Matt hadn't spoken the words aloud, but he knew his son—knew how to read between the lines. Having, led missions all over the world himself, he easily understood the word left unspoken: War

"Will you still be involved with black-op missions?"

Matt gave his father a slight head nod.

The wizened, old man dropped his head with emotion and closed his eyes. "You're so young."

In truth, McCormick felt about a hundred-years-old, considering all his recent injuries; but reading his father's angst, he offered, "I'm young in years, Dad, but I'm more than qualified." He shuffled his feet. "We have no choice … we have to protect our families, the homeland … our culture. For one crazy reason or another, we've lost many fine officers over the last few years … I'm next in line of command."

He continued, "I'll ask for the best men this country has to offer … Davy will be my first recruit."

Matt slid to the edge of his chair, and rested his arms on his knees, looking his dad straight in the eye. "Dad, the other thing is this: I'm going to ask Andi to marry me. I want a real life, with a real family. To be brutally honest, I'm not sure she'll even have me—there are still a number of things we need to work out." Matt paused, momentarily. "I know it's sudden, and probably too soon, but the two of us have been through a lot together ... we're kindred spirits ... we've bonded. Because of Bran, we've both lost out on a lot of the good things in life. I want ... I need her in my life. She understands me and the work I do ... I understand and know her in ways I could never know another woman." He laughed, and grimaced at the same time. "Hell ... I've investigated everything but her underwear drawer." He sat back in his chair and raised his brows, giving his dad a boyish, lopsided grin, "She even loves my dog."

The Reverend took a slow sip of coffee, his mouth puckering at its cold, bitter taste. He shook his head, and a worried expression crossed his brow. Finally, his eyes turned cold in a flinty-eyed glare. "Son ... it seems to me that a *good* investigator would have delved into that drawer."

McCormick's eyes began to dance. His dad always could spot an inaccuracy. He leaned forward, leveling his eyes, and shot the flinty look right back at him. "Old Man ... I'm a *damned* good investigator!"

The older McCormick kept a stern face as he settled back in his chair and began patting the upholstered arms, thoughtfully. "And she loves your dog, does she? Well, well, well ... that sure is a load off my mind. I was afraid you wanted to marry her just because she's such a hottie!"

Matt's head shot back, and roisterous laughter rolled up from his solar plexus. Images of an angry, coffee-splattered Andrea filled his mind and heart. "And there's that," he said, grinning wryly.

His dad rose and extended his hand, "My blessings to you both." Only half teasing, he offered, "If you're in a real hurry, the clerk's office should be open tomorrow morning ... you could get a marriage license bright and early ... you'll have to show birth certificates." He paused, preferring not to have to let go of his next comment, "and you'll need Lauren's death certificate ... and, of course, Bran's...." he cocked a mischievous eyebrow, "if the ink's dry."

Matt had thought it through, already: *Andrea would need time to grieve—and he would need time to heal—God, how he hated getting shot!* He gave his dad a head nod, "Already ahead of you."

A proud look crossed the old man's face. "You've always been ahead of me."

He continued, "I'll be available anytime, for either pre-nuptial counseling, or a wedding ceremony—for a fee, of course."

"What? You'd charge your own son a fee?" Matt teased.

He quoted the words of a time-honored sage. "Nothing of lasting value is ever free."

"Who said that?" Matt questioned.

His dad snickered, "Hell if I know."

Again, they laughed together, then the Reverend laid a firm hand on Matt's shoulder. "I can't begin to tell you how much I've missed you, son."

Matt swallowed the lump in his throat. "It's great to be back, Dad; but be prepared with a crying towel, in case Andi sees me as just another SOB."

"Nothing ventured, nothing gained," his father quipped, turning his head to hide his grin. The older McCormick felt no concern as to which way Andrea's answer would go. He'd seen the way the lovely, young woman, earnest and forthcoming, and beautiful in spirit, looked at his son.

The two men shook hands, and Matt left the study a better man. He walked back to the kitchen, to Andrea, and to his destiny—one way or the other.

The old man closed the door behind him, and walked across rustic, wooden-planked flooring to the window, thanking God for bringing his son home safely; and then he said a prayer of thanks for Andrea. She had managed, even in the throes of her own duress, to bring Matt back from his cold, dark past.

CHAPTER **53**

Large, fluffy flakes of snow fell peacefully outside the huge picture window, further whitening the cedars and pines in the dusky light. The inside lights were dimmed and only the candles burned, their flickering light dancing across the faces of everyone sitting around the large table as they joined hands as if on cue, bowing their heads. Andrea sat with David to her left, and Matt on her right. When Matt reached for her hand, her pulse quickened.

David leaned over and whispered to the two of them. "Fasten your seatbelts ... he's gotten very bold as of late," he said, nodding at his father. "We never know what he's going to say."

All was quiet as the patriarchal head of the family slowly rose and without a word of explanation, bowed his head and began talking:

"Father, today we come to you with grateful hearts for bringing our Matthew home again, and for keeping our David safe from harm ... and Stormy, our wonderful Stormy. We give you the praise for their successes, but mourn the loss of human lives. We thank you for keeping Andrea safe in her time of trouble, and for bringing her safely *home—home* to us. Father ... we already love her."

Matt's chin jutted up with a surprised, questioning look.

"Still Lord, we come to you with our hearts in tatters, and although we could have no greater love for each and every one gathered around this table, our hearts grieve for the one missing—our Clint. The last time he was with us—sitting at this very table—he shared the fact that he was ready to settle down, get married, have a family and give Stormy and me grandchildren. Father, we grieve for that unlived part of his life, and for the untold number of children who will never get a chance to sit at this table—to be a part of this family."

Andrea heard Matt take a deep, ragged breath, as sniffles came from

480

the women around the table. Sensing the depth of Matt's heartbreak, David slowly dropped Andrea's hand, and reached around the back of her chair to lay a consoling hand on Matt's shoulder, knowing that his brother had never shared the loss of his child with his parents—and probably never would.

"But we know, in our hearts, that our loss is your gain; and for you to have taken Clint out of this fight here on earth ... well ... you must have very special plans for him—for his eternal soul."

The Reverend cleared his throat. "We find it strange, Lord, that even in the midst of our sorrow; our hearts are light with that kind of unspeakable joy that you promised us so long ago. For a long time now—months and years—we've lived our lives in desperation, holding our breaths, and swiping the overflowing tears from our eyes, skulking around in the shadows, totally surrounded by darkness of every kind. You gave us The Garden, but you, in your infinite wisdom, knew that we mere mortals would screw it all up ... and we most certainly have."

His voice rose, "But now comes the good news ... you've offered us a way out. You sent us a Savior to forgive us our sins, lighten our load, stare down our demons, and light the pathway leading to a better way—if we'll only trust his words. Jesus said, 'I am the light of the world. Whoever follows me will never walk in darkness, but will have the light of life.'

"Today, Lord, we're in recovery mode and we're learning that, in spite of all our troubles, we have a far greater understanding of you, of your words, and their meaning. Now that we've groped alone in the darkness, we can better understand what the angels were all so fired up about when they hovered over the earth, flapping their wings, and singing, "Joy to the world, the Lord is come; Let earth receive her King." They were simply saying: He's here! He's here! Our Savior is here! The Bible tells us that he is the light of the world."

"The angels were sharing the secret of how to live our lives outside the darkness. Matt knows it, David knows it, and our enemies are finding out the hard way, as they, at this very moment, get schooled by the greatest teacher who ever lived. Lord, you were dead serious when you said, 'Greater is he that is in you, than he that is in the world.'"

The Reverend paused and wiped his eyes on a paper napkin of a Christmas tree design. He took a deep breath, "Family, do you hear me? The God in us was greater than Brantley Stone or Shaun Fitzgerald, or whatever name evil goes by!" A unified gasp rose from around the table, and both Matt and David reached for Andrea's hands and squeezed, sympathetically, as their father's voice grew louder. "Father, when you said, "Not by might, nor by power, but by the *spirit*," you were simply telling us to *use the force*." Slowly, he looked around at every person around the table. "What is the force, you ask. The force, beloved family, is the power of prayer! The angels were telling us to pray to our Savior … pray away the darkness … pray away the evil … because darkness can't exist, where there is light!"

He paused, again looking around the table, his gaze coming to a surprised halt on the slightly harried face of his daughter, Nicole, who arriving from Miami, had just slipped through the door, and taken her place at the far side of the table. "Father, we've had our losses, for sure. We've been beaten up physically, psychologically, and spiritually, but we gratefully thank you for walking beside us, lighting our path forward, and bringing us through the danger to the other side of fear, and we ask your blessings on each and every one at this table. On this Christmas Day, we thank you for the birth of the Christ Child, our Savior, our Light; and we ask that you help us all to seek *your* face, asking forgiveness of our own trespasses, as we forgive those who have trespassed against us. Amen."

"Amen," came the response in unison. A pall of silence settled over the table and hung heavy in the air. Andrea raised her gaze to Matt, seeing him, inconspicuously, wipe away a tear.

The joyful family gathering played out before Andrea, but her mind failed to focus on it, painfully aware of what she was missing in regards to her own family. Then her mind wandered to the first conversation she'd had with David, and the way he had described his missing, older brother. The pieces to the puzzle came together. Sitting here, at this family gathering between the two brothers, she realized that the missing brother had been Matt; and the problems David had shared with her that night in the newsroom had been Matt's problems—the aborted child had been Matt's own son. Clint had never married. Suddenly, she found herself grieving Matt's loss. Now, it was she who dabbed at the tears in her own eyes.

Then somebody—Andrea thought it was Matt—yelled, "Y-e-a-h … let's eat!" and all craziness broke loose as everybody started talking all at once, asking questions and making blanket statements. Andrea loved it. Matt noticed.

As the large casserole dishes were set out for a buffet, Andrea and Zoe gave each other questioning looks about the men they were with, each wondering how this had all come about. Everyone gleefully greeted Nicole, then settled back around the table while Orchard Bread and apple butter were passed around as everyone teased poor Missy, mercilessly, about anything and everything—especially the way she had delivered her mom's satphone to Matt at the restaurant. Matt spoke up quickly, rubbing his chin whiskers, mischievously. "Yeah ... Andi didn't actually call me a pervert ... but that's pretty much what she was thinking." Laughter roared around the table. Andrea covered her face with her hands and blushed as she remembered her reaction to the scene at the restaurant.

CHAPTER 54

Once the table had been cleared, Stormy cut into four more pies and shoved them to the center of the table for later, concerned at how thin her sons had gotten. She removed her apron and leaned across the table, whispering, "Andi, you must be exhausted. Matt said you spent the night on the couch. There's a fresh guest bed in the loft with a brand new goose down duvet. Why don't you go rest for a few minutes while the boys set up for a home-grown concert? I promise; it'll be a treat."

Andrea admitted to a headache, and Stormy went off to get her a pain-killer.

"Make sure it's an aspirin, Mom," Missy yelled over her shoulder, "She never takes anything stronger than an aspirin."

Andrea stiffened. Had Missy heard her speech, seen her husband, connected the dots? Suddenly, she remembered the face of the enthusiastic, young girl who had graced the front row of the gymnasium during her speech, and identified her for the first time—Missy.

Nicole introduced herself, offering Andrea help in any way she needed. Then she produced a cheerful, little plastic bag bearing holly leaves and bright berries, and the name of her shop. "I just flew in, so I haven't had time to wrap this, but I felt it was meant to be yours." Andrea opened the bag to find the cross-stitch sampler she'd picked up and discarded in the shop a few weeks ago." Andrea liked Nicole; she seemed to be a nice person, inside and out, but with a sharp, savvy look to her eye—like Matt. Nicole ended their conversation by saying, "My brother is a, genuinely, good guy ... clear to the bone ... he deserves the best."

Once she'd left, Andrea's heart took a nose dive. *The best,* she pondered, soberly.

Zoe slide into the chair beside her, giving her red, wind-burned face a look of concern. "Andi, are you really okay?" She furrowed her brow, and sighed in dismay. "Girl, you look so tired … and your lip's bleeding … and I get the feeling that you're upset with me about something."

Andrea dabbed a napkin to her lip, and started to deny her feelings, then stopped and came out with a heavy sigh. "Why did you tell Matt about our stupid Superhero conversations?"

Zoe looked up in surprise. "I haven't told Matt anything," she answered, sounding, not annoyed, but clueless. "Today's the first time I've ever talked to Matt … honestly," she looked at Andrea from the corner of her eye, "and WOW!"

Andrea gave her friend a big hug. "Yeah," she chuckled softly, "you should see him when he's not dripping blood." Now she smiled as though asking forgiveness. "Zoe, I'm sorry … I guess I'm just … being paranoid."

"You're not paranoid, Andi … you're in shock," her friend offered, kindly.

"So things are going great with you and David?" Andrea asked, genuinely interested.

Zoe blushed, "Yeah, they are … now that he's back from who knows where … I have no idea what he's been doing." Andrea smiled, but said nothing. Zoe slipped her arm through Andrea's. "Remember how you used to encourage me to have faith … that my knight in shining armor was on his way?" A soft, dreamy look came into her eyes. "Well, he's here … and it's David."

"I'm so happy for you, Zoe … and for David." She took a deep breath, letting it escape quickly. "Give me a few days to rest up, and deal with the results of Shaun's insanity … then we'll plan a shopping trip to the city, a girl's day out … okay?"

"Are you coming back to the *News*?" Zoe asked.

Andrea looked around the room, giving the question serious thought. At last she shook her head. "I don't think so."

Sadness came into Zoe's eyes, but she smiled, warmly, covering Andrea's hand with her own. "I understand … I'll catch you later, girlfriend," she said, softly.

Andrea returned the smile, in kind.

Stormy brought aspirin, and Zoe followed her back to the kitchen. Aunt Kat appeared out of nowhere, taking Zoe's place in the chair. "Well … everybody is mad as hell at me for hurting your feelings … and making a huge FOOL of myself," she said, bluntly in no uncertain terms. "Ms. Daye ... I'm sorry ... I didn't realize what all was going on ... and all that stuff I spouted in the library ... I just...."

Andrea laid her hand on the fretting woman's arm in a consoling manner. "You just had Matt's back ... besides, what you said in the library was absolutely true. I know a lot of women are after Matt ... and no ... there's nothing special about me." The two women looked at each other, eye to eye for a long moment; then Andrea thrust out her hand for a cordial shake. "My name is Andi, by the way ... and you can keep the proverbial finger ... if I had it back I'd probably just poke both your eyes out." She smiled, puckishly.

"Fair enough," Aunt Kat said, laughingly, as she stood up and shook Andrea's hand. Laying a gentle hand on Andrea's shoulder, she spoke, cryptically, "Andi ... I have a feeling you're a lot more special than what any of us knows."

Andrea washed the pill down with the last of her water, noticing that it was something much stronger than aspirin. She rose from the table and walked to the tree in the living room, admiring the gorgeous ornaments. David approached from behind, and sidled up beside her, studying the familiar ornaments. He reached around and removed one from the back side of the tree, and handed it to her, taking notice of her bruised, bleeding lip. "This is the one I made in kindergarten," he offered, laughingly. "Mom keeps everything."

Andrea studied the glue and cinnamon gingerbread man, smelling the cloves and spices, surprised at their pungency after all this time. She smiled warmly, and handed it back to David. "It's beautiful," she said, honest in her appraisal.

"Well, then," he grinned, "let's just put this little beauty right out here where everyone can appreciate this mighty fine work of art," he teased. He hung his humble contribution to the holiday on a prominent bough then stood back, admiring his creation.

"Andi, are you surviving this McCormick family Christmas? I know we can certainly be a motley crew."

Andrea gave him a weary, but pleasant look. "David, your family is awesome ... I just wish I had met you all much sooner."

David gave her an appreciative smile back, quickly followed by a look of regret. "Andi, I'm ... I'm pretty sure I was the one who busted your lip last night."

She shot him a circumspective look askance. "And yanked my hair out by the roots?" Her words were not teasing, nor were they venomous.

"Yeah," he said, showing even more remorse for his brutality. His voice took a downward spiral. "Matt let me work him over pretty good, as well."

"Let you?"

He nodded. "He could have stopped me the instant I approached him ... he had the skill."

As her forgiving nature finally surfaced, Andrea dismissed her friend's admission. Impressed by his honesty, she offered, "It's okay, Davy ... Matt says you saved our lives," she said gently.

David studied Andrea for a long moment, thinking what a very fine woman she was, then looked up at the top of the tree which stood several feet taller than his 6'2" height. "That's Matt's ornament ... up there."

She followed his gaze up. "The star?" she questioned, dubiously.

"Yeah. One year ... it was snowy and frosty, just like today ... Matt and I were in here tossing around a football, burning up excess energy, something Mom never allowed in the house. I caught Matt's gentle pass then let go with a long, hard pass back ... it went all a kilter, knocked the old, cheap, tin star right off the tree and clear through the window."

Andrea's eyebrows shot up. "That must have been some pass!"

A sheepish grin crossed David's face. "I was young and stupid ... I told Mom that Matt had thrown the ball ... I never did tell her the truth; but neither did he. He understood how terrified I was of Stormy—at that young age—and the consequences she would dish out for disobeying her house rules. Matt deliberately made himself the target for all her wrath." David gazed at the tree, remembering. "He had just gotten his driver's license a few days before, and Mom took the keys away for two weeks; but after that, he drove all the way to Burlington, signed up for a soldering class, and created this beautiful star out of stained-glass and light-weight, flexible metal—it's his own design. Then he gave it to her on Christmas Eve with both our names on the gift tag ... after threatening to knock the crap out of me if I ever lied, or tried to pull that stunt again."

David studied the star. "That's the kind of guy Matt is...." He rested his hands on his hips, "He would make one heck of a family man—and one hell of a father."

Andrea took another long, admiring look at the star, and then appraised the enormously large window. "Who paid for the windowpane?"

"Who do you think?"

"Matt," they answered in unison, grinning, knowingly, at each other.

David hung his thumbs over the side pockets of his jeans. "You know, Andi, I'd only had two short conversations with Matt before that ugly scene went down last night, but I can assure you that the most important thing on his mind, all these months, was keeping you safe."

"Keeping me safe?" She repeated, puzzlement clouding her eyes. "Why would he feel a responsibility to keep me safe? I thought he was investigating me."

"He was, but that was just one part of his assignment ... his orders were to investigate and protect."

"You're kidding ... they actually put him in that awkward position?" she questioned, defiance settling on her face. David nodded, and Andrea shook her head in disbelief.

"It was all a part of their corrupt, grand plan."

She let out a loud sigh, "David, I have a question for *you* ... when you were at the *News* ... were you," she stammered, hesitantly, "my friend ... or just an agent?"

Dismayed by the question, David turned, immediately, and grabbed her by the shoulders. Looking her square in the eye, he reassured her, "I was both, Andi ... I was both."

"So it's possible to be both?" she questioned.

"Absolutely ... you get a sense of who's trustworthy, and who's not!"

A look of relief crossed her face. She reached up and wrapped her arms around his shoulders, giving him a huge, sisterly hug.

"David, I'm so sorry you were put in a position that endangered your life, but I'm so grateful you were there, and for everything you've done. You've been a fantastic friend." She lowered her arms, "Thanks for sharing that information about Matt—it explains why he...." She paused, "it explains a lot." She gave him another warm hug.

David started to walk away, but turned back around. A circumspective look crept onto his face. "Andi, I feel I should warn you ... Matt knows

488

exactly how damned good looking he is, but he views it as more of a curse than a blessing. He has a tendency to shy away from people who try to make it a big issue … he's always been that way."

Andrea closed her eyes momentarily, and smiled her acknowledgement. "Got it," she answered. "Thanks for the heads-up."

Mischievousness began to shine in little brother's eyes, and he threw out a question with indifference. "Andi … has he told you he likes to dance?" She shook her head. "That's how he relaxes after a kick-ass mission."

She shot him a surprised look, "Ballroom?" she asked, thinking she knew the answer. He certainly had the posh and courtliness.

David had nothing else to say, but grinned, saucily.

Andrea pushed away. "Aw, Davy … please don't tell me he's a stripper," she whined, letting her voice drop with indignation.

"Oh, g-a-w-d no," David laughed. "At least I don't think he's added that to his skill-set. Matt's into the urban street stuff … and I heard him say, just recently, that he'd really like to learn the *Anaconda*."

Andrea batted her eyes shut, thinking she was dreaming. When she opened them, David gave her a knowing look, nodded and winked. "Make sure he tells you the story about the socks." He walked away grinning, scampishly.

Andrea's heart warmed, as she acknowledged how incredibly charming the McCormick brothers could be. The Reverend and Mrs. McCormick had done a magnificent job as parents.

Suddenly, a strong sense of guilt possessed her—guilt for all the violence Shaun had visited on this beautiful, loving family. A frenzied, feverish feeling came over her. Like the babies in the NAS unit at the hospital, she felt ready to crawl out of her skin.

She looked around the room, trying to hide her angst. Seeing that everyone seemed to be happily preoccupied at the moment, she sat down on the strategically placed loveseat, angled, just so, to create a private alcove and an observation point for both the beautifully decorated tree and the wintery snow scene outside the window.

She picked up a copy of *Log Home Living*, from the library table behind the couch, and began to mindlessly thumb through the pages. Not a single one of the pictures in the magazine compared in charm with the McCormick home.

She looked up from the glossy pages. Tracker was suddenly at her feet, playfully growling, dragging and chewing on the end flaps of a small, brown, cardboard box. A piece of hempen rope, knotted and frayed, lay on top of a stack of 5"x 7" photographs. Fearing that the dog would destroy the contents, she rose and grabbed the box away from him, noticing that the skunk odor had been replaced by the strong smell of vinegar. She sat back down on the couch with the box between her hands. Seeing that they were photos of Matt, she curiously began to sift through the stack.

The picture on top was of Matt, the DEA agent, tough and austere. She tucked the photo underneath the stack, and looked at the next one. This photo framed a multi-national taskforce unit, just returned from an important, secret mission. Andrea gasped. *Matt served on a multi-national taskforce unit? That was really serious stuff.*

The next one, in reverse chronological order, had him standing front and center in the White House Oval Office in full-dress uniform—as a Navy Seal. The President of the United States stood behind him, placing a blue ribbon around his neck. She recognized the dangling gold medal—the Medal of Honor. Andrea lifted her eyes from the photo, still gasping. Shaun had been right—McCormick was a War Hero. She blinked back tears as she reveled in his life-long service and dedication to his country.

She looked, again at the photo. The Reverend and Mrs. McCormick looked on, great pride showing in their demeanor. David stood behind Mom and Dad; but who was the woman, dressed to impress, standing next to Matt—a woman wearing a less-than-impressed expression on her face? The realization struck her hard—she was Matt's wife.

Andrea's green-eyed monster returned, then quickly dissipated. This was the woman who had aborted Matt's child, full-term, just for spite … the woman who had drowned!

She quickly tucked away the photo, and dropped her gaze to the next one. The sight of it almost sent her off the couch. It looked to be the original photo of the one run in the three-year-old newspaper article of the young war hero from Afghanistan, the one that had sat on her desk for weeks. The one she had eventually stuck in her desk drawer, and never gotten around to reading. "My God," she whispered, "this can't be happening!" Her front page hero was McCormick?

She sat frozen in incredulity for an endless moment.

Photos of his first and second tours in Afghanistan came next.

Beneath those photos, was one of a very serious Matt, the West Point Cadet, in military dress uniform, looking straight into the camera, with chin tucked, and mouth unsmiling beneath a low riding cap. Golden bars indicating his success at reaching 2nd Lieutenant, glinted in the bright sunlight; but his eyes shone just as bright as his newly attained butter bars. She could almost hear the spirituous Hoo-ahs in the background. Andrea sucked in a deep, full breath, wondering why these photos had just been tossed into a box. Then she saw the labeling on the side: *Media Photos*.

She sat in solemnity as the facts penetrated her senses. This funny guy, as his mother called him, might crack jokes and run around in holey jeans, but Matt McCormick was quite the accomplished man. She hadn't been aware that a warrior could move around from service to service the way McCormick had done. She let out a heavy sigh, and uncovered the last picture in the stack.

Suddenly, her heart skipped a beat, and her eyes froze on the image. Staring back at her, in full color, and full charm school personality, were the bright, smiling, intelligent eyes and wry, audacious grin of a fully decorated Eagle Scout—the very same boy who had saved her from the raging flood waters all those years ago.

As if by magic, Andrea shook off the veil of muddled thinking. At some deep level, she had been aware of this fact for months; but with all the grief, pain and chaos Shaun had caused in her life, her battered mind had suppressed and refused to accept what should have been obvious all along. Now, after all these years, she finally knew his name—Matthew Justice McCormick!

Sitting in a state of shock, Andrea was further caught off guard when Reverend McCormick walked over and sat down, not in the chair, but on the cushion beside her. He took the box from her hands, taking no notice of its contents, laid it aside. He gently lifted her hands and sandwiched them between his own. "Andi, I'm guessing that you're experiencing a feeling of guilt, about now, for your association with Shaun. Am I right?"

A wan, telling smile crossed her face. It was a very blunt question, but Andrea welcomed it. "How did you know?" She searched the room for Matt. He was nowhere to be seen.

"It's inevitable … for a good person to feel remorse when innocent people get hurt," he offered.

"I understand that, but the part I don't understand is how this family can even tolerate having *me*—Shaun Fitzgerald's wife, in this house, after everything he did."

This was the emotion he'd hoped would surface. The Reverend closed his eyes, and shook his head. "Sweetheart, you were never a part of Shaun's crime—you did no harm. From what Matt has told me—you were taken hostage."

Hostage? Andrea sucked in her breath. She had never considered her circumstances in that light; but yes, that was exactly what had happened. Shaun had moved in and taken control of her home, her money, and her life.

Now, Rev. McCormick moved to the edge of the couch and turned to face her. He reached for her other hand and held them both tightly in his own. "Andi, I can assure you … you have nothing to feel guilty about. Ask for forgiveness, if that would make you feel better; but don't take on the responsibility of paying for a demented man's crime."

Matt carried in a load of firewood, laid a log on the fire, and then stood by with one foot propped up on the raised, stone hearth, resting his arm comfortably on his thigh. With poker in hand, and with eyes trained on Andrea, he waited patiently as the new log caught fire.

He had watched her talk, first to Zoe and then to David, and now to his dad, feeling grateful that they were all here for her; but he could tell, by her demeanor, that she was more than exhausted. They would both need to sleep for the next several days—to heal. He wondered if it might be better if she stayed here tonight, where his mother could keep an eye on her. No, he decided, quickly. She needed to be with him—for both their sakes; but he would let her decide, whether or not, she wanted any further involvement with him.

Andrea locked eyes with Matt's father, and tried to swallow the lump in her throat. "And you can honestly say that you don't hate me for all that has happened to your family?"

The Reverend dropped his head in a manner reminding her of Matt when he was feeling strong emotion, "Andi, I preach forgiveness," he said simply, his voice taking on a richer, deeper tone, "but you're not to blame for what happened to this family—you just happened to be born to a man who owned a company ... a company that someone else wanted for nefarious reasons—it's that plain and it's that simple."

Sudden anger bubbled up in Andrea's chest and throat, and she thrust her chin forward in defiance. Her words came out, fast and furious, "I'm quite certain that I will *never* be able to forgive Shaun Fitzgerald for the harm he brought to the people I love!"

Reverend McCormick paused, and took a long look at the distraught, young woman, then raised his gaze towards the fireplace, to his son. He pursed his lips, "Andi ... there's something you have a right to know ... you're not in this thing alone." The aging, battle-tested minister prayed that the young woman was strong enough to handle what he was about to reveal. "Brantley Stone or Shaun Fitzgerald, as you knew him, once lived just down the road from here. Clint, Matt and he grew up together, played together as kids, and later played on sports teams together. He ate most of his meals right here with his feet under our table. He even went to church with us on Sunday mornings." Something groaned, inside the man. "Those three boys were inseparable ... they were the three musketeers, the three amigos, the three stooges. You never saw one without the other two. Often times, Donnie Donahue would join them."

"Sheriff Donahue?" she asked, awe-shocked.

"All and the same," he offered. And then one day, for whatever reason, Bran changed. He embraced a radical group and declared himself our enemy."

Andrea sat in dazed silence.

"We've *all* lost on this go-around." The experienced minister sucked in a deep, sorrowful breath, and let it out, slowly. Then he raised his chin with determination. "I'm going to tell you the same thing I would tell Matt, or anyone else in this family: if you can't find it in your heart to forgive the man, then at least, don't let him steal one more precious moment from you ... start living your own good life."

Too stunned to recognize the second shock wave as it steam-rolled over her, Andrea tried to imagine the whole tragedy through the family's eyes—through Matt's eyes. He had just killed two of his boyhood friends.

They stood, and he gave her a compelling smile. "Find your happy place, Andi—you deserve it," he said. Before walking away, he grabbed her hand, turned it palm up, and placed her smartphone in the middle. "You left this at the shop a day or two ago ... I took the liberty of charging it up."

Tracker circled the hearthrug a couple of times, then, finally, stretched out next to McCormick. Matt's grandmother came in, lifted the brown, Vermont Teddy Bear with its big, red bow from her favorite quilt-draped, antique rocker. She sat down, plopping the bear into her lap, as though it were a child. She started rocking away, gazing sadly into the fire.

Matt quickly finished his task, then shoved a leather ottoman up close beside her and sat down. He planted his booted feet firmly in front of him, as he prepared for serious conversation. He felt a need to apologize for being away so long. The observant Tracker, stretching and yawning, once again sought out McCormick, and lay down at his feet.

Looking into his grandmother's aged face, wrinkled but wizened, Matt recognized the look of loneliness.

"Hey you," he teased, playfully, raising his hands, shielding himself with a defensive move, lest she hurl the bear at him. She didn't. He nodded towards the fire, "Just exactly what is it that you see in those flames, Grandma?" He spoke in a soft voice, tender but upbeat.

Shook loose from her reminiscence, she raised her chin in the true McCormick investigative fashion. She gave him a wan smile. "Oh ... my boy ... I was just remembering all the joyful time your grandfather and I had together."

Knowing how much she had loved his grandfather, he scratched his neck and feigned embarrassment for its added effect. "You talking about all those nights the two of you set the sheets on fire?"

"Oh, no," she chuckled, color rising to her cheeks. "Young man, you should show more respect to old ladies," she teased.

Matt shot her his best, crooked, smartass grin. "I assure you, Grams, there's no old lady here, and I *am* being respectful." Matt gazed into the fire as though, he too, could see his grandfather there. "When I was a kid ... growing up, Grandpa would tell me stories about the hard times the two of you had in the military, early on; but he always spoke of you in the highest, most glowing, red-hot terms. He thought you were the smartest, most beautiful woman in the world ... you were his heartthrob ... his night and day ... the love of his life!" Matt looked into his grandmother's misty eyes, then turned his eyes back to the fire, lost in his own memories. "He always spoke of the two of you as though you were one person." He paused, thinking about what he had just said. "I was just a kid ... I didn't understand it then." He bounced a look off Andrea, then turned his gaze back to his grandmother, giving her a long, serious look.

Her pale, thinning lips had spread into a perkier smile. "I was quite the hell-raiser in my younger years ... I used to get so mad at him," she groused. "He was forever being chased by wild, loose women."

He chuckled softly, and reached for her hand. "You shouldn't have worried ... Grandpa knew how to handle that problematic situation."

The sound of regret crept into her voice. "I wish ...." she sighed, heavily. "I wish ... now ... that I had been a little kinder."

Matt pursed his lips, and gave his head a shake to the side, "Nah, you kept him sharp!" he offered, matter-of-factly, leaning into his elbows, "That's exactly what the General wanted." She slowly nodded in agreement. He shot her another wisenheimer look, "And just because you can't *remember* all those long, cold, winter nights," he deliberately teased, "it doesn't mean they didn't happen."

She sucked in a deep breath, "Ah ... but there lies the problem, Dr. McCormick." She finally confessed, "I actually do remember ... I haven't lost my mind, or my memory—yet!"

McCormick smiled, gently. "I know it's hard, Grandma; but those warm, loving memories of all those years of blessings ... that's Grandpa's *gift* for you, today." As he spoke the words, his hands shot forward, as though something special lay nestled in them.

She stared at his upturned palms, feeling as though her grandson had, literally, handed her a most precious gift. She sank deeper into her memories.

Soon, she shot Matt a ratcheted up smile. "Matt, you always did have a way of getting to the bottom line. Instead of seeing my memories as something that drains, and steals away my happiness today, I should view them as an addition to my life, like a gorgeous bow on a package."

Finding his emotions too raw to appreciate that particular image, McCormick quickly dismissed her analogy. "Or a humongous pay-off on a life insurance policy," he added, whimsically.

"Or like the gift of a clever, badass grandson," she laughed.

"There you go," he breathed out, softly, realizing for the very first time that he desired the presence of grandchildren at the end of a very long life. He flashed a tender smile, followed by an inquisitive look. "Grams ... I've always wondered ... is it hard for you to look at me? Everyone says I look just like Gramps."

Another wan smile crossed her lips, and she reached over to pat his jean-clad knee, feeling the prosthetic she knew nothing about. Her eyes batted shut for a long moment. When she opened them again, they were misty, expressing a new sadness. "Matt, your grandfather was a man of great integrity, strength, and character ... you not only look like him, but you're a lot like him...." She paused, "only better ... you've added humor to the mix." She looked deep into his eyes. "You wonder if it bothers me to look at you ... no, grandson, no ... you're the gift that keeps on giving ... *you* are the gift."

Matt dropped his head, feeling embarrassed by her words of praise. They sat together in silence, staring into the flames, feeling the bond that only a family member can offer.

At last, McCormick stirred, comfortable with his emotions. Thanks to his grandmother, he was finally beginning to get a handle on the man he needed to be from here on out, the man he was destined to be—his grandfather; and that was more than okay with him.

Thinking that it was time her grandson started making his own sweet memories, and realizing that she had ammunition to use in that regard, Grams shot back. "I can't help but notice, Matthew, that you haven't taken your eyes off that beautiful, young woman all day."

Matt's face flushed. Granny Mac had just turned the tables on him. But she was right. He hadn't been able to pull his eyes away from Andrea. He tried to change the subject. "I ... was really surprised to learn you two knew each other ... how well do you know her, Grams?"

She shook her head, "The only thing I know is that she's a talented, young journalist, an excellent speaker, and an absolute s-a-i-n-t." McCormick's eyes widened. "You should have seen the way that girl cared for all those drug addicted babies in the hospital the night the nurses all came down with the flu. Andi not only rocked the place, figuratively speaking, but she cooed, and sang lullabies. She changed diapers, and gave the poor little dears baths while they wailed and writhed. I understand it was almost daybreak before they finally found a nurse well enough to work the morning shift." They gazed across the room at Andrea just as his dad was rising from the couch, giving her a hug. Together they watched Nicole graciously deliver a cup of tea, cookies and a bright Christmas throw, before returning to the kitchen.

"Why is she here today?"

Not wanting to go any further into the sordid details, Matt rose to his feet, and shoved the ottoman back in place. With eyes a glimmer, he shot a wink and a nod at his grandmother. "Grams, I'll explain it all later; but I'm sure that if you stare into those hot, leaping flames long enough, you'll figure it all out yourself." He leaned over and kissed her forehead, giving her hand a squeeze, allowing time for her to squeeze back; then he took long strides across the mammoth-sized room.

Grams turned her face to the fire, her eyes alive with hope. She'd figured it out hours ago.

CHAPTER 55

Matt approached the couch from behind. He saw that Andrea had kicked off her boots and was leaning back against the arm of the couch. A cheerful cranberry and hunter-green Christmas pillow had been placed behind her back. She had one leg tucked under, and the matching throw covered the other. She held the delicate, china cup with both hands and sipped with a distant look in her eye.

"You okay?" he asked, trying not to appear intrusive. Curiously, he noticed the short length of knotted rope that lay in her lap, recognizing it as his own.

Looking up from the cup's rim, and over the back of the couch, she gave him a brief, exhausted smile, "Yeah … I'm just tired."

Now a pensive look settled on her face, as she avoided meeting his eyes, seemingly intent on exploring the view of the large, frozen lake through the window. He could tell something had her mind disquieted. He wished he was a mind reader. Was she about to start screaming at him like a Banshee?

Following her eyes with his own, he offered, "That's Lake McCormick—it's a private lake … I think, in the future, we'll need to take its name off all maps and signs … for security reasons." She shot him a puzzled look, but said nothing, unable to process anything further.

He walked around the end of the couch, took her empty cup, and set it on the end table. Then he offered her both his hands, and helped her up from the couch, suddenly taken aback as he glimpsed his Eagle Scout media photo lying atop a cushion. He hadn't seen it in years. Ushering her to the window, he pointed outward, "…and, that long, silver ribbon, meandering through the woods over there … that's McCormick's Creek." He chuckled to himself, "God … I used to tromp all up and down that *thang,*" he offered,

498

deliberately slaying the last word for her benefit. He shot her a crooked grin, "I all but lived out there … my grandfather actually called me McCreek."

Her face showed no expression, but like a sleeping volcano, emotions bubbled beneath the surface.

Concerned by her reticence, he quietly sucked air and jammed his fingers into his hip pockets, thinking he recognized a rejection coming his way. His eyes glazed as he stared out the window, and a sudden memory popped into his mind. Merely trying to make conversation to cover the awkward silence, he offered, "When I was about seventeen, I rescued a young girl from that swollen riverbank in the middle of a flashflood." He wondered why that particular memory had suddenly surfaced, then immediately regretted saying anything—he hadn't meant it to sound like bragging.

Andrea sucked in a deep breath, and let it out slowly. "And you did it using standard Boy Scout apparatus: ropes, knots, pulleys—and kisses."

McCormick's head snapped around. His sharp eyes narrowed as he looked at her askance. Now, his mind flooded with the sounds, the scents, and the emotions that accompanied the memory; and he slowly, blushingly, nodded his head in confirmation. How did she know? His jaw went slack as he came up with the only possible explanation. With color drained from his face, and already knowing the answer, his question came out as a mere wisp, "That was you?"

Like the ice-covered lake, the frosted creek and everything frozen outside the window, Andrea's eyes began to shimmer. "No...." she said softly, trying to smile through her swollen, bleeding lips, "that was you."

McCormick looked deep into her exhausted, misty eyes, and found staring back at him, the same young girl he had rescued all those many years ago—the girl with the teal blue eyes—the girl who had stolen his heart for a lifetime.

He closed his eyes and dropped his head—*Bitchy Reason Number Four*, he thought, as his heart dropped to the pit of his stomach.

He stood, silent, as though shell shocked. Details from the memory rushed forward in his mind. He remembered that day in late May, as though it were yesterday. It had been raining for hours in the higher elevations, and flash flood warnings had scrawled across the TV screen all afternoon. McCormick had felt caged, trapped inside the house.

Courted and recruited by Army's football coach, McCormick had been mentally preparing for Beast, West Point's first of two summer basic training camps, but his mother was still trying to dissuade him, going around and around about his choice of schools. She kept reminding him that he was too much of a "smart mouth" to make it through the extremely disciplined academy. *Thanks for the vote of confidence, Mother,* he thought.

She had wanted him to go to medical school—the area needed a doctor; she had argued. She had also been pushing him to cash in on his good looks, but that one really sent him into a state of delirium. He'd made his decision, made his commitment—he was going to West Point. In spite of his set goals, his mother had still remained diabolically opposed to his decision—the military already had her husband, and one of her sons, she argued. With his Dad away on a mission, their differences of opinion had left him feeling demoralized and emasculated, which was often his mother's way.

He had slipped out the back door to clear his head, and to walk off his frustration. Knowing that the bridge two miles downstream would soon be washed out, he went to check it out, as he usually did. He had approached the bridge and stood in the damp, dusky evening, listening to the wind swishing through the pines, feeling the raindrops beat against his face. He thrived on being outside in any kind of weather.

A sudden roar rose behind him, and with great force, a wall of water came crashing down upon him, instantly pushing his head and shoulders forward, as a strong undertow swept him off his feet, pulling him under. At last, he surfaced, gasping for breath—and for life.

He swam to the nearest tree, clinging to its limbs as the rapid force of the water tugged at him, threatening to pull his clothes from his body— threatening to pull him under a second time. He remembered praying. Having just barely escaped drowning, and being hit by debris, he felt muddleheaded.

Once the initial onslaught was over, McCormick had tried to swim away, when, suddenly, he heard the voice of a young girl, singing angelically from the top of a Weeping Willow tree nearby. He recognized her song—a Christmas carol.

With adrenaline coursing through his young body, he swam over to the tree, and with curiosity, climbed into its low-hanging branches, dripping with rain. Dazed, he looked up.

There she sat. Dressed in a gauzy white shirt and khaki hiking shorts and boots, the girl was tanned and beautiful, her skin glistening in the rain; but the thing that enchanted him the most, were her teal-blue eyes, intelligent and illuminate. When she spoke, her words took wings with depth and meaning—surely this was a wood nymph, he thought, if only for an instant. In his youthful imagination, he felt that he was being lured into the tree.

She was obviously bright, and she hadn't gushed on about herself, her nails, or about how handsome a guy he was; nor did she try to seduce him, as so many of the young, local girls had done. Still, her presence had made him feel like a man.

He remembered that she had been a little younger than he, but her replies to his questions were adroit and clever. She was extremely skilled at making meaningful conversation one minute, then becoming joyfully, light-hearted, and teasing the next. He could tell she was grounded in something other than the culture of their decade.

When she fell into the creek, he had dived in after her with no thought, what-so-ever, of the consequences to himself. So completely in tune with each other, and not wanting their time together to come to an end, McCormick had deliberately taken the long way around. He took fire trails, side trails, sunken trails, deer trails, forsaken trails—any trail that would prolong their walk into town; but their time together did, finally, come to an end.

Early the following morning, McCormick had hiked up to the campground, in search of her, but the family had broken camp and moved on. When his dad returned the following afternoon, he shared his story and the two of them had tried to track the family down. As luck would have it, everything had been paid for with cash, leaving no trail; but he had been haunted by her beautiful, young face, quick wit, and sparkling personality ever since that day. He had carried her in his memory, and in his heart, to West Point, to Afghanistan, and to Taxpayer Island, and back.

Now, he focused on Andrea's swollen face. *Welcome home,* he wanted to say to her; but when he opened his mouth to speak, his breath would go no farther than his throat, nor could he get the words past his dry, cracked lips, and jaw—now swollen to twice its normal size. He reached for her trembling hand, and held it tight. His heart raced when she gave his hand a hard squeeze in return.

When, at last, he could speak, he murmured, "I could never get you out of my mind."

His voice was so deep and rich that it sounded, to Andrea, as though he'd pulled it from the very depths of his soul.

With eyes veiled with emotional pain, and the dark shadow of agony across her face, she whispered in a faltering voice, soft and caressing, "You've been ... right here," she thumped her heart, "all these years ... and I've missed you so-o-o much!" Her long lashes, thick and dark, released hot, burning teardrops that skittered down the full length of her face.

"Matt!" David's commanding voice pulled them from their tenderhearted reunion, "You about ready to get started?"

"Give me a minute," Matt answered, a tinge of impatience sounding in his voice, his hungry eyes roving over Andrea's eyes and face.

"Go ... take care of whatever is needed," she offered. "I ... I need to lie down for a while," she said, her voice husky, and barely audible. Slowly, she turned and mounted the steps to the loft, reluctant to leave his side.

Reading her mind, he gave her a reassuring nod. "I'll be here," he promised, his deep, throaty voice croaking like an old man; yet suddenly, McCormick felt like a seventeen-year-old kid.

"Aw geez ... you guys all smell like smoke!" Missy complained, as she walked into the room carrying a bottle of deodorizing spray. From the top of the stairs, Andrea watched the teen spritz the air as her brothers set up musical equipment.

Spoken like a true sister, she thought, watching the sock-footed girl plop on to the couch with an elaborately decorated sugar cookie in one hand, her cell phone in the other. Andrea realized, at that moment, that Missy reminded her of her sister. She would enjoy spending time with her—once she found a way to break through the ice. Maybe she would invite her to go on the shopping trip with Zoe.

Matt strummed an acoustic guitar close to his ear, until satisfied with its sound, and then moved to set up a microphone to suit his own height, as the rest of the family came through the door.

"Hey, Matt!" the young girl yelled. "What did you do undercover?"

"Anything and everything," he answered, eluding details.

Before he could give her a better answer, the young girl asked, "Have you learned Dierks Bentley's songs, yet?"

"I'm probably a couple of years behind," Matt offered, giving his little sister a wry grin. "Which one are you talking about?"

"Riser."

McCormick shot a questioning look at his brother. "Know it?" David gave him an affirmative nod.

He does sing, Andrea realized, imagining his deep, sexy voice set to music.

Giving up thoughts of a nap, she returned to the railing over-looking the stage area.

"Every time I heard that song," his sister enthused, "it reminded me of you … and I'd cry … of course that was before I found out you weren't really dead," she quipped, deliberately teasing.

McCormick grimaced at her remark, but teased back, "Well I ain't dead yet, kid." His gaze bounced to the loft, still shell-shocked by Andrea's revelation. He was surprised to find her standing, frozen in place, at the top of the stairs, staring back at him with sober eyes. *I ain't dead yet,* he thought, determinedly.

"I'll give it a try," he promised his sister. He winked at the little duckling who had turned into a beautiful swan during his absence; but McCormick saw only the cute, little girl who, in times past, constantly begged him to push her higher on the rope swing. He wished he'd made himself more available.

A few minutes later, Andrea watched David go to the electric guitar and start tweaking the strings, all-the-while stealing nervous glances at Zoe, who was helping his mother set out punch and cookies for guests. Andrea enjoyed witnessing this other side of David.

She could hear the lively banter between brothers as they turned on the amplifiers and hooked up two more microphones. It was quite obvious that they had always been very close, even before Matt dropped out of the picture, but today they seemed especially so, following their close brush with death—and their early morning snowman caper. At one point, Matt had seriously rubbed his jaw, and groused to David, "Man, you must have packed a whole lifetime of frustration into that wallop, bro." The microphone clearly carried his voice across the room.

David had grinned back with a degree of satisfaction and answered his older brother, "Yeah, but will you stop whining. I had orders to shoot you ... I just couldn't find a spot on your freaking body that hadn't already been shot all to hell!"

Andrea wept at his words, but McCormick, for some reason, had found his little brother's comment hilarious, and accepted it as a sidesplitting joke. He'd laughed and grabbed his painful shoulder with his right hand, while raising the other to his brother's for a high-five. "That was a good one," the chortling McCormick offered.

CHAPTER 56

To Andrea's surprise, a line of friends and neighbors had learned of the fire, and hearing numerous rumors, began to file into the large room, mingling with the family in a convivial gathering. A glance out the window told her they had come by sleigh or snowmobile. The men approached Matt and David, shaking hands and having short, friendly conversations, offering their help. Then they sauntered to the back of the room to talk with Reverend McCormick before sitting down in folding chairs set up for the occasion.

Noticing that Farah was among them, Andrea watched her walk straight to Matt. Expecting him to give her a courtesy condolence, she was astonished when Matt gave the woman a big bear hug, and gently took her aside, guiding her to the loveseat, where the two sat in serious conversation. As the long minutes ticked away, Andrea wished she could listen in on their conversation.

Soon everyone was ready to begin, but suddenly, a long pregnant hush fell over the room. Finally, the restive audience began to stir. Whispered voices filled the room, as they sat staring at the empty drummer's seat— Clint had always been the drummer.

McCormick took a look around the room. Mom, Dad, and Grams sat in the back. They appeared to be grieving. With all the excitement, the obvious had escaped them all—it was time for a reality check. Deeply feeling his brother's absence, he took the stage, and leaned into the live microphone. He spoke in a gentle voice. "The family's all missing our brother Clint … wasn't he one heck of a guy?" Low murmurs of agreement traveled across the room. An *Amen* came from somewhere in the crowd. "Clint wore a lot of different hats … one of which was drummer. In losing him, we sadly lost a very fine musician; but, if there's a drummer in the house, would you please come help us out with our loss?" His voice crackled with emotion. A sad, uncomfortable moment passed between all the family members. No one responded.

Preparing to speak again, Matt returned to the microphone. Suddenly, from out of the stillness, came a small, thin voice across the large room, "I'm a drummer."

All heads turned towards the loft, surprised, thinking, at first, that it was a joke.

"I'm a drummer," Andrea repeated.

Matt leaned into the microphone and said in a surprised, serious tone, "Well then, Miss Daye, come join our band."

As Andrea descended the steps, Matt and David shot each other questioning glances. Seeing what passed between them, she gave Matt a challenging stare, her palms spreading upward, "What? I was in a band … in college."

Crossing the stage to the 5-piecee drum kit, she positioned herself comfortably and confidently on the seat. Warming up with a well-practiced, professionally accomplished drumroll, she then went smoothly into a rhythmic opening, setting the tempo for Matt's first song.

Matt and David cocked eyebrows that said: *who knew*?

Doubled-down on shock, but tamping it all down, Matt announced in a light, upbeat voice with a bit of showbiz flair: "Ladies and gentlemen, performing *l-i-v-e*, and together for the first time ever … I give you … the *Red Springs, Smoky Jeans Band*." Surprised at the name Matt had given the band, David and Andrea snorted, gagged, and fanned the air with their hands as though planned.

The music started, first David's electric guitar, then the drum intensified. Finally, Matt began to sing to his little sister in his baritone voice, deep and rich: *"Lay your pretty head down on my shoulder … You don't have to worry anymore…."* When sis's phone chimed out a loud suspenseful ring tone, she lost spoke loudly into the phone. "Hey, Zach, remember that *extinct* lady? She's here … you'll never guess what she's doing."

Matt shook his head in amazement, and smiled laughingly at his audience. Then he zeroed in on Andrea. *"I'm a riser, I'm a get down low so I can lift you higher."* They locked eyes, understanding and reliving the same memories of their creek crossing, cliff climbing adventures.

The music proved to be therapeutic for everyone. They had all sung the familiar carols, with Matt beginning to wrap up the session with *How Great Thou Art* on the acoustic guitar—by request from his mother. Matt, as it turned out, was an extraordinarily talented musician, and Andrea hung on every note, never having heard a finer presentation. She marveled that his injuries seemed not to affect his golden voice, clear and professional. His intricate finger work, up and down the strings, could not be improved upon—and his mother had sobbed through the entire song. When he transitioned into *It Is Well With My Soul* without changing cords, even his dad broke down in tears.

At song's end, loud cheers and plaudits filled the room.

Matt leaned in closer to Andrea, in order to be heard above the din of the crowd. He asked, "Andi, do you have a request?"

There was no need to think about it, so she answered immediately, "Do you know, *Mary Did You Know?*"

A smug smile crept across McCormick's bruised, cracked lips, and he nodded, as he recognized the song. It the tune he'd heard his little brother whistle through gutsy, puckered lips in the middle of the rain-drenched Peruvian rainforest, and the song that had cascaded over Andrea's shower curtain, just a few short weeks ago; but it was much more than that. This was the hallelujah, the song of praise he'd heard tripling from the top branches of the willow tree, while an enemy undertow threatened to pull him under, all those many years ago.

"Why don't you sing it with me—Pentatonix style," he urged.

Andrea searched his eyes, seeing something shimmering from within, something she'd never seen there before—hope. Her heart leaped at his request. The chance to sing with Matthew J. McCormick, aka, McCreek, once again, went beyond her wildest dreams; but as sudden doubt filled her eyes, she blushed and whispered, in all honesty, "I may not be able to do it … without tears."

His eyes smiled with golden tenderness, and he shot her that wonderful crooked grin she had grown to love. "Then let the good tears roll," he said.

Together, they began to hum the music without instrumental accompaniment. Matt turned, encouraging David to join them. As they began to lift their voices in song, Dad rushed forward to add his deep bass, and Zoe happily took the alto part, at David's behest. Matt motioned for

Missy, and she added her sweet, tender, soprano voice to the mix, singing an entire solo verse.

As the beat and spirit of the music filled the room, and Andrea's booming, angelic voice reached into the rafters and upper octaves, she slid off the stool, inviting the rest of the audience to join them. Soon everyone was on their feet, singing, clapping and rocking to the music. Even Farah's long skirt swished as she hugged herself and swayed to the music. From the stage, Andrea longed to throw her arms around the woman in commiseration, but she would leave that for another day.

As the song ended, they all began to rally around each other, but Matt yelled, "One more time!" Everyone, joyfully, repeated the song.

When the music ended, Reverend McCormick offered a prayer for those present, and the guests began to leave. With drumsticks still in hand, Andrea wandered over to the brothers, busily taking down the equipment. A pleased, happy look glowed on her face. Matt noticed.

"You two guys are, beyond a doubt, the best musicians I have ever had the pleasure to perform with," she said with enthusiasm. "How did you, with everything else you do, get so accomplished?"

"You tell her, Davy," Matt grinned, as he bent down to unplug the cord to one of the microphones.

"Well...." David stammered. "There's really not much to tell. When you grow up in this remote area, where the electricity is off for half the winter, you have to find ways to entertain yourself. Once you lose your power and your generator goes down, you pick up your guitar. Anything with strings is a Godsend. He bent down to pick up a guitar case. "It's either that or the sheep and goats," he smirked, over his shoulder as he nonchalantly walked away, carrying half the musical equipment with him.

McCormick turned to Andrea with just a hint of a smirk on his swollen lips. He added, "I'm sure that, by now, you know exactly where *my* proclivities lie."

She blushed, but said nothing as she walked to the drum kit, grateful that Matt was letting all her stupid accusatory goat remarks go unanswered. He followed with dogged steps.

As she laid the sticks atop the drums, McCormick reached around her shoulder, and gently covered her hand with his own, the heat searing through her. In a voice cracking with emotion and regret, he said, "Andi ... I was a stupid kid ... you were my first."

She looked up into his swollen face. Sometime during the day, he had trimmed his beard and mustache down to mere stubble; yet still, he looked so much the worse for his confrontation with Shaun Fitzgerald. His lips and taut jaw line, both bruised and bloody, were testimony to the strong force he'd stood up against, and defeated. The head area that had taken the butt of Shaun's rifle, had looked minor earlier in the day, but now showed indications of a deep, serious injury, marked by its dark purple coloring. The eye, itself, was red, presumably from a broken blood vessel, and was on its way to being completely swollen shut. He was much thinner, his body looking more like the young, warmhearted, seventeen-year-old kid she remembered. Her heart seared with jealousy, thinking of him with anyone else but her.

At last, she lifted hot, liquid eyes to meet his. "You were my only," she said softly.

Matt's mouth fell agape, as his mind immutably grasped the import of her words. His stare drilled straight through her—into that deep, dark corner of her soul. Feeling the complete ass, he collapsed to the drum seat, totally drained from the accumulated, emotional impact of the last several days. "My god, Andi ... I am so sorry." He reached out and pulled her to him.

Andrea parked, noncommittally, upon his knee; but he quickly gathered her up in his arms. Her head collapsed to his shoulder, and his cheek fell to the top of her head, his neck in dire need of support. Thinking he had destroyed the woman's life, he offered, "Andi ... I'm sorry."

Wrapping her arms around his diminished waistline, she rasped in a voice, completely depleted, "There's nothing to be sorry about, Matt ... I just never wanted anyone else—until I met you."

They snuggled closer, snickering softly at the conundrum, both fully grasping the illogical, unpredictable consequences of their unintended, youthful romp through the woods; but both realizing that their long search for the other was finally over. With tenderness, he raised her chin and looked deeply into her eyes, and slowly delivered a repeat performance of that first kiss—a kiss just like the one in the Writer's Block Lounge, months earlier; except for one difference. This time they knew each other—the good and the bad—they accepted and loved each other. This kiss had meaning, depth and promise ... and pain.

"Hey!" Once again, it was David's loud voice, sharp and scolding, that pulled them out of their dazed reverie. He entered the room, quickly closing the distance between them. Sounding every inch the tough, federal agent, he exclaimed, "Don't you two love birds realize you're sitting next to an open mic?"

In horror, they both looked up and around the room, appalled at who might have overheard their reminiscent divulgence of their youthful indiscretion; but, finding the room empty, their breaths collapsed in unison.

"Made you look!" David teased; but as he bent down and unplugged the microphone, shock had found its way to his face—he had heard every word! Now, his mouth broke into a slow grin as he came to understand what had been years in the making. He needn't have worried about the *shadow enemy* destroying their relationship. The enemy had been defeated years ago.

Now a female voice, strong and authoritative, suddenly spoke up from across the room. "Why don't you two *lovers* get a room ... one with all the amenities?" It was Stormy's voice. She stood holding the kitchen door ajar. Grams, Missy, Zoe and even Aunt Kat all stood, tittering with widened eyes, gaping mouths, and blushing faces. "I've made reservations for three glorious nights at *Forest Hills Regional Hospital*, Stormy teased. "That's the one for patients, who use their bodies as weapons of war. The *Christmas Goose* will pick you both up at your cabin. I'm in the process of baking more cookies right now, but be advised ... I'm your doctor ... I'll be on board ... any objections?" When no one dared speak a word, she said, "Good ... enjoy your very s-l-o-w sleigh ride home, but I want to see you both in my office before you leave here. Bundle up and stay warm; Dad's putting extra blankets in the sleigh ... he'll take care of everything around here."

Later, in Stormy's office, she handed Andrea an eight-hour painkiller and a bottle of water. After checking her vitals, she said, "Andi, what can I say ... you've literally been through hell and high water, and you need rest ... I can give you something to help you sleep. You still have some dehydration, and it's possible that you may have some smoke inhalation, as well—nothing serious, there. Your toes are recovering ... no frostbite damage." She paused, "but as your doctor, I'm afraid I do detect one very serious problem."

Andrea sucked in her breath, waiting for bad news.

"I'm sorry Andi, but I have found a very serious, acute case of lovesickness in all four chambers of your heart."

Andrea blushed, and her breath gushed out in a snigger. Stormy wiped the grin off her face and pulled down a frown. "However ... in checking Matt, earlier, I found that he is seriously dehydrated and needs to be on an IV drip. He's suffering from sleep deprivation, and needs several day's rest; but I need your help in keeping him awake for the next several hours ... he has a concussion and a cracked rib." Stormy wondered if she should say more. She decided to disclose everything. It was more than obvious that this young woman was madly in love with her son.

"Matt had started a round of antibiotics, but let'em slide while he was off chasing...." Stormy hesitated, uncertain of which name to use.

Andrea sighed, heavily, and finished the sentence for her, "Bran."

"As a result, Matt has pneumonia in his left lung; I've started a new round of antibiotics, but he needs to be hospitalized, stat." The doctor continued, "I've stopped the bleeding in his shoulder, but he needs a blood transfusion, and possible surgery; and he needs to take that prosthetic off for a while, for at least a couple of days. His jaw isn't broken, but we'll x-ray it, just to be on the safe side. His red eye is a direct result of both his head trauma, and his pneumonia ... I can fix all of that."

Stormy shot Andrea a wizened look. "But here's the deal ... Matt won't go to the hospital unless you agree to go with him; and girl, I have to add ... there must be a new pandemic going around this mountain, because he has the worst case of lovesickness I've seen in all my days of medicine!" She shot Andrea a smartass grin. "Bottom line ... he refuses to let you out of his sight."

Stormy reached for Andrea's hand, and her voice softened. "I should have acted hours ago, but Matt insisted that you both have the day with the family."

"I don't know how he was able to perform today," Andrea offered, commiseratively.

Stormy removed her stethoscope and laid it aside. "Girl ... I've got Matt so drugged up...." she chuckled, "he wouldn't know if he got sacked by a 300 pound linebacker; but, Sweetheart, he wasn't performing today ... Matt was praising."

A smile crossed Andrea's lips, and in heartfelt sincerity, she offered,

"Stormy, you do realize that you have raised a very, very good...." She started to say *man*; but seeing the twinkle in the older woman's eye, she amended her words, "Badass."

Wistfulness softened the lines on the doctor's face. "You know, Andi ... that's, actually, the highest compliment you could ever give me." A proud, radiant smile traveled clear to the bone as she plopped down on a stool. She chuckled, again, "But I'm afraid Matt deserves all the credit on that count."

Andrea shot her an understanding grin.

"Andi, let me have my son for three days, to heal his wounds ... and then the two of you can medicate, self-medicate, or whatever ... for the real problem ... deal?" The two women laughed and Andrea's hand shot to her lip, to keep it from splitting open again.

"Deal," she answered through her fingertips.

"Is there anything else I can help you with ... vitamins ... birth control?" Now the doctor appeared to blush.

"Andrea closed her eyes and shook her head. "No ... I want to give Matt children as soon as possible—if he'll have *me*."

A spirited moue of determinedness parked on the doctor's face, "Don't wait for him."

Andrea swallowed a surprised gulp. "Pardon?"

"Andi, Matt loves you ... more than life itself. And through," she chortled, "divine intervention, for lack of a better term ... the rest of the family has been more than apprised of the situation," she chuckled, again, "He's always loved you; but now he's got this crazy idea that marriage would be asking too much of *you*." She turned away and opened a cabinet, chattering, as though to herself. "Frankly, the pastor and I have been pining for grandchildren for over ten years ... and Grams swears she's not going to die until she's seen her beloved husband's likeness on the face of a great-grandson ... that would most likely be a child of Matt's."

Suddenly Andrea's mind quickened, giving birth to a, heretofore, unthinkable idea. She smiled, covertly, having stumbled upon a do-or-die mission.

"There's no better place to have a baby than right here in Vermont," the doctor was saying. She grinned, wryly, and plunked a bottle of pre-natal vitamins into Andrea's hands.

Finally, feeling sated with the tradition-filled celebration, Matt caught Andrea alone as she left his mother's medical office. Catching the far-away look in her eye, and suspicious of what had been discussed, he leaned close, and whispered in a low, ragged voice, "Still think you don't know anything about me?"

Andrea had succumbed to Stormy's homemade beeswax remedy for her painful mouth. Matt, on the other hand, had turned down his mother's offer. As they kissed, Andrea could feel the corner of his lip curl up, wryly, beneath her seriously, greasy ones. "I've wanted to do that ever since I was seventeen-years-old," he teased, returning an icepack to his jaw.

She thrust a water bottle into his hands. "You d-i-d do that at seventeen-years-old," she said, without subtly. Reading her mind, he gently brushed a slow hand across her cheek, her ear, and through her hair.

"I can't believe this is happening," she ruminated.

"Stop thinking so much," he offered, "and just drop into the chocolate." He gently dipped his lips to hers once more.

When his dad approached, dressed in barn clothes and boots, and carrying a man-sized snow shovel, they quickly shoved apart. Together, they all stepped out into the cold, frosty air.

Dad said, "Matt, that snowman sure meant the world to your mother." He gestured towards the stacked balls of snow.

"Davy and I had that all planned out before the Christmas I went AWOL," Matt answered, as all three pairs of boots clomped down the porch steps together.

Dad propped the shovel against the railing, and Matt and Andi started to crunch through the crusty snow when his dad called out to him. "Matt, I noticed that you have the old "fur ball" back.

McCormick froze. Not wanting to talk about it in front of Andrea, he answered, "Yup."

"Where'd he go?"

"Don't know ... guess he went looking for *me*," he said reticently.

"Where's he been all this time?"

Matt pursed his lips and gave his dad a hard, inquisitive stare, realizing that whatever the man was doing, he was doing it intentionally. Earlier, Matt had shared his dilemma, and a few laughs concerning the dog's behavior.

He answered, "Probably tried to swim the ocean, but I hear he ended up in a Husky Rescue center." Matt added, "I'm told some knock-out gorgeous wood nymph walked out of the forest one morning about a month ago ... and rescued him."

Andrea turned, and shot Matt a questioning glance, askance.

"And that one worked out alright?" His dad asked.

"So far."

His dad turned towards the house. "Well, Good-night, kids," he called from the porch, grinning like a Cheshire cat. He had helped Matt with many things over the years, and now, he'd helped him open up this particular— hard to approach—can of worms; but the two kids would just have to slug it out between themselves as to who, actually, owned the dog.

"Best to get *everything* out in the open," he advised, deliberately using the voice he used from the podium. Then he threw an unexpected taunt over his shoulder, "Of course, using a microphone is optional—unless you want the entire Green Mountain area to know where your proclivities lie." A huge, impish grin covered his face.

Matt and Andi shot each other discomfited looks.

"Say good-night, Old Man," Matt said through sniggers. "Merry Christmas!"

When they were out of earshot Andrea asked, "Why do you call him Old Man ... it sounds a bit disrespectful?"

"Not at all ... Old Man is a military term for a Commanding Officer," Matt offered. "Being called Old Man to an officer is like having a medal of distinction hung around his neck ... he served, he led, he conquered ... he survived; and that's great testimony to his skill as a soldier, and a leader. Dad certainly deserves that distinction ... I call him that out of great respect."

"So ... I could call you Old Man ... and not be disrespectful?"

"Never mind ... I'm not that needy ... yet."

Walking to the waiting horse and sleigh, Matt asked. "Andi, are you embarrassed by all of this attention?"

Knowing that he was referring to their youthful indiscretion being made public, she answered without hesitation, "Not really ... how about you?"

"Are you kidding ... I'm claiming bragging rights," he teased, shrewdly.

Andrea saw through the teasing, but threw him a captious warning glance, anyway.

"Are you sure you're okay with this hospital idea?" he asked.

"Yeah, sure ... as long as we don't have to share a bedpan ... "what did your dad mean about you getting your dog back? Fur Ball's my dog," she said adamantly.

"Well ... yeah, technically ... but he was ... *my* dog ... before he became *your* dog."

"I don't understand ... I got him from a rescue center."

"Yeah, but I lost him to a rescue center."

"You gave up your dog ... how could you do that?"

"I didn't *give up* my dog—I left him ... in a kennel." He was toying with her now.

"Why'd you leave him in a kennel?"

"I had to exit stage left, and I didn't know if, or when, I would be coming back."

"You didn't know ... *if?*" Suddenly, Andrea stopped short, understanding the situation for the first time. "McCormick, are you actually trying to tell me that Tracker is really *your* dog?"

"Y-e-a-h ... I am. I got him as a pup. When I went off to war, I left him with a military trainer. When I got back he was a well-trained, fighting machine. He fought with me in Afghanistan."

There was a very long silence, as Andrea digested this information.

"So ... you're saying ... you probably wouldn't want to give him up?" she asked, doubt shrouding her thoughts.

"Nope, we're best buds ... he's worth over forty thousand dollars, trained."

"What's he trained to do?"

"Dogs, in general, love to jump out of windows ... Tracker is trained to jump out of exploding buildings, and to locate and disclose concealed weapons under man-skirts." The implication went over Andrea's exhausted head.

"So ... you're saying, in essence, that he means the world to you," she commented dryly, sounding disheartened.

"Yep! He saved my life."

"How did he do that?"

McCormick leaned against the sleigh, slapping his gloves across his thigh. He paused, and dropped his head. His eyes turned to flint, and his jaw went to solid rock with gut-wrenching seriousness. He hated to talk about it, but Andrea deserved an explanation. Sadly remembering the lost lives of his military brothers, he began, "Tracker went out with me for night-to-light sentry duty one morning, and took off, chasing who-knows-what with a frisky tail. We'd walked for about fifteen minutes ... away from the camp. We got hit by an enemy missile ... all the members of my unit were ki... wiped out—all except Tracker and me ... that was the first time he saved my life." Andrea's mouth went agape. He continued in low, guttural tones, "The shock wave from the explosion threw me back against a boulder...." his eyes locked into Andrea's, "just like Pitys. I went unconscious, but Tracker brought me back to my senses just in time to prevent the diabolical bastards from doffing my head ... that was the second time he saved my life." He swallowed hard, as though trying to rid himself of the past. Now his low, ragged voice scraped the deepest recesses of his soul. "I've never been able to justify the fact that I survived, as if by ... divine intervention."

CHAPTER 57

Unsettled by his accounting, Andrea's gaze dropped, ruefully, to the tracks in the snow. It wasn't the fact that she'd never actually read the three-year-old newspaper article that bothered her, or the fact that she'd never recognized the warrior and his dog. Duh! No, it was the fact that, over the last three months, she had completely misjudged this honorable man. She asked softly, "Is that why you got your medal?"

"Nah ... they don't give out medals for not getting blown to bits ... Tracker and I took out the missile launchers—he has PTSD as a result."

He continued, "When I got home ... I learned that my wife had abor...." He stalled.

Andrea laid a gentle hand on his arm. "You don't have to go there, Matt ... I already know."

They stood staring at each other in silence as though the only members of a secret society.

Finally, she asked, "Do you have PTSD?"

He shot her a painful look. "Workin' on it," he answered, in all honestly.

Andrea considered all that had been said. "Do you suppose there's some way we could both take possession of a crazy war dog?"

McCormick's eyes met hers. "Maybe," he said, before looking away. Seemingly preoccupied, he turned and gave a loud whistle, then turned back to lift Andrea into the sleigh. He settled into the seat beside her, waiting for Tracker to find his way out of the woods.

While they waited, McCormick's head dropped, and he rested his arms on his thighs, staring solemnly at the floor-board between his sprawled knees. He had found someone worth dying for, fighting for and fighting with, but there was still something between the two of them that continued to rankle his soul—the wound that would not heal. He'd best address it now.

"Andi … I realize I'm not aging very well…." Their chortles were soon averted to tender commiseration. His chin shot up, "but do you … do you really see me as a … a crazy, inked up, peg-legged, bullet-riddled, geeky, sleuthing, gun-toting G-man?" Is that what I've become … in your eyes?"

Their eyes locked in bottom-line honesty.

Welcoming the opportunity to address her foolishness, Andrea searched for just the right words needed to apologize—special words—nourishing words that would serve him for a lifetime.

Finally, "Matt, those words were spoken in anger and fear … I was simply being a smartass, as I'm sometimes inclined to be."

"Sometimes?" he repeated, tauntingly, attempting to strengthen her veracity.

"Most times," she conceded. "I regretted them the moment they left my lips. Matt … I'm sorry … I'm d-e-e-p-l-y sorry; but I didn't exactly call you *peg*-legged, either. And yes … that's exactly the way I see you. I'm a realist, as well as a nurse; but McCormick, you need to know that whether you have one leg or twenty, makes no difference to me—it's your heart, your soul, your mind, and your character that's captured my respect … right along with your wry, smartass humor." She wanted to mention his million-dollar smile, his belly laugh, and his gentle touch. She wanted to mention his heart-stopping good looks, but she remembered David's warning about that sort of thing.

She looked him straight in the eye. "I've spent the last several years of my life without *any* kind of love…." McCormick nodded his understanding, "and years without that kid who first stole my heart, and set my body on fire while I was just a young girl—that kid had *just* those particular qualities. You touched my soul, Matt … and never a day went by that you were not front and center in my mind … and my heart." Her hand rested on his thigh. "You need to know that I will never be able to look at you again without seeing that young, energetic, seventeen-year-old kid, with long, tanned, brawny legs and a million dollar smile, who told me he was preparing for anything that came his way, never knowing that, all-the-while, he was preparing to save *my* life … over and over again."

Her throat tightened, and she whispered, "Special Agent Matthew J.

McCormick, you've not only saved my life, but you've made me safer ... stronger ... better."

The man's head dipped with humility. Adding a chuckle she continued. "Mac, don't think for a minute that I don't appreciate your gorgeous, good looks, your toxic masculinity, or your ever-changing hair styles ... because I do." She shook her head slowly, silently. "But for days now, I've witnessed you ... completely without camouflage or precept ... with your big heart hanging out there like the dewlap on a crazy bull moose, while you fight to save humanity where ever it's needed. I love the person you are, Matt ... and whether we be friends or enemies, I really don't want to live another day without you."

By now, McCormick's left eye had completely swollen shut, leaving only a tear to shimmer behind his thick lashes while his heart leapt with joy. She'd accepted him as the stupid kid he'd been in the past, the tough-minded, hard-assed warrior and sleuth he'd become; but more importantly, she accepted him as a man—she had stopped the bleeding!

McCormick gazed lovingly into her beautiful eyes. With a heart flooded with every emotion known to man, rendering him completely unable to speak, his only recourse was to caress her cheek, and comb his fingers through her hair with a gentle, loving touch. In this woman, he saw the stirring young lass who had tumbled out of a tree and into his life; the innocent girl who had been entrapped in the cultural depravity of the day. Like a shimmering butterfly caught in a labyrinthine web of evil, her heart sang out like the dawn of a fresh, new day in a forest filled with lightsome birdsong. She was a survivor, a woman capable of living a full, rich life, rich in happiness and full of love and joy—no matter what the circumstances. Her beauty could shame the mythological, woodland creatures, but he didn't care about that. Her heart glowed with an everlasting goodness.

If, and when he ever got his voice back, he would share these things. In the meantime, a full-blown tear skittered down his bruised and battered cheek as he reached for her hand in adoration, and unabashedly drew her fingers to his dry, feverish lips.

Andrea's heart filled with a warmth and joy she knew would last forever; but she soon pulled back, and a mischievous glint came to her eye, "I have to tell you, Super Sleuth ... during these last few months of being alone ... scared out of my boots, miserably cold ... even frozen, I never realized that all I had to do to find the kid of my dreams was to travel down to the fringe of my brand new, never-before-used, Christmas throw to those sexy, brawny legs."

Suddenly caught off guard by her comment, McCormick looked at her head on. His mind streamed back to the immediate action he'd taken to save her from hypothermia. "You've known about that?" he questioned, his hand dropping away with embarrassment. "I was warming ... saving your li... protect...."

She pressed her finger to his lips, bringing an end to his stammering. "I figured it out."

Tracker came running out of the woods as though being chased by the very Hounds of Hell. Wet and panting hard, he jumped into the back with a giant thud that shook the sleigh, causing even Windy to look back.

McCormick picked up the reins. A huge, satisfied grin crossed his face as he said the words. "Family ... let's go home."

A huge silver moon hung high in the sky, illuminating the snow and glittering ice crystals as the sleigh smoothly glided under twinkling stars and snow-flocked boughs. Andrea's heart raced joyfully with the happy sound of jangling bells. A sense of accomplishment filled her journalistic soul. She'd actually seen her plan through, be it by determination or by fate. She had found her phantom soldier and gotten her interview with law enforcement, in spades; and she'd found that special someone standing between the drug culture and the country's innocent children. She'd even gotten the opportunity to watch him at work, putting his life on the line with every breath he took; and he had literally lifted her out of her own private hell. Never again, would she doubt the effectiveness of law enforcement. Would she write her article? Hell no. This story, this hero, deserved a book.

"So, what else don't I know about you, McCormick? I just have this overwhelming feeling ... that there's much, much more."

Something similar to a growl escaped his lips. "Guess you'll have to stick around ... and ask a few more questions?"

"Have it your way," she teased, snuggling closer as bells jangled in the cold, crisp air.

Finally, "Matt ... how did the two of you survive on your own?"

McCormick looked at her askance. "Are you talking about Tracker and me ... or me and my toxic masculinity?"

"You and Tracker ... after the missile struck your camp."

Somberly, McCormick recalled his warrior experience, played out in a world of darkness. Looking straight ahead and speaking to the air, he growled, "I guess you could say that things got a little squirrely at that point."

Andrea gulped.

"I didn't know you were a professional singer."

"I didn't know you were the Little Drummer ... She-boy!"

"Are you the guy who put out the salt block at the cabin?"

"I thought you could use a little tongue licking, tail-flicking entertainment."

"McCormick ... is your name really ... Matthew *Justice* McCormick?"

"Yep."

"Are you ... by any chance ... the guy who mailed my necklace to me from Virginia?"

He shot her a long sideways glance. He tried for a lopsided grin, but, by now, his swollen jaw wouldn't stretch quite that far. "I am," he said softly, modestly.

A gratified smile crossed Andrea's lips.

Now his eyes began to shimmer, as he slowed the horse to a slow trot. He propped his left foot up on the front rail of the sleigh. "Andi, here's a question for you ... do you always keep a loaded pistol in your underwear drawer?"

"Always!"

She shot him a perspicacious glare, "Do you always go through women's underwear drawers?"

"Always."

Already knowing the answer, he asked, "Do you know how to use it?"

"Yeah, sure ... I took the training course ... still go to the range for target practice."

McCormick grinned. His life had just gotten a whole lot easier.

Mimicking the agent, Andrea propped her right foot up on the front of the sleigh, and threaded her arm through his, practicing what she was about to say. *Find your happy place,* his father had advised her. She remembered his mother's words of advice: *why wait for him?* Finally, she took a deep breath, daring and gutsy. "Hey, McCreek...." Her gaze trailed off for a moment, as she contemplated the mammoth decision she was making. Finally, she looked at him straight on. "Would it matter to you ... terribly ... if *I* was the mother of your children?"

McCormick shot her a shell-shocked look, askance. Even with pain shooting through his lips, he couldn't control the grin that spread wide across his face.

"Wut?" he asked, his tongue sharp and clipped. His brows knotted in feigned outrage. "You think I want a whole nut tree full of squirrely, gun-toting, badass kits with raging tempers, and long, tanned, brawny legs with the ability to kick ass, and dance the Anaconda in ballerina slippers."

"She laughed and added, "Or little bald-headed goons with baby Vandykes skulking in shadows, and painting murals with the bloody tips of their knives ... while Dad dozes with his loaded gun beside his chair?"

They rubbed their chins, pretending to weigh the options.

At last, they nodded their heads and exclaimed in agreement, "Yeah ... we could live with that!"

EPILOGUE

David had tracked down and questioned his young charge to the max, short of any kind of brutality, and now he wheeled his large, black, mud-streaked Suburban around the hospital parking lot. He'd been driving for hours, working straight through New Year's Eve, and the previous two days. He was hungry; his body was exhausted, but he didn't mind. His hair was still neatly trimmed, but his chin whiskers had grown scruffy and unruly, and his clothing was rumpled and dirty. He'd had little time to clean the mud off his Gortex boots, leaving a great deal still caked to them. He stopped at the front door and waited for Andrea.

Dr. McCormick's promised three-day hospital stay for Matt and Andrea had stretched into a full week. His brother had slept most of that time following surgery. But at last, his serious injuries were healing, and it was time to send the hero home on this New Year's Day. Andrea had healed quickly, spending most of her days tending to Matt's needs, rocking NAS babies, and returning phone calls, trying to get her life back on track.

David was prepared to drive them all back to the mountains, but first he had a job to finish while Matt got last minute tweaking on the myoelectrical parts of his leg.

Andrea climbed into the SUV, took one look at the draggled David and asked with widen eyes, "Been muddin'?"

David grinned, and answered in a manner reminiscent of Matt. "You could say that."

Still wearing McCormick's West Point jacket, Andrea needed warmer clothing from the Daye estate, so David drove there first, knowing they would have time for a serious discussion on the ride back to hospital to pick up Matt.

She showered and packed to the loud thumping drum beat, and sharp horn sounds of Chicago's *Beginnings*; the lively music hand-picked by David to set the mood for the day. Ordered to leave his boots at the door, he now investigated her extensive music collection in socked feet in the downstairs family room.

Foaming at the mouth with toothbrush in hand, she yelled down the stairwell, "That was my Dad's favorite."

Ready to leave, she noticed that the house didn't seem as haunted and morose with David present. Still, she looked around at her teal-colored room. Her life here was over; and she was more than anxious to move on, to get back to Matt.

As she descended the stairs and crossed through the kitchen, David yelled, "Better check your answering machine while you're here." He'd spoken nonchalantly, but quickly turned his face, in order to hide his devilishness.

"Thanks for reminding me ... I don't know where my brain went," she offered, as she began listening to the numerous recorded messages of the past four weeks, starting with the oldest, and writing down each name and number.

David asked, "Got anything to eat?"

"Doubtful ... check the fridge. There might be some stale cookies, or an apple or two in the crisper."

When she came to one particular call that had come in from Boston just hours earlier, she froze, and her breath caught in her throat. Vaguely recognizing the number, she hurriedly pushed the button and played the tape. David raided the refrigerator; then walked over and stood close, watching her face drain of color as she listened to an older gentleman's voice: *This is a personal and private call for Andrea Daye. If you are Andrea Daye, please return my call as soon as possible ... if you're still interested.*

If you're still interested. She shot David an unreadable look. "Let's roll!" As David reached for his boots, she spewed, "Go, go, go," pushing him out the door, while punching numbers into her cell phone as she jogged to the SUV. David tossed her bags in the back, atop a full arsenal of guns, ammunition, and bullet-proof vests then hustled around to the driver's seat, and quickly started the engine. As they drove down the driveway, through the open, unlocked gate, she returned the call amid the crackling radio scanner, issuing orders for an action taking place elsewhere. Chomping on his apple, David aimed his thumb at the radio. He turned down the volume. "Got to listen to this," he apologized, "I'm on duty."

"No prob," she offered, half-mindedly.

A sly grin parked itself permanently on David's face, as he listened to Andrea's one-sided telephone conversation, fully aware of the subject matter being discussed—after all, he had set it all in motion.

On the ten minute drive back to the hospital, and with an additional twenty minutes sitting outside in the parking lot, David reluctantly engaged Andrea in an extremely personal conversation. Embarrassment had crept across the agent's face as he'd flashed his creds, and began asking questions he was certain Andrea wouldn't want to answer—questions he already had the answers to. She had answered each one, honestly and forth-rightly, looking her friend and soon-to-be brother-in-law, straight in the eye.

At last, Andrea jumped out of the SUV, and ran into the hospital. David took the tape recorder from his pocket, and flipped it off—totally satisfied with all her answers.

She continued a fast-paced walk along the hospital corridors, until she found her hero standing, hale and hardy, at the Check-out Counter, still looking a little gaunt. He was dressed in brand new jeans, with a snug-fitting butt, the cuffs, knees, and pockets already distressed and frayed, but oh those sexy legs. The side of his face and jaw were still discolored from stitches and bruising. His demeanor was one of slight impatience as he signed off on his medical charges and release forms.

When he had finished, he folded the papers, then stuck them in an inside breast pocket as he turned around to greet her. Once his hands were free, he draped his arm across her shoulder, lovingly, immediately noticing the troubled look on her face. She had been crying.

"Whatzup?" he asked, concerned and unsmiling.

She looked up into his handsome face, "McCormick ... do you trust me?"

He snickered, and shot her a teasing, puzzled smirk. "Kid ... I just gambled life, limb, career and freedom on that trust," he answered, his deep voice crackling, as curiosity germinated in his mind.

"Well, yeah ... but that was days ago," she teased. "Do you trust me enough *today* to take a ride into Boston—no questions asked?"

"Boston?" His chin ticked up slightly, as he gave her a curious, hooded look. He noticed that her voice sounded thin and wispy, as though she could barely breathe. Intrigued, but questioning the adamant request, and thinking of all the miles between here and there, he answered, "Yeah, but do we have to go right *now*?" His Neanderthal roots had floated to the surface, and all he wanted was to eat an ox, and go home to his man cave—to be alone with his woman, and his dog.

Andrea shot him a playful, pleading, puppy-dog look that, years ago, had worked like a charm on her dad; but McCormick could see through it, to that unsettled something hiding behind her eyes—the deep, dark secret she'd never revealed to him as an agent.

She nodded, emphatically, and promised, "I'll buy you a steak dinner, a jug of wine—*and* a whole urn of black coffee."

McCormick considered her proposition. "Add deep-dish, blackberry cobbler, ala mode to the mix, and I'm in," he finally agreed, giving her a warm smile.

"David's in the car … he'll drive."

McCormick's antennae shot up, and his eyes widened, knowing that David had been on duty in Boston all week, investigating a head-on collision that had taken place the day before Christmas, and supposedly involved some kind of serious criminal activity. A determined sense of investigative challenge settled in McCormick's bones.

As he headed down Hwy. 89, David glanced into his rearview mirror at the handsome couple in the back seat, talking quietly amongst themselves, holding hands, laughing and giving each other private looks. Whether or not there had actually been divine intervention in this case, was anybody's guess; but it was more than obvious that these two were meant to be together, and that a powerful force had been in play to bring them together.

As their long drive neared its end, Andrea began to feel as though she had taken, and passed, Law Enforcement 101. The ride had included a lot of serious shop talk between the men, followed by a profusion of jokes and stories. She loved it all. Laughter came easily for all three as they genuinely enjoyed their time together. Matt was a natural entertainer; everything he said was fresh and exciting, making the hours in the car pass by painlessly.

When the sign announcing the turnoff to Boston off I-91 appeared, David flipped on the turn signal and once again glanced into the backseat.

Andi had laid her head on Matt's shoulder, and his brother had wrapped his arm around her as they whispered sweet-nothings to each other. They both deserved to be happy, he thought. His only regret was that he hadn't been able to spend more time with his brother; but he brushed the thought aside and wished that all his working hours could be this pleasant, and productive. Finally, he swung the SUV into one of the many parking spaces at the city's favorite indoor water park.

Totally disconcerted, McCormick looked at the towering building with huge, multi-colored water slides jutting out the roof and sides from every angle. Furtively, he glanced out the shaded, rear window at the two vehicles that had been riding their tail since entering the Boston City Limits. They had pulled in right behind the SUV, and quickly cut their lights. Had he been on the job, his gun would've been in his hand, at the ready. He turned to Andrea and asked, "Why are we here?"

David's phone vibrated and he got out and slammed the door shut behind him, creating an aura of privacy inside the vehicle.

Hesitantly, Andrea shot McCormick a tremulous smile, "McCormick, you once told me … no … twice you told me that you needed to know, for sure, that I had your back."

He studied her lovely face—a face healed of all its wounds, yet still wearing a veil of stress. She seemed restive, her hands growing more fidgety by the second. McCormick had never seen her in this state. He didn't understand why she was being so serious, so elusive. He waited for her to say more, dubiety growing in his mind.

At last she let out a loud sigh, "Matt … I've always had your back."

Their eyes locked. "I don't know what we're talking about here," he said, his frown lines deepening in vacillation.

A sly smile crossed her face, and she, lovingly, laid her hand on his upper thigh, "I know you don't, but you will … *trust me.*" She released the latch to the side door and slid it open. "Follow me … keep your mouth shut … and walk in my footsteps!" As she prepared to step to the ground from the high-riding vehicle, she glanced back over her shoulder, grinning impishly, while trying to suppress joyous, but restrained laughter. McCormick watched as she started to trot towards the building, seemingly in a hurry.

Once again, his steely eyes took in everything around him, including the building with its bright, neon lighting, trying to make sense of this trip. He called out, to her back, "You do know that I don't have swimwear." He got out on his side, and walked around the back of the Suburban, and followed, wondering why this whole trip had been shrouded in such mystery—and why was David with them, talking to headquarters on his satphone, and very obviously on duty? When he caught up to her, he spoke in a low, roguish tone, "Maybe they'll let *you* go skinny-dippin'."

The strong smell of chlorine hit their nostrils as soon as they walked through the entrance. Inside, near the door, stood an older gentleman wearing a dark suit, white collar, and the air of authority ordained to him by God. His pants were wrinkled as though he had been sitting, waiting a long while. Recognizing Andrea, he stepped forward and offered his hand. "Miss Daye, Rev. Jonathan Robbins, remember me? It's good to see you again."

She shot him a nervous, abbreviated smile. Yes, she did remember him.

Trying to shed a light on their reason for meeting, Robbins stated emphatically. "There's been a sudden turn of events." He looked long, and hard, at McCormick, then nodded his head towards the windows overlooking the water slides. "He's on the Mammoth."

McCormick shot Andrea a blank look. She ignored him. Rev. Robbins turned and led them to the window overlooking the large pool full of noisy, rowdy swimmers, their loud voices bouncing off the walls. The Reverend Robbins stepped back.

As Matt peered through the window, entirely clueless as to what he was looking for, he first noticed what was reflected back to him through the glass. David was exchanging a familiar greeting and handshake with the reverend. It was obvious that the two men had met before, and now stood talking in warm, somber tones a short distance behind him, trying to get glimpses of the swimmers over Matt and Andrea's shoulders.

Also from the reflections, Matt noticed that security was out in force. He quickly recognized military men in civilian clothing, their bodies erect, arms at their sides, and eyes forward. Fully trusting his brother, and because they were mostly young men, he figured this was some kind of training exercise. Whatever it was, David was, obviously, in charge.

Matt let his body relax as he turned his focus to the crowded pool. One boy immediately caught his eye when he swished out, torpedo like, from the bottom end of the largest tube slide, hitting the water with extreme force. Next, the lad dove down, touched the bottom of the pool, then rose and swam at full speed towards the pool's edge, as though his very life depended on it. Then, he hustled back up the ladder to have another go at the slide.

Wanting, first, to witness Matt's reaction, Andrea followed his gaze until his eyes locked onto the lad. When his jaw went slack, she turned her own eyes on the boy. She gasped. The kid was tall and slender. His hair was dark brown, almost black. His keen eyes, though red from the chlorine, had a thoughtful, intelligent look about them. A myriad of emotions surfaced as she remembered the softness, the lightness of the swaddled bundle she'd held in her arms thirteen years ago. She remembered, all too well, the sweet smell of her newborn baby, the lotion, the precious newness of life she had brought into the world at such a very young age. Tears flooded her eyes, and sobs gurgled up in her throat, racking her chest. She turned her head away from the window as the agony of deep emotions overwhelmed her. McCormick turned a concerned, questioning eye on her.

Cruelly, in retrospect, she had been allowed to watch the infant's birth in an over-head mirror hanging high above her delivery room bed, witnessing his tiny, thatch-covered head enter the world. As the doctor had laid him across her stomach, eternal joy had flooded her soul at the sound of his first, faint cry—but that euphoric feeling would not, could not, last. Forced to give up her child for adoption, the young, teenaged girl had been allowed to hold and nurture her son for only a brief time; but during that time the two had, unwittingly, bonded to each other—and she had grieved her loss every single minute of every single day. She turned back to the window, and for the second time in her life, gazed upon her son—*the kid was the spitting image of Matthew Justice McCormick!*

Rev. Robbins stepped forward, and from out of nowhere, produced a box of tissues. "Something very unfortunate has happened, Miss Daye," he began, his tone, steadfast, but commiserative. His voice dropped to a funereal tone, and he offered, "Peter's adoptive parents have been killed in an automobile accident. Their car was hit, head-on, as they returned from a shopping trip just the day before Christmas. Luckily, the boy wasn't with them, but was, instead, on a team bus, returning from an ice hockey game. Peter plays on a traveling team and is considered very talented and aggressive on the ice, I'm told."

He gave Andrea a compassionate look. "I thought you would want

529

to know … before he goes back into the system." He glanced at Matt. "Normally, we contact the father, as well—but no father was listed on his birth certificate." He took in a deep, regrettable breath and looked closer at McCormick. "Older children rarely get adopted—Peter will most likely be living with foster parents or at the Home until he comes of age."

The venerable old man turned towards the window again, and looked through the glass at the boy, who was, once again, climbing the ladder to the water slide for the umpteenth time, "Peter's a great kid … loving, caring, kind," the clergyman pointed out. The man had always personally thought that Peter deserved better than the adoptive parents he'd gotten, but he said, "He's a super student … working almost two-years above his grade level. He's a whiz on the computer, but he also loves to read. His adoptive father was an English professor, quiet and reserved; he's already read many of the classics. His mother was a dental hygienist, and so his teeth are perfect … and he's strong and in excellent health."

Disquietude settled over Matthew J. McCormick, hearing the kid sized up as though an animal.

The Reverend paused, not wanting to say anything negative, but being the professional, he knew he must. "There has been *some* trouble at home. Peter and his parents were not exactly cut from the same cloth. The Conrads, his adoptive parents, were mostly stay-at-home, sedentary types. She was a fretful woman, knitted Afghans; he played Bridge all weekend with neighbors, or graded essays. Both were in poor health, and I'm afraid neither one was actively involved in the boy's life. Peter, on the other hand, has a wide streak of wanderlust … he's run away from home on several occasions. He never quite gets into trouble with the law, but he seems to crave adventure … his family lived in a small house on a cul-de-sac with very little lawn space. They never traveled or took vacations … never had a pet. When he runs, he runs to the mountains. The last time he took off, he made it halfway up *The Long Trail* in Vermont before they found him weeks later."

He looked askance at Matt, observing his mannerly, genteel countenance and demeanor, seeing the boy's likeness in him; but he also noticed Matt's bruised face, his frayed, holey jeans, scuffed-up boots, and his evil-looking tattoos. He looked again through the window at the thirteen-year-old boy. "Andrea, I remembered that, at the time, you didn't want to give up your son, and that you've written, and even called several times just recently, about the possibility of getting him back … if you're still of that mind, you could take him home in a few weeks—after you've shown that you can provide a safe and financially stable environment for the boy."

Matt bristled and glanced at Andrea, waiting for her to reply, but she remained silent, refusing to meet his eyes. In Andrea's mind, she was *trusting* in the shrewd, astute McCormick's ability to do the math, and connect the dots.

Now, with heart pounding in his ears, McCormick stared, long and hard, at Andrea's flushed profile. His heart plunged to his stomach, doing emotional belly flops as he did the math. *You were my only,* she'd said on Christmas Day. At last, he came to the only rational conclusion—*he* was Peter's father!

He was Peter's father!

Along with that realization, came a full understanding of Andrea's mercurial temperament. He dropped his head and groaned inwardly, at last cognizant of Bitchy Reason, Number 5! He took a long, fresh, appreciative look at the woman, fully understanding the problems she must have suffered through—alone.

"I should warn you, also…." Robbins was saying, "He has a bit of a temper. He has a habit of going off on anyone trying to sell drugs … he beat up a kid, once." He stammered, "Actually … his school principal tells me that he has beaten up several kids … for that very reason."

Now, Matt and Andrea looked, mockingly, at each other, locking laughing eyes. Wry grins twitched across their lips, begging to be set free. David, standing behind them, took it all in. A wide grin ran across the full width of his mouth, as well. Suddenly, roisterous, unrestrained laughter shot out from all three.

Failing to see the humor in the situation, the Reverend's face clouded with a look of shocked be-wilderment.

Matt took a quick step forward, and offered the Reverend his hand in an act of apology. "I'm Matt McCormick. I've learned—just this very moment—that I'm Pete's father. I'm in … law enforcement." The corner of his mouth shot up, audaciously. "I beat up on drug dealers for a living."

"Oh," The Reverend finally got the joke, and quickly recognized Matt by name and reputation.

Now McCormick's jaw clenched tight, the tone of his voice impervious to any decision other than his own. "Peter's mother and I will be taking *our* son home *today*." He put strong emphasis on the last word.

"All right!" David cheered from behind, stoked by the outcome and feeling euphoric. He had already bonded with his young charge.

Hot tears streamed down Andrea's cheeks, but she was soon smiling and laughing through the deluge, quickly dabbing away the salty dampness. She had trusted Matt to make his own decision; he had most certainly made the right one!

A satisfied grin spread across Rev. Robbins's face as he watched McCormick pull the beautiful, young woman to his side, making things right. "Are the two of you married?" he asked with genuine interest.

McCormick dipped his head, and ran a hand of frustration through his hair. "Workin' on it," was all he could manage to say, his emotions overriding his tongue.

When Peter took a break and headed for the restroom, Andrea excused herself to freshen up. McCormick approached David, and the two men shook hands and gave each other a bro-hug. Nodding towards the bodyguards standing at various points around the building, Matt asked, "So, what else is going on here today, agent? What's with the two tails … the babysitters … the fire power?" He nodded towards David's shoulder holster tucked under his jacket.

David squared his feet and shoulders. "Sir, these men are here for *your* protection."

With eyes asquint in disbelief, McCormick looked at his kid brother as though the words had been shot from a missile launcher. He gave him a questioning frown.

"You're a big fuckin' deal, now … Sir," David answered, matter-of-factly, showing respect, with no flamboyance intended.

Continuing to report, David offered, "Soon as the kid found out his adoptive parents had been killed, he took off. A search of the family's personal files turned up Peter's adoption papers."

David continued, "Since you were off grid, having that shoulder operated on when Brantley Stone's involvement was discovered, I was pulled into the investigation."

McCormick's eyes fixed on his brother in a hard questioning stare. "Bran?"

"Yeah, turns out … the car that hit Peter's adoptive parents was registered to Brantley Stone … the jerk had assets all over the place."

A frown pulled down McCormick's face and his eyes narrowed.

"I was tasked with finding the boy. When I finally caught up with him, he told me that some weirdo had been contacting him, threatening to kill his parents if he didn't meet up with him … we figure Bran planned to grab Peter for nefarious reasons, but the kid took off before that could happen."

McCormick breathed out his answer, "Smart kid." His jaw turned to steel as the investigator in him began to unravel the rest of the story. Connecting the dots, McCormick summarized. "Let me guess … if Bran had gotten his hands on Peter … he would have sacrificed him in order to kill Andrea … in the cruelest, most onerous way possible."

"You got it. " David nodded in agreement. "Getting the facts about the kid's birth parents wasn't easy. I had to go heavy and threaten some people with jail time before I got answers. I questioned the doctor, who delivered the infant, and through his leads, I was able to trace the adoption and the child, back to the Daye's—back to Andrea." David continued, "When I caught up to Peter, he was halfway to Red Springs, camped out alongside a dirt road, in a water-logged pup tent, and up to his ears in slush and mud. His matches were wet, and he couldn't get a campfire going to save his soul. He'd eaten nothing for two days … and he was just minutes away from hypothermia." David locked eyes with his older brother, "but he'd read your book, Matt, and his plan was to hitchhike up Hwy. 91 to the mountains; he'd done it before…." David looked around before continuing. He lowered his voice, "Matt … he was coming to you … he wanted to meet you and Tracker."

McCormick lips pursed, and he went silent for a long moment. David gave him time to digest this latest news.

Finally, Matt looked at his brother in head-scratching puzzlement. "My investigation turned up nothing in regards to a child. How did Bran know?"

Again David grimaced, "There's the rub. Nothing turned up because there *was nothing* to turn up. According to what Andrea told me this morning, her mother had been extremely upset that she had refused to have an abortion. That's when Rev. Robbins was called in. As we all know, big money talks, and her mother's money made things disappear—things like records, supposedly all done in Andrea's best interest."

"How did Andi know about it?"

Continuing to reveal his findings, David added, "At some point before her death, dear ole Mother shared the story of Andrea's illegitimate pregnancy with Stone, who later tried to use it to embarrass Andrea, not realizing that she felt no remorse. When that didn't work he started making threats on the boy's life—she actually went through a living hell for the kid."

As McCormick's mind grasped the facts, putting the puzzle together, his eyes suddenly shot towards the ceiling in an "aha" moment, then came back to settle into his brother's eyes. "And it was a living hell because Fitzgerald threatened the kid's life … in order to get Andrea to marry him," he stated, matter-of-factly.

"I haven't gotten that far in my investigation."

McCormick explained, "Bran couldn't just kill Andrea like he had the rest of her family. In order to gain full control of the Daye dynasty, he had to first marry her, and locate her mystery child; if the kid surfaced, he would be in line to inherit—so he had to be eliminated, as well."

David's eyes widened.

McCormick rubbed his hand down the full length of a face gone pale with the realization of what might have come about had Stone been able to follow his plan to fruition—and had McCormick not stayed in hot pursuit of Stone. "Other than the attending physician, what led Stone to Peter?"

"The doctor knew nothing about the present-day circumstances, so that was a dead end." David remained silent for a beat. McCormick, recognizing his brother's time-honored stall tactic, shot him a flinty look.

Finally, David answered. "Peter wrote an article for a kid's magazine … they published it, and someone brought it to Fitzgerald's attention—probably Jolene Jorgenson at the *Forest Hills Daily News*."

McCormick's frown lines deepened as he questioned David, further. "What was the article about?"

Again David held his tongue.

"Aw, come on, Davy … out with it," an impatient McCormick urged. "What was the title?"

Finally, a reluctant David answered, "The Heroes I Most Admire … By Peter M. Conrad … he wrote about you, Matt, and your dog. The article included pictures of both you and Tracker ... it had a Boston dateline, and the boy's headshot—and as we now know ... the kid's the spitting image of you. Bran must've looked at the kid's picture and figured it out."

McCormick sensed more to the story, "And?"

David let out his hot breath. "And then there was the story *I* wrote as a sports editor for the *News*, about the young, aggressive kid playing hockey for a traveling Boston team ... I left the job before I got a chance to interview him, but I ran the initial article and included his picture in full uniform ... as well as the team's schedule."

McCormick sucked air, "Did Andrea play a role in any of this?"

"Aw, nah ... she's completely innocent. She had no knowledge of the adoption agency, who Peter's adoptive parents were, or where he lived. She only knew that he was out there—somewhere; but she had lost contact with Rev. Robbins until just recently. She had nothing to do with digital birth records being withheld. That was all done at the hospital."

David relaxed—the worst of it had been said. "They took the child away from her just hours after he was born. Shortly after her family was killed, she tried to get him back ... and then she had tried to contact Rev. Robbins from the hospital about a week ago while you were in surgery."

McCormick was speechless.

David continued, "She did get to name him, though; but he hates the name, Peter."

A pregnant pause hung in the air as McCormick's mind whirled like a Cat 4 hurricane. Finally, "What's his middle name?" he asked, trying to push down a melancholic, heartsick feeling, just now cognizant of the fact that he had missed his son's birth. *Hell ... he'd missed his son's whole life!*

"McCreek," David answered, "but he prefers to be called Creek."

McCormick's eyebrow shot up quizzically, "Creek?"

"Yeah ... as in swollen or muddy ... weird name, huh?" David baited. "Andrea got the name from that old dilapidated signpost on the edge of town; the one that points the way to McCormick's Creek Campground. "Hey, wasn't that Grandpa's nickname for you?"

"Yeah," McCormick answered, his tone guttural.

"The kid's known all along that he was adopted," David added.

"And Andrea knew nothing of her mother's misdeeds?"

"Not until Bran tried to control her with the information," he paused for a beat, "however, she had, without knowledge, continued to make large contributions to the group that handled the adoption ... turned out to be a shell company. Andrea claims, however, that she was only making annual contributions to her mother's favorite Christmas charity; but she assures me they were done solely in remembrance of her mother. I've got it all on tape ... it's quite a story."

David paused, shaking his head. "Since there are no records of Peter's birth, other than the actual paper birth certificate, her mother's little misdeed is going to cause the kid a lot of legal problems as he gets older ... Social Security number, and all of that."

"That was probably taken care of when he started school ... we'll get it straightened out." McCormick combed thoughtful fingers through his hair. "I've got some serious restitution to make at West Point, though ... Cadets aren't allowed to have kids."

David chortled, "Yeah, but you didn't know anything about it back then."

"Still happened ... you've shared all this with Andi?"

David nodded. "Had to ... I was ordered to interrogate her, but she didn't know any details. She'd never told anyone what happened ... or who. For all the parents knew, it was a virgin birth."

David's attempt at humor failed, miserably, and he tried to recoup. "She was just a kid ... her parent's just figured she'd been raped."

McCormick gave a diminutive shake of the head. "She wasn't *raped*," he offered in an incredulous tone. " Normally, McCormick wasn't one to explain himself, but now he spoke of things he would say only to his brother. "We were just young and stupid." *And in love*, McCormick thought. "I'd dragged her out of the creek ... saved her life, actually." David, the agent, studied his brother's stone hard face for micro expressions. "It was storming and she was scared and cold ... I was just trying to ... warm her up."

"Aw, really?" David guffawed with feigned sympathy. "Well ... brother ... I celebrated New Year's Eve by chasing that *warm-up* all through the mountains ... on foot ... up hill and downhill ... through the slush and mud ... for hours," he teased.

The muscles in McCormick's face remained sober and unchanged. He asked, "What's going on ... now?"

David's face waxed serious once more. "My orders for the day are to reunite Peter with his birth mother ... I hope you don't mind, but after

536

much discussion, Andrea and I decided to pull you into it, and let it play out, naturally. One look at that kid," he gave Matt a wiseacre look, "and I knew I was Uncle Davy."

Seeing a crack in his brother's stone face, David gave him a smug grin, "Hey big guy … I've been working the numbers … aren't you just a little young to have a kid that old?"

A light came into McCormick's eyes, and the corner of his mouth shot up in a devilish grin. In a rough, military growl, he barked, "Now … there you go again … tromping all over my proclivities!"

The two men laughed heartily, enjoying the joke, needing the stress-breaker.

David continued to razz, "You gonna pass out cigars?"

"Damn straight," McCormick shot back, proudly.

When Andrea returned refreshed, smiling and walking on sunshine, the guys immediately shut down the locker room mentality. She sidled up beside Matt. In a last-ditch effort, David baited his brother with one last, low-pitched chortle before walking away.

Once David was out of earshot, Andrea whispered, tauntingly, "Hey, McCormick … is this good for you?"

Serious resoluteness settled on his face. He looked into Andrea's beautiful eyes, tropical blue—and deeply happy. His appreciation of her as a person had grown by leaps and bounds since he had entered this noisy, smelly building. He hadn't known it was possible to love someone so deeply, so completely.

Looping her arm around his waist, she leaned into him, and whispered, "How did we not recognize each other?"

Matt's jaw flexed, then softened as he curled his arm around her shoulder. "Circumstances … I was the law, and you saw me only as an inked up, one-legged jackass; I could only see you as Bran's wife … our thoughts just never got out of the box."

She gave him a blushing grin, "And, if you'll remember … that night was especially dark."

"Especially…." He didn't even try to hide the roguish gleam in his eye, "And I do remember."

"Does any of this change your opinion of me?" she asked with incertitude.

He looked deep into her gorgeous eyes, giving her an aggressive, sexy grin, half-laughing and half-serious; it was a grin she'd never seen before. "Trust me … you've never looked so hot; and just to clear the record … I'm not injured."

Accepting the grin, his comments and the timbre of his velvety voice as a promise of things to come, Andrea's stomach did a complete somersault.

They both stood watching through the window awhile longer. Peter had returned to the ladder. Matt watched intently, determined to let him have all the time he wanted on the slides. He had never seen a kid work so hard at having fun—or was it just fun?

After three more times down the slide, McCormick watched him finally swim to the edge of the pool to rest, taking in deep gulps of air. He pulled himself out of the water and sat down at water's edge, exhausted. He was tall for his age, with long legs hanging well over the side of the pool. They reminded Matt of his own two legs—once. He dropped his head, as raw emotion swelled up, tightening his throat. When he looked up at Andrea, a flicker of doubt was in his eyes, "Now that you have the clone, I suppose you'll want to kick this old, shot-to-hell, bag of bones to the curb?"

Her eyes widened with disappointment at his words. Frowning, and adding an extra toughness to her voice, she snipped, "Agent … you know me better than that!" Then a slow, sensuous smile spread across her lips, as she gently rubbed her hand over his still-healing shoulder and down the length of his arm. "Matthew Justice McCormick … don't you realize, by now, that I have so much love in my heart for you that my only desire is to make as many *clones* of you as possible? Be warned, super sleuth … Peter is just the beginning!"

McCormick rubbed his still aching jaw, "Would it bother you if we dropped the Peter, temporarily, until he comes to a better appreciation of the name; and one of the Mc's and just called him Creek?" he asked.

She grinned back, approvingly, "Why not? He's your son."

McCormick grabbed her hand and shoved the heavy door open with his hip and thigh. Hot, humid air hit them in the face as they entered the pool area. Amid echoing voices, and the strong odor of chlorine, they walked poolside towards the boy, each basking in their young son's image, taking it to heart.

When his dark eyes, water-blurred but fiery, looked up, instant recognition flickered across his face. He smiled, and asked with innocent awe, "Hey, aren't you that war hero guy? We read about you and your dog in class."

A humble McCormick bent down, playfully tousling the kid's wet hair, letting his high-tech knee touch the pavement. He glanced over his shoulder at Andrea, giving her a long, rueful look that said: *How sad that this boy has only read about his father.* She read the look, and rested a consoling hand on his strong shoulder.

With empathy and cold, wet fingers, the strapping, young kid reached over, gently touching McCormick's discolored cheek. Frowning, he asked, "What happened?"

Emotionally stirred by the boy's concern, McCormick answered, softly, "I met up with some drug dealers."

A flash of alarm shot across the boy's veneer and deepening frown. "Did you win?"

"I did."

Already knowing, the kid asked, "Your name's Matt McCormick isn't it?"

McCormick nodded, "Y-e-a-h," he answered, "that's who *I* am...." He slowly rubbed a hand along his bristled chin, "but the important question here today is: who are you?"

A bereft, forsaken look came into the lonely boy's eyes. He swallowed hard, and dropped his head. Fully aware that his life had been suspended by circumstances and loss, and having no sense of a future, or control over what direction his life might take next, the young lad felt abandoned and scared; it showed on his long face.

McCormick tried to tamp down his feelings, but still, his voice crackled with emotion. "Don't know?" he asked, having experienced similar turmoil in his own life. "Then, let *me* tell you who you are," he offered, knowing that the words he was about to utter would bring new meaning to the young boy's life. "You are Creek McCormick—you're Matt McCormick's son." He let the words hang in the air, giving the lad time to grasp reality.

The boy's head jerked up, his face drained of color. McCormick looked him in the eye. "Son, I need for you to understand something. I've known of your existence for...." He glanced at his watch; then gave the kid a crooked grin, "just under twenty-seven minutes. If I'd known sooner, I would have been here in a nanosecond ... but let there be no doubt about it ... your dad is here for you now."

He nodded over his shoulder at Andrea. "I met this lovely lady, long ago, on the banks of McCormick's Creek ... sitting in the top branch of a willow tree ... in the middle of a flashflood ... singing, euphorically, at the top of her lungs." Instinctively, McCormick realized that only the truth would suffice here, "But, as fate would have it, she's been weeping ever since." McCormick raised his chin and looked earnestly at the boy. "Creek, I figure you're the one, and only person in the world who can bring an end to all those tears. This lovely, gracious, talented woman is your mother ... she loves *you* more than life itself." McCormick lifted his eyes, and locked into Andrea's as he continued to speak, "and I want you to know that not only would I go through high water for her ... but I would willingly fight the fiery flames of Hell." His eyes returned to the lad. "And I'd do the same for you."

Tears surfaced, and a sudden feeling of shyness crept over Andrea as the young boy stared at her for a long moment. Finally, a huge smile broke across his face. Flashing his beautiful, perfect whites in instant bonding, he jumped up and threw his arms around the first woman to ever lay claim to his heart. "You look just like I always thought you would," he gushed. She hugged him, but he hugged tighter; she clung, but he clung longer to the hands that had first held him with love and skin-on-skin contact.

Stoked by this mutual show of affection, McCormick stood, and pulled her to him, while laying an arm across his son's shoulder. "We're taking you home, Creek ... to the Green Mountains." He looked, promisingly, at Andrea, "and we're going to be a real, live, flesh and blood, kick-ass family."

The kid shuffled his feet and shyly dropped his head, "Can I meet Tracker?" he asked, holding his breath, awaiting an answer.

McCormick gave his head an astounded quarter shake at the question. "Creek," he answered with determination, "if you can love him, and show yourself responsible, Tracker can be your dog ... his life hasn't exactly been all slump."

"The boy gave them each a winsome smile, then once again, dropped his head, self-consciously. "I already love him," he admitted, as the corner of his mouth shot up in a grin, slow and wry, just like his dad's.

McCormick's eyes locked into Andrea's. Teasingly, he offered, "Then it's settled ... Tracker is Creek's dog."

McCormick's own eyes began to shimmer, as he drew his head back, recognizing and appreciating his fortuitous circumstances. He blinked away tears of joy. His loving God had, not only saved his life, but had moved mountains in order to make this all possible!

Andrea reached up, and with both hands pulled down her son's face to her level—he was already taller than she. With deep, heartfelt emotion, she placed a kiss on the dark thatch of wet hair at the very top of his head, ceremoniously claiming him as her own. After years of keeping her heart locked away, and the joy of her son's birth unexpressed, she let heartfelt tears roll, unabashedly, down her cheeks.

Seeing this new tsunami of fresh tears, McCormick groused, "Oh, my gawd ... it's going to be flash floods from now unto perpetuity!" Before Andrea could challenge him, he quickly shot her a hot, sexy wink with strong, suggestive implications, and added, "Trust me."

#

Lightning Source UK Ltd.
Milton Keynes UK
UKHW010733290920
370728UK00001B/12